CW00839815

Please follow Darke Industries on Facebook
or
@DarkeIndustries on Twitter

All feedback is welcome. It's what makes people grow.
darkeindustries@hotmail.com

For my Mum

Who has always been there for me,
and made me the man I am today

With all my love

David
xx

Epilogue – Part I

The two figures leaned into the steep incline as they climbed the barren hill, the hoods of their worn travelling cloaks pulled down over their faces against the drizzle blown on the wind. The figure in front was smaller; just a boy. The man behind moved at the child's pace, watching his own footing as well as that of his young companion. The rock and coarse, upland grass were slick with rain, and a tumble could send one or both of them breaking bones as they crashed down the bank.

To say the man watched over the child patiently was not entirely true. It was obvious that he was wary of the boy's safety, but the slow progress was clearly annoying him. His pale hands clenched and unclenched. He sighed heavily, the sound swept away by the wind.

"Where are we going?" asked the boy, pausing to look back at the figure stooping over him, half-protecting, half urging him onwards.

"Nowhere fast, it would seem." The voice was gruff, irritable.

"I'm soaked through."

One of those pallid hands reached out, urging the lad forward. "And you'll keep getting soaked until we find some shelter."

"I'm tired, though."

The man paused for a second, raising the hood out of his face slightly to peer up into the mist above them, smothering the summit of the hill. "I'm not carrying you, boy. You need to toughen up."

"I need to rest."

"No, lad," growled the man. "You don't. You need to push on. There's a cave up there. We'll shelter and get a fire going."

"How do you know there's a cave up there?"

"How do you know there isn't?" The response was angrier now, the fists squeezing an imaginary larynx.

The boy still wasn't moving. He looked up into the mist himself, staring for an infuriatingly long time. "I think you're right."

"I'm infinitely grateful for your agreement."

"I'm not looking forward to getting there, though."

"Why not? Afraid I'm going to throttle you and leave you there to rot?"

"You wouldn't do that," replied the boy, once more moving up the incline at his tediously slow pace.

The man didn't respond. The grip that was forcing the blood from his knuckles disputed the child's confident assertion.

"I'm just going to be bored, aren't I?"

He's stopped again...

"We'll eat and get some sleep."

"That's all we do," protested the lad. "Walk, eat, sleep. Ever since I can really remember."

"Lucky you." The shove was harder this time, accompanied by a grab of the collar of the youngster's cloak, heaving him forward.

"What's that supposed to mean?"

"It means, boy, that a lot of people did a lot more than be bored so that you can walk, and eat, and sleep, and *learn*..."

"What did they do? When?"

It was the man who paused now, staring down at the child before him. The silence went on, interrupted only by the occasional gust of wind and spray.

Maybe it's time he knew...

"I'll tell you, boy. But it's a long story. And I'm not for telling it out in the rain."

"A story is better than just eating and sleeping. It's not an old, boring story though, is it?"

"It's old, and it's new," replied the man, relieved that the lad was moving again. "I'll tell you when we get to the cave and get the fire lit."

"How old? Days? Years? Before I was born?"

"Time's a strange thing, lad," replied the man, placing a hand on the child's shoulder to steady him as they began to move at a decent pace. "Much of it happened just before your birth, and then after it. But it starts a long time before that. Before I was even born."

"Before *you* were born?" asked the boy warily. "How long ago does it start?"

"Long, long ago, boy. At the time of the birth of the New Gods..."

Prologue

He was enveloped in darkness. Not merely the absence of light, a blackness that pressed in on him, squeezing his form.

Mortis had never felt fear before. He was a god, after all, the God of Death, and most emotions did not come easily to deities. He did not know if it was fear he felt now, or more an absence of control. He was a New God, but since he had come into being he had always felt in control. That was the intrinsic part of being a god…

And yet now, as he moved slowly through the darkness that was the Great Enemy's territory in the Astral Realm, he felt almost helpless.

Not against the demons. They fought around him as he moved, dull flashes in the blackness as they struck each other. His servants and those of his allies, clashing with those of Lunaris. The Creature in the Darkness. The Lurker.

The Great Enemy.

Mortis, and those who had allied with him, were the New Gods. They had come into being as the prayers of the mortals had changed. The prayers fed the gods in the Astral Realm their power, and the mortals had moved away from belief in gods of the sun, of the sky, of thunder, of weather.

They had moved away from belief in the God of the Moon. Lunaris.

One by one, the Old Gods had begun to fade, until they could only be sensed as wisps of ethereal thread, fragments floating through the Astral Realm. They had been replaced, by gods such as Mortis. Gods of wealth, of compassion, of war. Gods of emotion and god of worldly desires.

But Lunaris had refused to go quietly into the ether. Lunaris had struck whilst he still had the power to do so. He had committed the cardinal crime. He had slain another god.

Lunaris had been worshipped as a protector, the moon that provided light in the darkness of night. It was only natural that he had lured the fledgling God of Fear, Termos, to his realm. The one who threatened his power the most, as the weak-willed mortals began to prey for Termos to spare them their worldly terrors, rather than Lunaris to protect them.

Termos' death had sent a shockwave through the Astral Realm. Mortis still felt the aftermath of the blast his mind had felt, as Termos' existence shattered sending shards like glass through the plane. Then, as quick as the explosion had spread, it sucked back into the centre, leaving a silence that roared in the minds of the gods.

Termos was gone. And not like the Old Gods. He was completely gone. Nothing.

The New Gods had come to confront Lunaris, but his realm had changed. He had absorbed the power of his prey. He was strong, and he was not in the mood for talk. And so, the battle had begun, demon versus demon in the black realm of Lunaris. There was no moon here to light the way. Lunaris was not what he once was…

Mortis had not chosen a form for his journey. He was invisible, nothing, a lack of form.

Other gods could sense him. It would not fool Lunaris. But it kept the demons away as he moved.

He did not fear the demons. He was a god, after all. Occasionally one would blunder into him in the darkness, suddenly surprised by the immense power they felt beside them. They scratched and clawed, but he smashed them with his will. They shattered easily, miniature explosions akin to the fate of Termos. He felt righteous.

He was getting close now. He could sense it, a red glow up ahead atop a black hill. He could sense Lunaris. And that meant Lunaris could sense him.

A shudder moved through his form. The sheer power of the new God of Fear weighed down on him. He was so *strong*. He pushed up the incline, each movement heavier and heavier. It was draining him before he even faced the Great Enemy. This did not bode well…

He spotted where the red glow was coming from. It emanated from a small entrance in the side of the hill. He pushed inside, gripping the walls of the passageway beyond to wrench himself onwards.

And then the voice came. A hissing rasp that echoed through the passage, and through his mind. The shuddered again.

"It doesn't have to be this hard, Mortis. If you wish to come before me, I can make it easier for you. Just choose a form."

Mortis shook himself, steadying his voice as his projected it down the corridor with as much force as he could muster.

"Why?" he asked. "You can sense me, as I sense you. We are gods. We don't need a form to fight."

"True," replied the voice of Lunaris. "But we do not have to fight. If that is your aim, you do realise that you *will* shortly cease to be? I merely wish to talk. But whilst we talk, I would like to see you. I would like to see how you see yourself. Of course, if you wish to fight, it would be wise to give in to my request, otherwise I shall continue to resist. By the time you face me, you will be on your knees. You *know* this..."

Mortis knew the truth of the Lurker's words. He was already drained from the exertion. He chose a form.

The headwind from the passageway abated immediately. He stepped forward warily, his old, bowed legs treading carefully. The Creature in the Dark could not be trusted. He was a murderer.

Mortis moved forward steadily, down the rough earthen corridor towards the red glow, the flowing, black, sackcloth robes shifting around his old, gnarled body. As he walked he leaned on the long, rough-hewn oak staff he carried in his right hand, using it to keep his balance. In his left hand he carried a clock, a simple wooden timepiece with a large white face that shone in the gloom, absorbing the red hue of the glow from up ahead. A brass pendulum swung from side to side, moving amongst the strands of his long grey beard. Its ticking was soothing, easing his apprehension at the rising sense of the impending doom he felt as he entered the chamber at the end of the passageway.

The chamber was a tomb. It was a simple, round room hacked out of the dirt. To each side a wall sconce held a torch, burning with a crimson flame that provided the flickering red glow. Directly ahead sat a simple stone sarcophagus. The lid leaned against it, the top carved with a simple sculpture of an old man in long, flowing robes, clutching a rough oak staff and a clock.

Mortis shuddered as he took in the form leaning nonchalantly against the stone coffin.

"I would greet you as 'my young friend', Mortis, but you seem to have taken the form of the owner of this sarcophagus," hissed Lunaris.

A smile played across blood red lips that barely concealed row upon row of razor sharp teeth and the forked tongue that flicked as he spoke. The face in which the mouth was set was slim and elegantly featured, the face of a beautiful mortal woman. The eyes were slit-pupiled and feline, but red as the light from the flames on the wall. The strange beauty of the face was offset by the complete lack of hair on the head, and the pointed, six-inch black horns that jutted forward from the forehead. Lunaris' torso and arms were also those of a slim naked female, although the nipples on the modest breasts had been sliced off and dripped blood down the flat stomach towards black-furred goat legs as he pushed away from the coffin and stood to his full height. Slender, clawed hands toyed with the stinger of a scorpion's tale that flickered around as if not under his control.

"How do I look?"

"As I expected the Creature in the Dark to appear," replied Mortis, moving forward to stand within a few feet of his foe, keeping his dark eyes trained on those of Lunaris. He could feel the raw power emanating from the Great Enemy, almost burning his skin like a flame.

"Oh please, Mortis, don't insult me. It was you and your kind that made me this, after all. If you hadn't stolen our existence, there would have been no need for this unpleasantness. Don't hate me because I didn't just fade away like the others."

"We get our power from the mortals, Lunaris, you of all should know this. I am a New God, and I know that it is their change of worship that altered the Astral Realm, not us."

"And you took it, no matter the consequence for me and my kind," spat Lunaris, his eyes flashing a brighter red as his anger peaked. Mortis could swear he felt his skin burning and peeling on his face and his grey beard singing to black wisps. It was as if Lunaris' power made him *mortal*. "I did what I had to do to survive. I suggest you and your kind accept that and leave me to my existence."

"Never!" Mortis lunged forward to strike the Great Enemy with his staff, jabbing forward towards the mouth of knives.

Lunaris didn't move a step. He raised one clawed hand, and suddenly Mortis was in a heap against the far wall. He sat prostate, shaking his head to clear the long grey hair from his face.

"Please don't make this unpleasant, Mortis. We must be able to reach some kind of understanding. Immortal life would be unbearable without the companionship of other gods. And in the spirit of understanding, please tell me, why did you choose such a boring form?"

3

Mortis reached over and grabbed his staff from where it had fallen, hauling himself upright and moving apprehensively back towards Lunaris.

"I am the God of Death. I shepherd the souls of the dead into my realm, to protect them from evils such as yourself. Death can be distressing for mortals. I adopt a form that minimises their discomfort and puts them at ease."

"But why?" pressed Lunaris.

Mortis paused for thought. "I don't understand your question."

"Why bother? They are just ants. They do not care for us. You've seen the result of their fickle beliefs. Why would you care for them? The ones who come to me are frightened at first, but they get used to it. Why make things easy for them, when they do not reciprocate?"

"Because we are gods. That is what we *should* do. They worship us, they give us our power, we should take care of them."

"Nonsense," snarled Lunaris, his eyes flashing red again. The heat on Mortis' face pulsed again, but seemed to be less powerful now. "They worship whether you coddle them or not. Until they tire of you, or choose a different god. I won't let that happen. I don't nurture them, I terrify them. *That* is the way to ensure they are loyal. And still they worship. They are praying now. Their world has become a frightening place, and they pray for me to make it stop."

"I feel their prayers," replied Mortis. He felt a slight rush of power flow up his spine, straightening his old bent back and shoulders. "More of them are dying, and as they die they pray for me to let their souls find solace. But why? Why are they dying?"

"Can't you see it?" asked Lunaris, the wicked smile returning to his face. "The Mortal World is at war. Armies move against armies. My demons roam the lands, summoned by my followers to spread fear and my word."

"You lie. We can only sense the Mortal World, and see through the cloud for an instant at a time. The barriers are too strong, we are too distant."

"I'm looking right now," smiled Lunaris. His eyes were glazed, staring somewhere over Mortis' shoulder. "They fear."

Mortis was about to scoff, but he hesitated. Maybe Lunaris was right. He *could* feel something... amiss. He closed his eyes, reached out with his mind. There were rifts, slashes in the ethereal plane. He focussed his mind, gritting his teeth.

He saw it.

He was watching from a hilltop, as two armies of mortal men clashed in the rain. Steel rang against steel, weapons hitting weapons, weapons hitting armour, weapons hitting bone with a crunch and flesh with a squelch. The mortals roared in anger, screamed in agony. Horses whinnied and fell in the mud, crushing their riders.

Then he was swooping down over the field, between the bodies writhing together in the mud, desperately trying to kill each other and not be killed. He felt their fear. He felt their prayers.

Before him was a noble, his retinue hemmed in at the centre of the field of battle. They were losing. A stray backswing from one of his own guards caught him across the face, smashing his ornate helm back into his nose. He stumbled to one knee, his arm across his face, blood flowing from beneath the chin strap. An enemy footman lunged forward with a spear, driving the point into the vulnerable spot at the groin of his plate armour. The noble screamed, splatting down into the mud as the opposing general shoved the spearman to one side, raising his sword in both hands.

Mortis felt the lord's prayers. He was calling out for salvation, for anything to stop the pain and the impending doom. The enemy general brought the sword down, severing his head and raising it aloft for all to see.

Mortis plucked his soul out and directed it to his realm, easing his passing. He felt a trickle of energy flow into him, a glow in his heart.

Then he was somewhere else. He didn't seem to be able to control the glimpses, they were given to him. The rifts were not made by him, they were made by the mortals and their prayers, as if when they reached bursting point the division between the planes split like a burst dam.

He was passing through a village, between the hovels and the animal troughs. There were no mortals around him, but he was not alone. Something was there. It was dark, malign, foreboding. He had felt the presence before, passing through the darkness of Lunaris' realm. It was a demon.

He looked down and saw them, the corpses. Dotted here and there, deep rents in their soft tissues and throats, as if they had been slain by a vicious animal. He moved past the corpse of a peasant woman, face down in the mud with her arms wrapped around a ball of rags. Mortis looked closer. It was a little girl, covered in mud and the blood flowing from her mother's torn body. He was quivering from terror and the cold, begging to be saved from this nightmare.

As he moved into the village square he could feel the residual prayers of the dead. They drifted above the corpses, cyan wisps of entreaties to Mortis to save their souls. They were slowly dissipating, merging into the Astral Realm, feeding his strength. He channelled the souls to rest. Once again he felt a rush of power through his form.

In the village square there was a small group of survivors, huddled together around the stone shrine that was the centre of the settlement. They cried out in fear, imploring the deity whose simple statue topped the stone plinth for respite from the nightmare. The statue was hewn rock many moons previously and had begun to lose its form, but he recognised it. He recognised the robes, the beard, the simple carving of a clock in his left hand.

One of the women screamed suddenly, jolting Mortis' view away from the shrine towards the shadows between the nearest hovels. He saw it as it moved out of the darkness, cloven hooves squelching through the mood as it stalked slowly towards the remaining villagers.

The demon. Its form was familiar. Its form was the same as that standing in the tomb with him beside the sarcophagus. A demon of Lunaris.

It bared its teeth and trotted towards the villagers, clicking its razor-sharp claws together, revelling in their screams for mercy.

Mortis had never been so close to the Mortal World. He wondered, could he…

He reached out his hand. It seemed immense in comparison to the creature. It made him realise his power, a god versus a demon. He grabbed the demon's head with all the power he could muster, squeezing, twisting, pulling.

The villagers covered their ears as its piercing scream rent the air, a chill wind blasting their cowering forms. He ripped its head clean off, crushed it to dust. It took a few more staggering steps before its body crashed into the mud, bubbling down into a primordial black goo that ate into the ground. Then there was nothing left but a dark, steaming puddle.

The rush of power was greater this time.

He was somewhere else. It was a different time. Time moved differently in the Mortal World to in the Astral Realm it seemed, sometimes grinding past as slowly as a glacier, sometimes flying by like a swift.

It was summer. The sun blazed down outside the temple in the town, streaming in through the stained-glass windows, but the glorious view was deceptive of the situation. The temple was packed with townsfolk. Some filled the pews, heads bowed in prayer. Others held their bodies against the barricaded doors as they shook from heavy blows on the other side. Something was outside, and it wanted to come in.

He floated over to the nearest window. As he did so the head of a Warhammer smashed through, sending shards of ornate glass and leadwork flying through his ethereal being. He looked beyond the weapon, out into the grounds of the temple.

They were filled with the dead. Not lying on the ground, but standing. They groaned and shuffled towards the temple, some bearing rusted weapons, some unarmed, but Mortis could sense all were consumed with maleficent intent. They ranged from skeletons clothed in battered armour or rotten rags, through semi-decomposed corpses, through to dead-eyed fresh corpses who were almost indiscernible from the living.

What is this abomination?

Then he saw the mortal at the rear of the assembled masses, clad in black robes and chanting as he drove the undead forward. His skin was pale, his eyes dark sunken hollows in this bony face. One of his eyes was white and blind, but the one that saw was focussed on the temple with bitter determination.

The doors shuddered again, and the head of an axe splintered through heavy black ebony. It struck again, chunks of wood flying amongst the men pressing against the entrance. One fell to his knees, screaming, clutching his eyes where the fragments had imbedded.

Mortis suddenly floated backwards, spinning to face the altar. Behind it against the back wall of the temple stood a ten-foot tall statue on ebony, much better preserved than the simple stone effigy from the village. It was him. On the altar lay the body of an old man in sackcloth black robes, immaculately kept apart from a jagged tear through which could be seen a sword wound to the heart. Townspeople knelt around the altar, as if imploring their only hope to somehow come back to life.

Could this man help them? Could Mortis help them? Surely he couldn't...

His eyes caught sight of a familiar figure. He recognised the boy from the village. He was a couple of years older now, no longer clad in mud stained rags but in similar robes to the old priest, although the hood was white rather than black. He was recounting the events of that day, of how Mortis had answered the villagers' prayers and smote the demon about to kill them.

The townsfolk began to shed their fear. He felt their prayers, he felt them swell within him.

He swooped towards the old man's body, kneeling astride it and breathing with all his might into the corpse's mouth.

And then he was pressed against the ceiling. He looked down as the old man twitched once, twice, thrice. His old, grey eyes opened and he drew in a long, rasping breath, coughing his way to sitting upright. Mortis felt a rush of strength as the mortals' thanks gravitated up towards him.

The old priest regained his feet as the great doors to the temple finally gave in, the townsfolk scattering before the undead horde as they clambered into the building. The old man reached out a hand for his staff, and the boy handed him the smooth, six-foot rod of ebony.

Mortis looked down as the townspeople parted like waves split by the hull of a speeding ship, split by the arrowhead of the undead heading directly for the priest. At their rear, the necromancer strode into the temple, his eye trained on the only threat before him, eager to slay him again.

The priest extended an arm towards the oncoming horde, slamming the ebony staff on the marble floor. A faint, purple wave of light flashed out along the ground from the impact, and Mortis felt a rush of power leave his form and flow with it. As it reached them, the front wave of the undead collapsed to the ground. As their trapped souls found release he felt the power flow back into him, the malignance leaving them as they escaped the control of the necromancer. An extra rush took him as the townsfolk took hope, dropping to their knees in thanks for their salvation.

The priest slammed the staff down again, and more of the undead shook free their tethers. Mortis felt the same recycling of energy, but he also felt something else. The priest was only a mortal, and he was tiring. There were many more undead, and already the staff shook as his weakened body leaned on it for support.

The necromancer arched his body back, purple wisps of energy gathering in his claw-like hand, and snapped forward, throwing a ball of malignant ire at the priest. Mortis snapped his hand down, slapping it back at the sorcerer. It hit him full pelt, knocking him onto his arse.

Some of the undead broke free of his bond. They were still trapped in the Mortal World, but they regained their old feelings, their old sense of right and wrong. They began to fight amongst themselves, some attacking those that were still rapt by the necromancer's evil control, some fighting to escape the temple and flee.

Mortis reached down and cupped his hand reassuringly on the scalp of the priest. The trembling left the mortal for a moment as he brought his staff down a third time, the heaviest blow yet. As he did so Mortis channelled his strength through him, caressing his fragile human frame, directing the flow of power, shielding his mortal state, using him as a conduit for the immense magical energy of a god.

The purple tide along the floor lapped forward relentlessly, releasing the undead from their tie to the Mortal World. He sent them to the next life in peace, the bound and unbound alike, feasting on their gratitude. The flow did not stop, and as it reached the necromancer he was thrown up into the air and pinned against the wall of the temple. He went limp, overwhelmed by the power of Mortis channelled through the priest. The youth in the black acolyte's robes snatched up one of the undead's rusted daggers and slit the necromancer's throat as he hung, pinned to the wall.

Mortis searched for the necromancer's soul, but it was not there to be absorbed. He had gone to another god...

Mortis pulled away. He was back in the crypt, face-to-face with Lunaris. Things were happening in the Mortal World, things that gave him power. He felt it, coursing through his mind. If it was fear he had felt before, it was gone. He could do this.

"I see it," he said.

Lunaris sneered. "I told you. You don't even know the power you possess. You are like a baby."

6

"But how? We have only ever been able to see glimpses of the mortals, at times of great prayer. How is it possible to see such detail? To influence the Mortal World?"

"When they pray hard, when the power builds up, sometimes there is a rift. Not just a slit for you to peer through, a gash that you can project through. You can't actually *go* there, but you can influence events. It just takes a burst of magical energy to tear the fabric. And I've made it happen..."

"How?" demanded Mortis. He needed answers, but he also needed to think. How could he defeat this creature? How did you kill a god? He felt the power now, but how did he harness it?

"The mortals fear, and they pray. I have created such suffering, such terror, such war. You saw the demons. They are causing chaos and division. And the humans do the rest, slaying each other over this trifling affair or that."

"You can't just send demons into the Mortal World."

"No, no," smiled Lunaris. He was enjoying this, enjoying educating the child. "The mortals summoned them. I whispered to them, guided them, and they summoned the creatures themselves. Unbelievable, aren't they? Orchestrating their own pain..."

"We can't talk to the mortals. They can't handle our thoughts, our voices. It crushes them."

"You aren't talking to them in the right way, Mortis. You can send a thought, a word, an idea. Drops of influence, slowly saturating their minds as they pray. Too much and they are driven mad, of course, or worse. But then I've done that too. Insane mortals, sewing discord and summoning demons. The being next to you collapsing to the ground dead as they pray, smoke billowing from their nostrils. It all adds to the effect."

"You're a monster..."

"Isn't that what you call me?" snarled Lunaris. "Monster? Creature? Lurker? You and your kind made me this way as much as the mortals with their fickle beliefs. Now I tire of this talk. I am willing to teach you, to teach you all, but you must cease this ridiculous action against me."

"And if I refuse your offer?" asked Mortis. His confidence was growing. The Lurker didn't seem as dangerous any more. His outline was thinning, become less defined in the flickering red glow. Mortis could feel the faith of his mortal followers growing as they overcame the evil stalking their realm.

"You see this coffin?" Lunaris' clawed fingers clicked across the lid as he ran his hand along the carving of the old man. "It is yours. If you persist, it will be your last resting place. You know you don't have the power to defeat me."

Mortis looked into the sarcophagus. Within was a blackness unlike that outside. This dark was pulling, not just oppressive but crushing. Lunaris had done something here, something Mortis did not understand. The sarcophagus contained doom.

Mortis looked down at the clock in his hand. The hands clicked backwards slowly. He smiled, focussing his mind. The hands moved faster, back towards midnight.

"But I do," he said. "Do you see this clock, Lunaris? It symbolises a mortal's life. It ticks backwards, slowly, as their days pass, until it reaches midnight. Until they die. Sometimes, things happen that speed up the movement of the hands, events that unfold in a mortal's life. Sometimes the hands snap round to midnight in an instant."

Mortis reached down with his wizened old finger and pushed the hands, driving them closer to midnight, stopping a minute away.

"What is this nonsense?" snapped Lunaris. His voice faltered slightly, the confidence draining from his demeanour. He felt it too, Mortis knew. He felt his power ebbing.

"This is your clock," smiled Mortis, tossing it into the sarcophagus where it disappeared into the gloom. "And your time is up."

"Your clock doesn't affect me."

"But it does," roared Mortis, a flash of light lancing out in all directions from his body before reforming round him as a dull white glow. The red torches sputtered and died. "It matters because I *believe* that it matters, and because I am stronger than you..."

Lunaris shook his head in defiance, but his eyes were wide with dawning realisation. Mortis was in control now. His glance turned desperately to the coffin, his eyes peering into gloom.

"No!" he screamed, clambering onto the rim of the sarcophagus, reaching inside, his hands searching for the clock.

Mortis didn't seem to move. He was just suddenly there, right behind Lunaris. He shoved with all his power and the Lurker disappeared into the coffin. His screams and curses struggled to reach Mortis, as if even the sound of his voice was being sucked back into the darkness. Mortis lifted the heavy lid with one hand and slammed it down, blocking the sound completely.

He turned and ran. He was filled with the euphoria of power, rushing through him as he absorbed it from the very fabric of Lunaris' realm. As he moved down the passageway out of the burial mound the light around him became blinding, leading his way out into the open. He dropped his staff and slammed his hands out to either side, imbedding them into the earthen walls as if they were hot coals pushed into butter. As he ran he left deep gauges in the walls, causing the passageway to collapse behind him.

And then he was out in the open. The light from his being flashed outwards one last time, illuminating the realm for an instant. Lunaris' demons crumbled to dust as the light touched them, leaving those of his allies to shield their eyes against the glare. Then it was gone. The realm of Lunaris was still dark, but not the all-consuming blackness of before.

Mortis fell to his knees as the barrow collapsed inwards on itself behind him.

It was done.

That was then...

Chapter One

She watched as the acolyte crawled on his hands and knees in the filth, drawing the chunk of chalk along the stone of the sewer floor. As he finished the star inside the circle that completed the pentagram he pushed himself to his feet, allowing the long sleeves of his flowing purple robes to drop down around his hands so he could use them to attempt to wipe the dirt from his knees and hands.

She shook her head beneath the hood of her own enveloping purple robes.

"Is it not bad enough that you've sullied your sacred garments enough around the knees? Why also dirty the sleeves?" she chided.

"I'm sorry, magister," replied the youth. "It's just... the filth... why a sewer?"

She didn't like it any more than he did. The smell from the effluent channel flowing beside them was so bad she could almost taste it inside the hood of her robes, and it wasn't even a quarter full. The rituals she had performed in her time as a magister were very often distasteful, but this sewerage was, to her mind, worse.

"Nobody comes down here. At least nobody without a very good reason. And the ritual you are honoured to be studying today is not one that is viewed favourably by the uninitiated."

"What about the cleaning crews? And the ratters?" asked the acolyte.

He asked pertinent questions. He was one of the more able acolytes of the sect. He was clumsy and lacked decorum, but his mastery of the lessons she had taught him already was impressive. At such a young age, his knowledge of the arcane lore books was immense. He was good. Maybe a little too good...

"Our companions will ensure we are not disturbed," she snapped. "Do you think it is right to question my preparations?"

"No, magister," he replied quickly, bowing his head low. He was aware of her lack of tolerance for even implied criticism, and was eager to avoid her ire. "I am sorry."

"Why is it that you apologise so often, acolyte?"

"I..." the boy hesitated, his head still bowed in deference. He shuffled his feet. "It is... er... it is polite when wrong to..."

"I did not ask why you apologise when you are wrong. I asked why you apologise so often."

"I... er..."

"Apology is a weakness. If you are constantly apologising, it shows you are lacking. You apologise so often because you make mistakes so often. So stop making them."

She didn't know why she was bothering to continue teaching him given the current circumstances. She supposed it was out of habit. The sect was so short of new blood, she felt that she spent every second of her day attempting to guide them in the right direction. It had become a habit.

The acolyte was talking. He was just standing, shuffling, head down. This made the decision she had already made easier. He was bright, but he wasn't suitable. He was too timid. He was afraid.

"Is the pentagram complete, acolyte?" she asked, more softly this time.

"Yes, magister."

She moved forward to inspect the sigil. She was a graceful mover, but the robes flowing down to the floor made it seem as if she glided along the stone. The acolyte looked up from beneath his hood, admiring her splendour. Even in a sewer, with her entire body and head enveloped by robes, she oozed beauty.

"What is this?" she asked abruptly, a leather sandaled toe protruding from the hem of the garment, pointing to a small scuff in the perimeter of the pentagram's circle.

"It is... err..."

"It is a gap in the pentagram, acolyte. A gap caused by your clumsy knee."

"I'm sorry magis..."

She reached out like lightning and cuffed him around the back of the head.

"You are apologising *again*, acolyte," she snapped. "Stop... making... mistakes. Especially ones with potentially dire consequences. What would this break mean?"

He was shuffling again. She wanted to reach out and strike him in the face, but she was becoming impatient. At this rate they would be here all night. She couldn't see his face beneath the hood, but she knew his eyes were rolled back in his head, regurgitating the writings of the ancient tomes he had studied by candlelight deep into the night.

"The entity that we summon, should it have malignant intent, would not be contained within the pentagram and could, should it wish, cause us harm, magister."

"It *will* have malignant intent. It *will* wish. And it *will* cause us harm," she snapped. He was not suitable. He read the lore, he memorised it by rote, but he did not read between the lines or question its teachings.

"But the tomes state…"

"How many summonings have you conducted, acolyte?" she hissed. She hit him again, harder, right across the ear. She spoke through the ringing she knew he would be hearing. "When you drag a creature from the Astral Realm to the Mortal World at your behest, it will be angry. It will be angry that you have put a sigil around it, seeking to control it. And it will be even more angry when it sees that the mere mortal that has pulled it forth has failed to even draw a line with a piece of chalk."

The acolyte was sobbing under the hood. She could sense it. He opened his mouth to apologise, then thought better of it.

"Repair your mistake," she said, softening again. As he knelt down to drag the chalk over the gap in the pentagram she moved over to a black jute sack they had left on the cleanest piece of ground they could find. She reached inside and pulled out seven small candlesticks and seven stubby black candles.

"It is done, magister," uttered the acolyte as she returned to the pentagram. She inspected the chalk, made sure it was unbroken.

"Don't mutter, acolyte. It makes you seem at worst like a petulant child, or at the very least weak. Strength of character is everything within our order, and with the entities that we consort. Place the salt. And do it properly."

The acolyte produced a pouch of salt from within the sleeve of his robes and slowly began to pour it, forming a line around the perimeter of the chalk pentagram. As he worked, the magister slotted each of the seven candles onto the spikes of the candlesticks and placed them on the ground. Then she stood and waited for him to finish. He was taking forever about it, obviously trying to make up for previous errors.

No, not suitable at all. Why couldn't he work quickly and *accurately?*

He finished pouring the salt.

"Are we ready?" she asked.

He hesitated, walking around the pentagram twice, stooped peering at the ring of salt. She sighed audibly.

"Yes, magister, it is done," he replied, stowing the pouch back inside the sleeve of his robe.

She walked around the pentagram quickly, eyes peering out from under the hood for weaknesses. As she completed the circuit and stood by his side, the acolyte flinched visibly.

Weak. He should know *it is right.*

"Good. Now, place the candles."

He worked quicker on this one, grabbing the candles from the floor and placing one at each corner of the pentagram star. He picked up the remaining two candles and stood, staring out from beneath his hood at the symbol.

"What is it?" she asked, her voice soothing.

"These two candles. I… I don't think I need them."

"Are you asking me, or telling me?" she asked, eyeing the youth keenly.

He shuffled his feet, then his confidence returned. His posture became more confident. She was impressed with him for a second.

"I don't need these two. The pentagram is complete."

He didn't flinch this time as she slid up beside him. She was impressed.

"Correct. Put them in the sack and bring the rest of the ritual items."

The acolyte scurried off, his confidence returned.

Too little, too late.

He returned carrying the contents of the sack, five collections of bones each wrapped in black cloth, and a blank piece of parchment. She took the latter from his hands.

"Place the ritual items on the pentagram and unwrap them," she said. As he did so, she pulled a quill and ink pot from the sleeves of her robes and wrote on the parchment in flowing, ancient script.

"It is done, magister."

She looked up. Just inside each candle at the points of the pentagram, the acolyte had placed and unwrapped the bones. Laying on the black cloth at each point was a tiny skull and rib cage, two piles of arm bones and two sets of leg bones.

"What are these bones acolyte?"

"They…" He hesitated. She sensed him taking a deep gulp in his throat. "They appear to be the bones of a child."

"Close," she replied, gliding round the pentagram as she spoke, checking the final setup. "They are the bones of an unborn child."

"But… why…?" asked the acolyte. She sensed another deep gulp, this time she suspected holding off the urge to vomit.

Weak.

"Our demon will want them. Do you know what type of creature would want these?"

The acolyte's hood shook. He was trying to regain his composure. She gave him credit, for such a frightened little thing he was doing as good a job as she had come to expect from him.

"I do not know," he said. "I am not given access to those lore books yet. I know that each god's demons require different ritual items for summoning, but not what totems."

"There are *no* gods," she spat. "There are different types of demons, but no gods. Understand that. *We* are the gods. So, what type of demon will this offering summon?"

"I… I do not know."

"Good," replied the magister, calming as she returned to the acolyte's side. "You are not afraid to admit your lack of knowledge. Hubris is a good trait in an acolyte. That is why you are not yet privy to the offerings required to summon an entity. Otherwise you might be tempted to try it without the correct control and attention to detail. The ritual items are gifts. To bring a demon into the Mortal World, you must tempt it, give it something. Our particular demon will want these offerings. An unborn child cannot pray, and therefore the power of its soul has not been claimed. It will want this."

"I understand."

He did. She felt it. He didn't like it, the very thought made him want to retch, but he understood. That was not enough to succeed in the Order.

She reached forward and took his hand gently. He enjoyed her touch, she knew that. He had seen her without her hood, and she felt his lust. She saw it in his eyes when she led study with him. He thought she wasn't looking across from her desk back at the Order, but she didn't need to look, his longing for her was tangible to someone with her mastery of the world around her.

She placed the parchment into his hand.

"Put it in the centre of the pentagram," she whispered.

The acolyte looked over his shoulder at the sigil, reluctant to leave her touch. She let go, urging him onwards.

He stepped carefully into the pentagram, lifting his robes to avoid damaging the symbol. He placed the parchment down gently. As his eyes took in the name written there they widened. He looked over his shoulder at her.

Idiot.

He was back at her side, quick but careful.

"But magister," he said. "This is a demon of the god…"

Her hand lashed out, fast and hard this time. Her slender hand shook free of the long robe sleeve as she struck, the heavy amethyst rings that adorned her fingers adding to the pain of the blow. The acolyte stood there, quivering. She knew beneath the hood his split lip was bleeding down his chin.

"*We* are the gods. Did I not tell you that only minutes ago?" Her tone softened, and she reached up, her slim hand reaching inside his hood and caressing his young face. "And I have told you of the need for secrecy in our order. I am impressed that you know the names of the demons so well. Your learning is a credit to you. But I know the demon that I am summoning. And you know it too, thanks to your learning. So why would you speak something that does not need to be spoken? Our enemies listen everywhere. We are despised. *Never* say what does not need to be said."

"I understand, magister." His voice was mumbling, which annoyed her. He was fighting back tears, which also annoyed her. But there was no need to hurt him further.

She pulled him closer, into her body. One hand on his cheek, she used her other to pull his bottom forward, pressing him against her. She felt his manhood swell against her hip. She didn't need him much longer, it was only fair to give him some happiness.

"I need to feel the magic in you," she whispered, pulling his ear close, pressing his cheek against hers. "You won't ready this in your textbooks. I have learnt this through countless summonings. Some demons like to feel magic. Not just the magic of power, but the magic of mortal binding..."

"Magister, do you mean...?"

She pushed her face under his hood and kissed him, pressing her cold lips against his. His penis bulged further as he pressed against her, sliding his thin hands around her tight buttocks. Her hand moved round from his rear, sliding up past his ground and up his chest. She pulled back her robe, revealing her pert left breast.

"Light the candles," she whispered.

She felt him close his eyes. His body tensed slightly against hers as he concentrated, pulling the magical energy from the ethereal plane into this one. A slight purple mist hissed around them as the five candles at the points of the pentagram burst into flame. She could feel the magic flowing through him, pumping in his heart.

Her hand slid the ceremonial dagger from the sheath beneath her left armpit. She flicked it in her fingers and plunged it up beneath her sternum into the acolyte's heart. He stiffened, his grip on her rump tightening and then releasing as he breathed his last breath and his body went limp. As he fell she pulled him forward so as not to damage the pentagram, guiding him down onto the ground on his back.

The magister leaned forward quickly, the razor-sharp dagger still embedded in his chest moving as she did so, slicing through flesh and arteries to carve out the heart. She pulled it forth triumphantly in a spray of black arterial blood, the slippery muscle writhing in her hands as she tossed it into the centre of the pentagram.

She stooped over and kissed the acolyte's corpse on the forehead. She didn't have to, it wasn't part of the ritual, but she did feel for him. It wasn't his fault he didn't have what it took. At least this way his service meant something.

She had let him light the candles. It wasn't always necessary to have a sacrifice to summon a demon, but the more you gave them the better proceedings tended to go. In her experience, a heart still laden with magical energy served best.

And besides, even the smallest use of magic took its toll on the human body and mind. It wasn't so bad for the clerics, who asked for the power they sought from the gods. Those, like her, who *took* it, they felt the effects more. Her hand pulled her robe back over breast and then paused for a moment over her abdomen. Yes, she knew the toll magic use could take...

The magister shook her head, bringing her concentration back to the moment.

She took up her position at the head of the pentagram, checking once more to make sure everything was in place and undisturbed. Then she opened her mouth and spoke the Words of Summoning, her usually lilting voice coming out as an unearthly deep rasp in the Demon Speech. As she spoke her eyes glazed over, purple energy running into them like iodine drops spreading in a vial of water. The power flowed through her, coursing down her spine to her feet. Her heart pumped hard, aching with the strain.

Tendrils of purple light flicked out from her feet, rolling across the floor and coalescing at the centre of the pentagram around the acolyte's heart. Crackles spat out, licking against the ritual items at the pentagram's corners. As the energy built within her the crackles became solid links, joining the bones into a star with the heart at the centre.

She roared the final word in the Demon Speech. The power rushed from her as the heart and skeletal parts in the pentagram exploded in a bright flash, throwing liquid and fragments in all directions. The dark blood and bone fragments hung in the air at the edges of the pentagram as though they had been hurled against glass.

It was done. She could feel it, there in the pentagram. The magister held her concentration, the purple glaze over her eyes fading back to just a haze in the vitreous humor. The pentagram was good, it was holding the demon, but it still required her fortitude to back it up.

She saw it. A malignant grey cloud of smoke, vaguely coalescing and shifting into the form of a human. Its eyes were the only feature, black slits in the grey.

"You are brave, mortal," came the croaking voice. "Brave, or foolish."

It was using its own language rather than the Demon Speech. It underestimated her. That was good.

"I am neither," she replied, choosing her words carefully. She had been told by the Order how this must play out. The creature needed to listen and heed her words, and it would not do so if it was vitriolic towards her. "I merely wish an audience with the most powerful of demons."

12

The croaking laugh echoed round the sewer chamber. It was like old boards in a house creaking under the weight of heavy feet.

"Flattery," said the demon. "Why do mortals always think that flattery will save them. You a right, I *am* powerful. And yet you seek to contain me with your chalk and salt and pathetic will."

An arm coalesced and slammed out from the figure as it threw itself towards her. It smashed into the invisible wall, cyan flashing across its surface. As it pulled away, she saw it. Her heart sank for a second. There was a crack, a punched impact mark in the barrier with hairline cyan marks spreading from the centre.

"You can't contain me, it seems. You have made a mistake, mortal. You will get your audience, but I don't think it will run as intended..."

The form moved back to lunge again.

"Halt," she roared, summoning all her strength of will. The demon felt it, paused for a second. "Read the parchment."

The form pulled inwards into a ball, the heard reforming peering towards the scroll on the floor at the centre of the pentagram. The slitted eyes pored over the script for a second. She felt a shift in the demon's mood.

"I know your name," she said as the demon reformed, standing upright again. "I have not used it, for a do not wish to cause you discomfort. I think you know I have the power to use it if needed."

"That is very... magnanimous..."

"It is right to give you the respect you deserve," she said, trying to hide the relief flowing through her body. She kept her mind focussed. She had to be alert. The demon was cowed, but that made it more dangerous. It knew that if it was to strike, it would have to be with brutal force. "I have a proposition for you."

"Indeed?" rasped the demon. It moved closer again, right up against the barrier, the eyes locking onto hers. "Come closer. *Whisper* it to me..."

The magister took half a step forward involuntarily before she could stop herself. She stiffened, shaking her head to get the creature out of her mind.

"No," she said, taking the half pace back. "I don't wish to have my head ripped from my shoulders. I will speak from here, if you would be so kind as to listen. It would be beneficial for all concerned."

"Fine."

"You have the ear of the gods. I would be most grateful if you would take our proposal to one of them."

The demon paused. It merely stared, trying to reach into her soul again, trying to use her like a puppet. It just wanted her close, another foot or so. Within reach. One punch through the barrier and *snap*...

It wasn't working. The mortal was too strong.

"Speak, mortal. I will carry your message, should I like what I hear. But know this; if you summon me to this cloying reality again, I will tear off your limbs before I devour your soul..."

"That is most gracious of you," said the magister, making sure to push any sarcasm from her tone. "I think you will like what you hear..."

The god moved across the barren landscape quickly, with purpose. There was no form, no gender, just a grey cloud, vaguely humanoid with black slits for eyes. It did not wish to be recognised, not if it was found here. It would be... difficult to explain.

It paused on a hill, looking all around it, ensuring it was not followed.

The landscape around was barren, the ground a grey dust that swirled around in the occasional, light breeze. The sky was dark, not black enough to absorb all light, but dull enough to make one peer in the gloom to see. It was predominantly flat, which helped when looking for any unexpected companions, as long as you could sense into the night.

No. No demons. No deities. Nothing.

It had not been here since the battle against the Lurker. None of them had.

Times had changed since then. Back in their formative years, they had all joined as one to fight the Creature in the Dark and his minions.

Over time, they had realised that they did not all share the same values. Destroying Lunaris had brought them together. After all, he had killed one of their number, and that could not be tolerated. But

13

in the following eons they had discovered that a God of the Poor could not abide a God of Wealth, that a Goddess of Healing was diametrically opposed to a Goddess of Blood and Murder. They had formed two factions, the Light Gods and the Dark.

In hindsight, it didn't know whether this was a true enmity, or just the way it had to be. It had been so long, that was just how it *was*. None of them could really claim that they cared enough about the mortals to hate those who represented the opposite of everything for which they themselves stood. Did gods care? If they did, it was hard to care so much when the view of the Mortal World was so hazy, so distant.

Maybe it was just simple practicality. After all, prayers to a god who stood for murder and death robbed power from a god representing peace and mercy. That was the way of things. Maybe it was just about survival.

And there had been no more wars in the Astral Realm. There was one thing that they all agreed upon; any god who slew another would be destroyed as a usurper.

The god moved on from the hilltop. Where was it? It was around here somewhere. The scene of the final battle, where Mortis had destroyed Lunaris. The last time a god was slain.

Perhaps it wasn't the gods who had made the factions. Perhaps the mortals had, their hatred of the deity that opposed their own flowing up through their prayers into the very beings of the gods themselves. Maybe the gods weren't the players, but the chess pieces. Maybe, for all their power, the gods were the controlled, not the controlling.

It certainly felt that way when some unseen mortal ripped the power from you to heal this person or smite that one. The worshippers weren't so bad, they asked for it. You could give it, or did not give it. *That* was being a god. The ungodless stole it like a rapist, taking with no gratitude or higher purpose.

That was why the god was here, looking for the site of the final battle. The demon had come to him with the proposition, and it had liked what it had heard. Maybe what Lunaris had said to Mortis was right. The mortals were fickle, aloof, unaware of the repercussions of their inconsistent worship. They were certainly ungrateful, disrespectful. The view of the Mortal World was so cloudy because they did not worship enough.

Maybe it was time to change that.

Maybe it was time to teach them where the power lay.

The god felt it before it saw it. A sense of doom. And as it looked upon the collapsed barrow, it also felt *him*.

Lunaris.

It was true. They had all been there when Mortis emerged from the tomb. As he collapsed to his knees they had run to him, cradled him in their arms, helped him to his feet. The conquering hero. It was only now, after hearing the demon's liaison with the mortals, that the god had started to question...

Why did Mortis need helping to his feet? When Lunaris destroyed Termos, he absorbed all that god's power...

Why did Mortis not control Lunaris' realm? Why was it still here? Not as dark, but still dim, dangerous. Not what it once was, but also not part of Mortis' domain. When Lunaris slew Termos, he had taken the God of Fear's realm and added it to his own...

The demon had spoken to the mortal. There were people who still worshipped Lunaris. Not many, but some. Their prayers would send power to the Astral Realm.

Why did Mortis not have the power sent to the God of Fear? Because Mortis didn't kill the Lurker...

It made sense. The god was, inside, disgusted that it had taken a mortal to point this out. The god had reached out, and sure enough still *felt* the Creature in the Darkness. Not in the wisps of the plane, like the Old Gods. He was still here. Weak, entombed, defeated, but still here. And now, standing beside the collapsed entrance to the barrow, it felt his presence.

It was simple, really. Back then in the dawn of their time, the New Gods didn't understand their own power. Mortis had said himself that he didn't know how he defeated Lunaris. He just knew that he had power, that it was growing, and that it was what he *wanted*.

But now the gods understood their power. They had had eons to play with it, shape it, learn to be a deity. And yet still, it seemed, they were learning.

The god concentrated for a second and the ground opened up, the passageway beneath pulling apart with a hiss like the throat of a mortal choked almost to the point of death and then released, gasping for breath.

14

The god moved inside. It could sense the Great Enemy. Not strong, not overbearing, just there. The god strode down the corridor, not fearful and apprehensive like Mortis all that time ago, confident and strong. It was powerful, and it knew it. Lunaris was weak, barely existing; a shade.

The grey cloud moved into the antechamber, causing the torches on the wall to burst into bright, cyan flame. It didn't need to approach to throw the lid from the stone sarcophagus, shattering it to fragments against the wall of the tomb.

It felt the Lurker now. Not a sense of power, just a weak little creature without a barrier between them.

Lunaris crawled from the coffin and collapsed on the floor of the tomb, gasping for breath like a strangled mortal. No, less than a strangled mortal. Like a fish, flapping on the floor by the river after being plucked out and tossed aside to die.

The Great Enemy was pathetic; a simple, thin, black humanoid form, the eyes plain pink slits instead of his beloved blood red. The god knelt beside him, the grey cloud tightening into a similar plain human form. A simple wooden chalice was gripped within both hands, pressed up towards Lunaris' lips. The Lurker drank deep, thirsty for the contents.

"Thank you," gasped Lunaris between gulps, the thin black arm drawing across his mouth to wipe it clean before pulling in for more.

"Oh, I wouldn't be so quick to thank me..."

Lunaris paused, the pink eyes now wide as he stared up over the goblet that he grasped with both skeletal, black hands.

The god moved like lightning, manacles of bright gold appearing in his hands as he clapped them shut around Lunaris' wrists. He worked quickly, slapping the ankles of the Great Enemy in chains as Lunaris threw down the cup, writhing against the bonds.

"I'm not here to free you, Creature, just place you in a different kind of bondage," sneered the god as it drifted away down the passage. "You weren't destroyed, so your power wasn't stolen. Those chains will give me your prayers. Don't worry, I'll use them well..."

As the god stepped out from the entrance to the tomb it collapsed again in its wake, drowning out the wailing of Lunaris as he felt the power of mortal prayer being sucked through him into his jailer.

The god looked around at Lunaris' realm. Yes, it was changing. It was becoming lighter.

Much better...

Chapter Two

Cecil Cramwall lay back nonchalantly in the chair beside the bed in the brothel room, watching the pasty white rump of his friend pressing between the legs of the whore. It wasn't a pretty sight, but then that wasn't the kind of thing that turned Cecil on. He liked women. He liked sex with women. Hence, he had fucked the prostitute first.

And he liked watching people have sex. He just didn't like the naked man part of it.

He took a sip of his wine from the gold goblet by his side. Good, Barralegnan red wine. Couldn't grow decent grapes like this in Castland, the weather was too shit...

He had brought the goblet with him of course. Brothels didn't serve in decent cups, they were liable to be teeming with disease and certainly not as beautiful. They also didn't serve decent wine, so he'd brought his own as well. He drained the goblet and held it out for his manservant to fill from the wineskin by his side.

"Thank you, Q'thell."

He spoke well. Of course he did, he was the son of the Lord Chancellor of Castland. One had to talk well. It was one of the things that separated one from the commoners, from the whores. Just because you fucked them it didn't mean you had to exist like them.

Cecil pondered his last thought as he readjusted his sated cock and balls as he sat naked. It was one of his strengths, his intelligence, his detailed analysis. It was one of the things that had eased his passage through the University of Regalla. That was why he and Toby Princetown were out celebrating. Graduating from the capital's university was something that eighteen-year-old heirs to lordships should do in style.

Perhaps he did envy the commoners' existence, in a way. Not the poverty and disease and lack of power, of course. But their freedom. They could act how they wanted, nobody was watching them. At least nobody who mattered. Or maybe people were watching, but the people who were watching didn't matter. And maybe the people who were watching who mattered didn't care...

He took another swig from his refilled goblet and looked back to Toby's arse. Obviously he wasn't watching Toby's arse, that would make him a homosexual. He was looking at the thighs wrapped *around* Toby's arse, at the buxom blonde he was riding.

She was beautiful, Cecil realised. Not just the long blonde hair. Not just the full red lips that formed in fake pleasure as she looked over at him whilst fucking his friend. Not just the dark brown eyes that stared into his as Toby humped away, squinting and eyeing him seductively.

It was here figure. Her breasts were large but firm. Her hips were ample but not childbearing. Her waist was naturally thin, not strapped in with whalebone and leather. Her thighs and calves were womanly but not chubby, muscle showing from gripping a man round the rump like a woman was supposed to do.

You didn't get this in the circles they moved in. A woman was meant to be comely but not exercised. Who in their circles would want a woman like this, formed from exercise of the basest kind? Formed from the exercise you *wanted* a woman for. It was a terrible conundrum.

Do you want to end up married off to a woman who looks like this but fucks for a living, or a woman who looks like shit but has never been fucked...?

Her skin was pale though. Not as pale as Toby's; he was as pasty as Cecil expected a vampire would look, but she had no colour. That was the problem. Common women were always covered up, working in one way or another or stuck inside. At least noble women had time to sit in the sun of Castland's summer and take in what was available, even if it was behind a screen held by handmaidens.

The girl squeezed her eyes at him as she shrieked another fake orgasm. Cecil was becoming annoyed. It had been endearing whilst she was writhing beneath him as he sawed his penis in and out of her, but now it was becoming irksome. The squelching as Toby stirred Cecil's porridge was also becoming more than a little sickening.

"I can love you both, sirs," she gasped. "I could keep you both happy. Take me home, make me your woman slave. Keep me in nice dresses and fine jewellery. Promise me... Oh fuck *yes*..."

She was staring into Toby's eyes now. Cecil had had enough. He stood up, draining his goblet and walking to retrieve his clothes.

"I can promise that I will be the last man to have sewn his seed in your cunt, my dear," he sneered, pulling on his undergarments. "Q'thell..."

Cecil's manservant slid forward again from the shadows. He was tall, six and a half feet, and moved with silent grace, like a panther. Well, Cecil had never seen a panther from the deserts of Altanya, far to the south, but he knew of them. Q'thell moved like a prowling like a cat, and a panther was a big cat. A big, black cat.

Q'thell was a Q'shari, so the black cat analogy fitted well. His skin was as black as the dead of night, his limbs long and slender. Cecil wouldn't say thin. He knew that beneath the dark brown leather armour in which he was clad Q'thell's muscles were knotted and hard as wire. The only parts of Q'thell that didn't suck the light from the room were his eyes, feline red slits in his face, no pupil, just red ellipses. And his teeth, when he chose to bare them; pearly white with slightly accentuated canines.

The Q'shari weren't human, despite the similarities. They were rare now in the world, so Cecil didn't know whether they all looked like Q'thell. Maybe some had different coloured eyes. Perhaps their skin was lighter. Perhaps it came in all different shades.

Cecil knew one thing. Q'thell was the deadliest being he had ever encountered. That was why he was not just Cecil's manservant, he was his protector. Cecil moved in the highest circles at court, amongst the fat lords who let others do the dirty business of war, amongst the knights who were skilled in combat, amongst the grizzled generals who had cut their teeth in the mud and blood of the battlefield. Q'thell made them all uneasy. They knew he was a predator.

There was a fencing sword and a parrying dagger at his belt, but Q'thell didn't reach for either. Under each armpit was sheathed a razor sharp, lightly-curved dagger, the hilt of each carved from the bone of some woodland creature he had obviously slain at some point. His left hand slid one silently out and slid it across the prostitute's throat.

The screaming became gurgling. Blood pumped up across Toby's face, causing him to spit and stop humping whilst he cleaned his eyes.

"Fucking hell, Cecil," he moaned. "What in the name of the gods did you do that for?"

"She was becoming tiresome," yawned Cecil, pulling on his breeches and shirt, fiddling with the buttons. "Pray you never bore me. Q'thell, sort this mess with the owner of the establishment. Finish up if you want Toby, you sick bastard. We need to get out on the town. There's more wine to be drunk."

Q'thell wiped his dagger clean on the bedsheets and replaced it in its sheath. As he turned to slide from the room, the squelching resumed as Toby continued where he had left off...

How had it come to this? he thought as he strode into the brothel corridor, heading for the stairs down to the main room.

He was a warrior, a deadly weapon from the noble Q'shari race. And yet here he was, babysitting this human pup and slitting the throats of prostitute women.

Q'thell was sure that Sanguis wouldn't mind. She was the Goddess of Blood, the Murderess. He knew that any killing would help sate her lust and glorify her name, but still, this all felt so... dull.

He ran his hand across his shaven black head, taking the steps down gracefully two at a time. He would like to grow his jet-black hair into one of the traditional styles of the Q'shari, perhaps the mohawk again, but Cecil disapproved. It wasn't becoming of a servant of the Cramwall family.

Humans. Short-lived vermin.

The pay was good, he couldn't deny that. It allowed him to purchase the best quality food and drink, when he wasn't dining at the expense of the Cramwalls and their noble friends, and his heightened senses meant that, unlike them, he appreciated it.

He could buy good leathers, the best available, even if they were made by humans. Inelegant, ugly, but practical. It wasn't like he could make his own in the Q'shari style, his path had been that of the warrior, not the artisan.

He also had a nice collection of weapons in his room at the Lord Chancellor's keep. They were running into the more exotic now; morning stars, flails, warhammers, battleaxes, halberds, a trident. Of course, like the armour they were rough, ugly, brutish. But he loved weapons. He never fought with them, but he practiced, learnt how to use them. It thrilled him, mastering another weapon. Feeling the different grip, figuring out the best way to hold it, to thrust or swing or parry. Listening to the sound it made as it moved through the air, as it struck a wooden or padded dummy.

Q'thell longed to know how they sounded striking a human body, but he would never get the chance. They were too ugly to use in battle, and in any case he hadn't seen a proper fight in years now. And you couldn't really carry them around the street waiting for this pair of brats to tire of a whore...

He didn't really need the money of course. His people were those of the wilderness, they lived in the forests and the hills and the mountains. If he chose, he could walk straight out of the door right now and leave the city, wander into the woodland and live comfortably. Hunt his own food, build his own shelter. As he strode into the main room of the brothel he looked past the grubby bar, past the dirty sofas, the gnarled tables, the whores and the lowlife men they serviced, towards the door...

He shook his head. No, he couldn't live like his people. It was too boring. He needed a purpose, something more than living amongst the trees. This wasn't much, but it was better than nothing. At least he was a part of something.

That was why he was a worshipper of Sanguis. The Q'shari were split in their beliefs, some following his path, most that of Faunis, the God of Nature. They still lived as one. They had to, for their own survival. Since the coming of the humans, the Q'shari had waned as a race, retreating further and further into the wilds to avoid contact with this new, aggressive upstart race. The Q'shari lived long lives. They were proficient warriors, skilled craftsmen and far better equipped in the ways of magic. They knew it, they understood it, and it did not take its toll on them in the same way as it did on humans. They did not get ill. They did not anger easily, or fight amongst themselves.

And yet, Q'thell suspected that this was why they were in decline. They were too passive. They retreated from humans, further into the wilderness, keeping themselves to themselves. Their pace of life was too slow. Their *makeup* was too slow. A Q'shari woman would carry a babe in the womb for three years. These humans bred like rabbits, and neither plague nor famine nor war seemed to cull them.

It was one of the reasons he had left. Not the main reason, but one...

He was Bloodkin, a worshipper of Sanguis. He favoured action, not passivity. And so he had left, to find something, to find purpose. He had found this...

Q'thell stood at the counter and banged his slender fist on the bar. The brothel keeper looked up at him, annoyance on his ugly, wart-covered face. He was a stocky enough man, carrying too much around the gut but still dangerous. Q'thell looked him up and down, even though he didn't need to. He had already sized him up on the way into the establishment. He reckoned he could put him down without weapons in around three seconds. He was too slow, carrying too much weight.

The brothel keeper shook his head and returned to whatever he was doing, fiddling around beneath the bar. He was muttering to himself now.

"Don't make me bang on this bar again," hissed Q'thell. His voice was low, soft, threatening in a non-threatening sort of way.

The brothel keeper hauled himself up onto his feet and tramped over, the nostrils in his flat, bent nose flaring. "What was that?"

"You heard me," snapped Q'thell. "Lose the bluster. The whores you beat might be frightened of you, but I'm not."

The man stared into the red eyes and lost some of his bluster. He was doing well to maintain a defiant air, Q'thell noted, but it was fading. He obviously hadn't seen a Q'shari before, and he could sense that this one was not to be trifled with.

"My companions have had a little incident upstairs," continued Q'thell, reaching to the pouch on his belt and pulling out a couple of gold coins. The brothel keeper's eyes widened in his fat face. "Your whore attacked one of them. I've dealt with it."

He tossed the two coins onto the bar. The fat hands enveloped them. Interesting. He was quite quick when gold was involved...

"Don't worry," slavered the brothel keeper. He was checking the gold coins between what teeth he had left. "I'll beat her black and blue. Fucking slut, attacking good customers."

Q'thell wasn't looking at him now. He was watching as Cecil and Toby swaggered into the main room, swilling yet more wine. Toby hadn't even washed the blood from his face.

"If you enjoy beating corpses then feel free," sneered Q'thell, catching the wineskin that Cecil tossed at him and gesturing for Toby to wipe his face. "Personally, I'd just get someone to clean that mess up."

"You fucking *killed* her?" snarled the brothel keeper. His nostrils were flaring again. Q'thell could sense it. "That's more than two fucking gold coins. Fuck that. These cunts can afford it."

"They can," replied Q'thell, watching as the two fops reached the door and waited for him. "But that's all you're getting."

"Fuck you. There's more gold in that purse. I seen..."

Q'thell's hand shot out without looking. The man's face was fat, but his fingers were long enough to clamp either side of it, digging into the temples like a vice. Q'thell turned, pulling the brother keeper forward across the bar on his tiptoes, pushing his face close and burning into him with squinting red eyes.

"How much will you see if I pluck out those beady little eyes of yours with my bare hands?" he hissed.

The man was almost limp now, beginning to sob, fat hands pulling at Q'thell's wrist, feeling the iron tensed sinews of the Q'shari.

"I would suggest you watch your mouth in future."

Q'thell let go and strode towards the door. The brothel keeper collapsed to his knees, leaning on the bar and clutching his hands to his throbbing temples.

Not three seconds. Two seconds. Maybe less...

The trio left the brothel, stepping out into the early evening streets of Castland's slum quarter. Toby was still rubbing the blood from his face. He had let it sit for too long, it had become stubborn.

"It fucking stinks around here," spat Cecil, swilling wine from his goblet. The gold was drawing attention from the locals, and Q'thell was acutely aware of this. He was also acutely aware of the stench from the sewer channel in the middle of the street, more so than the human whelps who had insisted on coming here. "How do these pigs live like this?"

Q'thell shook his head. This was going to be a long night.

"Come on, Toby," yelled Cecil, throwing the dregs of his goblet in the face of a passing common woman and tossing it to Q'thell. "The night is young and Regalla is our oyster..."

Chapter Three

Rage. That's what the demon was feeling. Rage.

Fucking mortals!

It was here, in this shit hole plane *again*. This was becoming tiresome.

It snarled, looking around quickly, searching for the culprit, black slits peering from the formless grey cloud of its body. It paused, realising with annoyance it was sat prostate on the stone cellar floor. You couldn't tell from the shapelessness of its body, but that didn't matter. It was a matter of dignity.

The demon heaved itself upwards, coalescing into the vague form of a man.

Heavy. It felt so heavy.

Why was the Mortal World so cumbersome? It stymied the demon's movements, making it feel slow and clumsy. The inside of its mind felt fuzzy. It resumed its search, peering into the gloom of the dimly lit cellar. Where was she, that fucking human cunt?

She had been summoning it, despite being warned. But she was strong. She resisted its attempts to shred her mind, to pull her within its grasp. She would slip up eventually, and then... snap...

It wasn't her, though. The demon saw the old man standing a few feet away. It assumed it was an old man. It was stooped and leaned on a staff for support. It was hard to tell. These mortals were always swathed in those fucking robes.

A different mortal. Who the fuck do they think they are?

It was in no mood for talking, for threats. It shook its head once to clear the haze, gathered its strength and flew forward against the pressure of the Mortal World, throwing itself at the barrier.

There wasn't one!

It roared forward, reaching out for the human. It paused, staying its outstretched grey paw inches from the old man's face. It looked around it.

No pentagram. Was this poor fool insane?

It pressed its face close to the old man, a gaping black maw filled with jagged razor teeth forming in the visage.

"I'm going to enjoy this, fool..."

The mortal was trembling now, struggling to contain his composure. And his bladder, from the sound of trickling piss on the stone floor.

"Wait, please." The demon was right, it was the voice of an old man. An old man who was feeling the extent of his mortality even more than on a usual day. "Your master... I was told you would not harm me. I was told that you would know why you were here."

The demon paused, pulling its hand back and clutching at its face. The mortal was right, there was something there. The shock of the summoning had blanked its mind, but it was coming back now. He had been told not to harm the mortal.

Fuck. Will I ever get to rend a human soul? Fuck.

"There, you do remember. Oh, thank the gods."

"Quiet," snapped the demon, probing at its temples. "I'm trying to think. Who are you, anyway, mortal?"

"I am..."

"Shut up. I don't care. Let me concentrate."

It was coming to the forefront now, coalescing in its mind. Yes, that was it.

At last. I will get to rend some souls...

The demon lunged at the old man, grabbing his throat and lifting him clean off his feet, the staff clattering to the floor. The piss was really flowing now, a dark river on the stone slabs.

"Maybe I'll start with you," it roared, letting out a crackling, maleficent laugh.

The old man was scrabbling at the solid smoke gripping his neck, choking for air and for words.

"I suppose I've waited long enough. I can wait a little longer."

Best not piss off the master.

These deities could be pretty vengeful, and at some point the demon would no doubt be back in the Astral Realm...

It dropped the old man, snorting derisively as his old bones clattered onto the floor, desperately clambering away in its wake. As it strode towards the steps out of the cellar its body began to solidify, taking shape. It knew just the form for this task.

This is going to be rapturous...

Charo stared up at the stars, trying to take his mind off the freezing cold night. They were beautiful up here in the hills, but he would rather he couldn't see them in all honesty. A crystal-clear sky meant one thing; it was ice cold.

He was sat on a sheepskin throw leaned against one of the long, uneven stone walls that marked the boundaries of their field. Well, not their field, the field that he and his older brother Mathias watched over for the landowner. The sheep were currently grazing the field furthest from the farm, high up in the hills, and it sloped steeply down from the tallest brow. The sheep didn't mind the incline, but it was murder on his ankles and knees. Still, it was work. It paid their way since their father had left them, and that was all a couple of lowborn youths could hope for in the bleak lands of north-west Castland.

Charo pulled the other two sheepskins up around his neck, desperately trying to keep the cold out. It wasn't working, the aching chill spread up through the fleece on the ground and into his back from the stone wall.

It was almost time for the next check anyway. The field was huge, it would take him an hour to zigzag across it checking on the sheep. He may as well start now, keep himself warm by moving.

He checked his sling was in his belt and grabbed his pouch of rocks, tying them beside it. He didn't know why he bothered, he couldn't hit a barn with it, never mind a wolf. Mathias could knock pans off a washing line at fifty yards. He was better at these things, better at everything really. Charo hoped someday to grow into a man like his brother, but he suspected that at sixteen already it wasn't going to turn out that way. He felt he would always be a burden...

He shook his head. Couldn't think like that. It upset Mathias when Charo spoke of it, even when he thought it. His brother seemed to be able to tell. Maybe it was the distant look in Charo's dark brown eyes as he stared into space, wondering how much better off Mathias would be if his little brother had never been born.

Charo checked the simple knife was tucked into his belt. It was a simple bone knife. He had whittled it out of sheep bone once when the landowner had paid them with a whole carcass instead of coin. He doubted it would be any use against anything, but it gave him some comfort.

He reached for his crook and used it to haul himself to his feet. He hated the thing. He was slight of build and below average height, and leaning on the hooked staff made him look and feel like an old man. Still, it was a necessity, helping keep sure feet on the uneven slope in the dark. He grabbed the three sheepskins and crept over to the stone shelter in which Mathias was sleeping through Charo's shift at the watch.

He peered inside, placing two of the fleeces carefully inside, out of the cold. Mathias was snoring softly under a pile of blankets. They didn't look alike for brothers. Mathias' blond hair and green eyes contrasted sharply with Charo's dark features. Sometimes Mathias joked that Charo wasn't his brother but an urchin he had found on the streets and adopted.

Charo smiled at the thought. Mathias. Always teasing but always there, always looking after him, gently guiding him on the road to manhood, filling the role of both older brother and father.

He pulled the fleece he had kept up over his head, wrapping it round his shoulders and upper body for warmth and moving quietly away from the shelter to start his check.

Charo always followed the same route. It was good to have a routine, to know where you were heading in the dark of the night. It took him a while each time the sheep moved fields to remember his chosen path round the new field, but they had been here for a week now so he knew where he was heading. Their shelter was halfway up the eastern boundary of the field, near the stile into the next. They had built them like that on purpose, it meant that each one could be used to cover two leas. No point in building more shelters than necessary. It had been Mathias' idea.

He headed up across the field first, towards the north-west corner. Most of the sheep congregated in the middle here for some reason during the night, which made it easier to keep an eye on them. It also meant he warmed up with the haul up the hill. From there he would head across the north perimeter. That was the greatest threat area, as the land beyond the brow of the hill was wild. The other side of the hill was untamed forest, and any unwelcome guests would likely come from there.

Next, he would cross the lea downhill from north-east to south-west. It meant he would be checking the beasts again, and at least moving with the land. He liked to think that was easier, but in actual fact the steep incline pulled at his thighs as he moved. He always did that bit slowly, leaning back against the gradient on his crook, making sure to keep a good footing.

He would then head back up to the shelter, passing the sheep a final time.

It was lucky the stars and moon were out tonight. He didn't have a torch. Oil was expensive, and they didn't have much coin left until they were next paid. If it was pitch dark out here tonight he would be stumbling around trying not to break his neck.

Charo knew that wouldn't happen, though. Mathias always had oil stored away, frugally saved up in case of an emergency. If it had come to it, his older brother would have done the trip without light so that Charo could have a torch with the last of the oil.

He smiled.

One day I'll make you proud, Mathias. One day I'll repay your love. One day I'll be able to look after you.

Charo made good time on the climb. He needed to, just to get some warmth into his freezing young bones. He moved amongst the dozing sheep, taking care not to stand on any of them. The landowner was not an unkind man, for a noble, but he wouldn't take kindly to any of his livestock being damaged. Mathias had once told him that this opportunity had only arisen because the previous shepherds had injured several sheep when driving them from one field to another and the landowner had had them run out of the village. Maybe that was just to make sure Charo didn't fall asleep on his watch, though...

He left the sleeping flock behind him, heading up into the night. He reached the north-west corner of the field quickly, pausing to rest at the wall. He leaned his crook against it and pulled some jerky from his belt pouch, chewing on it to warm his face with the motion. He blew on his hands, rubbing them together futilely against the cold. It was even worse up here, almost at the brow of the hill.

Charo stared at the brow of the hill, moving his gaze out past it and up at the full moon. It glowed in the black, speckled velvet of the night sky, a perfect white disc pouring out more light than all the stars combined.

What is it? he wondered.

Mathias told him that in the old days, before science, men had worshipped the moon as a god. Charo could see why. In the dark of night it was the light, a hole in the sky through which the daylight poured even at the darkest hour, until the hole ripped open and the morning brought back safety from the blackness. Men had grown out of favour with the idea of the Moon God, though. After all, it made no sense. What about the phases of the moon. It shrank and grew throughout the month, sometimes giving a basking reassurance in the fear of the dark, sometimes just showing a crack of daylight to cling to.

Charo had grown out the idea of gods at all. He didn't know whether he had even believed in the first place. He certainly didn't feel the need to worship them even if they did exist.

Why would he? What had they given him? His mother had died giving him life. His father had left he and Mathias when he was barely four years old. He vaguely remembered him. A drunkard and a wastrel. The only good thing in his life was Mathias, and Charo was just a burden on him.

Curse the gods.

A wolf howled in the distance. The shrill cry carried on the still air from over the brow of the hill, sending a chill down Charo's spine. It was a long way off, no threat. He felt himself glance up again at the full moon, panic beginning to niggle at the base of his skull. Mathias said there were no werewolves, that they had been wiped out hundreds of years ago by the priests of Guerro, the God of War.

A sudden gust of chill wind blew across him, causing him to grit his teeth against the cold.

Time to move on.

He moved along the northern border wall, steadying himself with his crook in his right hand and the wall on his left. He didn't want to be up here any longer. He was so far from Mathias, even in the still night he doubted his voice would carry to his brother in the shelter, certainly not loud enough to wake him. Charo contemplated leaving his usual route and just heading back down to the shelter, but fought against it. He couldn't let Mathias down, he had to finish his patrol. It was his last before Mathias' shift, he could crawl beneath the blankets in the shelter in less than an hour.

Then he noticed it. The mist.

It had come on without him noticing, sudden and swirling, making his vision fuzzy. The light of the moon and stars above had become hazy, his range of vision all around closing in. It didn't feel... natural. It was a cold mist, not humid, just pulling in around him, close and malignant.

It didn't make sense. He paused, clinging to the wall, making sure he had his bearings. Why in the dead of night? Why so cold?

He looked upwards again. The stars were gone now, the view a few feet above his head being just a blur of light. Around and below him his vision was blurred, he could only see a few feet, if that. Was this

his mind playing tricks on him? Was he just desperate for sleep? Had the cold got into his head and his eyes?

Charo was breathing rapidly now. He was panicking. The air chilled his lungs, making his chest ache. He crouched down, suddenly desperate for air.

He could feel it. There was something out there, something malignant. A noise carried on the air, a snort of breath, a snarl.

A werewolf!

He could feel it. He steeled himself, gathering all his courage, and peered up over the rough stone wall. The fog cleared for a second, giving him a glimpse of the brow of the hill, before reforming as thick as before.

Nothing. There was nothing there.

He sighed, trying to slow his breathing.

Calm yourself. Keep the wall to your left. The ground is sloping down, away from it. You're on the north wall. Follow it to the corner, then follow the wall down the hill. Get back to the shelter.

Charo gathered himself, crawled forward along the wall. Slowly, carefully, he pulled himself to his feet, moving as fast as he could through the fog. He had to get back, get away from this horror. He was trying to keep it subdued, keep his mouth from opening and whimpering out a yelping scream. There *was* something there, he wasn't imagining it. He couldn't see it, but it was there.

A scream split the air, tearing at his ears.

A primal, animalistic scream. A shriek of pure terror. The top stones of the wall beside him fell on him as something slammed into his side, snorting deep bestial breaths into his face. He felt its face close to his cheek, puffing warm moist air onto his cheek. The scream came again, right in his ear.

Charo fought the fear that was paralysing him. He dropped the crook and pulled the bone knife from his belt. He grabbed the head behind him, his thin fingers clasping around a thin animal snout. The fur was thin, short, smooth. He turned and went to lunge at the neck.

It was a deer.

Its head was bleeding from where it had hit the top of the wall full pelt, head first. It was struggling to scramble over the crumbling wall, screaming in fear. Its massive brown eyes met his, wide with desperation.

Charo dropped the knife. Summoning all his strength he reached under the beast, pulling it over the wall towards him. It clambered over him, staggering on the slope and rolling down the hill behind. As it regained its feet and stumbled down the hill the screams followed it into the thick mist.

He still felt the dread. It was eating at him now, clutching his heart, making it hard to breathe, hard to think. He pulled himself back up to his knees, staring into the fog over the damaged wall. This time it didn't clear. He was staring wide-eyed into the haze, into the nothingness.

A deep, malignant, throated growl tore through the night.

Charo shuffled backwards, feet flailing to try and get some purpose in the grass. Suddenly he was rolling head over heels down the hill, struggling to reach out and stop himself before he gained too much momentum. He bounced once, twice, three times, coming to a halt amongst some rocks. He gasped for breath, the cold air filling his winded lungs.

No time to stop. He had to get away.

He staggered to his feet and clambered down the hill as fast as he could, trying to keep his balance. He fell a couple of times, grazing his hands and knees as he descended from the mist. The night air was clearing as he spied the shelter in the distance.

"Mathias," he yelled with all the force he could muster. He ran up to the doorway and doubled up, gasping for breath. "Mathias."

The mop of blond hair stirred as his brother dragged himself from his sleep, looking up at Charo as the lad pulled air into his lungs on all fours. The sheepskin had gone, but he didn't feel the cold. His blood was pumping, thumping in his head, and sweat poured off him.

"What in the name of the gods are you doing, Charo?" he asked, kicking off the blankets and reaching for a flask of water. "Here, calm down. Drink."

Charo gulped at the water, coughing as the cold liquid hit his throat. He wiped his mouth on his sleeve, struggling to speak.

"There's something up there. A werewolf."

"A werewolf?" Mathias smiled gently. He pulled one of the fleeces from by the entrance to the shelter and hung it round Charo's shuddering shoulders. "Did someone fall asleep on the watch and have a nightmare?"

"No." Charo shook his head hard, making it spin. "No, I swear. It was at the north wall. It chased a deer into the wall."

Mathias cocked his head to one side, looking deep into his brother's brown eyes. Something had obviously scared the wits out of him, for sure. Werewolf or not, Charo was terrified.

"I'll go and have a look. The north wall, you say?"

"No, Mathias, stay here. I don't want you to go."

Mathias was already pushing the sling into his belt. He stooped in the low shelter, leaving his crook but grabbing the old iron sword he kept for protection. It was notched and rusted in places, but it had been all they could afford. He pulled the other spare fleece up over his head and shoulders.

"Charo, I have to go and take a look. Whatever it is that's got you all shaken up like this, we can't have it attacking the sheep now, can we?"

Charo knew Mathias was right. Suddenly the image of the previous shepherds being run out of the village crossed his mind.

"I know," nodded Charo, gulping deeply. "I'll come with you."

"Are you sure? Are you up to it?"

Charo nodded. He hurt all over. He knew underneath he was covered in grazes, and by tomorrow he would be black and blue, but he had to help Mathias. He had to be a man.

"Ok, let's go." Mathias ruffled his younger brother's thick, dark hair and headed out into the night.

Charo followed, eyes wide as he searched the night for the danger. He had his sling out, for what good it would do, a stone slipped into the belt. The fog had gone, and as they trudged up the steep hill he began to feel less wary.

There are no werewolves, he thought. *Mathias told me. Maybe it was just a normal wolf. Maybe I just imagined it.*

He was tired. *Very* tired. Maybe his mind had just played tricks on him.

There was no mist at the summit of the hill either. It didn't take long for Charo to lead them to the break in the wall. Mathias reached out and touched his arm, gesturing for him to wait.

"I'll take a look. You've got your sling ready, yes?"

Charo nodded.

"Good. Keep an eye out. Four swings and let fly, like I showed you. Don't take your eye off your target. Move and follow through with your whole body, shoulders down to waist down to feet. Yes?"

Charo nodded again. He wasn't confident.

Mathias moved forward slowly, the short sword raised in both hands. He didn't believe in werewolves, but something had scared Charo half to death, and there *was* a break in the wall. Maybe it was just a normal wolf or something else that had spooked the deer. Maybe it was poachers. But Charo hadn't imagined it.

He reached the wall, crouching down for a steady footing. He peered at the brow of the hill, searching for any sign of movement in the moonlight. Nothing. He spotted Charo's knife and crook by his feet.

"I don't see anything," he whispered. "Come on up here and get your things."

Charo obeyed. He had already spotted the fleece he had lost and tossed it over him for an extra layer of warmth. He slotted the knife into his belt and retrieved his crook.

"Right, keep watch while I just check for tracks."

"You're not going over there?" hissed Charo, shaking his head, eyes widening again.

"Charo, I'm just going to look for tracks. If something else has come through we need to be ready. You understand that?"

Charo nodded again. Mathias was right. He was always right.

"I'll only be a minute, and you can see me. I won't go more than a few yards."

Mathias clambered over the wall, stooping low to the ground as he searched for spoor. He moved quickly but warily, one eye flitting at the brow of the hill. He didn't want to be caught off guard if there was anything out here.

Charo watched, searching for any sign of movement. He was trembling again, the fear was rising in him again.

Mathias clambered back over the wall.

24

"Nothing, just the deer tracks."

"But there was something there," insisted Charo. "There was this fog, the thickest I've ever seen. And there was a growl."

"I believe you, Charo," smiled Mathias, cupping his brother's chin reassuringly. "But only the deer came close to the wall. You know how noise travels up here, especially on a still night. That noise could have come from far away. At least we know nothing else is in the field, yes?"

Charo nodded.

"Right, let's just stone up this wall quickly. We can fix it properly in the daylight. Then we'll check on the sheep and you can get some sleep, eh?"

They worked quickly. The rocks were freezing to touch, and the biting cold was back with Charo now that the excitement was over. With the wall patched, they headed back down the hill towards the centre of the field, checking on the flock.

"They're all here," said Charo after a quick count. "We won't get run out of the village."

Mathias smiled.

"We've even got an extra guest."

He gestured to the deer. It was nestled in amongst the sheep. Its ears were still pricked up as it looked around, eyes wide, trembling, but it was calmer than when Charo had first encountered it.

"We'd best let the baronet know in the morning," said Mathias. "It doesn't look harmed, but even so, they all belong to the king. We don't want to get accused of poaching."

"How do you know all this?" asked Charo, staring admiringly at Mathias.

"Life, little brother," replied Mathias. "Life. Now, let's get you back settled. You need some sleep…"

Chapter Four

It was too bright in here.

The Lord Chancellor's reception room in the Cramwall palace of Regalla only had a few tall, thin, crystal windows, but even so, it was too bright.

It was a shame, because Lord Drathlax would have liked to take in the splendour in comfort. His senses were at their peak at night. Oliver Cramwall would know that. This early morning appointment was almost an insult.

Maybe I'm just being overly sensitive. It's this blasted light.

Drathlax looked around him, squinting.

It was an opulent setting. He wanted to reach out and run his thin, pale hands along the sumptuous purple velvet of the curtains. Trace his nails along the smooth, polished oak of the tables. The blood red leather of the seats and sofas longed to be squeezed. The crimson would have excited him more if he hadn't fed last night...

And yet this light just bored into his skull like an awl through his eyes.

The intense smell of the sandalwood burning in the hearth stroked his nasal passages, but he couldn't appreciate it. The gold inlay on the wooden throne on which Cramwall sat glistered in the morning light through the windows, but not in a way that he could appreciate, more in a way that burnt his soul.

Drathlax was a Vampire Lord. There were still several of them scattered across the land, their estates usually high in the mountains where residences and settlements could be built in the shadow of the peaks. In a more comfortable environment.

The daylight wasn't dangerous as such. It burned. It was uncomfortable. But he could use the powers given to their kind by Sanguis' Gift to stave off the graver effects of the sunlight. Only a severely weakened or naked vampire would be harmed by sunlight alone. Even so, he was swathed in a flowing black cloak into which he could withdraw his hands, and sported a black, broad-brimmed hat.

No need to put yourself through unnecessary discomfort.

"Lord Drathlax," greeted the Lord Chancellor. "It is an honour to host you."

Not so much of an honour that you would stand up, meatbag.

Drathlax stepped forward and took a seat opposite Cramwall, smiling insincerely, fangs glinting in the morning light through the window. He winced.

"It is an honour to be here, Lord Chancellor."

"Leave us," said Cramwall, waving away the guard who had escorted the vampire in. As he strode from the room, the Lord Chancellor leaned in conspiratorially. "I'm sure we don't want the uneducated listening in on our conversations. They wouldn't understand."

"I'm sure even the educated amongst your people would not understand," replied Drathlax. "To business, if you would, Lord Chancellor. I find this setting... uncomfortable."

"Quite," replied Cramwall, gesturing to a carafe on the desk between them. "Wine?"

"Did it come from a vein?"

Cramwall laughed uncomfortably.

"Then, as I said, to business," replied Drathlax.

"As you wish. I have had complaints, my lord. It would appear that a village in the north has met an unfortunate end. A village under the protection of Lord Princetown of Snowgate. A village on the border with Lord Perlis, one of your own..."

"And you wish for me to ask Lord Perlis for assistance in dealing with the problem?"

"Alas, I fear Lord Perlis is the cause of the problem. The nature of the villagers' deaths seems to bear the, how should I say, hallmarks of your kind. And there are ferals running around in the forest. Lord Princetown has had to commit troops to hunt them down."

"I fail to see why I am here. Why have you not summoned Lord Perlis?"

"Well, my lord. You have always seemed a good contact with your people. You seem more reasonable, more of a leader amongst them."

"We have no leaders, Lord Chancellor," replied Drathlax, reaching out and pouring a goblet of wine from the carafe. He could still taste the metallic blood from last night's kill in his gums. The wine might draw it out a little. If he could savour it properly in this vile light. "We have a council, and I am but one member."

"Of course," replied Cramwall. The Lord Chancellor could sense the vampire's annoyance, was putting all of his diplomatic mind into his words. "Then perhaps you could plead our case to the Council? After all, we do have agreements with yourselves regarding this kind of activity. Deals that are mutually beneficial."

"We haven't seen many exiles of late, Lord Chancellor. A deal for cattle in exchange for not preying on your lands is not mutually beneficial if our people starve."

"I cannot be held to blame for the lack of exiles, my lord. That is, unless you count my strong control of crime in my country as guilt, in which case I fully accept that charge."

"Then may I suggest that you extend the scope of crimes for which exile is a punishment?" asked Drathlax. He was trying to be reasonable here, but the ruddy-faced, chubby little human was beginning to rile him. Vampires were not quick to anger, and Drathlax himself was famed for his immense self-control, but suggestions that his people should starve rather than upset their neighbours was beginning to grate on him.

Do we not have a right to live?

"I can look into that, my lord. An excellent suggestion. Anything that will bring an amicable continuance of our cohabitation. After all, war would be in none of our interests..."

"Is that a threat?"

Cramwall swore that red flashed in the vampire's dark eyes. His thin, exquisite features seemed for a second like those of a wild animal, snarling and hungry.

"No, my lord," he insisted. "Merely a statement of fact. We have lived together in harmony for centuries. You must remember, until Sanguis blessed your houses with the Gift, you were amongst the oldest and most revered families in Castland."

"Until?" asked Drathlax, raising an eyebrow. "Were? I was under the impression we are still noble houses in Castland. Just... different."

"Indeed you are, my lord." Cramwall could feel the tension in the vampire's voice receding. He was back in control. "I chose my words poorly, and for that I apologise. I just do not want any of us to jeopardise what we have. Nobody wants to be responsible for our mutual destruction. I will look into what you have suggested, if you would be so gracious as to raise my concerns with lord Perlis and the council?"

Drathlax smiled. The food was right. They both knew it. Sometimes, though, it was important to remind the human lords how unwise it would be for them to try to purge the remaining Gifted from the land.

"Thank you, Lord Chancellor. As always, your common sense prevails over my own. I will talk to the council. Please send Lord Perlis' apologies to Lord Princetown."

"I will, my lord. I will draft the law changes as soon as is practicable. After all, our friends must be supplied with fresh meat. It has always been the way."

Drathlax stood, shielding his eyes from the light through the windows. It was getting more painful by the minute.

"You are most gracious, Lord Chancellor. Now, by your leave, I will head back to my lodgings. As I am sure you can appreciate, this light is not helping my complexion."

"Of course, my lord. Will you be joining us this evening at the banquet? I trust you received the invitation?"

"I shall indeed, Lord Chancellor. The evening is much more my scene."

"Good news, my lord. We shall drink your health."

"Thank you. I promise that I will not try to drink yours..."

Drathlax smiled, turning with a swirl of his cloak and striding towards the door.

Time to get out of this light...

It was too bright in here.

Everywhere was too light.

Cecil Cramwall had the hangover from hell. His head swam, apart from when he moved, when it thumped like a drum. He swore each time his heart beat it echoed in his brain.

He didn't remember much of last night, which meant it must have been good. Toby was beside him as they approached the door to his father's reception chamber, swaying like a sapling in a storm. Cecil swore the lanky white-skinned fop looked even paler than normal, which was saying something. He looked like the fucking moon.

Cecil sniggered at the image of Toby radiating white rays out into the night.

"What?" asked Toby, starting to chuckle too. "What?"

"Fuck off, Toby," Cecil laughed. It was possible they were still very drunk. *Why the fuck would father call us here this early? Today of all days?*

Cecil swiped the flask of water that Q'thell was carrying, taking a huge swig and offering it to Toby.

Toby gagged, retching up watery red wine vomit all over the guard at the door's boot. The man didn't flinch, his eyes only slightly turning down towards the mess cascading from the young noble's mouth.

Cecil guffawed. Q'thell shook his head.

"Oh, gods," gasped Toby, wiping his mouth on the guard's tabard. Red vomit drool hung in strings from the Cramwall colours the sentry wore. "Don't just stand there, fool, clean up this fucking mess."

The guard stood, this time visibly uncomfortable. His eyes looked from Toby to Cecil, back and forth, looking for direction.

"Didn't you hear me...?"

Cecil smacked Toby right across the ear. Toby clasped the side of his head, soulless black shark eyes staring at Cecil.

"Don't tell him what to do," snapped Cecil. Raising his hand again. Toby flinched. "He is a soldier, and he is a soldier in the employ of *my* family. He does not work for you. He doesn't clean up your vomit. And he certainly doesn't clean your vomit off *my* family colours. Know your place, Toby, for fuck's sake."

The guard stood to attention, looking uncomfortable.

Toby crouched, covering his head in case there were further blows, ungainly and cowed.

Cecil panted, looking around for further signs of disrespect, his jowly face flushed at the cheeks. Blue eyes pierced out from black, hungover eye sockets, filled with pompous rage.

Q'thell leaned against the wall, a broad smile on his black lips. This was fucking hilarious. He was eager to see what happened next, what the whelps did. Would Toby fight back. Would he try to take his embarrassment out on the guard? Would he puke again?

"What are you smirking at?" snapped Cecil.

"I am a Q'shari," shrugged Q'thell. "I am a savage, remember. I find inappropriate things amusing. You don't pay me for my etiquette."

Cecil paused for a second before bursting out laughing.

"Wine, savage," he sniggered, grabbing the skin that Q'thell handed him and taking a deep swig. Maybe this would sort out his hangover. "Guard, get a servant to clean up this mess. And get them to clean you up while they're at it."

"Yes, my lord." The relief in the soldier's voice was evident. He bowed quickly and scuttled off.

"Come on, fool," smiled Cecil, grabbing Toby round the shoulders and kicking open the doors to the reception room.

A tall, thin apparition met them as they moved toward the doors he had booted open. A pair of dark, cold eyes met Cecil's, blazing out from beneath a wide-brimmed black hat. The face was white as a sheet, even paler than Toby's. Cecil always thought his friend looked like a vampire. Now he knew that he was wrong. A shiver went up his spine, chilling the humour of recent events instantly out of him.

"Are we not knocking any more, Cecil?" roared Oliver Cramwall, up on his feet now behind the desk at the far end of the reception chamber. "Lord Drathlax, my apologies."

"My lord," nodded the vampire, tipping his hat.

Cecil nodded, paralysed.

Q'thell took in the vampire, nodded. Drathlax nodded back, gliding out of the room.

The scene seemed to freeze into an uncomfortable silence. Cecil stood, still feeling the departed Vampire Lord's gaze in the back of his head. Toby swayed, looking from Cecil to the Lord Chancellor, whose face was turning purple with rage. Q'thell looked from human to human to human, taking in the situation with bemusement. He stepped back and closed the doors quietly.

"You're on the wrong side of those doors," snapped the Lord Chancellor. "Cecil, get your creature to wait outside."

Cecil opened his mouth to speak, but Q'thell was already moving. He pulled open one of the huge doors and slid outside, closing it silently behind him.

"Get up here now!" snapped Oliver Cramwall, thumping back down into his throne.

Cecil approached his father's desk, taking the seat left vacant by the Vampire Lord. He could swear it was ice cold on his buttocks and his back. Toby stood beside him, concentrating on standing up straight. He wasn't doing the greatest job of it.

"Are you both still drunk?" snapped the Lord Chancellor.

Toby shook his head so hard it must have made his head spin.

"A little," smiled Cecil. "We are celebrating our graduation, after all, father."

"Maybe you are celebrating a little too much if it causes you to forget simple etiquette, Cecil. You are my son, but you still knock before entering my audience chamber. And you, Toby. You are not my son. Remember that."

"Yes, Lord Chancellor," mumbled Toby, the black pits of his eyes falling to the floor, his head bowed submissively.

"I attend very important people in this chamber," continued Cramwall. "Much that we speak of is of the greatest importance and is private. Perhaps it is time for you both to take an interest in these affairs and the running of the realm. After all, in time you will succeed me, Cecil. And you will follow your father as the Lord of Snowgate, Toby."

"Yes, Lord Chancellor," repeated Toby. Cecil looked up at him. His friend was doing his best, but he was either going to vomit again or collapse. Or both. This would be amusing...

"Toby, pull up a chair," said Cramwall, his voice softening. "Before you fall down."

Toby hurriedly took the Lord Chancellor up on his offer, dragging a chair to Cecil's side and dropping into it with as much decorum as he could manage.

"What were you discussing with the vampire, may I ask?" enquired Cecil. His father had calmed down, and although he didn't want to set him off again, he was curious.

"Lord Drathlax, Cecil. Please, remember your manners."

"Manners?" asked Cecil. "He is a vampire, an animal."

"This, my son, is a prime example of why you are here. To learn. You need to understand the way of the world, and how the realm is kept together. The Vampire Lords are not animals, they are merely... different. All of us in this room can draw of family line back and it will connect with one or more of them. They are nobles of Castland, even if they have at some point been given the Gift of Sanguis."

"Doesn't that depend on your idea of 'noble'?" asked Cecil. Toby was becoming uncomfortable with his friend's challenging of the Lord Chancellor, squirming in his seat. "I can't recall the last time I ate one of our poor folk."

"Rest easy, Toby," smiled Cramwall. "There is nothing wrong with an inquisitive or challenging young mind, as long as you both heed my words when I answer your questions. Cecil, do we not walk amongst the commoners like wolves amongst the sheep? The Vampire Lords merely do this in a different manner. And you will find that they don't prey on their people. How would they maintain order in their lands if they fed on their peasants? There would be a revolt."

"Then why haven't they starved out of existence?"

"Because we supply them with food."

Cecil's eyes widened in disbelief. His mouth dropped open to speak, but his father interrupted him.

"What is the penalty for crimes such as military desertion, sedition, riot?" asked Cramwall, coaxing his students.

"Exile," replied Cecil, aware that his line of questioning had been broken. "But..."

"And how is exile carried out?"

Cecil played the game. "The criminal is tied to a board and dragged from the back of a horse to the border of Castland. There they are stripped of their clothes, branded with the mark of the exile, and ordered to leave the land, returning on pain of death."

"And you believe that?" smiled his father.

"It is the law of the land, father. Why would I doubt it?"

"Wouldn't they just return? Castland is a large country, there are plenty of wild areas where whole bands of these convicts could form outlaw colonies, plotting our demise. Or they could sow the seeds of invasion in foreign lands. We cannot spend valuable resources recapturing criminals who have already been sentenced and punished."

"Then what happens?" asked Cecil. The defiance had left him. Maybe politics wouldn't be such a boring life after all, if there was a level of intrigue involved...

"The onlookers, if any have journeyed to view the exile, are escorted back. The remaining exile guard chain the criminals in wagons and deliver them to the Vampire Lords. I am sure you can figure out where things go from there…"

Cecil shook his head. He was having difficulty taking this in.

"But…" he stammered, for once struggling for words. "But that's disgusting. Why would we feed these monsters? Why not just exterminate them?"

"Please, Cecil, maintain some diplomacy. Have you ever seen a Vampire Lord in battle? I have not, and I have no wish to. They are extremely powerful beings. Their lands are remote, the terrain is difficult. How would we 'exterminate' them? Would we even win? Besides, they are a part of Castland. They fought beside us in the Third Raskan War, and all of Castland's wars before then. They *are* Castlanders. As I said, they are just different."

"It all just seems a little barbaric to me," shrugged Cecil.

"Well, it is the way of things," replied the Lord Chancellor, his tone hardening a little. "And it is our role to maintain the way of things. Simple as that. And I must say, this protest seems a little hypocritical, given the fact that a whore with whom you both seem to be acquainted had her throat cut in the Northern Quarter last night…"

Toby had frozen beside him. His eyes were wide, his mouth gaping open like a mouthfish, holding its place in the river against the current and allowing the tiny water life to flow in.

"That brothel owning bastard brought a complaint!" snarled Cecil. "I'll have Q'thell gut him like a fish!"

"You will do no such thing," snapped his father, silencing him with an icy, blue-eyed stare. "The man didn't complain. Do you think I need commoners to tell me what is happening in my own city? This kind of nonsense must stop. It threatens the natural order of things, gets the peasants riled up. I ought to have that cur of yours hanged."

"It wasn't Q'thell, father. The girl attacked us, attacked Toby, isn't that right?"

Toby was still frozen like a marble statue. His mouth moved a couple of times, nothing coming out. He nodded frantically instead.

"I don't care, Cecil. That black creature makes me uncomfortable. It makes everyone around here uncomfortable. I must insist you get rid of it."

"But father, don't you want me to be safe? Q'thell is a loyal dog, he does exactly as he is told. Look at us, there's not a mark on us. He despatched the bitch before she even had a chance to stick a knife in us. I admit he is a little different, but he is exceptional in his work."

Cecil could see his opportunity, and he took it.

"And after all, father," he said. "The Vampire Lords are different, but we abide them…"

Cramwall paused for a second. He smiled.

"You learn well, my son," he said. "But you must be aware of these differences. Did you see the connection between your creature and Lord Drathlax on the way out? This could be of use to us. They are, after all, both devotees of Sanguis."

The Lord Chancellor paused, his mind working.

"Yes," he continued. "If Q'thell wishes to stay, he needs to prove this loyalty you insist that he demonstrates. We are all at the banquet for the visiting Barralegnans tonight. Bring your man. I want him to get close to Lord Drathlax. I want to know that the message I have given him has sunk in, that he is going to act upon it. Maybe Q'thell can verify that for me."

"What message, father?" asked Cecil.

"Let us discuss it," smiled Cramwall, pouring wine for the three of them. "We can also discuss how we are going to get this obsession with prostitutes out of your head. I have found you a woman to wed, a good match. Whilst your Q'shari is wooing the Vampire Lord, you will be wooing this girl…"

It was too bright in here.

He had been working all night, and the morning light streaming in through the open window of the room was starting to made his tired eyes ache.

It had been a rough night on the watch. In the early evening, he and his patrol had attended a murder. Prostitute, pretty girl, throat slashed by a couple of nobles in the Northern Quarter; the poor quarter. The brothel keeper had given a vague description. Two young fops and their bodyguard. Nothing to really go on.

But the disorder had followed the youths around the city, and the patrol had dragged in their wake, hearing stories of bar fights and peasant baiting. Then one witness had given a full description of the bodyguard. Dark leathers, two curved knives, skin as black as the night with eyes of burning red. A Q'shari.

Sergeant Rollo Yarner of the Regalla city watch had cut his teeth for three decades on the streets of the capital, and he knew when something was too hot for him to handle. He had a fair idea of who these youths were, and he knew better than to get involved. He had given his report to the Watch Captain and left it with him.

It would end there, no doubt.

And now this...

Another dead whore.

Yarner crouched by the side of the bed, trying not to lean on the dirty linen. It wasn't just the usual grime you associated with these establishments, there was obviously the blood from the neck wound. Her pale throat was caked in it as it dried, but it had run down her neck too, soaking into the sheets.

Nowhere near enough though. A neck wound like that, a fatal one, should have soaked the mattress through.

He squinted against the morning light. He peered at the prostitute's neck, trying to find the source of the blood flow. It wasn't a cut. You'd be able to see it, puckering open like glistening red lips. Like the other girl.

Yarner pulled a handkerchief from his pocket, dipping it in the ewer of water on the bedside table, using it to wipe the dried gore away. There. Bite marks. Two pairs of deep puncture wounds. Like an animal. But a gentle animal; her throat hadn't been ripped open. There was some bruising around where the teeth between the two pairs had been keeping a grip, but the skin wasn't broken there. She hadn't struggled...

They were human teeth marks. Not an animal, a sick fucking bastard.

Why didn't she fight back?

One of his patrol, Arnald Kroch, stepped into the room through the broken door. Yarner had sent the others home. They may as well get some rest, even if he couldn't. Arnie had volunteered to stay on and help finish up.

"Brothel owner didn't see or hear anything," he said, dropping down into a simple wooden chair by the window. "Says she had her last customer about four. He remembers checking on her as the clock struck. He brought her a jug of water. She was fine. Gave him his cut of the night's takings and said she was going to get some rest."

"Hmm..." Yarner dropped the bloodied handkerchief into the jug of water. The blood spread out from the linen, swirling in the jug slowly. He dipped his fingers in, rubbing them clean. "Very strange. What time did he find her?"

"Said it was about eight. She didn't answer when he knocked. He waited a while then kicked the door in. He said she was always up early for breakfast, didn't matter how late at night it was."

"Believe him?" asked Yarner, looking at the younger man. Arnie was one of the good ones. He hadn't been with the watch long, but he had the instincts of a much more experienced badge bearer.

"No reason not to," replied Arnie. "Why, you think he did it?"

Yarner paused, shook his head. The owner was one of the better ones. He looked after the women better than most. "No. He's got a good reputation with the girls round here. So, what happened?"

Arnie shrugged, looked at the window. "Some ne'er-do-well climbed in through the window and stabbed her."

"Except she was bitten in the neck, Arnie."

Yarner stood, prowling over to the window and looking out.

"Some evil buggers around, sarge," replied Arnie.

"Did he notice if the window was locked?"

"Didn't say, boss. I'll go ask him."

Yarner nodded his thanks. He was a good lad. Most of the others would be moaning like old women by now. He looked down into the street. The climb up was hazardous, sheer brick, no drains or ledges to cling to. Nobody could have clambered up. Even if they'd had a grapnel, they would have left footprints. The street all around was filthy, filled with spilt sewerage and animal muck.

Captain Graves was going to love this. He wasn't the most patient man. Graves didn't like open ends.

31

Yarner rubbed the copper badge pinned to his leather doublet, thinking, thinking. He gripped the edge of the window, leaning out further and twisting round, looking above him. His tired eyes searched, looking for...

Footprints. There was a set, scuffed into the walls. A trail coming down, then one going back up. The ones coming down were upside down. Whoever had climbed in had done the descent head first. The only hand- and foot-holds were the shallow gaps between the stonework.

A chill ran down his spine. Arnie strode back into the room, making Yarner jump.

"The bloke says he thinks it was. He always tells the girls to lock the windows. Says you never know what unsavoury types are knocking about. Ironic, really, for a man who runs a whorehouse."

"So, she must have let him in..." pondered Yarner.

Graves was not going to like this one bit.

"Just ask some of the neighbours if they saw anything. I'm just going to check the roof. Then I'll report in and you can get some rest."

"That's the best thing I've heard all night, sarge," smiled Arnie, heading out through the wrecked door.

Chapter Five

Charo followed Mathias up the long, winding path leading up to Baronet Wender's mansion. His eyes kept being drawn to the bloodstained sack that his brother was heaving over his shoulder. Each time he looked he could feel his eyes filling with tears. He kept having to sniff them back, be a man. It was hard. He was scared.

Mathias had done the final watch, and heard nothing. He was taking that very hard, like he had let them down. Charo didn't blame him, but that didn't matter. Mathias blamed himself. And although Mathias was always patient with his younger brother, he was not so forgiving towards himself.

Charo had woken and they had gone to check on the sheep before fixing the wall. But the sheep weren't there. The deer was.

Or rather, what remained of it. The poor creature had been ripped open from throat to loin, its neck and legs hanging at impossible angles. Charo had been sick. He tried not the think back to the sight, closed his eyes as they walked, but it kept jumping into his mind.

Poor thing. So beautiful, so graceful, so elegant. Snapped and rent open.

They had found the sheep in one of the south corners, still terrified. Some were covered with sprayed blood. They had been close by when whatever it was had struck. But why hadn't it taken them all, slaughtered the whole flock?

It had taken half the morning to calm them, settle them back. They would be alright now, in the daylight. The kind of creature that would do this was something of the night.

"Are you sure we can't just bury it?" asked Charo. He had asked the same question before, he knew Mathias' mind was made up, but it was worth the try.

"No, Charo," replied his brother, striding onwards purposefully towards the door to the mansion. "All the deer in the land belong to the king. If it looked like we were trying to cover something like this up, we'd be strung up. I know you're frightened, but the baronet is a reasonable man. We just have to be honest with him. After all, honesty is all we have."

Charo nodded, head down. Mathias was right. Mathias was always right.

The liveried footman at the door stepped forward as they arrived, looking them up and down, his face a disdainful sneer. "I'm sorry, gentlemen, but do you have an appointment?"

Mathias shook his head. "No sir, but we have urgent need to speak to Baronet Wender. We tend his sheep, and..."

"I am sorry, boys, but the baronet does not grant audiences with shepherds at their behest. I'm sure if he wanted to speak to you, let alone invite you to his home, then he would have sent word."

Charo looked at his brother. Mathias was slow to anger, but it had been a long night. And his head was heavy with self-blame.

"Fine," he snapped, dumped the sack off his shoulder at the footman's feet. "We'll just leave this here and be on our way."

Charo prayed that the footman would hold his ground, that they could just leave. But he didn't. He knelt down, pulling open the sack with forefinger and thumb and peering carefully inside.

"Wait here," he said, leaving the carcass and slipping inside the house.

The wait was long. Charo stared at the door, willing it never to open. Maybe if they waited long enough it would start to go dark, and they would have to leave to tend the sheep. Mathias' features softened. He cupped Charo's chin in his hand, smiling reassuringly.

"Don't worry, little brother. This is my fault. I'll take the blame and any punishment."

"I don't want you to get punished. It's not fair."

"Charo, the world isn't fair. But this is my responsibility. And a man needs to stand up and bear those responsibilities, not run from them."

The footman opened the door to the mansion. Baronet Wender stood there, his small frame enveloped in a cloak of bearskin. He had obviously been in bed. The hair atop his thin head was ruffled and his eyes looked tired. Tired and annoyed.

"What in the name of Argentis is this mess?" he asked. He spoke firmly, not angrily, just direct and to the point.

"My lord, it is a deer," replied Mathias, bowing to the baronet. Charo followed suit, quickly and awkwardly.

"I can see it is a deer, my boy. What is it doing in a sack on my doorstep?"

"It was killed last night in the sheep lea," replied Mathias, his head still bowed towards the floor in deference.

"In *my* field?" snapped Wender. He was concerned now. "You do realise these beasts all belong to the king?"

"Yes, my lord, that's why we thought it best to bring it to your attention."

"Wait. Look at my, lad. Did you kill it?"

Wender stared into Mathias' eyes, searching for lies, for any sign of hesitance. Mathias shook his head.

"My lord, if we had killed it, we would not have brought it here. It ran from a beast in the woods and took shelter in the field. We were going to bring it to you this morning. But when we checked, it had been ripped apart."

Wender softened slightly, his posture becoming less haughty.

"I believe you, lad. You have always been decent folk. But you do realise I must report this to the watch in the village. There will be a fine, as it was killed on my land. I shall have to dock you both this month's wages to cover said fine."

"But, my lord," protested Mathias. "That isn't fair. We didn't harm the beast."

"I understand that," replied the baronet slowly, his voice hardening again. "But it isn't fair that I should pay the fine either, is it? After all, I pay you to tend the animals on my land, yes?"

"Well, yes my lord," replied Mathias. His head had bowed again. He could see where this was going, that it was pointless to argue.

"And the animal was on my land, and you were aware of it?"

"Yes, my lord."

"And it came to harm. Are the sheep ok? After all, it could have been one of those that suffered due to your negligence, yes?"

"Yes, my lord. All the sheep are fine."

"I'm glad you understand." Wender turned to the footman. "Get someone to take this into the village to the watch. Let them know I will be down later to sort out the affair. I will plead the case of these two shepherds. That sounds fair, yes?"

Mathias nodded. "Yes, my lord. Thank you, my lord."

"Good. Be on your way, lads. And please, try to stay out of trouble. I do not need this kind of difficulty in my life, I am a busy man."

Mathias bowed again, striding down the path. Charo followed suit, scurrying to keep up with his brother.

The journey back had been silent. Mathias was striding fast, and Charo struggled to match his pace. He didn't complain. Mathias was obviously angry. He wasn't worried that his brother would snap at him. Mathias rarely lost his temper with Charo. But Charo knew he was obviously thinking over their options, and it was best to leave him to it.

Charo had gone to check on the sheep when they arrived back at the field, whilst Mathias took stock of their supplies in the shelter. When he returned, Mathias handed him a list.

"We'll be okay, Charo," he smiled, ruffling the lad's hair. "We've got enough of the basics to last until next month. Get these things from the village, if you would?"

Mathias handed him a purse with their remaining coin.

"I know we'll be fine," replied Charo, smiling back. "You always make sure of that."

"*We* always make sure of that. Whilst you're gone I'll get that wall patched up properly before dark. It might just be potatoes for supper, if that's alright?"

Charo nodded. He struggled to keep his smile, though. He hated potatoes.

"Pick some parsley on your way back. We'll try to give them some taste, eh?" said Mathias, sensing the fall in the mood. "We've got those rabbit bones knocking about, I'll brew up a stock using them. Then for the next few days you might need to look after the flock on your own during the day, while I catch us some more. I'll pick some herbs as well. We've got plenty of dry kindling in the shelter in the south-east field, so we'll be alright on that front. No treats for this month, but we'll just have to make do. Are you going to be okay carrying that lot?"

Charo glanced at the list. He could read, a rare thing amongst young, poor lads. Mathias had taught him, patiently scrawling letters and words on flat rocks using chalk. Mathias said he had picked it up really quickly. It had made him so proud to hear his older brother say that...

Charo nodded. It was all basics, more vegetables, the cheapest staples. He would just have to bear it, he supposed. Mathias could do great things with even the most basic of foodstuffs. Charo didn't like the idea of catching the rabbits, but there wasn't really much choice. They couldn't live off potatoes. Well, *he* couldn't live off potatoes, anyway.

"Good lad. Keep your chin up, Charo. We've got each other, that's all that matters."

Charo smiled.

"Hurry now," goaded Mathias, turning and heading up the hill towards the north wall. "You need to get back before dark."

Charo hurried off. The idea of being alone in the night suddenly filled him with dread, bringing back images of the broken deer.

We'll be alright. We've got each other.

The demon felt them approaching. Two of them. A boy and a girl. Young, in their teens. Their souls felt sweet, like honey. They were happy, in love, giggling as they approached the abandoned house on the outskirts of the village. They were trying to be quiet, to sneak, but they were too enraptured with each other.

Its senses were becoming accustomed to the Mortal World, attuning nicely. It could move more freely, not feeling as heavy and cumbersome. Feeding on the deer had helped. Something about devouring corporeal flesh made it stronger, bound it better into its shell on this plane. It wasn't as succulent as a human soul, but it helped. It had to be patient. There would be time for wholesale slaughter, soon.

These two will do for now.

It swept over to the window in the upper floor of the house, its powerful, bovine hindquarters bristling with power but making no sound on the rickety wooden boards. It peered through the glassless opening, eyes seeking out its prey, protruding out on raw, bloody stalks from the beaked human skull that topped off its form. It steadied itself with powerful, four-jointed arms that leant each side of the window, three chitinous claws on each hand digging into the wet, softened stonework. Two wizened human arms hung from its chest, short and pathetic, kneading at the window sill in anticipation.

It saw them. The lad was feigning rejection, clutching his broken heart with one hand, pulling at her hand with the other, cajoling. She was pretending to resist, shaking her head, giggling. He pulled her close, kissed her. A youthful kiss, sloppy and inexperienced. They turned towards the house, jogging inside through the dusk.

They needed to be quiet. Their parents would come looking if they didn't shut up. The demon didn't give a fuck if they got caught, it just wanted its meal. And now wasn't the time to be cutting down mortal after mortal if they came calling...

Unfortunately.

A playful squeal floated up the gap where the stairs used to sit. They had long since collapsed into a pile of sodden wood, weakened by the elements that battered into the roofless building. The demon dropped to all fours, scuttling over to the opening, the vestigial human arms dangling like drooping, mislocated testicles.

It peered over the edge. The young lovers collapsed in an embrace onto a blanket by the trapdoor to the cellar where the demon had been summoned to this plane. The lad pulled at the girl's dress as she giggled, sucking at an exposed nipple.

It had watched him bring the blanket earlier, lay it down and adjust it over and over, as if he was setting the table for a romantic male. Judging by his attack on the girl's breast, that's what he viewed this as. The demon had contemplated taking him then, but had resisted.

Two would be better than one.

The lad hitched up her dress as she pulled down his breeches. He pushed into her, pale buttocks humping eagerly. Her eyes were closed as she threw her head from side to side, gasping and pulling at his back. She didn't even notice as the demon slid through the gap, crawling along the ceiling, rotating its head through half a turn so that it could train its eyestalks on them.

The demon watched them fucking. Partly because it liked it; the meatbags who thought themselves above the animals behaving like beasts. Partly because, in its experience, humans in the thrall of rapture tasted better. Fruity. Zesty.

It clung to the wall, opening the beaked mouth, tasting the air.

Yes. That's it. Rich, fruit flavours rising up to it...

The demon dropped.

It twisted in mid-air, landed astride the copulating couple on all fours, claws digging into the floor. It thrust its pelvis forward, the huge bovine cock ripping inside the youth's pumping arse. He let out half a wail of agony before the beaked snapped forward, ripping out the back of his skull.

The girl let out a yelp from the forceful thrust that pushed the lad uncomfortably into her. She opened her eyes to find them gazing into the unblinking stalks as they bored into her mind. The beak chewed messily, spilling gore and bone onto her face.

She parted her mouth to scream. One powerful arm pulled back, slamming down towards her. A claw carved into each eye, scraping the back of her skull. The third closed through her throat. The demon pulled, yanking the head off with a spray of black blood across the blanket.

The demon reared back, savouring the taste. The beak took another bite, snapping through the boy's neck like an axe striking a twig.

Rapturous...

Chapter Six

Mortis leaned by the marble-walled pool, gazing into the still blue water. This was a favoured spot in the Astral Realm, a neutral area where the gods would sometimes congregate. He was here with Pharma, the Goddess of Healing.

He looked up from the water, took in her figure. A slim, middle aged human woman, perfect curves showing through the tight white dress that clung to her. She was playing with the long, flowing blonde hair that fell down to her waist, cascading down her back and across her breasts like a golden waterfall. Her kind eyes, blue as the water in the pool, met his. She smiled. It warmed him.

"What are you thinking, Mortis?" she lilted.

He shrugged. He had taken the form of a man, also middle aged. Not handsome, not ugly, just plain. Shoulder length dark hair, brown eyes, medium build. Nondescript in every way. It was the form he used most of the time now.

"I don't really know," he replied. "I just feel... something. It's been bothering me for a while now."

"What?" asked Pharma, touching the hand that leant against the pool wall.

Mortis snapped his eyes over to Contras, annoyance in his glare. The God of Chaos was giggling at the other side of the pool. He was showing something to Argentis, the Opulent One, God of Wealth. It looked like a mirror, half the size of the Mad One, sparkling silver ornately curled around the glass. Mortis couldn't see what they were looking at, but Contras' laughter cut through him like a knife.

Mortis reached into the pool, grabbing a handful of water, pulling it out. It clung to his palm like a ball, solidifying slightly. He squeezed it, rolling it round his hand, taking his mind off the pair of Dark Gods nearby.

"When the mortals pray, I'm sensing something amiss," he replied.

"In what way?"

"I'm sensing a name in some of their prayers. Not my name. Not any of our names. A different name. As if I'm receiving prayers that aren't meant for me."

"Interesting," smiled Pharma. The smile was distant, the hand had withdrawn. She was holding something back, he could tell. "Do you still feel the power of the prayer? Does the energy still fill you?"

He nodded.

"Then what is your concern? Any power is good power, surely?"

"It just doesn't sit well with me," replied Mortis. "I like order, balance, you know that. Have you felt it?"

He looked into her eyes, reading her response. They were close, they always had been. He would be able to tell if she lied.

"Yes." She nodded. "I've been feeling it too."

"And the name?"

"Yanara," she replied. "I hear the name Yanara."

"Me too," interrupted Argentis. "I get many of these prayers."

The Pleasure Bringer was walking around the pool to them. He was tall, his skin sparkling gold, eyes of emerald green looking them up and down as he approached. He was completely naked. His muscles rippled as he moved, the epitome of male elegance and beauty.

Contras was coming towards them too, the mirror slung under his arm. He was in the form of a money, clambering across the surface of the pool, his feet not breaking the surface of the water.

"And me," he cackled, eyes rolling in his head as he approached.

"Stay out of the water, fool," snapped Mortis. He dropped the ball of liquid back into the pool. It coalesced back into the water, the ripples of its impact spreading and fading quickly. The surface was still as ice again.

"I'm not *in* the water," laughed Contras, dropping down beside the two Light Gods.

Mortis shook his head, clenching his fist. Pharma placed her hand on his forearm, soothing him. She turned to Argentis, blue eyes staring into golden, pupilless orbs.

"How long have you felt these prayers?" she asked.

"Who knows?" Argentis replied. "Time flows so differently in the Mortal World. A decade? A millennium? What does it matter?"

"It unsettles me," Mortis intervened. "Changes in the Mortal World affect us all..."

"Mortis doesn't like the uncertainty," sneered Contras. "Maybe this is why he hates me so much."

"I hate you because you are an abomination," snarled Mortis, turning on the simian god.

37

Contras shrugged, turning his back, returning to staring into his mirror.

Pharma squeezed Mortis' arm, trying to bring him back to her and Argentis.

"What do you think, Argentis?" she asked. "What do you think it means?"

The God of Wealth shrugged, scratched his genitals, gave his fingers a casual sniff.

"The mortals are fickle," he replied. "We all know that. The lessons of the past have taught us. So, some of them have created their own little name in their tiny minds. So what? We are still getting their energy, because it's the *idea* that matters, what they are praying *for*. Not the name that they give to it. They can't create a god."

"They created us," said Mortis, calming. He could deal with Argentis. He was a Dark God, but reluctantly so. There had to be sides, and Almas, the God of the Poor, was a Light God. Argentis was more a victim of mortal contrasts than any of them. "The Old Gods weren't ideas, yet they had power. Then the mortals shifted their worship, and they ceased to exist. What if they create this Yanara?"

"Then we shall have a new playmate," smiled Argentis. "After all, as much as I love you all, your company does become tiresome."

Pharma's grip on his arm tightened again, pre-empting the flash of anger. It sent cool sparks arcing through his being. His vision clouded for a second, blue and blank as the water in the pool. He wouldn't tolerate such interference from anyone but her.

"Maybe that would be a good thing," continued Argentis, savouring the hate he felt as it saturated the air around Mortis. "Maybe we could dispense with all these factions and just be friends. I've never borne any of you ill will, after all, yet I am cast aside as a pariah."

Mortis felt Pharma's grip. He quelled his anger, for her sake, speaking through gritted teeth.

"Almas said something to me once, Argentis. That is why it is he who we welcome, and you who we despise. He said, 'The poor have nothing to pray for other than some comfort in life, and their inevitable death.' And yet your servants have the power to change that, and they choose not to do so."

Argentis looked him in the eye, his muscled hands clenching across his chest.

"You burn me to the core, Mortis. My worshippers are mortals. They pray to protect their interests. It does not make them evil, it just makes them fallible."

"Then change their view," snarled Mortis.

Pharma pulled at his hand now, drawing him away from the Opulent One. They moved without walking, drifting away from the pool. Mortis didn't resist, allowing her to drag him without protest.

"You know we can't," called Argentis, golden teeth shining through his grin. "The mortals don't listen. They see what they want to see, not what we tell them to..."

Pharma interlocked her fingers with his as they moved into the cloud, leaving the Dark Gods behind at the pool.

"He's right, Mortis," she said, her head bowed, avoiding eye contact. "You know he's right. I sent a son, and I lost him. They don't listen..."

Cecil strode down the hallway of the Lord Chancellor's palace, Toby to one side, Q'thell slightly behind on the other. On either side hung huge portraits of his forebears, gazing down on him with indignation from beyond the grave. He was in a foul mood, so much so that he hadn't even had any wine since his earlier audience with his father.

Toby was still struggling to keep that stupid grin off his face. He had been ribbing him since the news this morning, and it was making Cecil's blood boil. He could *feel* his face going red, his cheeks burning.

"She's going to be *so* ugly," giggled Toby. He had perked up during the course of the day, probably because he had not been put off wine by the earlier disclosure. Quite the opposite. "A fucking Yanari! She's going to white as a sheet. Hair just the same, like wire wool. Like a sheep with straight hair! Short! Thin as a stick. Like a fucking waif!"

Cecil span round, lashed out. Not a slap this time, a clenched fist. It caught Toby on the cheek, stopping him mid-guffaw.

Q'thell shook his head.

He even punches like a whelp...

Cecil glared, blue eyes piercing into the dark pits of his friend's. Toby stood up to his full height, glaring back.

Q'thell watched with amusement. This could get interesting. Maybe he'd get to gut a noble today...

Toby was taller. A pale, gangly youth, but definitely taller. His limbs weren't coordinated though, and he was definitely weak. Q'thell reckoned there was more bone than muscle under that black silk tunic.

Why black? It's just accentuates the human pup's pastiness?

"Stop looking down at me," snarled Cecil, getting closer to Toby, teeth gritted. "I am the son of the Lord Chancellor. Stoop like you usually do. I am six feet tall, the heir to this land. And *you* are my subordinate. Or have you forgotten?"

Q'thell stifled a snigger. It was true that he had read the newspapers whilst walking the streets of Regalla. Maybe that was what people wanted to hear, that their future ruler was tall and striking. But Cecil was five-ten at best. And he was unfit, even for a youth. He definitely had his father's features. Not as fat as the Lord Chancellor, but it would grow on him. Jowled. Saggy cheeks, rosy when angry. Big face, receding hairline even at eighteen. A classic case of human inbreeding. Q'thell had to admit, for a human his eyes were striking, just like his father's. Not the colour, but the intensity when angered. It was a viciousness, an animal cunning that even Q'thell respected.

He had been offered money to kill either or both in the past, from their enemies. He hadn't taken it. In a way, deep down, he respected them.

For humans.

Q'thell didn't understand humans and their denial of their self-perception. Cecil had a mirror. For fuck's sake, he watched the man-child preen himself in it every morning. Parting the hair at the side, flicking as much forward to cover the balding as possible, polishing his face to a sheen until he looked like a bulbous moon.

Can't he see what he's looking at? Can't he see that maybe that's why he has to pay for sex...

But it was the denial that perplexed him the most. Why lie about your height? Why deceive even yourself? Why not deal with the things that you could affect? Why not train, lose some weight, learn to fight?

How have these creatures put the Q'shari into decline?

Q'thell wanted to see them fight. He would let it carry on for a while before he intervened. The ghost-like pup had the longer reach, and the height advantage, definitely. He was also angry. Not the incredulous anger that Cecil was drawing forth. Proper rage.

But then he would know that even if he landed a punch on the Cramwall spawn, it would not end well for him. Or his father. That would hold him back. And Q'thell had seen Cecil fight, with a rapier at least. The lad couldn't punch for shit, but he was good with a blade, even if it was the weapon of a toff. And it wasn't like he was fencing with people paid to yield. Q'thell would have been able to tell. He was good, in fairness. That would give him balance. Reactions. Foresight.

"Answer me!" roared Cecil.

No, he'd win...

Toby's shoulders slumped. Q'thell could see the defeat in his body, without looking into his eyes.

"Sorry, Cecil," mumbled Toby, eyes diverting to the floor. "It was only banter."

Q'thell's mood dropped.

Fucking pussies. No noble blood spilt today, then...

Cecil stood for a moment, tiny fists clenched. Slowly the tension left him, a smile cracking across his chubby face. He snatched a wine flask from Q'thell's belt, drinking down a swig.

"You are a bastard, Toby," he laughed, shoving the wine at his friend. "Seriously, though, a fucking Yanari. By Argentis, I swear the old bugger's gone fucking mad. Do we all really want to be praying to Yanara?"

Cecil couldn't believe it. The times were changing if his father thought a Yanari could enter the elite of Castland.

The Yanari were a slave race, when it came down to it. Thousands of years ago, the Bandit Country to the south had been the centre of the Illicean Empire, at one point conquering much of the area now known as Castland. They had spread south, across the Jagged Sea into the deserts of Altanya. From there they had taken slaves from the pale-skinned natives, shipping them back across the sea to work the land and tend the houses of the Illicean nobles.

But the Illicean Empire had fallen. It took hundreds of years, but it had spread itself too thin, and made no attempt to pacify the regions that it conquered, preferring to rule with an iron fist. The tribes of modern day Castland had fought back in the north, as those in Altanya fought back in the south.

Altanya had fallen first. It was across the sea, and supplying an army to fight in the desert was a huge burden when fighting on two fronts.

The slaves had revolted. They had united under their worship of Yanara, the Slave God, a deity formed in the mines and the fields and the rape-beds of their oppressors. They had fought for their freedom whilst the Illicean army was engaged in a ravaging war. It had broken the empire. The Illiceans attempted to salvage the situation by granting the slaves their own lands, a territory in the empire; Yanar. The slaves accepted, and they fought beside their old masters to repel the invading tribesmen from Castland.

The tribesmen had relented. They had formed together, formed civilisation as Cecil knew it, the realm of Castland.

The Illicean Empire had collapsed. Its values, its organisation imploded. Their nobles formed townships, looking after their own people, becoming insular. The people grew angry. Law and order broke down. Their rage was directed at the nobles who had failed to protect them and their way of life. They chose their own leaders, forming what was now known as the Bandit Country; a realm of robber princes who preyed on the trade routes between Castland and Altanya and the east that passed through their lands.

The Bandit Country fell into chaos, and during that chaos the full collapse of the Illicean Empire's organisation was realised. They turned on the Yanari people, blaming them for the Altanyan uprising that had set in motion the demise of their empire. The Yanari were forced to flee Yanar. They spread throughout the world, looking for safe haven.

Now, Yanari could be found in enclaves across Castland, Barralegne to the west and Raska to the east. The welcome they received varied from place to place, but they settled nonetheless. And now, it seemed Cecil's father wanted to form a marriage bond with one of these families. *The* Yanari family, it would seem. He was to marry the daughter of Iluma Porwesh, the head of a banking family rumoured to have amassed wealth that rivalled that of the king.

"What's the bitch's name?" asked Toby, swigging deeply from the wine flask.

"Careful, Toby," smiled Cecil. "That's my future wife you're talking about. Her name is Kalyanit."

"Fucking mouthful," laughed Toby. "I hope for your sake she isn't hideous."

"Father assures me she is very pleasant on the eye. Fuck knows how, if she's a Yanari."

The Yanari were descended from the Altanyans, a short, bleached-skinned race of desert dwellers. The Altanyans all had pale eyes, fair hair, thin frames. Their bodies had adapted to living in the dry heat, developing calloused patches on their neck which drew in any moisture from the air, keeping them hydrated. Over time, the Yanari had lost this feature, and their skin and hair were darker than their southern cousins. Nobody knew whether it was the new environment, or their interbreeding with the northern races. Perhaps it was a product of both.

Their divergence from the Altanyans had been aided by the fact that no Yanari would ever choose one for a partner. The hatred was too deep. There was a racial animosity steeped in the Yanari blaming the Altanyans for abandoning them in the Bandit Country. The feeling was mutual. The Altanyans viewed the Yanari as weak for forming an entente with their old masters, and that their expulsion from the Bandit Country was a deserved price to pay for their lack of backbone.

"So if you've got to woo this creature, what am I going to do? I'll be bored stiff with all the old bastards."

"Don't be ridiculous, Toby. *Everyone* is here tonight. It's the banquet of the year. Trust me, you'll have more fun that I will. Now let's get a move on, we don't want to put my father in a bad mood again..."

People were arriving at pace now. It was almost time for the feast to be laid out, and from their table beside the top podium Cecil and Toby could see the nobles being announced by the herald as they entered the massive, high-ceilinged ballroom.

Of course, Cecil had a seat at the top table on the podium, beside his father, but currently Toby's sire, Lord Arther Princetown of Snowgate, was occupying it. He and the Lord Chancellor obviously had business to discuss, which suited Cecil fine. For now, at least, he could sit with Toby and get some wine down him.

Not too much, mind. Much as he would love to get drunk as a lord, he had to be on his best behaviour for meeting his future betrothed.

Cecil and Toby had been joined by Gideon de Pfeiff. Gideon and Toby had no such reservations about getting inebriated, much to Cecil's chagrin.

Gideon was only a couple of years older than Cecil and Toby, but he was already a lord. His father had died a few months previously, leaving him as the heir to the city of Westroad. It sat on the main route out towards the border with Barralegne, and now it was all Gideon's. And the young lord was obviously loving it.

"So I told the castellan, 'We're being far too soft on the serfs. Double the tax rate.' And do you know, the little shit had the audacity to argue."

Gideon's chubby face was all exaggerated incredulity. He banged one ham fist on the table, sending a couple of goblets skittering to the floor. He was short, his build somewhere between stocky and fat. His voice was loud and slurred as he spoke, probably from the amount of wine he had already put away, but then it was hard to tell. He was always loud and brash, and he had a tendency to run his words into a semi-intelligible babble as he blustered.

"What did you do?" asked Toby, laughing at their friend's ranting tale.

"What do you think I did?" roared Gideon, a big paw clutching at the messy mop of blond hair atop his head, his face turning red. "I lost my fucking rag, that's what I did. Had the impudent little whelp exiled."

Cecil shook his head. Exile. Did Gideon know what that meant?

"Does the Lord Chancellor know that you've doubled the tax rate?" he asked. Cecil was only a baby when it came to politics, but he was already beginning to learn that his father liked to know everything.

"Well, no," blustered Gideon. He went to stand up. "Maybe I should let him know..."

"I would do, but not now. I'm sure he'll be interested. The last thing we need is a peasant revolt. Things with the Barralegnans are a little strained at the moment, I believe. Wouldn't want to give them any ideas, would we?"

Gideon nodded enthusiastically, his developing second chin wobbling with it. "Right, old chap. Whatever you say."

"Anyway, enough politics," smiled Toby woozily, laying a thin, long-fingered white hand on Cecil's arm and pointing down the banquet hall. "It looks like the main event has arrived..."

Cecil looked up. Sure enough, a footman had entered bearing the coat-of-arms of the Porwesh family; a simple yellow Sun of Yanara on a cornflower blue backing. The herald was announcing Iluma Porwesh and his entourage. Cecil took a deep swig of wine, gulping it down as he stood beside Toby and Gideon as they clamoured for a better look at their friend's future betrothed.

His father was beside them, pushing through to Cecil's side.

"Behave, you pair," he snapped, turning to his son. "I hope you aren't drunk, Cecil."

Cecil shook his head. "No father."

"Good." His father's face softened into a smile. "Come, let us meet your young lady."

"Sweet Argentis, look at her," gasped Gideon.

Cecil's heart sank. What was that supposed to mean? He closed his eyes, gathered his resolve, followed his father into the parting crowds toward the arriving Yanari group.

A woman stood beside Iluma Porwesh, dressed in the classic, plain fashion of the Yanari. Her dress was pleated; blue, matching their family colours, trimmed with sunburst yellow lace. Her head was topped with a white, frilled bonnet that tied beneath her chin. Light brown hair fell down to her slim shoulders, adorned with yellow ribbons. She was pale, but not blanched white. She had more colour to her than Toby. Her eyes were sapphire blue, alert as they flitted around the room, presumably seeking him out. They looked out from above sharp cheek bones, which were set above smiling light lips that concealed teeth of white pearl. Her chin was thin, delicate without being fragile. Her figure was to die for, curved but not voluptuous, toned. She was of average height for a woman; not too short, not too tall. She moved gracefully, a small, delicate hand resting on that of her father.

She was older than Cecil, thirty perhaps, but that didn't matter. Her entire figure radiated elegance. It was as if she had been carved from cut glass. She seemed to shine.

She was beautiful.

Oh, in Argentis' name, please let that be Kalyanit, thought Cecil, desperately looking amongst the entourage for any other Yanari women. *Don't let it be his fucking wife!*

"Porwesh, it is an honour as always," smiled the Lord Chancellor, extending his hand.

Iluma Porwesh was more classically Yanari. He was short, fragile and pale. His eyes were as blue as fresh water, and ice cold. Being in his sixties, what remained of his white hair was so thin it was almost invisible on his scalp. His face was lined, drooping, the lips almost unmoving as he smiled.

Thank fuck she got her mother's looks...

"The honour is all ours, Lord Chancellor." Porwesh bowed before taking the outstretched hand, shaking it with that mirthless smile. "It would appear your son has lost control of his face."

Cecil realised his mouth was agape. He slapped it shut, his teeth clicking together with a snap. He could feel his father's eyes burning into his temple.

"My lord, it is a pleasure to meet you," he said, bowing slightly and extending his hand.

Porwesh took it, the smile returning. "I am no lord, my lord, I am but a simple Yanari, but your sentiment is much appreciated. May I introduce you both to my daughter, Kalyanit."

Cecil waited for his father to kiss the lady's hand, before doing so himself. He stared into those eyes, deep pools of blue, smiling. "It is most definitely a pleasure to meet you, my lady."

"Oh, my lord," laughed Kalyanit. Her voice was smooth, as elegant as her demeanour. Her laugh was like babbling water. Her smile melted something in Cecil's chest. "If my father is not a lord, I am no lady."

"Oh, but you *are* a lady, Kalyanit," purred Cecil, fixing her with his most adoring stare.

"You flatter me, my lord," she said, the smile flowing across her lips again.

"Well, you two seem like you will get along well," smiled the Lord Chancellor, placing an arm around Porwesh's thin shoulders. "We have much to discuss. We'll let you pair get acquainted before the food is served. Join us at the table when you are ready. No rush..."

Q'thell glanced over the Vampire Lord's shoulder to where Cecil was dancing with the Yanari girl. The feast had gone on for hours, and he was feeling full, sleepy. Even so, he felt it his duty to keep an eye on his charge.

He had been seated with Drathlax and his entourage, despite technically being a servant. He didn't know whether it was to slight the Vampire Lord, or just on the proviso of them being similarly-minded devotees of Sanguis. Probably the former.

They had made small talk over the food, picking their dishes carefully. They had similar tastes. The venison flank and the beef fillet had been brought to them rare and bloody, and they had both eaten their fill. Most of the other courses they had declined, instead filling up on the heavy Barralegnan red wine served in honour of their guests.

Q'thell shifted his gaze, taking in the Barralegnans. It was difficult to tell them from the Castlanders at first glance, to be honest. It wasn't just that all humans looked alike to him. They came from similar stock. Dark hair, dark eyes. The main difference was that Castlanders tending to get fairer and lighter eyed as you headed north and east, towards Raska, where the bloodlines had been more diluted with those of the humans in the east.

You could tell by their clothes though. Frilly, delicate, fancy. Even Barralegnan men seemed to dress like their women. Although the beards marked them apart. Not the beards of woodsmen or herdsmen, waxed and trimmed facial hair of all shapes and sizes, the bigger and more audacious the better it would seem.

The Barralegnan ambassador was still on the podium, sitting beside Cecil's father, deep in conversation. He was a brute of a man, well over six feet tall, even taller than Q'thell, and much stockier. His muscles bulged through the delicate silk shirt and tight breeches, so much so that Q'thell reckoned they would split if he properly exerted himself. He would love to fight him, feel a blade slide into that heavy muscle. It would be like stabbing on ox...

"So, tell me, Q'thell," lilted the Vampire Lord, interrupting his thoughts. Drathlax gestured for his entourage to join the dancing and leaned in close to the Q'shari, dark eyes set on his own. "Why are you really sitting here with me?"

Q'thell shrugged. The wine was swimming in his head a little now. He wasn't drunk. That would take a lot. He could just feel it, hazing his mind ever so slightly. He liked this feeling, from time to time. He was usually tense, like a coiled spring. Sometimes it was good to let go, to relax. Not too often. Not often enough to get sloppy. Just occasionally.

"Cramwall wants to know if you're going to sort this border incursion business out or not."

Q'thell had never been one for diplomacy. Sanguis only knew why Cecil's sire had thought that this was the task for him.

Drathlax leaned back, his eyes still trained on Q'thell. There was a cloud in the vampire's eyes now, a slight purple haze seeping into the pupil, swirling at the heart of the blackness.

"Interesting. Does he not trust me?"

Q'thell shrugged, staring back. He could feel an itching at the back of his head. Perhaps it was the drink. "Do you trust him?"

The vampire seemed annoyed. He leaned forward again, staring harder. "That wasn't what I asked you, Q'thell. Does Cramwall not trust me?"

Q'thell felt the itch intensify. It became a burn, scalding the back of his skull, on the inside. It wasn't the wine.

"Don't try that shit," he snarled, leaning forward, eyes blazing red. Drathlax recoiled, as if he had been caught staring at the haze of the sun behind a cloud that suddenly cleared. "My race taught you to hold people in thrall when you were just savages eating carcasses."

Drathlax shook his head, a dark smile crossing the deep red lips that carved his pale face in two. He reached for his goblet of wine, took a deep swig.

"My apologies, Q'thell. That was... rude."

"Accepted," snapped Q'thell, leaning back in his seat. It felt good, putting the vampire in his place. They were powerful creatures. He let out a self-satisfied grin. "So, do you trust him?"

Drathlax paused for a second, turning the wine goblet in a pale, slender hand.

"As much as I trust any human," he replied. "The Q'shari know as well as we do what men are capable of."

"True. That's why I don't understand why you're going to sort Cramwall's little problem for him. You are going to sort it, aren't you?"

Drathlax nodded, himself leaning back in his chair. "But, of course. It is to our mutual benefit. Peaceful coexistence is the best option. It has been so for centuries."

"Does that not make you sick to your stomach?" hissed Q'thell. "Here we are, members of two once great races, and yet we must bow and scrape to the humans?"

"We bow and scrape to nobody," snapped Drathlax. He was feigning outrage. Q'thell could tell. Deep down, he knew it to be true.

Interesting...

"Nevertheless, Drathlax, your people are in decline, just like mine. A shadow of their former glory. Do you not think that together the children of Sanguis could reverse these fortunes? Could we not put the humans in their rightful place?"

"What you speak of is treason, Q'thell," warned Drathlax. There was no malice in his voice, no threat, just a statement of fact.

"For you, maybe," shrugged Q'thell. "I'm a Q'shari, a savage, not a subject of Castland."

"Well, we *are* subjects of Castland, my friend. Not just that, we are nobles of the realm. We are vampires second, not foremost. It has always been the way."

"And Sanguis?" asked Q'thell, raising a brow so that the red slit of his eye posed a questioning expression. "Do you not belong to Sanguis, before all those other trifling matters?"

Q'thell smiled. The vampire was hesitant, pondering. He had sown a seed.

"Anyway," he continued, gesturing to the podium. A herald was calling for order, the room quietening as he announced that the king was about to speak. "Your master demands your attention..."

Cecil yawned widely. The king's rambling speech had finally finished, after over an hour. A full hour of the old bastard going on about the glory of the realm. His great leadership passed down through the Lord Chancellor. The Third Raskan War, even though it had been over with for years now. Keeping alert to the threat, not just at the Raskan border to the east, but also the enemy within. Raskans and their spies preaching empowerment of the common folk, threatening the natural order. The importance of strong relations with Barralegne, their shared values, their interlinked aristocracies. Compliments on their fashions, their horse stock, their weapons, their wine.

The wine had been the only thing that held Cecil's attention. There had been countless toasts, and he had been drinking deep at each one. The Barralegnans did do great wine, whether it was this full-bodied red from the border regions that was currently being gulped down by the flagon around the room, or the crisp whites from their southern coastal areas that had been served with the fish and poultry courses at the feast.

Finally, the old bugger had sat down. They were talking amongst themselves now at the high table, the musicians playing light background music. The table had been split down and rearranged so that they could sit in a circle round it, discussing lighter matters. The politics had been concluded for tonight, it was down to small talk.

Cecil was drunk. He had done his dancing, done his wooing, done his compliments. He had done his duty, not that he had minded. Kalyanit was not only beautiful, she was interesting. Cecil had asked her about herself, shown an interest, complimented her. A perfect gentleman. She had been well schooled at her father's home, and attended the Academy of Dance and Song on the island of Massapine, far to the west of Barralegne. It showed in her skill on the dance floor. Together they must have looked brilliant, the most up-and-coming couple in all the land.

Kaly, as she had asked him to call her, had never married as her father had insisted she wait for the right match, the best man in all of Castland. She had made it perfectly clear that she felt Cecil was that man. Her mother had been a Castlander, and on her deathbed Iluma had promised that he would ensure their daughter was only given to her perfect match.

Cecil assumed that was why Kaly didn't look like a typical Yanari. He had politely asked if she felt accepted by the Yanari, being a half caste. Her response had been simple: "Any child with a Yanari parent is accepted. There are not enough of us to be precious about it, and history has been cruel to us."

So intelligent. Even her responses were elegant. They matched her looks, her movement, her entire demeanour. He lounged back in his chair, his hand reached across onto her arm, his hand on the back of hers. Perhaps it wasn't appropriate, but he didn't care.

They were in esteemed company. The Barralegnan ambassador, Lord Alain du Chanchat, the guest of honour, was loving the attention. Quaffing back the wine, bellowing jokes and friendly taunts while slapping people on the back and grabbing their thighs with his bearlike hands. *What does he look like?* That beard, long and waxed, trimmed and shaped into a pair of neat curls at either corner. That hair, again waxed, shaved short on the sides, long on top. Swept sideways across his head so it looked like a black, crested wave, frozen in time.

King Jaros had originally been sat beside him, but the Barralegnan's inappropriate physical contact had caused him to pointedly swap places with Toby's father some time ago now. He was uncomfortable with this situation. Even Cecil in his inebriated state could tell. Jaros was used to being listened to, giving rehearsed speeches, leaving the running of the realm to Cecil's father, who in most cases ignored the ruler's rantings and did what he thought was best. Jaros was not good with people, and du Chanchat was certainly a very *big* personality.

This buffoon actually thinks he controls the realm…

Gideon was seated next to the Barralegnan on the opposite side to Arther Princetown. As a lord of his own city, he was entitled to be there, and he was not as intimidated by du Chanchat as the others. From time to time he would hit back at one of the ambassador's jokes with a slurred, unveiled insult, sometimes accompanied by a punch to the massive man's arm. Luckily the Barralegnan was taking it in good heart.

Kaly's father was there too. He was spending time chatting to Lord Oskar Tremelowe of Kassell, Castland's eastern city. Both were seemingly eager to avoid the attention of du Chanchat, content to have their own conversation within a conversation. Cecil was interested to hear what they were talking about, but the background noise of the room, the minstrels, and the roaring laughter of the Barralegnan ambassador were making it impossible. It didn't help that he was pissed.

Cecil's father completed the table's occupants. Cecil could feel him, glaring at him disapprovingly. Maybe it was the drink, maybe it was the hand on Kaly's soft skin, Cecil didn't know. He didn't care. Feeling Kaly beside him made him feel strong, feel invincible. He was going to marry the most beautiful woman in the realm, in the world, and become the Lord Chancellor of Castland. His father could fuck off.

"I just don't understand where it all went wrong for you Castlanders." Du Chanchat was in the middle of another of his drunken rants. "Our countries used to be so alike, but you've lost your way."

"How so, old chap?" asked Gideon, raising a bushy blond eyebrow. His beady blue eyes rolled in his head and swivelled towards the Barralegnan.

"Well, you pander to your peasants, for a start," laughed du Chanchat. "I mean, elections. In Argentis' name, what is all that about?"

"My lord," smiled the Lord Chancellor, steepling his hands and resting his jowled chin upon his fingers as he fixed the emissary with a glare. "I don't think you truly understand how to run a stable country. The elections give the result we want them to give. We hold them when we choose, and the Establishment Party has won every seat in every election to date. And the members of the house do exactly as they are told by their ruling lords. And the ruling lords do exactly as they are told by me."

"And Cramwall does exactly as he's told by me," piped up the king, shuffling his old bones in his seat.

"Yes, quite, your majesty," smiled the Lord Chancellor thinly. Cecil let out a snigger, prompting another glare from his father.

"What's the bloody point, then?" asked du Chanchat, filling his cup again. Red wine splashed over the table, running onto the floor.

"It keeps order," said Cecil, pulling himself up in his chair. He could sense a row, and he was in the mood for one. This bearded pig was making his skin crawl. "The commoners think they have actually decided who is ruling the country. How can they complain if they voted it?"

His father nodded approvingly. "Order. Stability. Obedience."

"Seems weak to me," shrugged du Chanchat. "It seems your poor folk don't know their place, otherwise they would just do as they are told. You've strayed from the old ways, the pure ways. I hear you even let them serve as cavalry."

Oskar Tremelowe broke off from his conversation with Porwesh, slamming his hand on the table. He was a stocky man, not the size of the Barralegnan and years older, but his strength was enough to send goblets of wine over. Servants scurried over, righting the spilt vessels, refilling them.

"Did you fight in the Third Raskan War, my lord?"

Du Chanchat shrugged again, some of his brashness receding. "Why would I fight in a Castlander's war?"

"If you had, you would understand what those peasants achieved. Especially the cavalry. You see, the thing about the Raskans is that there are so many of them. And they have so many horses. If we had sent nobles only on horseback, they would have been outnumbered thirty to one. Have you ever led a cavalry charge against those odds, my lord?"

The Barralegnan was silent. He swigged at his wine, not meeting Tremelowe's stare.

"I thought not. Our ancestors learnt that in the two previous wars. Those men took back lands taken from us by Raska almost a century ago. Noble men and poor men alike."

"It just seems to me," said du Chanchat, choosing his words carefully. "That if you had more nobles who actually fought at the head of your armies, you would have more well-bred cavalry. From what I hear, your knights and lords don't generally lead your people into battle any more. You've even elevated commoners to titled positions, for fuck's sake."

"Those men are heroes," snarled Tremelowe, hauling himself to his feet, sending his chair skittering onto its back. "I fought. My men found, and I led them. My *son* fought. My son died."

Tremelowe turned, storming across the podium and down the hall. There was an awkward silence before the Barralegnan spoke again.

"I will send my condolences, and my apologies. I just find it difficult to understand why you would leave your country inviting exploitation of your weakness, from within or without…"

"Is that a threat?" snapped Cecil, pulling himself to his feet. His chair didn't fly over like Tremelowe's, as he had intended, just teetered backward.

Du Chanchat paused, before bursting out into bellowing laughter.

"Calm down, lad. We're drinking and talking here, not fighting. And certainly not declaring war!"

"Then why insinuate it?" Cecil was glad the word had come out right. "Maybe we would be better demonstrating our strength by taking the Marralot region from Barralegne. The wine's good, after all, and it sounds like we could do with a buffer area on your side of the mountains, lest you get any ideas about invasion."

"Cecil, calm down," hissed his father. The glare was back, but Cecil was past caring. This foreigner couldn't just waltz into the heart of Castland, insult them and then threaten them without being challenged.

"Don't worry, Lord Chancellor," laughed du Chanchat. "I am not thin skinned. The boy's obviously had a little too much of our fine Marralot red. Or maybe he's not getting the carnal pleasures he desperately needs from this girl…"

"How dare you insinuate that I would take advantage of this noble lady?" Cecil's blood was boiling, he could feel his heart thumping in his ears. His face had gone the colour of beetroot, his loose cheeks scarlet red.

45

"Fair enough, maybe it's your boy lord who isn't giving you what you desire," shrugged du Chanchat, jabbing a thumb at Gideon. The young lord of Westroad was dumbstruck, sat there beside the Barralegnan with his big mouth hanging agape.

"I beg your pardon?" Cecil was lost for words, his mouth flapping like a fish, foundering for an insult.

"Don't tell me you've not fucked each other. Neither of you is the image of Argentis, but I'd give you a go."

Du Chanchat wasn't laughing now, just leaning back in his chair, sipping at his wine. The dark brown eyes fixed Cecil from beneath bushy brows, an uncomfortable lust burning in them.

"I am not a homosexual," snapped Cecil, finding his tongue.

"Neither am I," smiled du Chanchat. "But sometimes you have to scratch an itch. I mean, women are all nice and soft and wet in the right places, but sometimes you must want something different? And you wouldn't fuck your woman in the arse now, would you?"

"What..." stammered Cecil, his eyes wide, his head swimming. The wine was catching up with him, the adrenaline had subsided. "What are you talking about?"

"It's only natural," said du Chanchat, his eyes still fixed on Cecil. His thick fingers slid around the rim of his wine goblet seductively. "Sometimes it's the tedium in the field, dull periods of inaction. Sometimes it's the cold. Sometimes it's just for a different kind of pleasure. You think Argentis gave you an arsehole just to shit out of?"

"That's disgusting..."

"Oh, not at all. We tell the commoners that, obviously. Can't have them indulging in the full range of carnal delights. After all, we need them to breed, not enjoy themselves. But for the nobility, surely you must recognise it is one of the many privileges..."

"You are an animal," hissed Cecil, the rage returning. What was this Barralegnan pig insinuating? How did they live in that shithole country of theirs?

"I'm confused," said du Chanchat, feigning bemusement. "You don't want to fuck the girl, you don't want to fuck your friend here, you don't want to fuck me. Have you taken a vow of celibacy, boy?"

"How dare you continue to insult my honour?" roared Cecil, the rage flowing through him again. "I demand satisfaction."

"Cecil," hissed his father, struggling to gain his attention.

"I can give you satisfaction," laughed du Chanchat, unlacing the strings on his breeches.

"A duel!" shrieked Cecil, hurling his goblet of wine at the Barralegnan. It sprayed across his face, staining his silk shirt. Du Chanchat didn't even flinch, just licked the wine from his face and carried on laughing. It pushed Cecil further into his rage. He felt Kalyanit's hand on his forearm, slapped it away. "Tomorrow, after breakfast. Send your man with the venue and I'll be there."

"Cecil, you retract that right now," roared the Lord Chancellor, himself now on his feet, striding round towards his son.

Cecil ignored him, barging past his father on his way out of the banquet hall. "Send your man. I'll be there."

"Retract that this instant," screamed his father, his fists clenched in frustration.

It was too late. Cecil had stormed from the room.

"Don't worry, Lord Chancellor," smiled du Chanchat, quaffing the contents of his goblet down and reaching to slosh more in to replace it. "I won't kill your son tomorrow. What would that do for diplomatic relations?"

Chapter Seven

The cleric of Mortis rested by the well at the centre of the village, leaning against the stone wall, catching his breath and his energy. It was early, only just past dawn. Too early for an old man to be out in the cold. Certainly too early for him to be traipsing through the spray of morning rain. He thought of his bed back at the chapel, lonely and empty after he had been woken from his slumber.

It was hard to leave it now. It got more difficult each day. Soon he wouldn't rise at all. Mortis would take him to the Astral Realm, to serve at his side with the rest of the faithful.

Not today though. Today he had been roused by one of the sheriff's deputies. The village wasn't big enough to justify having a watch, so law and order was left to the sheriff and a handful of part time deputies, mostly young lads who liked the excitement of wearing a copper badge before or after their work in the fields or in the forest.

The boy had looked pale, like he had eaten something the previous night that hadn't agreed with him. He was quiet today. He worked in the alehouse when he wasn't deputising, and he was usually loud and brash, a confident youth. Today he was awkward, his eyes wide, sullen.

"Father Pietr, perhaps we could move on?" he asked, looking around nervously. The village was just coming to life, women beginning to gather at the well to collect water for washing their families and making breakfast. "Sheriff Wrathson was quite insistent that you come urgently."

"I am old, boy," replied the cleric curtly, more sharply than he meant. He smiled, his thin, wrinkled features apologetic. The lad was obviously rattled. "I am sorry, son. But I have used a day's worth of urgency already since I rose. I need to rest, just for a minute. Why don't you tell me what this is all about?"

"As I said before, father, the sheriff was insistent. Bring the priest, talk to nobody."

Pietr knew what he would be needed for. There was only one thing clerics of Mortis were summoned for, and that was a death. It could be the Pallons, both of them were old, older than Pietr. One or both of them might not have made it through the night. Or perhaps the Ghents. Their babe was ill with the fever. He hoped it was the Pallons. They had had their time, spent all of their years together. The Ghents had been trying for a child for years. He was accustomed to dealing with death, to comforting the bereaved and helping the souls of the departed to pass unto Mortis, but sometimes it was sadder than others...

Whichever it was, Pietr didn't understand the urgency. Wrathson was not a godly man, he had never shown any urgency in summoning the priest before. Pietr had chastised him for it. His tardiness delayed the rituals, made preparing the body harder if it had already gone stiff. Maybe the stubborn, self-important bastard had finally listened. Pietr almost wished he hadn't.

But that was wrong. He closed his eyes, said his apologies to the Keeper of Souls.

"Come then child," he said, pulling himself upwards, supporting his weight on his ebony staff. He held out an arm. "Help me along, lad. We'll get there faster. At least tell me where we're heading."

"To the old Starling house, father," replied the deputy, taking the priest's arm and helping bear his weight.

Pietr's heart sank. An accident, then. The house on the outskirts of the village had been abandoned for years, and had fallen into disrepair. He had urged the mayor to have it fixed up or torn down for months. Perhaps now people would start listening to him.

By the time they got there they were soaked through. The rain wasn't heavy, but it seeped into everything. The hem of his long black robes was caked in mud, and his simple leather shoes were waterlogged. If he didn't get back in front of the hearth at his chapel soon, the village would need a new cleric of Mortis. The apprentice was only ten years old. He would have liked to finish the girl's training before he left the Mortal World, so she was ready to take his place.

Pietr sensed it the second he crossed the threshold into the old, derelict building, past the pasty deputy standing guard at the door. The malice was overbearing, almost tangible. There was a scent on the air. Not just the smell of death, not just the tinny smell of blood. There was something more, the aroma of ammonia, like cat's piss.

He felt fear. He was old, he had seen much in his long life, death in all its grisly detail, but he felt his heart rattling against his fragile ribs as he stepped towards the bodies on the floor.

Sheriff Wrathson was stood over the remains, staring at them, or rather through them. He didn't seem to notice the pair approach, lost in thought, his hand resting on the pommel of the longsword at his belt. Not resting, gripping. The knuckles on his hands were white. He was not the leanest of men, a paunch and neck fat testifying to long evenings enjoying the hospitality at the inn for free due to his position within the village, but he looked to fit his uniform better today, such was the tension in his body.

"Sheriff," whispered Pietr, anxious to keep away from the swing of an arm or a blade if he startled the man.

Wrathson turned his head towards the priest slowly, as if it was an effort, as if his neck had fused into place from staring at the gory sight before him.

"Father. What the fuck is this?"

Pietr shook his head, casting his eyes over what remained of the corpses. A girl and a lad, in their teens he reckoned. He couldn't really tell who they were, as their heads were missing. They had been ripped off, not cut, bone and torn sinew trailing across the floor. The bodies had been laid out, naked, and the fronts opened with ragged tears from throat to crotch. From just a cursory glance Pietr could see that not all their organs were present.

"You were right to keep this quiet, sheriff," said Pietr, kneeling to examine the bodies more closely. His knees cracked. He might not be able to get up again after this. "Who are they?"

"Jacob, the lad who milks the sheep, we think," said Wrathson. "His parents came knocking on my door in the middle of the night. They'd checked at his girl's house, but he wasn't there, and neither was she. I got the lads up and we did a search, and found... this..."

"Help me up, lad," said Pietr, gesturing to the deputy. The youth scurried over, as did Wrathson, the pair helping the old man to his feet. "What else have you found?"

"We thought maybe it was an animal," offered the deputy. "A bear, maybe?"

"This is not the work of something of this world. You both know that. Maybe you can't sense it, *smell* it like I can, but you know it wasn't a bear. What else have you found?"

The sheriff's eyes flitted over to the trapdoor in the corner. "It's in the cellar."

Pietr sighed. This was going to be an ordeal.

It took some time for the pair to help the priest down the slippery stone steps, taking great care to avoid him falling. The cellar stank of mildew and damp, but cutting through it all Pietr could catch that smell again. The scent of the demon.

A couple of lanterns had been set up by the sheriff and his men, illuminating the simple store room. Pietr paced back and forth, sensing the residual swirls of energy in the room.

"The moss on the stairs has been disturbed," said Wrathson, matter-of-factly. He seemed more in his element here, recounting his investigations. "And on the floor. It's recent. And then there's these."

The sheriff knelt down. Pietr hadn't seen it until Wrathson pointed it out. His eyes weren't what they used to be. The lawman grabbed a handful of fine soot from a pile on the floor, lifted it and let it fall through his fingers.

"There's more piles around the room," he said. "What does it mean?"

"It means that someone has dabbled in something beyond belief. This is a summoning, sheriff, and a very basic one at that."

"A summoning for what?" asked the deputy. His eyes were wide, and not just through struggling to see in the dark.

"A demon," replied Pietr. "But I don't understand. Were there no chalks marks? A pentagram?"

"A what?" asked Wrathson, dumbfounded.

"A circle on the floor, a five-pointed star within," replied Pietr patiently.

"No, nothing."

"Interesting," replied Pietr, looking around the cellar, peering into the shadows. It wasn't a big room, there was nowhere to conceal anything. "And you didn't find another corpse down here?"

"No, why would we?"

"Because, sheriff, somebody summoned a creature from the Astral Realm in this room, and didn't bother to bind it. They had no control over it. Either they were inept, or certain that it wouldn't eviscerate them on the spot."

"Maybe it was the sheep milker and his girl?" offered the deputy.

"No," pondered Pietr, his eyes turned upward for inspiration. "Whoever did this was naïve, but it still required some knowledge. This kind of ritual can be taught, but nobody within a hundred miles would be able to show them it. And neither of them could read. So they couldn't have discovered the lore for themselves."

There gathering was interrupted by footsteps on the steps. They turned as one, their eyes wide, fear gripping them.

It was the mayor. The village's elected representative was a short man in his early fifties, his greying hair swept back over his delicate skull. His bespectacled eyes were beady and betrayed an animal cunning that sent a shiver down Pietr's spine whenever the man looked upon him. His lips were thick and moist with saliva as he spoke, always sharp, always condescending. Pietr found him thoroughly arrogant and unpleasant to be around. Mayor Kove reminded Pietr of a slug. A particularly nasty slug.

"What in Argentis' name is going on in here?" he asked, moving down the final step and striding up to Sheriff Wrathson. He completely ignored the priest and the deputy. They were beneath his acknowledgement.

"There has been a murder, Mayor Kove. Two, in fact. A couple of the local youths, a lad and a girl."

"Jumping to conclusions, sheriff?" sneered Kove, looking up at the burly lawman with those piercing eyes. The sheriff was uncomfortable, Pietr noted, like a child being scolded by a teacher. "I saw the corpses upstairs. Looks more like an animal attack to me. And it will do to anyone else that comes looking. I spotted your deputy hanging around outside the door from across the village. Do you really want to raise a panic?"

The sheriff was stumbling for words, unsure which probing criticism to address first.

"Mayor, an animal would have fed until it was sated," intervened Pietr. Kove turned on him, looking him up and down disdainfully. "And it certainly would not have laid them out after removing their clothes."

"The priest speaks. Tell me, Pietr, why are you here? Are deaths no longer investigated by the authorities? Have we gone back to the times of church rule?"

"I called the cleric to attend to the remains, mayor," said Wrathson, finding his voice.

"Then why is he not upstairs attending to them?" snapped Kove. "Why are you holding a meeting down here, like a coven of witches?"

"Look around you, mayor," said Pietr, gesturing to the piles of ash on the floor. "These deaths were not the work of mortals. Someone summoned a demon here."

Kove's eyes widened. For a moment Pietr thought it was with fearful realisation, but it became quickly apparent it was disbelieving dismissal. "A demon. I have never heard anything so preposterous. Tell me, priest, how many budding demonologists do we have in the village?"

"Look at the signs, mayor," sighed Pietr, exasperated by the man's arrogance. "Can you not smell? Can you not sense it? I don't know who, but somebody pulled something from the Astral Realm here."

"I see some ash and I smell mildew," snapped Kove, turning once again to the sheriff and poking a skinny, manicured finger into the bigger man's chest. "And the only thing I sense is an air of naïve superstition. I expected better of you, sheriff. Please tell me you do not believe these fairy tales?"

"Well, it does seem a bit fantastical," pondered Wrathson, avoiding eye contact with Pietr.

"At last, rationality has returned. I thought we'd lost you there for a while, sheriff. I was beginning to wonder who would replace you. So, is it animals? Or do we have a killer in our midst?"

"I do agree with the priest on that front, mayor," said Wrathson, choosing his words carefully so as to avoid further prods in the chest. "Animals wouldn't have laid them out like that. And an animal would have eaten more. Certainly not just run off with the heads. Not the meatiest bit of a human, that's for sure."

"We have a murderer then? Who?"

Pietr shook his head. He opened his mouth to speak, but both men stared him down.

"I don't know, mayor," muttered Wrathson, expecting further jabs of the finger. They came as the mayor continued to speak.

"Then find out, sheriff. And quickly. Does anyone else know about this, other than us and your deputy upstairs?"

"No, sir."

"Good. Keep it that way. We don't want to cause alarm. Search the houses, under the proviso of searching for the missing youngsters. Nobody is to mention the details of this to anyone, understood? But first, get these bodies over to the cleric's place. *Discretely*. And light the old man his hearth, so that he feels comfortable enough to stay in the chapel until we have resolved this."

"Yes, sir," replied Wrathson, turning to Pietr and the deputy. "Come on you two, you heard the mayor. Let's get moving."

Pietr obliged. It was obvious more talk would be a waste of breath. He had preparations to make, and not just with the remains...

Watch Sergeant Yarner took a long swig of dark ale from the pewter tanked, leaning back in his chair as he drank deep, his feet up on the table in the brothel. The brew was shit, thick and brown, with dubious looking floaters, but it did the job. He needed it after the night shift.

The Copper Badge was their regular haunt. Putting aside the variable quality of the ale, it was hospitable enough for a whorehouse. It was open all hours, so perfect for when they came off the night shift, and it was safe for watchmen to frequent. Old Edna, the owner, didn't even mind if you just drank rather than bed the whores.

Yarner didn't partake, of course. He had a wife and kids at home. He was lucky he was allowed to go for a few drinks after his watch ended without pushing his luck further than that.

Magnus, sat beside him, was not so weighed down. He had a wife, and kids, he just didn't seem to have many morals. He was counting out coppers from his pouch eagerly, green eye darting around the room from weasel features, weighing up the whores. The other eye was white, blind from breaking up a bar fight years ago. A wicked scar lay testament to the incident, carving down across his forehead, through the brow, down his cheek to his chin.

"I might bed that whore that Arnie's sweet on," he sneered, licking his thin lips. "What's her name?"

"Lucy," replied Yarner, fixing Magnus with a fierce glare. "And you better hadn't."

"We've clocked off, Yarner," smiled Magnus. "I don't have to take your orders."

"How about I just smash you through that door, then?"

Magnus shrugged, but backed down. "Fine. She's fuck ugly anyway."

"Look who's talking," laughed Yarner, gesturing for two more tankards of ale. Old Edna brought them over, shuffling across the room, stooped from her twisted back.

"Rough night, gentlemen?" she asked, her throaty voice creeping out from a toothless mouth.

"You could say that," said Yarner, tossing a few coins her way.

"Why don't you tell me about it?" she asked, laying a wizened hand on the watch sergeant's shoulder. "Let me take your mind off it. Take anything else you want to give me. For you, it would be on the house, love."

"It's alright, thank you," smiled Yarner politely. "Just the ale, as always."

"Pity," sighed Old Edna, shuffling away. "You'd never forget an hour with me. There's benefits to a woman having no teeth, you know..."

Yarner shuddered. Magnus chuckled, taking a swig of the beer in front of him.

"So, Yarner, what the fuck's going on here? Dead whores two nights on the run?"

"I thought we'd clocked off?"

"Well, need to talk about something. I'm a little short of coin, need to wait for the others, see if anyone wants to share a girl with me."

"You're a degenerate," said Yarner, shaking his head. "If you hadn't been working with me the last two nights, I'd think maybe the bodies were down to you."

"Hey, I ain't never killed no whore," snapped Magnus. "I know you don't think much of me, but I ain't a murderer. And certainly not by biting their fucking neck open. There's worse than me about, Yarner. You should know that, you've served long enough."

"You're right, Magnus. I hate to admit it, but you're right."

The girl had been found in almost exactly the same state as the previous night. Dead in her room, throat bitten deep. No signs of forced entry. No witnesses. Nothing to go on. Captain Graves had been less than impressed. His mood had not been lightened when one of Sergeant Napier's lads had barged in, reporting another girl dead in an alley down by the docks. Yarner had sent Derron, his unofficial second, over to have a look.

His thoughts were interrupted by the doors to the whorehouse being flung open. Griegor stomped in, blocking the morning light for a second, his huge frame crashing down beside Magnus. Griegor was the muscle in Yarner's squad, six feet five and pure power. Bald head, overbearing brow, bent nose, front teeth missing, he had the effect of halting most potential confrontations in their stride. His huge dog, Reaper, a Castland Mastiff, trotted in beside him and curled up around the legs of his chair, promptly dozing off into a deep sleep.

"Griegor, fancy sharing a girl?" asked Magnus.

Griegor stared at him for a second. Magnus deflated like a punctured pig's bladder.

Griegor didn't say much. Most of the time he didn't have to. He turned his gaze to Reaper, ruffling the fur on the snoring dog's back.

Arnie followed him in, looking around the room eagerly. "It's starting to piss it down, sarge. Why can't we have the lamplighters back? Why do we have to go round and light the bloody things, then put them out again every morning? We're supposed to be the watch."

"You ask this every time we do a night shift, Arnie," groaned Magnus. "Fucking whinging about the lamps. The council got rid of the lamplighters a fucking year ago to save money, and you're still fucking moaning."

"Just seems like we've got better things to be doing," shrugged Arnie. "Nothing wrong with asking questions. What will they get rid of next, the rat catchers? How many people's jobs are we going to be doing?"

"Don't ask too many questions, lad," said Yarner, smiling at the youth. "Keep your voice down. The powers that be don't like being challenged, in any way at all."

Old Edna creaked over with two more tankards. Yarner tossed some coins her way.

"Not for me," smiled Arnie. "Anyone seen Lucy?"

"Yeah, just fucked her," smiled Magnus as Griegor drained one of the tankards in one go, pulling the second closer with a massive paw. "She's shit, don't know what you see in her."

Nobody laughed. Arnie ignored him. "She'll be upstairs. I let her know I'd be in today, she'll be in the bath, getting ready."

"Arnie, I've told you to be careful, lad," chastised Yarner. The lad was too naïve still. Eager, but naïve. "Don't let people know too much about yourself. Do you want to end up with your throat bleeding like those whores?"

"Sorry sarge," mumbled Arnie, head lowered. "It's just, I trust Lucy. You have to let some people in, otherwise what's the point?"

"Just be careful, Arnie. Remember, she *is* a whore, after all."

"Not for much longer," smiled Arnie. "I'm going to take her away from this life. She'll live with me. We talk about it all the time, after... Well, after. Soon as I've saved up enough money, I'm going to marry her."

"You'd save up your coin faster if she didn't keep charging you by the shag, lad," sniggered Magnus. Griegor joined in, his bellowing laugh shaking the room. Even Yarner let slip a smile.

Young love. Maybe the lad was right, you had to let someone in. Otherwise, the world was a lonely place, especially for a watchman.

Arnie glanced towards the stairs to the bedrooms, seeming to sense Lucy's presence. She was there at the bottom of the stairs, leaning against the wall, clad only in a white towel. Her long, red hair was wet from the bath, sticking to her porcelain shoulders. Her eyes were warm and hazel. Yarner took in the gaze as she looked at Arnie, pink lips smiling, revealing cute dimples in lightly freckled cheeks. Yarner had a sense for these things, and the girl did genuinely seem happy to see the lad.

It wasn't true what Magnus had said. Lucy wasn't ugly, quite the opposite. She did bear a scar, similar to Magnus' but not as deep and jagged, across her cheek, but it didn't detract from her comeliness. Besides, Arnie wasn't the shallow type. Yarner wondered whether he was really cut out for the watch. Maybe he had too gentle a soul...

"Sarge?" asked Arnie, smiling.

"You don't have to ask me," smiled Yarner. "Go see your woman, lad."

Arnie didn't have to be told twice. He almost skipped across the room, grabbing Lucy's hand as they stumbled upstairs, giggling.

The doors of the whorehouse burst open again, Derron crashing in to escape the rain. He shook his head, sending spray across the room from the tumbling locks of blond hair. He was a good-looking lad, too pretty for getting his face punched every other night by drunken dock workers and thugs. A few more years would sort that out...

"Hey, Derron, fancy going two's up on one of these bitches?" asked Magnus, his eye alight. "They'll do a discount if they're using their time more efficiently..."

"Fuck off, Magnus," snapped Derron, hanging his grey rain cloak over the back of the chair nearest the fire and dropping into it.

Old Edna plonked a tankard of ale in front of him, cooing at the handsome youth. Yarner paid her, waiting for her to shuffle away. "Same as our dead girl?"

51

"No," replied Derron, taking a deep gulp of the beer. "Killed around the same time, the cleric of Mortis reckoned, but not the same. Throat cut first. Some bite marks, on her neck, her breasts, her thigh."

"Similar, then," said Yarner, rubbing his temples. He was tired again, and the ale on an empty stomach wasn't helping his thought process.

"There's more," continued Derron. He was swigging the beer deep, halfway through the tankard already. "She'd been cut open. The priest reckoned her liver was missing."

Yarner sat back in his chair. "Not similar, then."

Magnus shrugged, his mood souring. It was obvious he wasn't getting laid this morning. "Maybe the sick fuck just felt like experimenting. It ain't like he's got to stick to any rules, is it?"

"They usually do…" pondered Yarner.

"They do," said Derron. "It could be, Magnus, that we've got two sick fucks to deal with."

The watchmen sat in silence for a while, swilling their drinks. Old Edna brought more. Yarner paid.

"So, what next?" asked Derron. "What if there's more?"

"Find them," stated Griegor, slamming another empty tankard down. "You guys have the smarts. Find them. Then I'll feed them to Reaper."

"He's right," agreed Magnus. "I ain't got no sentimentality for whores, but this ain't right."

"I've just got a feeling that if we dig into this, the captain isn't going to be happy with what we find," said Yarner. His head was fuzzy from the ale. He needed to get home, see his family, take his mind off this.

"I think you're right, sarge," said Derron, standing and moving over towards the prostitutes gathered near the stairs. "But then, me and you have upset him before. Now, if you'll excuse me, gentlemen, I need to take my mind off all this…"

Magnus grunted, his eye filled with jealousy as Derron was mobbed by the eager whores, like crows round a particularly sumptuous carcass.

Yarner drained his ale.

Graves isn't going to like what we find at all…

Cecil's second hangover was worse than the previous morning's. His mouth felt like he'd been sucking sandpaper throughout his brief sleep. It had been late by the time he had stormed back to his room, and he had not drifted off to sleep quickly. He had been too angry.

Then Q'thell had woken him at dawn. His father was demanding to see him.

And so he sat opposite the Lord Chancellor, who was busily perusing and signing papers, handing them one at a time to his castellan to seal. The smell of the sealing wax was making Cecil nauseous. His head was light, swimming, as though full of water. It didn't move in relation to his body the way it should.

He sipped at the mug of Altanyan coffee in front of him. Black, of course. He needed to sober up, he had a duel to fight after all. He plonked the mug back down, starting to become impatient. Why had his father summoned him here to just ignore him? He should be getting ready. Did the old man *want* him to lose?

"Use the coaster," snapped the Lord Chancellor, without looking up from his papers.

Cecil adjusted the mug, swallowed deeply. There was a lump in his throat. The coffee wasn't helping. "Father…"

"Quiet boy," roared the old man, picking up a ledger and hurling it across the table. It caught Cecil on the forehead, making his brain lurch agonisingly inside his skull. The castellan stifled a smirk.

Cecil did as he was told. He knew better than to argue when his father was in this mood. The blue eyes were burning with barely suppressed rage. The Lord Chancellor was not a big man, but his temper could flare and cause the burliest warrior to wilt like a moth in a candle flame.

The Lord Chancellor reached the last of the pile of papers. He read it slowly, carefully, before signing it and placing it to one side. He gestured to the rest and addressed the castellan. "Take these. Close the door on your way out."

"Yes, Lord Chancellor," the man replied, gathering the large pile and doing as he was ordered. The old man waited for the door to close before turning those piercing blue eyes on his son.

"What, in Argentis' name, was that ridiculous display last night?"

Cecil paused, considering his response carefully. It took longer than he would have wished, his mind was not at its best this morning. "That man insulted our realm. I was defending our honour."

"No, Cecil, he did not. He is a Barralegnan, their humour is different to ours. Gods, every nation's humour and customs are different to ours. That is what makes us better. That is what makes us Castlanders. So, try again..."

"He insulted my honour. And that of my soon to be betrothed. I defended that..."

Cecil knew straight away he had rushed that one, even before his father slammed his hand on the desk. The echoing crack reverberated in Cecil's head. "Do you think I would just sit there if that were the case? Do you think Porwesh would have accepted it? Different humours, Cecil. Different customs. Are you even *listening*?"

"I am sorry, father." Cecil bowed his head. It made his eyes droop. He was tired, far too tired for this. "I was drunk. I was angry."

"At last, realisation dawns," cried the Lord Chancellor, exclaiming to the otherwise empty room. "It must stop, Cecil, before it even starts. Anger is a powerful emotion, but it must be channelled correctly, used appropriately. It must not be allowed to rashly affect your judgement."

"But isn't anger rash by its very nature?" asked Cecil. He regretted it instantly, this could lead to another book or worse heading his way.

"Not if you control it, lad," replied his father. He had calmed, he was adopting the demeanour of a teacher with a difficult student again. "It can be your friend, if you control it. Otherwise, it will be your enemy. Every warrior knows that, though I do not profess to be one. Every politician knows it. Everyone who is successful in any walk of life knows it. Do you have any comprehension of the trouble you could have caused? The diplomatic repercussions? And as for the king..."

"So what if the old bastard's angry," shrugged Cecil. "He has no power. You wield the power in this country."

"But he *wants* power, Cecil," replied the Lord Chancellor softly. "He wants to threaten our democracy, to take back absolute rule. The realm is finely balanced. The poor are becoming vocal. They read *newspapers*, for Argentis' sake. Newspapers aimed at them and their woes, encouraging them to disrupt the natural order. And those who can't read, which is most of them, have them read aloud to them by demagogues and agitators. The king knows this, and he sees it as a weakness in our system. Didn't you see how his eyes lit up when you mentioned invading the Marralot region?"

"I was a little drunk and a little angry..."

"You were *very* drunk and *very* angry, son. But they did. He liked the idea. And that is dangerous."

"The Barralegnans would deserve it," replied Cecil. "What is wrong with a little national pride. Maybe putting du Chanchat down in a duel will send them a message..."

"We cannot afford another war, Cecil. The people are tired. It would cause a revolution. And you will not be duelling with du Chanchat, I have dealt with that."

"But my honour..."

"Will be no use to you if you are dead," replied his father curtly.

Cecil pulled himself upright in his chair, puffing out his chest, attempting to recover some elan. "I am excellent with a rapier, father, you know that. I have no equal. And some gorilla from Barralegne certainly isn't capable of besting me."

"Those are fair points, Cecil. But once again, you demonstrate the anger clouding your judgment. And the wine. Tell me, who chooses the weapons in a duel, according to Castland law?"

"The challenged party." Cecil's answer was confident, but as he spoke he understand where his father was going with this.

"And you think du Chanchat would choose the rapier, or the foil, or the epee?"

Cecil sat in silence. What little colour was left in his hungover face had drained away.

"No," continued his father, gesturing at the weapons adorning the walls of the audience chamber, brutish weapons of war used by Cramwall's throughout the ages. "He would choose the battleaxe, or the greatsword, or the flail. And that massive brute of a man, that *killer*, would pulverise my only son in front of my own eyes. I already lost your mother. I won't lose you too."

Cecil nodded.

"Luckily, du Chanchat is not only a warrior but also a diplomat. He knows that whichever of you had won, the repercussions would have been unpleasant for both countries. He was happy to allow you to rescind your challenge when I spoke to him."

"Thank you, father." Cecil meant it. His heart was beating heavily in the chest just imaging the fate that could have befallen him.

"You are my son, Cecil. You are not a warrior. You are a politician. You are the future Lord Chancellor of our great country. You have many great qualities. You just need to hone them. Which bring us to our next item of business."

The Lord Chancellor picked up the paper from by his side, folding it crisply. He dripped wax from the red candle on the table onto the join, pressed the sealing cylinder into it, forming a neat Cramwall crest in the claret. He tossed it across the desk to his son.

"What is this, father?" asked Cecil, eyeing the document suspiciously.

"It is a declaration that you are on diplomatic business in the name of the Lord Chancellor, and are to be given every assistance required or requested. You are to go on a visit for me, Cecil. It is time you learned to be a man of politics and negotiation."

"But what about Kaly?" asked Cecil. He couldn't be away. He had only spent one evening in the company of his future betrothed, and he yearned for more time to get to know her. He was surprised at himself. He didn't realise he felt so strongly for this woman after such a short space of time.

"Kalyanit will happily wait for you, Cecil, I have already discussed that with Porwesh."

Cecil sighed. He didn't dare let his father see that his disappointment was due to personal rather than political feelings. "What do you need me to do, father?"

"I need you to go to the east. Have you heard of Lord Tomas Bannar?"

"A martial lord. One of the soldiers who fought in the Raskan War, raised to the nobility and given lands for his service. You want me, the son of the Lord Chancellor, to meet with a glorified commoner?"

"Do you intend to behave like this in his presence, Cecil? Are you even interested in learning to be the Lord Chancellor, or should I find myself someone willing to learn diplomacy?"

Cecil shook his head. "No, father. I will be the embodiment of politeness."

"Good," smiled his father. "Because you will need to combine that with the delivery of a very definite message."

Cecil was interested now. He sat forward, listening intently.

"You see, Cecil," continued his father. "Lord Bannar is, so I hear, planning to give land to his common folk. I do not know how, and I do not know why, I just hear rumblings. I need you to find out what he is doing, and why he is so intent upon upsetting the natural order of things. And I need you to let him know that this is... frowned upon."

"You want me to threaten him?" smirked Cecil.

The Lord Chancellor sighed. "Are you still drunk? I want you to let him know that his ideas are neither welcome nor supported. He is new to the nobility, he probably doesn't understand how things work. Setting him straight should be sufficient."

"I understand."

"Good. Are you sure you are capable of this task, Cecil? I am putting my trust in you."

Cecil nodded. "I won't let you down, father. Lord Bannar will get the message."

"Excellent," smiled the Lord Chancellor. "You will leave tomorrow morning. Take your Q'shari with you. I have already debriefed him on his task this morning. It appears the vampire will acquiesce to our wishes. The east can be a rough journey, I would rather he was at your side."

"Can I take Toby with me?"

"No, lad," replied his father. The blue eyes did not meet those of his son, he was looking past him, thinking. "Toby needs to stay here. I have a task for him too..."

Chapter Eight

He was hunting. His senses were keen in the night. He smelt the blood of the few humans that still walked the streets below in the dead of night. He could hear their hearts thumping in their chests, smell the alcohol on their breath and oozing from their pores as they moved amongst the streetlamps, heading home in the early hours.

He paused at the edge of the guttering, crouched on all fours, peered down into the street. It was dim; virtually every house had extinguished their lamps by now as their occupants were long in bed. Just the streetlamps stood out, casting circles of light beneath them as the people shuffled between them.

It didn't matter, he could see perfectly, even into the shadows. The prey were all crisp and clear as they moved, some staggering, some shivering against the cold, some laughing, some sobbing. He liked the cold. It tingled on his pale skin. He smiled as he felt the hairs raise, trapping heat that he did not need.

He looked between the humans, selecting a victim. A group of youths, arms around each other as they sung bawdy songs as they staggered down the road. The noise echoed in his ears, assaulting his ear drums. They were out of tune, awful. He grimaced, watching as they moved away, trying to focus his senses away from their wailing.

A pair of young lovers, hand-in-hand, the lad walking his girl home after she finished her work at the tavern. Was he hungry for two? He would have to kill them both, it would be unnecessarily cruel to part them, leaving one to mourn the other. No, it would be a waste if he could not consume them both. Life was sacred, it was evil to snuff it out for no reason.

Prostitutes, one in a doorway, one on a corner, plying their trade. He didn't think he could handle another whore. Their blood was always rich, full of lust and sex. Heavy, like game. No, not another whore, he fancied something different, something leaner. Besides, he didn't want to draw attention to himself. Another dead whore would start to make a pattern, the humans would form assumptions, make up their own stories...

He would have to dispose of the body this time. The river maybe. Or a sewer.

Then he saw her. Not a whore this one, smelt too pure. Plain. Innocent. No smell of alcohol. Out on an errand for her master. He could hear the faint jangle of coins, too many for a common maid. What kind of monster would send a young girl out on her own with a purse full of coins at this hour? Through this area of the city?

But it wasn't the girl who interested him. As she passed beneath him he leaned further over the edge of the rooftop, fingers gripping the guttering like iron clasps as he took in the man following her. Dark clothes, soft shoes. He could hear the footsteps, but his senses were extraordinary. The girl wouldn't. He kept to the shadows, avoiding the street lamps, moving from doorway to doorway. His movements were lithe, nimble, quiet. Footpad? Cutpurse? Rapist?

It didn't matter. He could sense the malice, smell the avarice as the man too passed underneath.

Perfect.

He moved quickly, silently, scurrying across the rooftop in parallel with the two humans. The girl passed by an alleyway. The man followed, slipping out of sight behind the wall as the girl looked over her shoulder for a second.

The vampire made ready to pounce, but he was too slow, the stalker had moved on. Instead he leapt, black cape flowing behind him as he crossed the alleyway with ease, landing noiselessly on the opposite rooftop.

He could feel it now; the shadowy character was preparing to make his move. The man's muscles were tensing, creaking like a coiled spring as he prepared to strike...

Drathlax threw himself flat on the rooftop as he reached the next alley, his hands gripping the edge, pulling his head over the edge for a better view.

The man struck. He was up behind the serving girl in a flash, his hand clasped around her mouth, pulling her back into the alley beneath the vampire. She squealed in fear, her nostrils flaring in terror as she tried to draw breath.

"Make another sound and I'll cut you, bitch," hissed the man. It was a whisper, but Drathlax could hear from the rooftop. It was a vicious threat, driven by avarice rather than anger. Controlled, cynical, a statement of fact.

They were well into the alley now, directly beneath Drathlax. The man's hands were all over the girl, feeling round her breasts, her waist, between her legs.

"Where's that purse, bitch?"

Footpad, then...

The girl brought forward a trembling hand, slowly, not wanting to antagonise the thief. She reached inside her blouse, pulling out a small leather pouch of coins. The footpad snatched it roughly, stuffing the purse down his trousers.

"Now," sneered the thief, spinning the girl round and holding her by the shoulders in a vice-like grip. "That should see me through the night. Now my work's done, I can have a bit of leisure time. What else you got for me?"

The girl whimpered, her lip curling as she began to sob.

"Show me those tits, bitch."

She shook her head, beginning to whimper again. The footpad struck her across the jaw with the back of his hand, reaching forward and ripping open her blouse to reveal her pale, pert breasts.

"Not much more than a mouthful there," he laughed, pulling her closer and tearing at her skirt, pushing his hand down towards her crotch. "You're lucky I'm not choosy..."

A footpad and *a rapist. He'll taste good. Pungent, mouldy, like mushrooms...*

Drathlax had seen enough. He threw himself over the edge of the rooftop, the cloak billowing out as he landed silently behind the footpad. The girl's eyes widened even further in terror as she watched his ghost-like landing, staring at the vampire's pale white face. He wouldn't kill her, she had been through enough. He would breach her mind, wipe her memories clean like a chalkboard. She would probably thank him if she knew he had done it.

The footpad sensed the girl go rigid in fear, her feeble struggle ceasing. He turned slowly. The girl fell away from him into a cowering heap on the floor.

"What the fuck have you come as?" sneered the thief. His features were thin, pale from working at night. Spiteful, cold grey eyes met Drathlax's dark, black gaze. He wasn't fazed by the vampire. The footpad was, in his own mind, the thing to be feared that stalked the night. It was no use trying to hold this one in thrall.

"Them clothes are nice. They'll fetch a pretty penny once I pull them off you. You made a big mistake interfering in my business, you pasty cunt..."

The man lashed out, his fist screaming towards Drathlax's face. The vampire watched it come, felt the rush of air, heard the whoosh as it split the wind. In an instant, a thin, pale hand caught the blow. He squeezed, feeling a satisfying grinding as the footpad's bones protested. Then he pushed, sending the thief sprawling beside his victim.

"Bastard," snarled the thug, pulling himself upwards quickly. Drathlax heard the grate of metal sliding from a sheath. A dagger glinted in the moonlight. "Shame to stab holes in those clothes, but you just made this fucking personal."

The man lunged. Drathlax twirled, the cloak swishing behind him as if he was engaging in an elaborate dance. As the thief stumbled past the vampire caught him a winding blow with the back of his forearm, right into the floating ribs.

The footpad turned quickly, gulping for breath. The knife span in his hand and he pushed forward again, bringing it down in a chopping motion towards Drathlax's chest. The vampire was almost caught unawares. He wasn't expecting the attack to come so quickly, he had struck the human pretty hard. Was he on drugs? Maybe that filth they called Gunpowder that was becoming popular amongst the poor folk? If he'd been snorting that dirt up his nose that could explain the pale complexion...

Drathlax caught the forearm with his left hand, the blade an inch from piercing his chest. The man's left hand came across, punching him in the temple once, twice, three times. Drathlax shook his head and then launched his right arm upwards, clashing his hand around the footpad's throat. He lifted him from the floor, pinning him against the alley wall.

"What... the fuck... are you?" gasped the footpad, struggling for breath as his feet kicked beneath him, trying to find some purchase.

Drathlax snarled. His left hand gripped, twisted. The footpad's arm snapped, the dagger clattering to the floor. He screamed, the sound reverberating through the night.

The vampire punched him in the stomach and dropped him. The footpad fell to the ground on all floors, the scream dying in his throat as he gasped for air. Drathlax punched downwards with all his strength, right into the small of the man's back. The spine snapped with a deep crunch.

Drathlax rolled him over, kneeling down as the footpad lay beneath the whimpering serving girl's feet.

"Hungry." He opened his mouth wide to reveal the glinting fangs, pausing for a second to allow the footpad's wide eyes to take in what was about to befall him. He threw his head forward and bit down on the man's throat, the fangs piercing deep into the jugular.

The spray was minimal. Drathlax drank deep, plugging the wound with his lips, eager not to waste a drop. The feeding was disappointing. The blood was thin, weak, tainted by sulphur.

A fucking drug addict.

Drathlax drank nonetheless. He had a long journey tomorrow, back to his lands, and he didn't know when he would next be able to feed. When visiting the capital the Lord Chancellor turned a blind eye to the odd dead peasant, but in the smaller towns and villages along his route home the authorities would not be so accommodating. The arrangements with the Vampire Lords were limited to the top echelons of society, and provincial rulers were not privy to them.

His feeding was interrupted by the sound of footsteps approaching. One person, light shoes, wary gait. The watch, alerted by the footpad's screaming?

Drathlax pulled his head up, eyes searching the alley. Blood oozed from the thief's throat, running down his neck onto his chest.

Nothing, but they were coming closer.

He scrabbled to his feet, placing his hand beneath the serving girl's chin and raising her to her feet. He stood before her, his eyes boring deep into hers. She was weak, tired, afraid. He found his way into her mind easily, sliding between the thoughts like a seeping cloud of smoke.

The footsteps reached the opening to the alleyway. He turned, saw the silhouette of a man in the light of the streetlamps. He turned back to the girl quickly, pushed into her mind, squashed the memories of tonight like grapes beneath a vintner's foot. No time to be gentle.

Then he was gone, clambering up the sheer stone wall of the alley like a sailor up the rigging...

He was hunting. And he had found his prey.

The night was cold. He had pulled his thickest cloak out of the wardrobe and wrapped it tight around himself, moving silently into the night. He had been walking for what seemed like hours, the chill seeping into his bones.

Through the rich district of the South Quarter, passing the tall, elegant houses wrapped in their lush gardens. Amongst the numerous guards providing safety to the inhabitants; the personal retinues of lords and knights and merchants, interspersed with frequent watch patrols.

Through the merchant district that sat astride the Regal River. The buildings here were more practical, no towering minarets or intricate archways and pillars. No gardens, just yards filled with crates or carts or equipment. Some of the buildings were still impressive, in a functional way. Less people here. Some of the artisans lived above their workshops, but many had residences further afield. The odd light in an upstairs room, that was all. A few watch patrols, a few hired guards keeping an eye on the security of their patrons' properties.

As he neared the river the shops and workplaces gave way to warehouses, large and imposing on either side. The road was wider, allowing more cart access. Hooks hung from ropes above gantries used for loading stock into the upper floors, ensuring every available square yard of space was utilised.

The smell grew as he approached the river; fish and sewage. His nose crunched up as he approached the Knacker's Bridge that forded the wide, Regal River. He paused before crossing, looking out across the massive breadth of water, flowing slowly underneath him, black as the night sky above it. He took in the docks; a couple of large goods barges were being unloaded even at this hour. The stevedores worked in silence, eager to get the job done and get back to their beds or the whorehouse.

He moved out across the bridge, careful to watch his footing. The bridge was wide enough, but the lamps were infrequently placed. The cobbles were stained black in places, where blood from one of the many animal carcasses loaded onto carts during the day had dripped out, leaving a trail along the bridge on the journey to the abattoirs on the other side. As he walked the smell of death grew stronger, a further assault on his nostrils.

The watchmen guarding the opposite side of the bridge paid him no heed. They were there to keep an eye on those moving from the poor districts towards the rich ones, not the other way around.

He strode quickly through the abattoir buildings, eager to get clear of the smell. As he approached the Northern Quarter he heard the sounds of people, of bawdy song, laughter, drunken brawling, vomiting. The smell began to change again, back towards sewage, mixed with sweat and poverty.

It was dangerous here at night. He paused, pondering the cold, the stench, the sense of impending violence. He considered turning back, but only for a second. He had to do it again. The girl by the docks last night have given him a taste for this. It was as if he had an itch that he could not scratch during the day. Only at night, here in the forgotten areas of the city, could he satisfy his basest desires.

He had done his best to keep to the shadows of the buildings, avoiding the streetlamps and the other people moving through the night. The threat of violence was ever-present in the night of the poor districts, but he was left alone. His cloak was pulled tight around him, the collar pulled up and wrapped around the lower part of his face. It seemed to ensure his was left alone. He gave the demeanour of someone who did not want to be recognised, and people who didn't want to be recognised tended to be dangerous.

As he prowled, he had become aware that he was not alone skulking amongst the shadows. There was another man, lithe and cat-like, slipping from doorway to doorway, alley mouth to alley mouth. He felt the malice coming from the footpad. The man was trailing a serving girl. He felt a certain sense of power knowing that the thief was unaware of his presence. The hunter himself was being stalked. The possibility of discovery made his heart rush in his chest, although he did not know what he would do if the footpad turned and spotted him.

Then the thief had struck, dragging the girl into an alleyway. He dropped into the shadows of a doorway, breathing deeply. From the alley he could hear the girl whimpering, hushed threats, the sounds of ripping clothing, a scuffle.

Should he go around there? Could he kill the man? Would the thief rape the girl first? Would he kill her? Could he just observe, would watching give him the same thrill as he had felt last night?

He steeled himself.

Be a man. Go around there. Test yourself...

He let the cloak fall looser around his shoulders. He pulled the long duelling dagger from his belt, gripping it tight in his right hand, keeping it under the cloak. He gritted his teeth and strode out from the doorway, heading toward the alleyway.

What he saw as he turned the corner was not what he had expected.

The serving girl was stood against the alley wall, stiff as a board. Her skin was drained white, eyes staring widely through the opposite wall. Her breathing was shallow and fast, her bare pert breasts pulling in and out quickly. At her feet lay the footpad, his throat ripped out, blood pooling on the stone around his neck.

He entered the alley carefully, crouched ready to defend himself. He shook the dagger free from his cloak, the forked blade glinting in the moonlight as he approached. The girl seemed oblivious to his presence, staring into nothing. Had she killed the thief?

He knelt, looking over the man's corpse. The footpad's arm had been snapped like a twig and was bent at right angles by his side. His torso had crumpled to the floor awkwardly, as if his spine had been broken.

He looked up at the girl, cocking his head to one side. She hadn't done this, she wouldn't have the strength. And she would have been covered in gore.

Interesting...

He stood, walking up to the girl. Slowly, carefully, he slid in front of her, trying to look directly into her eyes. She just stared through him as if he were invisible. No blood on her. She hadn't killed the thief. The only colour to her face was a bruise forming on her delicate jaw.

Slowly, tentatively, he reached out his left hand. He touched her shoulder gently, feeling the chilled, soft flesh. He moved it down, over her chest, the breast, the nipple. He cupped the tit, gave it a gentle squeeze.

Nothing. The girl didn't move a muscle, didn't flinch, didn't alter her breathing or her gaze.

He smiled, moving the hand lower, across her belly. He eased her skirt down around her waist, letting it fall down to her ankles. Gently he pulled the bloomers forward, using the knife to cut through them. He let the tattered undergarments drop to the floor and stepped back, looking the girl up and down.

He liked to look on the naked form of a woman. All were different, all interesting in their own way. The girl had a mole by her navel, he noticed. Maybe he would cut it off, take it with him as a keepsake. How long would it be before it spoiled, he wondered. Perhaps he could dry it out, salt it like the provisioners salted meat and fish.

He stepped forward again, slipping his hand down into her crotch. He slid a finger into her womanhood, moving slowly, gently. He forced his way in deeper, looking deep into the blank eyes. Yes, this was different, better than paying for it. It felt... purer.

The girl didn't react at all. This irked him. He was used to women squirming when he played with them, screaming and gasping. This was no good. No good at all.

"Time to see what you look like on the inside," he hissed, pressing his mouth close to her ear, hoping to feel her flinch in fear.

Nothing.

He brought the dagger up and pressed the point of the longest blade against her stomach, just above the mole. Slowly her pushed forward, slipping it into her flesh, pressing deeper.

The girl's eyes narrowed to slits. She screamed, an agonising, piercing shriek that echoed through the dead of the night.

He brought his left hand up quickly, clasping it over her mouth, trying to quell the noise. Everyone in the Northern Quarter would have heard it...

The girl started biting. As he pulled away her teeth clamped shut around his little finger, digging deep in fear and pain. He screamed, pulled his hand away. His finger didn't come with it. There was a spurt of blood across her face. *His* blood.

"Fucking bitch!" he roared, throwing his head forward and clamping his jaws around her cheek. He bit down, pulled away, tearing a chunk out of her face.

She was screaming now. It reverberated in his head, accompanied by the thumping of his adrenaline-fueled heart. He spat the chunk of flesh out, grabbed the hilt of the dagger in both hands, thrust it in and out of her torso one, twice, three times, four. Blood was splattering forth on his body and arms. The grip on the knife became slippery, sticky.

He stabbed again and again in a frenzy. Her screams were becoming gargles now, her body growing limp. As she slipped to the ground her jumped on top of her, digging the blade into her stomach and dragging it across the skin, cutting her open in all directions. The girl's eyes slipped shut as her twisted the knife and pulled it free, her entrails dragging behind it.

He would have liked more time with her, the chance to look at her insides in more detail, but he could hear noises in the street. People were shouting to one another, running down the street.

He stood up and ran, clutching his wounded left hand close to his body as he fled the scene.

Charo picked up the pace of his walk as he commenced the final stage of his patrol, desperately trying to get some warmth back into his limbs as he headed back towards the flock of sheep. The cold seemed to bite harder due his rumbling stomach. Mathias could do wonderful things with the most basic of ingredients, but that didn't make up for their lack of quantity. It was going to be a tough month...

It was good that his brother was in charge of the rations. If it had been him doing the cooking, no doubt their supplies would quickly be depleted. He liked his food, he always had. Mathias laughed that he could eat a whole ox each day and still not put on any weight. It was true. For all he ate Charo was slight of build. His brother assured him that he would fill out as he grew older, but Charo wasn't so sure. He would never be as strong as Mathias, he was sure of it.

He looked up to the night sky, glad that it was a crisp, clear night. It meant that it was cold, but it meant that he could see. After recent events Charo was apprehensive enough about moving about the field at night on his own, and pitch blackness would have made it worse.

Then he heard it. A distant sound coming from up the hill, a low humming, it seemed. A woman's humming.

He shook his head, listened again. Was he just tired? Surely nobody would be out here in the dead of night. He and Mathias were only in the desolate spot because they had to be. He strained his ears, listening again.

He could the humming, gentle and tuneful. It was definitely there, and it seemed closer now. He could almost make out the tune. He started up the hill, using his crook for balance as he tried to ascertain the source of the sound.

He was heading in the right direction, it was definitely coming from up the hill. He must be near the sheep now, he could hear some of them shuffling and bleating softly as they huddled together, sleeping. He hurried further on, trying to distance himself from the noises they made so that he could concentrate on the sound of the woman.

As he left the animals behind, the humming became clearer, louder. He could make it out. It was the tune of a lullaby, hummed softly without words. He knew the song, everyone did. The Hands of Mortis. A child's tune, used to soothe infants to sleep in their cribs.

But it was more than that. As he approached and the tune became clearer, he swore he recognised it. Not just the song, but the voice. Gentle, loving, but somehow tinged with sadness. He *knew* the person humming. He just didn't know *how* he knew her…

"I love you, Charo." The voice whispered gently in his ear, so close that the breath on his face made him jump.

He span round, almost losing his footing, looking all about him for the woman. But there was nothing. Preoccupied with the sound, he hadn't even noticed the mist rising up from the ground around him, enveloping his legs up to the knees. He began to panic, panting for breath as the fog rose.

Charo retraced his steps towards the flock, resisting the urge to break out into a run.

I'm just tired. I need my bed. It's been a difficult few days, my mind is in a mess.

He moved steadily, carefully. The mist had risen around him now, clinging round his face and blocking out the light from the night sky. The stars were distant blurs in the fog above him, barely lighting his way as he approached the sheep.

He had to finish his patrol. He couldn't let Mathias down, not again. A tear rolled down his cheek, forming an icicle at the base of his chin as he moved amongst the animals. They groaned and nuzzled at his legs as he moved. He checked a few, made sure they were alive and well. He moved in a hurry, prodding his way through the flock and moving quickly towards the shack.

He began to run now, heaving in lungfuls of ice cold air as he rushed through the mist. He could *feel* something in the night, watching him with a hungry avarice. He didn't know what it was. He didn't want to know what it was. He needed to get back to his brother.

Charo was sobbing as he arrived back at the shelter. The mist seemed to clear behind him as he stumbled to the door, ducking his head and scurrying inside. He threw down his crook, pulled a pile of blankets over himself, peering out through the opening into the night, looking for the source of the malice that was still causing the hairs on his neck to stand on end.

"Everything ok, Charo?" Mathias sat upright amongst his own pile of blankets, rubbing his eyes free of sleep. He smiled.

Charo nodded, wiping his wet eyes with the blanket and sniffing deeply. "The fog… It's back…"

Mathias crawled over to the entrance to the shelter, pulling the blankets with him. He looked out into the night, at the fog bank rolling across the field and breaking a few yards from them.

"It sure is," he smiled. "Lucky me, getting to head out into that. You need to get some sleep. Last patrol before morning. You get to sleep through to dawn."

"Please," urged Charo, reaching out and placing a thin hand on his brother's lean, muscled forearm. "Stay a while. Don't go yet."

Mathias' green eyes fixed him with a concerned glare. "What's wrong, Charo? Don't you want to get some rest? You'll need to sleep, otherwise you'll be ill. It's cold. You've got to keep your strength up."

"I just wanted to talk to you." Charo avoided the gaze, trying to hide his fears from his brother. He didn't want Mathias to go out into the fog, not with… *It*… out there.

"What about?" asked Mathias, playing along. Charo didn't know why he bothered trying to fool his brother, he always knew, even if he didn't let on that he did.

"What was mother like?"

Mathias smiled. A sad smile. His eyes looked past Charo, as though he was looking into the past. "She looked like you. Slight build, dark hair, eyes dark as oak. You remind me of her."

"I thought you said I was an orphan," said Charo, forcing a weak smile.

Mathias laughed. "You know I'm just joking with you. You look like mother, I look like father…"

"Don't mention him," interrupted Charo, his eyes narrowing.

"Now, Charo," said Mathias, taking his brother's hand in his own, the rough skin grating gently against Charo's. Mathias' gaze returned to his brother. "You don't remember anything of father other than the bad times. He was a good man, before the drinking. Before mother died."

"Before I was born, you mean."

"Unfortunately, those things happened close together, so to you it might seem that it was you that made him that way. But it wasn't. He loved you very much. He just couldn't cope with mother's passing."

Charo changed the subject. He didn't want to remember to drunkard he remembered. "But what was she *like*? Not her appearance. What was she *like*? How did she sound?"

Mathias shrugged, the smile returning. "She sounded like a woman. Like a mother. She was kind, beautiful, loving. I remember her singing, she was always singing to us. She cared so much for us, Charo. For both of us. Why do you ask?"

"I think I remember her," muttered Charo, feeling stupid. "But, that's stupid..."

"It's not stupid, Charo," said Mathias, cupping his brother's chin in his hand. "She didn't die birthing you, not during. She held you in her arms afterwards. She loved you. She sang to you, just as she sang to me. You were her world, right until the end."

Mathias' eyes had welled up. Charo reached up, wiped a tear from his older brother's eye.

"Now, I need to get moving," said Mathias, patting Charo gently on the head and getting to his feet, gathering his things and heading to leave the shelter.

"Mathias. Did mother ever sing the Hands of Mortis to us?"

Mathias paused in the doorway, his eyes looking to the ground. "Yes, lad. She hummed that as she held you in her arms. She hummed that as she passed away..."

Mathias headed out into the night.

Chapter Nine

Yarner knelt beside the two corpses, massaging his temples deeply. He was knackered. Another night shift, two more murders, and another morning no heading home on time. The lads in the squad were getting pissed off, he could feel it as they tramped around the alleyway, looking for evidence. They were all tired, and they were all angry in their own way.

Arnie was pining for his whore. They had arranged to go for breakfast together. The lad had been going on about it all night. Derron was angry that someone was stabbing shit out of whores and now cutthroats on their patch, and he wanted someone to hang for it. Magnus was angry because he basically didn't like being at work, and wanted to spend as much time away from it as possible. And these murders were eating into his personal time, which could be spent being a miserable bastard elsewhere. Griegor was angry most of the time anyway, and was currently taking it out on the crowd of ghouls at the alleyway entrance who were attempting to get a good look at the corpses.

Yarner winced as Griegor punched one of the onlookers across the cheek. The sound was ugly, brutal, a crack that signalled a broken face bone. In fairness, if the idiot had just listened to the monster of a watchman it wouldn't have come to that.

"Derron," he called, his concentration broken. "Crowd control, please."

Derron dropped the dislodged cobble he was staring at. He didn't really think it was anything of interest, he was just trying to look busy whilst mulling over the murders in his own head. He strode over to Griegor and the crowd of busybodies.

"What's going on here, then?" he asked, addressing nobody in particular.

"This bloke's just broke my husband's face, copper," spat a woman who was currently cradling the latest victim of Griegor's rage in her arms.

Derron looked up at the massive watchman. Griegor just shrugged.

"Maybe your husband should have just done as 'this bloke' told him, then," said Derron. He pointed a finger at each of the crowd in turn. "And maybe each of you should do the same, and go about your business. Do you see that dog?" He gestured to Reaper, growling deeply and pulling against the chain leash gripped by Griegor. "That dog will do you all even more damage than this brute of a man, I swear to Almas. And in one minute, I'm going to take the leash off them both if you are all still here."

The peasants began to disperse slowly, spitting on the floor and grumbling about watch brutality. Derron watched as they moved away before turning to Griegor. "What have we said about your temper, big man?"

"Breach of the peace," shrugged Griegor, patting Reaper on the head as the dog sat down quietly at his heel. The big man raised a bear-like paw, the thumb gesturing at one of the crowd who remained.

Derron turned, taking in the straggler. A plain man, medium build, medium height, light brown hair, hazel eyes. Nondescript in every sense. The man smiled a disingenuous smile, nodding to Derron with feigned politeness.

"Fuck off, Jaspar," said Derron, shaking his head. "It isn't the time."

Jaspar Ratcliffe faked a shocked expression, pulling up the rough paper and stick of charcoal he held in his hands. "Can I quote you on that for the Gazette, watchman?"

"If I have to tell you again, agitator, your quote will be Reaper's growling and your screaming. Not sure how you're going to spell all that in your rag..."

"Threats of violence from the watchmen who are supposed to protect us," pondered Ratcliffe, looking at the departing crowd of poor folk as they headed down the street. "Maybe that would make a story. Maybe I should speak to some of those people down there? Or maybe Sergeant Yarner will talk to me?"

Derron sighed deeply. He would be the first to admit that he had no idea how to deal with this man. Yarner seemed able to handle him, understood how to talk in a language the troublemaker understood. The Gods only knew why. Captain Graves had displayed significant interest in the known agitator's activities, and yet Yarner humoured him. Still, Derron knew better than to question the sarge's judgement.

"Sarge," he called. "Ratcliffe's here, wanting to speak to you."

Yarner looked up from the corpses, cursing under his breath. "He'll have to wait. I'll speak to him when I'm finished. No more interruptions, I'm trying to concentrate."

Yarner peered at the dead footpad's neck, taking in the deep neck wounds. Bitten, like the previous two. Blood pooled around the body, sticky and coagulating. Nowhere near enough for the depth and location of the wound. Same killer. More brutal though.

"He got royally fucked up, sarge," observed Magnus, standing over his shoulder as he knelt. "Look at his fucking arm."

Yarner nodded. The arm had been snapped, the splintered bone protruding through a rough tear in the skin. "I haven't seen anything like that since that pissed noble fell off his horse onto the cobbles."

Magnus sniggered. "Yeah, that was funny. Not the kind of wound you see in an alley brawl, though. And look how he's twisted."

"Broken spine?"

Magnus nodded. "I ain't seen no man broken up like that. Not since that bloke kicked Ranger when he was a pup. Remember, breaking up that riot at the docks? Griegor picked that bloke up like a doll and brought him down on his knee."

"I remember," replied Yarner absently. Same killer, just more brutal. A fitting end for a man who stalked the night, spreading fear and brutalising people. Stalked in the night and brutalised.

"What about the girl?" asked Arnie, moving over. He was still pale. He'd been sick by the alley wall on arriving on the scene. Yarner pondered on how much that was to do with his unfamiliarity with death. The lad wasn't weak. Perhaps it was more down to his worry for his Lucy. "Another prostitute?"

"Nah," came Magnus' response, beating Yarner to it. "Not dressed for it. Too boring, too drab. Not enough on show."

"She's fucking naked," snapped Arnie.

"But her clothes are right there, boy. Serving girl's clothes. Anyone can see that. What whore wears bloomers you could use to cover your whole body?"

"So what was he doing then?" asked Yarner. He was interested in what his men could do, what they could put together for themselves. He wouldn't be around forever, after all. "Rapist?"

"Could be," replied Magnus. "I'd fuck her."

"You'd fuck your mother," snapped Yarner.

Magnus smiled. "Aye. And she's dead. Got a decent bulge in his pants, there. Maybe he was ready for the deed when he copped it. I've heard your cock can stay hard hours after your dead."

Yarner looked down. Crude as he was, Magnus was observant. He reached down, pulled a pouch from the man's trousers. He dropped them on the ground, spilling the metal. Gold glinted in the early morning light.

"You were right, Magnus. Not a whore. Who pays a whore that much gold?"

"Maybe she was *really* good…"

Yarner shot him a glare. "You were doing well, Magnus. Don't fuck it up now."

"So why did she let him rip her clothes off before she killed him?" asked Arnie. Too desperate for approval, too eager to jump in before thinking things through.

"You think *she* did that to *him*?" laughed Magnus. "You been paying any attention lad? Griegor over there would struggle to do this to him."

Arnie opened his mouth. Nothing came out. He stopped, looking over the scene again. "So, he must have killed her…"

Yarner hid his disappointment, coaxing the boy on. "With what, Arnie?"

Arnie looked around him, searching for the weapon. He cast his eye on the dagger nearby, clean steel flashing back at him. "His weapon's clean. No blood. So, he didn't kill her. And she didn't kill him."

"Good, lad, good," encouraged Yarner. "So, who killed her?"

"A third person," blurted Arnie. He realised that wasn't enough. He needed more. "He watches the man hold the girl up, steal her money, then he strikes and kills them both."

"I don't think you get where the sarge is coming from, lad," said Magnus. He wasn't his usual brash self now, something was dawning on him. "Why would a bloke who can snap a guy all to pieces need to stab the shit out of a little girl?"

Arnie shook his head, the pieces coming together in his mind.

"Two killers…" The three of them spoke at once.

"Exactly," said Yarner. "The girl was killed by the one who slaughtered the woman at the docks last night. The thief was killed by our whore murderer. Luckily, we've got a bit of a lead on the former."

"How do you mean, sarge?" asked Magnus.

63

Yarner leaned forward, gently pulling the girl's jaws apart and pulling a finger out from their grip. He turned it in his hand, taking in the emblem on the ring that still adorned it.

"Maybe unluckily…" he said, standing and striding toward Derron and Griegor. "I need to talk to the captain. Help the clerics get the bodies out of here and then get home. Ratcliffe, I'll see you later at the Badge if you still want to talk…"

Charo bounded across the field. Mathias' yelling had reached the shelter, loud enough even at that distance to wake him from his slumber. He had grabbed his sling and ran towards the sound of his brother's voice. As he moved his eyes flitted through the dawn, searching for rabbit holes and other trip hazards.

"Charo," called Mathias again. "Get your things."

Charo could see Mathias now. He was pale as a ghost, staggering back towards his younger brother, his rough hands tearing at his blond hair as he moved. Mathias looked around himself as if in shock, eyes flitting this way and that. Was he injured? Charo saw no marks, but his brother was reeling as if from some terrible blow. As he approached, Mathias bent double, retching on the grass.

"Mathias," he called, grabbing his brother under the arms, helping him stand.

"Don't go back there," gasped Mathias. "Get your things. Gather all the food and kindling you can carry."

"What is it?"

"Don't go back there."

Charo wriggled free, Mathias too slow and weakened to grab hold of his skinny body. He retraced his brother's steps, his run slowing to a jog as he saw the mist gathered low around his ankles up ahead. He stopped dead as he began to make out the shapes rising like islands out of the low fog. White woollen hillocks, torn and bloodstained. Pieces here, pieces there. The fog itself seemed stained with gore.

His jaw dropped, the strength seemingly seeping out of it. He felt water in his mouth, rising before the vomit. He bent over, throwing up what little of last night's meagre meal was left in his stomach.

It couldn't be. The sheep had been fine when he left them. And now they were… dismembered.

Looking down through his watering eyes he saw that his thin vomit had spattered across a string of bloody entrails strewn across the grass. He heaved again, his body shuddering with the effort. There was nothing left to bring up. He dropped to his knees, closer to the innards.

Mathias hand grabbed his shoulder, pulling him to his feet. His brother spun him round, holding his face in both hands, speaking close to him.

"We have to go, Charo. Now."

He didn't argue. Mathias' strength had returned, necessity driving him now. He pulled Charo along, striding urgently back towards the shelter.

I need to be strong. I need to be a man.

Charo pulled his hand free, jogging by Mathias' side to keep up. As they reached the shelter then began gathering their meagre possessions, stuffing them into backpacks and jute sacks.

"Only take what you need," said Mathias, grabbing two of the sacks and tying them to each end of his crook. He grabbed the sword in its battered leather scabbard, clipping the rust-stained chain to his belt beside the sling and pouch of stones.

"I've got the food," replied Charo, stuffing the last of the vegetables and herbs into a sack along with the last rabbit.

"Take the skins too, we can sell them," said Mathias, grabbing the sack of food and tying it to the end of Charo's crook. "Bring an empty sack, we'll use it for the kindling from the south-east shelter."

Then they were outside, tramping down the hill. Mathias carried a backpack on one shoulder, the crook balanced across his back with the gunny sacks suspended on either side for balance. Charo carried his own pack, his crook slung over the opposite shoulder, the provisions bag dangling behind him.

"Shouldn't we tell someone?" he asked, his eyes wide with apprehension. "I mean, we didn't do anything wrong."

"Nobody will believe us," replied Mathias, staring straight ahead as they pushed on down the field. "They didn't believe us before. They certainly won't now. There's nothing left for us here."

"Is this what happened the last time?" asked Charo, bewildered.

"This isn't the time, lad," replied Mathias, reaching over and pulling his little brother along by the scruff of his rough, brown tunic. "We need to move. Faster."

64

Yarner sat opposite Captain Graves as his superior looked at the finger on the desk in front of him. He hadn't touched it, picked it up. Just grimaced at it. Staring, shaking his head.

He's not happy.

The watch captain's office was sparsely furnished. Many of his rank in other areas of the city had luxurious rooms, decked out in oak panelling and adorned with stuffed animals, plush chairs, elaborate desks, swords and shields and scrolls of honours. Yarner knew that, he had seen the office decked out by the previous captain.

Graves wasn't like the previous captain. His tastes were far more spartan. Yarner remembered the captain's first day, helping rip out all the previous furnishings and decorations. Graves had sold them, putting the money into the Northern Quarter Watch's funding pot rather than his own pocket. Yarner didn't particularly like the man, but he wasn't a parasite like the previous captain. He wasn't some noble's youngest son who had been sent to the watch to keep him out of his father's purse. He was awkward, difficult to get along with, quick to anger, but he wasn't an idler.

Yarner looked around the office. He had seen it plenty of times, but he knew that this staring and head-shaking would go on for some time. Graves was methodical, predictable.

The furnishings were basic. A simple table sat by the window, surrounded by uncomfortable wooden chairs. It doubled up for the captain's dining and for meetings with the sergeants. The desk sitting between them was similarly dull, cheap and functional. The chairs on which they sat didn't match, other than the fact that they hurt your back and your arse when you were stuck on them for too long.

A couple of cushions couldn't exactly be called opulence...

Yarner shifted in his seat. The creaking caused the captain to shoot him a critical glance. He gave a suitably apologetic look, shifting his gaze upwards to the only adornment on the walls of the office; a framed copy of a certificate from the Regalla Watch Academy, announcing that Otto Graves had graduated with honours.

Yarner didn't doubt it. The man was uncompromising in his devotion to keeping the peace. What he did doubt was how interested Graves was in upholding the *law*. Graves wanted stability, the natural order. In Yarner's extensive experience of policing the capital, the two did not always go hand in silk-gloved hand.

The sergeant shifted again, letting out a sigh. He knew he shouldn't, but he was tired. He hadn't seen enough of his family over the last few days, and it was looking like today was going to drag out into the next shift.

"For Guerro's sake, man," snapped Graves, reaching into the drawer of his desk. He pulled out two crystal glasses and set them on the desk, before pulling out a bottle of Westroad whisky. The captain poured two small measures, pushing one towards Yarner. It was the only extravagance allowed in the captain's office. "Drink that, it might keep you quiet."

"No, thank you, captain," replied Yarner. "I've just finished another long night. It might put me to sleep."

"Good." Graves gave a mirthless laugh. "Then I might be able to concentrate."

Yarner obliged, swilling the amber liquid around in the glass and taking a sip. It was good whisky, in fairness. Smooth, with only a slight afterbite. It was the only indulgence the captain allowed himself.

Graves resumed staring at the digit on the desk in front of him, peering closer warily, as if he feared it might reach up and poke him in the eye. He reached forward and turned it gently with his forefinger, careful to touch the ring that encased it rather than the dead flesh.

"It's a finger, sir," said Yarner, before he could contain himself.

Graves shot him a glare, ash grey eyes glinting in the morning light from the window. Yarner knew he could get away with more than most with the captain. He was good at what he did, and Graves knew it.

"I can see that, sergeant."

Graves went back to staring at the body part. This could go on for some time. Yarner knew he had to speed things up or he would be heading straight out from the office to his next night shift.

"We pulled it out of the dead girl's mouth. We ascertained that it belongs to the man who killed her."

"By 'we' I take it you mean 'you'," said Graves matter-of-factly. "Your men couldn't deduce their way to the nearest brothel, let alone solve a murder."

"They're learning, sir," replied Yarner. "They made plenty of observations themselves. No man is born into this world knowing how to be a watchman, in the same way new-borns can't weave, or smith, or piss into a bucket. You know that…"

He gestured to the certificate above the captain's head.

"Quite," replied Graves, sitting back in the chair and staring across at his sergeant. "So, tell me what happened. That is what you're here for, isn't it sergeant? To educate me?"

Yarner ignored the jibe. They both knew that Yarner was the experienced one. There was no need to make it more difficult than it was.

"The footpad was killed by the same person who did the two whores in their rooms. Throat bitten out. Resistance this time, and shocking strength in response. The one who killed last night's girl also cut up that girl by the docks the previous night. Same butchery, same savagery."

"*Two* murderers, sergeant? That doesn't bode well when the commoners get wind of it."

"I know, sir, but that's the way of it."

"So, sergeant, how do we deal with this?"

Yarner hesitated. The question shouldn't really have needed a response. "We catch them and get justice, sir."

"But you aren't giving me names, sergeant. *Who* did this? That's what I need to know. I recognise this crest, sergeant…"

Graves reached out, pulling the ring off the finger, careful to touch the dead digit as little as possible. He wiped his hand on his tunic in disgust.

"We both do, sir," replied Yarner. He didn't like the way this was going. "That's the problem…"

Yarner paused, rolling the ring between his fingers, deep in thought. In a second it was gone, slipped into his pocket. "I'll deal with this. Don't you worry about that. What about the other killer?"

Yarner nodded. This was the difference between justice and keeping the peace.

"If I had to make a guess, sir, you would laugh at me."

"When have I ever laughed at you, sergeant?" asked Graves. "You know that I hold you in the utmost regard. You're one of mine. And you're one of my best."

Yarner took a sip of the whisky, letting it roll across his tongue. "If I had to guess, sir, I'd say we have a vampire in the city. Throats ripped out. Too little blood at the scene. The footpad last night had been pulled apart like a child in the grip of a bear."

"Fairy stories, sergeant," replied Graves, fixing Yarner with a stern stare. "I have never laughed at you before, but you are pushing me close to the limits. The same man killed them all, and I will deal with it. I suggest you tell your men the same. And tell them to keep their lips sealed."

Yarner sensed that he was being dismissed. He drained his glass, placing it gently down on the desk and pushing it back towards the captain as he stood.

"And is this justice being served, sir?"

Graves' stare hardened. "Sergeant, I asked you earlier what we should do. The answer is simple; we make it stop. *That* is the best course of action."

"But sir…"

"But *nothing*," snapped Graves. He didn't stand. He didn't shift at all. He just glared. "You are very good at what you do, sergeant, but you do not understand what I do. It is my job to look wider, to look at the potential ramifications, to look at the larger politics. We have three dead whores, a dead thief and a dead serving girl. Is that worth upturning the apple cart?"

"So their lives mean nothing?"

"I didn't say that, sergeant," replied Graves, his tone becoming gentler, more coercive. "But you deal with dead commoners most days. If it's not a whore, it's a sailor stabbed in a barfight, a drunken mouthpiece beaten down in a riot, a stevedore crushed by a faulty crane. It happens, and the poor folk get on with it. So should you. Can you imagine what would happen if the truth came out? What would be asked of us in keeping it hushed up? How many people would need to be made silent? Isn't it better that you and your men just keep their mouths shut and get on with their lives, and let me deal with the grittier side of things?"

Yarner paused. He thought of his men, their lives. He thought of Arnie and Lucy, of Griegor and his dog. It wasn't his place to put them in danger. He understood exactly what the captain was saying, he had policed Regalla long enough.

"I understand, sir."

"Good," replied Graves, draining his own glass. "You and your men are due back on the day shift in a few morns. Take the intervening time off. Sergeant Billings and his squad will relieve you. It's the least we can do after the rough few nights you've all had. Come back relaxed and ready for work, like nothing has happened..."

"Thank you, sir."

The words stuck in his craw as Yarner strode from the room, slamming the door behind him.

There were ripples in the pool. Mortis didn't like it. It made him feel unsettled, watching his reflection in the clear sapphire water crack and distort. Was it a sign? A sign of his power, his very existence, being undermined? Or was it just water, moving in the breeze?

"Did you see that?" he asked.

He was flanked by Guerro and Almas at the edge of the pool. He looked from one to another, a questioning frown on his face.

Guerro, the God of War. The Martial Lord. The Honourable One. His lower body that of a warhorse, strong flanks and rippling muscle. His upper torso human, strong, powerful, but scarred. His face was strong, bearded, but honest and open.

Almas, the God of the Poor. He took no other names. He wanted to have as little as the mortals who worshipped him. Thin, wiry, sickly almost. A kind face, but one wrinkled with many burdens. His face could change in appearance in an instant, displaying fear, anger, confusion, envy. Of all of them, Mortis believed that Almas truly felt the ebb and flow of mortal prayer and fear most intuitively.

"See what, old friend?" asked Almas, a sad smile crossing his lips.

"The ripples. Do you see them, or is it just me?"

Guerro looked down into the pool, shaking his head. "No, Mortis. It must just be you. What do you think it means?"

Mortis looked from one to another. Could a god panic? He believed so. It was a sign. A sign of his power waning, his very existence threatening to fade to nothing. Or worse than nothing; something, but something with no power or influence or presence. He switched his gaze between his fellow Light Gods again, his head moving quicker now. Almas smiling sadly, a grin beginning to creep across Guerro's face.

"He jests with you, Mortis," laughed Almas. Guerro burst out laughing, a deep, bellowing sound. "We see the ripples. It is nothing, I'm sure."

Mortis shook his head. "You mustn't jest, you two. You know I fear for the stability of the world. Of our world, and of theirs."

"You fret too much, Mortis," teased Guerro, a thick, powerful hand clamping down on the God of Death's shoulder. "I fear Lunaris get inside you all that time ago? Does he still eat away at you?"

Mortis paused, thinking back into the distant past. The feeling of dread. The triumph, but also the taste of defeat. The realisation of what *could* have happened. What could *still* happen...

"His touch made me fear for what could happen in the future, my friends," admitted Mortis.

"How did he touch you?" asked Guerro. "Did he touch you the way a priest of Argentis touches a young boy?"

Almas shook his head.

"In a way, yes," replied Mortis. "I do feel defiled. He did take something from me, all that time ago. He did take my innocence. He showed me what we can do. He showed me what the mortals can do. And I worry about both of those things to this day."

"Things have changed since then, old friend," reassured Almas, also placing a thin hand on Mortis' shoulder. "You won. *We* won. All of us, Light and Dark. No god would do that again. Even if they knew how. We would all unite against them. We might argue, we might not even like each other, but we understand that there has to be balance."

"He's right," insisted Guerro. "The Mortal World has been stable since the defeat of the Lurker. Things change; they war, they have peace, they fight, they fuck, they die. But there are no great shifts, no great lurches. We have equilibrium, which is good for us, and good for them."

Mortis smiled, a warmth spreading through him. "I thank you both. Sometimes I don't understand why you have patience with me. Especially when I often take souls that should have ended up with yourselves."

"We still get their worship throughout their lives, Mortis," replied Almas. "But in many instances, a mortal's prayers at the time of their impending doom fall to you, not to us."

67

"It is true," nodded Guerro, returning his gaze to the pool. "I've known many worshippers, so devout that I see through their eyes, feel their thoughts and their feelings. I have gazed thought their own eyes upon their wives as they make love, their thoughts straying to me above all else. I have watched as they fight on the battlefield. Their prayers are so *intense*, neither of you would believe how strong they pull me into themselves, wishing for honour and glory and survival. But when a pike splits their ribs, or a battleaxe lops off a limb, I often lose that connection with them. They think of you, the Protector of Souls who will guide them safety into his realm."

"Does that ire you?" asked Mortis, looking the God of War up and down.

Guerro returned his gaze to Mortis, as if shocked by the question. "No, my friend. You are good. You are pure. You defeated the Lurker."

"The Honourable One is right, Mortis," said Almas, squeezing his friend's shoulder. "Sometimes even gods need faith. And we have faith in you. The poor pray to me, and I do what little I can to guide their way, to ease their suffering. They wish for a little luck, a morsel of good fortune, and I give them what I can. But in the end, on their deathbed, they turn to you for salvation."

"I feel like a thief..."

"You're nothing of the sort, Mortis. We are just two sides of the same coin. After all, the poor have nothing to pray for other than some comfort in life, and their inevitable death."

"And yet I steal from my own, it seems," replied Mortis, reaching up and touching the hand of Almas in appreciation. "Does this not threaten the balance? What if the Dark Ones gain power from this? Would you trust them not to follow in Lunaris' footsteps?"

"The flow is more complex than that, Mortis, and you know it," replied Almas. "Pharma heals the sick when they pray to her, rich and poor alike. The power flows between us. The followers of the Dark Gods pray to you at their death, just as ours do. In battle, a worshipper of Sanguis will let slip an utterance to Guerro. One of Contras' loons will fire off wishes in all different directions. It all balances out."

"And you are the strongest of us all, Mortis," said Guerro. "You banished the Great Enemy. Nobody would stand against you."

"Any you are committed to stability," added Almas. "Which means we are assured of balance. The balance you crave."

Mortis smiled, buoyed by the words of his companions. He reached down to the pool, pressing his hand through the surface of the water, sending ripples of his own. He pushed his hand deep, hoping to find something, pull it out of the liquid. There was nothing. He pulled his arm back, watching the water drip down in random trails, dripping off the ends of his fingers.

"It just worries me that I don't see the Mortal World clearly. I don't feel I know enough about what the humans are doing. What they are thinking. What they are feeling. That is where the threat lies."

"But you have a mortal son, Mortis," said Almas. "Are you not in tune with him? We all sent out our people, Light and Dark alike, to find the Portal Stones so that you could birth him. It was the one thing you asked of us, after banishing the Lurker."

Mortis nodded. "He was born. His mother died. She never told him his heritage, never pushed him towards me. I don't know if he prays, but he doesn't pray to me..."

A tear rolled down the God of Death's cheek. He didn't know if it was voluntary or not, it just seemed to be the right response, and it happened. Did gods feel sadness, feel loss?

Almas ran his hand down Mortis' arm soothingly, taking his hand. "I am sorry, Mortis. That must pain you."

"I think it does," replied Mortis, staring into the pool, willing its waters to clear and show him the Mortal World through the eyes of a human. "I see little of people's lives. I see their deaths. I sometimes see what is killing them. I feel their pain and their fear, but I don't see what is causing it. I fear for the stability of the Mortal World, and yet I know nothing of what is truly happening other than that people are dying."

Guerro pressed in on his other side, bear-like arms embracing him from behind, pulling him close. "Then we will tell you what we see, my friend. Hopefully that will put your mind at rest."

Mortis smiled. "It would help, my friends. It would help..."

68

Chapter Ten

Yarner took a swig of the ale from the tankard in front of him, avoiding the eyes of the man sitting opposite him at the table in the Copper Badge. The place was empty, which was for the best. He hadn't left the captain's office until mid-morning, so even those drinking after the night shift had left by now. His wife was going to be furious. He hadn't seen the children for days now, but that couldn't be helped. It had been a difficult time for a watch sergeant in the Northern Quarter.

He hadn't said a word since he arrived, just sat down opposite Jaspar Ratcliffe and drank the beer Old Edna had plonked in front of him. Ratcliffe would know to leave him be, to wait for him to speak. Yarner just had to get things straight in his head, figure out what it was right to tell, and what needed to be left unsaid.

Yarner looked up at the agitator who was patiently waiting for him to speak. He did this every time they met, searching for a distinguishing feature, something that would set Ratcliffe apart. It was Yarner's job to describe suspects, to describe people. Ratcliffe was just... A man. A male Castlander. There really wasn't much that set him apart, make him recognisable, make him distinctive.

Yarner eyed the pewter badge on Ratcliffe's plain brown tunic, a simple emblem of the People's Gazette; a rolled-up parchment.

"Take that off, would you? I'm in serious trouble if I get seen talking to the likes of you."

Ratcliffe smiled, pulling the brooch from his chest and pushing it into his pocket. "You do understand that everyone around here knows who I am, sergeant?"

"I think you have ideas above your station, Ratcliffe," replied Yarner, draining the dregs of his ale and signalling for another. "You having one? I take it you're paying, you may as well."

Ratcliffe shook his head, waiting for Old Edna to drop down another tankard before speaking. "So, what's the news?"

Yarner shook his head. "It doesn't work that way, you know that. You're the newsman, you tell me."

Ratcliffe smiled. His eyes narrowed. He did know the game, and he was good at it. "Rumour has it some noble's carved up seven whores and a footpad."

"Four *women*," replied Yarner, raising his tankard to drink and then pausing, sensing the trap. "And we don't know it's a noble. We don't know who it is."

"You got me there," smiled Ratcliffe. He was scribbling on the parchment he had on the table. The words were delicate despite the charcoal stick he was writing with, not the script of a commoner who had learnt to write in the same hovel room as his family ate and slept.

"Where did you learn to write?" asked Yarner, bringing the tankard to his lips. He wasn't drinking, he was looking intently at the newsman, gauging the reaction. It was guarded, the swagger had dropped for a moment.

"This isn't an interview about me, sergeant."

"This isn't an interview at all," snapped Yarner. "My name comes into this, or even any mention of the watch, and I'll find where you live and break you in half."

"Why sergeant, you know you can count on my discretion," gasped Ratcliffe, a look of feigned, shocked disappointment crossing his face. "There's no need to threaten a scholar."

Yarner almost spat out his ale. "Scholar!"

"I am a scholar of humankind, sergeant. I study the activities of the people, highborn and low. I examine their motives, make sense of their actions. And I tell people what they need to hear. What they deserve to hear. Not like those other rags."

Yarner didn't answer. In truth, that was why he gave the agitator his time. Ratcliffe was unrelenting to the point of annoying, but he did indeed tell the poor things that the more 'upmarket' newspapers would not. He rooted out and imparted what was really happening, rather than what the establishment wanted them to think was happening. And Yarner held a begrudging respect for that. It certainly came at a personal risk to the reporter himself.

"So, sergeant," said Ratcliffe, calmly settling into his rough chair. "Tell me what you can. As always, your anonymity is assured."

Yarner took a deep swig of his ale, pondering his next statement carefully. He wanted the truth out, and he had a feeling that most of it was going to be brushed under the rug. But he had to protect himself and his men. Too much information would put them all in jeopardy.

"We've got five murders over the last few nights, all in or around the Northern Quarter. Three whores, a serving girl and a footpad."

"I could have told you that," sneered Ratcliffe. Yarner shot him a glare. "I'm sorry, sergeant. Please, continue."

"They're bad, Ratcliffe. Some of the worst I've seen. Throats ripped out. Hacked apart in some kind of frenzy. Guts pulled out. Savage."

"Tell me more." Ratcliffe was barely containing his excitement. "This is going to be a great story. The Regalla Ripper..."

Yarner shook his head. "You didn't get this from any of us, remember. You were at the scenes and you saw it with your own eyes, ok?"

"Of course," replied Ratcliffe. "Just tell me where I was..."

Yarner imparted the locations of the murders. Ratcliffe was excited now, struggling to sit still in his seat.

"So, any leads on who's doing the killing?" asked the reporter.

"That's the thing, Ratcliffe." Yarner paused, letting his words sink in. "It looks like it's a noble."

Ratcliffe paused, his mouth agape. He sat for a second, the charcoal trembling between his fingers. "How do you know?"

"The serving girl had bitten the culprit's little finger off. I pulled it out of her mouth. There was a signet ring on it."

"In Almas' name, Yarner, this is unbelievable," gasped Ratcliffe, licking his lips. "Which noble? Which family?"

"I didn't recognise it," lied Yarner. That would be too much. "And you didn't see it clearly enough, remember. But it was definitely a family sigil."

"The bastards will try and cover this up, Yarner, you know that?"

"I know," said Yarner, staring into his ale. "It will be as if those people just disappeared. Their lives would mean nothing. No justice. No truth. That's why I'm telling you."

"Thank you, sergeant. I appreciate this. The people will appreciate this. You've done the right thing."

"I know," replied Yarner, standing and draining his tankard. "If I can tell you any more I'll find you. Now remember, keep the watch out of your story."

He didn't wait for the reporter's reply. He pulled the collar of his leathers up and headed out into the daylight.

At least he had a few days rest with the family...

The carriage was as comfortable as could be expected. It was the best money could buy, after all. The inner sides were packed with stuffing beneath the ornate oak panelling to keep as much heat in as possible. He ran his fingers over the inlay, admiring the delicate carved scenes that ran up the walls and came together at the centre of the roof. They took the form of a hunt, hounds and horsemen flowing up the walls towards a carved boar that projected down from the ceiling. A lantern hung from the boar's tusks, unlit at present due to it still being early afternoon.

The seating and armrests were soft, padded velvet, but even with extra cushions they could not completely protect against the movement of the coach along the rough road. Cecil shifted his numb arse again as the coach's wheels hit another rut.

"Apologies, Master Wulska," he said to his guest. "I'm afraid even the best coaches are at the mercy of our roads when it comes to comfort."

"Nonsense, my lord," replied the middle-aged Yanari sat opposite Cecil. "It is infinitely more comfortable than our wagon."

Cecil's retinue had come upon the Yanari family only a few miles out from Regalla. Wulska was an artisan from the capital, travelling with his family in their wagon along the road east. Cecil had invited the artisan to join him in his coach. He could do with the company, and besides, he was the Lord Chancellor's son. It was only right that his retinue provided protection for citizen craftsmen travelling the roads of Castland.

"It is most gracious of you to offer us your protection, my lord," said Wulska. He was shifting in the seat, uncomfortable in the presence of nobility. He didn't seem to know how to position himself.

"The roads are safer than ever, Master Wulska, but even so there are still bandits. Fear not, though, you will have no finer protection than my personal guard."

Cecil smiled, pulling down the window and pushing his head out to look. Up ahead Q'thell was leading half of the mounted men, the Q'shari's sharp eyes scouting the road ahead and to the sides. They had entered the Old Forest, but this close to the capital the trees had been cut back some way from the road. As they got deeper in, the Q'shari's job would become more difficult, as the trees closed in on them like a smothering green blanket. Still, Cecil was confident his man could handle their safety. Nobody would be stupid enough to attack such a large, well-armed group anyway.

He looked back. Master Wulska's wife was driving their wagon behind Cecil's coach, and beyond that were a couple of his own carts loaded with provisions. Behind them road the other half of his personal guard, protecting their rear from any danger in the woods.

Cecil pushed the window shut, closing out the brisk afternoon air.

"You will be safe as long as you travel with us, Master Wulska. Tell me, where are you headed?"

"To the north, my lord," replied the artisan. "A couple of days on this road, then at the Green Man Inn we'll head up towards the Red Cairn Hills."

"A little bleak for the likes of a master craftsman from the capital, isn't it?" asked Cecil, raising an eyebrow.

"You flatter me, my lord," smiled the Yanari gracefully. "Alas, I am no master craftsman."

"But you are an artisan, are you not? I take it you are a member of the Artisan's Guild?"

Wulska nodded quickly. "Oh yes, my lord. I would not trade as an artisan without paying my dues, I promise you."

"Rest easy," laughed Cecil. "I am not trying to ensnare you, Master Wulska. I just assumed you would be advanced in the guild by now, given your age."

"Alas, I am a humble Yanari," replied Wulska, his eyes diverted to the carriage floor. "I am merely grateful that I am allowed to be a member of the great Artisan's Guild. A Yanari cannot be granted the title of Craftmaster, and should not aspire to it."

"Hmm…" Cecil had never realised that this was the case. He supposed it had never interested him before. His thoughts strayed to Kaly. He was missing her already, he realised. Did she, too, suffer this type of barrier in her life? "Tell me, Master Wulska, what do you craft?"

"I work with leather and animal hides, my lord. I also perform taxidermy."

"And would I have seen any of your work?" asked Cecil, pushing thoughts of Kaly from his mind. He would see her again soon enough, he had to be patient.

"I believe a boar I prepared for Iluma Porwesh was given to your father the Lord Chancellor, my lord."

Cecil knew the beast. It was displayed in his father's study. It was a magnificent specimen, and its preservation was immaculate. Cecil had seen some terrible efforts at taxidermy. He remembered one at Toby's father's townhouse in the capital; a fox, it's legs spread wide at impossible angles, the glass eyes wide and crossed, the mouth agape and twisted. Cecil had remarked it looked like it was being fucked up the arse.

"Your work is brilliant, Master Wulska. I find it hard to stomach that you are not able to be called a Craftmaster, for you display all the skills required of the title."

"You flatter me, my lord," smiled Wulska, bowing his head stiffly a couple of times in thanks.

"Tell me, why are you heading to the north? I do hope you aren't taking your skills away from the capital?"

"Yanara's grace, no, my lord," gasped Wulska. "I love Regalla. It is my home. But is my duty as a Yanari to observe Illumination at least once every five years."

Cecil cocked his head inquisitively.

"My apologies, my lord, it is not for me to burden you with my culture."

"No, no, my good man," insisted Cecil. "Please, I am interested. Tell me about this Illumination."

Wulska proceeded slowly, cautiously. "Well, the Yanari are not an abundant people. It is taught by Yanara that we must never be complacent with our lot in life. The Yanari have been beset by many misfortunes over the course of history. Yanara teaches that each of us must continue to develop their skills and expand their knowledge throughout their life, to ensure we are always prepared for the challenges ahead."

Wulska paused, seemingly gauging how these words have settled with the noble in front of him.

"Go on," urged Cecil, leaning forward intently.

"Hence the Illumination," continued Wulska, more comfortable now. "Every five years, at least, a Yanari must learn a new skill, or broaden their knowledge. They must make themselves a better Yanari."

"Interesting," pondered Cecil. The rest of the Castland population could benefit from his activity. "But, why have I never heard of this?"

"Alas, many Yanari do not follow these tenets strictly, my lord," shrugged Wulska. "It would not be obvious to someone who was not a Yanari. Many these days pay lip service to Illumination. They will read a book, or learn to juggle, or something equally inane."

"That is a shame," replied Cecil sincerely. "And what is it that you intend to do for Illumination?"

"We have not travelled much, my lord," replied Wulska. "In our youth, my wife and I worked hard. We needed money, a home, a life together. We put aside the excitement of youth, of revelry, of seeing the world outside the capital, and concentrated on building a future instead. Then came the children, and the responsibilities only became heavier. Now the children are older, and business is good. We have enough money to take some time away from the capital."

"So you are going to travel and get drunk? Live the youth that you missed out on?" Cecil smiled gently, teasing. "Sounds a little inane..."

Wulska returned the smile, bowing his head briefly. "No, my lord. We are going to look upon the Red Cairn Hills. Sketch the stone burial mounds. Take rubbings of the engravings. When we get back to the capital, we intend to research, to see if we can discover any further insights into the history of the area and the men who lived and died there all those years ago."

Cecil nodded. "Very admirable, Master Wulska."

"Thank you, my lord."

"Tell me, my friend. Do you partake in wine?"

"Very occasionally, my lord. We try to save our money for the business, and for the children."

"Don't worry, my good man," smiled Cecil, pulling a dripping wineskin out from a wooden bucket of melting iced water beneath his seat. "I'm not going to charge you..."

Cecil produced two goblets from a cabinet above the Yanari artisan's head and filled them with the crisp, golden white wine from southern Barralegne. He handed one to Wulska, clinking them together in a toast.

"To your Illumination..."

The Yanari skulked in the corner of the tavern, observing the room. Grey eyes peered out from beneath the hood of the rough sackcloth tunic, darting from patron to patron, taking in the intervening scene as they moved.

He was like all Yanari, short and pale. A gnarled white hand lifted the tankard of ale to his hooded face, the rough lips taking a sip, spitting the liquid back into the vessel rather than imbibing it. Tayuk didn't drink. Ever. It made you loose. It made your tongue loose. It made your movements loose. It made your mind loose.

Tayuk was the opposite of loose. He was like a taut spring, ready to snap like a bear trap at any moment. Not out of control; calculated, like the trap, ready for the correct pressure to be applied at the opportune moment.

There was something that set Tayuk apart from the other Yanari in the tavern. He was not slight of build. He was short, yes, but he was stocky around the shoulders. His arms weren't thick and muscled, they were tight as wire and hard as steel. It was what had set his path in life, long ago as an orphan child. Someone had seen his potential, and now this was what he was...

Tayuk. The Knife.

The Truth in the Sun was a Yanari tavern. Nestled in the north of Regalla, separated from the poor district of the Norther Quarter only by the North Gate to the capital, was the Yanari area known as Little Yanar. A quiet area. A miniature city within a city, with poor areas, merchant zones, artisan streets, opulent mansions.

The Truth was in the poorer area. Most Yanari didn't drink to excess, and those that got inebriated in public tended to be poor. It wasn't a shithole, not like some of the dives in the Northern Quarter, and there was never any violence. Yanari knew that it was in their interests to stick together. Their history taught them that.

Tayuk's eyes swept the bar again, searching for the street pedlar. He found him in the corner. Panil had just arrived and joined his friends at their table. He had bought a round of drinks.

As he should. He's made a fair profit today; his purse will be heavy.

It was Tayuk's job to know the business of all the Yanari, rich and poor. He moved among them. He listened. He overheard.

He also knew the people that the Yanari dealt with. The people they bought from, the people they sold to. He knew whether they were happy or displeased.

And on the streets of the Old Market this afternoon, Panil had sold a set of steel finger rings to a merchant. Eight rings, sized in pairs for each finger. Intricate engravings. Polished to a sheen by Panil overnight, over and over until you could see your reflection.

Panil blacked up his teeth when he was peddling his wares at the market. Scruffed up his white hair, ran soot through it so it turned grey. Rubbed ash into his skin, under his eyes. Walked with a stoop and a limp, gimped his arm a little. It added thirty years to his age, maybe more. Nothing like the thirty-year-old man who sat in the Truth now, downing a tankard of ale, bright eyes flicking around the room alertly.

Panil was a good actor, too. He could act stupid, like an old man who had lost his mind and sold trinkets without realising their value. The rings *were* steel, but they were polished up like silver, maybe even white gold. And the merchant had spotted them, glinting in the watery afternoon sun. Tayuk had heard him talking with his assistant: "Nobody makes rings out of steel."

And Panil had not tricked the merchant. He had been honest. He'd told him the rings were steel. But the merchant had thought he knew better, thought he saw a quick profit. He had paid over the odds. Not much, but a tidy profit for Panil.

Tayuk had watched, had heard the trade. He had followed the merchant to his valuer, who had given him the unfortunate news. And the merchant had not been impressed.

And now a man was coming. Tayuk didn't know who, but he knew he was coming. He sipped at the tankard again, spitting the warm liquid back into the mug.

The tavern door flapped open. The man entered. Tayuk knew it was him. He was a Castlander, not a Yanari. Not that outsiders didn't drink at the Truth. There were a few there now. But Tayuk knew them all, recognised their faces, knew their business. He didn't know this man.

The hired thug wasn't tall, he was just bigger than a Yanari. He wasn't heavily built, medium at most, but again he was thicker set than a Yanari. His hair was dark, his eyes brown. An outsider.

Tayuk eased along the wall slowly, looking into his mug, eyes peering out from under the hood as the man moved into the room, looking from Yanari to Yanari. One hand was behind his back, under his tunic. Tayuk saw the bulge of a cudgel or a blackjack.

The Knife didn't move yet. He leaned by the door, watching. Couldn't strike now, had to be sure. Maybe the guy was just lost...

The thug spotted Panil, laughing with his group in the corner. He took a few seconds, looking closer, checking his was sure it was the right Yanari. Panil's appearance was different now he had bathed, the man was double-checking, sizing up the face, the eyes. He seemed to have made his decision. He was walking over.

Tayuk slid across from the door, getting behind the man. How could a man walk into a room full of Yanari with a cudgel and beat one to a pulp? The Yanari were not a violent people, that was the reason for Tayuk. But surely, this wasn't right? Was this why his people had been so badly treated in the past, because they did not stand up for themselves?

The thug was at the table now, pointing at Panil.

"You're the pedlar from the market, yeah?"

Panil's eyes widened, his head shaking, his mouth moving but no words coming out.

The man brought his hand out from behind his back, the candlelight shining off the polished wood of the blackjack. "You fucked with the wrong man, milky..."

Tayuk gritted his teeth. The word stuck in his head for a second, bringing back memories that threatened to engulf him in rage.

Anger is bad. Anger makes you rash. Anger leads to mistakes.

He regained his composure, staggered forward in a drunken gait, one foot finding the floor, then another, slowly, ungainly. He bumped into the back of the thug, dropping the tankard and letting the contents spill down the man's tunic.

"Sorry..." he mumbled, head down beneath the hood.

The man spun round, raising the blackjack. "You fucking..."

73

The Knife struck. The blade flashed forward, sticking beneath the ribcage, across into the liver. His hand grabbed the man's armpit, squeezing the muscles there, an iron grip pinching nerves. The blackjack clattered to the floor.

The thug was gasping in pain, struggling to speak. The Knife pushed the blade, wriggled it slightly. He pulled the man towards him, stepping backwards, leading him towards the nearby corridor that led to the back yard of the inn. This was all planned. Panil and his friends always sat here, next to the corridor. The man followed, struggling to keep his feet as his eyes began to rise up into the back of his head.

The Knife bore his weight, pulling him down the corridor and out into the yard. They were alone. He pushed forward, twisted the blade through ninety degrees, ripped it out. Dark blood followed, pumping across the cobbles and the Knife's trousers.

The thug was gone. He crashed forward onto the stone with a sickening thud.

Tayuk worked quickly. He didn't want to leave too much blood for the Truth's owners to clean up. He hoisted the corpse over his shoulder, throwing it onto the back of the cart he had left in the yard. He pulled the pile of sacks there over the body before jumping up into the seat. He grabbed the reins, flicking them gently and clicking his tongue. The cart lurched forward, out into the street.

Now Tayuk had to tidy up. One of the abattoirs had just received a herd of pigs for slaughter tomorrow. Pigs got shipped in live. Pork didn't keep well. And pigs would eat anything...

"Where is that thrice-damned priest?" screeched Mayor Kove, clenching his clammy little hands in theatrical rage and slamming them down on the desk in front of him.

Sheriff Wrathson averted his eyes from the official's glare, shuffling towards the window of the mayor's office. He was careful to avoid the plush Altanyan rug that lay in the centre of the room. He had already been admonished for traipsing mud on it when he had arrived with the news of the dead sheep. The mayor was livid enough without intensifying him further.

Wrathson peered through the glass, looking out over the village from the commanding vantage point of the mayor's house. "I can't see him coming. He is old, mayor. It will take the deputies some time to get him back from the hills."

Kove hissed his displeasure. "The sooner that old fool dies so we can get a younger cleric the better."

The sheriff busied himself inspecting a spider, busy tending its web on the outside of the window. He watched as its legs moved, gently spinning thread like a small, black hand wriggling its fingers in some intricate, stationary dance. He wished he was the spider. Concentrating on building, maintaining, catching flies. Not dealing with... this.

"Get away from that window, sheriff," snapped Kove, searching for something to lash out at with his tongue. "Staring won't bring them back any quicker."

"Yes, mayor," replied Wrathson, skulking over and taking his place at the edge of the rug in front of the desk once more. It was like being back in the schoolhouse, being chastised by his teacher. That had happened a lot. He had been a poor student, always stood in front of a desk, a tongue or a ruler lashing out at him. Unsurprising he had left before his twelfth birthday.

"Why would the ungrateful little bastards do it?" snarled Kove, glaring again at the sheriff. He was playing with a silver-plated letter opener now, scratching angrily at the desk. Wrathson pondered whether the little man was going to try and stick it in him. He hoped so. The sheriff took the verbal abuse, the withering scolding. It was a job, and it paid well. But if the little shit tried anything physical, Wrathson would pull him apart like a straw doll. He had never let anyone hit him and get away with it, not since school, not since the teachers. Not since he had become a man at such a young age.

"We'll have to find them and beat it out of them, I suppose," he replied. He realised his fists were clenched at his sides. He relaxed them, flexing his thick fingers.

"Baronet Wender took them in when they arrived here. I remember the day. Some sob story or other. He gave them work. A future. And this is how they repay him. Killing a deer, killing two youngsters, killing his sheep."

"We don't know that they..."

A withering stare from the mayor cut Wrathson off mid-sentence. "They did it. All of it. And they need to hang for it."

A timid knock came from the door. Wrathson sighed with relief, hurrying over to open it. The two young deputies waited outside as Father Pietr shuffled slowly in. As Wrathson closed the door the old priest approached the desk, his muddy shoes leaving a trail across the rug before he plonked himself down heavily in the chair opposite the mayor.

"Have a seat," growled Kove through clenched teeth.

"You made better time than I expected," said Wrathson as he moved over to stand behind the priest, trying to ease the tension. He couldn't tell whether Kove was more incensed about recent events or the hammering his beloved rug was taking.

"Your lads brought a cart for me, sheriff," smiled the old priest thinly. "Although I fear the journey has jolted my old bones all out of place…"

"*Nobody gives two fucks about your bones, old man!*" The mayor finally boiled over, screaming at the top of his voice and jamming the letter opener into the already-scarred wood of the desk. It bent on impact. A cheap piece of shit. Wrathson stifled a smirk.

Pietr paused for a moment, cocking his head to one side and looking first to the letter opener and then to Kove, who was visibly seething now. His pale, blubbery lips had gone red, slobber gathering on them.

"You appear to have broken your little knife," said Pietr, meeting the mayor's stare.

Wrathson burst out into a snigger. He brought his forearm across his face, resuming his position at the window and staring intently out at nothing whilst he regained his composure.

Kove was breathing heavily now, his little knuckles turning white as he kept his hand gripped around the broken tool. Was he actually going to try to use it to stab the priest? Again, Wrathson hoped so. If he tried to kill a man of the gods, the sheriff would punish him for it. He realised that his tolerance for the little runt had reached the end of the line. He would sort this business out in the village, then it was time for him to move on, before he got himself into trouble.

"What did you see, father?" asked Wrathson, walking over and standing on the rug beside the cleric.

"I'll ask the questions, thank you very much," snapped Kove.

"Ask them then. If we're going after these lads they've already got a head start on us." Wrathson met the mayor's stare this time. Pietr sensed a defiance in the sheriff that he hadn't seen before. He wasn't the scolded child from the cellar. Something had changed in him.

Interesting…

Kove broke eye contact first, turning his glare on Pietr. "What happened up there, old man?"

"The sheep have all been ripped apart, just like the new milking lad told the sheriff," replied Pietr. "The stench of the demon was thick on the air, just like at the Starling house."

"Enough of this demon nonsense," snapped Kove. "Where are shepherds?"

"Mathias and Charo are gone. The deputies checked their shelter. They've taken their belongings and fled."

"See, sheriff?" smirked Kove. "Innocent men don't run. Get your deputies and go after them."

Wrathson nodded. The mayor was right. He loathed to admit it, but the lads *had* told the baronet about the deer. Maybe that had been an accident. But this time they had ran.

"I'll need trackers," said Wrathson, heading towards the door. He could feel the rush already. He hadn't seen any action in this village, other than domestic disputes and the odd drunken brawl.

"I'll send word to the baronet," said Kove, joining the sheriff at the door. "I'm sure he'll be happy to lend you the services of his gamekeeper, given the circumstances. I'll have him in the village square within the hour."

"I'll take Willem, too," nodded Wrathson. "He's the best hunter in town. Supplies half the meat for the butcher. I'll have to pay him, though…"

"Of course. Deputise him if you have to, just be ready to leave in an hour."

"I should go too," said Pietr, struggling to turn in the seat to face the men as they hurried to leave the room. They paused in the doorway.

"Is this some kind of sick joke?" sneered Kove, a disdainful grin spreading across his rubbery pink lips.

"Seriously, father, we need to move quickly," said Wrathson. "The trail would kill you."

"But you'll need me if they have their demon with them…"

The sheriff paused, looking between the priest and the mayor.

A demon… Their demon…

Kove burst out into a snigger. "I thought we had been through this, sheriff. There's no demon. Now move. Be ready in one hour, no longer. I want these bastards swinging from the balcony of my house…"

Wrathson paused a second longer. His eyes met those of the priest, a gentle look of sad concern on his face.

The sheriff shook his head and strode from the room.

There are no demons...

Chapter Eleven

The Green Man was one of the busiest coaching inns in Castland, so Cecil had heard. He had not travelled much, devoting his time to his studies and his leisure pursuits in Regalla, so he did not have much basis for comparison. It was certainly bustling as they stepped through the doors, having arrived after dark. The Yanari family's wagon had broken a wheel around midday, and it had taken some time for his wainwright to fix it.

Cecil was surprised that Master Wulska had not had the good sense to bring spare wheels. After all, if his wagon had broken one after only a day or two's travel on the relatively well-kept East Road, how did he expect it to have made the journey into the Red Cairn Hills?

As it happened it had given them a chance to have lunch beside a babbling brook in the Old Forest. The early afternoon had been surprisingly sunny in the clearing around the stream, and they had set out a trestle table and eaten the last of the soft bloomer bread before it went stale, accompanied by cheese from around Castland; hard goat's cheese from the north, bitter sheep's cheese from the east, the strong mature cheddars of the central regions around Regalla and Westroad. Master Wulska's wife had supplied some Yanari cheese from their wagon, a soft and creamy rinded goat variety that put Cecil's own Snowgate offering to shame. He had made a mental note to ask Kaly about it when he saw her next.

They had washed it down with Panda Port from the Bandit Country. A rare vintage of fortified wine that was, technically, illegal in Castland, Cecil brought it out only on special occasions. It had played off against the cheese flavours delightfully as they ate and listened to the world around them; the trickling and splashing of the water, the calls of animals and wild birds. They had even managed to grab a basket of crisp, bitter apples from a tree in the forest.

They had whiled away half the afternoon by the brook. The wainwright had had to adapt one of the numerous spare wheels carried for Cecil's coach to fit the Wulska's wagon, and he had insisted the man also made them four more so that they had a full set for the rest of their journey. After all, he was in no hurry. He wasn't expected in Bannar for a couple of weeks, and if the upstart lord had to wait, then he had to wait…

Dusk had been upon them as the retinue pulled up at the walls of the coaching inn. The gates had been locked up; it was well past time that any sane traveller would be on the roads. But Cecil had adequate protection, and the setting of the sun had not caused them to befall any harm. The hired guard at the gate had been suspicious, but the Lord Chancellor's note had ensured them entrance.

The innkeeper greeted them at the door, a barmaid offering to take their travelling coats. Cecil declined politely, taking in the scene before him. The Green Man had seemed grand from the outside; a large, stone and timber building surrounded by high-walled yards and outbuildings. Inside did not disappointment. The main room was huge, larger than any inn that Cecil had frequented. The bar was set in the centre, able to serve any of the several smaller rooms into which the interior of the inn was split. Fires roared in each room. The heat was immense, and welcome after the cold of the Castland evening.

The rooms were a thunder of noise. Men and women of all types were crammed on benches, chairs, barrels. The space between them was filled with people standing. They were laughing, arguing, drinking, eating. The odd lesser noble or knight had grabbed a booth, their retinues gathered around them like a keep's defensive wall. Caravaners and traders discussed deals over ale. Travelling mercenaries argued, told stories, arm wrestled, spat and cursed. Commoners travelling huddled together, keeping their packs and their children close, uncomfortable hemmed in by more worldly-wise folk. Virtually every walk of life, packed into an inn.

Cecil both loved it and loathed it. The heat, the noise, the smell of food and beer and sweat. It made him feel alive, pressed into the brutal reality of life in all its different facets. And yet it was ugly, uncouth. Where was the segregation? Why should the upper classes be pushed up to the stench of poverty and baseness? Cecil didn't mind it whilst out gallivanting in the Northern Quarter, but that was a choice. This was the only place to stay, and yet the wealthy were forced to mingle with the poor and their filth.

"What can I do for you, Lord Cramwall?" asked the innkeeper, bowing deeply.

"My lord will suffice, inn keep," replied Cecil. "Lord Cramwall is my father. I need rooms for myself, my manservant this family. My men will sleep in the common room."

The innkeeper was looking from side-to-side, avoiding Cecil's gaze. This did not bode well.

"My lord, as you can see I am stuffed to the rafters." His hands were twisting uncomfortably, the fingers trying to strangle each other. "Even the common room is full."

Cecil glanced around, taking in the various groups cramming the rooms.

"I am sure if you ask around some of these fine people will give up their rooms and sleep in their carts. Tell them I will reimburse them double, and pay for all their food and drink for the evening."

"I will try, my lord."

"Good man. As for my men, there are roughly the same number as those mercenaries over there. Tell them we are on the Lord Chancellor's business and I will give them a gold piece each if they vacate their beds in the common room and sleep in that barn out there. They look pretty drunk already, no doubt they won't even notice the difference by the time they take to their beds."

The owner looked less convinced by this. "I will try, my lord."

"Now, we need some space to eat and drink. My men will set up trestle tables outside. The Yanari and I will take that small room over there."

Cecil gestured through an archway to one of the rooms off the main bar area. It was bustling, like the rest of the inn.

"But, my lord, it is full."

"No statement of good news ever started with the word 'but', my good man," smiled Cecil. "Just shift some people around. Get those lot out here. There are a couple of knights and lesser nobles in here, they can move into our room. We don't mind sharing with them. Some of these merchants don't look overly shabby, they can come too." The innkeeper was looking to the floor. "Honestly, man, you can't expect us to dine with pig farmers and travelling sellswords."

"You are right, of course, my lord."

"Good," said Cecil. "I shall see my men are stowing the horses and getting set up whilst you rearrange the room."

Cecil washed down a chunk of pumpkinseed bread with a swig of wine, wiping his mouth with a handkerchief embroidered with the emblem of the Cramwall family; a simple, strong, stone wall topped with a crown.

The food was good, in fairness to the inn keep's wife. He had ordered them a whole roast chicken each. The flavours were excellent, the flesh plump and moist, the stuffing hearty and chunky with safe and chestnut. The skin of the birds was crisped to perfection, infused with just the right amount of taste from the sprigs of thyme pressed into the skin.

The wine wasn't bad, either, for a backwater inn. He supposed it was the best-placed inn in the country outside of a major city. The Green Man sat on the point where the East Road from Regalla to Kassell met the major trading road that headed northwards up from the southern ports of Castland and the Bandit Country. After crossing the East Road it headed north and then west, up towards Snowgate. The inn sat at the intersection of two of the most well-used roads in the country. A prime spot.

There had been some filthy looks from the patrons when the group had re-entered the inn and taken up their spot in the newly-set up back room. Cecil had laughed them off. Q'thell was standing by the door, chewing at a chicken leg and watching for any sign of dissent from the rest of the inn's inhabitants.

The select few sat with them looked relieved to have been segregated from the mixed crowd. They were talking amongst themselves now, occasionally passing a smile or a nod of respect Cecil's way.

This is how it should be...

"Is the food to your liking, Master Wulska?" asked Cecil, chewing down on another morsel of melt-in-the-mouth breast.

"It is delightful, my lord," nodded Wulska, taking a small sip of the wine. "You really have been too generous to our humble Yanari family."

"Nonsense," smiled Cecil. "We should value our artisans and the families that support them. When I get back to the capital I intend to raise the issue of your Craftmaster rank with the Guildmaster personally."

"Please, my lord, that is not necessary."

"Of course it is. I had no idea of this situation. I cannot understand why no Yanari has brought this before me sooner."

Wulska shrugged, losing himself in his food.

"It is because too many Yanari equate humility with apathy." The words came from Wulska's wife, Esme. She was looking at the artisan with a mixture of sadness and disgust. "It is our failing."

"Forgive me, good lady, but I do not understand," said Cecil, placing his fork down gently and giving her his most sincere look. "Why would your people just accept this injustice in silence?"

Wulska shook his head, placing a hand on his wife's arm. Esme shook it off gently.

"The lord asked, Alit," she said, turning back to Cecil. "History has been cruel to our people, my lord. *Men* have been cruel to our people. In the old times, back in the Illicean Empire, the Yanari fought for their freedom and their rights. But this led to them being scattered throughout the realms of men, guests in the countries of others. Since then, the Yanari have become placid, weak. They do not fight, they remain 'humble'. They keep their heads down like dogs, hoping the master who hit them will not do so again if they remain docile."

"You are not guests. You are Castlanders. A Castlander who is as skilled as your husband deserves his rank in society, in the same way as any other. He should demand it, it is his right."

"Alas, Alit is a Yanari. He is too meek to demand. He accepts his lot in life. He abides."

"Master Wulska is a good man," insisted Cecil, sensing a slight towards his travelling companion.

"He is," admitted Esme, taking her husband's hand and gazing lovingly at him. "He is. I could not have asked for a better husband, a better companion, a better father for our children. I am not insulting him when I say that he is weak. He is what he is; a Yanari. *We* are Yanari. Powerless Yanari."

"You have friends who will support you. There are enough Yanari in the country, in the capital, for you to be heard."

"Really, my lord?" asked Esme. Her tone was harder now. Piercing grey eyes met his own. "Are *you* a Yanari? Do you walk the streets of Regalla and get called milky? Milker? Corpse? Linen skin?"

Cecil, for once, was speechless. Did this happen? Did his dear Kaly suffer these insults?

"I thought not, my lord," said Esme, her tone softening. "I, too, am guilty of being a Yanari when I say that these things will never change. We are here, we are tolerated, but we are not welcome. We are powerless..."

They were interrupted by a commotion at the doorway to their back room. Q'thell had tossed down his gnawed chicken leg at the approach of three of the mercenaries Cecil had spotted upon arrival. The Q'shari was blocking the doorway, looking down at the men, red eyes blazing.

"Let me past, blackman," snarled the biggest of the men. His gnarled, scarred face was full of drunken rage as he stared up at Q'thell, gritting his teeth. "Where's that fucking fat little lord?"

Q'thell smiled, his fangs glinting orange in the flickering light of the hearth fire. He didn't move, but looked over his shoulder to Cecil. "I think he's talking about you, my lord."

Cecil's face reddened as he pulled himself to his feet. He strode over to the door, making sure to keep Q'thell between him and the mercenaries. How dare this thug speak to him, the son of the Lord Chancellor, like that? In front of his guests...

"Do we have a problem, sir?" asked Cecil, his hand resting on the hilt of his rapier.

"Looks that way," sneered Q'thell, returning his stare to the man in front of him. "This fool's still got his chain mail on. Must be very uncomfortable. Probably grated his nipples off. Probably what's making him act so rashly."

"I'm not going to tell you to fuck off again, tree dweller," spat the mercenary, shoving Q'thell with both hands in the chest.

The Q'shari didn't move. He raised a hand, planting the palm in the mail-shirted mercenary's chest, pushing him back a couple of steps. "You're right about that. You tell me to fuck off again, or lay those paws on me, and I'll dice you right here."

Q'thell was sizing the men up now, slitted red eyes darting from one to another. Only the biggest one had his chain mail shirt covering his leathers, the others just had the hide. Decent quality leathers, too. They must earn a fair amount of coin. Which meant they were good at what they did. All bearing arms, swords strapped to their belts. All ugly, which meant they had been in plenty of fights. All drunk, which would make it easy.

"Q'thell, please, calm down," laughed Cecil hollowly. "Let us see what these lads want."

"Lad?" sneered one of the men, spitting on the floor at Q'thell's feet. "I've got ten years on you, fatboy. Ten years of fighting, not eating and sitting."

"Then why, pray tell, are you behaving like a petulant child?" asked Cecil. "What is it you want? You are interrupting our supper."

"These men are sergeants in the toughest mercenary outfit this side of Regalla, boy," said the first man, stepping back up toe-to-toe with Q'thell. "Not wise to call them children."

79

"And you are?" asked Q'thell, his tongue playing with his fangs, tasting the air. No fear coming from the human, he would have been able to taste it. Probably too drunk to know he was in trouble.

"I'm Captain Denger Kral of the Old Foresters." The man was obviously expecting recognition. Q'thell didn't oblige. He had heard of them. Middle of the range hired soldiers. "Veterans of every way since our founding 200 years ago."

"You're 200 years old?" sniggered Cecil.

Kral paused for a second, the words sinking in through the drink, his face turning slowly purple. "The Foresters' name is, yes. And we bring honour to that name with our skill in battle. These men here fought in the Raskan War. Your father hired us. That's how good we are."

"And, did he not pay you?" asked Cecil, feigning bemusement. "I am struggling to figure out why you are interrupting our meal."

"Because nobody insults my men by telling them they'll be sleeping in a fucking barn. And nobody insults me and my sergeants by telling them to sleep outside in a cart."

"I see where there has been a misunderstanding," smiled Cecil. "I'm not *telling* you to move for my men and I, who are, I hasten to add, on the Lord Chancellor's business. I am *paying* you to move. I thought all you people loved coin? Is it not coin that motivates you?"

"Not when we want a fucking bed for the night, no," snapped Kral. "We're keeping our spots."

"No," said Cecil. His voice was firm, bolstered by the wine and the afternoon drinking port. He watched Q'thell's body tense as he sensed what was coming. "I am offering to pay you to move. If you will not, then I have plenty of men outside who will put you to sleep in the ground rather than in the barn."

"Trouble for you is," sneered Kral. "Like you said, little boy, they're outside. And we're in here..."

Q'thell sighed with disappointment.

Why say that? Why telegraph what you're doing?

The three men rushed him. He knew he couldn't hold them all. He grabbed Kral by the scruff of his chain mail shirt, pulling him forward and peeling off to the side. As he span away the other two men staggered forward, put off balance as the resistance they expected from the Q'shari did not manifest. Cecil stepped back, whipping the rapier from his belt.

Q'thell turned with the mercenary captain, helping his momentum carry his head into the wall. He pulled back the collar of the chain mail.

Too loose. Should have got it fitted more tightly. Less comfortable, more use.

In a flash Q'thell had one of the daggers sheathed beneath his armpits in his hand. He drove it down into the flesh of Kral's exposed shoulder, between the clavicle and the back of the rib cage. It slid down into the mercenary's chest easily, deep and fatal. Q'thell twisted, pulling it out in a spray of black blood.

He turned quickly. Cecil was waving the rapier in containment strikes at the two mercenary sergeants, who were struggling drunkenly to unsheathe their swords. The young noble moved well, Q'thell noted. Textbook, predictable, but well enough.

Q'thell struck the nearest man, the dagger penetrating the side of his neck, between the spine and the windpipe. He pulled forward, slashing the mercenary's throat open. More blood pumped forth, covering the carpet at Cecil's feet.

Q'thell pushed the body to the floor. The final mercenary had his longsword out now, bringing it up to bear. It didn't matter about Cecil's skill with the rapier now, one big two-handed strike would snap that rapier in two. Q'thell twisted forward, slashing his blade across the back of the mercenary's arm just above the elbow, severing the tendons. His fingers went limp, the blade dropping to the floor. Q'thell arced round behind him, spinning to deliver the finishing blow...

Cecil lunged forward, leading knee bent, back leg pushed straight, fencing stance strong and true. The rapier pierced the mercenary's throat, the thin blade protruding from the back of his neck. By the time Q'thell completed his spin and buried his dagger in the man's eye, he was already dead.

Q'thell smiled. The teeth glinted. He hated to admit it, but he was quietly impressed.

Cecil stood, rigid, the weight of the dead man weighing on the rapier. Q'thell stepped forward, pushing the corpse of the mercenary off the end of the blade. It crumpled to the floor with a thud.

Q'thell put his face close to Cecil's ear, whispering. "First time?"

Cecil nodded. The colour was draining from his normally ruddy cheeks.

"Feels good, yes?"

80

The young lord didn't respond. Q'thell turned away as the inn keep scurried into the room, waving his arms frantically. "No, no, no."

"It's all done, little man," said Q'thell, knife in hand as he walked over to the corpse of the mercenary captain. "How many rooms did they have?"

"Two," replied the innkeeper, shaking his head in disbelief as he took in the blood pooling on the floor of the room. "One for Captain Kral, one shared by the sergeants."

Q'thell reached down, gripping the captain's ankle. He turned to Cecil, snapping long, thin, black fingers. "Two rooms, my lord."

Cecil shook his head, regaining his composure. "Yes. Two rooms. I'll have Q'thell share with me. Master Wulska, you and your family have beds for the night, it would seem."

Q'thell smiled, dragging the corpse of the mercenary from the room, dagger still in hand. A trail of blood followed them. "I'll deal with the bodies. And I'll tell the mercenaries they're sleeping in the barn after all."

Cecil nodded, a smiling crossing his face slowly. He walked across the room, confidence returning to his gait. He sat down beside Esme, looking her in those pale blue eyes.

"I have power," he said, reaching over and taking a swig from his goblet. "Which means that you are not powerless."

The little girl plodded through the dusk, her movements slow and clumsy. The shadows cast around her by the pale moonlight shifted and moved as the tall trees drifted lazily in the night wind. It was cold, but she did not feel it. It was dark, but she was not scared.

Well, a little scared.

She clutched her straw doll closer, pulling it into her armpit. She stroked its straggly hair, ran a tiny finger across its simple face.

How had she gotten here? She looked back over her shoulder, brushing her thin hair from her eyes. Through the trees, the lights in the windows of her family's homestead were distant already, tiny pinpricks in the distance.

She remembered saying her prayers, climbing into her cot. Her mother had kissed her goodnight. He father was dozing in the rough rocking chair by the fire downstairs. He hadn't bothered to come up. He never did. He was always too tired, too worried about the crops. Sometimes she heard them arguing downstairs.

They had been arguing tonight. The memories were hazy. She had buried her head under her rough straw pillow, trying to drown out the voices. Angry voices.

But she had heard it.

The tapping at the window. At first she had been scared, had kept her head under the pillow, willing the noise to go away, to be drowned out like the raised voices.

But the tapping hadn't gone away. It had gotten louder. She had peered out, seen the eyes at the window. Thin, black slits in a misty grey cloud. Not red, the colour of anger and blood. Not envious, greedy green. Not cold, heartless blue. Just black, set against harmless, passive grey. Her own eyes were dark brown. Her mother said they were nearly black, beautiful eyes where the pupil was hardly visible.

He remembered rising slowly, carefully, pulling the rough blanket around her nightdress to shield against the cold as she timidly approached the window.

There was a gap then. She vaguely remembered a feeling of pain, a crunch in her ankle as she had dropped down from the upstairs window to the ground below. The blanket had fallen from her hands a few hundred yards from the farmstead, but she wasn't cold. She was moving. She needed to be somewhere.

Blackness. Nothing.

She came to her senses again, stumbling on the rough ground beneath the trees. She skinned her knee on a protruding tree root. She sat for a second, looking at the broken, furrowed skin, trying to decide whether to cry. There was no blood. She decided not to.

As she stood, the broken skin on her knee tightened up. She looked down, peering into the darkness. The trees were thicker here. She was further away from home than before. A lot further. The lights were no longer visible even in the difference. The land was different, wilder.

The girl returned her gaze to her knee. The blood was coming now, oozing from the breaks in the skin. She shook her head, tears welling in her eyes. Where was she? Why was she here? It was cold, and she was scared. Her knee hurt. Her ankle clicked as she moved it, bone grating against bone.

She pulled back her head and opened her throat, a piercing cry splitting the cold night air, leaving in its wake a haze of cold breath.

The demon was losing its temper. It was nestled in the back of the girl's mind, hiding amongst the thoughts, slipping between memories, trying to evade her consciousness. It had taken control occasionally, pushing her onwards, guiding her in the right direction. It knew how this worked. Taking a mind was intricate. Too invasive and the human would break. And this was just a child, so much more delicate.

But this was ridiculous. The girl was weak, trembling, pathetic.

It had broken her ankle jumping from the window, it was pretty sure. Or at least a bone in the foot. It had hoped the fear would drive the child on, the sense of purpose. If it was being honest, it was out of practice. Usually it could take time on a possession. Feel the human's fears, their motivations, what would push them on, make them more susceptible.

But it didn't have time for that. It needed this girl, and it needed her now. The master had set it a task, and the girl just happened to be in the right place to push it along.

Not even the right place, really. Too far away, but the nearest available host. It would be difficult; the girl's body was weak.

She was crying deeply now. Making too much noise. Curled up in a ball like every pathetic human, wanting the gods to save her but willing to do nothing to save herself.

It had had enough.

The demon surged into her mind, taking control again. Puppeteering humans was so cumbersome, like having half your brain removed. It got the feeling for her movements again, flailing a foot out wildly as it figured out how to move the heavy limb.

Slowly, awkwardly, the girl clambered to her feet. The ankle cracked again as it bore weight, but the demon didn't care. It didn't feel her pain, it wasn't linked to her that closely. And she wouldn't be feeling it. The girl's mind had been pushed to the back now, squeezed out by its own oppressive power.

It concentrated, finding its balance. The demon tested itself, pushing the youngster's arms out behind her body, then twisted them back against themselves. The joints cracked as it brought the palms of her hands round in front of her head, touching her face from behind.

It was amazing what the mortals could do with their bodies, if only they were brave enough to try, to let go...

The demon released the arms, letting them fall away behind the girl's back and return to her sides.

It needed to move. It concentrated, the girl plonking one foot in front of the other, stomping awkwardly across the uneven forest floor. With every other step the ankle cracked.

82

Chapter Twelve

Charo and Mathias huddled round their small fire, shivering beneath their sheepskins. The remains on the thin, tasteless vegetable stew bubbled in the cooking pot, the only sound in the still, cold other than the spitting of the last twigs dying in the receding flames.

They had long since stopped trying to warm their hands on the fire, it was too close to dying now. The best approach seemed to be to keep your arms and hands under the sheepskins and keep your legs as close to the fire as possible, but as the flames guttered out the cold began to seep into their feet, creeping up their calves and thighs quickly.

Charo kicked his legs to try to keep warm. It was late, the dark of the night drawing closer through the trees, creeping in to envelop them as the fire reduced itself to glowing embers, but neither of them felt like sleeping. They were dead tired, but the prospect of curling up on the cold ground and trying to get another broken night's sleep was enough to make Charo cry.

The shadows of Mathias' face broke into a weak attempt at a smile. "You should try to get some sleep, little brother. We've been pushing pretty hard."

Charo nodded, not moving. "My feet hurt."

"I'm sure the cold will numb them soon enough," joked Mathias. Except it wasn't a joke. They both knew it was true. "I'm sorry, that wasn't funny."

"It's okay." Charo forced a smile to reassure his older brother. "How much further do we need to go?"

"I don't know," admitted Mathias. "I don't know the land this way. I don't know where there are villages or towns. We just need to get as far away as possible, start over again. We've done it before."

"I remember," nodded Charo. "You carried me."

"I did," chuckled Mathias. "But that was a long time ago. You were a lot smaller then. Don't start getting any ideas..."

"I won't," laughed Charo. "I'll keep up, I promise. I have to. I'm sorry, Mathias. This is all my fault."

"Why would you say such a thing?" asked Mathias, shaking his head. "You didn't kill the sheep."

"I know. I just feel like I brought this on us. I was looking at the moon that night, thinking of werewolves. Maybe I woke it, whatever it is. Maybe I brought it down on us."

"Rubbish," snapped Mathias. "Don't think like that. I don't know what killed those sheep, but it wasn't your fault."

"Maybe," said Charo, looking absently over his shoulder into the thick darkness amongst the tall, powerful trees of the forest. "I can still feel it, you know. It's still here."

Mathias didn't answer. He shivered suddenly, a chill running up his spine. The hairs on the back of his neck stood on end.

"Why did we run last time?" asked Charo, returning his wide, fearful eyes to Mathias. "Was that my fault too?"

"No, Charo," replied Mathias. "This isn't your fault, and neither was last time."

"Why did we leave, then?"

"Father stole a loaf of bread. He was trying to feed us. You probably don't remember, but he was desperately trying to stay off the drink. I'd never seen him so determined. He shook most of the day, it was obviously torturing him, but he tried. But nobody would employ him. People thought he was unstable, unreliable."

"He was," said Charo, his eyes staring at the forest floor.

"True. But he was trying, this time, Charo. He couldn't feed us, so he stole a loaf of bread from the market. Father was many things, but he wasn't a thief, and certainly not a good one. He got caught, and they dragged him to the square to throw him in the stocks."

A tear rolled down Mathias' cheek. He wiped it away quickly, impatiently.

"When they asked him why he did it, he said it was to feed his children. And do you know what the sheriff said, Charo?"

Charo shook his head. He was thinking about bread, his stomach groaning.

"He said, 'So it's all *their* fault? Maybe we should throw them in the stocks with you. It might discourage them from becoming drunken thieves like their father.' So I grabbed you, and we ran. Not like this time, we didn't have any supplies, we weren't prepared. We just ran, for days. Until we got here."

"But why would they blame us? We were just children."

"Because, little brother, the world is cruel. People are cruel."

Charo looked at Mathias, his head hung towards his knees, shivering in the chill night.

"Thank you, Mathias," he said, reaching over and touching his brother's knee. "Thank you for everything."

A cry, distant and wailing, drifted through the still air to them. They sat bolt upright, looking around, eyes wide.

"What was that?" asked Charo. He peered into the gloom, searching for any sign of movement.

"I don't know," said Mathias. "A wolf. A forest cat. It was a long way away, thank Almas."

The cry came again. Still distant, but clearer. Not threatening. Fearful. A young girl.

"What's a girl doing all the way out here?" asked Charo, reaching for his knife and his sling.

"I don't know, Charo, but we need to stay clear of other people."

The girl wailed again, a primal noise. Pain. Terror.

"We need to help her," said Charo, standing and heading towards the sound.

Mathias hesitated. "Charo…"

"The world may be cruel, Mathias, but we aren't."

His brother nodded, pulling the sword from amongst his belongings and clipping it to his belt. He rummaged for his sling and stones. "Light a torch. We'll need it."

"Come on, you pair," hissed Wrathson at the two deputies. They were lagging behind, dragging their feet, mumbling to each other. "And be quiet."

Wrathson wasn't as fit as he once was, but he could sense the end of the chase. They had been on the road for two days now, but he could sense they were getting close. The tracks were getting fresher. He had hardly let them sleep or rest, eager to gain ground on the two youths who had a decent head start on them.

He was tired, and he did feel for the two deputies. Benjamin, the older one who worked at the inn, had turned his ankle in a rabbit hole this afternoon. The hunter, Willem, had strapped it up good and tight, but it must still be giving him grief. The other deputy, Lucas, was helping him bear the weight. They must both be knackered. But sometimes part of being a man was pushing yourself when you needed to. They would have to learn that someday, it may as well be today.

"How far?" the sheriff asked, whispering to the trackers ahead of them.

Willem knelt, resting some of his weight on his bow, examining broken brush on the forest floor. He swung his lantern around, scanning the ground further afield. A few yards ahead crouched the gamekeeper for the baronet's estate, a tall, lean man named Warwick.

"Close," replied the gamekeeper, standing and moving further down the trail.

Willem nodded his agreement. He was a taciturn man, probably a benefit in his profession. Less talk reduced the risk of disturbing the prey. Besides, he spent long periods of time in the wilderness with nobody to talk to anyway. He moved after Warwick. The gamekeeper moved slowly, quietly, but Willem was something else. His steps across the twigs and crisp leaves didn't make a sound. It was as though he was weightless.

"They were slowing down," whispered Warwick as the sheriff moved closer to them. "Probably camped soon, not too far ahead. They're young lads, they probably need rest."

"*We're* young lads," groaned Benjamin.

Wrathson turned, quickly for an overweight man. His finger lashed out, stopping just short of the young deputy's nose. "I know you're tired, lad, and I know you're hurting. But if you open that mouth of yours again and nothing useful comes out, you're going to hurt a lot more. Do you understand?"

Benjamin nodded slowly. Wrathson turned back to the trackers.

"Shutter those lanterns, gents. Only as much light as you need. Nothing more. We take them by surprise and we can do this quick, without anyone getting hurt."

The trackers obliged, the light from their lanterns narrowing to thin slits as they cast them across the ground and the trees, working their art in the darkness.

"I hope they run," said Warwick, tapping the yew bow slung around his shoulders. "I haven't fired in anger on a man in years."

Willem shook his head. "You'd shoot a boy and enjoy it?"

Warwick shrugged. "We both kill things for a living. Don't tell me you don't enjoy it."

Willem paused, inspected a broken sapling on the forest floor. "I enjoy the skill. The death is just the way of making a living. And I don't make a living killing people. Certainly not children. I can put a deer down at 100 yards. I don't enjoy it. It doesn't sicken me. I'm just good at what I do."

"Interesting," pondered Warwick, turning his cold eyes on the hunter. "You've killed a deer?"

"Only when on a hunt with the baronet's men, sanctioned by the king," replied Willem, avoiding the gamekeeper's gaze and brushing past him, searching for more spoor.

"I hope so," sneered Warwick. "You don't want to make an enemy of me. Remember, you might think you're good, but you aren't me. If you were, you'd be tending the baronet's lands and I'd be snaring rabbits like a poacher."

"I don't snare rabbits," said Willem absently, his head cocked to one side, his ear searching the night. "I shoot them. What was that...?"

The group stopped as one, listening. A slight breeze had picked up, biting at their cheeks and fingers as they concentrated. The leafless branches of the huge forest trees swayed, seeming to sweep a faint sound towards them.

It was a cry. A young girl, crying for help.

"Was that...?" started Lucas, his voice trailing off as the sound came past them again.

"What's a little girl doing out here?" asked Wrathson. "It can't be."

The sound came again.

"It is," hissed Willem, sprinting off into the night. He flicked the shutters on his lantern open again to light his way as he bounded nimbly across the uneven ground.

"Come on," yelled Wrathson, running after the hunter.

Warwick pulled open the shutters on his own lantern and followed, his long, lean legs quickly outpacing the overweight sheriff. The deputies followed, struggling to draw their weapons.

As he struggled to keep the bobbing lantern lights in sight, his heart thumping in his chest, Benjamin realised he was no longer thinking of the pain in his ankle...

The demon watched the girl scrambling through the brush on the forest floor. She stumbled through the darkness, her breathing heavy, falling to all fours every few steps. Her ankle was hurting her, but she was fighting it. The fear was gripping her.

The demon was quietly impressed. Maybe she was a fighter after all...

Between the panting the girl would occasionally cry out. The wails had been quiet at first, sobbing pleas for help, but they were getting louder. It didn't try to stop her. It needed her to yell out now. It whispered to her, projecting its voice as a hiss in her little ear. She yelled out again, louder this time, tears streaming down her face.

Good. Good.

It was moving behind her, out of sight in the darkness. It slipped from one flank to another. It was capable of moving almost silently, despite the twigs and leaves under foot, but it was making a noise on purpose. It moved like a sheep dog guiding a lone animal back towards the flock, rushing a branch here, stamping a hoof there, sometimes letting out a low, ominous growl.

They were near. It could sense them closing in, coming to find the girl.

The demon paused, dropping to all fours, cocking its head to listen as the girl moved away into the night. Two groups, closing in fast. It could hear them now, not just sense them. It was time.

It bolted forward, powerful flanks crashing through the undergrowth. It bore down on the girl, the two wizened arms set in its chest grabbed her shoulders from behind, stopping her in her tracks. It stood over her, feeling with satisfaction her trembling as it shuddered through his limbs. It looked down at her, stalked eyes taking in her tiny frame.

Scream for me now, child.

Slowly, the whimpering girl turned her head upwards, wishing that if she didn't look then she would wake from her nightmare, at home on the farmstead in her bed. Her eyes were closed as she tilted her head back. She had to see what was behind her. This wasn't a dream. Her eyelids gradually unscrewed, the pupils widening in the dark as she looked up at the beaked human skull.

She opened her mouth and shrieked.

The scream rang through the chill night air. It hit Mathias like a slap around the ears, causing him to stop in his tracks. He shuddered, the sword hanging loosely in his hand, terror gripping him round the heart.

Charo carried on running into the night, straight towards the sound.

Mathias steeled himself. He didn't want to see what had made the sound. More to the point, he didn't want to see what had made the girl make the sound. But he had to go. If his little brother could be so selfless, so brave in the terror of the night, then so could he. He started forward, gripping the hilt of the sword as he caught up to Charo.

And then they saw it. A creature. An abomination. Eight feet tall, staring down hungrily at the little girl it held in its grasp. The dark of the night seemed to recede around the pair, as if the creature was giving off its own dim light source, a faint glow surrounding them.

Mathias froze to the spot again beside his brother. He reached out a hand, grabbing at Charo's shoulder, holding him back. What was it? Not a beast of the forest. Not a creature of this world. It oozed malice, so thick that it seemed to cling to Mathias' skin. The stink of ammonia assaulted his nostrils, causing his stomach contents to churn and rise in his throat. His eyes stung, water beginning to gather in them.

The girl turned her head to them slowly. She stared at them, eyes wide but no longer terrified, instead filled with resignation. She met Charo's gaze.

"Help me…"

Charo shrugged Mathias' hand from his shoulder. It fell limp to his brother's side as he took a step forward, raising the bone knife in front of him.

The monster moved quickly. The atrophied human hands released the girl. Powerful, sickeningly-jointed arms moved down, razor claws digging into the girl's shoulders. It let out a roar, throwing its head back as it pulled the arms away, tearing the girl in half down the centre like a butcher halved a pig.

The stalked eyes stared at Charo as he continued to step forward. It dropped the two pieces of the girl to the forest floor and hissed at him, the beak wide and threatening. Mathias found control of his body again, ran forward after his brother, raising the sword. He knew it would do no good, but he had to do something.

Then it was gone. The glow around the creature faded, and it was away silently into the night.

Charo knelt beside the remains of the girl, shaking his head in disbelief. Mathias stood beside him, his eyes wide, staring into the gloom after the creature, searching futilely.

Neither of them noticed the crashing movements of the men closing in on them.

Willem reached them first. Both of the lads, one kneeling down, one standing. Both armed. The younger one had a knife whittled from bone. The older one was stockier, the bigger danger. He was upright, ready for a fight, a sword in his hand.

He dropped the lantern to the floor, nocking an arrow in his bow in a flash. He levelled the bow at the older one. "Hold right there, Mathias. I don't want to hurt you, but I will if you do anything stupid."

The two lads hardly moved. They turned their heads slowly, staring wide eyed at the hunter as he covered them. Neither moved to attack. Their faces were haunted and distorted in the light from the lantern on the floor.

Warwick reached them, raising the lantern to cover the fugitives.

"Weapons down, you little fuckers," he snarled. He unclipped a hatchet from his belt, feeling the weight as he sidled up beside Willem. "Drop them or you're dead men. You don't want to be fucking with me."

The lads stared back, not moving to attack, not dropping the weapons. They just stood like ghosts in the night, unresponsive.

"Drop the big one," growled Warwick, gripping the axe and moving forward.

Wrathson arrived now, the overweight sheriff panting for breath as he joined the two trackers.

"Listen to him, boys," said Willem, ignoring the gamekeeper but keeping the bow trained steadily on Mathias. "Drop the weapons. Nobody needs to get hurt, here."

"Do as they say," panted Wrathson. He hadn't bothered to draw his sword. Charo was no threat, any of them could best him even if he came at them with his bone knife. He was a runt. Mathias was bigger, stockier, but the sheriff knew he wasn't a proper fighter. Wrathson wasn't in the best shape, but he would be able to draw his sword and put the lad down before he got a strike in. "We just want you to explain what happened back there, that's all. Drop the weapons and step away."

Charo seemed to come out of his trance first. He turned his head slowly to the sheriff, looking at the outstretched, calming arm being held towards him. He nodded slowly, dropping the knife to the forest floor. He turned to his brother, moving over and touching his arm gently. Mathias responded as if he had been scalded by hot water, jerking to his senses.

"Slowly, boys," urged Wrathson gently. "Drop it and back off."

"It's alright, Mathias," whispered Charo, squeezing his brother's arm. "It's alright."

Mathias looked to Charo, nodded, dropped the sword. Slowly, the pair of them moved away, covered by Willem's bow.

"Right, you little bastards," snapped Warwick, spinning the axe in his hand and moving to strike with the blunt of the blade.

"You touch them and I'll break your legs and leave you for the wolves," said Wrathson calmly, unslinging his backpack and rooting for a pair of manacles.

Warwick had paused, looking at something on the ground where the lads had been stood. He was kneeling down now, casting his lantern light across the forest floor.

"What's this?" His hand reached down, pulling at a mass of hair on the ground. He gripped a handful, turned it over to reveal the face of a girl. He recoiled in disgust, playing the light across the rest of the remains on the floor. "You fucking bastards..."

"Is that...?" asked Wrathson, stepping up to the gamekeeper and snatching the lantern. "Is that a girl?"

"You fucking bastards." Warwick was striding towards the shepherds. The hatchet had spun around again.

Wrathson was staring at the two halves of the child's body, torn apart like a rag. His eyes took in the entrails, the blood, black in the night, soaking into the forest floor. He turned his gaze to Charo and Mathias, his eyes wide and disbelieving. What had they done?

Charo was shaking his head. "It wasn't us..."

"You fucking bastards."

"Calm it, Warwick," warned Willem. He still had his bow levelled at Mathias, but he was trying to keep an eye on the gamekeeper now, and weigh up what had the sheriff so rattled.

"*You fucking bastards!*" Warwick dropped his lantern and ran at the shepherds, the blade of the hatchet glinting in the meagre light as he raised it to strike.

Then something hit him. Not someone, *something*. Something huge and powerful, but fast. Wrathson and Willem watched as the massive shadow charged out of the night, a massive footfall crushing the gamekeeper's lantern underfoot as it struck him at pace.

The force of the impact took Warwick with it. The thing and the gamekeeper were yards away before either of them had time to react. All that was left was Warwick's arm, twitching on the ground like a beheaded snake, still gripping the hatchet.

The huge shadow burst its way through the two approaching deputies as they breathlessly arrived at the scene, knocking them aside. As it moved it tossed Warwick's head over its shoulder to bounce a few times across the forest floor.

Willem released, an arrow slicing the air between the two lads as they recovered from the impact. He was sure it struck home, he never missed, but the mass didn't even flinch. There was a sickening crunch as Warwick's body was thrown against a tree trunk, dropping to the ground in a crumpled heap.

Then it was gone.

They stood in silence, staring into the dark after the creature.

Benjamin and Lucas slowly turned to look at one another, backing away from the path the creature had taken towards the older men. As they approached the guttering light from Willem's lantern on the ground, Wrathson noticed the dark patches on their trousers. He didn't mention it. He was surprised he hadn't soiled himself, there was no need to embarrass the lads. His first brush with death hadn't involved... whatever it was.

"Willem, get that lantern up and lit properly," he said, slipping his sword from its sheath.

The hunter nodded, dealing with the lantern and holding it out for the sheriff.

"What the fuck do I want with it?" snapped Wrathson. He didn't look at the man, he was too busy scanning the night, searching for signs of movement, listening for sounds of approach. Not that they had had any warning the last time.

"I figured you'd want my bow nocked, sheriff," replied Willem. "Takes two hands to wield a bow."

Wrathson nodded, taking the lantern. "You're right, Willem. You're right. Ben, bag up the girl's remains. Lucas, you're going to have to get what's left of Warwick together. Tie up the sacks and drag them if need be."

Benjamin knelt by the two halves of the girl, busying himself pulling a sack from his pack. He was heaving already, his stomach trying to spill its contents on the ground. Lucas stood still, looking over his shoulder into the dark, eyes wide with fear.

"No, sheriff," he said. "I'm not going out there."

"Listen, boy," started Wrathson, feeling his temper boil. He held back. The lad wasn't even looking at him. There was no threat he could utter that would penetrate Lucas' fear right now. The sheriff moved forward, gripped the deputy's shoulder firmly. "It's ok, Lucas. We'll do this together. Help Ben get the girl sorted. Then we'll all go and gather up Warwick. Ok?"

Lucas looked at him, nodding. The lad was petrified.

"Good lad. And give me your manacles. I need to..."

Wrathson stopped, shocked by his stupidity.

Never turn your back on an enemy...

He span round, sword ready. Willem followed his movements instinctively, the line of his arrow directed at where the shepherd lads had been stood.

They were still there. Charo and Mathias stood together, staring off in the direction the creature had taken, silently keeping watch.

Wrathson moved over with the two sets of manacles, covered by Willem. Both of the lads extended their hands to receive the cuffs as he approached. Wrathson slapped them on firmly, leaving the foot locks to dangle loose and heavy from their wrists. He needed them to be able to move, and from the looks of them they weren't going to be running away.

Why didn't they run.

The younger shepherd, Charo, looked up, dark eyes meeting Wrathson's. "We didn't do it, sheriff. We didn't do any of it."

"Every man of the law hears that a lot, lad," replied Wrathson. He turned away from the boy's gaze. He wasn't afraid of Charo's empty-eyed stare. He was worried that he actually believed him, and he didn't want the boy to know that. It was a weakness that could be exploited. "Just walk with us, and don't even think about trying to run."

"What's the plan, sheriff?" asked Willem. The hunter had his bow trained on the shepherds, but his concentration was elsewhere. That worried Wrathson. Willem was a man of the woods, he was used to being alone in the wilderness at night. And he was scared.

"Walk with me, Willem," said Wrathson, taking the hunter out of earshot of the others. "Can you follow the girl's trail? We need to get to shelter, to her home. Give her parents the bad news. Get some rest. Then at daybreak we can strike for home."

"I can, sheriff," nodded Willem, his eyes moving about them, scanning the gloom. "But we're two days from the village. Do you think we'll make it back?"

Wrathson stopped. He didn't really have an answer. Certainly not an honest one he could give. "Why wouldn't we make it home, Willem?"

Willem stared into the night, still searching. He raised his head, sniffing at the air distractedly. "I hit that thing, sheriff. I'm sure of it. Gauged its movements, the lope of its gait, its height. Shot to the neck. Back of the neck. Jugular shot. Definite bleed out. At that range, even if it hit the neck bone it would have gone through, paralysed it. Yet it carried on. Threw Warwick around like he was a rag doll. Smaller than that, like he was an insect."

"What are you trying to say, Willem?" asked Wrathson.

Willem looked him straight in the eye. "That shot would have put down a bear, sheriff. A *bear*. I'm saying that it was... something else..."

There are no demons.

"Whatever it is, Willem, we can stay here or we can move. I'd rather move."

Willem nodded.

"Let's get everything gathered up and get on the move, then," said Wrathson, turning back to organise the deputies in their grisly tasks.

Chapter Thirteen

Yarner sat with the lads in the Copper Badge, leaning back in his chair and taking a deep gulp of his ale. It was late. Most of the regulars were heading home for the night, but Old Edna was still serving ale, so the watchmen were still drinking it.

Yarner was tired. Days at home with the family were almost as knackering as working the watch shifts. He didn't get many days off, so he forgot how exhausting the children could be. And the list of chores he had to catch up on seemed to grow rather than shrink. Tomorrow he would be spending the last day before returning to work fixing the leaking roof as best he could. He wasn't a carpenter, but on the wages of a watchman with mouths to feed it was difficult to justify paying one to do a job he could botch with his limited skills.

His wife had given him some earache for going out drinking, but it was good natured. He had done his jobs around the house without moaning over the last few days, and he had earned a drink or two.

Secretly, he longed to get back to work. He needed to know what was going on with the murders. Ratcliffe's People's Gazette had spread the word of the killings, and the writer's agitators had been around Regalla, standing on crates and carts to read the story to crowds of peasants for a few coppers each.

Yarner hoped it was enough to stop the whole affair being swept under the carpet, but he doubted it.

"What are you thinking, sarge?" asked Arnie, catching Yarner's distant look.

Yarner smiled at the lad, gesturing for Old Edna to bring over another round of drinks. "Just wondering if they've caught that murdering bastard, yet."

"Doubt it," sneered Magnus. "Your pet reporter's being telling some interesting stories, Yarner. Says it's a fucking noble. Wonder where he got that idea..."

Derron shot the scarred man a warning look. "Watch your tongue, Magnus."

"He's not my pet reporter," said Yarner. "And I didn't tell him anything, if that's what you're insinuating. I suggest you remember that."

Magnus shrugged, taking his newly-filled tankard from the table. He drank deep, wiped his mouth with his sleeve. "Whatever you say, Yarner. You keep on getting the drinks in and maybe I'll remember to forget, eh?"

"You should shut up, Magnus," said Griegor, his mouth stuffed with beef brisket and hard bread. Old Edna had knocked him up some food, even at this time of night. When Griegor was hungry it was best to oblige him. Not that he would harm the old woman. He just wouldn't stop mentioning his rumbling belly every couple of minutes until he was fed.

"The brains of the group speaks," sneered Magnus.

"I have got brains," said Griegor matter-of-factly. "I know my numbers. And I can read some. Derron taught me."

Derron nodded supportively. "That's right."

Magnus sniggered. "For fuck's sake. Alright, my learned mate. There's nineteen districts in the capital. Each of them's got, say, seven patrols. Each with five men, just like us. How many watchmen have we got on our side to try to keep order when the sarge's non-pet agitator stirs up the peasant folk into a fucking revolt?"

Griegor paused in the middle of chewing his food, grease dripping down his chin as he cocked his head to one side.

"I don't understand," he said after a long pause. "What do you mean?"

"Fucking genius," laughed Magnus, gulping back more ale.

"Griegor," said Derron coaxingly. "What's nineteen times seven times five?"

"665," replied the big man, without hesitation.

"See, dickhead," smiled Derron, turning his gaze on Magnus. "You just need to word your question right."

Magnus shrugged.

Derron was right. Yarner had been guilty of thinking the giant was simple when he had been assigned to his squad. He had been happy to have the muscle onboard, but training Griegor had started off as a major pain in the arse. It had been Derron that had broken the deadlock. Griegor wasn't thick, he just saw the world differently it seemed. Things had to be explained to him differently. He seemed to struggle understanding what human behaviour was acceptable and what wasn't, which was an

89

important job for a watchman. Even now in many instances one of the others had to name a crime being committed before Griegor would move into action.

Griegor's awkwardness with the intricacies of human behaviour did not extend to his interactions with animals. Griegor loved them, seemed to have a bond with them. Reaper had been an unexpected bonus of having the beast of a man on the patrol. Again, it had been Derron's suggestion when he observed Griegor's affinity with animals. The pair had been trying to catch a dog that was running wild in the market, attacking anyone who got within biting range. Derron said Griegor had just called the animal over, knelt down and rub its head behind the ears. The animal had calmed instantly.

And so, Yarner had asked Captain Graves for a dog for the patrol. Not many watch squads had a dog handler. It was hard to find a watchman who could train one adequately. But Griegor had not made Yarner regret the effort it had taken to persuade Graves.

The big man was smiling now, proud of himself. He reached down with a moist chunk of brisket, slipping it into Reaper's mouth. The massive dog took it gently, wolfing it down. "Good beef, eh boy?"

Magnus smiled spitefully. "I thought you didn't eat meat, Griegor?"

"I don't eat chicken," replied Griegor, washing down the last of his meal with half a tankard of ale. "Chicken comes from animals. From a chicken."

"And where do you think that brisket came from?"

"Magnus…" Derron stared at the weasel-like man opposite him threateningly.

"Brisket comes from beef," replied Griegor. "Everyone knows that."

"And where does beef come from?" asked Magnus, smiling wickedly.

Griegor looked from Derron to Yarner and back again, starting to deflate, his face showing earnest worry.

"Magnus I swear to Guerro I'll knock your fucking teeth down your throat," growled Derron, moving to stand.

"Sit down, Derron," snapped Yarner. "Magnus, keep your mouth shut. Griegor, beef's just beef. You're fine with beef."

Yarner thought back to the day Griegor had discovered that the roast chicken he was eating was a dead animal. The big man had been distraught, stuck his fingers down his throat to throw it all back up. It was the only time he had seen Griegor cry. And he had. Like a baby. Yarner and Derron had had to convince him that pork, mutton and beef didn't come from an animal. After all, a man the size of Griegor with his appetite couldn't live off fruit and vegetables.

Griegor was still looking uncertain. Yarner changed the subject quickly. "Where's that young lady of yours, Arnie?"

The young lad smiled at the mention of Lucy. "She'll be down when she's ready. She's probably just getting ready for me."

"Lady…" sniggered Magnus into his ale.

"Magnus, I have no fucking idea why any of us watches your back out there, you evil little bastard," snarled Derron, his eyes angry again.

"Because I watch yours," shrugged Magnus.

Yarner knew he was right. Despite being an awful human being, Magnus was a good watchman. "That's a fair point. Maybe you could try being less of a cunt about it, though."

Magnus smiled insincerely, turning his empty mug upside down. "Only way I know how to be. My tankard's dry."

"Well, I'm sure we can have another round for the road whilst we wait for Arnie's Lucy to collect him," said the watch sergeant, calling Old Edna over with more drinks.

He skulked through the night, pulling the black cloak around him against the cold as he hurried past the late-night revellers on their way home. He hadn't been back to the Northern Quarter for days. The incident with the girl had shaken him up. He had told the physician that a dog had attacked him, bitten his finger off. His hand was strapped up tight, the wound cleaned and stitched. The night seemed foggy from the laudanum he was taking for the pain.

He giggled to himself for no reason, his body feeling light as he stopped to stare up for a second at the streetlamps. The light seemed to streak out from the lamps in lines. If he squinted it cracked out across his vision like a white spider web. As he moved his head from side to side the beams of light span like a kaleidoscope.

It hadn't been the pain that had kept him away. It was how close he had been to being caught. He had considered giving up his night time activities, but had found the draw of it grew stronger each day he stayed at home.

He was a hunter. A hunter didn't stop taking prey because he was a hurt. He got back in amongst the prey, otherwise he would starve.

He felt the same. He had a taste for the hunt, for the kill. To give up on it would cause him to die inside. He would be nothing, a shell.

Besides, surely the risk of getting caught was part of the thrill.

But there was something else that drove him back to the poor district. He hadn't seen *enough*. He needed to know what the inside of a person looked like, and he had not yet cut deep enough. He had seen the entrails, but not the core of the being. He hadn't had time to delve deeper, and the light in the alleys and by the docks had been poor. He couldn't see what he was cutting, what he was holding, slippery and sticky in his hands.

So tonight he would need more time. The streets were too dangerous, but also the risk of getting caught was too high. The thrill of the risk was good, but actually getting apprehended would be the worst of all scenarios. And he needed light, so he could see what he was doing, the damage he was causing.

He knew just the place.

He pulled the collar of the cloak up around his face as he approached, passing the front door of the whorehouse quickly. Above him a copper sign in the shape of a shield creaked as it swung in the gentle, biting breeze. He moved fast, slipping into the alleyway adjacent to the building.

This place had a side door. He knew because he had used it before. Some patrons liked a little discretion in their dealings, and being from a noble family he had often felt the need to cover up his private forays into the seedier side of the city and its nightlife.

A pale hand reached out from beneath the cloak and tried the door handle. It turned and the door opened before him, revealing the back hallway and the stairs that led up to the girls' rooms. He checked for any signs of movement and then slipped into the warmth, closing the door gently behind him.

He moved slowly up the stairs, placing his feet carefully on the creaking boards, hunting.

On his walk past the front of the whorehouse he had checked for lights in the rooms, noted one in his mind. He found his bearings quickly, slipping over to the room third from last in the corridor. He knelt quietly. Yes, candlelight flickering in the crack under the door.

He would have to be quick if he wanted to be left undisturbed. The prey mustn't have time to make a sound. He drew the three-pronged parrying dagger from his belt, slowly, quietly, holding it behind his back under the cloak. He would need to get within striking distance and move quickly, stick the main blade straight through the throat to kill any scream or cry for help. It meant that if he felt like fucking her before getting to work she would be dead. He'd done it before, it felt the same as with a live girl, just without the noise.

He reached out his bandaged hand, taking it in for a second, hesitating.

Yes, kill her quick, lest she wounds you.

He knocked gently on the door.

Lucy paused pulling the ivory-handled brush through her thick, flowing red hair on hearing a knock at her door. She finished the draw of the brush and bent down to look at herself in the mirror of her dresser. Her hazel eyes took in the beautiful brush in her porcelain white hand. It was the most expensive thing she owned, a gift from Arnie. He had bought it from the dockside markets off a trader from Altanya. It was made from the horn of some great creature they had far to the south across the seas, a massive cow-like beast with huge ears and a long nose. The handle was made in the shape of the creature. She forgot the name of the beast. Arnie had told her, but she had not been listening. She had been too busy trying to stifle the tears welling in her eyes. Girls in her trade didn't cry, and yet she had never experienced an act of kindness like that before.

She ran the brush through her hair again, making him wait. He shouldn't come up here, he should wait for her. He needed to accept that. She would go down to get him when she was ready.

She felt harsh for a second. Was it her own insecurities that made her annoyed at him for coming upstairs uninvited?

She was a strong young woman. She had had a difficult life, an orphan girl growing up in Regalla thrust out of the poorhouse and onto the streets at fourteen and forced to earn her keep in a rough world. She expected people to follow the rules that she set, if they wanted to be in her life.

But it was more than that. She wanted to be ready for him. She had spent the evening in the company of other men, and she wanted to be bathed and cleaned up for him when she saw him. She wanted to be pretty. Not in the way that attracted paying customers, in the way that attracted a man who genuinely loved her. A man that she was scared of losing.

She shook her head.

You're leaving yourself exposed, girl. You're the first girl he's fucked, sooner or later he'll get bored and move on.

Lucy realised she had stropped brushing. The tears were gathering in her eyes again. She shook her head, brushed again.

"Come in," she called, more abruptly than she intended.

The door opened and closed slowly as a man stepped into the room. It wasn't Arnie. He was heavier, she could tell by the tread of his feet. And taller; he blocked more light from the hallway as he entered.Lucy leaned forward again mid-brush, casually adjusting the mirror on the dresser to cover the door behind her.

The man in the room was tall, about six feet. He had a thin frame beneath the black cloak that was hanging from his shoulders. His hair was jet black, set off in contrast against his, which face pale as a ghost. He had his right hand behind his back, which caused Lucy to be instantly wary. His left hand was bandaged tightly, covering some wound. Dark brown eyes, almost black, looked her body up and down in the light shift she wore.

The way he stood and stared unnerved her. She ran the brush through her hair once more and opened a drawer of the dresser, placing it inside. Her hand stayed there for a second, moving gently through the contents, before she half turned to look at the visitor side-on.

"I'm finished for the night, mate," she said, smiling insincerely. "Maybe one of the other girls will still be up for you..."

"My lord," said Toby Princetown, stepping forward towards Lucy.

"Beg pardon?" asked Lucy. Unseen by Toby, her hand tightened its grip on the object in her hand.

"My lord," repeated Toby, taking another step forward. "You should address me as 'my lord'."

Lucy shifted sideways slowly, trying to open up the distance between her and Toby. It wasn't just the hand behind the back that unnerved her, or the rigid posture, or the blank dark eyes. This man seemed almost devoid of emotion, as though possessed by some malevolent demon from a fairy tale to scare children.

"Well, my lord," she said, moving around the edges of the room. "As I said, maybe you should find someone else."

"No, my dear," said Toby, his voice hollow. "You'll do."

He lunged. Lucy saw the blade whip out from behind his back, thrusting towards her throat. She span away nimbly, twisting towards the door, slashing away with the knife she had in her hand. She didn't make contact, and she hadn't intended to. She just wanted to keep him back, maintain distance between them.

"You little bitch," snarled Toby, turning on her. There was emotion now. Rage. He came at her.

Lucy screamed. She turned and fumbled with the door handle desperately.

"Someone's having fun," sneered Magnus, looking up at the ceiling of the brothel's bar area.

Old Edna didn't seem to be so amused. She was fumbling under the bar, heading towards the door to the whores' rooms.

"That's Lucy," cried Arnie, dropping his ale and stumbling to his feet, heading after Old Edna.

"How can that little wetling tell one girl's scream from another?" sniggered Magnus, taking another swig of his beer.

Yarner laughed for a second, before the mirth died in his throat. He had a bad feeling, a sense of foreboding suddenly rising up within him.

"Come on lads," he urged, shaking his head to clear the ale haze from his brain as he found his feet and moved after Arnie.

Arnie bounded past Old Edna at the bottom of the stairs, taking them two at a time in his effort to reach the upper floor. On the landing Lucy ran past him, a knife in her hand, her hazel eyes wide with fear.

The adrenaline caused his heartbeat to thump in his ears as he stood on the landing. Who had attacked his girl? He had never seen Lucy so scared. He had never even seen her scared. She had run past him in blind fear, not even recognising him.

He saw the man then, running out of Lucy's room and across the landing towards him. His watchman instincts kicked in, taking in the particulars, just has Yarner had trained him. A few inches taller than Arnie. Thin build. Black clothes, black cloak. Pale skin, white like marble. Black hair, neatly cropped, widow's peak. Black eyes, soulless. Left hand in bandages. Right hand clutching a duelling dagger.

Duelling dagger. Always check the hands first...

Toby thrust the dagger into Arnie's stomach. The watchman was an obstacle, and he needed to escape. And to do that he had to go through the man blocking the stairs. All thought of the prey had gone. The hunter was dead. Toby was scared, and he needed to escape.

He pulled the blade out, leaving Arnie to fall to the floor clutching his stomach, blood running through his fingers.

Toby descended the stairs in three bounds, almost turning his ankle, landing unbalanced. Old Edna was there already, her gnarled, wrinkled hands clasped around a cudgel. She struck while he was off balance, a surprisingly strong blow catching him around the temple.

He reeled for a few seconds, bouncing from wall to wall in the corridor, his ears ringing. The laudanum killed the pain in its tracks, but it did nothing for his balance. He reached out both hands to get purchase on the walls, dropping the dagger to the floor, desperately trying to find direction. His legs were still moving, but his brain was steering him properly. He ricocheted down the corridor towards the side door, pulling it open and stumbling out into the cold of the night.

Yarner heard the commotion as he approached the door, the others close on his heels. As he entered the corridor he threw himself to his knees at the base of the stairs beside Lucy and Old Edna. Arnie had tumbled himself down the staircase, patches of blood marking his trail, and now lay with his head in Lucy's lap, clutching his punctured stomach.

"Almas, please, don't take him from me," wailed Lucy. Tears ran in streams down her pale cheeks, gathering in the furrow of her scar as she cradled Arnie's head, caressing face.

"That way," spat Old Edna, gesturing towards the side door with the cudgel before pulling off her headscarf and pressing it to Arnie's wound. The lad groaned deeply as she used all of her delicate frame to apply pressure. "Hold still, lad. I know it hurts."

"Lucy, get a physician," said Yarner. The girl didn't move, throwing her head back in a waterfall of red hair as she let out a soul-splitting wail. Yarner grabbed her face with both hands, staring deeply into her hazel eyes. "Lucy. If you love him, get a physician, or he will die."

The girl nodded, steeling herself and running through the bar into the street. Yarner pulled himself to his feet, yanking his short sword from its sheath and running out of the door. "Come on lads."

The chill of the night took the breath from their inebriated lungs as they ran out into the alleyway, turning quickly and following the receding footfalls into the main street. The temporary loss of breath was worth it. Yarner's head began to clear of ale as the cold hit him.

The watch sergeant peered into the gloom between the streetlamps as they ran, focussing on the fleeing figure in black, cloak trailing out behind.

"Griegor, get Reaper after him."

The big man slowed his run, dropping to one knee in the street. The rippling muscular form of the mastiff running at his side slammed to a halt, sitting obediently, lightly panting as Griegor met his eyes. The watchman unclipped the chain leash that had been clattering along the cobbles from the dog's collar.

"Reaper," commanded Griegor, pointing a thick finger at the dark figure disappearing into the gloom. "Stop."

The dog paused for a second, his eyes flicking in the direction of his master's finger. He seemed to nod before loping off down the street past Yarner, Derron and Magnus.

"You're fucked now," called Magnus as he watched the black mass of Reaper gain steadily on the figure of the fleeing man.

They were gaining on the figure anyway. Reaper just made the inevitable apprehension quicker. The fleeing man turned as he sensed the mastiff bearing down on him, putting in one final spurt of pace before the dog lunged forward and clenched its jaws around his calf. Then he was down, skidding across the cobbles. The scramble of man and dog came to a halt after a few yards, Reaper releasing and standing over the felled fugitive, hackles raised, growling deeply.

"Good boy, Reaper," called Griegor as they approached. He fell to the dog's side, leaning into his flank, muscle pressing against muscle. He rubbed Reaper's ears, the dog groaning with satisfaction.

"You're in deep fucking shit, mate," snarled Magnus. He took a step back, booting the stricken form of Toby straight across the cheek.

"Calm it Magnus," said Yarner, gesturing to Derron to take charge. "Get this bastard up, boys."

Derron and Magnus hauled Toby to his feet, one on each armpit. The noble's eyes were wide with fear, dark unreflective pits of black in the dim light of the streetlamps.

"Seems like you tried to kill the wrong whore this time," said Yarner, stepping up and staring Toby right in the eye. "Your head's going on a spike for this, you toff bastard."

Toby turned his eyes away. His head span on his neck, trying to shake off the kick to the face, the cudgel blow to the temple, the laudanum pumping through his veins. The stars in the sky above swirled into one, a speckled black blanket becoming a mess of light. How was he going to get out of this?

"Help," he said, his voice hollow and light. The dark eyes returned to meet Yarner's, staring deeply. He shouted louder. "Help. Help me."

"Fuck that shit," laughed Magnus, punching the young noble in the ribs. "We're the fucking watch, mate."

Toby spluttered for a second, catching his breath from the blow. He looked at Magnus for a second with disdain, then shouted again, louder this time. "Help me. Please, help me. I'm being attacked."

Yarner shook his head. "You're coming with us, little Lord Princetown. You're going to answer for this."

He turned to lead the way back towards the watch house. Ten men had gathered in the street around them, standing silently watching them. Their feet were planted apart, arms folded in front of them. Rough men, with bad body language.

"Nothing to see here, people," said Yarner. "Watch business. This man is under arrest for murder."

"Murder," confirmed Griegor, standing up to his full height beside Reaper. "Move along, or you'll be in breach of the peace."

The big man looked to Derron for approval. The blond watchman nodded his head encouragingly.

"They aren't the watch," cried Toby. "They attacked me. I am a nobleman and they are robbing me."

"Speak again and I'll cut your throat," snarled Magnus, scarred face pressing up towards Toby's chin.

"We are the watch," announced Yarner, fumbling at his belt for his pouch where he had stowed his copper badge. Shit, had he left it on the table at the whorehouse?

One of the men stepped forward, his hand falling to the hilt of a sword at his belt. "They *are* the watch. Yarner here got me put in the stocks for three days for hitting a tavern wench with a mead bottle. Cunt spilled hot fucking soup all over my gods-given crotch, and I gave her a slap. And I got fucked for it."

"This isn't your business, Johann," warned Yarner, peering into the dark at the man ahead of him. Local troublemaker. Tough man. Popular in the Northern Quarter, for some reason.

"Wulli here got his nose busted by the big simple fucker over there a few months back," continued Johann, gesturing to Griegor. "Nose and face. Couldn't stand up for three days without puking his guts up. He got the sack from his job at the docks. Had no work since."

"Breach of the peace," shrugged Griegor. "Should have kept his mouth shut."

"He was drunk in the street because his wife miscarried that afternoon," snapped Johann. "So the question here, *my lord*, isn't whether they're the watch and whether they can find them copper badges. The question is, what's it worth to get you off the hook you're currently wriggling on?"

"Johann, don't," urged Yarner. He realised he was still carrying his short sword. He lowered it, held out his other hand with the palm open. "You don't know what this bastard's done."

"I know what you lot have done," replied Johann. His companions were spreading out now, circling the group of watchmen.

"Twenty gold pieces each," called Toby.

Johann turned his gaze to the noble, shaking his head. "Twenty gold? Fighting a watchman's going to get us in serious shit, *my lord*. Which means we'll have to kill them. And make a good job of hiding the bodies."

94

"Are you seriously thinking about sticking up for this cunt?" snarled Magnus, drawing a dagger from his belt. "You know he'd piss on you as soon as look at you? You know he's been cutting up whores all round this fucking quarter?"

"I'm sure he's scum, Magnus," spat Johann. "But so are you. And so are we. And we've got kids going hungry."

"Fifty gold," shouted Toby. "To each of you."

Magnus stuck an elbow on his jaw. His long, thin fingers clutched at his face, blood bubbling from his split lip.

Johann's avaricious eyes met Yarner's, the gaze steely and angry. "Deal, *my lord.*"

The men closed in quickly, clubs and daggers in hand. Johann made a charge at Yarner, the sword now in his hand, swinging it heavily in an arc at the watch sergeant's chest. Yarner parried it easily, but the strength of the blow put him off balance. Johann recovered quicker, raising the blade again.

Reaper hit him full in the chest, sending him sprawling to the ground, heaving for air. Johann was a tough man, but the mastiff weighed as much as him, if not more, and he was pure muscle. The huge dog crouched, hackles raised, growling deeply as Johann struggled to his feet.

Yarner looked about him quickly. Derron had dragged the noble away from the group and was fending off two assailants, swinging his short sword quickly in defensive arcs to keep the thugs at bay. Three of Johann's gang were trying to get in close to Griegor, circling the big man, who was swinging Reaper's heavy chain at them desperately. His jaw was set in frustration. They were keeping their distance, preparing to attack from different angles. Griegor roared, the chain arcing out surprisingly quickly and smashing one of the men's jaws. He collapsed to his knees, spitting blood and teeth.

Two of the men were helping Johann to his face, keeping their eyes on the menacing dog.

"Fucking kill the thing," snarled Johann, shaking them off.

Where's Magnus? That little shit better hadn't have run.

Yarner turned his attention back to the fray slightly too late for comfort. One of the men lunged at him with a knife from the side. He took a step back, striking the man's weapon hand with the flat of his blade as he passed. The weapon skittered across the cobbles. Suddenly Yarner was caught in a tight bear hug from behind, strapping his arms by his sides. His assailant squeezed, crushing the breath from him, the sword dropping from his fingers as he struggled.

The injured thug approached, nursing his wounded arm. "You fucking bastard."

He planted a headbutt on Yarner's nose. Blood streamed down his lips and chin, his face throbbing from the impact. He struggled to bend forward against the weight of the man on his back, attempting to bow his head as punches rained down on him.

One of the men with Johann lashed out with his club, catching Reaper across the nose. The dog yelped, backing off slightly as Johann and the two thugs spread out around him.

"Reaper, kill!" roared Griegor, his attention turning away from the two men attacking him. He started towards the dog, both of the men raining cudgel blows down on him from behind as he moved. Griegor didn't seem to notice, his focus purely on Reaper.

The mastiff heard the command and leapt forward, his jaws clamping shut around the neck of a dagger-wielding thug. The man fell backwards, Reaper tearing and ripping at his throat, blood spraying across the floor. The other man was smashing his club down on the animal's haunches as Johann looked on, aghast.

Yarner pulled forward with all his weight, dropping to all fours, still in the clutches of the bear hug. The man attacking him had trouble landing blows now without striking his friend and was resorting to ineffectual kicks to his ribs. Yarner looked round desperately as best he could.

One of the men got to close to Derron, trying to charge him. He ran straight onto the watchman's sword, the weapon impaling him through the stomach. As he fell his weight twisted the weapon from Derron's hand. The other man closed in, dagger glinting in the lamplight. Derron grabbed Toby with both hands by the shoulders, desperately trying to use him as a human shield.

A sickening crunch sounded as one of Griegor's pursuers landed a heavy blow on the big man's head. The force of the blow snapped the club in half. Griegor staged the last few yards towards the thug assaulting his dog, tackling him heavy to the ground. The giant hauled himself up the man's body, grabbing his head and smashing it repeatedly into the ground. His movements slowed as the two men behind battered him with club and fist and boot. Reaper turned and lurched at one, grabbing his ankle in those vice-like jaws.

This was going badly. Yarner had to get out of this grip, one way or another. He summoned the last of his strength, rolling over. The man on his back moved with him, now lying underneath him on the cobbles. Yarner butted backwards with his head, desperately trying to get a blow in on the man's teeth or nose, anything to loosen the grip. As he lay, his belly exposed to the air like an upturned beetle, the other assailant came across his fuzzy vision, raising a boot to stamp down on his head.

This is it. Almas, take care of my family...

The thin, blurry form of Magnus flashed across his vision. The watchman thrust his dagger straight into the thug's eye, whipping it out almost instantly. The boot didn't crash into Yarner's head, it just disappeared out of sight as the man crashed to the ground, dead.

Yarner flinched as Magnus kicked out at his face. His foot caught the man behind him the temple. The grip loosened and Yarner rolled away, gulping in lungfuls of air. He pulled himself upright, there was not time to rest.

"You alright, sarge?" sneered Magnus.

Yarner didn't answer, his eyes staring wide at the scene across the street. Reaper was getting the better of the man attacking Griegor. The man's foot was now hanging from a thread, and the big man now had him in a headlock on the ground, twisting hard. The man's face was going purple. His neck would snap any second. Johann stood over them both, his sword raised above his head, ready to dig it into Griegor.

Magnus flicked the dagger in his hand. Gripping the blade he reached back, threw his arm forward, released. The weapon glinted as it span in the air, flying towards Johann as he started to bring the sword down.

The hilt of the weapon caught him on the forehead, knocking him back, dazed. Magnus shrugged. "I'm not a fucking circus act."

He turned and ran at Johann, making the distance up quickly. Yarner struggled after him, mustering all the speed he could gather. Magnus lunged at the off-balance thug, wrapping both arms around his sword arm, pulling the weapon up into the air. Yarner bowled into him with all the strength he could muster, his feet leaving the ground as he landed the tackle. The pair crashed to the ground, Johann's head cracking on the cobbles with a sickening crunch as the sword clattered away.

Yarner gathered himself as quickly as he could, clambering on top of Johann and raising his feet. There was no need. Blank eyes stared upwards at the night sky. A dark patch of blood was already spreading across the ground from the back of his skull.

The neck of the man in Griegor's grip snapped noisily. The big man rolled onto his back, gasping for air. Reaper stood over him, nuzzling at his master's face, whining.

"Here boy," urged Magnus, retrieving his dagger and jogging towards Derron. Reaper followed reluctantly as Yarner knelt by his master.

"You're in big fucking trouble, boy," snarled Magnus, striding forward as the man ceased lunging at Derron.

He lowered the knife as he saw Reaper at Magnus' heels, dropping it to the ground and raising his hands. "I'm sorry. Take me in."

"Fuck that," replied Magnus, stepping up to the thug and sticking his knife in his stomach. The man groaned, sliding to the floor.

"What the fuck was that, Magnus?" asked Derron, shaking his head.

"These cunts tried to fucking kill us, Derron. Didn't you fucking notice the knife he was trying to stick in you?"

"He fucking surrendered."

Toby was shaking his head in disbelief as he stood in Derron's grasp, the fear wide in the dark eyes. "You're supposed to be the watch..."

"You're fucking next, your lordship," spat Magnus, pressing the blade of the bloody dagger against Toby's white neck.

"Magnus. No," called Yarner as he helped Griegor to his feet. "We're going to get in enough strife about all this, without that bastard ending up dead."

Magnus pressed his scarred face up to Toby's, the one seeing eye boring into the noble's dark pits. A trickling sounded from the cobbles as Toby voided his bladder in the street. Magnus spat in his face. Thick phlegm dripped down Toby's trembling bottom lip.

"Get this cunt away from me," growled Magnus through gritted teeth.

Derron pulled the noble back slowly, away from Magnus' blade.

Yarner and Griegor limped over, each groaning from their injuries.

"What now, sarge?" asked Derron. He glanced over to Magnus, who was still glaring at the noble. He shuddered. He had never seen his fellow watchman so angry, so dangerous.

"You run to the watch house and get Captain Graves. *Only* Graves, do you understand? The less people know about this the better. He needs to make the decisions about this. Give Magnus this bastard."

"Magnus?" asked Derron, returning his gaze to the seething little man.

"Yes," said Yarner, turning to Magnus. "Get this scum in that alley and keep him there. He's not to be harmed, you understand? But if he tries anything, and I mean *anything*, cut his throat. Not too deep, mind. Let him feel it bleed out."

Yarner stared at Toby, his eyes firm. The young lord was trembling across his entire body now, tears streaming down his cheeks.

"Aye, sarge," said Magnus, grabbing Toby's arm and dragging him towards the nearest alley. "Me and you are going to have a little quality time, cuntling."

"Only Graves," said Yarner, squeezing Derron's arm. "Me and Griegor will get all these bodies and wounded off the street. We'll be waiting in the alley when you get back. Hurry now, lad."

Derron nodded, running off into the night.

Chapter Fourteen

Alit Wulska urged the horse along the dirt track gently, careful to take it slowly. The Green Man was several days behind them now, and they had left the Snow Road, the main route north, some time ago as they branched off towards the Red Cairn Hills. The thick forest had receded as they travelled, giving them a better a view of the land around them; barren heath patched with thickets of gorse and heather. The road was poor, and the added inclines were making it tough going for the wagon.

Of course, Lord Cecil had been very kind in giving them spare wheels, but fitting them would be a problem should one of theirs break. Lord Cecil had given him a signed parchment stating that anyone they encountered should extend them all the hospitality expected of a guest of the Lord Chancellor, and that any bills or requests for recompense should be sent to Regalla for settlement, but the problem was that there were no wainwrights up here to show the document to. There was nothing for days around, according to the map he had weighed down with rocks on the seat beside him.

They could, of course, rely on one of his sons. Alitain, his older child, was to enter the family business. Alit smiled, taking a nibble of the smoked, cured sausage he clutched in one hand. He longed for the day that Alitain gained the skill required to join him. He would rename the shop Wulska and Son. The lad was good; he learned quickly, he was diligent, and he concentrated solely on his work and his learnings.

Tanis was like his mother. He was impetuous, questioning, rebellious. His spoke his mind too freely for a Yanari, without thinking of the consequences. Without thinking who might be listening. At fourteen he was two years younger than his brother, but much further behind in his mastery of crafts. Alit had managed to find him an apprenticeship with another Yanari artisan, a carpenter, but he was told the lad was not learning as fast as he should. An apprentice's wage was minimal; after all, he was being given the benefit of teaching and experience; but often Master Sennet sent word that Tanis' monies had been deducted or withheld in full.

The boy didn't concentrate, that was his trouble. He said Master Sennet was spiteful and mean, withholding his wages for minor lapses, but Alit doubted the truth of it. He had known the old Yanari for many years, since Alit himself was a youth, and he was not a miserly man. Ali found himself wondering if, should a wheel break, Tanis would have learned enough to be of any use in repairing it.

How terrible, to doubt one's own son. I should pray to Yanara for forgiveness in slighting my own child.
Alit shook his head. It was Esme's fault. He loved his wife, but she filled the boys' heads with thoughts that should not be contemplated by a Yanari. She had pressed him to let them have their childhood. He loved her, and he had relented. They had not had theirs, after all, and wasn't it the role of a parent to make a better life for their children than they had experienced? Alit had entered into his trade at the age of ten, and at a similar age Esme had been sent into the employ of a local artisan as a maid.

So, they had not sent their children to work until they were thirteen. They had been allowed to stay at home, to enjoy their childhood, to study and play and develop their imaginations.

But Esme had filled their heads with stories of the Yanari of the past. She had told them of Palla the Dawnlight, who had led a Yanari slave army against the Illiceans and conquered insurmountable odds at the Battle of the Meandering Snake River. And of Lika Tryesh, the Sunchild, who at fifteen brought together the Yanari children of a town in Barralegne that had incarcerated all of their Yanari parents. Lika and his group gathered the Barralegnan children of the town for a secret party, and slit their throats one by one, leaving the corpses piled in the square for their parents to find. Lika and the rest of the Yanari children were nailed to trees in the cemetery and their corpses left for the crows.

Alitain had benefitted from the time. He had researched the stories, made his own way, made his own mind up. Of course, the story of Palla was one of the Old Stories, from the Book of Yanara, so its veracity was in no doubt. But Alitain understood that the Yanari in Regalla were not slaves, and there was no longer a need for such violent thoughts. The story of Lika was a fable. Historical records showed that there had been a Yanari lad called Lika in a town in Barralegne who was put to death for murder. He had poisoned a local family who had had his father jailed for embezzling from them.

Alitain had become a good Yanari. He knew that the best way to live was to observe the rules, make a living, stay unnoticed.

Tanis, on the other hand, had descended into a world where the Yanari were an oppressed warrior people, who needed to break the shackles that he imagined bound them. His mind was on bloodshed, on rebellion, on vengeance. This was not the Yanari way, and yet Alit did not know how to talk sense into him. He was making this path for himself, failing in his studies so that his only way to make a living would be to succumb to these primal urges, a cause that did not exist.

Alit's only hope was that he would grow out of it. Esme herself seemed unable to control the boy she had created with her stories. It was true that Esme was not as at ease with the Yanari way of life as Alit, but she was not a revolutionary. Esme was proud of her heritage, just as Alit was. She was just proud in a different way...

Alit stirred from his musings as he noticed a gate ahead, blocking the dirt track. There was no wall to either side, but the ground there would be impassable to the wagon. He flicked the reins with one hand, finishing off his cured sausage as the wagon came to a gentle halt.

As he climbed down from the seat, Esme emerged from the back of the wagon. She pulled her shawl around her as she approached. The air was colder as they got higher into the hills, and the barren land provided no shelter from the biting wind.

"What is it, dear," she asked, moving over a pushing against him for warmth. He pulled her close under his thick, woollen travelling cloak as they headed over to the gate.

"Just a gate, my love," he said as they approached. The wood of the obstacle was new, freshly-sanded and erected. The latch that held it shut was locked firm with a large steel padlock. "What's this?"

"Are you sure you brought us down the right path, Alit?" smiled Esme gently, her grey eyes teasing as she looked upon her husband. "You aren't used reading a map. Perhaps this Illumination isn't teaching you all the skills you wanted it to..."

Alit shook his head, reaching up to the seat of the wagon and pulling down the map. "There aren't enough roads to confuse me, Esme. We are here."

His pale finger pointed to a spot on the map. Esme pressed back into his side, peering at the parchment.

Tanis had jumped down from the back of the wagon now. "What's going on, father?"

"There's a gate, lad," replied Alit, looking the map up and down again. "I can't understand why it's locked up. This is a common road, it says so here."

Esme checked the map, nodded her agreement. "Is the map reliable?"

Alit shot her a look of feigned disappointment. "Do you know your husband at all? I bought it from Master Jinnis, the cartographer. He is an artisan, and a Yanari."

Esme nodded. "I'm sorry, Alit. So, we should be able to pass."

Alit hesitated, looking over his shoulder at the gate. The track beyond wound a twisting path in to the hills, cold and desolate. He began to feel hesitant. Maybe this was a mistake? Maybe a more comfortable Illumination could be had nearer to Regalla.

"Then we should go," insisted Tanis. The lad skipped back to the wagon, reaching inside a producing his carpenter's saw.

"What are you doing, lad?" asked Alit, shaking his head. "Calm yourself. Whoever owns this gate will take a dim view if we damage it."

Tanis slipped past him, poising with the saw at the cross beam of the gate beside the padlock. "Nonsense, father. If we just cut this beam, the gate will fall open. If this is a common road, we have the right."

"What are you talking about, boy?" snapped Alit. The lad was out of control. A Yanari would not think of damaging another's property.

"Honestly, father," insisted Tanis. "It's the law of the land. A common road is for all to use. Anyone blocking a common road is committing a crime punishable by incarceration in the stocks."

Alit looked to Esme questioningly. This was her influence.

"The lad reads," shrugged his wife, smiling gently and stroking his cheek. "If it is our right, then we can pass."

"It is, father," said Tanis. "I promise. I read it before we left Regalla."

"Tanis," said Alit gently. "It is not for us to upset the apple cart. Whoever put that lock there, it is not for us to decide to remove it. We are humble Yanari..."

"Alit," said Esme, bringing his face round to face her. "We are *Castlanders*. The lord, Cecil, said the very same. He gave you a note to that effect. If this is our right, it is our right."

Alit hesitated, looking from his wife to his younger son and back again.

"Alright," he said, smiling superficially. "We are on Illumination, after all. It should not be blocked by a padlocked gate if we are doing nothing wrong. Be careful though, Tanis. Do as little damage as possible."

The grinding of Tanis' saw began as soon as the words left Alit's mouth.

99

The vampire moved quickly through the brush, keeping low to the ground. The humans on the wagon wouldn't be able to see him at this distance. He was right on the limits of his own, far superior, vision and he was clad in greens and browns that blended perfectly with his surroundings. Even so, it paid to be careful. There were others prowling the hills, he could smell them. They were following the wagon too.

Xavier had watched the humans at the gate. At least, he assumed they were humans. He had never seen their like before. Short, slight of build, with skin as white as his own. An adult male and female, and young lad who sawed the gate so that the padlock holding it shut fell to the ground. There was another child in the wagon. Xavier had scented him. The tender smell of youthful meat.

He had watched them head off and then inspected the gate, running cold, white hands over the smooth, new wood. Recently erected. No pockmarks or blemishes, the hinges free of the taint of rust. He had breathed in the scent of the wood, savoured it.

But who had put it up? Lord Perlis needed to know about this. The Vampire Lord was insistent on being informed on everything that Xavier discovered on his scouting trips.

Xavier had followed the wagon, ensuring he kept off the path and well in amongst the hillocks and heather. At first he had meant to overtake them. The track they were following would lead them through the Red Cairn Hills to the north, and into Lord Perlis' lands beyond. The journey would take the humans days with their cart, but Xavier could cover the ground much quicker. He didn't need rest, and it was mid-afternoon already. When night set in he would be able to move faster, his senses more attuned, his body stronger, swifter.

But then he had felt the pursuers' presence, and it had roused his curiosity. He had sniffed the air, flicked out his tongue to taste it. Eight men, on horseback. They had picked up the family's trail at the gate and were following them. They would be here soon. Xavier could already hear the faint fall of hooves on the path as they cantered after the wagon.

He turned his dark eyes to the south, squinting down the path. Yes, they were coming. Outriders in the livery of Lord Zachary Unstead, whose lands bordered the Red Cairn Hills on the west.

Xavier moved closer, still low to the ground. He needed to see what was happening here…

Alit held the reins of the wagon in one hand, his other resting on Esme's thigh as she sat beside him. She looked over at him, smiling as she met his gaze.

"What is it?" she asked.

"Nothing," smiled Alit. "Can't a man look on his beautiful wife without a reason?"

"Stop it, Alit," she giggled, looking away bashfully, her cheeks blushing slightly. She was beautiful, even given the effort she had put into working long hours as a maid and raising two children. She had tended their home whilst he spent hours in the workshop, labouring to make a decent life for them all.

He suddenly realised how little he told her of his gratitude. "I love you, Esme. You know we all owe our happiness to you."

Esme shook her head, giggling again.

"You make this humble Yanari very happy."

She shook her head, feigning annoyance. "If you don't stop with all that 'humble Yanari' rubbish then you will find yourself very *unhappy*, Master Wulska. We're not in the capital now, there's just us here. You don't need to bow and scrape."

Alit paused.

"Yes, mistress," he said with a teasing smile.

Esme punched him gently in the arm. He pulled away, clutching his bicep as though mortally wounded.

"You there." A voice from behind the wagon called out, firm and serious.

The two Yanari looked round over their shoulders. They hadn't noticed the horsemen approach. As they watched two of the men rode round to the front of the wagon. One of them grabbed the horse's bridle, pulling it to a halt.

Esme's eyes were wide with panic as she looked to Alit. The eight armed men surrounded the wagon as their leader paced his horse up alongside the driver's seat on which they perched.

"It's alright, Esme. Look, they're liveried. They aren't bandits."

The lead outrider shook his head as he overheard Alit, greasy black hair flapping across his face as it fell loose from beneath his helmet. He was lean and weathered, a cruel-looking man with rugged features and piercing green eyes. He sported a beard that attempted to cover the pockmarks on his face left by some childhood pox.

"We certainly aren't bandits, love," he said. "We're outriders in the service of Lord Unstead of Hearth Hill. We stop people like you getting robbed by those filth."

"Then we humble Yanari are most grateful to you," said Alit, bowing his head slightly, ignoring Esme's sigh of disapproval.

"Yeah, yeah," said the man, waving his hand dismissively. "What are you doing on this road?"

"We are heading to the Red Cairn Hills, sir," replied Alit, pointing down the track.

"Do you hear that, lads?" laughed the man, looking around his crew. "I've been knighted by a fucking Yanari. Thank you very much, my lord."

The men burst out into raucous laughter as their leader performed a deep bow on his horse, his arm held elegantly out to one side.

Esme shuffled in her seat. Alit squeezed her thigh reassuringly, trying to hide his own discomfort.

"Now, mate, I don't need you to point out where the Red Cairn Hills are for me. I know this land like the back of my gnarled hand. I want to know what your business is on Lord Unstead's land." "I was under the impression that the Red Cairn Hills were common land," said Esme. "Given to the people for their enjoyment of their history and natural beauty by Lord Perlis."

The man stopped dead, the beady green eyes burning as he stared as Esme. "I don't remember talking to you, woman. I was talking to your husband. Lads, if this milky bitch opens her mouth again, stick a quarrel in her."

To Alit's amazement, two of the men raised their crossbows, levelling them on the back of their forearms at Esme. He raised his hands in a calming gesture. "Please, please. We are heading into the hills as part of our Illumination."

"Illumination?" piped up one of the outriders, shrugging. The leader shot him a look to keep his mouth shut.

"Yanara demands that, at least every five years..."

"Yeah, yeah, heathen bullshit," interrupted the man, gesturing to the wagon. "What's in here then? No illicit goods for trade, eh?"

"No, sir, I assure you," insisted Alit. "Just our sons, and our provisions."

The man turned and nodded to the men at the rear of the wagon. They dismounted and pulled open the back of the wagon, clambering inside. There was the sound of a clamour as the men rummaged through the Wulskas' belongings, pans crashing to the floor of the wagon, sacks and bags being ripped open. The men emerged, throwing Alitain and Tanis to the dirt of the road.

"Get your hands off me," screamed Tanis, turning on one of the men. The outrider pushed him to the ground again, landing him on his backside.

"Anything?" asked the lead outrider. His men shook their heads, their disappointment evident. He turned back to Alit, pulling his horse close against the cart and leaning into the Yanari's face. Alit smelt stale whisky on the outrider's breath. "This road, and this land, is off limits to everyone without the permission of Lord Unstead."

"But, sir, I was under the impression the Red Cairn Hills were common land," said Alit meekly, avoiding eye contact. He squeezed Esme's leg again, willing her to be quiet.

"And they are, mate," said the man, still staring. "But you aren't in the Red Cairn Hills. At the minute, you're on Lord Unstead's land."

"But this is a common road," yelled Tanis, striding up defiantly to the outrider.

"There's a fucking gate back there, isn't there boy?" snarled the man, turning his horse so that its flanks pushed the lad aside. "And you fucking milkers damaged it. I've had enough of this shit."

"But sir, we have been given the blessing of Lord Cecil Cramwall," cried Alit, reaching desperately for the pack sat beside him on the seat. The crossbows snapped round to train on him, the outrider slipping a dagger from his belt and holding it to his pale throat. Alit gulped visibly, feeling the sharp steel scraping against his skin.

"Slowly, mate," said the outrider menacingly. "Would be a crying shame if you cut yourself."

Alit moved carefully, pulling the sealed roll of parchment from his backpack and holding it out for the outrider. The man snatched it, pulling it open and reading slowly, his mouth moving as he struggled with the words.

He shrugged. "This doesn't say nothing about giving you the right to roam across private land, mate. Just offers you assistance if you need it. And that's what we're doing. There's worse than bandits in those hills and beyond. We're saving you from that shit."

"But this isn't a private road," insisted Tanis. "You can't do this."

"If he talks again I'm going to slit his throat," said the outrider, not looking up from the parchment.

Alit glared at Tanis pleadingly. The lad stared back defiantly, his fists clenched at his sides.

"You lot can tell all this to Lord Unstead," snapped the man, reaching to his belt and taking a swig from a metal hipflask. "It's his gate you've fucked up, anyway. And I'm sure he'll be interested to hear you've been dragging the Cramwall name into all this. Boys, get these fuckers of the wagon. Get them all in the back. One of you drive it. We're heading home."

The rest of the men dismounted, dragging Alit and Esme roughly from the wagon. Esme cried out as she fell to the dirt, her dress ripping as it caught on a protruding nail.

"Get off me, you filth," she screamed, pulling away from the man pawing at her.

"You were fucking warned, milker," snarled the man, striking her across the cheek with the back of his hand. Alit broke away from the outrider gripping him, wrapping his arms around his wife and pulling her towards the back of the cart.

"Esme, please, please," he pleaded, dragging her into the wagon.

The lead outrider spat on the ground. "Fucking Yanari. Fucking animals."

He looked down to where Tanis was standing, staring up at him, hatred burning in his glassy grey eyes. "I'm going to kill you."

The outrider laughed. He pulled his foot free of his stirrups and booted the lad across the face.

Faunis, the God of Nature, ran through his territory in the Astral Realm. The Lord of Beasts had taken the form of a deer, swift and sure footed. He ran hard and fast, leaping gracefully over the obstacles in his path as he moved between the tall, thick-trunked trees that towered up into the sky above him.

The wind rushed against his face as he sprinted, the cool air soothing as he worked up a sweat. Was this what it was like, to tear through the thick soup of the Mortal World, splitting the heavy, clogging atmosphere with your form? He didn't know. He imagined this was how it felt.

He stopped, tilting his head to sniff the air.

He wasn't alone. There was another here. He looked around, wide brown eyes searching for the slightest hint of movement, eyes flicking as they nervously sought out any sounds.

Sanguis emerged from behind a tree, her movements delicate, noiseless. Her lean, black, Q'shari body seemed to entwine itself around the trunk as she moved into view, clad only in a blood red loincloth and scarlet veil that flowed down over her pert breasts. The Murderess ran a slender hand through her flowing, jet black locks of hair before waving, the crimson slits of her eyes settling on Faunis.

"What are you doing here?" asked Faunis. His form changed as the Dark God approached. He raised up on his back legs, his upper body shifting in a green mist, twisting into the shape of a wiry male Q'shari. The leaf green eyes settled on Sanguis suspiciously.

"I come here often," smiled Sanguis, white fangs glinting even in the small amount of light penetrating the thick canopy above them. "I like your realm. Or, more to the point, I like to understand why the Q'shari hold it in such regard."

She reached out a hand, running it gently down the bark of the tree. She stroked again, harder, splinters digging into the palm of her hand. She pulled back, as if burnt.

"The Q'shari who worship me are a pure people, and old race who understand the intricacies of life, but also its simplicity."

"Overly complex as always, Faunis," smiled Sanguis, sauntering over to him seductively. She reached out, running her hand down his flat stomach. "Were all the Old Gods so boring and vague?"

Faunis looked at her for a second, taking in her sensual lips, the tingling in his groan as she moved her hand lower. He brushed it away. "We understand. We had an eternity to learn. I don't expect you children to understand."

Sanguis huffed at the rebuff, staying close to Faunis, pressing against him. "And yet you are the only one left. Doesn't that worry you? The Old Gods all gone. Maybe you didn't understand at all..."

Faunis shook his head. "I still have prayers, Sanguis. The others lost their followers to the likes of your kind, but my people stay faithful. There are not many, now, but they are loyal. It is not the quantity of prayers that matters, but the quality."

"So you admit that the mortals control your fate. Interesting. Doesn't that make you feel vulnerable?"

"I do not understand," said Faunis, taking a step back from the Murderess. She followed, pressing herself against him again, leaning close.

"I don't have a large number of worshippers, Faunis. I feel vulnerable. I have some humans, the assassins and the killers. But they are shunned by their kind."

"Because they are evil," snapped Faunis, leaning his head back as Sanguis moved forward to lick at his face.

"Evil?" She span away from him, incredulous. "When a man kills, it is evil. When an animal kills, it is nature. Hypocrisy of the worst order."

"A man has a choice, Sanguis. That is the difference."

"And you made them that way, Faunis. A mortal is just an animal, after all."

"I didn't make them, Sanguis," said the Life Giver, spreading his arms wide. "They were just there. Like all of nature. Like the Astral Realm and the Mortal World. Like us."

"And yet we, the New Gods, were created. So obviously the mortals have the power to make something. And I have created. I still remember their prayers, thick and heavy, all that time ago. They wanted it so badly, to live forever, to be better than they were. And their prayers were so powerful I was able to grant their wishes, to give them the Gift. And yet you have created nothing? Maybe you do not understand at all, Faunis. Maybe you are more vulnerable than I, even?"

Sanguis moved closer again, wrapping her long limbs around his waist, pulling him close against her.

"Maybe you are alone, and we should protect one another," she cooed, pulling his head close and whispering in his ear.

"I don't understand," said Faunis, placing his hands meekly on her waist.

"But I thought you *did* understand?" she said, smiling as she kissed his throbbing black neck. "You are alone, Faunis. Where were you when we fought the Lurker?"

"Nature does not take sides," said Faunis. He wanted to push her away, but her warmth against his chest was soothing. He felt her push her pelvis in against him.

"So you didn't fight. When the Lurker caused chaos in the Astral Realm and suffering in the Mortal World, you stayed to one side and watched. All that suffering. And you say my people are evil?"

"Nature does not take sides," repeated Faunis, weaker this time. Sanguis leaned back, her hands stroking up his ribs and chest, resting on his cheeks as she stared into his eyes.

"You are neither Dark nor Light, Faunis. You are alone. And if your worshippers are slain, you will disappear like the rest of the Old Gods. We need each other. We have the Q'shari, between us. Some are yours, some are mine. You have some woodsmen, some herbalists, some backwater villages who turnover animal dung for a living. I have those that you call evil, who are despised by the fellow humans. I have the vampires. They are strong, but they are few. Other than that, we are exposed. The others have worshippers across the Mortal World, in vast numbers. Pyra, the Flame, has the entire realm of Altanya devoted to her."

"You know much of the Mortal World," said Faunis, gazing into the blood red slits of Sanguis' eyes.

"It is the quality of the prayer, my love, that matters," smiled Sanguis, stroking Faunis' cheek with her thumb. "My people in the Mortal World are angry, and their prayers are intense. Sometimes their power makes me dizzy, lose all sense of self control."

Her hand ran down Faunis' chest, finding his nipple. She squeezed it gently, moving her head down and caressing it with her soft lips. He moved his hand to her head, running his fingers through her mane of soft, black hair.

"We need to be there for one another, my love," said Sanguis.

Then she disappeared. Faunis felt her move away through the trees, unseen but not unsensed. He looked after with dark, wet, brown eyes. He missed her presence.

He had never felt so alone.

The hall of Lord Perlis' castle was a step back into the past. It was typical of most of those of the Vampire Lords. The cold, bare stone was the most noticeable feature. A single, long rug sat on the floor, faded with immense age. It bore a simple depiction of a battle long forgotten by men, back in the ancient days of Castland's founding. Long forgotten by men, but not by Lord Perlis. He could still taste the blood in his mouth from the mace blow that had smashed his face.

A pale hand wandered up to his cheek and jaw, touching the mangled bone beneath the white flesh. The wound had been suffered whilst he was still mortal, and those injuries tended not to heal so well. His left eye still had a squint from the distorted, ridged bone beneath his skin. He had lay there, dying in the morning light, feeling his life flow away. That was when he had been given the Gift.

He looked over at Lord Drathlax, sat beside him. The seats were ancient but elaborate, carved from the bones of bears and wolves that the two of them had hunted in the time after Perlis' elevation to vampirehood. They had been close, through all these centuries. After all, Drathlax had saved Perlis' life that day.

Drathlax cocked his head slightly as he saw his old companion running his fingers down the cracks in his face. Perlis brought the hand down quickly, turning his attention back to Xavier, who stood before them in the hall, describing what he had seen on the road.

The walls of the hall were similarly bare, decorated with threadbare tapestries that were only as preserved as well as they were due to the shutters that were bolted shut on most of the windows. The simple, wooden candleholders that hung from the vaulted ceiling were empty, the only light coming from the single fire in one of the hearths, and the weak light of midday that shone through the slats in the shutters. Lord Perlis' lands beyond the Red Cairn Hills were bleak, the daylight was weak at the best of times, but the vampires did not need it to see. The darkness was their ally, it hugged them like a thick blanket.

"Then Lord Unstead's men took them away, father," concluded Xavier, sitting on the edge of the long, heavy table that ran the length of the hall.

Of course, Xavier wasn't Perlis' son, not in the mortal sense of the word. Xavier had only had one child, a girl. She had refused the Gift when Perlis had offered it, choosing instead to die when her time was up. Cara had insisted that she would rather her flame burnt twice as bright for half as long, so that she made the most of her time in the Mortal World. Her flame had burnt bright, but for much less than half as long. Perlis had lived on, through years that he could not count. Time passed strangely for an immortal, it was hard to keep track of years running into the past when you counted your life in centuries and decades. It was long ago, but it still hurt him to think back. The humans that knew of the vampire legend assumed they were heartless, unfeeling beasts.

Nothing could be further from the truth. Perlis' emotions burnt with an intensity that matched those of his physical senses. He could not place the number of years since Cara's death, but he could still picture her; the platinum blonde hair, the deep blue eyes, the delicate cleft chin. She had been his image. He had changed little over the years, apart from the eyes. The Gift had darkened them, to an indigo that was almost black. It was those eyes that had fallen upon Xavier a few decades ago.

Perlis had found the youth when he joined the castle's small group of servants. He was working in the stables with the horses when Perlis had gone to collect his mount for a hunt. The dark indigo eyes had taken him in as he led the beast out; the shoulder-length, silver hair, the eyes blue as the deep sea, the dimpled chin, the sharp cheekbones that reminded him of his own before his face had been pummelled. Surely they were related, some distant relative from a bastard child of his forebears?

Perlis knew he had to have him. He had to have a child again. His heart had swelled and pumped at the idea. It was forbidden to give another the Gift without the agreement of the other Vampire Lords. Their kind needed to keep a balance; food was scarce and their existence relied on a delicate relationship with the humans. But Perlis could not resist. Drathlax, his old friend, knew about Xavier, but the others were unaware. If they found out, they might slay him, send his soul to oblivion. A tear ran down Perlis' broken cheek at the thought...

Drathlax cleared his throat, bringing Perlis back to the room abruptly.

"Interesting," he said, pausing as he gathered his thoughts. "What do you think, Lord Drathlax?"

"I think it is not our affair, Lord Perlis," replied the older vampire.

"The plight of the humans is not our affair, certainly," said Perlis, his hand once more straying to his face. "But their misfortune could be used to our advantage, old friend."

"How so?" asked Drathlax warily.

"I hear rumours of dissatisfaction, even out here. The people of Castland are tired. The war with the Raskans hurt the people hard. They want some comfort. But the years have passed and the measures taken to aid the war effort haven't been revoked. They are hungry, and they feel downtrodden."

"Where do you hear such things?" asked Drathlax, his black eyes settling on Perlis.

"I hear them," said Perlis. He smiled, the undamaged side of his face rising gently, leaving the left hanging behind it. "Do not tell me one who travels as much as yourself has not."

Drathlax shrugged, taking an elegant sip from the human skull goblet in his slender hand. The wine was tangy, fermented with human blood in Perlis' own stores for a decade. An excellent vintage. He moved it around his mouth, savouring the tastes.

"You know the truth, Lord Drathlax," said Perlis, sipping from his own cup. "I opened up my lands, the Red Cairn Hills, so that the people, rich and poor, could look upon our heritage, upon the burial sites of our relatives. They wouldn't know what they were looking upon, of course, but the point is moot. I gave to the people, and Unstead is taking from them. That will cause a stir."

"It is his land that borders the hills to the south, Lord Perlis. You know that."

"I do," smiled Perlis. "But it is a common road. Do not pretend you do not know the laws of the land, old friend. We were present when they were made, remember. We helped form them."

"That is true," said Drathlax guardedly.

"Then it is settled," said Perlis. "We will make some mischief for the human lords. Xavier, send a pigeon to our friend in the capital. Let him know of this gross injustice."

"Yes, father," said Xavier, slipping off the table and heading from the hall.

Drathlax watched him leave before turning slowly to Perlis. "We should consult the Council first, Perlis."

"Why, old friend?" laughed Perlis. "Those old bastards don't need to know about our little game. Why let them share our amusement?"

"*Is* this just a game, though?" asked Drathlax. His eyes settled on Perlis, dark and suspicious.

"Of course," replied Perlis, avoiding the gaze. He stood, moving over to a side table and replenishing his goblet.

"And what about the village?" asked Drathlax.

Perlis stopped pouring, placing the old, rough-glass decanter down gently. "So that is why you are here. Not a social visit to an old friend, then?"

"You admit it, then?"

"I would never lie to you, old friend. We are hungry here, Drathlax. My *family* is hungry. We can't live on goats and sheep. We are supposed to be lords, the immortals, the Chosen of Sanguis."

"You left ferals amongst them," snarled Drathlax, up on his feet now. His eyes glinted red with anger.

"Yes I did," growled Perlis, his own eyes flashing crimson. "We fed, because we were hungry. And that cunt Unstead called in Princetown, and his soldiers slaughtered an entire village under my protection. Burnt them at the stake. Man, woman and child. So I went back, and I gave them some ferals."

Drathlax shook his head in amazement. Every human bitten by a vampire wasn't given the Gift. The hunter had to *want* them to have it. He thought back to his own turning; the confusion, the pain, the bloodlust, the pain of the sunlight on his newly-immortal flesh, intense and incandescent. A new-born vampire needed to be nurtured, to be shown how to survive, how to control the pain, how to come to terms with the fact that humans were your new food source. They needed to be taught the balance, how to *survive*. Not having that nurturing hand led to feral creatures, awakening as a new being buried six feet underground in a box and punching and clawing their way towards the scorching daylight.

Creating ferals was forbidden.

"The Council will hear of this and they'll want your head," shouted Drathlax. He felt sick to his stomach. "And the Lord Chancellor..."

"Listen to yourself, Drathlax," roared Perlis. "The fucking Council. How would they find out if you did not tell them? They live in castles in the hills and the mountains. They don't know what's happening in their own villages, never mind the rest of Castland. The Lord Chancellor? You mean Cramwall. He's just a fucking human. You used to be fearsome, Drathlax. You used to tear through the meat like it was hay in the field. Now you're nothing more than a lackey."

"How dare you?" snapped Drathlax.

"I dare because I want to *live*, old friend," said Perlis, the glare in his eyes fading. He turned and walked over to a painting, hung behind his chair in pride of place on the wall. "Do you see this?"

Drathlax looked upon the painting, a crude portrait of Perlis. It had been made before his injury, his thin, simple face painted without the battle injuries that he now sported. "I've seen it a hundred times, Perlis."

"Cara painted it when she was just a girl," smiled Perlis. His hand moved close, hovering over the surface of the ancient, dry paint, desperate to touch it but wary of the damage the contact would do. "It is amazing. The brushwork; heavy and deep. The colours; vibrant and bold. The frame. She made it herself, took her weeks."

Drathlax's old eyes looked over the picture, took in the dilapidated frame where it had come unglued in one corner. "It is a child's painting, Perlis. It is not great art. I have a portrait by the great master Unnanis in my hall at home..."

"And it is sterile, old friend," interrupted Perlis. "It is a perfect outward likeness. It shows your features, but the eyes are just black pits. They don't show your soul. This picture shows me as I truly am; vibrant, intense, *alive*. How you used to be. She wasn't the best at drawing, but she carried on until the day she died. I have a gallery of her paintings upstairs, beautiful works that show passion and life. The important things. I want to *live*, old friend. Not just exist, fed by human masters who throw scraps from their table as if to a pet dog. It is our place in the world."

Drathlax looked at the painting for a long time, staring at the deep, passionate, clumsy brush strokes. *Maybe Perlis was right...*

"I shall have to inform the Council," he said, turning to stride from the room.

Perlis stared at the painting, dark blue eyes flicking over detail he had not noticed before in years staring at its beauty.

"Do what you think is right, old friend."

He reached out a finger, gently touching the surface of Cara's painting. A piece of dry paint broke away, floating gracefully to the floor. As Perlis stared down at it, a tear rolled down his broken cheek.

Chapter Fifteen

Yarner raised his lantern high, trying to see through the murk of the sewer tunnel. The nauseating smell of the effluent channel seemed to give off a warm fog of its own, thick and cloying even in the cold Regalla morning. He could swear it was green.

"Do you smell gas?" he asked, preparing to blow out the lantern flame.

"All I can smell is fucking shit," groaned Magnus. His scarf was wrapped around his scarred face, muffling his voice. His beady eyes peered into the darkness past Yarner.

"Fucking rat catching in the sewers," spat Derron, pulling his own scarf around his mouth and nose. "We should've listened to young Arnie. He said this would happen. I almost envy the lad for getting stabbed."

"Right you should," said Magnus. "He's laid up in bed getting fucked better by his whore while we're stuck down here."

Yarner stifled a laugh. His ribs were still sore, and even breathing caused him pain. He was lucky too, in a way, having had his nose broken. The stench of the sewers was struggling to penetrate the thick crust of clotted blood in his nasal passages.

He looked back at Griegor, shuffling behind them at the rear of the group. "Are you alright, big guy?"

Griegor nodded, groaning with each step.

The giant man was hurting, but he wouldn't admit it. He had taken even more of a beating than Yarner. His ribs were bust up and his whole body was covered in deep grazes and bruises. There was a lump the size of an apple on his forehead, and another on the back of his skull. They had had a couple of days to rest up, but despite Yarner's protests Griegor had insisted on coming back onto the shift with them.

It wasn't just that Griegor was in pain. Yarner knew he was missing Reaper. The big dog was stuck at the watch house recovering. Even if he wasn't, they wouldn't be able to get him down here. He wasn't a ratter, he was a fighting dog. Griegor was used to having him around every hour of the day, and the absence of his canine companion was making him sulky.

Captain Graves had arrived quickly once Derron had filled him in on events. They had taken the Princetown boy and the survivors of the fight to the Lord Chancellor's palace. Graves had woken up the captain of the Cramwall guards and handed them over, explaining the situation. Yarner and the lads had waited outside for an age before the Graves returned and sent them home to rest.

The following afternoon Yarner had been given the news. The Lord Chancellor himself would be dealing with the situation. There was to be no further talk of the matter. Yarner had had to vouch for the lads. They had been given a hefty pouch of silver each, and warned in no uncertain terms as to the repercussions if they divulged the night's events to anyone.

Then had come the cherry on the cake. They were to take on some less conspicuous duties. The city had a rat problem, and the Clerics of Pharma were worried that it could lead to disease. Yarner and his men were put in charge of the unenviable task of culling the rats in the sewers.

His wife was already complaining. His stinking clothes piled up on the kitchen floor every evening ready for the wash were starting to seep the smell of shit into the very fabric of the house. Yarner knew why they were down here, though. Graves had had to vouch for them, otherwise they would have been made to disappear. He wanted them out of the way, where they couldn't let him down.

Yarner didn't like the burden. He had explained things to Arnie. The young lad wouldn't talk now he understood. He was too busy planning what engagement ring he was going to buy for Lucy with his hush money.

Griegor did as he was told. He hardly spoke anyway, and when he did it was only to his friends in the patrol. Derron was smart, he knew to keep his mouth shut, especially when it came to the business of the aristocracy.

Magnus, though. Magnus worried Yarner at the best of times. The little man had saved his life, there was no doubt about that. But Yarner had never really trusted him. He just had to hope that the weasel's animal sense of survival kicked in; if he spoke of last night and was discovered, he surely knew what would happen to him...

"There's one of the little bastards," called Derron, raising his lantern to catch the scurrying creature in its light.

"Little?" laughed Magnus, raising one of the crossbow pistols they had been supplied with. He squinted his good eye, following the creature. "It's as big as a fucking cat."

107

Magnus squeezed the trigger. The creature squeaked and rolled across the floor, the small bolt skewering it through the midriff. Griegor shuddered, shaking his head.

"It's okay, Griegor," said Derron, reassuring the big man. "Rats are bad. They eat all the dogs' food. They even bite babies in their cribs. Then the children get sick."

Griegor nodded reluctantly.

"At least you got the sharp end into it this time," smiled Yarner. "Not like with Johann."

Magnus sneered, pulling back the wire and snapping another bolt into the miniature crossbow. "Next time I won't fucking bother trying."

"Don't be like that, Magnus," said Yarner. "Come on, bag it up. We don't want Graves thinking we're just messing around down here."

He forced another smile, but it was insincere. This wasn't work for a watchman in the capital.

Still, at least they were alive...

Lord Chancellor Cramwall steepled his stubby fingers beneath his chin, the beady blue eyes staring across the desk in his audience chamber at Toby. The young noble was avoiding the glare as he sat before Cecil's father, manacles clinking as he rubbed at his eyes, trying to get used to the light.

Toby dragged his dark eyes upwards to look at the Lord Chancellor, revealing the dark bruising across his face where the watchman had elbowed him. He looked the Cramwall's chest, still trying to avoid the stare. "I'm not sure..."

Captain Charles Capethorne of the Cramwall household guard stood behind Toby. A gauntleted hand clamped down on his shoulder, squeezing tightly to stop his protests. "I don't believe the Lord Chancellor addressed you, Princetown."

Toby swung his head round to look at the soldier. He opened his mouth to demand respect, but thought better of it. Capethorne was stern, stocky, the greying hair on his square head testament to a man who had fought for a living and survived into middle age. If he struck Toby, it would make a mess. Especially with those studded gauntlets. He thought better of it, returned to looking down at the desk in front of the Lord Chancellor.

"What were you thinking, you fool?" asked Cramwall, sealing a document and pushing it across the desk at Capethorne. The captain reached over Toby's shoulder and picked it up, cold chainmail pressing menacingly across the young noble's cheek.

"I don't know what you mean, Lord Chancellor."

The short, chubby man's cheeks went red with rage in an instant. "Don't you lie to me, you little bastard," he screamed, spit catching Toby's face even from across the desk. "I'd catch Cecil across the face for lying to me, and he's my son. My flesh and blood. What do you think I would do to you?"

Toby didn't answer.

"You killed those women, you little degenerate. Like a savage. Like an animal. You have besmirched the name of your house, of your father."

Toby turned his gaze to the floor.

"Do you have any idea of the unrest you have caused? Do you have any idea how much worse it could have been if this got out? A boy of noble birth, slaughtering commoners in the street?"

Toby didn't answer. He didn't know what to say to make the shouting stop. The noise was a sharp contrast to the silence of the palace dungeon, locked in the quiet dark with only the drip of the leaking roof to keep him company.

"*Answer me!*"

"I... I did not mean to cause trouble, Lord Chancellor..."

"*Trouble!*" roared Cramwall, spreading his arms out to the audience chamber. "This isn't youthful folly, boy. This is a sickness. You have left a trail of devastation that *I* am having to clean up. I have a captain of the watch who knows more than he should, and I have to trust him to keep quiet. I have good men of the watch working in the sewers to cover your trail, and I have to trust them too..."

"They assaulted me," cried Toby, tears streaming down his cheeks. "A nobleman, assaulted by commoners."

"If he interrupts me again in front of my guest, then knock some of his teeth out," snapped Cramwall, addressing Capethorne. The guard rubbed his fist against the palm of his hand, relishing the idea.

"If I may ask, Lord Chancellor?" said Toby meekly, his lip trembling as he took in Iluma Porwesh sitting beside Cecil's father. "What is your guest doing here?"

"You may not ask," snapped Cramwall. "I am tired of you, Princetown. You have led my son astray for too long. You have been a constant pain in my behind. I thought maybe Cecil had some sickness in his head when I heard of the incident with the whore before he left, but now it seems that it is *you* who was born with a tainted soul."

Toby opened his mouth to protest, then clamped it shut again quickly. There was a rage in Cecil's father's eyes that was best left to die down naturally. Fanning the flames would cause him more pain.

"Are you ready for your sentence?" asked Cramwall, calming in an instant and leaning forward across the desk, seeking out eye contact from the young lord.

"But..." Toby stammered, looking from Porwesh to the Lord Chancellor and back again. "But there has been no trial..."

Cramwall laughed mirthlessly. "A trial? Put you up in front of a court, with commoners and the middle classes watching? Let it be told in the journals that the only son of Lord Princetown of Snowgate is a degenerate murderer? That the nobility is prone to the same base behaviour as the peasants? Jeopardise the balance of order by threatening the belief that we are better than them? Never."

"But when my father hears of this..."

"He *will* hear of it, lad, because I will tell him. I will tell him myself that his son has been exiled because he is a murderous stain on the seat of the aristocracy's pants."

"*Exile?*" Toby's span, his thoughts straying to the hazy, half-drunk conversation in this same hall regarding supplying the Vampire Lords with food. He looked from right to left, searching for a way out, but his legs had turned to jelly.

Cramwall smiled. "Not that kind of exile, boy. You are a noble child, even if you are twisted one. This is Castland. We do not send our little lords to be the food of vampires."

Toby fell back in his chair, gasping for breath.

"I need an envoy to go to Altanya. You will have to suffice. It is an honorary position only. Drink their drink, eat their food. Listen, learn, and represent Castland. Maybe it will make a man of you."

"Altanya is halfway across the world," said Toby slowly, still struggling to catch his breath.

"Exactly," smiled Cramwall, leaning back in his chair. "You will go, and you will not come back until I send for you. And this sick hobby of yours will cease immediately, do you understand? Otherwise Captain Capethorne here will separate your head from your body."

Toby heard the leather of Capethorne's gauntlets creak as his hands rubbed together in anticipation.

"If I refuse...?" he asked meekly.

"Then the good captain will separate your head from your body right here in this very hall. A court would not be so lenient as to sentence you to exile, Toby, believe me. I am merely trying to limit the damage to this great country's order. In the process, I am giving you a chance to redeem yourself. To purge yourself of this curse that you have developed."

Toby nodded, defeated. "Thank you, Lord Chancellor."

"Good," said Cramwall, gesturing to Capethorne. The guardsman hauled Toby to his feet. "Remember, boy, you are representing Castland out there. Listen, learn, report."

Toby nodded as he clanked his way from the hall, dragged by the soldier.

Cramwall and Porwesh sat in silence for a moment, both staring at the doors through which the young lord of Snowgate had departed.

"I do mirror young Princetown's thoughts on one matter, Lord Chancellor," said Porwesh gently, the pale, wrinkled face turning inquisitively towards Cramwall. "Why am I here to witness such delicate affairs of state?"

Cramwall smiled, turning to the Yanari and pouring them both a small goblet of sweet red wine. "You are my friend, Iluma. And soon our families are to be joined by the marriage of our children. Then we shall be more than friends. We shall be allies."

"You flatter me, Lord Chancellor," smiled Porwesh, sipping gently at the wine with pale lips bloated from a lifetime of rich food and drink.

"Not at all, Iluma. You are an intelligent man. You are rich, and that means you are powerful. Even more so, you have accrued your wealth despite being a Yanari, which I understand can be a significant barrier in the world. That means you are shrewd."

"You flatter me further," shrugged Porwesh, feigning discomfort.

"I need shrewd men as allies, Iluma," sighed Cramwall, leaning back in his chair and gazing upon the Yanari. "The balance in Castland is delicate at present, and yet I seem to be surrounded by lords who lie fat and complacent. What is worse, their children are imbecilic. Their fathers do not discipline them, do not guide them on the path required to maintain order in our great country."

"And Lord Princetown concerns you most..." said Porwesh, his blue eyes peering over his cup as he drank. It was a statement, not a question. Cramwall liked that. Honest, intuitive, to the point.

He didn't answer the question. "Lord Princetown has involved me in a dispute that he should have resolved himself. One of his pledged men, Lord Unstead, had some unfortunate dealings with one of the Vampire Lords. He called on his liege for help, and Lord Princetown... escalated... the situation."

Porwesh raised his thin, white eyebrows. "Escalation is no good for anyone, Lord Chancellor."

"Quite," replied Cramwall. "If he had been more diplomatic, some unpleasantness could have been avoided. Instead, I had to extend an invitation to a Vampire Lord and invite him here to ask for his help in calming matters. I had to invite a *vampire* into my house, into my city. And I had to *ask* him for favours."

"A most untrustworthy breed of creatures," agreed Porwesh, sipping again at the wine. It was sweet enough to tantalise even his old taste buds. He swilled it across his tongue, savouring it. It reminded him of the wine he imported from the Bandit Country, in the old lands of his forebears.

"True, Iluma, but a necessary understanding needs to be maintained to keep order. Alas, Lord Princetown appears unable to control Lord Unstead. Either that, or he does not understand the delicate balancing act required to keep our great nation peaceful. Whichever, he is displaying most undesirable traits. A bird brought this news this morning..."

The Lord Chancellor passed the old Yanari a piece of parchment. Porwesh reached inside his simple blue tunic and pulled a pair of thick-rimmed spectacles out, perching them on his bulbous nose. He read the paper once, then again, shaking his head.

"Lord Unstead has taken it upon himself to block the common road leading to Lord Perlis' lands," said Cramwall, taking a deep sip of the wine. He didn't usually partake, but recent events were forcing him to find a way of calming his nerves. He was used to a calm control of the state's affairs, but he felt that his grip was slipping, through no fault of his own. "I imagine this is some attempt to strangle any trade route for the Vampire Lord, but if word of this gets out, the poor folk will not look kindly upon it. They are already... ungrateful."

"It appears he has incarcerated a Yanari family from the capital," said Porwesh, still staring intently at the parchment. "An artisan, his wife and children. I feel that I see why I am here."

"Partly, my friend," said the Lord Chancellor, smiling. "Once again, you demonstrate that you are astute. I would like you to ensure that, should word of this come out, the Yanari do not take this incident personally."

"We humble Yanari are not minded to take offence so quickly, Lord Chancellor."

"I know, Iluma." Cramwall leaned closer to the Yanari. "But your assurance would be most appreciated anyway. And there is more to it than that. Lord Princetown, as you quite rightly observed, is becoming a liability. If it were required that he be replaced, I would like that to be with someone who I trusted. A wise man, bonded to my family by blood."

Porwesh's eyes widened, wrinkled lids folding back into his thin face. "Lord Chancellor, I am but a humble Yanari..."

"Which is why you would be a good fit, Iluma. You are smart. You see things that others do not. Soon we will be family. And the Yanari understand the importance of stability, of humility, of obedience. If it comes to it, I would like you at my side."

"I am honoured by your implication, Lord Chancellor," said Porwesh, bowing his head deeply. "But Lord Princetown is..."

"Fuck Arther Princetown," snapped Cramwall. Maybe the wine was going to his head quicker than he expected. "He has caused me enough problems. He acts irrationally. He allows his lords to do as they please. And his son has lumbered me with a potential fiasco in the very capital of our country, and prisoners in my dungeon who attacked the watch defending him. My dungeon is for *my* enemies, not those of Toby fucking Princetown."

"What of those men, Lord Chancellor? They will talk if they are let loose. Cutthroats and thieves cannot be relied upon." Porwesh swilled the sweet wine around his tongue again.

"Capethorne ripped out their tongues the night they were delivered," replied Cramwall, gulping back the last of his wine. "I am going to miss that man. Another thing that little shit Princetown has deprived me of. The criminals will be hanged this evening and their heads mounted on spikes outside the watch house in the Northern Quarter. Nobody attacks the watch in my city."

"Without order, we have nothing," agreed Porwesh, draining his own wine, smiling beneath the lip of the goblet.

Jaspar Ratcliffe stood atop the balcony of the Troubled Traveller Inn, looking down on the assembled crowd in the street below. The latest issue of the People's Gazette had been a rushed affair. A carrier pigeon had arrived only last night with some extremely interesting news, and Ratcliffe and the others had worked through the night to get the story into the crude printing press in his basement.

He looked down at the parchment before him, checking it over again as more of the common folk continued to join the crowd. A few spelling mistakes, but that was to be expected. They had been working quickly, the letters must have been loaded incorrectly. No matter, most of the poor couldn't read anyway. They relied on Ratcliffe and his agitators to proclaim the news to them. The *real* news. He didn't need to read the story out from the paper anyway. He knew what it said. He had written it. It *was* him...

News had spread fast. He had sent out his army of urchin runners, giving them a copper each to spread the word that a new and important article was ready. Below him, one of his vendors was hawking copies of the newspaper to those that could read. They stood amongst the crowd, poring over the words, pointing at the parchment and nudging those around them. Most weren't interested. They wanted to hear it from Ratcliffe.

A couple of his assistants were still in the basement, printing more copies. The rest were out in their usual spots, gathering crowds of their own.

"Come on Ratcliffe," called out a man from the bustling people below.

"What's the news, Jaspar?" called another.

They were becoming impatient, but Ratcliffe knew how to hold his audience. He held out a calming hand before pointing to the great timepiece set in the tower of the temple of Pharma. It was approaching seven o'clock, the twilight closing in and the air beginning to cool. Not too cold, not too dark. Most people would have finished their toils and would be on the way home. Hungry, but not too hungry to stop by and hear his proclamation before eating and drinking.

The huge brass bell in the tower began to strike the hour. The crowd fell silent, waiting for the dongs to pass, their eyes staring up expectantly at Ratcliffe. A few of the watch had gathered, keeping an eye on the throng. There weren't enough of them to stop him speaking, there were too many peasants wanting to hear what he had to say. Besides, the watch were commoners too. They wanted to hear just as much as the others.

Ratcliffe cleared his throat into the silence, holding the parchment out before him for effect.

"Brothers and sisters of Regalla, fellow Castlanders," he proclaimed. "A matter of great interest has come to the attention of the People's Gazette, and it is my privilege to tell you the facts as they lie in our corrupt land. You won't hear this in the Castland Times, because it is owned by the rich, and the truth would threaten their stranglehold on you and your families."

The crowd looked up in thrall, their eyes wide. Ratcliffe smiled inwardly, warmth spreading through his body even in the cold of the evening.

"Several days ago, a common family from this very city, the *capital* of Castland, were travelling the common road that leads into the Red Cairn Hills. There they were set upon by the minions of Lord Unstead of Hearth Hill, and dragged off to be imprisoned. The People's Gazette is not sure if they are alive or dead, but one thing is certain; this is yet another example of the lords of this land abusing their power and abusing the common people.

"The Red Cairn Hills are an area of historical interest, of bleak beauty. They were given to the people by Lord Perlis of Bloodstone. He wanted the common folk, especially those of the towns and cities, to be able to experience some of our great nation's history. He wanted them to be able to visit and see their stunning beauty. But Lord Unstead and his master, Lord Princetown of Snowgate, want to deny you this. They want to deny you your *rights.*"

The crowd was beginning to clamour now, alive with mumblings of anger and disgust. The glow in Ratcliffe's chest grew warmer.

"The road that leads to the Red Cairn Hills is a common road. No man, not of high birth nor of low, has the right to stop you travelling that road. Yet Lord Unstead has done just that, with the backing of Lord Princetown. He has put up a gate, a barrier, in the same way that the nobles of this city block you from living your life, from dragging yourselves from the gutter in which *they* put you."

The men and women were heaving now, fists raising in defiance.

"If they are not putting you in the gutter, they are putting you in the grave. Only earlier this very month, a noble prowled in the Northern Quarter, preying on poor folk and butchering them like pigs. And has this been met with justice? Has anyone heard of punishment for this aristocrat?"

Cries of "no" and "murderer" erupted from the crowd.

"No. He has been allowed to kill at will. Because he is one of them, and the people he killed were deemed to be of no matter. Of no worth. And what will you do about it? What will we do about it? They are few, and we are many. We have the power, not them, and yet we allow them to walk this realm as if it were the other way around.

"The People's Gazette will be organising a trek to the Red Cairn Hills. We will be finding out what happened to those poor common folk, and we *will* be exercising our *right* to walk that road. The People's Gazette is with you. The only question is, are you with the People's Gazette?"

The crowd roared. Ratcliffe smiled, letting the parchment free from his hand. He watched as it floated down into the sea of upraised, pumping fists.

The time would come, soon enough…

"I am not sure why you are telling me this, Porwesh," said Ceva Mardich, gently placing his knife and fork down on the delicate china plate in front of him and setting his light, inquisitive eyes on the man opposite him at the dining table. "I have heard this news already, in the gutter rag they call the People's Gazette."

Porwesh took in the owner of the Castland Times, taking a sip of the sweet wine in his crystal glass. Mardich had brown hair, a slight tan to his skin. It was testament to him being half Yanari. But that meant he was a Yanari, simple as that. He was a difficult man, but Porwesh knew how to get what he needed from him. Mardich would play the game, insist that anything Porwesh requested was a great chore, but he would acquiesce in the end.

It helped that Porwesh owned a large proportion of the newspaper, unknown to most in Castland. His money made the publishing house run by Mardich turn over day-to-day, and the gold flowing in was the most important thing to the man.

"Was the food to your liking?" asked Porwesh. It was uncouth to talk business so directly this soon after dinner. He had raised the story of the arrest in the east over the meal, planting the seed, skirting the issue gently until the food was finished. It was the Yanari way. One did not catch a snake by charging it from the front.

"Excellent," replied Mardich. "Your chef never fails to source the best smoked meats and cheese from the old country."

"He has a talent for it," admitted Porwesh, smiling thinly. "I don't dare ask how he obtains it."

"Your lodgings aren't up to the usual standards, though."

Porwesh shrugged, looking around the dining hall in which they sat. It was true, the rented townhouse was not as opulent as his own mansion, but then most places in the world weren't. Porwesh was only visiting the capital, and he did not agree with parting with huge amounts of gold for something that he would not own after the deal. The townhouse was adequate for his needs.

"It will suffice for a humble Yanari," he smiled.

Mardich nodded, laughing slyly.

"The story in the People's Gazette is not the whole of the matter, my friend," said Porwesh. "The detained family was Yanari."

Mardich raised an eyebrow as he sipped from his own glass. "Interesting."

"Not really," shrugged Porwesh. "Our people are persecuted every day, in this country and the next. Maybe not so directly, but slighted nonetheless."

"Alas, what are we to do about it?" asked Mardich absently.

"I want you to print the story," said Porwesh. "Give some credence to the tale. As you say, the People's Gazette is a common rag, but the Castland Times has a much loftier reputation."

Mardich almost spat out his wine. "Why would the Times agree with the filth in the Gazette?"

"To tell of the Yanari plight," said Porwesh. "To let both the rich and the poor know what Lord Princetown and his friends have done."

"I will admit, Porwesh, I am at a loss here," said Mardich, his eyes wary. "For years you have advised me of the importance of order, of maintaining the stability of the realm. That the rich should be assured of their place. For the poor to be reminded of theirs."

"That is true, Mardich. You will need to trust me. Perhaps it is time that we also made a little noise about the position of our people in the natural order."

"This will cause... unease. It most unlike a Yanari to cause trouble. That is what my mother taught me. By Yanara's tears, it is what you have always told me. Writing of sympathies for the Yanari will not be popular. It will place me in an uncomfortable situation."

"Nobody knows you are a Yanari, Mardich."

The man shrugged. It was true. He was small in stature, but he did not stand out as one of Porwesh's people. "Even so, it may affect my readership. My profits would fall. It would be a risk for me."

Porwesh smiled behind a sip of his wine. As expected, he had penetrated to the crux of the matter. "I will compensate you double for any loss of revenue, my old friend. And I will make adequate reparations for any other discomfort you may feel if there is any repercussion from the story."

"You are a good man, Porwesh," sneered Mardich. His eyes were already away from the room, calculating a flow of gold coins in the back of his head.

"All Yanari are good men, Mardich," said Porwesh, placing his glass down slowly on the table. "It would make an old man very happy if the Times could be printed and ready for the morning..."

Mardich drained his glass, pulling himself to his feet with a slight bow. "Then I shall make you happy, my friend."

Porwesh slumped his old bones down in the chair, his tired eyes watching as Mardich slunk from the room. He reached out a wizened hand and rang a small, silver bell that sat on the table before him. The door opened quickly, his young Yanari valet rushing in.

"How can I help you, master?" he asked, scurrying up to Porwesh's side.

"Get hold of the Knife for me, please, lad," said Porwesh. "Tell him it is urgent."

Chapter Sixteen

The thin morning light shone weakly through the slats in the shutters, casting delicate lines across the rough blanket on the bed. It was cold in the bedroom, but that was the east. It was always cold. The light was always weak. Lord Tomas Bannar looked on the bed, on the slender figure beneath the blanket. He stood naked, a hard-muscled man of six feet, his body scarred from battle in the Raskan War and before. His hair was dark brown, almost black. His hazel eyes took in the woman in the bed. Her arm was pulled under her feather pillow, the only sign of comfort in the otherwise basic room.

She wasn't sleeping. She was pretending to sleep. Tomas knew. He didn't know how, he could just sense it.

He placed his bear, rock rump on the foot of the bed beside her feet gently. He reached a powerful hand, gently running the rough skin along the blanket, running it up her leg and settling it on her shapely behind. As it moved the thin light broke like the silky strands of a spider's web.

"Not again." The woman groaned, tired blue eyes turning to him with mocking annoyance. Her left hand emerged from the covers, a simple silver band adorning the ring finger. She ran it through the flowing blonde hair, trying to pull out the tangles. "Isn't twice in the night enough for you?"

Tomas smiled. His features were hard, rugged. His nose had been broken too many times to count, his forehead was scarred from a horse running him down in the field. A couple of his teeth were broken, his lip had a chunk taken out of it. He wasn't a pretty man, he was a soldier. And yet gazing on her softened him, melted his features gently.

"I'm sorry, my love," he said, squeezing her arse gently. "I didn't mean to wake you. I just went for a piss."

Talia's eyes widened in shock, teasing him. "Are lords supposed to speak so crudely?"

Tomas pinched the arse cheek gently, clambering over and spooning in beside her on top of the covers, pulling her close. "Less of that. I've told you about this lordship bollocks before."

"I'm sorry, my lord," giggled Talia, biting her lip as she looked over her shoulder at him.

"Stop it," warned Tomas, grabbing her wrist pulling her out from under the warmth of the blanket, pulling her close in the cold morning air. "We'll have enough of all this etiquette bullshit when the little lord of Regalla gets here."

"You mean, you will," she laughed. "I won't be meeting him, will I?"

"Of course, you will," replied Tomas, his eyes meeting hers. "You are the most important thing in my life, Talia. You know that. I thought we'd been through this before?"

The mirth in Talia's eyes ebbed away. He stopped pretending to fight his iron grip, instead twisting her wrists free. "This won't work, Tomas."

Tomas' own eyes saddened. His rough hand reached up to her face, cupping her cheek. "You are my wife, Talia. You should stand beside me as my wife. If I have guests, you should greet them. I want to show you off to the world."

"This wasn't what we agreed, Tomas. I married you to shut you up, not to be dragged into all this..." Her voice faded away.

He looked at her, a tear welling in his eye. "Why marry me if you don't love me?"

Talia's eyes squinted, fire burning at the centre of the light blue loop of her iris. "I love you more than life itself, Tomas. But I worry. I worry that this is just a passing fancy for you. I worry that you don't understand. And I worry that I will not fit in. You're a lord, and I'm a woman of Raskan descent. What will your fellow lords think of that? What do the common folk think of us? Why do you think I live here, rather than at the keep?"

"The keep is my home, Talia," said Tomas, wrapping his strong arms around her and squeezing tight. "It is *our* home. You're my wife, and everyone else can go fuck themselves bloody. Especially the lords. I'm a lord because I killed a load of people. Do you think I'm like them?"

"No, I don't," replied Talia, nestling her head into the base of his neck. "And that worries me too. You care about the peasants. I worry that is because of you care about me. Either way, these ideas will not be popular. I'm thirty-five years old, Tomas. I've seen these lands change hands, seen the difference between the rule of Castland and Raska. In Raska it would be different, but we are not in Raska. We are in Castland, and the poor are expected to know their place."

"I'm not of noble birth, Talia. I can marry who I want, and I have done so. I love the people because I am one of them. I love you because of who you are. That is the end of it, and it will be the end of anybody who challenges that."

Talia looked up at him, smiling weakly. "You say you aren't of noble birth? How old are you, Tomas?"

Tomas sighed, rolling onto his back. "You ask this most mornings. I don't know, Talia. The physician reckons I'm around forty."

"When is your birthday, Tomas?"

"I don't know. Do you think I will just wake up one day and remember? Do you want that?"

Talia rolled up beside him, leaning on her elbows as he looked at him. Her hand moved over his body gently, softly resting on the scar on his forehead. "Where did you get this?"

"At the Battle of Dead Man's Gate. The Raskans stormed our position. We were outnumbered eight-to-one. A horseman ran me down. I stuck a spear in his stomach but his mount trampled over me, back hooves went straight over my head. Do you know how much a horse fucking weighs? Believe me, it feels more when it stands on your face, even for a second in the soft mud. I got back on my feet, still killed more than I can count."

"And here?" asked Talia, her finger resting on his lip.

"The Pale Field. Raskan general caught me with a punch to the face. Had a decent gauntlet on, thick leather and metal stud. Smashed some teeth up good too." Tomas pulled back his lip, revealing the jagged, broken pre-molars."

"Here?" asked Talia, her soft lips kissing a pockmark above his right nipple.

"Arrowhead Pass," he replied, feeling his loins swell at the touch of her lips. "Leading a cavalry charge. Never been any good on a horse. Hit the man I was charging good, especially for me. Took him clean out. The crash was like nothing you've ever heard. Lost my balance though. Landed on my own broken lance. Took the cleric of Pharma two hours to pull out all the splinters."

"And this one?" Talia kissed again, a faded slash across his left ribs.

"I..." Tomas hesitated. "I don't know."

Talia moved her face lower, licking a pebbled graze scar across his stomach, below the navel. "This?"

"I don't know, Talia."

She climbed astride him, leaning forward and kissing him on the lips. Her finger played with the patch of hairless scar tissue on the side of his head, above the temple. "Here?"

"I don't know," he said, returning her kiss. "You know this. You ask me as if the memory has come back, as if it's my fault."

"Not at all," she replied. "You tell me you aren't a noble, but how can you say that? You don't remember anything before the war. You have wounds all over, wounds that you got in battle. Some you remember, some are from before. You can fight like no man anyone knows. A man who can get a lordship in one war, despite remembering nothing from before it. Like no common man can fight. Do you see why this scares me?"

She reached down, pushing him insider her.

"I love you," insisted Tomas, moving with her as she rode him.

"And I love you," she gasped between thrusts. "That's why I worry what will happen if you remember what you really are..."

Cecil stood at the bar of the inn as the owner boiled the heavy, black kettle over the fireplace. They had made decent time along the East Road, but from here it would be a different story. They were staying overnight in the village of Tanner's Mere, a small settlement beside a beautiful, still lake. The inn was quiet, and he could hear the sound of water fowl settling for the night outside.

Tanner's Mere was set at a fork in the road. The East Road turned south here, towards the city of Kassell. They would not be keeping to the main road, though. Bannar lay to the east, across the Bleakthorn Hills that had marked the border of Castland before the Third Raskan War. The scouts warned that the road from here was rougher, and the travelling would be more arduous. As such, Cecil was abstaining from alcohol for the night. He wanted to see how difficult the journey onwards would be without a hangover first. There were no inns or villages for days along the road, so it was important he didn't start this leg of the journey feeling worse for wear.

"Pour it in here when it has boiled," said Cecil to the inn keep, gesturing to the pewter mug in front of him. The man didn't have coffee, so Cecil had got some from his own supply.

"Certainly, my lord," said the elderly man, wrapping a thick cloth round the handle of the kettle and pulling it out of the fire with both hands. He was weathered, his skin tough as leather, but strong for his age. The muscles in his arms were like taut wire as he poured the hot water into Cecil's cup.

115

The innkeeper reflected the village perfectly, right down to the eye patch on his face. A tough, rugged village surrounded by a ditch and spiked, wooden wall. A village for tough, rugged people who had seen conflict in the border wars with Raska.

"Now, some milk if you would, please."

The innkeeper shook his head reluctantly, wary of causing offence. "Sorry, my lord, I could not dream of giving you the milk. It isn't fit to serve to a noble."

"Nonsense," laughed Cecil. "I can put up with it, even if it is poor."

"It's not that, my lord. The milk is sour. The cattle, the sheep, the goats, all their milk is off. Putrid."

"How odd," mused Cecil, stirring the coffee and taking a delicate sip.

"It's cursed," spat one of the few patrons, sitting on a stool at the bar near Cecil. Another sturdy man, lean and rough. A hunter, by the looks of him. A bow and quiver were slung over his shoulder as he took a deep swig of the thick, dark local ale. "Faunis has deserted us here. We have angered him somehow."

"Faunis," smiled Cecil under his breath. He had heard that there were still yokels who worshipped the God of Nature. Deniers of science, of progress, living in the dark ages. "Why would the Lord of Beasts curse you, man?"

"Ignore him, my lord," insisted the tavern owner. "He's drunk."

"The Life Giver does not curse us, my lord," said the ranger. "But men have angered him, and he has withdrawn his protection from the folk of these parts. Without it, our crops will fail, our livestock will sicken and die."

The barkeep shuffled his feet awkwardly, finding himself a job to do tidying the tankards on the shelves beneath the bar.

"Surely a man of the wilds does not fear these superstitions?" asked Cecil, taking in the hunter. "You must spend many a night out there in the dark, alone."

"I do," said the hunter, a drunken, distant stare fixing Cecil. "And that's *why* I fear the curse, my lord. I see things out there, things that shouldn't be. There are evils abroad in the wilds, and they look at our village and our homes with greed and envy."

"You make me nervous about heading into the hills," smiled Cecil.

The hunter's eyes widened. "No, my lord," he insisted, shaking his head wildly. "You must not go into the hills. It is not safe. There is only death out there."

Cecil laughed, but it was forced. The hunter was beginning to worry him. "Then it is lucky I have my men to protect me."

"They can't protect you against what's out there, my lord."

"Then I shall have to protect myself," said Cecil, tapping the hilt of the rapier at his belt, then moving a ringed finger to the stock of his pistol.

The hunter looked puzzled, taking in the weapon suspiciously. "What's that?"

"It is a pistol, my friend. Have you never seen one before? It is a gunpowder weapon. The future of warfare."

"What does it do?" asked the hunter, spitting on the floor again.

"I've seen them," came the barman's voice as he pulled himself back up into view. "They were first used at the Battle of the Silver River, in the war. The King's Household Musketeers set up on the banks of the river, where it was at its widest. Bigger weapons than that, though, almost as long as a man. Had to have a second bloke holding a stand for the things. The Raskans charged us on horseback, across the ford. Three volleys the Household got off. Cut men and horses down like wheat in a field hit by a scythe. The Raskans couldn't get to them, the river was too deep. They had to try and go through us. But they were fucked when they reached us. They'd lost the stomach for the fight, seeing the smoke and fire from those things. We broke them, and the Household got off two more volleys in their backs."

"You see?" smiled Cecil, tapping the weapon again. "The future of warfare."

"Not so good in the open field, though," said the innkeeper, reminiscing. "The King's Household Musketeers were slaughtered almost to a man at the Killing Plain. Two volleys they got off before the Raskans closed on them. A volley of arrows from horseback hit them from close range, then the fuckers got in close and mopped up the rest with spears. Too slow to load."

"Well, there have been major advances since then," spluttered Cecil.

"How long does it take to load that thing, then?" asked the hunter, spitting again. Cecil grimaced.

"Well, a little while," he said. "But it doesn't matter. This is a pistol. It is used for close quarters combat, before drawing the rapier."

"I can fire twelve arrows in a minute with this," said the hunter, tapping the bow at his shoulder. "And I hit every time I loose."

"I'm sure you can," replied Cecil. "But I can draw and fire this much quicker than you can ready that bow."

To demonstrate he whipped the pistol from his belt, pulling back the hammer as he levelled it at the kettle hanging in the fireplace. He pulled the trigger. There was a bang as the gunpowder ignited, smoke billowing out from the barrel of the gun. The iron bearing ricocheted off the kettle, smashing a bottle of brandy behind the innkeeper's head. The acrid stink of sulphur wisped across the air.

"Fair play," sniggered the hunter, spitting on the floor again. "I couldn't smash a bottle of good liquor like that."

Cecil shook his head, dropping a few coins on the bar to pay for the broken bottle.

"Q'thell, load this for me," he called, looking about the room for the Q'shari. "Q'thell. *Q'thell*. Where in Argentis' name is that beast?"

Q'thell jogged through the night, one hand resting on the rapier at his belt to stop it jangling as he moved. The horse couldn't have got far, and it wouldn't run mindlessly into the dark. It would stop soon, once it realised it was all alone out here.

He resolved to beat the guardsman who had let Cecil's favourite mount run off when he got back to the village. The village deputy on the gate was going to get a thump too.

Why have walls with a gate if you leave it open at fucking night?

He looked back over his shoulder. The lights of the village were still in sight. The land around the village had been cleared of trees to give a good line of sight in the event of attack. He was beyond the clearing now though, passing the tree line again. He pricked his keen ears up, listening for the horse.

Another sound came to him on the still air. Not a sound he had been expecting. He listened again, moving gently across the undergrowth, moving close to the trunks of the trees for cover. Not that anyone would see him out here. His skin was black as pitch, his leathers equally dark. Only the red eyes stood out, slits as they pierced the darkness, searching for the source of the sound.

For the source of the chanting.

Male voices, chanting in a low, undulating drone. He didn't understand the words. He knew the tongue though. The Demon Speech.

He saw them ahead in a clearing. Light from a single torch flickered over them, mounted atop a wooden post driven into the ground. Tied to the post was a young woman, clad only in a thin shift that was open at the front, exposing her cold, goose-bumped flesh from neck to groin. Her nipples stood erect in the freezing air. Her head lolled from side-to-side, struggling to stay still and upright, as though she were drugged.

Five men stood around her at equal intervals, chanting in the Demon Speech. They were clad in robes of different colours, roughly spun from a variety of materials. In places they were patched with other shades, obviously where their owners could not source matching cloth. A sixth man stood in front of the girl in the centre of the circle, his back to Q'thell, a crude stone dagger clenched in his hand.

Q'thell moved silently, crouching beside a tree at the edge of the clearing.

Humans really are fucking weird...

The chanting was reaching a crescendo now. The men began to move anticlockwise around the pair at the centre of the circle, twisting and turning in a rhythmic, hypnotic dance. Q'thell caught sight of one of the men's faces as he passed, the eyes wild and unseeing as they bulged beneath the hood.

The man in the middle of the spinning crowd pulled at the cord round his waist. His robes fell open as he approached the girl, still with his back to Q'thell. A hang reached out from beneath the flowing cuffs of the robes, gripping the girl's chin and forcing her to look into his face. He pushed himself closer to her, pulling her legs apart.

Q'thell had seen enough. He stepped out from behind the tree into the clearing, drawing the rapier and parrying dagger silently. It was a shame he didn't have his two Q'shari swords with him. He carried them whilst travelling, cross-sheathed across his back, but when they were in civilised company in the evenings Cecil insisted he carried the trappings of a noble's retainer.

"What have we here?" he asked, plunging the knife into one of the circling cultists. It caught on a rib as it slid in. He brought his sword hand forward, helping push the dead man from the blade.

That'll need sharpening again tonight...

117

The man at the centre of the group looked over his shoulder, vacant eyes looking distractedly at Q'thell. "Kill him," he said dismissively.

The other four charged Q'thell, reaching inside their homemade robes. Only one had even drawn his dagger by the time they were cut down, their blood seeping into the forest floor.

The leader turned to face Q'thell, his eyes wild. His robe fell open revealing his naked body, his cock erect, ready to desecrate the girl before she was sacrificed. He took a step forward. The rapier flashed out, glinting in the flickering torchlight from above. It caught the man's knife hand, slicing off the thumb. The stone dagger fell to the floor.

The man's face had barely registered the pain when Q'thell slashed out again, severing the hard member. It dropped to the ground, the man screaming as he fell to his knees after it, grabbing the penis from the ground desperately as if he was somehow going to be able to reattach it.

Q'thell stepped up to the girl, standing close, red eyes trying to make contact with hers. He sheathed his knife and gripped her jaw, forcing her face towards his. The eyes stared through him, as though looking into the Astral Realm.

Q'thell shook his head, cutting her down from the post and slinging her over his shoulder. He grabbed the lead cultist by the collar, dragging him along as he screamed.

"Fucking humans. You're no better than dogs..."

Chapter Seventeen

Mayor Kove banged the gavel on the small desk at which he sat, bringing the draughty village hall to order. The assembled common folk stood as one as Baronet Wender strode into the room through the back entrance, taking a seat on the small stage. Once he was seated comfortably the congregation took their seats again, staring up at Wender as one from the rows and rows of chairs.

Sheriff Wrathson and the two deputies sat behind Mathias and Charo, who were positioned at the foot of the stage to one side. Charo was fidgeted in the uncomfortable chair, causing it to creak. As he shifted the manacles joining his hands and feet clinked noisily, breaking the silence. He wanted to stand, stretch his legs after days in the cramped cell at the sheriff's station.

"Mathias Culler," said the mayor, looking down at a stack of papers in front of him. "Charo Culler." Wrathson prodded the two lads in the back gently, urging them to stand.

Charo felt the eyes of the entire village fall heavily on him and his brother as they stood, the chains clinking. There was anger, disgust, shock on the faces of the people. The parents of the young girl who had been slaughtered in the forest were filled with hatred. The woman hissed, her eyes filling with tears. She buried her head in her husband's chest, sobbing uncontrollably.

Others in the crowd were sobbing too. Warwick the gamekeeper's wife. The parents of the lad who milked the sheep, and those of the girl he was knocking around with. What was happening? The sheriff had refused to speak to them on the journey back. They had called at the farmstead to collect the girl's parents, and then started the arduous journey back to the village. It had rained day and night, soaking them all to the bone. The mood had been grim, sombre. Mathias had tried to find out what was going on, but Wrathson had threatened to gag them both if they didn't keep quiet.   Charo was scared. He didn't know what was going on, but he knew it was serious. They had been thrown in the cells on arriving back at the village, nobody explaining to them what was happening. Their only human contact had been when one of the deputies thrust a meagre portion of bread and water through the bars of their cell before walking away without speaking.

"You stand accused of demonology. Your actions have led to the deaths of Jacob, the sheep milker, and his girl Jennifer. They have led to the death of Maria, whose parents sit over there, a girl of only five years. They have led to the death of Warwick the gamekeeper. As a result, you stand accused of their murders. Your actions have led to the death of one of the king's deer, and as such you stand accused of grand larceny. You have also caused the deaths of an entire flock of the Baronet Wender's sheep, leading to charges of sheep rustling. How do you plead?"

"What's demonology?" asked Charo, his eyes wide with confused fear. He looked from Kove to Mathias desperately. Mathias placed a hand on his arm, trying to reassure him.

"It is consorting with, and summoning of, creatures from the Astral Realm." Father Pietr spoke up from the front row of chairs, his old voice filled with grim disappointment.

"But..." started Charo, trembling.

"How do you plead?" snapped Kove, cutting him off abruptly.

"We didn't do it," shouted Mathias, shaking his head sharply.

"Let the record show a plea of not guilty," said Kove, dipping a quill in an inkpot and scrawling on the parchment. The movement of his hand was abrupt, filled with annoyance. "This hearing will present the evidence of your crimes. You may then speak in your defence. Baronet Wender will then rule in the name of the justice of King Jaros III of Castland, and justice will have been seen to be dispensed."

Charo felt Wrathson's strong hand on his shoulder, pulling him back down into his seat. He submitted, slumping down with a clunk. Mathias was more reluctant, his eyes blazing with anger.

"Sit down, lad," whispered Wrathson, close to Mathias' ear. "Don't make this any harder than it is." Mathias glared at him before sitting slowly.

"Let us deal with the facts in order," said Kove. "The matter of the dead deer has been witnessed by Baronet Wender, and is therefore not open for challenge."

"We didn't kill it," called Charo.

Kove shot him a glare of annoyance. "You delivered the carcass of one of the king's deer to Baronet Wender, did you not?"

"Yes," said Mathias. "But..."

"Then the deer was killed. That is the fact. Sheriff Wrathson, tell us what occurred with young Jacob and Jennifer."

Wrathson pulled himself to his feet. "I was alerted to the fact that they were missing last week by their parents. It was just after midnight I think, maybe one o'clock. The lad wasn't home, so his parents had checked at Jennifer's home. Neither of their families had seen them, so they woke me up. I gathered my deputies, Benjamin and Lucas here, and we began a search. It would have been early morning, maybe five o'clock, when we decided to check the old Starling house. It's been in disrepair for a while and we thought..."

"Sheriff, please could we move this along a little quicker," sighed Kove. "I'm sure none of us wants to be here past lunch, with our bellies rumbling."

Wrathson glared at the mayor. Yes, he was definitely out of here after this business was dealt with. Maybe he'd punch the insufferable little cunt in the face before he left, do everyone a favour.

"We found the kids in the old Starling house. They'd been ripped apart, butchered. We summoned yourself and Father Pietr. In the cellar of the house some sort of ritual had been performed."

"What kind of ritual was this, father?" asked Kove, turning to the cleric of Mortis.

Pietr leaned heavily on his staff as he stood to address the hall, supported by his young apprentice. "It was a summoning, mayor. A demon had been summoned in that cellar. I could smell it, sense it. A malevolent entity."

"Could Jacob and Jennifer have summoned this creature?"

"It is possible, mayor. The summoning was basic, and did not bind the demon to prevent the caller suffering harm. I find it unlikely, though. The creature seems to have spent a significant time around Mathias and Charo. I can still smell it on them. They reek of its foulness."

Mathias shook his head. Kove shot him a stare, daring him to speak out of turn.

"Sheriff, what of the sheep?" asked Kove.

"The sheep were found slaughtered to a one. Mathias and Charo had fled."

"The flock, too, stank of the taint of the demon," added Pietr.

"And why do you think these lads would kill the animals, sheriff?"

"I don't know," shrugged Wrathson. "Maybe they were pissed off that the baronet docked their pay for the dead deer."

"That's not true," yelled Mathias.

"Is that so?" sneered Kove. "You weren't angry about having your wages cut? It seems you have a bit of a temper, boy."

"He was angry," said Wender, looking down on the boys from the stage.

Mathias could see the way this was playing out. His eyes flitted around the room like an animal caught in a snare, searching for an escape.

"Then you ran," said the mayor. It wasn't a question. "You ran because you were guilty."

"I knew what people would think," said Mathias desperately. "I knew you would think it was us."

"Because it *was* you," said Kove. His beady eyes squinted at Mathias. "Innocent men don't run. You fled to avoid justice. You caught them in the forest, sheriff?"

"Yes," said Wrathson, nodding slowly. He winced as the memories of that night came back. "We tracked them and caught up with them in the night. As we approached, we saw that the little girl, Maria, had been... torn in half like a rag..."

The girl's mother let out a haunting wail. Her husband clutched her tighter, tear-filled eyes staring balefully at Mathias and Charo.

"I'm sorry, love," continued Wrathson. "The lads were standing over her. When we apprehended them, it came out of the dark at us. Tore Warwick the gamekeeper apart. I've never seen anything like it. The way it moved. The sheer power."

"You all saw it?" asked Kove. "All of you witnessed it? A demon?"

The two deputies stood and nodded. Willem called out his affirmation from amongst the crowd in the hall.

"Both of their remains bore the marks and essence of the creature," confirmed Pietr.

"So, sheriff, in your mind, Mathias and Charo Culler summoned this demon?" asked Kove, sneering at the two youths.

"I wish to Guerro I didn't think that," said Wrathson. "I just can't see any other explanation. It didn't harm them, only others. Why didn't it kill them when it killed the girl?"

Tears rolled down Charo's cheeks. He clung to Mathias, his brother shaking his head, pulling him close.

"I would have to concur with the sheriff, mayor," said Pietr. "It is uncommon, but not unknown, for a creature of the Astral Realm to be grateful to its summoners for freeing it upon the Mortal World."

"So you, too, agree that Mathias and Charo Culler brought forth this demon and all the suffering it has caused?"

"I do," said Pietr, his sad eyes turning on the youths.

"Do you have any evidence you wish to bring?" asked Kove, pig-like eyes settling on Mathias and Charo.

"We didn't do it," roared Mathias defiantly.

"That is not evidence," sneered Kove. "In that case, it falls to the baronet to make his decision in the name of the king. Baronet Wender, have you heard enough?"

"I have indeed," said the noble, taking his feet. The assembled crowd stood with him. Wrathson dragged the youths upright, Charo still clinging to his brother. "In the name of King Jaros III of Castland, I find Mathias Culler and Charo Culler guilty of demonology, murder, grand larceny and sheep rustling. The sentence is death."

"No," wailed Charo, pushing his face into his brother's chest. Mathias stared up at the baronet, green eyes blazing with hatred.

"The verdict has been given," said Kove. "I have already sent for an executioner, he will be here within the week. Mathias and Charo Culler will be held at his majesty's pleasure until his arrival, at which point they will be taken to the village square and hanged from the neck until dead. May the gods bless King Jaros III of Castland."

Kove banged the gavel on the table again, signalling the end of proceedings. The only sound filling the hall was that of Charo wailing into his brother's ribs.

Talia led the mule through the streets of Bannar, laden with kegs and bottles of Hope Meadery's finest wares. She paused by one of the water troughs dotted around the town square, letting the animal drink. As it quenched its thirst, she ran her hands through her golden hair, teasing out the tangles. The sun's weak light played across her face, warming it slightly.

It was cool, but not as cold as it could be. For the time of year, in the lands to the east which bordered Raska, it was actually an unseasonably warm day. Not that the cold bothered her. She had Raskan blood. She came from hardy stock.

She was tall for a woman. Not stocky, but strong. She had worked her whole life, and life in the bleak east had not been easy. The lands were used to warring and fighting between Castland and Raska, and both the terrain and the people bore their scars. The soil was poor, only good for the hardiest of crops; potatoes, turnips, and the like.

Talia stroked the mule's nose gently, looking around her fellow townsfolk as they bustled about their business. The life was hard, but the people didn't complain. Tomas was a good lord. He spent time with his people, cared about them. That made a tough life more bearable. The people were poor. Bannar had little in the way of trade or exportable goods, other than the mead produced by the local brewers. There was plenty of honey out here, supplied by the great apiaries that dotted the land around Bannar. They supplied the meaderies, and also local candlemakers who produced some of the finest candles in the land. That was the sum total of production for Bannar and the surrounding villages.

Talia gently pulled at the mule's bridle, coaxing it back into motion. She moved amongst the people, smiling as she passed, greeting each one in turn. They smiled back, nodded to her pleasantly. It wasn't because she was Tomas' wife, it was because they were her friends. She had grown up here, knew every man, woman and child in the town.

She tied the mule up outside the Happy Raskan, the inn at the centre of town. The cellar boy greeted her as she arrived, moving to offload the mule's load. Talia patted him gently on the head and went inside the inn.

The tavern was simply furnished, the mismatched benches, tables and stools all rough and functional. The fireplace lay unlit; it wasn't cold enough for the innkeeper to light it yet. Above the hearth were mounted two crossed Raskan spears, adorned with tattered old tassels beneath the iron heads.

Ivan, the owner, stood at the bar, scrubbing at the rough wood with a tattered rag. He was a couple of year's older than Talia, thick set with hair the colour of straw. His bright blue eyes lit up as he looked up to see her standing in the doorway. He smiled.

121

"Talia." He walked with a slight limp as he moved over to her; a reminder of the Third Raskan War. He clamped his strong arms around her, pulling her close and kissing her cheek. She hugged him back, smiling.

"It's like you didn't see me yesterday," she laughed.

"You say that every time I see you, girl," said Ivan. "Is it wrong to show affection for your oldest friend?"

"It isn't polite to call a lady 'old'," she said, chastising him mockingly.

"You know what I mean, girl," said Ivan, pulling out a chair for her to sit on and giving a deep, exaggerated bow. "You've been spending too much time with his lordship."

Talia sat. Ivan plonked himself down opposite her. "A woman's place is with her husband, isn't it?"

"Not all the time, it seems," replied Ivan. "Seems he's too high and mighty to have you living at the keep. And you're still working at the meadery. Seems to me his lordship doesn't you like I do."

"We've been through this before, Ivan. I choose to live in the town. I choose to work. I don't want to be some pampered lady sitting on a velvet cushion in a castle. My place is here, with my people. With you."

"Exactly right," said Ivan. "You should have married one of your people, not some Castlander."

"Ivan," snapped Talia. She was sick of this conversation. He was her oldest friend, they had grown up together, but sometimes she just wanted to smash him round the head with a pan. "Tomas isn't like a Castlander. He's more like us than you realise. He's a good man. That's why I love him."

"He's still one of them, though. He's a conqueror."

"Are you saying you preferred living under Raskan rule, Ivan? Where nobody owns anything? Where nobody is any different to anyone else?"

"It wasn't so bad…"

"Really?" Talia reached out her hand quickly, pulling back the sleeve on Ivan's right arm. The skin was scarred, furrowed, deeply tattooed with a crude Raskan coin. The punishment for being an embezzler; a man who had not paid his dues to the local elder. "Seems to me you didn't like Raskan rules too much."

Ivan shrugged. "There were some drawbacks."

"Drawbacks," she scoffed. "We all ate the same shit food. We all wore the same shit clothes. We all thought the same shit thoughts. You hated it, that's why you kept back money for us."

"At least there weren't Castlanders all over our town."

"You've said it for yourself, right there. *Our* town. Mine, yours, theirs, Tomas'. This is everyone's town now, Ivan. These are good people. They don't look down on us, they are our friends. We have Tomas to thank for that. I hear stories of how Raskans are treated in other domains, by other lords, and those stories make my blood run cold. Tell me, did you own this place under Raskan rule?"

"Of course not," said Ivan. "The elder owned it, in the name of the realm. They owned everything."

"And do you own it now?"

Ivan hesitated. He had been trapped, and he knew it.

"Exactly," she smirked. "Tell me, how did a peasant inn keep save up the coin to buy his own inn?"

"Your husband totted up the rent that I had paid him for the land, and let half of it count towards payment for ownership."

"And that meant you had enough to buy the inn from him?"

Ivan nodded.

"And yet you still speak ill of Tomas…" She shook her head.

"I don't trust him," said Ivan. "I know you love him, but I don't trust him. He's a Castlander. Your brother made me swear on his deathbed that I would look out for you, and now you're married to one of the fuckers that killed him. That killed our friends, our people…"

"We killed plenty of theirs," snapped Talia. The fire grew in her eyes. "No doubt many of them were Tomas' friends. And yet he treats us well. He treats everyone well, no matter their blood. He doesn't hold grudges, look down on you. The war was years ago, it is time it was forgotten about. This is our life now, and it's a better one. I'll hear no more of it, or else you can consider our friendship finished."

"You'd choose him over me?" asked Ivan, the hurt evident in his eyes.

"If you make me," she said, meeting his gaze with a steely stare.

Ivan looked away. "I'm sorry, Talia."

"No, you're not," she said simply, smiling gently, the warmth back in her eyes. "Try to see the good in him, that's all I ask. Trust my judgement, if nothing else. Don't let your mind be blinded by a hate that needs to die. It will drag you down if you nurture it."

Ivan nodded.

"Now," she said, reaching out and placing her hands around his. "I have news for you. You are the only person I have told this, so you must keep it to yourself."

Ivan raised an eyebrow. He could sense what was coming. He held his feelings in a vice-like grip within himself. Talia was not one for making empty threats, he knew that from years of friendship.

"I am carrying Tomas' child."

Ivan forced a smile, moving his hands to grip hers. "Congratulations, Talia. I am truly happy for you."

"Tomas doesn't know yet," she smiled with uncharacteristic shyness. "I don't know how to tell him, so you must keep it secret for now. I wanted to tell you first."

"Why?" asked Ivan. A tear was welling in his eye. He fought it back. What was he thinking, a grown man getting soppy like a wench?

"Because you are my oldest friend, Ivan. And because I would like you to be our child's godfather."

"I... I am honoured, Talia. I would love to. But... Isn't it the tradition with these nobles that their liege lord should be the godfather of their first child? Won't Tomas want Lord Tremelowe, or whatever his name is?"

"You don't know him at all," she smiled, relieved that the conversation had not twisted back into an argument. "Tomas will do as I wish. He and Lord Tremelowe are close, but Tomas isn't exactly one for tradition, is he? You will be our child's godfather. If you agree?"

Ivan pulled Talia to her feet, gently wrapping his strong arms around her and hugging her. "Of course I agree, Talia. Of course I do."

"Good," she said.

A tear rolled from his eye as he pulled her close, his cheek resting against hers.

Chapter Eighteen

Lord Zachary Unstead ran a freckled hand through the shock of red hair atop his head, grabbing a tuft at the back in frustration. The outrider's report was a surprise, and Unstead did not like surprises. He was the victor of many battles, during the Third Raskan War and before, and victory in war relied, in most cases, on there being no unexpected variables.

"When you say a group of commoners, Sergeant Tumoore, how many do you mean?" he asked the leader of his outriders. His light brown eyes settled on the ranger, conveying his usual air of disdain.

"Upwards of fifty, my lord," replied Tumoore nervously, scraping the greasy black hair out of his eyes. "A carrier pigeon arrived just now, from my scouts to the south. They're headed towards the Red Cairn Hills. The lads said they got close enough to hear them talking."

"And of what were these dangerous common folk talking?"

"Of breaking down the gate, my lord. Of heading to the Red Cairn Hills. Of asserting their rights."

"So, they were talking of trespassing on my lands?"

"Yes, my lord," replied Tumoore. His hand strayed to the hipflask at his belt then retreated as if burnt. He wrapped his fingers together instead, kneading them jerkily.

Unstead stood, rising gracefully out of the elaborate ebony chair at the head of his hall and walking purposefully down the steps from the dais. He was clad all in black, his tunic and sleeves hemmed with scarlet. The front bore the symbol of his house; a single drop of claret blood.

The Lord of Hearth Hill was tall, slender, elegant. He stopped beside the outrider, nostrils flared beneath the long, pointed nose as he sniffed at Tumoore.

"Have you been drinking, sergeant?"

Tumoore hesitated, shuffling his feet. "I had a swig earlier, my lord. Just to clear the airwaves. Got a cold coming on. Hazards of being an outrider, my lord."

Unstead shrugged, moving on past Tumoore. He reached the centre of the hall, turning theatrically and taking in the captain of his guard, a portly, red-faced man who stood to one side of the lord's seat.

"Captain Peacock, do you let your men drink on duty?"

The fat little soldier shook his chubby face, his eyes full of apprehension. "No, my lord. I'm sure the sergeant here's just using it for medicinal purposes. He's a good soldier. Reliable. Does as he's told. Isn't that right, Tumoore?"

"Yes, captain," nodded the outrider furiously, turning to face Unstead. "Always."

"That is good to know," smiled Unstead. His fingers stroked his smooth chin inquisitively, each one bearing a ring set with a blood red ruby. "If your judgement isn't impaired by drink, I'd like your advice, sergeant. What should I do? Peasants are aiming to invade my land, challenge my authority, in direct contradiction to the laws of Castland. What would you have me do, sergeant?"

Tumoore cleared his throat, glancing at Peacock. The captain was avoiding his gaze, trying to distance himself from the question. "I'd slaughter them like pigs, my lord. They are vermin."

"I like your thinking, sergeant," said Unstead, turning his gaze to Peacock, the eyes squinting disconcertingly. "What say you, captain?"

"I... My lord, the balance with the poor folk is a delicate one at present. Perhaps unprovoked violence would have... unexpected consequences."

"Hmm," pondered Unstead, strolling between the two men. "Were you both with me at the Battle of the Red Cairn Hills during the war?"

Peacock's head nodded, dropping to take in the black stone floor of the hall. Tumoore nodded too, longing to grab the hipflask and drain it down as his mind flashed back to the day.

"Lord Perlis had a simple job that day," recalled Unstead, looking into the past as he stared at his black chair. "Five hundred Raskan prisoners of war. Take them to his lands in the Red Cairn Hills. Set them up in tents. Set up picket fences. Keep them there. Not a difficult task."

The lord turned his gaze on Tumoore. The outrider looked to the captain, searching for guidance. Peacock was still looking down at his paunch. Tumoore shook his head in agreement, hoping it was the right answer.

"But Lord Porwesh only left fifty men to guard them," continued Unstead, shaking his head. "The Raskan captains had promised their men wouldn't cause trouble. Lord Porwesh took them at their word. Set them to work building their own prison, their own picket fences and accommodation. And what did they do that night?"

DAVE GRAY

"They rose up and killed Lord Porwesh's men," intervened Peacock, grabbing the easy question like a beggar snatched an offered coin.

"And we had to tidy up that mess, didn't we? We took a company of men-at-arms and knights, and we cut down men armed with hammers and saws. We cut them down to a man."

Unstead was looking between the two men, searching for a response. Both heads were bowed, nodding, trying to push the memories from their heads.

"What would they have done if we hadn't?" asked Unstead, his long arms spread wide in a questioning embrace. "Look at me, men, look at me. I know it was a hard day for you both, because you don't understand the way of the world. You are not lords. You don't have my vision, my knowledge of the world. If we hadn't killed them all, they would have seen it as weakness. We would have put them in a stockade, and they would have risen up again and killed more good Castlanders."

Tumoore and Peacock nodded slowly.

"As it was, how many of those Raskans caused us any further issue?" smiled Unstead. He didn't expect an answer. "None. Because we shoved their corpses into a huge hole in the ground and filled it over with earth."

Tumoore shuddered. He could still hear the cries of the wounded as they shovelled mud onto them as they lay. It wasn't only corpses that had been buried that day.

"The poor are the same as the Raskans. For Argentis' sake, the Raskans are just a nation of peasants. We keep control of the commoners through fear, and in most instances it works. But when they lose that fear, there is no going back. You can hurt them, kill their families, brand their bodies, but it doesn't quell their rebellion completely. It festers, turns to hate within them. They never forget it. You can't cure a dog of the rabies by beating it. It has to be culled."

Unstead looked between the two soldiers again, gesturing with the outstretched arms. They moved in closer. He embraced them, one on either side, walking towards the door to the hall.

"Sergeant Tumoore here is right," he said, releasing the men and pushing them towards the exit. "Captain Peacock. Take all the men you can rally and join Sergeant Tumoore's outriders. Cut the peasants off and cut them down. Invoke the spirit of the Battle of the Red Cairn Hills."

Peacock looked back over his shoulder, nodding meekly.

"And sergeant," called Unstead. Tumoore stopped in his tracks, his bladder trembling with fear. "Get a new tabard. You are representing the Unstead family out there. Can't have you looking like a pile of dung."

Tumoore sighed, nodding as he hurried from the room. The doors hadn't swung fully shut before he ripped the hipflask from his waist, gulping the contents down.

Father Pietr woke in a cold sweat, crying out into the chill air of his room. His bedsheets were soaked, clinging to him like the amnion of a new-born puppy. He writhed, getting a frail leg free from the twisted linen, letting the cold air play on his clammy flesh.

Dread filled him. His nightmare had been close, real. He could still feel the warm, foetid breath of pure malignance on his wrinkled cheek. It had been a simple dream. He had been watching from above as he slept, viewing his own body from the outside. He had watched as his own form tossed and turned in the darkness, groaning incoherently. Except he wasn't him. He was... something else...

He was bulky, powerful, rippling with maleficent strength. He had knelt down beside the old man sleeping in the bed, pressed his mouth close, inhaled the air and tasted the flavour of human sweat.

Then he had been back inside his own sleeping body, feeling the breath on his face. As he breathed, even though asleep, he had dreamt the acrid smell of ammonia in the blackness. The scent of the demon.

He was awake now, he was sure of it, but his old nostrils could still smell the stench. No, that couldn't be. Surely he was still dreaming?

He pulled himself upright in the bed awkwardly, old eyes straining in the dark of the night. A wind kicked up outside, rattling the loose glass in the window. His attention flicked to it with a start, trying to reassure himself that it *was* just the wind.

It had come for him. He knew it would. The stench was definitely there, strong and overpowering. Was he still dreaming?

A low growl came from the corner of the room, near the door, faint and otherworldly. His heart pounding in his chest as he reached for the staff leaning beside his bed, clutching it close to his chest to summon his power. He closed his eyes, concentrating hard. The candle on his bedside table burst into flame with a puff of violet smoke. The effort made him feel faint. He was old, and even the most basic drawing of magical energy took a lot of energy from him.

He didn't want to open his eyes. There was a rustling now. His old ears struggled to tell whether it was inside the room or not. He felt like his chest was going to burst open, the thumping in his head making it hard to discern sounds and their distance.

"I know your name, demon," he said, his voice faltering. It was a hollow threat, one that was unlikely to discourage even a mortal foe, let alone a creature of the Astral Realm.

He heard the door creak open. He forced his eyelids apart, dreading the sight he was about to behold.

His apprentice stood in the doorway, her skinny, young form shivering beneath her nightdress. Pietr looked around quickly, searching for signs of the beast. The smell was fading, the overbearing presence receding.

"Are you alright, father?" asked the girl. "I heard you cry out."

"No, child," said Pietr, his eyes falling on the window. It was open, the freezing wind gusting into the room, causing the candle flame to flicker and die. "Get me up. It is here."

Sheriff Wrathson woke from his slumber, his neck clicking awkwardly. He had fallen asleep in his chair in the jail office, his feet up on the table, and his whole body was paying the price. His feet were dead and his back ached like shit. He grunted as he moved, struggling to get to his feet and stamp the life back into his legs.

What time was it? Dead of night, judging by the cold and the blackness outside. His breath frosted on the air as he moved, lighting a new candle to replace the one that was guttering out on the table. Yes, well into the early hours, given the dying wax stub.

Wrathson looked around the room, spotting Lucas sleeping on the floor near the cold, black fireplace. He smiled. He liked to keep one of the lads with him at all times whilst he had prisoners in the cells. That wasn't very often, so the lads didn't mind. Even so, he didn't expect them to sleep on the floor. There was simple bed set up for them in the corner of the office.

He prodded the lad gently with his boot, coaxing him awake. The youth yawned widely, rubbing the sleep from his eyes. "Sorry, sheriff. I must have dozed off."

"Don't worry lad," laughed Wrathson. "So did I. There's a bed over there for that though. I might be a cunt, but I don't expect you to sleep on the fucking floor."

"It was cold, sheriff," said Lucas, getting to his feet clumsily, his movements still heavy with sleep. "I must have nodded off by the fire."

"Get to bed, lad," smiled Wrathson. "I'm heading up to mine…"

He turned as he heard a noise coming from the cell where the Culler boys were being held. A clumsy shuffling, feet scuffing on the floor as if one of the lads was sleepwalking.

"Keep it down in there, you pair," called Wrathson.

The lads had behaved, in fairness to them. They talked, they sobbed, but they didn't smash the cell up or bang the door or throw their meals around like many of those Wrathson had seen sentenced to death. Wrathson had upped the quality of their food, giving them whatever he and the deputies were eating. After all, they didn't have long left, it seemed only right. The executioner had taken longer than expected to arrive, but he had finally turned up the previous evening. Later on today they would be delivered to Mortis…

A pair of small hands came into view, gripping the bars of the cell door. They squeezed hard, the knuckles turning white with the effort.

Lucas looked to Wrathson inquisitively. The sheriff shook his head, striding over to the cell door.

"Listen, lad," he said. "I know it's shit, but this will all be over soon."

He looked through the barred opening in the door as Charo stared back blankly, the dark eyes staring straight through him. The boy's expression was blank, distant, like those of a criminal hanging dead at the gallows. Wrathson shuddered.

"It's coming," whispered Charo emptily.

Wrathson looked to Lucas. The lad was shivering, his hand resting on the sword at his belt. He was looking to the sheriff for reassurance, but Wrathson had little to give. He had seen things he wished he could forget over the last weeks. He shook his head gently, trying not to show the apprehension that was rising in his stomach.

A gust of wind rattled the shutters on the windows. One flew open, shattered glass sprinkling onto the floor of the office.

Just a tree branch? Or a stone thrown up in the wind? Surely.

"It's coming," repeated Charo, still gazing through the sheriff towards the door.

"That door is locked, isn't it, lad?" asked Wrathson, the fear tremoring his voice slightly.

Lucas grabbed the large, iron keyring from his belt. He moved over to the thick, iron-bound door slowly, reaching out tentatively and checking the handle. He turned to Wrathson, nodding with a reluctant smile.

"Good," said the sheriff, turning hesitantly to look at Charo's pale face staring through the opening in the cell door. There was no fear, no tears, no sobbing. The face was emotionless, the eyes empty.

"It's here."

Wrathson turned to Lucas, his eyes wide with fear. The young deputy didn't have time to move before the door to the jailhouse smashed inwards. Splinters and twisted iron engulfed the lad as a huge shape stooped in through the gap, hurling him across the room. Lucas' head smashed hard against the wooden floor as he landed, the keys spilling from his limp fingers and skittering across the floor past Wrathson's feet.

He heard Mathias moving in the cell behind him as he stood, watching the huge form of the demon stand to its full height within the office. The stench of cat piss filled the air, a cloying evil sticking to the sheriff's skin as the eyestalks settled on him. The beak seemed to sneer hungrily.

Mathias' face pushed Charo's aside at the door to the cell, his eyes taking in the full horror of the creature in the room. "Let us out of here, sheriff."

Wrathson stood, frozen, as the creature took a couple of heavy steps forward. Behind him, Charo's small hands emerged in the gap beneath the cell door, reaching for the bundle of keys, trying to tease them closer.

The sheriff found control of his body again, pulling the sword from his belt and crouching. He was out of shape, but if he had to die he would go down fighting. He knew it was hopeless, but then he had felt that way before in a scrap.

Wrathson charged forward. The demon cocked its skinless head to one side inquisitively as the mortal approached, as if amused by the effort. It certainly wasn't something it was used to. The mortals usually shit themselves, or curled up into a ball of concentrated terror. It reached out a long, powerful arm to grab him.

Wrathson batted it away with the sword, deflecting the grasp downwards and exposing monster's shoulder. He planted his feet for balance and raised the sword above his head, bringing it down hard on the demon's arm, close to the joint. The blade bit deep, striking thick bone and sticking. Wrathson pulled the blade loose, raising it to strike again.

The creature moved quickly, batting the sheriff aside with a heavy backhand. Wrathson staggered across the room, falling to one knee before recovering. He regained his feet, panting heavily. Fighting was hard work, and he was unfit.

The demon stood for a second, the eyes turning to the deep wound on its arm. It hissed angrily, charging forward, the bovine hindquarters pumping with raw power. Wrathson swung once, twice, landing two slashes across the demon's skull before it hit him, crushing him up against the wall of the jail. He felt the stone give a little against his back as the air was crushed from his lungs, a couple of ribs popping audibly.

The monstrous entity took a step back, allowing him to slide to the floor. The sword dropped from his grip as he hit the ground, his reflexes causing his arms to clutch at his crushed chest. He looked up as the huge, dark shape crouched over him, the slavering beak moving down towards his face.

So this is it. At least I wasn't killed by a man. There's not many that can say it took a demon to see them off...

A pair of skinny arms wrapped around the creature's neck, gripping tight. The beast stood up to its full height, spinning around to try to dislodge Charo from its back. Wrathson pulled in as much breath as he could muster, his sides splitting with pain as he reached for his sword.

Mathias knelt down, snatching up the blade before he could reach it. The youth turned on the beast, his eyes angry and wild. He swung the blade, the blow clumsy but strong. It dug deep into the demon's rump.

Not the best choice of targets.

The lad leaned on the blade, dragging it heavily as he withdrew, leaving a long, vicious gash in the creature's hindquarters. It didn't flinch, jumping upwards once, twice, thrice, smashing Charo against the ceiling of the office. Debris rained down on Wrathson as he crawled for the door. He had staggered to his feet as Charo landed on the floor heavily. The sheriff turned for a second, hesitating in the broken doorway.

"Run," gasped Charo, rolling slowly onto his back, winded. Beyond him, Wrathson saw the demon turn on Mathias, wrenching the sword from his grip and bending it like a plant stem. It lashed out, throwing the youth across the room. He struck the wall hard, landing in a dishevelled heap.

Wrathson stumbled out into the village square, calling the alarm with all the heaving breath he could muster.

Charo stared upwards, struggling to force his limbs to obey his commands. His head was light, spinning, his vision dotted with blinking patches of light. In between them, the demon's hideous visage coalesced above him as it stooped down, coming to rest astride him. The powerful front limbs bore its weight as it leaned close, black ichor dripping down on his face from the wound on its shoulder. It stank like piss, was sticky as tar.

The beaked skull pressed close to his, foetid breath making his face damp. The wizened little arms grabbed his chin as the eyes stared into his, an inch separating their gazes.

His vision went white. Was he dead? Was this what it was like, the Astral Realm? He wanted to pray, but he didn't know which god to plead with. Was he too late? Was this what happened if you were too slow to pledge your soul?

He heard a voice. It was hollow, echoing in his brain. It wasn't passing through his ears, it was *inside* him.

"The mayor did this to you, Charo. Mayor Kove. He summoned a demon of the god Lunaris, the Lurker, the Creature in the Dark. The God of Fear. That demon killed your people, your sheep, and ruined your life. He ruined the life of your brother, Mathias. Then he let you take the blame."

Charo tried to speak, but he could not open his mouth. He realised he could not even feel his mouth. He could not feel anything.

This is death, then; an unfeeling eternity of bright light and taunting...

"Why would he do such a thing?" asked the voice gently. "He is a worshipper of Lunaris, Charo. The Lurker has returned, and his following grows. Mayor Kove wanted to spread fear, and he has succeeded. But he has also failed."

Charo tried to move, to feel his body again. His mind was working, but his body was limp, floating in the whiteness.

"It seems he does not understand Lunaris, Charo. He has failed the God of Fear. Do you know what they call Lunaris in the Astral Realm, Charo?"

He tried to shake his head. He felt nothing.

"No? They call him the Great Enemy. The other gods fear him, because he threatens them. They do not care for your kind. They have no interest in your lives, in your pain. They care only about worship. Worship gives them power. Lunaris loves you, even though you have turned your back on him. The God of Fear draws power from the fears of mortals, and he uses that power to ease your fears. Mayor Kove did not understand that. He loved the *power* of fear. He revelled in causing terror. Lunaris requires that the circle is completed. The fear of your people gives him strength, and that strength must be used to protect you."

Charo tried to kick his feet. He felt the sensation returning. He could feel his limbs, distant and tingling.

"What does Lunaris want with you, Charo?" asked the voice, becoming more insistent. "He wants nothing *with* you. He wants *you*. He will give you power, if you are his champion in the Mortal World. Mayor Kove did not hold true to the values of Lunaris. He did not care for the people, only for causing torment and pain. For that he must pay the price. And the baronet. He knew of the mayor's actions, yet he did nothing. You, on the other hand, understand the agony of mortal suffering. You care for your fellow man, yes?"

Charo nodded. He felt it this time, his head moving back and forward.

"Good, Charo. Good. Spread the word of Lunaris as his champion. Make a better world for your people. Let them understand that to fear is mortal. Their fear and their prayer will be their salvation."

Charo nodded again. His vision cleared, the white blanket receding. As the cloud wisped aside he saw the haunches of the demon as it moved away from him, leaving him lying on the floor of the jail. He felt his hands, clenched and unclenched his fists to regain the feeling.

He knew what he had to do…

The demon stomped into the night, its hooves falling heavily, purposeful. It opened its beak to the sky, roaring loudly. The time for stealth was gone. It was time for the demonstration. It loved killing in the dark, the nuances of playing the complex instrument that was mortal fear. But it also relished this. Wholesale slaughter, in full view of the frightened, pathetic beings of this place.

The people of the village were already out in the streets. They were running from their houses at the call of the sheriff. Some came armed with pitchforks and household items. Others were just fleeing mindlessly, running in one direction and another aimlessly. All bore expressions of panic, and as it screamed into the night and they laid their eyes upon it, the panic turned to terror.

It snatched a passing villager, picking it up by the ankle and holding it before its face, staring into the wide, panicked eyes. It looked like the deer it had killed; frail and scared. It swung it about like a rag doll until the leg came off at the hip, the rest of the human crashing to the ground some yards away.

So fragile. So pitiful.

It had carried out its orders. It had sown the seeds. It had given the boy mortal the vision; the master had been very insistent upon that. It had left the child's brother alive, as commanded. At least, it hoped the human still lived. The blow had been pretty hard, but it had been angry. It was wounded, and although it did not feel pain, the gashes in its corporeal form hindered its movements, made it feel heavy and impeded. The spindly little creature better had live; the god was not prone to being disobeyed.

The demon shrugged, reaching out and twisting the head off a passing woman as she ran. The legs carried on pumping for a couple of yards before the body realised it was dead. It sneered, stomping into the centre of the village square.

The god wouldn't be able to see if the mortal had survived. The gods couldn't see much of the Mortal World. It was here now, experiencing the full glory. The gods sat in the Astral Realm, tinkering like disinterested children with a toy with which they had already grown tired.

The rest of its master's commands were vague. It was to let the boy defeat him, to voluntarily return to the Astral Realm. It didn't mind. It could slaughter this whole place first, then return with a host of boastful stories to tell its fellow demons. Its tongue flicked out and licked its beak with satisfaction.

The eyestalks settled on the sheriff from the jailhouse. He was slumped against the well, gasping for breath, struggling with the wounds from the impact inside the building. That had felt good, listening to the crack of ribs as it crushed him against the wall. It was sure the outline of his body was immortalised in the stonework.

That fucking piece of meat actually attacked me…

The demon charged forward, reaching out to tear the insolent mortal limb from limb. The man's arms raised, his eyes terrified as the huge form bore down on him.

It felt a slight impact as a small weight threw itself against his muscular hindquarters. It stopped its charge reluctantly, turning its gaze with irritation on the human gripping the thick trunk of its leg.

The fucking boy. Great! Not yet, you little shit. Daddy's not finished playing.

It reached down, swotting the mortal child away. It took a couple of blows to dislodge him. It didn't dare strike too hard, it had already bashed him into the ceiling and killing him would lead to an eternity of torture in the Astral Realm.

It had more people to kill first, and it wasn't ready to go home. It turned menacingly on the sheriff, clasping a clawed hand round his throat. It looked around, something else springing to mind. That fucking priest. Where was the old bastard? It saw the old man, leaning on his young apprentice, chanting nonsense and circling his staff at the demon.

Yes. You're next, you old fucker.

The boy was on him again, clambering up his chest.

Tough little bastard. Didn't give you enough credit.

The demon reached up, the razor-sharp claws clenching gently around the boy's arm, trying to pull him away. It longed to rend him apart. It contemplated for a second just pulling him to pieces, staying in the Mortal World for the rest of time. But it wasn't worth the risk. The vengeance of the god would catch up with him in the end. He would always end up back in the Astral Realm, and an eternity of agony was a long time. Either that, or eventually the master would come to the Mortal World and find it...

The lad pulled back a skinny arm to lash out, dark eyes filled with concentrated hate.

Fine, boy. Hit me. I'll put up a fight and then go home. But I won't make it easy for you...

The young human brought the skinny fist forward, connecting with the demon's bony jaw. It made to sneer the mortal, finding it didn't have the necessary features. The pain caught up with it, a burning sensation it had never before felt during its existence.

It held the mortal at arm's length, one of the atrophied human hands reaching up to its beak. The bottom jaw was gone, smashed to nothing by the boy's blow. The demon felt weak for the first time in an eternity. It dropped forward, still gripping the child, the other main arm bearing its weight on the cold, hard ground.

Cold. I can feel the cold. The master lied to me.

The lad punched at the arm still gripping him. The demon screamed in agony as the small fish cut straight through the powerful limb, the severed forearm falling as dust to the ground around him. The demon's eyes widened on the stalks, an unknown emotion causing through its form; fear.

Charo reached out, grabbing one of the eyestalks and pulling forward. The demon's head followed, propelled towards the youth before it snapped off, crumbling to ash in the lad's hand.

It screeched again, the cry splitting the cold night air, causing the dumbfounded mortals watching to clasp their hands over their ears.

Charo lashed out again. The first smashed straight through the demon's skull, like a warmed spoon making its way through butter.

The demon collapsed to the floor, its head a cloud of smoke before it hit the ground. It felt a wrench in its chest as its essence was ripped from the Mortal World. The sucking sensation enveloped it, consuming it. It was in a tunnel, dark walls pressing in on it as it was dragged towards the blackness. Not the Astral Realm. Nothingness.

I served well. I did as I was asked.

Then it was gone. Not returned home. It was nothing.

Charo stood in the silence of the night, looking down on the crumbling remains of the demon. Foetid smoke rose from the collapsing ash form as it disintegrated into nothing. The villagers looked on, jaws dropping in quiet awe. Wrathson struggled to his feet, gently prodding the remains of the demon as they fell in on themselves.

"What in Guerro's name fucking happened?" he mumbled, looking around at the villagers as they gathered cautiously around him and Charo.

Mathias stumbled through the crowd, sword in hand, shoving the shocked peasants aside. He grabbed Charo in his arms, pulling him close, the weapon pointing warily at Wrathson.

"Are you ok, brother?" he asked, wildly looking around the crowd that surrounded them. "Are you hurt?"

Charo shook his head gently, turning his attention to the assembled villagers. Father Pietr had found his way to the front and was kneeling beside the smoking ashes of the demon. He leant close, sniffing the remains. He picked up a handful of dust, letting it run between his fingers.

"Is it gone, father?" called out on the peasants, clutching his wife and children close and looking warily around the dark village square.

"Yes," replied Pietr, struggling to his feet. He looked at Charo warily. "The demon is destroyed."

"Charo saved us," said one of the crowd. Others joined in slowly, calling out their thanks to the boy before them.

Wrathson stepped forward slowly towards Charo. Mathias trained the point of the sword on the sheriff's chest, but the bulky man reached out carefully and gently pushed it away, his hands open and outstretched. The placed a hand on Charo's shoulder and knelt down, bowing his head.

"You saved my life, lad," he said. "I owe you everything."

"But how...?" asked Pietr, his voice weak and hollow.

"Lunaris," replied Charo simply, squeezing the sheriff's shoulder and helping him to his feet.

"The Lurker?" pondered the cleric of Mortis, shaking his head. "I do not understand."

"Lunaris sent me a vision and gave me the power to destroy the demon. He wants me to lead the people of this land to their salvation. For too long they have been oppressed by the wicked. They live in fear, and only Lunaris can save them from that."

"Why would the Creature in the Dark care?" asked Pietr, looking amongst the people of the village. "He feeds on fear, revels in it."

Several of the people began to murmur threateningly. Wrathson and Mathias stood in front of the boy, shielding him from the crowd.

Charo moved them aside gently. "Lunaris gains power from the prayers of the fearful, and uses that strength to protect them. He is the light in the darkness, the moon in the night. He will be our saviour."

The crowd's protests grew louder. Pietr shook his head, backing away and pulling his apprentice close. "No, boy. The Lurker is not to be trusted..."

"Lunaris is the way to your salvation," insisted Charo, stepping forward from between Wrathson and Mathias.

"He is a lord of demons," cried one of the crowd. Others shouted their agreement. They moved forward as one, then stopped in their tracks.

A faint blue glow was centring on Charo, circling his feet. It rose higher, illuminating his body in an eerie blue light. It spread around him, shining down on all of them, growing to illuminate the whole of the village square, pushing back the blackness of the night.

"Look," gasped Willem, the hunter pushing his way to the middle of the crowd and pointing upwards to the heavens.

Above them the moon was large and full. It shone intense and bright, blue light beaming down into the village. The glow did not touch the surrounding land, it merely bathed them in its radiance, forming a beacon in the cold darkness. Slowly, it faded, leaving them staring at Charo by the light of a few lit torches carried by villagers.

Willem was the first to speak. "Charo, I am with you. The woods have been dark of late. Not just without light, there has been a malice to them. If Lunaris is the way to fix what is broken out there, then I'll stand by you."

The hunter knelt at Charo's feet, leaning on his bow.

Wrathson knelt beside him. "You know I'm with you, Charo. You saved my life. If that means I'm destined to help you on your path, then I'll do it gladly."

Several of the villagers called out, dropping to their knees on the cold ground and praising Charo and Lunaris. Others stayed on their feet, confusion on their faces, looking to Pietr for guidance. The old priest stepped forward slowly, his old gaze falling heavily on Charo's dark eyes.

"I am a cleric of Mortis, Charo. I will not break with my faith and worship another. It does appear, however, that I have wronged you. I accused you of a crime, and yet you saved us here when I was powerless to defend my flock. For that, I apologise with all my old heart. Mortis works in strange ways, and I will not be arrogant enough to say that I understand them. It would seem that it is his will that I atone for my mistake by helping you. If your aims are as pure as you say, then they are also the goals of Mortis himself. If you will have an old fool, I swear by the Keeper of Souls that I will do everything I can to assist you."

The old priest slowly took to his knees, supported by his apprentice. One by one the rest of the villagers knelt, pledging their allegiance to Charo, the champion of Lunaris.

"I'm yours to command, little brother," said Mathias, dropping down beside Charo. "You've followed me all your life. You're a man now. It's time that I followed you."

Charo shook his head, looking around the bowed people of the village. Was this really happening? What did he know about leading men? He only knew what was right in his heart, and it seemed that was what these people wanted. It seemed it was what a *god* wanted.

"Stand up, please," he insisted. "This isn't what Lunaris wants, you all grovelling on your knees. It certainly isn't what I want. For too long, people have kept you down, oppressed you. We are going to make that stop. Not just for us, but for all the people of Castland."

The crowd took its feet, cheering Charo's name. Pietr was the last to stand, his knees aching in the icy wind. "One question, though, Charo. If I may?"

"Of course," replied Charo.

"If yourself and Mathias didn't summon the demon, who did?"

The crowd looked on expectantly. Many were apprehensive that the boy before them was going to admit to the crime. He was Lunaris' champion, after all. Had he done this to gather support for the Lurker's cause?

"Mayor Kove," replied Charo. "He summoned the beast, and set it loose upon you. Upon *us*. Baronet Wender knew of this, and did nothing. They murdered your children, your husbands, and then blamed two poor shepherds. They sentenced us to death for their crimes."

"That fucking weasel," snarled Wrathson, smashing a thick fist into the palm of his other hand. The pain in his ribs stabbed into his side at the effort. "I'll fucking kill him."

"Lunaris does indeed want justice," said Charo. "These men summoned one of Lunaris' demons to this world. They used it to spread fear, with no thought given to the suffering of the people. Their motives were selfish. They didn't want to spread the light of Lunaris. They just wanted to see the terror in the eyes of the poor. That's not the way of Lunaris."

"It's settled then," said Willem, turning to the crowd. "We string Kove up, just like he aimed to do with these lads."

The crowd roared its approval.

"Charo," uttered Mathias, the worry on his face in the flickering torchlight evident. "The mayor's an elected official. If we do this..."

"Who elected him?" asked Charo simply.

Mathias looked around the assembled crowd, shrugging his shoulders. "Well, we did."

"It appears he has been un-elected," said Charo. The crowd yelled its agreement again. "I know you are frightened, brother. So am I. But we have to start somewhere. These men tried to kill us. They killed women, children, and blamed it on us. Across the land, these men are sowing the seeds of misery and terror. They did it to us when they ran us out of our home before. It's time *they* felt fear."

Mathias nodded reluctantly. Charo was right.

"It's settled then," said Wrathson, raising his fist to the night sky. "Light torches. Gather what weapons you can. We hang Kove."

The people cheered as one.

Chapter Nineteen

The magister looked out from beneath the hood of her purple robes at the other senior members of the Order. They sat around an ornate octagonal table, carved from polished black stone. The surface of the table was carved with numerous gullies, twisting this way and that before sinking into holes at each of the eight sides.

Eight sides. Eight magisters of the Order. Identically dressed, hooded so that only the voices differentiated one from another. They had names, of course, but they weren't their real ones. They were those assigned for use when within the Order. Nobody knew the true identities of their fellow members. If you didn't know who your fellows were, you could not betray them after all.

She was sweating beneath her robes. The fires in each of the hearths in the room were lit to guard against the cold of the night. The acolytes had piled them high with fragrant logs before leaving the session to discuss their business. She supposed she should be glad of the warmth. Sitting on a stone chair in the small hours of the freezing morning would have been more uncomfortable than this heat.

Outside, a distant clock struck four o'clock. The dead of night was best for their meetings. Their business was not fit for the bright light of day. None of the magisters complained about lateness of the hour. The members of the Order rarely slept. It was a waste of time, and time was a precious commodity. They understood that. The fact that others did not gave them one of their many advantages over the weak and the foolish.

The Grand Magister stood in front of his stone throne, calling the session to order. They took their feet as one as he spoke.

"I hereby open this session of the Head of the Order," he said simply, his voice low and dark. He reached out a small, pale hand and took hold of the handle of the small, ornate iron kettle that sat in the brazier beside his chair. The touch of his skin on the hot metal handle caused a hiss to pass through the room, but he did not flinch. He lifted it and poured the deep red contents into a jewel-encrusted golden chalice before him. He placed it back in the brazier gently, his hand unseared by the burning iron. He took the chalice in both hands, drinking a gulp of the warm liquid down. "Let us drink."

The magisters passed the cup from one to another, each drinking from it in turn. When it reached her she breathed in the heady aroma. Herbs, spices, red wine, and the rest. One swig made her feel instantly giddy, the subtle blend of ingredients working on her mind. It clouded her thoughts, made her eyelids heavy and her mind dull. Her perception of this world dulled, as any increased understanding of the realms beyond pushed it to one side.

She turned to look on the flickering flames in the fireplace, watching as they licked up at the roof of the hearth. They made faces as they moved, the uppermost tendrils of flame becoming hands that tickled the stone, their touch blackening it gently with sooty fingerprints. She watched as the others drank as their turn came around, the rubies and amethysts on the goblet winking at her sneakily as the cup moved.

This was her world, her place. This was where the Mortal World was run. Order stemmed from here. Chaos stemmed from here. Pampered kings and lords sat in their halls, drinking and eating their fill and guffawing at their perceived control over all around them. But it was the Order that ran the world. It was the Order that let them think that they did. The Order saw all, weighed up the consequences of action or inaction, allowed things to happen or prevented them from occurring.

She was an eighth of the power that ran the Mortal World, and the Astral Realm beyond it. Maybe she was more than an eighth of that power.

Yes. I am more than that. They just don't know it yet...

The chalice had returned to the Grand Magister. He placed it beside the thick tome sat in the stone lectern carved before his seat at the table. "We sit in the dark, and shine the light."

"We sit in the dark, and shine the light." The magisters repeated the verse as one, taking their seats together.

"The Head of the Order is in session," proclaimed the Grand Magister.

She sensed a wooziness in his voice. She did not know his age as she had never seen his face, but she knew he was old. His voice was old. His posture was old. The heady cocktail took its toll on him, more than it should. He was weak. She found her finger toying with the ceremonial dagger inside her robe and moved it away quickly. Her eyes darted out beneath the hood, searching for any sign the others had seen her action.

"How goes our most important interest at present?" asked the Grand Magister, addressing the room in general. Did he not know one magister from another? Were his senses that dulled?

Interesting.

She waited a moment, letting an uncomfortable silence spread through the room.

"Everything is running smoothly, Grand Magister," she spoke up. "The demon has played its part as intended."

"How can you know this, Magister Cinquis?" asked the Grand Magister, his hooded head slowly turning towards her. "These events are many leagues away from here."

Several of the magisters murmured their scepticism, backing up their leader.

"I can sense the demon's presence, Grand Magister," said Magister Cinquis. "I have summoned it before. I know its name. I can feel when it is returned to the Mortal World. Surely you all have this perception?"

She smiled beneath her hood. Some of the others would not like that. They did not have her strength, her perception. She knew that, she felt their trepidation towards her.

I am strong and they are weak.

"So the demon is here," said Magister Trius, her voice cutting and disdainful. "What of it? How do you know it has completed its task?"

"I never said it was still here," replied Cinquis, turning a baleful gaze on her fellow magister. "It is because it has now gone that I know its role has been completed."

"It has been banished to the Astral Realm?" asked the Grand Magister.

Cinquis shook her head gently. "No, Grand Magister. It is gone. It is nothing. I feel it no longer. I called it before this session, just to be sure. It is in oblivion."

"Even if what you are saying is true, Magister Cinquis, I do not see how it confirms that all goes to plan," said Trius scathingly. Cinquis thought the magister was old, too. Not as old as the Grand Magister, but still, she was weak. "So what if the creature was banished?"

Cinquis paused, feeling the inquisitive eyes of her fellows on her. "It has met the child. It has given the message. It has been banished. Who else but one with power could destroy a demon? Who else could cast it into oblivion?"

"I was under the impression that our order dealt in facts, not presumptions," scoffed Trius, throwing her arms up in exaggerated exasperation. The sleeves of her robes slid down. Cinquis caught sight of a thin, white wrist and hand. The veins were dark and raised. A liver spot marked the skin.

Old. Weak.

"Magister Trius is correct," said the leader of the Order, reaching out to the side for his mahogany staff and banging it heavily on the stone floor. "We need a scrying. We need proof. Magister Trius, this is your forte. If you would be so kind..."

The heavy doors to the chamber opened slowly, an acolyte scurrying in with a bundle of cloth in his hands. The Grand Magister extended a wrinkled hand, pointing to the centre of the stone table, where the spider web of carved channels converged into one. Another acolyte moved quickly between the magisters, placing a simple stone cup at their right hand, and a small purple candle at their left.

The first acolyte had clambered onto the stone table, careful not to tear his robes. He crawled to the centre and placed the bundle of cloth down, gently unwrapping it to reveal a new-born baby. The child lay naked, its weak legs moving without coordination, gurgling gently. The acolytes retreated from the room quickly.

"Let the candlelight show us the way," intoned the Grand Magister.

Cinquis shook her head. This was distasteful. Unnecessary. She glared at ungainly form of Trius as he crawled up onto the table with difficulty.

Old. Weak. Sceptical and jealous.

Cinquis concentrated for a second, feeling a tingling in her body as he made the candle at her side burst into flame with a puff of purple smoke. The candles beside the other members of the Head of the Order shot into life. Trius knelt over the babe, turning her head to her own candle, lighting it with a point of her robed finger.

"We wish to see," proclaimed Trius.

Cinquis' lip curled beneath her hood as the older magister pulled the curved dagger from within her robe, sliding it deep under the baby's ribcage. The gurgling continued for a moment, dying away to nothing. Trius pulled the blade downwards, slicing open the child's belly. Blood pumped from the wounds, pouring into the carved furrows in the stone table. Cinquis watched as it approached, a dark flow in the troughs, flowing closer. She took the stone cup in her hand and placed it beneath the mouth of the gargoyle carved in the stone beside her, watching as the child's life blood dripped into the vessel.

She raised the cup to her lips in unison with her fellow magisters, drinking the babe's blood down. Cinquis hissed at the metallic taste in her mouth, fighting the urge to gag.

Trius was bent down over the child now, the knife flicking through the open belly. She reached inside, pulling out the entrails, pressing her face close to the intestines in her grip.

"What do you see, Magister Trius?" asked the Grand Magister, delicately wiping the sticky blood from his lip with the sleeve of his robes.

"Nothing," said Trius. "I see nothing, Grand Magister."

Lying bitch.

Cinquis composed herself, glaring at the old magister crouched on the table before her. She longed to reach out with her mind, throw back the hood and gaze upon the fool who opposed her. She longed to know the face of her enemy.

"Perhaps if the magister is struggling, I should look?" she said, moving to stand. "It would seem Magister Trius' vision is not as sharp as it once was."

"No," snarled Trius, bending down over the frail body again. The knife moved deep, cutting at veins and sinew. She reached inside, pulling the child's heart out and holding it close to her face, almost within the cowl of her robes. As she peered, a haze of purple began to gather around the organ, faint and shimmering. Trius breathed deep, pulling it into her lungs.

Old cunt. She didn't even try. She lied to the Head of the Order.

Trius head fell back awkwardly, her frail body arched backwards. Her arms dangled behind her, not bearing her weight on the table, just hanging freely. When she spoke her voice was a hiss, an empty whisper.

"I see the boy. He despatched the demon. The people of the village are with him. They are filled with hope. They are filled with anger. A word is coming through… Lunaris… Lunaris… They are following the boy. They are following the Lurker. A small sea of torchlight, heading to the mansion. Anger in their hearts. Vengeance. Justice."

Cinquis shrugged. "It is amazing what one can see if one tries."

"There is more," came Trius' rasping voice. "The anger is rife. Anger and discontent. Across Castland. I see the woods, the hills, the villages, the towns. The city. Anger amongst the poor folk."

"Word has spread already?" mused the Grand Magister.

Cinquis smiled broadly. It was her plan, and it was coming to fruition. Persuading the Head of the Order had been difficult, but they had given her the chance. She could not have hoped for a stronger start.

"No," hissed Trius forcefully. "Anger hasn't spread from the village. Not yet. This is different. Many streams, flowing from many sources. The Red Cairn Hills. Regalla. The east. Separate springs, the waters bubbling over, forming tiny babbling brooks. But they are flowing together. From small streams, mighty rivers are formed. And the rivers form the raging waves of the seas."

Magister Trius went completely limp, rolling onto her side on the table, a pile of purple robes. The Grand Magister looked on, his emotions hidden behind the hood of his gown.

Cinquis smiled, her tongue flicking out over her teeth beneath her own garments.

Old. Weak. Pathetic.

The magisters were murmuring their approval now. They were with her again. She felt a rush of elation through her body, the sensation heightened by the wine of the opening ceremony.

"All appears to be going well, Magister Cinquis," said the Grand Magister reluctantly, raising his arms to quiet the group. "Perhaps too well. Can we control this raging sea, should it pool up around us?"

"Of course, Grand Magister," said Cinquis, her voice brimming with confidence.

"I should hope so, magister," replied the Grand Magister. He was apprehensive. Overly cautious. "How long will things take to run their course?"

"It will take some time, Grand Magister," she said. "Emotions in the people of Castland are not quick to boil over. Even when they do, the nobility is good at suppressing the masses. It could take years before the poor gather enough resolve to fight for change."

"Years?" pondered the Grand Magister sceptically.

"Yes, Grand Magister. Is patience not one of the very columns upon which our order stands?"

"It is indeed," said the Grand Magister, fixing his glare on her. The headiness was beginning to wear off a little. She felt vulnerable, exposed. She struggled to push her feelings aside. "Our order is also based on success. Failure is met with… consequences…"

She nodded, slipping her hands into the sleeves of her robes to hide her trembling. The threat was real, she could feel it in the sweat seeping from her pores.

"We will not fail, Grand Magister. *I* will not fail."

Mayor Kove stared out into the night through his window, watching as the crowd of bobbing torches approached through the darkness from the direction of the village. The commotion had woken him, the noise of screaming and shouting from the commoners.

He had been annoyed at first, until he crept over to the window and opened it, listening to the sounds that carried on the frigid air up to his home. They were not sounds of revelry or raucousness. They were sounds of terror, of pain.

The din had died down after a time, but the eerie silence had been worse. Eventually it was replaced by cheering and shouting, of preparations being made and people gathering. Torches had flickered into life around the village, one by one. The people were gathering, and they were heading this way.

He had summoned one of his guards, sent him down into the village to investigate. He watched from the window as the hireling approached the crowd. They were close enough now for him to make out some of the faces leading the assembled populous of the village. Wrathson. That fucking priest. And the two murdering shepherds. What were they doing out of their cells?

Kove shuddered. It wasn't the cold, but he slammed the window down regardless. This did not bode well. He didn't know what was happening, and that made things worse. He was used to being in control. Torch-bearing yokels in the night converging on the governor's house could only mean one thing…

The mayor watched as his hired guard reached the villagers. He could hear raised voices, Wrathson jabbing his finger at the man, pointing accusingly up at Kove's home. The guard raised his hands above his head as Willem the hunter stepped forward, fixing him in the sights of his nocked bow.

"Shit."

Kove moved quickly, grabbing his clothes and rushing to get dressed. He reached under his comfortable bed, fumbling in the dim light of the candle on his dresser, pulling out a heavy pouch of gold coins and a bundle of cloth. He opened the latter, perturbed at the shaking of his own hands as he loaded the duelling pistol with shot and pulled back the hammer.

Wrathson strode up towards the entrance to the mayor's house, the crowd on his heels. Kove's other two hired men were already outside, breastplates hastily pulled on, hanging lopsided. One was doing up the chinstrap on his helmet whilst the other fumbled to draw his sword.

"I wouldn't do that, lads," said Wrathson, fixing them with a stare. "There's too many of us for just the two of you. We've got business with the mayor."

"Can't it wait until morning?" asked the one with his sword out. It hung by his side, pointing at the floor. Wrathson could tell her wasn't going to be fighting tonight.

"No, mate," said the sheriff, gesturing for them to move aside. "He's a murdering little runt, and he needs to answer for it. It was him that summoned the demon, that got all those people killed."

The men looked around the crowd, their eyes eventually settling on Father Pietr.

The old cleric nodded grimly. "It is true. Mayor Kove called forth the beast."

"So you're either with us, or you're against us," said Wrathson, standing before the two men. "You willing to lay down your lives for a murdering scumbag?"

The guards shook their heads, moving aside to allow the crowd through. They poured through the elegant doors, traipsing mud into the entrance hall of the mayor's opulent home.

"Split up," ordered Wrathson. "Find the mayor and bring him outside. Keep him alive, though. He won't put up a fight."

The villagers fanned out, rooting eagerly through the rooms. Mathias and Lucas bounded up the stairs, heading for Kove's study, and the bedroom beyond. Charo followed behind, struggling to keep up.

Mathias and the deputy burst through the study doors, swords in hand. Kove whimpered as they barged in. His beady little eyes flitted left and right, searching for another way out of the room. He was trapped, the only exit was back into his bedroom. He slunk behind his desk, trying to keep anything between him and the youths.

136

"Best come quietly, mayor," said Lucas, raising an open hand, strapped up by Father Pietr due to the sprained wrist he had gotten when thrown by the demon. He and Mathias advanced slowly towards the mayor.

The little man shook his head, spittle gathering at the corner of his rubbery lips. "What's this about? You have no right to be in here. No right. I'll have you flogged."

"You know what it's about," snapped Mathias, taking another, larger step forward. "You summoned that creature and blamed it on us."

"No," yelped Kove, raising the pistol he held and pulling the trigger.

Mathias lunged into Lucas, throwing them both to the ground as the shot whistled past them. There was a sickening splat as it imbedded in flesh. Mathias looked up to see Charo fall to his knees, blood oozing between the fingers he held clasped over his belly. His little brother fell forward onto the soft Altanyan rug, groaning as the crimson liquid spattered its ornate thread.

"Charo," cried Mathias, grasping at his brother's face as the lad struggled to breath. His face had drained of all colour instantly from the shock of being shot.

Mathias looked up, his eyes blazing hatred. Behind the desk Kove was fumbling in drawers, searching for more gunpowder and lead to reload his weapon. Mathias jumped to his feet, raising the sword aloft and bearing down on the mayor.

"No boy," roared Wrathson, the sheriff striding into the room. Mathias stopped in mid swing, turning to face the lawman, breathing heavily. "Lucas. Get Father Pietr up here to tend to Charo. *Quickly.*"

Wrathson moved forward, rubbing his hands together as the deputy scurried from the room. Kove had found a pouch of black powder and was desperately tapping it into the barrel of the pistol, his hands shaking like poorly fitted cartwheels. Most of it was hitting the floor.

"Sheriff," warned Kove, attempting to summon forth some semblance of authority. "I order you to stand down."

Wrathson smiled. "I don't think so, you little cunt. You're under arrest for demonology, murder, killing one of the king's deer and sheep rustling."

His blocky fist lashed out, smashing the ugly little man across the nose. Kove collapsed backwards to the floor, the pistol and gunpowder flying across the room.

Wrathson turned to Mathias, sat on the rug, cradling Charo's head in his lip. "You'll be alright, Charo. I promise."

Charo nodded, his eyes distant. "I know I will..."

Chapter Twenty

Oliver Cramwall sank deeper into the marble bath, leaving only his sagging face above the warm, fizzing water. The bubbles intensified as the physician kneeling beside him opened several pouches of multicoloured salts, pouring the crystals into the water in careful measures. The popping and bubbling clouded the liquid, protecting his modesty as he sighed out loud. His old skin creaked with pleasure, the soothing oils and powders tickling at his nerves and soothing his aching joints.

"You are a master of your art, Doctor Pallius," said the Lord Chancellor, closing his eyes for a second to savour the moment.

"That is why you employ me, Lord Chancellor," smiled the little bespectacled man, dipping a fingertip into the water and looking to the ceiling as he measured the temperature. "Needs more heat."

He stood and moved over to a large brass cauldron sitting on the nearby firepit. He delicately filled a steel jug a couple of times, pouring the boiling liquid into the bathwater.

The Lord Chancellor winced a little, the hot water stinging his skin before spreading out evenly through the rest of the bath.

"I am sorry, Lord Chancellor," crooned the doctor gently. "It is important you get the full benefit."

"Quite, quite," nodded Cramwall, turning to the High Priest of Pharma who sat in a nearby chair. "My apologies for receiving you whilst my physician is attending to me, father, but my schedule is extremely tight and my old joints ache in this accursed cold. I fear I am close to seizing up."

"I am grateful for your time, Lord Chancellor," replied the cleric. He was an old man, easily seventy, and yet his movements were more fluid and easy than Cramwall's. His hair was white and flowing, with a matching beard that hung down the front of his cloud-white robes. His eyes were blue and gentle, his skin only slightly lined despite his great age. The only part of his dress that set him apart from any other cleric of Pharma were the ornate gold chain hanging round his neck and the slender, silver staff that leaned on his chair, topped with a clear diamond the size of a man's palm.

"Tell me, father, what is it that required my attention so urgently?" asked the Lord Chancellor, swishing a wrinkled hand around the effervescent water.

The High Priest shuffled uncomfortably. "The priesthood is worried, Lord Chancellor. I am worried. The health of the realm, in particular the poor, appears to be in dire straits."

"How so?" asked Cramwall absently.

"My priests are struggling to keep up with the flow of the sick stretching from temple and chapel doors. In some of the outlying areas, I am getting word that our houses have had to be closed to new supplicants."

"I would not worry, father. The poor are a hardy breed. Those fit enough will survive. If they don't... well, there are enough of them to keep the country running smoothly, are there not?"

"That..." The High Priest looked confused, his demeanour flustered. "That is not how Pharma teaches us to view the world, Lord Chancellor."

"Indeed?" mused Cramwall. "Well, that is your faith, and I am sure Pharma has her reasons for seeing the world in that light. I have to view things with a wider lens, I am afraid."

The cleric paused again, pondering his next words carefully. "I fear that, if we fail to treat the sick, we may see an outbreak of illness, Lord Chancellor. It is well documented that, in times where the priesthood as lacked the resource to tend the afflicted, disease spreads through the land. The Green Plague, the Black Plague, the Red Plague..."

"And a whole other rainbow of plagues, I imagine?" laughed Cramwall mirthlessly.

"Pheasant Pox," continued the priest, obviously perturbed by the Lord Chancellor's response. "Blood-Burst Eye. Split Bowel. All of these blights cost many lives, rich and poor, when they were allowed to spread. Disease does not recognise the border between the rich and poor quarters, Lord Chancellor."

"Are you saying I should build some walls, then?" asked Cramwall, fixing the older man with his steely blue stare. He raised a shiny eyebrow.

"No, Lord Chancellor. I need more resources. The priesthood of Pharma needs more resources."

"I cannot give you more clerics, father. Perhaps you should incentivise joining you order more invitingly."

Pallius smiled to himself at the Lord Chancellor's remark. The High Priest shot him a look of disdain. "Our numbers are adequate, Lord Chancellor. We need more resources. Ingredients for salves, potions, poultices, infusions. These are not inexpensive..."

"Ah," sneered Cramwall, raising his arms from the bath in exasperation. "The play reaches its final act. You are asking for gold."

"It would help significantly," admitted the High Priest. "We need more raw materials. And people have become less generous with the giving of alms of late."

"You sound as though you are disappointed that people are not giving you money hand over first, father. We have just fought a difficult war. An *expensive* war. Perhaps people are entitled to keep hold of their hard-earned gold in these times of uncertainty, rather than waste it away."

"Charity given to the works of Pharma is not wasted, Lord Chancellor." The old priest's eyes were sad, perhaps even a little angry.

"I beg to differ, father," snapped Cramwall. "Doctor Pallius here is my personal physician, a man of science graduated from the University of Regalla. He tells me that you waste your ingredients by using them in their raw state. Is that not correct, doctor?"

Pallius smiled condescendingly, nodding his head. "It is true that most materials are more productive if dried, ground, concentrated. Less is required, and one herb or root can treat up to ten times as many patients. There is also less wastage. No fresh ingredients rotting on shelves in old men's laboratories."

"Pharma teaches us that ingredients must be used in their natural state, Lord Chancellor," insisted the High Priest. "Powders, compounds, crystals. These are the trappings of drug addicts and criminals."

"Perhaps Pharma should teach you to be more practical," pondered the Lord Chancellor. "Tell me, father, how many people survive Split Bowel in your care?"

"Well," spluttered the cleric, shrugging his shoulders. "It depends when they are treated. Advanced cases are impossible to treat. In the early stages, if captured, infusions of nightshade had been known the kill the canker."

"Doctor Pallius has cured numerous advanced cases by cutting out the infected part of the gut."

"*Surgery?*" exclaimed the High Priest, shaking his head vigorously. "*No man's skin shall be cut by any of the faithful.* The Book of Pharos. The Tenets of the Priesthood."

"Even if it saves his life?" Cramwall shook his head, tutting. "What about Blood-Burst Eye, Doctor Pallius?"

"Death only occurs when the pressure of the blood in the head causes the brain to seize," said the physician simply. "I have cured every case I have come across by popping the eye from the socket under general anaesthetic. The blood build-up can be released, and the eyeball pushed back in. That does not involve cutting the skin, High Priest."

"*Pain is part of the salvation of the afflicted,*" quoted the cleric. "*To be rendered senseless during the cure will cause weakness to set in.* The Book of Pharos. The Tenets of the Healer."

"Tell me, High Priest," said Pallius, rubbing his chin thoughtfully. "How many of your afflicted die of shock when you pop their eyeball out without anaesthetic?"

"It is known to happen. But it is part of the process. Healing is not based on numbers and butchery. It is about strength and faith."

"Faith," smiled the Lord Chancellor, sitting up in his bath as Pallius draped a downy white towel around his shoulders. "In that case, use magic. You do not need the people's money for that. Neither that given by alms, nor that secretly taken if I hand you their taxes from the coffers of the state."

"Magic is difficult, Lord Chancellor," sighed the High Priest. "It requires prayer, and for Pharma to hear those voices and answer by donating her power. Even when she does answer, the toll on the human body and mind, even channelling energy that is given freely, is gruelling."

"Sounds like your god cares less for the suffering of the people than my fellow physicians and I," sneered Pallius.

"*Blasphemy!*" cried the High Priest, rising out of his chair and pointing an old finger at the physician. "This man is a heathen and a heretic, Lord Chancellor."

"Easy, father," said Cramwall gently, dabbing at his arms with the towel and turning his gaze to Pallius carefully. "I think the good doctor makes an interesting point, even if he has worded it rather clumsily. How can you expect the people to give money to Pharma, if she will not lend her power to save them? Or if her priests have more concern for their own health than those of their faithful flock? You bear your age well, father. How often have you channelled these immensely damaging forces for the good of the sick?"

The High Priest lost his resolve, his head bowing towards the floor. These men would not listen. "May I at least ask that food donations to the poor are increased? I am sure your physician would agree with me that hunger makes the threat of disease worse by damaging a man's constitution?"

"Food is a resource that we must protect, father," replied Cramwall, standing up in the bath. Pallius knelt down, wrapping another towel around his waist as he stepped from the bath. "There are troubles brewing, inside the realm and without. I would remind you that you only have to worry about the sick. I have to worry about the health as well. I have to worry about the rich *and* the poor. I have to take into account the near *and* the far. I have to repair the damage caused by the past, and plan for the damage caused in the future. The balancing act of maintaining order is a delicate one, and there is no gold to spare.

"If you need gold, I would say this: I have never seen a poor cleric of Pharma. Your robes are always white and soft. It has been established that you are wasting your ingredients, and your healing methods are not the most efficient. That diamond atop your staff is, I imagine, worth more than the palace in which we sit."

"The Tear of Pharos..." started the High Priest.

"Is just an exquisite piece of glass," snapped the Lord Chancellor. "It is beautiful, it is rare, and it is expensive. But it is just a rock. I hope I have given you some valuable guidance as to how you can make what you have stretch further in these troubled times. That is worth more than just handing you gold from the coffers of the people."

The High Priest nodded reluctantly. He could tell his audience was over.

"Thank you, Lord Chancellor," he said pointedly.

"It is my pleasure," smiled Cramwall, striding past the old man on his way to the door.

"The evidence has been presented," said Wrathson, his loud voice projecting chair across the assembled villagers in the square from his position standing on a chair beside the simple gallows that had been set up by the executioner. He turned to Mayor Kove, standing beside him on a stool with the noose hanging loosely around his neck. "Do you have anything to say in your defence?"

The executioner was looking uncomfortable at the events unfolding before him. The fat, stunted man had been present at the events in the square in the early hours of the morning, but he had not accompanied the villagers to Kove's house. It was not his business, and even though he was wearing his black hood today, he was perfectly aware that people had seen his face yesterday. Especially the travelling trader who was stood at the back of the crowd, and who had also avoided the storming of the elected official's home.

"I didn't do anything," whined Kove. The drool was dribbling from his lips in a waterfall, only rivalled by the tears streaming from his piggy little eyes. His face was more than just clammy now, it was positively soaking.

"It is time for the judgement of this court," said Wrathson simply.

"The baronet is not here to make judgement," whimpered Kove desperately.

"You're right," said Wrathson. "Because he's involved in this. His judgement wouldn't be just. You'll be judged by your fellow citizens, the men who elected you. Those assembled here."

"That is not the law of the land," cried Kove. Wrathson raised his hand to silence the mayor, threatening another ham-fisted smash across the face.

"I find you guilty," said Wrathson. He looked down into the crowd, pointing to Mathias standing at the front, his eyes filled with hate.

"Guilty," said Mathias, staring into the mayor's pig-like, tear-stained eyes. "Charo agreed."

"Guilty," said Willem solemnly as the sheriff's finger moved to him, standing beside Mathias.

"Guilty," said Father Mathias, sad eyes falling on Kove as he trembled on the stool. The apprentice of Mortis spoke up too, despite being too young to vote and being a girl.

Wrathson took the decision of each of the villagers in turn, each one proclaiming the same. He took the votes of the women and the children, even though they weren't allowed to vote by law. Only the trader and the executioner abstained, insisting that this was none of their business.

The sheriff turned to the mayor. "Looks like you're fucked, Kove. You've been found guilty and you're sentenced to death. In the name of the king I order that you be hanged by the neck until dead."

"Wait," sobbed Kove, a dark stain spreading across the crotch of his breeches and spreading down the leg. "I am an elected official. I demand an appeal to a higher body. It is my right."

140

Wrathson shrugged as Mathias moved over, standing in front of the mayor, the green eyes boring into the man who had shot his brother.

"You didn't give the Culler boys that right, Kove," said Wrathson. "I don't see why you should get it. We all piss out of the same place. You're proving that while you stand there."

Mathias kicked out a foot, knocking the stool from beneath Kove's feet. The mayor's legs kicked out, his face moving through increasingly dark shades of red as the muscles in his shoulders and neck tensed in an attempt to hold his body weight. After a few seconds the executioner moved forward, his arms open to ready to wrap them around the mayor's legs and pull him downwards, hastening his end.

Wrathson reached out an arm across the fat man's sagging breasts, stopping him in his tracks. "He wouldn't do it for you, mate."

All of the village stayed, watching as the mayor's movements became slower, weaker. Many looked away, their heads in their hands, but they all stayed. Mathias stood where his was, his back straight, staring at Kove intensely as the little man's life slipped away with a gasping that became a gurgle.

Fair play, lad. It's not an easy thing to watch.

After a few minutes the mayor's body stopped moving. His toe twitched disconcertingly, but Wrathson could see that he was gone. The stare was still cold, icy, but it was empty now. Kove was staring into nothingness.

"Cut him down," he said to the executioner. He looked over to Pietr. "Father, do your thing if you feel the need. Or don't. I couldn't care less either way."

Wrathson spat on the floor and led Mathias away by the elbow, heading back up towards the mayor's former residence.

Charo was propped up on the mayor's feather pillows in the official's bed as Wrathson and Mathias stepped in. The young initiate of Mortis had returned before them and was checking him over, gently rinsing his various cuts and grazes with clean, cold water. Charo winced at the icy liquid on his skin.

"Never mind all that shit, lass," said Wrathson, sitting heavily into the chair by Charo's bedside. "How's his stomach?"

"Father Pietr is tending to that," said the young girl. She was a weird looking little thing. Small for her age, skinny, with disconcertingly crossed eyes, one brown, one green. Her hair was mud brown and cropped short. She rinsed the cloth in the bowl of water, squeezing off the excess and repeating her cleaning. "He got the shot out pretty quick, so that's a good thing. He says it didn't hit anything important, just puppy fat."

"This skinny lad hasn't got any puppy fat on him," smiled Mathias, perching on the bed beside Charo and gently poking his fist at his brother's jaw.

"Is it done?" asked Charo. He didn't smile. Mathias didn't know whether it was the pain or recent events, but it seemed an eternity since he had seen that cheeky grin.

Mathias looked to his lap and nodded.

"Don't go getting soft on us Mathias," said Wrathson. "That cunt got what was coming to him. Simple as that."

"You're right," said the older Culler brother, running a hand awkwardly through his bedraggled blond hair. "I just..."

"Never killed a man, eh?" said Wrathson, his voice softening. "It doesn't get any easier, mate. Not unless your soul's got bits missing from it. But sometimes it has to be done."

"The sheriff's right, Mathias," said Charo sombrely, placing his thin hand on his brother's knee. "It took courage for you to do it yourself. But there will be more. We have to change Castland for the better."

"Is that wise?" asked Mathias. "Word will get out about what we did here. The lords will come for us. They won't believe talk of demons and murder. They'll see commoners who killed their fellow nobles, and they'll string us up like Kove."

"Let them come," said Charo. "These nobles won't give up what they think is theirs. Not without a fight. Nobody ever gave anybody anything. People have to take it."

"Mathias is right, though, Charo," said Wrathson gravely. "They'll send soldiers. Now those people out there will follow you. I'll follow you. But these men have armies of killers at their backs."

"We must trust in Lunaris," said Charo simply. "He has saved us from the demon. Why would he do such a thing only to let us be killed by the nobles?"

"I trust in you," smiled Mathias weakly.

"Me too," added Wrathson, clapping a meaty hand on Charo's shoulder. "You saved my life, and you did it by smashing a demon to pieces before my very eyes with those skinny fists. If you say Lunaris gave you that power, then I trust in him too."

Charo smiled. It was fleeting, but it warmed Mathias' heart. "Then we must deal with Baronet Wender."

Wrathson nodded. "Sooner rather than later would be best. If he finds out what's happened, he'll send for help. He's only got five men up there, all hired. They'll turn on him if we show up at his gates. Tonight would be best."

"Then tonight it is," said Mathias, nodding as he looked into his brother's dark eyes.

"Can I go with them?" Charo asked the initiate.

The girl shook her head quickly. "No, Charo. You need to rest. Upsetting your wound could cause it to fester. You've been lucky so far."

"It's alright, lad," smiled Wrathson. "They won't have demons at their side this time. Me and your brother can deal with this."

The sheriff's hand strayed to the stabbing in his ribs as he moved to stand.

If they do put up a fight, this might turn out the wrong way for all of us...

"Once it's done, we'll need to leave the village quickly," said Charo. "I need Father Pietr to get me ready to travel as soon as possible. Is the blacksmith able to craft as many weapons as possible while I recover?"

"He'll get on it, I'm sure," said Wrathson. "He's a good man."

"We'll need to harvest the crops that are ready, take them with us for the journey. Gather as many carts and beasts as possible. Anything that will help us out there."

"Where will we go?" asked Mathias, taken aback by Charo's newfound confidence.

"Regalla," replied Charo, as if the answer were obvious.

"The capital?" gasped Mathias. "They'll hang us."

"Not with the people on our side," smiled Charo, squeezing his brother's knee reassuringly. "Trust in Lunaris, Mathias. If we want change, it needs to come from the heart of Castland and spread out from there."

Mathias nodded reluctantly. He was looking to his lap again, avoiding his brother's gaze.

A knock came from the door, quiet and hesitant. The initiate moved away from her patient, opening the door slowly to reveal the executioner and the travelling pedlar.

"What is it?" asked Wrathson, addressing the fat headsman. "The mayor paid you, didn't he? Maybe not for the job you carried out, but he did pay you."

The man nodded, multiple chins wobbling below the ill-fitting black mask he still wore on his face. "And now, if it's alright, I'll be making my way..."

"Me too, gentlemen, by your leave," intervened the trader, stepping into the room, his hands clasped awkwardly together in front of his chest. "I have goods to ply, and the market here seems to have dried up somewhat."

"You aren't going to fight with us?" asked Wrathson. "You saw what happened last night? The creature summoned by the mayor? The way the rulers treat us like toys in their sick games?"

"I..." The executioner hesitated. "I feel I've seen justice done for that. But I've other jobs to get to. I didn't come here to fight the aristocrats. I came to do a job, and the way I see it that job's been done."

"And I have a business to run, gentlemen," said the trader, wringing his hands. "I have a family to keep. Goods to sell. This is not my fight."

"It's everyone's fight," said Mathias, taking in the two apprehensive men. "It wasn't my fight, or Charo's fight, or this village's fight, until *they* brought it to us. Are you both of secret noble birth?"

Both men shook their heads, looking to the floor. The pedlar spoke first. "Your ideals are noble, gentlemen. I wish you all the luck of the gods. But I am not a soldier, and I am not an ambitious man. I have mouths to feed, and I like my breath in my body where it belongs."

The executioner nodded his agreement under Mathias' gaze.

"Where will you go?" asked Charo gently.

"South." The men responded in unison.

"They'll tell people what happened here," hissed Mathias.

"Your brother's right, Charo," said Wrathson. He looked the two men up and down. "They should stay... or..."

"Tell the people," said Charo, addressing the men now stood fearfully at the foot of his bed. "But tell them the truth. Tell them of the demon. Tell them what the nobility did to the poor here. And tell them what happened to the beast and its master. Let them know that a wind of change is blowing towards them. Towards Regalla."

The men nodded eagerly, backing towards the door.

"We'll tell it true," said the executioner as they fled from the room to gather their trappings.

"This is dangerous, Charo," said Mathias, shaking his head ruefully.

"Make sure the headsman leaves the gallows," said Charo. "Reimburse him from the mayor's purse."

Lord Perlis walked through the town, Xavier moving at his side. No guards walked with them as they moved through the streets, flanked either side by the red buildings that gave the settlement of Bloodstone its name. They didn't need protection. This was Perlis' town. These were his people.

The humans moved about their business diligently, unloading wagons, skinning carcasses, hammering metal, planing wood. Their master rewarded them well for their endeavours, but they were expected to work. They ate well, they were free to spend their money as they wished, marry as their hearts led them, bear as many children as they wanted. There were no beggars in Bloodstone and the surrounding villages, no poorhouses, no workhouses.

And their lord did not feed on them.

Perlis placed his arm around his son, pulling him close so that their thin silver hair merged into one flowing fall. He smiled. He was happy. His people were happy. And soon his enemies would be unhappy.

"Why so glum, my son?" he asked, pulling Xavier's chin so that their eyes met. "It is a glorious day."

Perlis extended a long arm to the grey sky, filled with thick, ominous cloud. Up in the mountains beyond the Red Cairn Hills the land was bleak, and the weather equally drab. The sun and its pesky light rarely penetrated the thick clouds.

"The traders in town are unhappy, father," said Xavier. "They have seen no caravans for weeks. Nobody to buy from, nobody to sell to. Some of the artisans are struggling for materials too."

"Did you reassure the people that these issues were in hand?" asked Perlis.

Xavier nodded. "Yes, father. I just thought you should know."

"Correct," smiled Perlis, ruffling the young vampire's hair gently. "You learn well. A lord needs to know everything. Send the traders a goat each. Alive. They can keep it or they can eat it, it is their choice. Find what the artisans need and give it to them from our stores. Free of charge; a gift."

Perlis led his son across the street, heading to the domed, red stone building before them. Its supporting beams and frames were of ebony, black and polished. As they approached, two figures in flowing crimson robes opened the black doors, inviting them into the darkness of the interior.

The temple of Sanguis was unlit within, the only light provided by the delicate wisps filtering in through the window slits in the stone. The vampires slid along the ground gracefully, stepping out from the entrance corridor into the domed main room. Rows of red stone pews rose up on either side of them, carved out of the floor into simple furniture. The entire temple had been built from a mound of stone, hollowed out into a magnificent place of worship.

"Are our people at Unstead's pathetic little gate?" asked Perlis, sniffing the air as they walked down the aisle between the pews. The smell was faint but still tangible. Blood. Old, slightly stale, but it still caused his heart to pump faster. He flicked out his tongue, tasting the air hungrily.

"Yes, father," replied Xavier, his own eyes widening greedily at the scent. "Fifty of them."

"And nobody saw them approach from our lands?"

"No, father. I escorted them myself. No outriders came near the group. They were too busy tracking the party from Regalla. A group of Unstead's men arrived after us and formed a blockade. Not many of them, less than ten. I instructed the people to camp and wait. They chant the songs you told them by day, songs of rebellion and freedom. The man I left in charge negotiates for free passage through the hills, as is his right. Unstead's men refuse him each morning."

"Excellent," sneered Perlis as the pair stepped up onto the dais at the head of the temple, standing around the rough red stone altar. Perlis ran a slender finger through the blood-collecting gutters, gently running the digit up the leg of the exiled man strapped to it. The man struggled against the leather bindings, his muscles bulging as he strained to free himself.

Perlis moved round to the man's head, brushing past the red robed priestess of Sanguis who stood waiting with her sacrificial dagger. He leaned in close to the man, the thin fingers gripping his chin, indigo eyes fixing him with a stare that locked his eyes to Perlis' own. The vampire swayed his head from side to side, focusing his mind, like a snake hypnotising its prey. The exile's struggles abated, his body went limp.

"They know to wait for the Regallans and to follow their lead?" asked Perlis, licking his lips hungrily as his eyes fell on the man's throbbing jugular vein.

"Yes, father," nodded Xavier, his own eyes drawn to the pumping blood vessel.

"Good," said Perlis. "Then we shall have a feast in celebration."

"What of Lord Drathlax, father?" asked Xavier. "He left shortly after your talk. Will he and the Council not disapprove?"

Perlis shook his head absently, gesturing to the priestess of Sanguis. "He will never betray me, son. He is with us. He just doesn't want to admit it yet."

The cleric stepped forward, sliding the razor-sharp blade across the sacrifice's throat so that the vampires could feed.

Chapter Twenty-One

Q'thell sat bolt upright, tossing back the mound of furs covering him. The walls of the tent flapped gently in the cold, early morning breeze of the Bleakthorn Hills. He rubbed at his blood red eyes, the wiry muscles in his forearms rising from his black skin like lengths of strong rope.

Dreams again. He wasn't used to dreams. He hadn't dreamt since he was a child.

Bad dreams. They had started the night after he had dealt with the crazy humans in the woods near Tanner's Mere. The peasants had strung the surviving cultist up immediately once Q'thell had handed him over. Cecil had authorised it, and he was the son of the Lord Chancellor, so it wasn't exactly a lynching. The young lord himself had stuffed the dangling man's severed cock in his own mouth.

The dreams had started gently at first. Hazy recollections of the night's events; the cultists dancing round the girl, the blank look on her face as Q'thell cut her down. Whispers in the dark wood around them. He hadn't heard them at the time. Was it his mind adding them to the memory, or had they been there and he hadn't noticed?

But the dreams were becoming nightmares. Nightmares strewn with the spray of blood, the scraping of blade against bone. Screams. Whispers. Growls. Last night the faces of the cultists showed beneath their hoods. They were people Q'thell knew; Cecil, his father, Toby Princetown, Gideon de Pfeiff. Q'thell didn't care for these people, killing was in his very nature, and yet the visions unsettled him. Was he being haunted by the dead? Was he cursed?

He remembered now. The girl's face. It had clouded before his eyes, taking on the visage of the blonde whore from Regalla, the one he had killed at Cecil's behest. Q'thell had found his hand raising, the fencing sword in his hand pressing against the girl's throat as she hung from the post in the clearing. He couldn't control it. He slashed the blade across her throat, the blood spraying in his face, into his eyes.

Then he had woken.

Q'thell shook his head, looked down at his hands in the light of the dawn. No blood.

Obviously, you fucking fool. You've killed hundreds of people. Stop going soft.

He hissed at himself, pulling his leather armour on quickly and stepping out into the early morning light. The camp was still sleeping, the tents circling the remains of last night's fire. The stripped-bare carcass of a boar caught by one of the scouts still sat skewered on the spit above it. Q'thell moved over, picking at the bones, pulling off what little meat remained and stuffing it in his mouth.

The Q'shari moved quietly. He always did, but he took extra care now. Cecil's tent was beside his, and the fat little fucker had been in a torrid mood of late. Travelling in the barren hills was not something he was used to. Sleeping in a tent was not improving the noble larva's temperament.

The two men on the last watch were still patrolling the perimeter dutifully, yawning as they did so. Their limbs looked heavy, their skin and armour slick from the fine drizzle falling from the sky. Q'thell gestured for them to come over.

"Get the men up," he hissed. "*Quietly.* Don't wake his lordship yet. Start packing up."

"But it's only just dawn," said one of the men, his simple face puzzled.

"And I want to get on the road," said Q'thell. "I'm sick of these fucking hills. The longer we ride, the quicker we get to Bannar. Don't you want to get the sleep you're craving in the back of the supply wagon?"

The two men nodded, setting about raising the retinue.

Q'thell climbed the nearest hill, standing atop it, staring out over the land below. Barren mounds, interspersed occasionally with thickets of thick briars that gave the place its name. The inclines were becoming gentler, the ground less difficult. They could be out of this accursed place by nightfall if they got a move on.

He shuddered visibly, turning and striding back down into the camp.

"My arse is numb as a peasant's brain," moaned Cecil, shifting in his saddle as he rode beside Q'thell.

The Q'shari sighed. The drizzle had not let up. It didn't bother him, he was a creature of the wilds, but it made the ground difficult. A horse slipping or one of the wagons sliding down a bank would delay them, so they had to be careful, but he was becoming impatient. To make his day worse, the fat lord-baby had decided he wanted to ride with them, rather than sit in his little coach and doze.

"Perhaps you have saddle sores, my lord," he said, the impatience evident in his voice. "Maybe you should ride in your coach?"

"No," said Cecil absently. "That seat is hard as a homosexual's cock in a boy's schoolroom."

145

"The similes are in full flow today," sneered Q'thell. "They're rivalling this fucking rain."

"What would you know of literary technique?" asked Cecil testily.

"You're right, my lord. I'm just a savage. Maybe we should ride in silence so that my pigeon speak doesn't rile you further."

Cecil huffed moodily, staring ahead through the grey drizzle as they rode. Below, the gentler plains of Lord Tomas Bannar's lands were becoming visible through the haze. A day away, possibly less. He could make out the stonework of walls separating fields, the odd line of smoke rising from the chimney of a farmhouse. Some of the fields didn't appear sown with crops, but were instead dotted with white dots.

"What are those white things?" he said, turning to Q'thell again. "Are they sheep?"

"So you wish to listen to my ignorant talk again?" asked the Q'shari with a smile.

"Suit yourself. I'll use my spyglass."

"They're beehives," said Q'thell, eager to finish the conversation.

"Nonsense," scoffed Cecil. "Bees build nests. Ugly yellow things in the eaves of houses and hanging from trees."

"True," said Q'thell. "But they'll also nest in those. A beekeeper sets a queen up in a wooden hive, and they make honey. A man can then safely gather the honey, without having to smash the hive open and get stung all to shit."

"How do you know this?"

"I am a creature of the wilds, remember, my lord. We Q'shari taught you humans to build these hives. We have them ourselves, although ours are more elegant. More natural."

"So we are near civilisation then?" asked Cecil, his little blue eyes lighting up. "I long for a night in a decent bed."

"Not a good idea to keep bees near a settlement," smiled Q'thell. "Wouldn't want a swarm attacking people. The scouts reckon we'll hit a village in a couple of days. Not long after that we'll be at Bannar. At least by tonight we should be out of these fucking hills."

Cecil laughed. "I thought you were a creature of the wilds?"

"Not these hills," said Q'thell, looking over his shoulder. The clouds behind them were dark, gathering for a storm. They needed to beat it, or they'd be bogged down for a while. At least the road on the even plains below was supposed to be more passable.

Cecil guffawed, his jowls rolling in time with his heaving sides.

Baronet Wender's men had surrendered to Wrathson and the villagers, as expected. They stood amongst the assembled crowd in the village square, as did Kove's hired men. Charo looked at them suspiciously as he leaned on the young initiate of Mortis for support. There was no sign of revolt in them. All had listened to Wrathson recount recent events, and they seemed satisfied that he was telling the truth. They were men of action, as was the sheriff. He had no reason to lie to them.

"You shouldn't be out here, Charo," said Father Pietr. "You need to rest."

"I need to be here," replied the lad, staring up at the gallows as Mathias kicked the stool out from under the baronet's feet.

The noble thrashed against the strain on his neck, spittle bubbling between his lips as he struggled against the death that was closing in on him. His eyes were wide with terror, the blood vessels widening and bursting with the struggle. Charo longed to turn away, but he couldn't. This was the judgement of Lunaris, and he was bound to watch it. Even so, it seemed to go on forever. The man was suffering, his face turning purple, snot spraying from his nose as he thrashed.

Is Lunaris cruel? Am I cruel? We must deal with our enemies, but we mustn't become them...

Charo moved forward, shrugging off the young girl's support. The crowd parted as he walked, watching as he stepped past Mathias and stood before the kicking baronet. He reached to his belt, pulled out the bone knife in a skinny, trembling hand.

"Don't bother," said Wrathson, stepping forward and placing a hand gently on Charo's shoulder. "He deserves this."

Charo looked at him, the dark eyes filled with sadness. "No, sheriff. He deserves to die, but not to suffer. It makes us as bad as him."

The youth turned to the baronet and thrust the knife forward, plunging it under the ribcage into the noble's heart. The kicking ceased almost immediately, blood running down Charo's sleeve as he stood before the dead man. He left the blade in place, turning to the villagers.

"The justice of Lunaris has been served, as it will be served to all those who oppress us. We shall serve this justice until those people give up their cruel ways and allow all to live their lives free from fear."

The crowd cheered, calling Charo's name, praising Lunaris. Charo wiped his hand on his tunic, careful to avoid the painful wound in his stomach.

"Now we must prepare," proclaimed Charo. "Edgar is working to provide us with weapons. We will need them to defend ourselves. We must gather our provisions. Make sure we take everything useful from the baronet's mansion. As soon as we are ready, we will head to Regalla. I will take our case before the king in the name of Lunaris."

The crowd was silent. Charo looked amongst them, trying to gauge the looks on their faces. There was fear, apprehension, anger, support, all in fluctuating measures as they pondered the implications of their planned course of action.

Will they follow? Please, Lunaris, they must *follow...*

Another cheer went up among the crowd. They burst into life, each man, woman and child spreading through the village to make the preparations that most suited their skills.

Charo smiled as Mathias placed an arm around him, looking down at his little brother with pride.

Sergeant Tumoore rode beside Captain Peacock at the head of the group of armed soldiers. Twenty men of Lord Unstead's household guard, a good quarter of the garrison from the keep at Hearth Hill. Tumoore looked back over his shoulder, taking in the stiff young warriors, clad in their pressed, clean black tabards and shining chainmail. Had they ever been in a real fight? Most of them looked too young for the Third Raskan War.

"Shouldn't we have brought more?" he asked, turning to the captain. "I was under the impression Lord Unstead wanted us to raise a levy of the common folk."

"There are only fifty peasants," replied Peacock curtly. He'd got a bee in his breeches, Tumoore could tell. The older man wasn't comfortable with the idea of slaughtering commoners. The outrider wasn't a principled man, but the idea turned his stomach too, if he was being honest. He took a swig of his hipflask. "Twenty mounted soldiers will be adequate. It would be a bad idea to bring our own poor folk along to witness what we are about to do. Plus, we have your men already at the gate."

Tumoore shrugged. "When you put it like that..."

The outrider squinted, eyes trying to make out the men at the gate ahead. He could see them, gathered around, some sat on the floor beside their horses. No sign of the crowd of peasants. Maybe they had got tired of standing around in the rain, fucked off home. Tumoore hoped so. Thunder clouds were rolling in, it was going to throw it down. All this over a fucking gate. You could just walk round the bastard thing, for fuck's sake.

The first heavy spots of rain were beginning to fall as they approached the gate. The sky blackened the afternoon sky above them, the light dropping suddenly as if sun was setting in the evening. A rumble of thunder sounded ominously in the distance.

Tumoore pulled off his helmet, shaking the greasy black hair free, and hung it from his saddle. He wasn't getting struck by lightning. He didn't much believe in the gods, but if they were there they wouldn't like what they were about to do. He was glad he was only wearing leathers. He wouldn't like to be the men behind him right now.

"Sarge," called one of his outriders, waving his arms as they approached. "Thank fuck you're here." Tumoore didn't like the sound of that.

Where the fuck are the peasants? Why's Tom lying on the floor like that, with a fucking blanket pulled over his head?

"Your men are a mess, sergeant," chastised Peacock, taking in the dishevelled outriders. "Their tabards are worse than yours was. Make sure they get new ones, for Guerro's sake, before Lord Unstead sees them."

Tumoore shot him an annoyed look. "What the fuck happened here?"

"They rushed us, sarge," said the outrider. He gestured to two of the men, groaning as they leaned against a nearby boulder. "Dragged these pair from their horses, gave them a right kicking. Tom fell from his horse. It went wild, booted him in the head. He's fucking dead, sarge."

The captain was looking at Tumoore, the portly man's annoyance evident. Tumoore took another swig from the hipflask.

"Why didn't you just stab a few of them?" he snarled. "You've got fucking swords, haven't you? And horses. They're just peasants, they would have fucking run at the first sight of blood. Eight outriders against fifty unarmed men…"

"There was over a hundred," insisted them man, shaking his head. "We had to run. We came back to get these lads when they'd gone."

"You sent word that there were fifty," snapped Peacock anxiously. He was sensing failure, and Lord Unstead had no patience for anything but success. The lord of Hearth Hill had never lost a skirmish, let alone a battle. His reputation was everything to him.

"We saw fifty-odd on the road. But when we got here ahead of them, about the same again arrived and set up a kind of camp. They were pretty peaceful at first, just chanting and asking to be allowed past. We told them to fuck off, obviously. But this morning, the group we had been tracking showed up. And they weren't much for talking…"

"A hundred of them, now," exclaimed Peacock, shaking his plump head.

"Hey, it was you who chose to bring twenty fucking men," replied Tumoore. A crack of thunder rang out, nearer now. "This is just fucking great."

"We still have enough, sergeant. One charge and they'll scatter to the winds."

"You want to charge horses in this weather? By the time we catch up with them it'll be a quagmire out there."

"These men are trained to fight in all conditions," insisted Peacock. A few of the lads nodded enthusiastically. "I trained them myself. Get your outriders together, we need to stop these peasants before nightfall."

"What about Tom?" asked one of Tumoore's men, gesturing to the body of their fallen comrade.

"Fuck him," snarled the sergeant. "Get on your fucking horses, all of you. You've embarrassed me enough."

Tumoore had a bad feeling about this. A flash of lighting lit the air for a second. His gaze fell on the remains of the gate, smashed apart by the baying mob. The thunder came again, growing nearer still. He took another swig of cheap whisky.

We're going to end up like that fucking gate if we're not careful…

Ratcliffe looked around at the assembled common folk as they marched along the road into the Red Cairn Hills. The land was bleak, the sky dark and teeming rain down on them, but their spirits were high. They sang songs of rebellion and freedom as they walked, hoods and cloaks pulled up against the storm.

There had been a group already at the gate when they had arrived. He didn't know where they had come from, but obviously they had heard his rallying call in one of the sister newspapers. It didn't matter who they were. They were with him, and that was what mattered.

He had stood before them at the gate. They had lapped up his words, cheered his every proclamation as one of his agitators scrawled the speech down for posterity. Eight outriders against over a hundred of the righteous poor. Ratcliffe had turned to stare them down, watching as their courage waned in the wake of the anger of the oppressed.

Ratcliffe had called on them to charge, and they had done it. The rush had been like something he never felt before. Not power. He didn't crave power. Acceptance. Brotherhood. Belief. These people believed in him, in his words. They believed in themselves.

The outriders had scattered. A few had taken a bit of a battering, but that was to be expected. There would always be casualties, on one side or another. There were casualties every day amongst the poor; starved to death, beaten to a pulp, hanged or beheaded at the word of some noble or rich landowner. It was about time the ruling classes started to feel the pain.

They had wrecked the gate. They could have gone around, but destroying it was symbolic. It was a sign of their oppression, and they had destroyed it. The people around it carried pieces of it, some as trophies, others as crude clubs. He felt inside his pouch where the heavy padlock he had claimed sat. He stroked its surface, a corporeal representation of the breaking of invisible shackles.

148

It was throwing it down now. The huge drops of rain were heavy, like balls of lead falling from the heavens. The water streamed down his face, making hard to see in the darkness of the storm. He blinked a few times, trying to wipe the droplets from his brows and eyes.

Then he saw them. The group came to a halt as they all laid eyes upon the men blocking the road ahead. Eight men on horseback, outriders by the look of them, bearing the colours of Lord Unstead of Hearth Hill. They were accompanied by an armoured soldier, a portly man, presumably their leader. The noise of the lashing rain and the thunder had allowed them to approach unnoticed.

Nine men? Do they think they can stop us?

Ratcliffe moved to the front of the group, his collar pulled up against the driving rain. It was then that he saw them. Twenty more men, armed and mounted, swords drawn, stood off the rough road behind the outriders. The horses' hooves splashed on the waterlogged ground, their riders testing the balance of their weapons, ready to charge at their leader's command.

Ratcliffe hesitated. Could they beat a charge by mounted soldiers in chainmail? There were plenty of them, but would they hold their ground? They weren't warriors, they were just common folk. Some had pitchforks, scythes, sickles, clubs made from pieces of gate post. A few more carried swords; Almas only knew where they had got them from, but they carried them nonetheless.

He doubted they would withstand the charge. Was it all in vain? Was their glorious act of defiance destined to end here?

Almas, please stand with your people.

"I am Captain Peacock of Lord Unstead's household guard," announced the round man on horseback, his voice fighting to be heard against the thrashing of the storm. "In the name of the lord of Hearth Hill, I order you to surrender your weapons and turn back."

"I thought we were just going to butcher them like pigs," snarled one of the outriders, a wicked-looking man with menace in his jade green eyes. The captain glared at him to be silent.

Why haven't they just charged? We did a good number on their friends. Are they not certain of their own chances?

Their hesitance gave Ratcliffe renewed hope. He stood forward, rubbing the padlock in his pouch for reassurance. "I represent the people. The people of Regalla. The people of Castland. You hold a family of our own, just for attempting to exercise their right to cross this land. In their name, we are going to exercise the right that you denied them. Surrender *your* weapons, and leave us to our journey."

"I do not recognise your authority," called Peacock. "It is the lords who rule this land, not... whoever you are."

"Not any more," replied Ratcliffe, his eyes meeting the stare of the captain. Yells of approval came up from the mob at his back as they raised their weapons above their heads defiantly.

Peacock looked to Tumoore uncertainly. The outrider shook his head, drawing his sword. His men followed suit, preparing for battle.

"Charge," roared Peacock, raising his own sword and dropping it to his side.

To one side the soldiers spurred their horses, the animals splashing into motion through the slashing rain. The crowd around Ratcliffe hesitated, their shouts of defiance fading.

They're going to run. Almas, please, let them stand and fight...

An almighty crack split the air around them. Ratcliffe fell to his knees, his vision white as a great flash blinded him for a second. Around him the crowd staggered about, their ears ringing from the lightning strike. The outriders on the road fought for control of their rearing horses, similarly stunned.

In the waterlogged ground off the road, the mounted soldiers had crashed into the puddled ground. Smoke billowed from their armour. Horses screamed in pain and fear, splashing around in the mire to find their feet and flee the scene. Some of the men lay in the bog, lifeless. Others clutched at their heads, grasping their temples or trying to pull off their metal helmets. One man succeeded, revealing a charred, smouldering face.

The crowd surged forward towards Lord Unstead's men. A rock flew out from the group, catching Captain Peacock on the head, spinning his helmet through ninety degrees with the force of the impact. He sagged forward in his saddle, dazed.

"Stay on your fucking horse," yelled Tumoore, grabbing the reins and spurring his own mount. The pair galloped off the road, their horses' hooves leaving a trail of spray behind them.

The other outriders were not quick enough. Ratcliffe watched from his knees as the crowd fell upon them. Those who had not already been tossed from their horses were dragged to the ground, blows raining down on them heavier than the pouring rain.

Other members of the crowd broke off towards the soldiers in the mire, still reeling from the bolt of lightning that had crashed to earth amongst them. Pitchforks lashed out, sickles slashed. The men with swords moved efficiently, sliding blades into the unarmoured areas round the neck, armpit, groin.

It was over quickly. Ratcliffe struggled to his feet, his ears still ringing like the bells of the temple of Pharma back home in Regalla. The rain poured down, washing away rivers of blood that spread from Lord Unstead's fallen men.

What have we done? How will we survive this?

"We have struck another blow for freedom, Jaspar," gasped one of his agitators, his voice also faltering slightly as he realised the enormity of their actions.

Ratcliffe looked around at the crowd that had centred about him, the rain rinsing the blood from their hands, their faces, their weapons. Their eyes were wide, expectant, waiting for guidance. He didn't know what to say.

Two of the bastards had escaped. Unstead would find out what had happened, and he would send more than a couple of dozen men after them. The lord of Hearth Hill's reputation went before him...

"We need to get to safety," spoke up one of the crowd. He was tall, slim, dressed in brown ranger's clothes, an ornate steel sword in his grasp. He shook his thin, silver, shoulder-length hair in the rain, fixing Ratcliffe with intense, blue-purple eyes. He was flanked by a couple of the men bearing swords. Beneath their rags Ratcliffe caught a glimpse of chainmail. "Lord Perlis' lands lie through the Red Cairn Hills. We will put some distance between us and Lord Unstead's men, and shelter at Bloodstone."

Why were they wearing chainmail? What commoner could afford it? And that sword...

"Lord Perlis will hand us over to his fellow noble when he finds out what happened here," said Ratcliffe, looking around the crowd for support. His protest was weak. He had no other ideas.

What have I done? I am not a leader of men. I just tell them the truth, so that they can lead themselves.

"Don't worry, Jaspar," smiled the man, a flash of lightning illuminating his pale face and glinting white teeth. "I think you will find Lord Perlis is not the same as other nobles..."

A flash of lightning illuminated the corridor. The windows in the black stone walls of the keep dungeon were high, nothing more than slits up at the top of the room where it met ground level, but the brief glare from the heavens penetrated the whole room. For a second the Knife could see clear as day the soldier lying face down before him, the pool of blood from his cut throat spreading quickly as his life pumped out on the dark stone floor.

Then the cellar was dark again, lit only by a couple of guttering torches in the sconces on the walls. The Knife moved back into the shadows against the wall, skulking down the corridor towards the iron-bound door to the cells. He slunk up against the door silently, pulling back the hood of his tunic slightly, pressing a white ear against the thick ebony.

Movement. One man, in mail. Moving away from the door. The door would be locked. He knew it. He had his lockpicking tools, but it would alert the man on the inside if the storm didn't mask the sound properly.

Time to take a risk.

He would get in there eventually, but hopefully this would be cleaner.

The Knife paused for a second, listening to the storm outside. It was close, but not overhead. He waited, judging the distance of the guard's movements, waiting for the thunder. It would come soon. He rapped his gnarled knuckles on the heavy door.

The thunder clapped. He heard the man within turn, the tinkle of chainmail approaching the door. He slid to one side, his back flush with the wall.

The small hatch in the door slid to one side, just as the lightning flashed, illuminating the corpse on the floor in the corridor. The Knife heard a gasp from within.

Thank Yanara for the lightning. Will he come out to investigate? Is he a fool?

The Knife smiled mirthlessly beneath the hood as he heard a key turn in the heavy lock. The door creaked open slowly, the guard emerging cautiously into the room, sword in hand, his eyes fixed on the body in the corridor.

The Knife lunged forward, reaching under the chainmail coif and grabbing the man's ear. The soldier yelped, powerless to resist as the Yanari pulled him forward, exposing the back of his neck. The Knife's dagger slid under the coif, sliding between the vertebrae in his neck. The guard slumped to the floor, dead before the Knife let his weight take him down.

The Knife slipped into the room beyond quickly, the keys from the door in his hand. He looked at the cells before him, searching for the right one.

"Wulskas," he hissed. "Where are you?"

The face of a young Yanari lad appeared instantly at the bars of one cell, pale in another flash of lightning. The Knife sidled over, slipping the key into the lock and pulling the door open. His eyes flicked over the occupants quickly, checking they matched the description. Yanari, a man, a woman, two male children. It was them, the Wulska family.

"Who are you?" asked the woman, her eyes angry in the dark.

"I am the one who watches over you," whispered the Knife. "I have come for you. I have come for my brethren."

The Yanari didn't question him further. The youngest lad was already out of the cell, grabbing the fallen guard's sword. It was heavy in his young grip, but he pulled it upright nonetheless. The Knife smiled beneath the hood. It wasn't often he saw a Yanari willing to fight for his freedom. It wasn't often he saw a Yanari who even realised his freedom had been taken.

The woman was dragging her husband and older son to their feet, hissing at them to move. The Knife heard a noise from the adjacent cell, a scuffling as the occupant threw himself at the bars of his prison. He moved over as a flash of lightning illuminated the man before him. Skin and bone. Toothless grin. Dark hair straggly across his face, brown eyes mad from months in the cell. A Castlander.

"Help me," screamed the thing in the cell, an emaciated hand grabbing hold of the Knife's collar through the bars, a wild stare meeting the grey eyes.

"I am a Yanari," whispered the Knife, meeting the manic glare. "Would you help me?"

The prisoner hesitated for a second. A second too long. "Of course I would."

The Knife span his blade upwards, slashing the wrist gripping him. The arm retreated inside the cell, the bag of bones curling up on the stone floor, nursing the wounded limb. The Knife moved away silently.

"We need to leave," insisted the woman, dragging her family out into the corridor. "He comes in the evening. He comes to taunt us. He gives us our meal, tells us what he has done to it. Pissed on it, shat on it, rubbed his cock in it. Yet we eat it, because we are starving. My *family* eats this filth."

The Knife's eyes shot towards the opposite door to the corridor, beyond the bodies lying on the ground. His ears pricked up, catching the sound of footsteps on the stairwell that spiralled down into the dungeon...

Lord Unstead watched as his son descended the steps to the castle dungeons in front of him. Young Zacharus was only seven, but he resembled his father already. He was tall for his age, lean to the point of being gangly. He would grow into his frame though. Unstead had been the same. As they reached the bottom of the stairwell the lad tripped, the metal bucket he was carrying crashing to the ground, spilling chunks of fatty meat across the stone.

He has his mother's graceful movements, though...

The young boy looked up at his father, the green eyes apprehensive as they peered out from beneath the mop of unkempt red hair. "I am sorry, father. I..."

"It does not matter, child," smiled Unstead. "Scrape it up. It is only for the Yanari."

Zacharus set about shoving the chunks back into the bucket, trying to dust off the dirt as best he could. "Should we not have chef prepare more? This is spoiled."

"This is slop for prisoners, boy. They are our enemies. They are lucky we are feeding them at all. Would we show them mercy on the battlefield?"

"No father," replied Zacharus dutifully, standing and reaching for the handle to the heavy ebony door.

"Wait, lad," said Unstead, kneeling down to his son's level and looking him in the eye. "You are with me to learn how to be a lord, understand? One day, these lands will be yours. It is important that you understand how to keep order. These Yanari trespassed on our lands, and we need them to stand trial for that. But first, we need to know that they will admit to their crimes in front of a court. The youngest one, and the woman, they are stubborn. How do we convince a stubborn mule to move?"

151

"We beat it?" ventured Zacharus reluctantly. The boy was soft, he had his mother's heart. That was not a bad thing, if he learnt to control it, rather than let it lead him.

"In a way. We break its spirit. Let it know who is in control. We must break the spirit of these Yanari."

"What is a Yanari father?"

Good. Inquisitive. Eager to learn.

"They are filthy, ugly, white creatures from the south, lad. They have infiltrated our society, ingratiated themselves with the people of Castland with their bowing and scraping. But they are dangerous plotters. Never turn your back on a Yanari, boy."

"I will not, father," nodded Zacharus. "But if they are our enemies, why don't you just do away with them? You are always telling me we should deal with our foes swiftly and with lethal force."

"Those are wise words, boy," smiled Unstead. "I made the mistake of informing the Lord Chancellor that I had taken them prisoner, and he has stayed my hand. It is not an error I will repeat. Sometimes it is best to keep things to oneself. But there is more than one way to skin a cat. They will admit to their crimes in front of a court. The Lord Chancellor cannot deny me justice if they are seen to confess."

"But first you must break their spirits," pondered Zacharus.

"Exactly, lad," sneered Unstead. "Are you ready to see the little milkers? I warn you, they are ugly."

Zacharus nodded, pushing the heavy door open and stepping into the chamber beyond.

The Knife held his breath as the door open, his back pressed against the wall. The Wulskas were on the opposite side, obscured from view as the thick wood creaked towards them. There were two of them, a man and a boy, both dressed head to toe in black silks. The Knife watched their backs as they entered the chamber, taking in the scarlet red locks on their heads.

Lord Unstead. The Knife had read of him. The lad must be his son. They moved quickly to the middle of the room when they saw the corpse of the guard, the lad kneeling beside the corpse.

"Father, what is this?"

Unstead was reaching for his sword, turning towards them.

"Run," hissed the Knife. The family scurried towards the open door, the parents bustling the children along.

They hadn't crossed the threshold before the Knife had pulled out a slim throwing dagger from his tunic, sending it flying towards Unstead. It swooshed through the air, slicing it as easily as it would any flesh that it struck. It was a perfect throw. The Knife was an expert, and the weapon was weighted especially for him by the best Yanari smith in Regalla.

Unstead threw himself to one side as the blade span towards him, just in time to avoid it. It imbedded in Zacharus' eye as the lad stood and turned to face the Knife.

Both men stood, mouths agape, staring as the boy collapsed in a heap on the floor. Unstead moved first, lunging at the Yanari, a strong had grabbing his tunic.

"You fucking bastard," he roared, a first pounding into the Knife's temple.

The lord was strong for such a lean man. The Knife put all his strength into a shove, trying to use his low centre of gravity to get loose. Unstead's grip pulled the Yanari's hood loose. The man stood, angry hazel eyes boring into the white face before him.

"What the fuck are you?"

The Knife lashed out with another blade. He rarely missed, but he didn't catch Unstead's throat as intended. The dagger bit deep, slicing the chin and along the jaw to the bone. The lord screamed out in a blend of pain and rage, his grip loosening.

The Knife broke free, scurrying nimbly for the door and slamming it shut behind him.

"Run," he yelled up the stairway, bounding up the steps behind the Wulskas. As he moved he pulled the hood back over his head. He took the lead as they emerged at ground level, urging them onwards. "This way. Hurry. Can you ride a horse?"

"Yes," panted the woman, Esme. "So can Tanis."

"Good," replied the Knife, leading the way out into the courtyard towards the stables. He had dealt with the guards along the route on his way in, stuffing their bodies out of sight in the shadows, but even so he moved cautiously. He held his main knife out in front of him defensively, ready to strike. In his left he clutched another of the throwing blades from the collection sheathed around his chest.

He could throw and stab with both hands. He wasn't naturally ambidextrous, it had taken years of practice. But he had begun to train when he was a child. It was one of the first skills he had been made to hone.

The Knife stepped over the corpse of an ostler in the stables, gesturing to the three horses he had prepared. He clambered up onto the back of one, waiting whilst Esme helped Alitain up behind her. Tanis scurried up into the saddle nimbly, holding the beast steady as Alit struggled to join him.

"Hurry," insisted the Knife. He turned as he heard the sound of movement from the entrance to the stable. A guard came into view, silhouetted asking the fading evening light.

"What..." The voice was drowned out by gurgling as the Knife threw the dagger, the blade burying itself up to the hilt in the man's throat.

"Move," he urged, kicking his horse into motion.

They galloped across the courtyard as quickly as their riding skills would allow them. The gate was open. It was only just going dark, and the castle was not expecting attack. Besides, there was nobody manning the gatehouse to close it; the Knife had dealt with them already.

He sighed as they rode out into the fading light.

We're going to make it...

A thud came from behind him, dull and wet. He looked over his shoulder. A hundred yards away, at the gate, Unstead dropped a crossbow from his hands, reaching to grab another from one of the nearby guards.

"Alit," cried Esme, halting her horse.

The Yanari man slid from the saddle behind his youngest son, crashing to the wet ground below, a quarrel sticking out from between his shoulder blades. As he keeled over the Knife watched the gentle blue eyes roll into the back of his head.

"Alit," sobbed Esme again, moving to dismount.

"Keep riding," hissed the Knife, reaching over and grabbing the bridle of her horse. "He's gone."

"*No,*" she screamed, the pain in her voice tearing at his heart. He pulled at the bridle as another crossbow bolt whistled between them, splatting into the damp earth ahead of them.

"Keep riding," repeated the Knife, spurring his horse along and dragging Esme's with him. "You too, lad."

Esme wailed as they galloped across the sodden ground, putting as much distance as possible between them and the keep at Hearth Hill. The Knife hoped they had enough of a head start. He reached for the dagger in the scabbard at his belt, toying with the hilt as they rode.

If he catches up with us, I'll have to deal with us all. We can't go back as prisoners to that beast.

153

Chapter Twenty-Two

Tomas watched as the retinue of Cecil Cramwall approached the gates of Bannar, the hooves of their horses and the wheels of their wagons caked in mud as they splattered along the road. They looked drenched. The storm had passed, but it was still drizzling steadily. The sky looked like it hadn't finished yet, either. Another stack of black cloud was gathering to the west, following the young noble's group towards the town.

Ominous.

Tomas reached out for Talia's hand as she stood beside him, distrusting eyes watching the men approach. She took it reluctantly, tensing as he interlocked his strong fingers with hers.

"I can't believe I agreed to be here," she said. "I'm not coming tonight."

"You are," he said. "I love you, and I need you there. You'll be there because you love me."

"Do I?" she asked, smiling meanly at the hurt in his dark brown eyes. Her face softened as she reached a hand up and ran it across the course, black stubble on his cheek. "I'll think about it."

"I'll make it worth your while," he smiled, leaning over and kissing her hard on the lips.

"Stop it, my lord," she giggled, pushing him away gently. "We have guests. If I have to play the good wife, then you have to play the good lord."

Tomas slapped her arse playfully, looking around his entourage with a smile. "You hear that, boys? We have to behave like proper folk. Your lady has commanded."

The soldiers behind them broke into laughter. They were hard men, but they were good souls with it. He had kept on fifteen of his comrades from the war as his personal guard, men he had stood shoulder-to-shoulder with on the battlefield fighting the Raskans. Plus his sergeant, now *Captain* Farrell Ginspot of Lord Bannar's household guard. They still laughed about it over drinks. They all did.

He had only brought ten of them down to meet the little lord. The others were back at the keep. They had moaned, but he had made them dress in their full gear; chainmail, breastplates, helmets, light grey tabards bearing the simple sword motif he had drawn up as his emblem.

Don't want to ruffle the little brat's feathers.

"I wish they'd told me why he's coming here, of all places," uttered Tomas as the group came to a halt before them. A soldier dismounted and opened the door of Cecil's carriage, allowing him to step down carefully into the mud.

"As long as he isn't going to take you away from me to fight in some stupid war, I don't care," said Talia.

"Don't worry," smiled Tomas, stroking her cheek gently. "I'm done with killing people for money. I'm done with killing people for lords and their ambitions. I'm not leaving you. Ever."

"Good," she said, the worry in her bright blue eyes not subsiding.

"Greetings, Lord Bannar," said the young noble, splashing carefully through the mud as he approached and extended a soft hand. "Cecil Cramwall, son of the Lord Chancellor."

"Call me Tomas." He took the hand, shaking it firmly. The grip was weak, almost slimy. "It is a pleasure to meet you, my lord."

"I don't think that would really be appropriate, Lord Bannar," replied Cecil.

"Allow me to introduce my wife, Lady Talia," said Tomas, hurrying through the introductions.

Cecil smiled through the rain, kissing Talia's hand. Tomas smiled at her discomfort as she conducted an uncoordinated curtsy. "It is a pleasure to meet you, my lord."

"And who is this magnificent specimen?" asked Tomas, turning his attention to the tall, sleek, black form stood beside Cecil, clad in dark leather.

"This is Q'thell, my personal bodyguard."

Tomas looked Q'thell up and down, his eyes taking in the swords strapped to the other's back. Slender, sharp, deadly. He got the same impression of the red-eyed figure bearing them.

"A Q'shari, yes?" asked Tomas, extending a hand.

"Indeed, my lord," replied Q'thell, taking the hand. The men gripped each other for a second, each measuring the other. "It is a pleasure to meet a real warrior such as yourself."

"I've never met a Q'shari before," said Tomas. "I hear you guys are the real warriors. No doubt you have interesting tales to tell, Q'thell."

"You have no idea," sneered Q'thell.

"Captain Ginspot here will set you and your men up with lodgings in the barracks at the keep, Q'thell. I am sure you are tired from your journey and eager to get out of those wet clothes."

"Thank you," smiled Q'thell, giving a slight bow.

"I've had a room made up for you at the keep, my lord," said Tomas, inviting Cecil to join him as they walked through the gates of the town. "I've arranged a feast in honour of your visit. No doubt you'll be wanting the warmth of a hearth and a belly full of decent food after your jaunt through the Bleakthorns."

"Indeed," said Cecil, looking about him as they strolled through the mud. "The rain has been incessant. I long for some... rustic... hospitality."

Tomas smiled. "Our town is basic, I'm afraid, my lord. Not what you are used to in Regalla. The land is bleak, we are remote. We cannot help the weather or the resources we have at our disposal, but hospitality is something we have in good measure."

"I am sure," smiled Cecil distractedly. It was raining heavier again now, falling on his thinning hair. "How far is the keep, may I ask?"

"Less than half a mile, my lord."

"Good," said the youth hesitantly. "I could do with a bath. A feast sounds just the thing to raise my spirits. Tell me, what delights are served at Castle Bannar."

"We have stuffed chicken and the best mutton available in these parts," replied Tomas.

"Mutton? I prefer lamb, if I am honest."

"I don't see the point in slaughtering a good animal before it has had chance to live, my lord. To breed and to live. We have to be frugal with our resources out here."

"You're not one of those weird Pharma worshippers, are you?" asked Cecil, his lip curling disdainfully.

"No, my lord," said Tomas through gritted teeth. He felt Talia squeeze his hand gently. "The mutton is cooked to perfection, I assure you. My cook works wonders with the most basic of supplies."

Cecil didn't bother to respond.

Tomas looked to Talia, finding the calming blue pools of her eyes.

This is going to be a fucking nightmare.

Tomas Bannar's hall was, no doubt, to Cecil Cramwall's liking. He hadn't said anything, but the young noble had a habit of letting his disappointment show on his smug face. Tomas didn't much care. It was his home, and better than anything he could ever have imagined when he came round in a field physician's tent at the outbreak of the Third Raskan War, not even knowing his name, let alone where he came from.

He hadn't been recognised by any of the Castlander soldiers. He wasn't wearing any of the coats of arms of the various lords massing for battle. Not a Raskan; his hair was dark as night, his eyes equally so. Lord Oskar Tremelowe's men had found him by the side of the road as they headed east. A black eye and a scabby burn on the side of his head, but otherwise unharmed.

His injuries had healed quickly, and he had had nowhere else to go, so he had fought alongside them. Besides, he felt he owed them something for patching him up.

From unknown soldier to a lord of Castland. He felt ungrateful when he admitted to himself that he didn't feel comfortable in the hall. It was too big, too open. He felt exposed, inadequate.

The furniture was rough and functional, locally sourced. There were a few tapestries, basic and inelegant, mostly gifts from the local common folk. The candles that helped the torches in the wall sconces light the room were tallow, apart from the ones on the top table. Tomas had laid on a few of the best beeswax ones from a nearby candlemaker. He wouldn't normally bother, but he had company, and it would be expected.

It wasn't that he was miserly. Tomas had no interest in money, really. He allowed his castellan, Robert Edens, deal with most of the financial affairs in his lands. He kept an interest, but he trusted Edens to administer things as he would like. They knew each other well enough, having fought side-by-side during the war.

It had become apparent to them both that the new martial lords, raised from amongst the commoners in recognition for their service during the war, were not intended to be as rich as the established aristocracy. They were needed to take ownership of the lands wrested from Raska, and provide a competent buffer against retaliation. A couple had taken lands closer to the heartlands of Castland, handed the estates of families who had completely perished with no heirs during the fighting, but those men were high ranking officers before the war, and were distant relatives of longstanding nobles.

Tomas and Robert had pored over the finances, making savings where possible. They kept the tax rate low; much lower than the tithes set as standard by the Lord Chancellor in Regalla. Was that what Cecil was here about? Low taxes lessened the burden on the people, but it meant less money coming into Tomas' estate. Letting the tenants buy their lands was also an indirect drain on his funds.

He didn't want the gold for himself. His main worry was the outer wall of the keep; solidly made of strong oak, but still a lot more vulnerable than cold, hard stone.

Tomas broke away from his thoughts as Cecil took his first taste of the mutton stew, placing it delicately in his soft mouth, the shiny cheeks moving as he chewed. He took a glance at Talia and Robert, said to his opposite side, raising his eyebrows. Robert's kind eyes squinted as he burst into a gentle snigger. He raised the hook that replaced his left hand, lost in the war, in a vain attempt to cover his laughter. Cecil's cold, blue eyes settled on the castellan.

"Is the food to your liking, my lord?" asked Tomas, scowling gently at Robert.

"It is adequate," said Cecil, continuing to chew. "What do you say, Q'thell?"

"It's meat," shrugged the Q'shari from his chair beside the young lord, stuffing it down. "It's overcooked, but you humans overcook everything, so that's the be expected."

Tomas was surprised that Cecil had insisted his bodyguard sit with them at the top table. He had no rank or title, after all, and the Lord Chancellor's son seemed obsessed with such things. It didn't bother Tomas, he would happily sit and eat with anyone of any standing, but he suspected the action was intended as some sort of slight. If it was meant to offend, it hadn't worked.

"It's better than this stuff you call wine," said Cecil, gesturing to the simple pewter goblet before him. "Is it off?"

"It is mead, my lord," said Tomas, taking a swig from his own drink. It was dry, spiced, warming as it passed down his throat in the draughty hall. "Produced locally. The apiaries supply the honey, and the brewers make this fine beverage."

"Mead?" said Cecil, aghast. "But that is a drink for commoners. Do you have no wine?"

"Alas, we are a long way from the south, my lord," said Tomas curtly. "As you have seen and no doubt felt, the climate is a little cold for growing grapes."

"You are not wrong, Lord Bannar. It is bloody freezing in here." Cecil waved a hand in the direction of the nearest hearth. "Why in Argentis' name are these fires not lit?"

"It is not yet dark, my lord," replied Tomas patiently. Talia placed a hand on his thigh beneath the table, feeling the gritting of his teeth creaking through his powerful muscles. "We do not light the hearths until it is night. If you wish, we can get them stoked up for you. I forget that others are not used to the cold of the east."

He didn't wait for Cecil to respond. He raised his hand, beckoning over one of the serving lads. "Would you light the fires, please, lad?"

"Some hospitality at last," murmured Cecil, raising his eyebrows at Q'thell. The Q'shari didn't respond, turning his attention back to the food before him. "It is a shame it did not extend to ordering in some decent wine..."

"I am no expert in etiquette," snapped Tomas. He felt Talia's hand tighten on his thigh. "But I wouldn't dine at another man's table and pour scorn on the food and drink that he served. I wouldn't do it, because it is rude."

Cecil glared at the martial lord. Tomas picked up his bowl, draining the dregs of the juices and wiping his mouth with the back of his sleeve. He met Cecil's stare, the dark eyes hard and unflinching. Q'thell shifted absently, smiling as he picked up his own bowl and poured the gravy down his neck.

"I apologise, my lord, I forget my manners," said Cecil eventually, the words sticking in his craw. "Tell me, how fare things out here? Are all things well in the town of Bannar and the surrounding lands?"

Tomas grimaced at the town's name. It sounded so vain, naming a town after yourself. It hadn't been his choice. The martial lords hadn't been given the freedom to name their own lands, after all. Each was named after the newly-appointed lord. "We are as content as we could hope, my lord."

"No problems with the Raskans?" asked Cecil.

"What is that supposed to mean?" asked Talia, her own restraint faltering now.

"Oh... Well, I didn't mean the townsfolk. I meant invaders. Raiding parties from across the border. Your wife is a... er... a Raskan, Lord Bannar? Interesting."

"She is of Raskan heritage, yes," said Tomas carefully. It was his turn to place a calming hand on Talia's leg. "What of it?"

"Nothing, my lord," insisted Cecil. "I meant no offence. Lady Talia is a lovely woman, and you seem very happy. This makes me happy. It is good to see the newest additions to the Castland flock mingling so seamlessly."

"That is down to the man you see before you," said Talia, kissing Tomas gently on the cheek and standing. She added the afterthought with her back to Cecil as she left the table, holding up the hem of the flowing grey gown that Tomas had presented her with before the meal. "My lord."

"I meant no offence, my lord," said Cecil. "I was merely enquiring as to whether you require any assistance from the Lord Chancellor when it comes to the security of the realm? To the security of your lands? *Our* lands..."

Tomas raised an eyebrow suspiciously.

What does he want?

"As you can see, my lord, the outer wall of the grounds around the keep is wood. I would very much like to replace this with stone, but I can afford neither the materials nor the masons. If the Lord Chancellor would like to..."

"Interesting," pondered Cecil, interrupting the martial lord. "I will raise this with my father when I return to Regalla. Although we have much to discuss before then. It may be that the capital has needs too. A reciprocal arrangement may in everyone's interests."

"What do you mean?" asked Tomas hesitantly.

"We can discuss the boring details another time," smiled Cecil. "Free from the ears of bodyguards and castellans. I thought tonight was about celebrating? I blame myself for darkening the mood. Please, is there any entertainment?"

Tomas nodded. Robert left the table, heading off to organise the act they had prepared.

"Do you hunt, Lord Bannar?" asked Cecil cordially, his tone reconciliatory.

"I don't," replied Tomas. "I've killed enough in the life that I remember. I don't feel the need to do so as a hobby."

"Shame," sighed Cecil. "I do love to hunt. I was hoping we could head out tomorrow. The wilds of the east must contain some good sport."

"If you wish to hunt, I will accompany you my lord, as a courtesy. We can serve your kill up as tomorrow's supper."

"I hear there are bears in the east," smiled Cecil. He was rubbing his small hands together now avariciously. "I have never hunted a bear before. A magnificent beast. One would make a magnificent trophy; a memento of my visit to the eastern wastelands."

Q'thell's interest in the conversation had returned. The slender black figure leaned in close again, listening intently.

"Will you be eating bear tomorrow evening?" asked Tomas, watching as Robert returned with the entertainment.

A young lad entered the room, accompanied by several of the girls from one of the nearby villages. His name was Iain, the son of one of the apiarists. He was only twelve, but his skill with the bow he carried was like nothing Tomas had ever seen. Tomas clapped his strong hands together as the lad began to set up.

"Who in Argentis' name eats bear meat?" asked Cecil, a look of disgust crossing his rosy cheeks as he took another deep swig of the mead he had been deriding only minutes before.

"Nobody I know," replied Tomas. "If you aren't going to be eating it, then you're not hunting it. We'll track a boar. That'll make a nice meal for supper."

Cecil nodded reproachfully. Q'thell deflated slightly at his side.

"Watch this lad, my lord," said Tomas, leaning in closer to Cecil. "Every man over fourteen in my lands trains twice-weekly with the sword or the spear. We need to be ready for attack, every one of us. On top of this, every man, woman and child over the age of five trains twice-weekly with the bow. This lad is only twelve years old..."

Cecil watched, his mouth dropping open as the lad levelled the weapon at one of the young girls who stood in front of them, and apple balanced delicately on her head. Tomas smiled as Iain closed his eyes, releasing the bowstring.

The martial lord didn't flinch as the arrow flew between their faces, pinning the apple to the wall behind them. His dark eyes met Cecil's as they slowly opened, the tense flinch loosening the young lord's muscles.

Tomas smiled hollowly.

Take that in the manner it's intended, you little shit...

To Cecil's side, Q'thell was clapping his slender hands together loudly, his sharp, white teeth flashing behind his laughing black lips.

"You shouldn't rile him," smiled Robert, leaning back in the chair beside Tomas' bed. "He's a dangerous man to offend, Tomas."

"*Man?*" Tomas burst into raucous laughter, draining the goblet of mead before him and reaching to refill the men's cups. He sat on the bed, looking at his old companion. "He's a fucking boy. Every ten-year-old in these lands is more of a man than him. Did you see his fucking face when Iain shot that apple off the girl's head? You'd think it was balanced on his noggin!"

"Quiet, Tomas," laughed Robert into his drink. "Sound travels in this keep. He'll hear you."

"Fuck him," said Tomas. "The boy's a whelp. If I was a haughty son of a bitch then I'd be insulted that the old man sent him to speak with me. What do you think he wants?"

"I think he wants to hunt bears and get pissed on good wine," said Robert. "It's not what he wants you should be worried about. It's what the Lord Chancellor wants that should worry you. He's sent his only son halfway across Castland to speak with you."

"Maybe he wants to build a wall around my keep," shrugged Tomas. "Guerro knows we'll need it if it all goes to shit with the Raskans again."

"He won't give you a wall for nothing. The old man's as tight as an eel's cunt. And as slimy. He'll want something in return."

"What?" asked Tomas, gesturing to the bottle on the bedside table. "Young Cramwall didn't seem too impressed with the mead. It's pretty much all we've got. Unless you mean he's found out about the tax rates..."

"Possibly the rest too," said Robert, staring at the liquid in his cup as he swilled it around drunkenly. "Letting peasants own land isn't going to be popular, Tomas."

"Well if that's his price, he can go fuck himself."

"Be careful, Tomas. It wouldn't be wise to defy the Lord Chancellor."

"I'm a lord too, aren't I?" shrugged Tomas. "I can do what I want with my lands. I pay my gold to the crown's coffers. What I do other than that is my business."

"You don't know how these men think, Tomas," warned Robert. "They don't like change. They don't like being defied. You might be a lord, but you aren't like them. You don't think of yourself as one, not really, and that's your choice. But you need to remember, just because you suddenly decide to act like one, they won't accept it. To them you're still a commoner. A jumped-up commoner, but a commoner nonetheless."

"Are you calling me a commoner?" roared Tomas, draining the last of his mead and throwing the empty goblet at his old friend. He paused for a second before bursting into laughter.

"Yes, I am," laughed Robert, throwing his own empty cup at the martial lord. "Just be careful, Tomas. I know what these bastards are like. I've seen it first hand."

"Here we go," smiled Tomas. "Robert Edens, squire to knight whatever-his-face was of wherever. How did you end up fighting with the likes of me if you were a fucking squire?"

"The knight died. You know that, Tomas."

"Well, I hope you do a better job defending me, Robert." Tomas reached out a strong arm, slapping it on his friend's shoulder with a smile.

"I'm a one-handed castellan with a knackered back," laughed Robert, squeezing Tomas' shoulder with his hand. "You can fight better than any man I know. You don't need me to defend you. But you do need me to watch your back. You don't know these men, and you don't know what they're capable of. Defy them if you must, but don't insult them to their faces."

Both men turned to the door to the privy as Talia emerged, her toned figure wrapped in a towel after her bath. Her damp blonde hair stuck to her shoulders as he looked the pair of old friends up and down. "I'm sorry if I'm intruding on your clinch."

"Get out of here," smiled Tomas at Robert, pushing the man towards the door gently. "I have to make my apologies to my wife."

"Do you want me to rebuild the fire, Tomas?" asked Robert. The three of them turned their eyes to the dying embers, the remains of Talia's smoking dress still recognisable after she had tossed it into the fireplace.

"When have I ever asked you to sort my fire?" laughed Tomas, shooing his friend from the room. "Besides, we won't need the heat in here."

He closed the door behind Robert, getting to his knees and moving back towards his wife.

"You'd better beg, you bastard," snapped Talia, her face softening as he reached her, pulling the towel loose from her body. "He's a fucking cunt, and you made me dress up for him like a prize mare."

"I'm sorry, my love."

She gasped as he pressed his face into her womanhood.

"This place is a fucking shithole," groaned Cecil, sitting on the bed in his chambers. He reached out to the bedside table, refilling his goblet with mead and taking a sip. "Shit food, shit drink, shit women, shit weather."

"You seem to be getting that down you," said Q'thell absently, leaning back in the chair across the room, using the razor-sharp knife in his hand to trim his nails.

Cecil sensed the smile on the Q'shari's face. He let his rage subside, breathing deeply, a smile slowly crossing his face. "In fairness, it is quite good. But listen to me, Q'thell. This place has got me appreciating a drink made for commoners. What was my father thinking?"

"Didn't he brief you on what was expected?" asked Q'thell, red eyes squinting as he looked at the nails on his black, slender fingers. He nodded, satisfied, swapping the knife between his hands with a flourish and beginning to work on the other one.

"Bannar needs to stop coddling his peasants," said Cecil, leaning back in the bed, nursing the cup. "Tend the fire, would you?"

Q'thell sighed irritably, moving over to the fire and throwing a few logs on. He stabbed at it with the poker, imagining it was Cecil's head, before returning to his seat.

"I've got the leverage," pondered Cecil. He turned his attention back to the Q'shari. "You saw how I did that, yes? Found out what he wants. Father always says the most important thing in a negotiation is getting to the crux of what your opponent wants. You can work with that."

"Yes, it was very clever. Tell me, what does he want, then?"

"He wants a wall," declared Cecil. "I can use that to manipulate him. He can have it, in exchange for putting his people back in their place."

Q'thell sighed. It was like dealing with a child. "I don't think you really understand what he wants. Why does he want this wall, do you think?"

"To hide behind if there is an invasion by the Raskans," said Cecil bluntly. He shook his head, sipping at the mead delicately. "To defend himself. Honestly, Q'thell, do you know nothing of human culture."

"*Culture?*" hissed Q'thell under his breath, shaking his head. "Is it to defend himself? Or is it to defend his people? The man gives them land, keeps their taxes low. You told me these things. And yet you think he wants a wall to hide himself behind whilst they suffer?"

Cecil paused for a second, quaffing the remnants of his cup whilst he mulled Q'thell's words over in his head. He poured himself another drink thoughtfully. "He cares for these commoners. You're right. Did you see the servant? He actually *asked* him to light the fires. He said please, for Argentis' sake. This simple fool actually *cares* about these people…"

"So," said Q'thell coaxingly, sliding the dagger into a sheath beneath his arm and leaning forward on his knees. "His motivation is protecting his people. If you tell him he can have a wall, as long as he fucks them over, what do you think he will say?"

"He will refuse," mused Cecil.

"Or he'll agree, until his wall is built. Then he'll go back to his way of doing things."

Cecil tutted. "Q'thell, that would be dishonourable. A man's word means something to us humans."

Q'thell leaned back, resigning himself to the fact that the fat human cub was a slow pupil. "I don't really think he gives a fuck about your honour or your ridiculous etiquette. He's a warrior, not some breastfeeding pup."

"So, I should prey on that which motivates him," pondered Cecil, ignoring the Q'shari's disdainful tone. "If he will not acquiesce, I will allude to the fact that he is putting his poor folk in danger."

"I don't think that's going to work," said Q'thell. "He's a hard man. He's strong, and he's stubborn. And if he treats his people as well as it seems, they will fight for him, because he will be fighting with *them*. You don't think tonight's entertainment was just a little fun? It was a threat."

"He wouldn't be so stupid as to threaten the son of the Lord Chancellor."

Q'thell shrugged. "When you look into a man's eyes, do you actually see anything other than pupil and iris? Look harder next time. Don't concentrate on staring yourself. Read what he is telling you in his gaze. Bannar will do what he thinks is right. The consequences are immaterial."

Cecil paused for a while before draining the goblet. He nodded to Q'thell sincerely. "You give good counsel, my friend. I will try to appeal to his better nature, to his sanity. If Bannar will not listen, then it may be that we need to remove him as a threat."

"You're going to kill him?" chuckled the Q'shari. "Another duel? I think you'd have stood a better chance with the Barralegnan."

"If we have to kill him, then you will be the one doing it," said Cecil, pushing himself down beneath the thick blankets on the bed. "I cannot fail my father. He expects me to return with news that this matter has been resolved. I will not let him down again. I cannot abide the humiliation, and I certain cannot abide the bruises."

Q'thell leaned forward in his chair again as the young lord curled up in bed, his muscles tensing with anticipation. Was it anticipation? He lived to fight, to spill blood, and yet this martial lord unsettled him somehow. It wasn't just the physique, although the man certainly was intimidating. Not the biggest of men, but he appeared made of iron. It wasn't just the eyes; the man's mind was strong, it showed in his glare. It showed in the way he carried himself. Bones clad in thick muscle could still break. Muscle and bone clad in metal could still be torn and battered. But it took a certain kind of steel on the inside of a man to make him truly deadly. Bannar looked like the kind of man who would try to rip out your throat with his teeth even if both his arms were severed.

And there was more. There was an air about the man. Q'thell could sense it. It played across the hairs on his skin, seeped into his eyes, filled his lungs.

He stood slowly, slipping out of the door into the corridor of the keep.

Is this anticipation? Or is it trepidation...?

Chapter Twenty-Three

Lord Perlis hugged Xavier as he strode into the hall, gripping him tightly. It pained him that his son insisted on spending so much time out in the hills, away from his home, but this time it had been necessary. He had needed someone he could trust in the midst of the peasants, to guide them in their actions, steer them in the right direction.

"Thank you for keeping him safe," said Perlis, turning to the two soldiers flanking Xavier. They had removed their peasant garb and were back in livery no that they were in the safety of Bloodstone.

"It is he who keeps us safe," replied one of the men, bowing to his lord. "And you, my lord."

Perlis smiled, turning his attention to the man who accompanied them in the gloomy hall. "And who might this be?"

"This is Jaspar Ratcliffe, the leader of the group from Regalla," replied Xavier, gesturing gently for the man to step forward.

"It is an honour to make your acquaintance, Lord Perlis," said Ratcliffe, bowing his head slightly.

"I am glad to finally meet you in person, Jaspar," said Perlis, gliding across the floor to the reporter and extended a pale hand.

"I..." Ratcliffe faltered as he took the hand. The grip was strong but cold as ice. He struggled not to flinch, avoiding the urge to pull away. "In person, my lord?"

"Yes, Jaspar," smiled Perlis. Ratcliffe shuddered as he noticed the prominent, glistening canine teeth in the lord's mouth. "I have sent you much correspondence over the years. News I felt that would be of interest to the People's Gazette."

"That was you?"

Xavier laughed, patting Ratcliffe on the back reassuringly. "I told you my father is not like other lords, Jaspar."

Ratcliffe nodded gently, his head limp on his neck. Lord Perlis was different, and not just in his views, it would seem. The graceful movements of the man were almost disconcerting. It was difficult to keep the eyes focused on him, as if he shimmered as he slid into motion. There was an almost otherworldly aura about him.

"But why?" asked Ratcliffe, finding his voice.

"Partly mischief," admitted Perlis, gesturing for Xavier and Ratcliffe to sit at his table. He dismissed the two soldiers as a servant scurried in, placing a cup of water and a bowl of steaming root vegetable soup in front of the agitator. "Eat, please, Jaspar."

Ratcliffe didn't need to be asked twice. He was famished. His clothes were wet from the rain and his stomach growled as he tore a chunk off the hard bread placed on the table, dipping it in the hot broth and stuffing it down.

Perlis noticed his shivering and gestured for the servant to like the fire in the hearth. "You see, Jaspar, it is partly that myself and Lord Unstead do not get along. I enjoy causing trouble for him. That is why I sent you some of my peasants, to bolster your numbers."

"It's more than that, though, isn't it?" asked Ratcliffe, pausing in devouring the food before him. "Some of the news you've sent me isn't related to Unstead. The generous nature of Lord Bannar in the east, for example. Why tell me of that?"

"You are astute, Jaspar, I will give you that. The truth of the matter is that I do not admire the established order of this land. It is unjust, balanced in the favour of a few noble families. The rest of us suffer, to some degree or another."

"You are a lord, though," said Ratcliffe warily. "I don't see you suffering like the poor folk."

"It is true, the oppression in this land of ours affects some more than others," admitted Perlis. He poured wine for himself and Xavier, offering the carafe to Ratcliffe.

"No, thank you, my lord. The water is fine for now."

"But many of the nobility are bonded into a form of miserable slavery by the system of government in Castland. In most cases, unhappy lords pass this unhappiness down on their people, because they are powerless to challenge the natural order of things and it is the only way they know to ease their own plight."

"And you don't do that?" asked Ratcliffe, still wary of the almost ethereal man before him.

"Ask around my people," shrugged Perlis. "You are free to talk to them, and they are free to speak honestly with you. My people are happy, content. That is because I care for them. And I understand that

I am the same as all lords. I cannot fight the machine of Lord Chancellor Cramwall alone. We need to give power to the people. They need to *take* their freedom. There are men like myself who will support them."

"You want the people to revolt?"

"Against the right foe, yes," nodded Perlis. "That is why I give you information. The common folk need to realise that they are many, and the establishment are few. But nobody can force that view on them. They need to figure it out for themselves."

Ratcliffe felt Xavier's gentle, purple eyes settle on him. As he looked at Perlis' son, he felt something else. A scratching in his head, not an itch on the scalp, but a gentle irritation *inside* his skull. He shook his head, trying to clear the flashing spots that briefly gathered in his vision.

"I can tell you are sceptical, Jaspar," smiled the silver-haired youth reassuringly. "But my father is genuine. He has given you no reason to doubt his veracity. He has helped you at every turn. How do you think you got the money to start your journal?"

"I took out a loan with a low-level banker in Little Yanar," replied Ratcliffe, suddenly doubting his own words.

"And who do you think facilitated that loan?" asked Xavier. "Why would a Yanari take the risk of lending gold on a risky investment. A man who wanted to upset the status quo. Most unlike a humble Yanari, yes?"

Ratcliffe didn't paused. Xavier made a strong point. He decided to divert the conversation. "Assuming you are genuine, my lord, what do we do now? It will be dangerous for me and these people back in Regalla, once word spreads of what happened here."

"And yet you must go back, Jaspar," insisted Perlis. "You have important work to do. These common people have important work to do. You all need to spread word of the injustice that happened to the south. You need to let the poor folk know that they *can* challenge the order, and that they can win."

"Hard to do that with your head mounted on a spike…"

"I will come with you, Jaspar. My men will keep you safe from Unstead's malicious intentions, and I will plead your case to the Lord Chancellor."

"I thought you were also one of the oppressed masses, Lord Perlis," said Ratcliffe, more curtly than he intended.

"Indeed," smiled Perlis, sensing the agitator's discomfort. It was, indeed, an undesirable position for a man to find himself in. "But I am still a lord. Cramwall will listen to me. And Unstead has imprisoned a family from the capital for doing nothing more than travel a common road. The Lord Chancellor is many things, but he is aware of the threat to his precious order if the poor folk take exception to this. And the word is already out, thanks to you and the People's Gazette."

Ratcliffe had forgotten about the imprisoned family. Events had gotten out of hand very quickly, so much so that his concern for his own welfare had pushed the original reason for their march out of his mind. Were they alright? What would happen to them now?

He was interrupted in his reverie by the doors to the chamber opening, one of Lord Perlis' men striding in. He marched up to the table quickly, urgency in his steps. "My lord, we have more visitors."

"Who?" enquired Perlis, catching the soldier looking suspiciously at Ratcliffe. "It is alright, sergeant. Jaspar here is a friend."

"A man called Tayuk has arrived at the gates of Bloodstone, my lord. He insisted you would recognise the name. Says he's rescued to Yanari family from Lord Unstead and needs shelter."

Perlis' lip curled up into a gentle smile as he cast the indigo eyes over Ratcliffe. "So now we have witnessing to Unstead's crimes. A strong case, would you not say, Jaspar? Get them into the warm, sergeant. Feed them. Once they are settled, bring the man of the family to see us."

"The father didn't make it, my lord. Lord Unstead himself put a crossbow bolt in his back."

"The plot thickens," pondered Perlis, his hand moving to his shattered face, the smile on the opposite side creeping up into an avaricious leer. "Get them all fed and nourished. The Regallans too, including Jaspar here. Ready the men. We head for the capital at dawn. The Lord Chancellor will have no choice but to listen to us now."

Tomas sat opposite Cecil at the desk in his small study, wiping the sweat from his forehead. It was only late afternoon, but the little lord has insisted on the fires being lit. Tomas watched as the youth took a deep gulp of the mead that he had only yesterday being disparaging, before pulling his leather jack off pointedly and tossing it across the room onto a simple leather couch.

The hunt had gone as planned. Tomas didn't want to be spending days out in the rain trailing an animal just so Cecil could quench his bloodlust. His own trappers had netted a boar that morning, and released it just ahead of their group once they were a few miles from town. The trail was fresh, even the little lord could track the animal. They'd come upon it in a small clearing.

In fairness, the lad wasn't a bad shot with that ugly gunpowder contraption at his belt. He had hit the animal dead-centre, the weapon just didn't have enough stopping power to kill it. The Q'shari had despatched the injured beast quickly, and they had hauled it back. It was being prepared for this evening's meal as they sat.

Cecil was shuffling some papers in front of him on the desk. Tomas drained his goblet impatiently, pouring himself more mead. He was glad he was far from Regalla, where no doubt this drudgery was a way of daily life.

"A wall will cost a significant amount, Lord Bannar," pondered Cecil, the beady blue eyes settling on the martial lord. "My father will want certain assurances if he is to set aside gold from the crown coffers to build one."

"What assurances would those be, my lord?"

"The Lord Chancellor would need to be certain that your allegiance to the realm was absolute."

Tomas' eyes widened at Cecil's comment. "It is," he said bluntly, the anger in his voice tangible in the room.

"I am sure," smiled Cecil insincerely. "In the interests of good faith and honesty, though, I must admit I have some concerns. You have taken a Raskan woman into your bed, something that is most unusual."

"My personal affairs are exactly that, my lord," snapped Tomas. His patience with this boy was growing thin. Robert's advice seemed distant, fuzzy, muffled by the irritating presence of Cecil Cramwall. "Talia is as loyal as any of my citizens, and my people are as loyal as any other Castlander. Because they *are* Castlanders."

"And yet they do not hold to our values, my lord," said Cecil. "This is because you do not hold to our values. It is a question of leadership. You do not set the correct tithes. Word has spread as far as the capital that you are allowing commoners to own land. Not only that, you are actually *enabling* it. These are dangerous precedents, ones that are not in keeping with the natural order of this country."

"You question my leadership, Cramwall?" snarled Tomas, standing up to his full height, slamming his heavy hands on the desk. "When have you ever led men, boy? I don't mean those toy soldiers who followed you here because they were told to. When have you ever led men into battle? Led men to their deaths?"

Cecil shuffled uncomfortably in his chair, watching as the martial lord grabbed a two-handed greatsword down from above the hearth. "I was too young during the Third Raskan War, my lord."

Tomas swung the sword above his head, bringing to down towards Cecil. The youth flinched as it slammed down, burying itself in the desk. Tomas left it there, quivering with the force of the blow, pointing thick fingers at the nicks and scratches on the blade.

"Each one of those marks is a death, boy. A catch on a bone, an impact with armour. There's more men fell to this blade whose passing didn't even make a mark. I don't use it any more, never wanted it repairing. It hangs up there to remind me of the men I killed, and the men I lost. All in the name of Castland. Don't you ever insult my honour or my leadership again, or I swear to Guerro I'll tear you apart with my bare hands. I represent the values of Castland better than you, you fucking whelp."

Cecil pulled his eyes away from the sword, levelling them on Tomas. He felt his own outraged anger bubbling in his chest as he stood. How dare this thuggish brute speak to him in this way? The heir to Lord Chancellor Oliver Cramwall of Castland.

"I will have you know, my lord, that I can trace my lineage back to the first king of Castland. The blood of Castor runs through my veins, pure as any of the noble houses of this country."

"I can tell," sneered Tomas, moving close to the spoilt brat, pressing his grizzled features close to the shiny face. "It shows in that receding, thinning hair. It shows in that weak jaw. It shows in those soft, waxen cheeks. Most of all, it shows in that smug, self-entitled, arrogant fucking attitude. I've had enough of that shit. I've got more than most, and I earnt it. These people earnt it for me. I'll never forget that. It seems you have, generations of bullshit ago. You need to leave my lands at dawn, otherwise I'll cleave off that fat head of yours and sent it back to your inbred father."

Cecil opened his mouth to speak. He struggled to find the words. Tomas shoved his head forward, causing the youth to wince visibly.

163

"Don't say a fucking word, *my lord*," growled Tomas. "Get out of my fucking sight, before I do something you regret more than I do."

Cecil tried to meet the stare, but the burning anger was too heavy. It seemed to sear his face. He couldn't summon the energy required to lash out himself. He didn't know if he had the courage. He backed away from the martial lord slowly, fumbling for the handle of the door before slinking out into the hallway.

Tomas stood for a second, breathing heavily.

What have I done?

He turned quickly, downing the contents of both goblets on the table before upturning it with a bestial roar.

Tomas sat at the table in the town hall, flanked by Talia and Robert, as the various men and women filed in. They took their seats quickly as a couple of servants attended to their drink requirements, pouring mead, ale, water, herbal tea.

"You didn't listen to an old friend's advice, then?" asked Robert gently. He could tell from the look in Tomas' sad, dark eyes that the meeting meant strife for them all. The martial lord was slow to anger, but once the cork was out of the bottle, it was difficult to stuff it back in.

Tomas didn't answer. He turned to Talia, placing a comforting hand on her lap as the congregation finished taking their seats and fell silent. She was not herself, he could sense it. He had thought she, of all people, would understand his anger, would have supported his words. Her reaction had been tepid. He stroked her cheek gently, urging her to look at him. She forced a smile, her deep blue eyes filled with worry.

"Why are we here, Lord Bannar?" called one of the crowd. "We're all missing a good meal. I hear there's boar for us up at the keep."

Gentle laughter spread through the room. Tomas insisted on keeping senior members of his people informed of events, and gauging their opinion on matters that involved them. Mayor Pennant of the Establishment Party, sat beside Robert, didn't like it, insisting that he should be on the only representative of the people consulted on such matters, but Tomas couldn't care less. He liked the views of the representatives. Some of them only had one person nominating them, but that didn't matter. Every person's view mattered and deserved to be aired.

Tomas stood, moving round to the front of the table. He looked around the assembled people. *His* people. Artisans, innkeepers, watchmen, and many others. He would consult with the representatives from the outlying villages later. This was urgent. There wasn't time to summon them.

"There is boar at my table," he said, raising his hands for order. "And you are welcome to it once Cecil Cramwall has finished eating. We'll eat after him. I don't want to be in his presence."

"This will be viewed most unfavourably by the Lord Chancellor," called out Mayor Pennant.

"That's why I've called you together so urgently," replied Tomas, glancing at the mayor and then returning his attention to the hall. "This afternoon, Cecil Cramwall insisted that I alter the way in which I administer these lands. He told me that the taxes must be raised against all of you. He demanded that I cease allowing you to purchase your lands when you have the necessary funds."

"What did you say?" called out Ivan, the owner of the Happy Raskan Inn.

The assembled townsfolk awaited the response eagerly.

"I may have inadvertently told him to go and fuck himself."

"Inadvertently?" called Pennant, attempting to make himself heard over the supporting cries of the townsfolk. "Inadvertently? I cannot imagine how one would inadvertently say such a thing, Lord Bannar."

"Alright," admitted Tomas. "I told him to fuck himself."

The supportive shouts of the people died a little as the mayor took his feet, calling for order. "This is a most precarious situation, people. We are citizens of Castland, and therefore the Lord Chancellor is our master. To insult his envoy, his *son*, is to invite the wrath of the country down upon our heads."

"So you've put us all in danger, Lord Bannar?" asked Ivan, the blue eyes looking questioningly at the martial lord.

"I admit that I have," replied Tomas, his gaze settling on the innkeeper, his face open. "That's why I have brought you all together. It's your necks that my words have put on the line, as well as my own.

Castellan Edens feels that the Lord Chancellor will not accept my defiance, and will move to snuff it out. In that case, we may have to fight."

"He wouldn't dare," called out Farrell Ginspot from the back of the hall in his position guarding the doors.

"He would," snapped Pennant, reaching out to the assembly. "And he will. I have warned against these ideas from the start. We must fall into line with the rest of Castland."

"You've warned against these actions because they don't fall into line with the views of your paymasters," snapped Tomas, turning on the mayor.

"And you did not listen, my lord. I am the elected representative of these people, and you have ignored my counsel. It is an affront to our democracy…"

"What's an affront to democracy, mayor, is that only you and your party were on the ballot paper when these people cast their votes," growled Tomas. He turned to the people. "How many of you would have voted for Mayor Pennant if there was another on the paper?"

The murmurings of the crowd were angry, their dislike of the mayor tangible. Tomas smiled.

"I put my proposals before you before I enacted them," said Tomas. "Robert warned that the nobles in the capital would not like them, but you voted for them anyway, and I followed through on your decision."

"*I* didn't vote for them," called Pennant. "And my vote is the one that matters."

"You were the only one who voted against," roared Tomas. "Your democracy is fucked, mayor. The people, the ones who matter, chose to have some freedom over their own affairs, over their own lives. Now the consequences of our decision are emerging, and I'm back asking you again; what do you want to do? If want to fall in line with the rest of Castland, reverse all that we've achieved, then I will go now and beg forgiveness of the fat Cramwall boy. If you want to maintain what we have built, then we may have to fight."

"Fight for Castland?" scoffed Ivan. "I fought against you in the last war. Why would I fight for you now?"

A reluctant murmur of agreement spread through some of the crowd, uncertain but audible.

"I'm not saying you'd need to fight for Castland, or for me," replied Tomas, his eyes pinned on Ivan. "You would fight for yourselves. For your families. For the way of life that *we* built here."

"My lord, we cannot fight the capital, the nobility." Robert spoke up reluctantly.

"Everyone trains at the martial pursuits," said Farrell. "The pampered little lord saw Iain's skill at the feast. He'll spread word to his father."

"Tell me, old friend," said Robert quietly. "Is every man, woman and child as proficient with the bow as young Iain?"

"Doesn't matter," insisted Farrell defiantly. "They can draw a bow. One man can judge the angle of fifty archers, make sure they're aiming true. In a battle, you don't aim *at* the enemy, you fire into the air."

"How many cavalry do we have?" asked Robert. His voice was sad, heavy with defeat. "The Lord Chancellor will have heavy cavalry. Only the Raskans have ever won a battle without heavy cavalry, and what they lacked in armour they made up for in numbers. How many warriors can we muster against the might of the capital?"

"So we just let the establishment fuck us in the arse, then?" snarled Farrell angrily.

"Friends, friends," called Tomas, looking from man-to-man. "How long have we known one another. You both raise good points, that's why we're here. To make a decision."

"What do you think, Lord Bannar?" called out one of the representatives.

Tomas turned to Talia, sitting uncharacteristically quiet at the table. She avoided his gaze, her beautiful blue eyes falling to the floor.

"I think we are doing the right thing in our small part of Castland." He turned to his people, pacing in front of them as they sat at the tables. "The lords scorn our way of life, because it threatens theirs. They have brought this row to our gate, not the other way around. Some of you were born Raskans, and this way of life is better for you. It was thrust upon you, but we have made it better for all. Some of you were born Castlanders, and your lives too have changed for the better. We have cast aside some of the shit that comes with being under the Lord Chancellor's yoke. You didn't realise it was shit until you saw how things *could* be.

"If we give up now, we'll go back to the old ways. It won't affect me much, I'm a lord after all. I'll be fine. But it *will* stick in my craw, because we had the chance to change things for the better. Those of

Castland birth will see the progress we've made slip away. Those of Raskan birth will hate something they see as new, but something that is actually how Castland has been run for centuries.

"We can give up all we've achieved and step meekly back into the past. Or we can be defiant. It's your choice, and either way you need to know I'll stand by you and play my part. If we choose to stick to our way of life, I will head to Kassell to seek Lord Tremelowe's support. He is our liege lord, and a good man. He's aware of what we are doing, and has never questioned me. His support, I am sure, will force the Lord Chancellor to leave us be."

"What if he does not support you, my lord," sneered the mayor, raising an eyebrow.

"Then I will reconvene this group and allow you to amend your decision. I will go down on bended knee and beg forgiveness. If you decide now that you don't want this, then I'll do the same this instant. The choice is yours."

Ivan limped forward, his eyes moving between Tomas, the mayor, Talia, Robert. "Are you certain this won't come to war, Lord Bannar? I have a family. I won't see them butchered like the Raskans in the war."

"Nothing's ever certain, Ivan," said Tomas. "I am sure that Lord Tremelowe will give us his backing, and I am sure that it will be enough. I'm asking if you all want to take the risk, and I am being honest, as always, that the path is uncertain. You think it's easy for me. I'm a lord, I've fought before, I have experience. The opposite is true. Being a lord isn't something I asked for, and it means that your lives weigh heavy on my mind. I've fought before, and I never want to have to do it again. If I thought this would lead down that path, then I wouldn't be standing here. I've seen the blood, heard the screams, felt the blows. It sucks the soul out of a man.

"But I do not have a family. Many of you do. So you must make your own decision with that in mind."

Ivan's eyes searched over Tomas' shoulder, seeking out Talia. She avoided his gaze, a tear trailing down her cheek.

"I am with you, Lord Bannar," called out one of the crowd.

Others followed suit. Farrell raised his hand in a fist, shouting from the back of the hall. "In peace or in war, I'm with you, Lord Bannar."

"I vote against this course of action," called Mayor Pennant, his voice already being drowned out by the cries of support. "As the elected representative of the Establishment Party I cast the only relevant..."

The people were on their feet now, crying out their backing. Tomas looked to Ivan, stood before him.

"I hope that you're right, Lord Bannar," said the innkeeper. His eyes flicked to Talia, but she had already turned her back, slipping out of the hall with her face in her hands.

Cecil gulped down the goblet of mead as he stood before the dresser in his room, staring at the simple mirror before him. He broke away from inspecting his reflection for a second to refill the cup, before resuming looking over his features; the ruddy cheeks, the loose jowls, the signs of a double chin gathering beneath his mouth, the hair thinning and receding.

He blamed his father. It was the Lord Chancellor who had given him these features. At least he wasn't short. People said he had his mother's height. He didn't remember, she had died when he was young.

"Am I ugly, Q'thell?"

The Q'shari was drying his black hair and skin on a towel after slipping in from the rain outside. He tossed the cloth onto the couch, shrugging his shoulders. "You are all ugly. Graceless. Inelegant. Too much meat on your bones, too little muscle."

"That is very reassuring," sighed Cecil, draining the goblet again and reaching to refill it.

"Why are you humans so obsessed with your appearance?" asked Q'thell, moving over to the window and staring out into the twilight, watching the rain hammer against the glass.

"It is important," said Cecil, confused by the question. "Especially when you are of high birth. People expect you to look presentable, a paragon of physical and mental excellence. It reminds the lowborn that we are better than them."

"This country is doomed, then," sneered Q'thell. "The nobles of the realm are amongst the ugliest of you humans. Physical perfection deserted them a long time ago. Most of them look like they're made of wax and got left too close to the fireplace."

"It doesn't matter I suppose," mused Cecil. He was thinking aloud, not really taking in his bodyguard's responses. "I am promised to the beautiful Kalyanit, so I have landed on my feet. It would just be nice if she looked upon me as a comely partner."

"So that's what you are worried about," laughed Q'thell. "Find a mate. I would not worried, my lord, your human women seem more interested in gold and status than finding a man who doesn't look like his face has melted."

Cecil drained the mead again, replenished his goblet, staring absently into the mirror. He swayed slightly as he stood.

"I take it Lord Bannar didn't take your point of view regarding the negotiations," said Q'thell.

"No, he did not."

"I told you as much. Too proud. Too righteous."

"What were they talking of at this little meeting?"

"He wanted the townsfolk to back him in telling you to… What were the words…? 'Go fuck yourself.'"

"And did they support him?" asked Cecil. His eyelids were heavy as he turned his gaze on Q'thell.

"Apart from the mayor. But he's one of your kind, isn't he? It's to be expected. They took some persuading, though. Some were less convinced than others. One of the innkeepers in particular seemed a little reluctant."

"So there is some dissent in this perfect little land he has created for the poor?"

"A little. But they did back him. They backed themselves. He gave them the choice."

"Then he leaves us no option. You will have to deal with him tomorrow. After we have set off for Regalla, double back with as many men as you need and rid us of this upstart martial lord. I cannot go back to my father and tell him I have failed."

"You think he'll prefer to hear that you had a lord of the realm murdered in the street?" asked Q'thell. There was a heavy weight in the pit of his stomach.

Eagerness or apprehension…?

"It needs to look like the common folk rose up against him," said Cecil, finishing his drink and crawling beneath the blankets on the bed. "You said it yourself, there was dissent at the meeting. The mayor will back those assertions, I will see to it. Lord Bannar was killed by some of his peasants who were disgruntled at his course of action. That will be the story."

"As you wish, my lord," nodded Q'thell, slipping from the room and heading back to his own lodgings.

Once in the room he locked the door. He slunk through the dark, rooting in the backpack stowed under his bed, pulling out a set of blood red candles. He arranged them in a line on the simple dressing table, kneeling before it to light each one in turn.

He hummed an incantation to himself as he passed his hand across the flames, before reaching again into the pack. He pulled out a small, silver knife. It was too small to fight with, he had never used it in battle before. Along the blade the name of Sanguis was etched in the old tongue of the Q'shari.

"Sanguis, hear the prayer of your servant," he hissed, running the razor-sharp blade across the tip of his thumb. Dark blood dripped from the wound. He held his hand over each candle in turn, praying in the ancient Q'shari language as, one-by-one, the blood extinguished the flames.

Q'thell knelt there in the dark as the last candle went out. "Sanguis, hear the prayer of your servant…"

Chapter Twenty-Four

The villagers trudged down the muddy road. At their head, Charo stopped in his tracks. Ahead the trees parted gently like natural curtains, thinning to reveal a village in the dip down the path. The people pushed in close behind him, following his gaze ahead. Charo looked to Mathias and Wrathson at his side, before glancing up at Father Pietr, sat awkwardly up on the only horse that wasn't pulling a cart.

All of them were cold and wet. It was slightly warmer than it had been previously, the frosts clearing, but that brought the driving rains. Charo didn't know which was worse. They didn't have enough tents. They were saved for the old and the infirm, along with the limited amount of space amongst the supplies in the wagons. Most of them slept beneath the elements, wrapped up in blankets, furs, cloaks, anything they could gather.

They needed a few nights beneath a roof. They had gold to pay for it; there had been a decent amount at the mayor's home, and more in the baronet's mansion. The question would be whether there was enough room for them. This village was larger than their own, it might have space if the common folk let them share their homes. But there were a lot of them.

Charo uttered a prayer to Lunaris under his breath. The God of Fear wouldn't let him down. He would provide for them. With any luck the people of this village would join their cause.

"Where is this?" asked Charo, calling ahead to Willem.

"Woodhaven," said Wrathson, before the hunter could answer. "Population: 237."

The group looked at him curiously. The sheriff smiled, pointing to the rough sign nailed to a tree at the edge of the cleared area surrounding the village.

"You don't remember it?" asked Mathias, looking to his younger brother.

Charo shrugged, shook his head.

"We used to live here," said Mathias. "This is where you were born, Charo. This is the village we used to live in."

"Then the people will remember you," said Father Pietr hopefully. The old priest slept in one of the wagons each night, but even so the travelling was already taking its toll on his old body. "They will let us stay for a while, under cover of a roof."

"It would be best if they didn't remember us," said Mathias. "We had to flee. Our father was put in the stocks for stealing bread, and they were going to do the same to us."

"Villagers always remember a face," said Wrathson gravely. "They'll recognise you, lads. They won't get many visitors passing through. Maybe this is too big of a risk."

Charo shook his head. "We need the rest. If the villagers recognise us, so be it. We have business with the sheriff here, anyway. If he's still around, he needs to answer for trying to punish two young boys for the crime of having a drunk for a father."

"So be it," said Wrathson. "It might be best if me and Father Pietr arrange lodgings first. We can sneak you lads in later. We're all tired, and if there's going to be a fight, it would be best if we all rested first."

"That sounds like a good plan, sheriff," smiled Charo. "We'll wait here for your return."

With that the young lad headed back amongst the villagers, advising them of the situation, ensuring they got settled and rested. Men cast off their backpacks, spreading blankets across the floor and leaning against the heavy bags as they rested. Families gathered together, huddling close for warmth. Mathias watched proudly as his younger brother moved amongst his followers.

You are becoming a man, Charo...

Q'thell watched from the shadows of the outbuilding as Lord Bannar strode across the yard through the dusk. This would be the last of his visits before he headed back to his wife's home in the town. The mayor had been forthcoming with the information. As he had suspected, the official had no respect for the lord of these lands. Bannar planned to visit each of the representatives again, the check that they had not changed their mind after thinking on their decision. He would then be setting out tomorrow morning for Kassell, calling at other villages on the way to ensure their representatives agreed with the course of action.

His last stop would be the bakery on the edge of the town. Q'thell knew this would be the best place to strike. There would be less chance of being disturbed out here. No witnesses. Plenty of places for him and his two accomplices to hide, to observe, to plan their strike. Kill the upstart lord, hang the placard written by Cecil around his neck, leave the body to be found.

"You still have the sign?" hissed the Q'shari to one of Cecil's guardsmen.

The man nodded, pulling it from the peasant rags he was wearing.

Our lord was a traytor.

Q'thell sneered. Cecil had insisted the misspelling would further demonstrate that Bannar's common folk had risen up against him. The Q'shari wasn't convinced, but then that didn't matter. He had a job to do, it was as simple as that. It would be a shame to extinguish the light of such a magnificent specimen; there weren't many humans that he classed as such. But Sanguis did not approve of sentiment, so he cast the thought aside.

He looked out into the yard of the bakery as Bannar approached. Leather armour. Longsword at his hip. He felt a shiver of adrenaline. His guts felt light.

"Are you ready?" he hissed at the two soldiers.

The men nodded reluctantly. He had briefed them, they knew what they were about to do. Maybe they were nervous about killing a lord of the realm. Perhaps they feared for their lives. Bannar would be a formidable opponent, by all accounts. And the Q'shari hadn't let them wear their armour, even under their rags.

Q'thell didn't particularly care. They were here to make the attack convincing. After all, one peasant couldn't very well kill a martial lord. Nobody would believe that. It would be him doing to killing, but three men had to be seen fleeing. He would silence the two men out in the wilds, to make sure their tongues never got loose about the evening's events.

"Come on," he snapped, pulling up his hood and striding out into the yard quickly, the two men at his heels.

Bannar looked up as they approached. He raised a hand in greeting. "Good evening, lads."

Q'thell stopped a few yards away, gesturing to the two men. They stepped forward, drawing swords.

"We're sick of you defying the crown, Lord Bannar," said one, struggling to remember his lines. "You must die."

Q'thell sighed at the man's stumbling words. He watched as they at least followed his guidance, spreading out to move in on the lord from both sides.

They were too slow though. Bannar had his sword out before they got into range, parrying the first one's swipe and deflecting him towards his counterpart, allowing his momentum to carry him onwards. The man looked on wide-eyed as the staggering soldier's sword plunged through his stomach. He groaned heavily, crashing to the muddy ground of the yard.

Q'thell shook his head.

Who trains these fucking idiots?

Bannar moved in, smashing the hilt of the blade against the off-balance guard's face as he was trying to dislodge his weapon from his comrade. The soldier dropped to all fours, blood flowing into the muddy puddles from his flattened nose.

Q'thell reached up, drawing the two slender, curved swords from the sheaths across his back. Bannar looked at him as he approached, the dark eyes taking in the figure before him.

"There are only two men in town your height," he said, circling away from the two stricken soldiers. "Both of them are much heavier built, though. So, you aren't from town, are you?"

Q'thell sneered, shaking the hood down to reveal his sharp, black features. "You'll be dead soon, so I'll allow you the courtesy of seeing the man who cut you down."

"The chubby little inbreed sent you, then."

"He did," nodded Q'thell. He tested the weight of the swords, slashing the air between them a couple of times. The razor-sharp blades sliced the air with a whoosh.

"Why?"

"Perhaps because you insulted him," shrugged Q'thell, moving from a casual stance to a testing strike in the blink of an eye. Bannar deflected the blow, holding his ground, ready for another. "Perhaps because his brain is addled. He has an unhealthy relationship with his daddy, maybe it has made him unhinged. I don't much care. I do as I am paid, as long as it suits me."

Q'thell lashed out again, both swords flashing together at Bannar's face. The martial lord moved quickly, backing out of range, his feet moving carefully in the mud.

Fast, for a human...

"I always heard the Q'shari were a proud race," said Bannar. His eyes were everywhere, watching the blades, the feet, the upper body movement, the eyes. "How did you become a lackey to a pompous oaf?"

Q'thell slashed again. Bannar caught the weapon in an arcing parry, twisting his blade quickly. The Q'shari pulled back, only just avoiding losing his grip on the weapon.

Impressive...

"I am proud," he said, trying to hide his surprise at nearly being disarmed. "I'm here because I *want* to kill you. Sanguis will favour me for sending her your soul."

Bannar struck quickly, the longsword swinging towards the Q'shari. Q'thell backed away under a flurry of blows, swords clashing and sparking. He struggled to find an opportunity to counterattack, but the martial lord was too quick, too relentless. It was all he could do to keep his footing and fend off the attacks. He caught Bannar's sword in a block in the cross of his weapons, leaning forward with all his strength to push the man back, regain some distance between them.

How is he so strong...?

The two figures stood ready, breathing heavily in the dark as they stared at one another.

"You can still leave," said Bannar. "My fight isn't with you."

"The words of a fearful man," sneered Q'thell. He lunged forward, a low drive at Bannar's waist with his right hand. The man deflected it, as expected, but there was no force in it. Q'thell saved that for the strike with his other weapon, bringing it down towards Bannar's head. The human was too quick again, his weapon back up in position, both hands gripping the hilt of his sword as he absorbed the heavy blow.

Q'thell grunted, trying to keep his momentum. He preferred to be on the attack, moving forward. He brought the first sword up again, trying to hack at Bannar's chest. The lord sidestepped away, spinning quickly and bringing his sword down on Q'thell's back. The blade dug deep into the leather, down to the skin. A long gash opened up as Bannar drew the sword along the wound, withdrawing again.

The Q'shari gasped in pain, feeling the unfamiliar cold of blood soaking his armour from an open wound. He regained his posture, trying to conceal his discomfort from his opponent.

"I'm not scared of you, Q'thell," said Bannar, his gaze pure steel. "I'm not scared of any man."

Q'thell's eyes glowed red, intense and pulsing. He could feel his heart beating in his chest, heavy and fast. He heard the blood rushing through his veins, flooding his muscles with power, gathering in the gash on his back. He allowed the red rage of Sanguis to fill him, his vision hazing over with righteous red fury.

The Q'shari roared forward, swords sweeping in a storm of slashes. Bannar backed off under the onslaught, deflecting blows as best he could, his footing uncertain in the churned mud. A blow caught him on the side, not biting deep enough into the leather as he twisted, but winding him all the same. Another strike slapped into his neck, but it was the flat of the blade. He managed to get his sword up for the next couple, but he was in retreat now. He stumbled, losing his footing in the slippery sludge.

Q'thell's eyes flashed, smelling victory. He struck, his sword cutting deep into the bicep of Bannar's sword arm. The wound opened up, deep and bloody, the leather around the gash puckering like moist brown lips. He moved in for the kill, teeth glistening in the growling mouth.

But Bannar's sword was back up, blocking the blow. He powered to his feet, meeting the next blow with his own weapon rather than parrying. He struck again and again, clashing each strike of Q'thell's swords with his own. The man's eyes were angry now, the impact of the blades crashing together causing the Q'shari's arms to ache. He could feel his grip weakening, his lungs struggling to inflate as he breathed. The rage within him weakened, something else seeping in to take its place.

Fear? How is he so strong? How is he so quick? He's just a human...

He fell back under the assault. Bannar had the longsword in both hands, smashing forward relentlessly. He roared in defiance, a primal battle cry. The impact of sword on sword dislodged Q'thell's grip, sending the ornate Q'shari blade flying into the mud with a splat. The next blow smashed the other one loose. Q'thell's red eyes with no longer slits, they were wide, staring helplessly at his empty hands.

Bannar brought his weapon down on the Q'shari's shoulder. The steel dug deep, the leather armour saving him from a fatal blow. He felt his collar bone crack, his left arm falling limply to his side as the force of the impact pushed him to his knees before the human.

No. Sanguis, not like this...

He lunged forward on all fours like an animal, grabbing Bannar's wrist with his right hand. He sank his teeth in to the hard muscle and sinew, the fangs sliding through the thick leather. He clenched his jaw, desperation rallying some primeval strength from within him. He felt the grip loosen, Bannar roaring in pain as the sword dropped from his hand.

The martial lord fell on him, raining down blows on the Q'shari's temple until he released his bite. They rolled in the slippery mud for a few seconds, each trying to get a decent grip on the other. Q'thell's slender fingers on his working hand slid across Bannar's face, trying to slip their way into the lord's screwed-up eyes.

Bannar came out of the struggle astride the Q'shari. He pushed the hand away, smashing at Q'thell's temple with his other hand. Once, twice, three times, each blow sending a tremor through the Q'shari's lean body.

So strong… So fast…

Q'thell's vision wasn't red with blood rage now, it was fuzzy, grey, fading in the gloom.

Bannar's thick hands were round his slender throat now, squeezing hard. As Q'thell gasped for breath, he almost felt sorry for the victorious man astride him. He didn't know the full depth of Q'thell's abilities. He didn't know that Q'thell had a tail…

Not many Q'shari were born with them these days. They seemed to be a throwback from their more primitive days living in trees and their branches. It had been a source of much mocking when he was young. Children were cruel, and Q'shari children could be *very* cruel. No human had ever seen it. It was thin, muscular, a black, furred, prehensile cord that he kept coiled in his trousers or round one of his legs.

He uncurled it now, the thin appendage slipping up to his armpit through the mud as Bannar pushed his full weight against his windpipe. Q'thell took a deep breath as the tail unclipped the sheath of the dagger under his arm. He just needed to hold out a few seconds longer, fight the flashing blackness as his vision narrowed like a tunnel ahead of him.

"Die, you fucking bastard," snarled Bannar, squeezing harder still.

"You… first…" gasped Q'thell, a sneer spreading across his face.

He slid the razor-sharp blade into Bannar's chest, the point slipping easily through the leather. The muscular tail tensed, shoving it straight into his heart. The man's eyes slid up into his head, as he fell to one side, his hands falling away from Q'thell's throat.

The Q'shari lay there in the mud, breathing deeply, the red eyes staring into the black sky. He was still alive, he was sure of it. He had won. The human was dead, and he lived. It felt a hollow victory, but he had won. His senses were dulled from the fight, from the choking, from the wounds, but his vision was beginning to clear now. His hearing started to tune into his surroundings. There was distant shouting, the sound of people approaching. He felt the pain of his wounds. His back was slashed, mud sucking up into the gash as he lay. He couldn't move his left arm. His collar bone ached dully. Blood soaked his shoulder. His throat ached from the squeezing, his face throbbed from the blows.

But they were distant pains. The adrenaline was still in him, and he was still alive. He had won.

Thank you, Sanguis, for protecting your servant.

The surviving soldier's blood-soaked face swam into view, eyes wide with fear as he shook the Q'shari desperately. "We need to go, sir. The baker, he's gone for help. There's people coming."

Q'thell pulled himself to his feet, searching for his swords. He saw one nearby, pulled it out of the mud. He couldn't see the other. His eyes flicked around the scene, saw the crowd approaching quickly.

"Let's go," he hissed, sliding into the darkness as quickly as he could. His movements were awkward, ugly.

What has this fucking human done to me?

He paused as they reached the shadows, turning back to watch as the crowd of villagers descended on the baker's yard. Most were distraught, their eyes searching the shadows, filled with grief and rage. Q'thell watched as Bannar's wife fell to her knees in the mud beside the body of her husband, desperately ripping the white shawl from around her shoulders and pressing it against the wound in his side. It soaked quickly with blood, black in the darkness of the night.

The woman arched her back as she knelt, her eyes staring vengefully up into the black sky, a howl of agonising grief splitting the air.

The noise sent a shiver down Q'thell's spine. He hesitated for a second, watching the human mourn her soulmate. He had killed that man, and it seemed from her screams that he had also killed her.

Is this the will of Sanguis?

Q'thell watched for a second as the people gathered round, letting out their own howls of mournful pain. He felt the grip of Cecil's guard on his arm, shook it away.

She should be proud. Her husband had fallen to the will of Sanguis. He had fought well against the greatest warrior ever to walk the Mortal World. But Q'thell realised that she didn't know that. It would appear to her that he had been killed by some peasants, some of her own kind.

But that wasn't his fault. It was the little Cramwall shit's fault. Q'thell had done his part, given his offering to Sanguis. He had never met his equal before, and it seemed that he still had not. The man had come close, but he had still been defeated. Sanguis was with him, and that was all he needed.

"We need to leave, sir."

Q'thell stared into the eyes of the frightened man, angry and disdainful. He'd deal with this whelp as soon as they got out into the countryside.

"Come on," he snarled, striding into the darkness, away from the wailing crowd.

Charo knelt by the simple grave, running his hand over the simple, mouldering wooden headstone. He could barely make out the words engraved in the warped wood as Mathias stood over him holding a lantern:

Raechael Culler
Dutiful wife of Paull Culler
Loving mother to Mathias and Charo
Taken during child birth

"Mother?" asked Charo, looking up at his brother with wide, tearful eyes.

Mathias nodded solemnly, running his hand gently over the moist wood. Beside him, Wrathson looked around them at the tombstones, his eyes warily checking the route from the village.

"We shouldn't be out here, Charo," he said. "What if someone sees us?"

"It's late, sheriff," said Charo, his eyes staring at the rotting marker over his mother's grave. "Nobody will be around."

"Charo doesn't remember visiting our mother's grave, sheriff," said Mathias. "Please, give him a moment. I haven't visited since we left, either. It has been too long."

Wrathson nodded, his hard features softening. "Hurry though, lads. If we're found out here there'll be trouble. I get the sense from talking to the locals that they're a bit on edge, and finding us creeping around the graveyard won't ease the tension."

Charo smiled gently, his sad eyes still focused on the wooden tombstone.

Wrathson and Father Pietr had done well. They had managed to source lodgings at the village's two inns, even if some were in stables and barns. The elderly and children had taken the best rooms, but even a hayloft or shed was adequate for the rest. A roof was all they really needed.

"I miss her," said Charo, tearful, dark eyes looking up at Mathias.

"Me too," replied his brother, kneeling down beside him and putting an arm around his thin frame. "She would be proud of you, Charo."

"Do you think so? Do you think she would approve of what we're doing?"

Mathias nodded. "She was a good woman. She was kind and gentle, Charo. You are trying to help people. She would be proud."

"Even though there will be violence?" asked Charo. "The nobles will not give up without fighting, Mathias. Would mother be in favour of that?"

Mathias hesitated. "She was a gentle woman, Charo. But I'm sure she would fight for what was right, if it came to it. I'm sure she would fight for us."

Charo sighed, looking down at the soft, rain-sodden earth in front of the grave marker. He pressed his small hand into the mud, pushing it deep, as though trying to get closer to his mother. "I just wish I knew for certain. I wish I could see her just one last time. I *need* her. I grew up without her, and that's fine, because I had you. But at this moment, I need *her*. Is it wrong that a man needs his mother in times of trouble? Does that make me weak?"

"No, lad," said Wrathson. "Every man needs his mother, sometimes. A mother gives you counsel you don't get from a father, or a brother, or any other man. Most men get married so they've got that influence in their life. Those that don't still yearn for their mother's hand on their shoulder."

The youths settled their gaze on the sheriff. He turned away quickly, staring back out into the darkness, uncomfortable.

172

"I wish she were here," said Charo, returning his gaze to his hand, buried up to the wrist in the earth. He felt a gentle shudder through his body, a slight rush that made his shoulders tremble. A slight purple haze seemed to come across his buried hand, violet smoke wisping up from the ground in the lantern light.

"What was that?" asked Mathias warily, jumping to his feet, gripping at his brother's shoulder.

"I feel something," said Charo, resisting Mathias' pull. He felt a trembling in the earth, gentle, a shifting in the mud. He squeezed the soil between his fingers, opening his hand again. The movement was soothing, welcoming, gentle. "Something in the ground."

"Get back, Charo," urged Mathias. The soil was moving now, trembling slightly as though being shifted beneath the surface. He reached for the hilt of the steel sword made by Edgar, the smith, before they had left the village.

Charo fixed him with a gentle smile, shaking his head. "No, Mathias. I can feel her. She is here, with us, now."

Wrathson looked to Mathias, reaching for his own weapon. They could feel it now, both of them. A presence in the dark of the graveyard, besides the three of them. It both soothed and unsettled Mathias, familiar and otherworldly. The hairs on the back of Wrathson's neck stood on end as a gentle wind rustled up out of nowhere, causing the flame in Mathias' lantern to gutter out.

"She's here," said Charo absently, his eyes seeming to give a purple glint in the light of the moon as he stared past Mathias and Wrathson. There was a tug at his arm as the soil shifted again, seeming to pull him towards it. The pair watched as he got to his feet, pulling upwards with his meagre frame. His hand emerged from the dirt, clasped around skeletal fingers.

Mathias drew his sword, raising it behind his head. "Get back, Charo."

"No," said Charo, fixing his brother with the flickering purple stare. "It's alright."

The ground shifted heavily as Charo stood upright, a delicate skeleton forcing itself from the earth before him. The limbs moved desperately, like a man swimming through the soil to the surface. Charo dropped to his knees beside the skeletal figure as it pushed itself close to him, a faint purple fire burning in its eyes as it hugged him close to its chest, mouldering bones wrapping around his back and head. Charo nestled into the empty ribs, a smile on his face as the glow subsided from his eyes.

"It's mother," he said, wrapping his arms around the hip bones of the skeleton before him.

The old corpse caressed Charo's dark hair gently with one hand, reaching out the other to Mathias as he stood, staring.

"What the fuck have you done, Charo?" gasped Wrathson, drawing his sword and looking to Mathias.

The skeletal figure turned its gaze to Mathias. Mathias looked into the purple eyes, the sword slipping from his grasp to the ground. He took the outstretched hand, allowing the skeleton of his mother to pull him down into her grip. She clutched them both tight, hugging them to her chest.

"It's alright, sheriff," said Mathias. "It *is* her. It's our mother."

Wrathson stood, sword raised, his jaw agape. "You've raised the fucking undead, Charo."

"I've done nothing, sheriff," said Charo, gazing into the faint purple glow within the eye sockets of the skeleton's skull and extending a pale finger to the moon overhead. "Lunaris has brought forth my mother, to guide me on my journey."

Wrathson looked up to the moon, shining down bright in the night sky. As he watched it hazed, a purple glow shimmering across the perfect disc in the heavens. He moved his gaze down slowly, meeting the matching violet light in the eyes of the apparition before him. He dropped to his knees, the sword at his side.

"I've missed you, mother," smiled Charo, looking up into his mother's empty eyes. "Tell me, are we on the right path?"

Chapter Twenty-Five

Magister Cinquis placed the polished human skull in the centre of the dark wood table in her chambers. The shiny wood was already engraved with a pentagram, saving her the effort of forming one. Magister Octus finished pouring the salt from a pouch around the circumference of the symbol and took his seat beside her.

Cinquis nodded her thanks, casting her eyes around the rim of the protective ward. Octus was perfectly capable, but it was prudent to double-check everything. She opened one of the large jars by her feet, a delicate hand slipping into the cloudy yellow liquid and pulling out the human heart stored inside. She waited for a few seconds, allowing the liquid to run off into the jaw, before she pushed the shrivelled organ inside the skull.

Octus opened another jar, producing several strips of flayed flesh. He carefully wrapped the skull in skin, covering as much of the bone as possible.

Cinquis smiled. They were ready. The flesh was important. It was vital to fool the summoned demon into thinking it was possessing a living behind, rather than a lifeless skull.

"Light the candles, my friend," she lilted.

Octus nodded. He was attracted to her, she could sense it. Most men were. He had never seen her face, but her elegant figure and graceful movements were enough to ensnare him. He waved his hand, the black candles bursting to life in a slight haze of purple smoke.

"Are you sure this is wise, Cinquis? Summoning without a name is risky."

"The tomes in the archives detail only the most well-known demons, Octus. They are noteworthy because they are powerful. The last one took much energy to control. We only want information, so there is no need to summon such a mighty creature. It is a waste of our strength."

"If you are sure…"

Cinquis took his hand, focusing her attention on the skull. She felt the power flowing through her as she rasped in the Demon Speech, merging with that of her fellow magister as she drew on his strength. He shuddered gently, his grip weakening slightly as she pulled from his resources. She took more of his energy than she donated of her own. He wouldn't know. Octus gasped out loud beneath his hood as she tugged one last strand of power from him, her vision flashing purple for a second as she dragged the beast into the Mortal World. Violet flames burnt away the flesh from the skull, smoke billowing out from the eyes and mouth.

Octus swayed in his seat. She reached out to steady him, keeping her eyes trained on the skull. The sockets had flickered to life, twinkling with orange light.

"It is here," said Octus, wiping the sweat from his brow beneath the robes.

"Tell me, who has answered our call?" said Cinquis.

A low, grumbling laugh emanated from the skull. The jaw didn't move as the demon spoke, its voice a malignant hiss. "I am insulted that you think I would give you my name so easily, bitch."

"You are wise. I apologise for any perceived slight."

There was a long silence. Cinquis shuddered as it closed in around her. The candles seemed to dim slightly, the shadows in the corners of the room appearing to writhe and shift. The skull trembled slightly on the table, as though trying to move across the wood.

"What is this prison?" rasped the demon. "You offered me a body to possess. You have given me a dead skull."

"Again, I must apologise for the deception. I need information. I need your sight of the Mortal World. I wish to know of distant events."

"Why would I give you anything, mortal? You have deceived me, and you have affronted me. I do not feel inclined to assist you."

"I am willing to bargain. Assuming you are able to give me what I need."

"A bargain." The demon paused, tangible malice creeping through the room. "Interesting. I can see the Mortal World from the other side. The view is clouded, but it is becoming clearer. My master may be able to clear it for me. If the price can be agreed."

"What do you want?" asked Cinquis, smiling beneath her hood. She had its attention.

The demon paused again. The orange glow in the eye sockets of the skull waxed and waned as it pondered. "A soul. Your soul."

Cinquis laughed gently, shaking her head beneath the hood. "No."

"His soul, then."

Octus turned his gaze on Cinquis. She could sense his fear. She pondered the demon's offer for a second. Her fellow magister was weak from the summoning, she could make the pact and he would be powerless to resist. She squeezed his hand gently, turning her gaze back on the skull.

"No," she said. Octus let out a sigh of relief.

"A sacrifice then," hissed the demon. Its patience was wearing thin. She could sense it pulling against her will, teasing apart the threads of the Mortal World, preparing to head back to the Astral Realm. "A death."

"I can give you a death," nodded Cinquis, careful not to seal the bargain. "Stay with us, I will call for a sacrifice to be brought down…"

The demon cackled. The noise seemed to crackle across the magisters' skin, causing the hairs to rise of their own accord. "No," it chastised. "I will choose the offering. Not a peasant. The sacrifice must be worthy of my attention. It must be appropriate. It must merit the attention of my master."

"Who?" asked Cinquis warily.

There was a long silence now. Cinquis flinched as something brushed past her foot, seeming to caress her ankle hungrily. She kept her concentration focused on the skull. A breeze moved through the room, causing the candle flames to dance and recede. One went out…

Bastard.

She reached out a handle, pointing at the candle. It burst back into flame. She concentrated, the candles flaring up in bright, purple-tinged pillars of fire.

"I thought we were making an accord," she scolded.

The cackle split the air again, louder this time. "My apologies. You are strong, for a mortal. I wish for you to sacrifice the King Jaros III of Castland."

Octus shook his head, looking to Cinquis. "We should consult the Grand Magister…"

She shot him a look. Even without seeing the blaze in her eyes it silenced him.

Cinquis stared into the orbits of the skull, fixing her gaze on the orange glow. She paused for effect, making the demon wait for her response.

"It can be done," she said. "If you agree to give me the information I require, as and when I require it."

"I shall promise to give you the information you request, as long as it is within my vision. The pact would be in place as long as you live."

The doubt within Octus was tangible. She ignored it. The demon would be bound to complete its part of the pact. It would not be able to lie to her. It would destroy itself.

"It will take time for me to arrange the sacrifice."

"Time is only a concern to mortals," hissed the demon. "I am not a slave to it, unlike you."

"The sacrifice is large," she continued. "I will require an act of good faith. You would need to begin providing me with news even before it has been completed."

"Too vague, I am afraid," spat the creature. "There would be no incentive for you to complete your side of the bargain. I will allow you three requests. There will be no more until the sacrifice is made."

Cinquis nodded. "That is fair. And I will require your name."

"Do you think I am stupid, bitch?"

"Not at all," said the magister. "But I will need your name to call you back to the Mortal World, so that you can tell me what you have seen."

The glow in the eyes became gentler. Cinquis smiled. She had it.

"I will give you my name. When you call me, it will be a proper summoning. No more occupying rotting body parts. If you use it for anything other than to summon me, then the pact will be broken, and I will destroy you."

"You may try," she said.

"Seal the bargain, woman," spat the demon.

Cinquis steeled herself for a second, calming the trembling of her hand. She stood, reaching into her robes and pulling out the ceremonial blade. She pricked the skin on her thumb, extending her slender arm into the pentagram. Octus tensed, wary in case the creature dragged her into its grip. She held her hand over the skull, squeezing the thumb until a few drops of crimson blood fell onto the crown. They hissed on landing, as if the bone was a hot pan over a stove.

"It is done," she said, pulling her arm out of the pentagram as quickly as she could without showing fear.

"It is done," hissed the demon. "My name is R'jhal'chqk. Tell me, mortal, what is it that you wish to know...?"

Larcenara, the Goddess of Thieves, sat in the wall of the pool, reclining gently, her svelte hand dangling in the cool water. She watched as the God of Chaos giggled, staring into his silver mirror with manic, crossed eyes. He was in the form of a human, the limbs twisted as though snapped and then poorly healed. He poked a bent finger at the glass, the tip seeming to penetrate the surface with a flash.

Maniac laughter split the serene air. Pyra, Goddess of Fire, looked to Larcenara, shaking her head. She was a tall, statuesque figure, her naked body flickering as though aflame. Her long hair was made of intense fire, the warmth playing on the skin of Larcenara's cheek.

"What are you doing, Contras?" asked the Flame, even her voice seeming to crackle as though it was burning in her throat.

"Touching the humans," giggled the lunatic god, staring intently into the mirror.

"You can see the Mortal World that clearly?" scoffed Larcenara. She brought her hand out of the pool, flicking water from her fingers playfully at Pyra. The droplets hissed into vapour as they landed on her incandescent skin.

"Sometimes," smiled Contras. "The mists are parting more often of late."

"You shouldn't touch them," said Larcenara. "The mortals can barely handle it if we speak to them. Laying a finger on them will break their fragile little minds."

"Exactly," laughed Contras. "Sometimes they just curl up and die. Pathetic. But most of them just go mad. Beautifully, completely insane. It is exhilarating."

"You truly are an idiot," snapped Larcenara, gazing into the clouded waters of the pool.

"Guilty," laughed Contras, poking again at the surface of his mirror. "Damn it. Missed."

"Can you see the Mortal World more clearly, Pyra?" asked the Goddess of Thieves, squinting at the pool.

"I don't spend much time at the pool," replied Pyra, moving over to stand beside Larcenara and looking disdainfully down into the liquid. "The water makes me feel ill. I can see Altanya. It is clearer by the day. They pray a lot."

"I don't think I have ever seen Altanya," mused Larcenara.

Pyra laughed, a roar of flame at the back of her throat. "There are not many thieves in the land of the little white people. They treat them harshly."

"Worse than the rest of the mortals treat them?"

"Much worse. The Altanyans do not need Contras' touch to make them mad and angry."

"And yet their worship does not make you uncomfortable?"

"Why should it?" asked Pyra, smiling wickedly. "Even if it did, I could not stop it. And we need it to survive. I am not sure what it feels like to not exist, but I know that I am not anxious to give it a try."

"Why do they worship you so heavily, though? In most parts of the Mortal World we all have followers, to a greater or lesser degree. Altanya seems to be dominated by you."

"I think it stems from the volcanoes," said Pyra. She caught Larcenara's confused look. "Alas, you do not see much of the Mortal World, do you? Your followers pray to you in secret shrines in cellars, or as they sneak around in the dead of night. Your contact with the Mortal World is skewed, minimalist. The volcanoes in the east of the Altanyan desert are great mountains that spew fire out into the world."

"It is no surprise that they call out to you, then, if you rain fire down upon them."

"You speak as if I have any more control over the Mortal World than you. The volcanoes rain fire as they wish. I do not influence the mountains. Mountains do not pray, so they are free from our touch. The Altanyans pray, though. They summon my demons. They ask them questions."

"Of what?" asked Larcenara. She was growing tired of the conversation. She sometimes envied the contact the other gods had with the Mortal World, and Pyra's revelations were making it grow. Contras howled as he made contact with another human. "It would be a shame if someone were to steal that mirror from you, freak."

"I would just make another," laughed Contras. He reached into his tattered white shirt, producing another mirror identical to the first. He dropped it absently. As it fell it dissipated to nothingness, vanishing before it hit the ground.

"The Altanyans ask how to harness the power of fire," said Pyra. "And my demons tell them. They make metal tubes that they stuff with black powder, and when they set it alight iron balls fly from the end and cut down their foes. Ingenious, really. I get the impression they are planning a war."

"So your followers are going to upset the balance, and you are giving them the means to do it."

Pyra shrugged. "I honestly have no interest in the affairs of the mortals. But if they are going to kill one another, I would prefer that my worshippers are on the winning side. As I said, I have no interest in not existing."

Larcenara sighed, staring intently back at the pool's surface. Would her followers survive such events? They were not warriors, and they were not numerous. Pyra's words repeated in her head as she looked, willing the waters to clear. She didn't want to stop existing either. She didn't want to go the way of the Lurker...

The Lord Chancellor looked around the table at the assembled men, the look of annoyance on his face purposeful. He felt like a school teacher with a class full of particularly disobedient children.

Iluma Porwesh sat to his right, the only man in the room who wasn't annoying him. The old Yanari had pushed his chair back from the table, distancing himself from the others, making it clear that he was only there as an observer.

Beside him was Lord Princetown, the portly ruler of Snowgate clearly uncomfortable at being summoned yet again to Regalla. His dark eyes glared occasionally at Lord Unstead beside him, blaming him for the latest arduous journey to the capital.

King Jaros sat opposite the Lord Chancellor, seemingly allowing the government to create a dividing line between the opposing parties to the discussion. Facing Lord Princetown and Lord Unstead was Lord Perlis, accompanied by his eerily-similar son, Xavier. The Vampire Lord's indigo eyes were fixed malignantly on Lord Unstead, who returned the stare angrily.

Lord Drathlax completed the assembled men, sat to the Lord Chancellor's left, his dark eyes fixed on Lord Perlis and his son. His vexation imitated that of Lord Princetown, although his demeanour was less tired.

"I am astounded that I have to summon nobles of the realm to the capital to discuss events such as these," announced Cramwall. "Do any of you understand the implications of your actions on our delicate natural order?"

Lord Perlis spoke first. "I have done nothing to upset the balance, Lord Chancellor. I have merely escorted some poor folk back to the capital, where they belong. Poor folk who were attacked by Lord Unstead."

"Those people invaded my land and destroyed my property," snapped Unstead, scratching at the stitches holding together the deep wound along his jaw. "One of them assaulted me and killed my son."

"I know nothing of this," shrugged Perlis, sneering at the red-haired lord. "A family of Yanari turned up on my lands shortly after the Regallans. They had escaped from Lord Unstead's unlawful detention. Lord Unstead killed the father of the family, an artisan from the capital."

"I am aware of what happened," snapped Cramwall. "I read the missives you sent. I summoned you here to explain to me *why* this mess occurred."

"Quite," spoke up King Jaros, fiddling absently with the heavy, jewelled crown atop his head. The thin hair hung down from beneath it, grown out to shoulder length to attempt to disguise its recession. He was around the Lord Chancellor's age, but time had been even more unkind to the king. His face was thin to the point of being gaunt, his eyes lined and tired. The jawline was weak, the only strong feature a long, hooked nose. "This is indeed a mess."

"Your majesty," said Cramwall patiently. "There really is no need for you to be here. I can deal with these issues."

"I do not doubt your competence, Lord Chancellor," said the king insincerely. "I am, however, trying to take more interest in matters of state. I hear unsettling rumours from Barralegne. I hear they have increased training of their troops. Their smiths are pouring out armour and weapons. And now we have a crisis within our own nobility."

"It is hardly a crisis, your majesty," protested Princetown.

Cramwall slammed his hand on the table, causing the lord of Snowgate to jump visibly. "It *is* a crisis. We have enemies within, and enemies without, and our own lords are involving themselves in dangerous and very public disputes. It concerns me more that one of the most senior members of our aristocracy does not even realise that this is a crisis."

Princetown looked to the table before him, cowed by the chastisement.

"I want to know why this situation developed," snapped the Lord Chancellor.

Perlis stared defiantly at Unstead, daring him to speak.

"I am unsure if you are aware, Lord Chancellor, but Lord Perlis defiled one of my villages."

"I am aware, Lord Unstead. Your liege lord brought this to my attention. I spoke to Lord Drathlax, who agreed to address my concerns with Lord Perlis."

"That is correct, Lord Chancellor," said Drathlax guardedly, his gaze still fixed on his fellow Vampire Lord. "I have already spoken to Lord Perlis. There will be no more indiscretions."

Perlis looked up, his eyes meeting those of his old friend. He nodded. "I apologise for the misunderstanding. It will not happen again."

"*Misunderstanding*," roared Unstead, taking to his feet and smashing his freckled hands into the table.

"Sit... down..." growled Cramwall through gritted teeth. He waited for the man to settle back in his seat before continuing. "The matter was settled. Is my word, and therefore the word of the crown, not good enough for you, sir?"

Unstead shifted in his seat, his light brown eyes moving between the king and the Lord Chancellor. "I was not aware that the matter had been addressed, Lord Chancellor."

"I told you..." started Princetown, turning towards Unstead.

"I was not aware," said Unstead bluntly. "I apologise for my ignorance. Until the matter was resolved, I intended to block the road to Lord Perlis' lands, to punish him by denial of trade."

"So you blocked a common road and imprisoned a family lawfully passing along it," said Cramwall.

"My men were over-eager," replied Unstead. "For that, I also apologise."

"We Yanari are an unassuming people, my lord," said Porwesh, his glassy eyes settling on Unstead. "They will accept your apology over this misunderstanding."

"Lord Unstead killed a man," snarled Perlis. "You accept that?"

"The bastard milker who broke them out of my castle killed my *son*," roared Unstead.

Porwesh didn't flinch at the insult. "We are not a vengeful people," he shrugged.

"Wrongs were done on both sides," said the Lord Chancellor simply. "Lord Unstead imprisoned the Yanari family unlawfully. His son died in the rescue. He killed one of the Yanari in anger. Iluma Porwesh bears no ill will. The matter is settled."

"Settled?" cried Unstead, up on his feet again. "The life of my only heir laid equal against the life of a common Yanari pig? Are those the values set on a noble life by the Lord Chancellor of Castland?"

"I will not tell you to sit again," growled Cramwall. Unstead retook his seat reluctantly. "The lives are, of course, not of equal value. But laid against the life of your son is also the fact that you imprisoned these people, contrary to the laws of the land. And your men then attacked citizens of the capital travelling lawfully along a common road."

"Those commoners killed soldiers in my employ," yelled Unstead. Princetown was staring at him now, urging him to be silent, but the red-haired lord ignored him.

"Your soldiers were acting against the laws set by the crown. It is by the grace of Argentis that they did not succeed in harming those people. Otherwise this matter would have caused irreparable damage to our relationship with the commoners. The matter is settled."

Perlis sneered across the table at Unstead, his fangs glinting in the light. Unstead stared viciously at him, breathing heavily, his chest heaving with rage.

"What of the man who killed my son?" he asked, fighting to keep his anger under control. "I want that piece of Yanari shit."

Cramwall glanced at Porwesh. The old Yanari again didn't react to the insult.

His composure puts the nobles of Castland to shame.

"The rescuer disappeared after handing over the family," lied Perlis, smirking again at Unstead.

"If he is ever found, he will be handed over to you, Lord Unstead," said Cramwall. "The common folk from Regalla have been given a purse of gold each to keep their tongues from wagging. Those monies have been paid from crown coffers. Lord Unstead will reimburse the treasury, in light of his wrongdoings."

Unstead moved to protest. This time Princetown placed his hand on the man's arm, staying his words. "Lord Unstead agrees."

"What of the agitator who led these people?" asked King Jaros. "I hear he writes that rag, the People's Gazette. A treasonous rag. The poor have no right to knowledge. This gives us an opportunity to cut the head from the snake."

Lord Princetown nodded his agreement. Perlis shook his head, looking to Drathlax. His old friend avoided his gaze, turning his attention to the Lord Chancellor.

"It would be unwise to take action against him, your majesty," said Cramwall, thoughts moving through his brain as he pondered the implications. "The poor are angry at present, our control over them is delicate. To arrest this meddler would cause unrest. Making a martyr of him is not in our interests."

"But he must be silenced," insisted the king.

"I agree, your majesty," said Cramwall. "But you are new to the intrigues of state. Please, let me guide you through this. We must let the dust settle. At some point, this agitator will meet with an unpleasant accident. But now is not the time."

The king relented, his attention slipping away from the talks. "If you will excuse me, then, gentlemen, I must find out what is for supper."

The men stood, waiting whilst the ruler of Castland made his way from the audience chamber. The Lord Chancellor watched him leave, the disdain evident on his face.

"Don't sit back down," he snapped as soon as the doors fell shut behind the king. He looked between the assembled nobles, his voice stern. "This nonsense will desist immediately. Lord Princetown, Lord Drathlax, you will ensure that these men keep the king's peace, or there will be consequences. I would urge you all to remember that no man is above the security of the realm. Lords can have accidents too. They are not as easy to arrange as those that might befall an agitator, but they can occur nonetheless. Now, get back to your lands, and remember my words."

The men nodded. As they turned to leave, the Lord Chancellor reached out an arm. "Not you, Lord Princetown. Take a seat."

Cramwall watched the men leave, noting the baleful glares exchanged between Lord Unstead and Lord Perlis. The enmity was raw now, but he didn't feel that it was likely to recede with time. He had no doubt that he would have to intervene at some point. He resolved to work through the potential outcomes tonight, decide on the best course of action, ascertain who would live and who would die.

The doors closed once again. The Lord Chancellor looked between Porwesh and Lord Princetown, concern in his voice as he spoke. "I have had word from Bannar. My remarks about lords and accidents are not as hollow as they might seem."

"I do not follow you, Lord Chancellor," replied Princetown. Cramwall wasn't surprised.

"Lord Tomas Bannar appears to have died at the hands of his disgruntled peasantry. At least, that is what the mayor is telling me. Other sources indicate that it was my son who arranged for his demise."

"Why would he do such a thing, Lord Chancellor?" asked Porwesh, leaning into the conversation.

"Because he is rash, and has much to learn," pondered Cramwall, leaning back in his chair and resting his hands on the slight paunch of his belly. "I will deal with that when he returns. Lord Bannar was making some highly unsavoury alterations in his lands, rebalancing the relationship between the rich and the poor. These reforms needed to stop. I am not sure I agree with Cecil's methods, but he has put a halt to these developments. But word will spread, and the commoners will not like it. Combined with recent events in the Red Cairn Hills, significant unrest will ensue."

"These sound like troubling times," said Porwesh. "No doubt you have a plan, Lord Chancellor."

"Of courses, my friend," smiled Cramwall. "We shall cut off any revolt before it happens. Rip the weed out by the root."

"Round up the ringleaders," nodded Princetown, rubbing his hands together. "Hang them from the walls as an example to the rest."

Cramwall tutted, shaking his head. "No, Lord Princetown. The old ways will not work. The people are becoming educated. They have ridiculous, self-entitled views now, spread by people like Lord Bannar and this troublesome agitator."

"So what do you have in mind, Lord Chancellor?" asked Porwesh.

"We shall have an election," replied Cramwall.

"Will that be enough?" asked Princetown. "If the people are as informed as you believe, will they accept the process?"

"Probably not," admitted Cramwall. "That is why we will change the process. This will be an election like no other. The Establishment Party will not be the only option. We will allow other parties to stand. Parties that the poor folk see as representing them."

"This sounds dangerous," said Princetown warily. "The nobility is bound by law to respect the will of the elected representatives. How will we keep control if the representatives are sympathetic towards the commoners?"

"The Establishment Party will still win, Lord Princetown. The people will feel that they have a choice, but we won't let them exercise it. They will vote for the Establishment Party, because to do otherwise would be... unwise..."

"I don't..."

"Understand, Lord Princetown?" interrupted the Lord Chancellor. "That does not surprise me. The election will take place by district. One of the poor quarters of Snowgate will go first. The votes will be counted, and no doubt they will not vote for the Establishment Party. As such, a number of common folk equivalent to the unsavoury vote will be punished."

"Punished, Lord Chancellor?" asked Porwesh, his interest aroused.

"Yes, Iluma. Flogging, hanging, it would depend on the level of disobedience. I will let Cecil organise it. It shall be his last chance to prove himself."

"How can we decimate the poor folk and expect the realm to still run, though, Lord Chancellor?" asked Princetown.

"We will not need to. Word of the consequences of disobedience will spread, thanks to the very tool that the commoners see as their emancipator. The People's Gazette and other rags like it will inform the peasants of the penalty for revolt."

"It is a bold plan, Lord Chancellor," nodded Porwesh.

"Troubled times call for strong leadership," admitted Cramwall.

"They do indeed, Lord Chancellor," said Princetown, eager to ingratiate himself with Cramwall. He looked suspiciously at the old Yanari beside him, sensing him to be a threat. "May I ask that Toby is allowed to assist Cecil in his duties? The lad needs to learn the workings of politics in our great country."

"Your son is already learning," smiled Cramwall. "He is on his way to Altanya to act as our ambassador. I needed him out of the country."

"But..." floundered Princetown, his mouth moving without words coming out. "But... Why was I not consulted...?"

"Your son is a degenerate, murderous little bastard, Lord Princetown," replied Cramwall. "I wanted rid of him, for the good of the realm. If he was not the son of a loyal servant of Castland, I would have had him executed. You can thank me for that later."

"I..."

"Do not understand?" snapped Cramwall. "You do not need to. You just need to do as you are told, and make sure that this election goes as planned. Cecil is not the only one who has a last chance to redeem himself, Lord Princetown."

Chapter Twenty-Six

The temple of Almas in Regalla was, in all honesty, overstating its grandeur by using the word to describe itself. It was bigger than most places where the God of the Poor was worshipped, but it was still little bigger than a tavern. The hall was simply furnished, rough wooden pews lined up facing the basic oak altar with an aisle splitting the room. There were some crude hangings and paintings donated from poor folk who had the most basic of artistic leanings, but apart from that the décor was drab. The roof leaked when it rained, and one of the windows had been broken and never fixed.

The acrid smell of the cheap tallow candles did not bother Yarner like it once had. Spending extended periods in the city sewers had caused him to develop a hardier sense of smell. He smiled as the cleric of Almas pronounced Arnie and Lucy man and wife. The small congregation broke out in applause, Yarner's wife and children throwing a few handfuls of flower petals over the newly married couple.

They looked good together. Arnie was still tender from his wound, but he was putting a brave face on it. Lucy looked radiant in the emerald green gown Arnie had bought her, the colour setting off her vibrant hair and eyes perfectly. Yarner's smile widened as they walked past him down the aisle. He nodded to them both, slapping the young lad on the back as they headed for the door to the street.

The ceremony had been short. They had had a whip-round to pay the priest. Almas' clergy would do a wedding for free, but it was polite to give a donation.

Yarner turned his attention to Ratcliffe, standing beside him. He sensed that the ceremony hadn't been short enough for the reporter.

"Can we talk now?" asked the agitator, twisting the pewter badge on his tunic absently.

"Why are you here?" enquired Yarner, waiting in the pew as the rest of the congregation began to file out of the temple after the couple.

"For the Gazette," shrugged Ratcliffe. "The people need good news stories as well as grim ones. What better than the wedding of one of our heroic city watch?"

"And that's the only reason?" asked Yarner sceptically.

"Well, whilst I'm here I could do with talking to you about something else," smiled Ratcliffe.

Yarner shook his head, glancing over to the cleric of Almas. He was busying himself at the altar now, tidying up his religious items. An initiate had made himself busy sweeping up the flower petals. Yarner led the agitator by the arm to the back of the hall, out of earshot.

"I'm not a stooge for you and your newspaper, Ratcliffe," he hissed. "I have a family. Talking to you is risky."

"So you heard about my little escapade in the Red Cairn Hills?"

"How could I *not* hear? Your men are preaching it from the rooftops. A dangerous thing to do with no witnesses backing you up."

"Cramwall and his lackeys paid the peasants to keep quiet."

"I know," whispered Yarner. "Some of the other watchmen had to deliver the purses, convince people it was in their interests not to rock the boat. You would be wise to take a leaf out of their book."

"And why is that?" asked Ratcliffe, his eyes sparkling with interest.

"Because you're making powerful enemies." Yarner's eyes flicked around the room again, checking that the devotees of Almas were occupied fully with their chores. "Worse than you usually do. Look, Ratcliffe, I don't particularly like you, but I do sympathise with what you're trying to do. But sometimes a man has to cut his losses and keep his head down if things get too close for comfort. The word is that the watch has been ordered to bring you in if you do anything that constitutes breaking the law. *Anything.*"

"Then I must be getting to them," smiled Ratcliffe. "It's nice to be popular."

"Trust me, you won't like the attention if you give them cause to arrest you."

"I don't doubt that. Have you heard about Lord Bannar?"

Yarner shrugged. "Who's he?"

"A martial lord from the east. Fought in the Third Raskan War. Man's a hero, by all accounts. I hear he was letting his peasants by land. Until he met with an unfortunate accident after the Lord Chancellor's son paid him a visit. It appears I'm not the only one making himself unpopular."

"I'm glad you're finally realising how much trouble you are in."

"I'm going to run the story in the People's Gazette."

Yarner sighed. "Are you fucking stupid?"

"I understand why you don't stand up and fight, sergeant. You've got a decent job. You've got a wife, children. I don't have those concerns."

"You're not concerned for your own life?"

Ratcliffe paused. He had been scared in the hills. He had thought about it over and again since his return to the capital. Had he really feared for his own safety? Or had he feared that he was not going to finish his life's work? He genuinely felt it was the latter. He had taste for making a difference now, a sample of what it was like to take the fight to the enemy.

"You asked me once how a man like me wrote in such elegant script," he said. "Would you like me to tell you?"

"If it makes you leave me alone," shrugged Yarner. "I need to get to the pub, get celebrating with my friends."

"Friends," pondered Ratcliffe. "I haven't got many of those, sergeant. Nobody to tell this story to."

"It's probably because you're a cunt."

"Probably." The reporter gave a sad smile, a vulnerability creeping in that Yarner had not seen before. "I was born into a noble family, sergeant. Not a grand house, a minor baronet, but still the landed aristocracy. Classic Argentis worshippers, selfish and proud. No interest in the poor, in their struggles. I was interested. I fell in love, not even fifteen. One of the serving girls."

Yarner hesitated. He swore he saw a tear forming in the agitator's eye.

"When my parents found out, they had her sent away. I found out where to. I've always been good at getting information out of people, it's my gift. I was so angry with them. I did the one thing I could that would hurt them more than anything."

"I'm not going to have to arrest you for any of this, am I?" asked Yarner warily.

"I took away their only son and heir."

"You don't mean…"

Ratcliffe laughed mirthlessly. "*Me*, sergeant. I left. I went and found my love, and we fled to live out our lives together in peaceful poverty. Even then I loved to write. I dreamt of creating novels, plays, poems. She wanted to be an actress. I taught her to read, so she could fulfil that dream. But my parents sent a man after us, the head of his guard. He caught up with us too easily. We hadn't tried to hide our tracks.

"I had known him since I was a boy. He could see we were in love. He could see that we were happy, living in a hovel but at least having each other. And do you know what he did?"

"I dread to think," said Yarner, his eyes falling to the floor.

"He let us go," smiled Ratcliffe. "He was a good man. He let us live our lives. And when he told my father what he had done, he was cast out of the village. No job, no recommendation, thrown out after a lifetime of service. All for being a good man. That is what the nobility does. He hanged himself. He couldn't fine work, and the shame was too much for him.

"So I wrote about it. I started the People's Gazette, and it is the first story I told. My parents were shamed, but obviously not enough for the Lord Chancellor to strip them of any land or titles. I did it as a warning. If they didn't leave us alone, I would tell more of their dirty little secrets. So they let us be."

"You see, Jaspar," said Yarner. "You've got a reason to keep yourself safe too."

"She died."

Yarner met the reporter's eyes in time to catch a single tear trail down his cheek. He clasped the man's shoulder in his hand, squeezing it gently. "I'm sorry."

"Why?" asked Ratcliffe, the wooden demeanour returning. "You didn't kill her."

Yarner paused, looking at the man before him. He had always had a grudging respect for the agitator, but now he seemed more real, more human.

"I hear there's going to be an election," said Yarner. "Don't ask who told me, and don't bring me into any of your stories. The watch has been put on standby to police it. I don't know when, so don't ask. But rumour has it that the people will be allowed to put forward their own candidates."

Ratcliffe's eyes brightened as his mind kicked into gear, weighing up options in his head quickly. "This is great news. I'll need to raise funds. We can finally overthrow the Establishment Party. No violence, no revolt, just democracy."

"I'm telling you so you can get ready," said Yarner. "Don't publish it. And be careful. In my experience, when the rich give something to the poor, it very rarely comes without a cost."

"I'll be careful," nodded Ratcliffe. "Promise me, sergeant, if you hear anything else, you will let me know."

Yarner nodded reluctantly. "*If.* It's hard to hear much from the sewers."

"Thank you, my friend."

"I'm not your friend," smiled Yarner weakly, squeezing the agitator's shoulder again before moving past him through the doors of the temple.

Illeaka, the High Priest of Pharma, ran an old hand through his flowing, white beard, resting it neatly upon the polished marble table before him. He looked around the assembled head priests, taking in their pristine white robes and ageing faces. The youngest amongst them was almost sixty; Head Priest Lexis, the Keeper of the Lore. Lexis was based in the temple of Pharma in Regalla, along with Illeaka. The rest had travelled from the far corners of Castland to answer his call.

An initiate moved amongst them, filling their crystal glasses with wine or water as they requested. The room contained no candles, instead being brightly lit by the light of a single skylight that reflected from one polished silver mirror to another within the chamber. The light split into rainbow beams as it passed through the drinks onto the bright, white meeting table.

The assembled men fell quiet as Illeaka raised his hand slightly, calling them to order.

"I thank you all for making the journey to the capital. I understand for many it will have been an arduous trip. I am sure you are wondering why I have called you together."

There was a gentle murmur of agreement from the elderly priests.

"As discussed at our last assembly, we are all concerned at the state of the nation's health. The poor are suffering, and as per our agreement I managed, eventually, to find a gap in the Lord Chancellor's busy schedule in which to plead our case."

"Did he listen?" asked one of the senior clerics, skewering a fat, fresh, white scallop from the silver platter at the centre of the table with a delicate fork and slipping it into his mouth. "Are the nobility going to open their moth-infested purses to help us aid the peasants?"

"Alas, the Lord Chancellor has informed me that there is no gold available from crown supplies."

A grumble of protest sounded from the group. The High Priest raised his hand again, quietening the men gently.

"I share your concerns, my brothers. I am sure we all see the growing dissatisfaction of the poor folk. Their woes grow heavy, and this threatens the peace of the land."

"It is not just the peasants," spoke up one of the head priests. "One of my chapels near Westroad was looted for its silverware last month. It seems it was the local militia, trying to raise money to feed the garrison. A church of Pharma, raided by the nobility."

"Where was this?" asked Illeaka.

"Some village or other," shrugged the head priest. "I do not remember the name."

"This increases the weight on my shoulders," said the High Priest. "Some of the Lord Chancellor's words already bear heavy on my mind. He intimated that there may be conflict brewing. Another war. This will hurt the poor and the sick, as it always does. There are rumours of an election, and I fear that if the result does not address these issues, there will be open revolt."

"The church of Pharma does not involve itself with politics, Father Illeaka," warned another of the clerics, supported by the mumblings of his fellows.

"I do not presume to involve myself in politics," insisted the High Priest. "But only a fool would ignore the rumblings of discontent reverberating through Castland. We cannot help the sick unless we are prepared."

"How do you propose that we prepare, Father Illeaka?" spoke up one of the men. "Without gold we will struggle to be of any use to the wretched."

"Father Lexis," said the High Priest. He paused for effect, turning to the man beside him. The Keeper of the Lore stood out from the others. His hair was black as coal, shaved short on his head. His beard was neatly cropped. His brown eyes rested on Illeaka as he sipped from his wine, unsettling the High Priest. "What do we know of the Portal Stones?"

"The Portal Stones?" said one of the clerics mockingly. "Your idea is to pursue a fairy tale, Father Illeaka?"

Lexis placed his glass down gently, clearing his throat. His eyes settled on the scoffing priest, silencing him instantly. "The Portal Stones are not a fairy tale, father. To infer that they are is to cast doubt upon the existence of Pharos himself."

"I meant no blasphemy," blustered the old man. "I merely meant..."

"One hundred and twelve years ago, the clerics of Pharma scoured the known world for the Portal Stones. These were troubled times. The lands of men were in crisis, and the clerics longed for the guidance of the Merciful One. With the correct rituals, the shards of the Portal Stones can be combined to create a gateway between the Mortal World and the Astral Realm. Those priests sacrificed much to gather the fragments and perform the ritual. At the summit of Mount Split Peak, to the south, they summoned Pharma into the world."

"We know the stories of our mother god, Father Lexis," snapped one of the head priests. The Keeper of the Lore's eyes flashed out again.

"Pharma proclaimed that it was for mortals to be their own saviours. She sent her son into the world; Pharos. Born of a mortal woman, he was sent into the world to teach us the true way of Pharma. His preachings form the basis of our religion today. He taught us much. His life taught us that mortals are fragile and fickle beings. Jealous men took the son of our beloved mother and nailed him to a tree in the wilds. They poured pitch on him, and set him alight. But we will never forget him."

"I still fail to see what your proposal is, Father Illeaka."

The High Priest smiled gently. "We shall be the next generation of the clergy to collect the Portal Stones. We will summon Pharma to the Mortal World and plead for her help. She will guide us. At the very least the nobles will see the Merciful One in all her glory and provide us with what we need to continue our work."

"With the greatest of respect, Father Illeaka, we are old men, and our order is in crisis," said one of the head priests. "The world is a dangerous place."

"The world was a dangerous place back then," said Lexis. "Our forebears sought the fragments despite the perils."

"Do we know where the Portal Stones are?" asked another priest.

"The details are not recorded in the Library of Knowledge," admitted Lexis. "But the old tomes do refer to a place called the Library of Souls. The details of the combining ritual are held there, and possibly the locations of the Portal Stones. On creating the door that allowed Pharma to pass in the Mortal World, they were cast to the corners of the world."

"Where is the Library of Souls, Father Lexis?" asked Illeaka gently.

"Across the seas, to the south-west, Father Illeaka. The journey would be difficult, but I agree with your proposal. It is time the faithful made sacrifices for the afflicted once again."

The assembly descended into discussion, argument, protest. Most agreed to the principle of the High Priest's idea, but lacked the conviction that their goal could be accomplished.

"We do not have the resources," cried one of the head priests. "We are spread too thin. We would require help from men who know how to travel the wilder parts of this world, and those men would want gold."

"Perhaps we should ask Pharos for help," suggested Lexis, smiling knowingly at the assembled senior clergy.

"You are right, Father Lexis," said the High Priest, bowing his head. The others followed suit as the Keeper of the Lore looked on. "Pharos, the humble servants of your mother, the Merciful One, pray for..."

"With respect, Father Illeaka," said Lexis, interrupted the prayer. "I did not mean by prayer. I meant that we should ask him to accompany us."

A silence spread across the heads of the order. Lexis took in their bemused gazes, looking from one to another, a mischievous glint in his eyes.

"I do not follow you, Father Lexis," ventured the High Priest.

"Pharos did not die at the hands of the men who sought to execute him, Father Illeaka. Killing the child of a god is not something that can easily be accomplished."

"Blasphemy," cried one of the priests as the rest clamoured in support.

Lexis shook his head assertively. "I understand your apprehension. It is natural. It is not the version of the truth that has been relayed to the world. But I am the Keeper of the Lore. The Library of Knowledge contains the full truth of events."

"Why have these truths not been revealed sooner?" snapped one of the men, tugging at his beard in annoyance.

"Please, calm yourselves," urged Illeaka, raising his hands to bring order to the room. "You know the way of things as well as I do. The Keeper of the Lore is a position handed down from one man to the next. They alone have full access to the Library of Knowledge. It has always been the way, to ensure the teachings of Pharma remain pure and consistent."

"Why have we not been informed of a point of such importance?" challenged a head priest.

"It is the role of the Keeper of the Lore to prevent a shockwave moving through the faithful," said Lexis, fixing the man with his unnerving stare. "Knowledge must only be unveiled as required, when it is beneficial to the faith. Sometimes, it will never be appropriate to divulge information. It seems to me that today is a good day to reveal the fact of Pharos' existence."

"Then we should assemble a party to seek the Portal Stones," said the High Priest, sensing he had the backing of the majority of the head priests. "They shall seek the guidance of Pharos. I assume we know his location, Father Lexis?"

Lexis nodded. "It is written."

"Then we shall need a leader for this expedition," called one of the priests. "It should be a head priest. One strong enough to undertake the journey. One with the knowledge to complete the task."

Lexis felt the eyes falling on him, heavy and challenging. He smiled humourlessly. "I will need the strongest of our flock. They must have faith. The trek will be arduous. And meeting with Pharos may not be... as they expect it to be..."

"What do you mean, Father Lexis?" asked Illeaka, his kind eyes showing apprehensive curiosity. "What could be more of an honour than to meet the son of the Merciful One?"

"I do not imagine Pharos will be as you imagine him," said Lexis slowly. "Would you be of good temperament if asked to help the very people who had impaled you and tried to burn you to death?"

Chapter Twenty-Seven

Charo marched at the head of his people as they gathered around the sheriff's home. Mathias strode at one side, sword drawn. His mother walked on the other, her skeletal frame wrapped in a long, brown cloak. The hood was pulled up, leaving her face in shadow. Apart from the eyes. The violet glow from the orbits of her skull shone in the dark as they came to a halt.

It was late. The few villagers around had viewed them with suspicion as they moved through the night. Charo had only brought those of his people able to fight. Most had a weapon now, a sword or an axe forged before they left home by Edgar. A few had helmets, simple tin pot armour without a faceguard, but they had been in a hurry. The blacksmith and Wrathson pushed their way to the front now, taking in the sheriff's jailhouse.

It was a simple affair, two stories, the front door heavy and banded with iron. The windows were dark, the interior unlit. The sheriff was sleeping.

"How many men do you think he'll have?" asked Charo.

Wrathson shrugged. "Ten at most. Probably deputies, young lads like Lucas and Ben here."

"Can we beat them?" asked Mathias.

"Shouldn't be too difficult," replied Wrathson. "Assuming they even put up a fight. We've got the numbers."

"Can our people fight, though, sheriff?" asked Charo. "They're woodsmen, farmers, craftsmen."

"No point a craftsman making a weapon he can't use," laughed Edgar, hefting the heavy, double-headed axe he held in his powerful grip.

"The ones here can swing a blade, Charo," nodded Wrathson. "I've been working with them, every evening. And the lads who worked for the mayor and the baronet are soldiers. We'll be more than a match for them. Even so…"

The sheriff turned to Willem, gesturing to the balcony above the door to the jailhouse. The hunter nodded, slinging his bow over his shoulder and beginning to climb deftly up the trailing plants to the vantage point.

"I don't want anyone to get hurt," said Charo.

Wrathson shook his head gently, placing his hand on the lad's shoulder. "Listen, Charo. If there's a fight, people will get hurt. That's how it works. And if you want to change the way of things, there's going to be fighting. Now I'll follow you anywhere lad. If you want to leave, give up on this idea, I'll be with you. But if you want to do this, and I hope to Lunaris you do, then you need to understand that people will get hurt. Some of those people will be your friends."

Charo's dark eyes moved to Mathias. His brother nodded encouragingly, forcing a smile across his face. His mother reached out, her cold, bony hand stroking his cheek. She nodded, the purple light in her eyes warm and soothing.

"Let's get this done then," said Charo, pulling the bone knife from his belt. "Please, sheriff, try not to hurt anyone. We only want the man who forced us to flee our home."

Wrathson nodded, rubbing his dully aching ribs. He hoped it didn't come to a fight. He still wasn't at his best. "You just keep away from any unpleasantness. We need you safe, Charo. You're the only one of us that really matters."

With that he drew his sword, striding up to the door of the jailhouse and banging on it heavily with his fist. "Open up in there."

They stood in the black of the night, waiting for a response. Charo noticed uneasily that some of the villagers had begun to turn up, intrigued by what was going on. Wrathson banged again. "Open the door."

A candle light sparked into life at the window of the balcony. Willem dipped out of sight just in time to avoid the gaze of the silhouetted figure as the glass opened a crack.

"Who the fuck's making all that racket?" growled a voice, heavy with sleep.

Wrathson stepped away from the door, re-joining the others so that he had a better view of the window. "I represent Charo Culler. *We* represent him."

"Any relation to the stone mason Culler?"

Wrathson looked to Charo. The youth shook his head.

"No, mate," called Wrathson irritably. "When Charo and his brother were boys, you threatened to lock them in the stocks, for a crime their father committed. They were forced to leave their home, because of your twisted idea of justice. We're here to see you pay for that crime."

"Fuck off," snarled the voice. "You don't come into my village ordering me about. You're lucky it's late, or I'd come down there and throw you all in the cells."

"If you don't come down here, these men are going to throw torches through your windows and on your roof until this whole building's ablaze, mate. So I suggest you get your arse out here."

The window slammed shut. The silence returned. Wrathson shrugged at Charo.

"What now, sheriff?" asked Mathias, staring at the jailhouse. He remembered it. His father had stood here, before those doors, when he was sentenced to the stocks. He shuddered, remembering his panic, the blind need to flee the village, to protect his brother.

"Get some rocks together," said Wrathson to the two deputies. "We need to break some of these windows."

As the two youths began to look around the torchlit ground around the sheriff's house, Charo noticed the faint light of a candle moving around the ground floor of the building. A heavy key found its place in the lock of the thick door, turning slowly. The door opened angrily, the sheriff and three deputies striding out into the cold of the night, swords at the ready.

Wrathson had been right. The deputies were little older than Charo. They were confident, though, as they lined up beside the sheriff. They had the air of the naïve, who felt that being on the side of the law was being on the side of the righteous.

The sheriff was a tall man, rough and unshaven. He was thickset, giving off the air of a man who would take no nonsense. He rubbed the last of the sleep from his eyes, glaring through the darkness at those who had dared to defy his authority.

They had all taken the time to dress themselves in their leathers. They were ready for a fight.

Charo shuddered. "What is your name, sheriff?"

"Osborne. Who the fuck's asking, you little whelp?"

"Is this him?" Charo asked Mathias, ignoring the man's insult. "Is this the one?"

Mathias looked the sheriff up and down, taking in the sneering lips and impatient stare. He nodded.

"Listen, you bastards," snarled Osborne. "There's a lot of weapons here, and I'm not liking the way they're pointing. I'm the law in these parts, and I order you, in the name of the king, to lay down your arms and submit to arrest."

"I order you, in the name of Lunaris, to lay down your arms," hissed Charo. "Nobody will be harmed. We merely seek justice."

Osborne laughed, his deputies tensing at Charo's threat. "I dole out the justice here, boy. The *king's* justice. Not in the name of some old, dead god."

"Then you should deliver it upon yourself," said Charo, meeting the man's stare. "For trying to put two young boys in the stocks just because their drunken father stole a loaf of bread to feed them."

The sheriff hesitated for a moment, realisation dawning on his face. "That was you pair? I remember you, vaguely. You never did receive your punishment. Why come back? You're fugitives."

"We are passing this way to spread the word of Lunaris. It seems he has granted us the chance to also serve his justice upon you for your past transgressions."

"So the pedlar was telling the truth," mused Osborne. "He passed through a few days back. Stories of some lad leading an uprising, killing the village mayor and the noble, heading this way. I thought he was just mad from being in the wilderness too long."

"He wasn't mad. We are heading to the capital, to change the wicked way of things in Castland. Starting with you, sheriff, and your twisted brand of justice. I find you guilty of your crime, seeing as you offer no defence."

"And I find you guilty too," shrugged Osborne. "You admit to killing an elected official and a baronet of Castland. Not to mention all that bullshit about demons the addled trader was babbling about. The penalty under the justice of King Jaros III is death."

"My judgement is not show harsh," said Charo. "In the name of Lunaris, I sentence you to the stocks. You shall feel the humiliation and pain that our father suffered. Your sentence shall be three times as long, to take into account the unjust punishment you declared that Mathias and I should suffer."

"Sounds like Lunaris is a bit soft, boy. I wouldn't leave me alive if I were you. Even if you were able to dish out the punishment, I'd come back for you afterwards."

"Lunaris' justice is fair. It isn't tailored to the future risk of retaliation. Besides, I only need you out of the way long enough to take care of the mayor and the noble of these lands. I will unite the people and we will be on our way."

"That's enough for me, you little fucker," snarled Osborne, readying his sword. "Now you're threatening my village and my betters. Time for your punishment."

"Stand down, sheriff," roared Wrathson as Willem emerged from the shadows of the balcony, his bow covering Osborne and his men. "You're covered from above, and you're outnumbered. Just give it up."

"Outnumbered?" sneered Osborne, gesturing to the village folk gathered around the group. "This is *my* village. Sound the alarm. Bring the rest of the deputies. These people threaten your home."

Wrathson charged forward, sword raised, Mathias and Edgar on his heels. A arrow split the air ahead of them, striking one of the deputies in the calf, dropping him to his knees as he writhed in agony.

Wrathson's blade clashed heavily with Osborne's, sparks flying in the dark of the night. The struck at one another again and again. The man was strong, maybe a little lighter than Wrathson, but he was carrying more muscle. Wrathson felt himself tiring straight away, struggling to breathe as his ribs tightened with the effort of blocking the blows.

Edgar closed on one of the deputies, swinging the heavy axe in a wide arc. The lad's confidence disappeared instantly as the force of the blow ripped the sword from his hand, sending it flying into the night. The blacksmith pressed his advantage, shoving the haft of his weapon under the youth's chin and pinning him up against the wall. Edgar was a heavy man. The lad's face began to darken from the strain on his throat as he fought desperately for breath.

Mathias flailed with the sword at the other deputy, his movements clumsy and poorly aimed. Their weapons clashed sporadically, the youth concentrating on evading the ugly but ferocious attack. As they parted for a second Willem's bow struck again, an arrow to the gut putting the youth on the ground.

Wrathson wrestled with Osborne desperately, their swords hanging limp and useless as they gripped each other in close quarters. Wrathson dropped his first, grabbing the sides of Osborne's head with both hands and butting him hard. He didn't catch the nose or the mouth, their skulls smashing together with a dull thud. Osborne dropped his own sword, bringing his fist up under Wrathson's arms and landed an uppercut on his chin.

Wrathson fell onto his back, the force of the blow reverberating through his skull. His vision blurred as Osborne closed in on top of him, pounding him with blow after blow. He felt his nose pop from one punch, the familiar warmth of blood streaming across his lips. There was no point trying to defend himself from these hits, he needed to get this bastard off him quickly, or he was done for. He was getting *another* kicking.

He brought his knee up as hard as he could, hoping to find a bollock. It wasn't the result he was hoping for, off centre, but it distracted Osborne just long enough for him to slip a thumb into his eye. He couldn't hold onto his foe, drive it any deeper, but the man wailed, his weight shifting.

Wrathson summoned the last of his desperate strength, feeling the healing process in his ribs reversing with the strain. He clawed his way up Osborne's chest, sinking his teeth in the man's neck. He bit hard, pushing until his teeth met, pulling his head away so forcefully he ended up banging the back of his skull on the ground.

He spat out the chunk of flesh as he lay there, Osborne's blood spraying down on his face and chest. He pushed the sheriff off him, felt him crash to the ground beside him. Wrathson lay there, his vision spinning from lack of breath, the clamour of a crowd of approaching villagers seeming distant.

Wrathson knew they weren't noises from far away though. The alarm had been sounded, and the village was coming out in force...

Father Pietr sat at a pew in the cold of the small chapel of Mortis, resting his old limbs. He was wrapped in a wolf skin as well as his robes, but it was not enough. The cold was seeping into his bones, he could feel it. Once it was there, it set in for good, that was the way of things. The journey would be the end of him, he knew it.

Mortis, why give such a task to an old, infirm man?

Pietr's sad eyes looked up at the cleric of Mortis before him, stood perplexed at being awoken at such a later hour. He was younger than Pietr, but then that was not to say he was young enough to rise joyfully in the middle of the night.

"I do not understand the urgency," insisted the cleric. "Could this not wait until morning, Father...?"

"Pietr."

"I am Father Undor," said the cleric, hugging a mug of nettle tea he had brewed on being roused from his slumber. He hadn't offered one to his fellow priest.

"Unfortunately, Father Undor, I have a matter of the utmost urgency to discuss," said Pietr, eyeing the hot beverage enviously. "Events are unfolding in your village, and you need to be made aware of them."

"What events, father?" Undor paced before his brethren, stamping his feet on the cold stone floor to keep warm.

"The villagers with whom I travel are on a quest. They intend to bring about change in our country. They aim to realign the balance in Castland's society, force the nobility to treat the poor more fairly."

Undor paused for a second at this, sipping his tea cautiously. "A travelling headsman passed through recently. He referred to these events when we spoke. You know how headsmen like to feel they are the agents of Mortis. I assumed he was delusional."

"Not at all, Father Undor. These people have indeed overthrown their betters. Hanged them for the crimes they perceived to be committed against them. You see, the nobles summoned a demon of Lunaris to terrorise the common folk..."

"A demon?" gasped Undor. "One of the Lurker's creatures? If this is true, then I can understand their actions, but they must seek forgiveness, not exacerbate their sins."

"It would seem that they are inspired by Lunaris. He protected them from the creature, you see? Helped one of their own, a peasant lad, slay the creature in order to save them. They believe that Lunaris has sent the lad to lead them to a better future."

"Your flock has turned away from you, father?" sighed Undor, his eyes full of pity for the old man before him.

"Not entirely," said Pietr carefully. "They believe that Mortis is happy for the Lurker to guide his flock. After all, would our lord not want the people to lead a fulfilled life before entering his domain?"

"Your people have lost their way, father," insisted Undor, his eyes straying to the doors of the chapel. "Thank you for this information. I must inform Sheriff Osborne. He is running the town of late, the mayor being on his deathbed. He will know what to do to stop these heathens."

"May I?" asked Pietr, gesturing to the cup in his fellow cleric's hands and leaning on his staff as he stood. He took a sip of the tea passed to him by Undor, savouring the warm fumes on his face. "I did not come to warn you of these events so that you could inform the sheriff, father. I needed to ask you your opinion on the matter. Should we not, as clerics of Mortis, support these people in their endeavours?"

Undor's eyes widened with righteous disdain. "Absolutely not, Father Pietr. They are heretics, and their blight must be cut out of the world without mercy."

"I feared you would say that," mused Pietr, staring into the enraged eyes of the priest. His body jerked suddenly, the gaze widening, glassing over slowly. Another shudder passed through Undor's body before he slid forward to the ground, blood flowing from the deep knife wound under his shoulder blade.

"Come, Harat," said Pietr, placing his arm around the shoulders of his young initiate as she stood looking down at the bloody stiletto blade in her tiny hands. "I will go and check on Charo. Perhaps you should go and attend to the mayor? Ease his suffering..."

The villagers circled Charo and his group, shouting hostilities. They were gathering quickly, their numbers swelling. Mathias pulled his brother close, backing them towards the jailhouse. The deputies had struggled away to join their people. Edgar was supporting Wrathson as he stood, shaking his head to try to clear the haze.

"They killed the sheriff."

"Send word to the baronet."

"String them up."

The calls were coming thick and fast now. Not many of the villagers were armed, but they outnumbered Charo's people. He pulled away from Mathias, urging his followers to move aside as he stepped forward to address the angry crowd.

"The sheriff refused to come quietly and answer for his crimes. We tried to treat him justly, but he refused Lunaris' judgement." His voice was strong now, more confident than Mathias had ever heard.

"Lunaris?"

"What crimes?"

"Our father stole bread to feed us when we were children," proclaimed Charo. "He was punished for his crimes, but the sheriff insisted that my brother and I should also be put in the stocks. That is not justice. It is cruelty. Now we've returned, to lead you out of this life of servitude and poverty."

"Is that Charo?" came a voice.

"And Mathias."

"The stone mason's lads…"

"Told you they'd fucking recognise you," mumbled Wrathson beneath the bloodstained rag he was pressing hard against his streaming nose.

"Our father was not a mason," said Charo. "But yes, it is us. Charo and Mathias. We have come to help you."

A man pushed his way forward through the crowd of villagers. His hair was thick and blond, greying at the temples. His eyes were light blue, lined and tired, but filled with awe. His grey-blond beard was neatly trimmed, his shoulders broad and muscled. The wrinkles on his face and the fading of his hair made him look older than Charo suspected he was.

"It's your boys, Paull," cried one of the peasants.

Mathias moved up beside Charo, his jaw dropping. "Father?"

"Mathias," cried the man, tears welling in his eyes, glinting in the flickering torchlight. "Is it really you? And Charo. Little Charo…"

Charo looked to Mathias, shaking his head. "Our father wasn't a stone mason. He was a drunk."

"I *was* a drunk," said the mason, taking a step forward. Several of Charo's people raised their swords, sensing the youth's apprehension. "I fell down, I admit it. For a long time. I let you down. When you left, it almost destroyed me. But I found the strength to live, to learn a craft, to get back on my feet."

"Why didn't you come and find us, then?" asked Charo, his words hard.

"Why would you want me?" asked Paull, wiping back the tears from his face with his sleeve. "I thought it was best that I stayed here, with your mother. Stayed part of your past. Let you make yourselves a better future without me."

Charo looked to Mathias, his dark eyes untrusting.

Their mother moved forward, brushing past them gently. Her cloaked figure walked towards Paull, her arms outstretched.

"Raechael?" he asked, his voice cracking. "But…"

"How do you know…?" asked Mathias, shaking his head.

"It is her," gasped the mason as their mother reached him, standing before him, her arms outstretched. "I'd know her walk anywhere. I can *feel* her. Raechael, how I've missed you. But how?"

Their mother placed a hand on his cheek, stroking it gently. Paull looked at the skeletal fingers without flinching, leaned into his wife's touch. He reached up gently, pulling back the hood of the cloak, gazing into the purple glow in the empty orbits of the skull. He pulled her close, embracing her with all his strength.

"What is this sorcery?" cried out several of the villagers, clinging to one another for comfort.

"Send for Father Undor. He'll know what to do. We must seek the guidance of Mortis."

"Father Undor is dead," came a gentle voice from behind them. Pietr moved slowly through the crowd, his movements pained and stooped. "Your priest was a failed servant of the Keeper of Souls. In our village, the mayor and the local baronet summoned a demon to torture the poor folk. It was your cleric who gave them the means to do so."

Pietr reached the front of the crowd, standing beside Charo's parents and tossing down a heavy, leather-bound tome onto the cold ground.

"You won't be able to read it," said Pietr. "It is written in the Demon Script. A grimoire detailing the rituals for summoning a creature from the Astral Realm. I found it in Father Undor's quarters."

"Where is Father Undor?" called out one of the villagers.

Pietr fixed him with a steely glare, the usually kind eyes hard as steel. "The penalty for heresy is death."

The crowd were silent now, taking in the sight before them. Slowly, they began to murmur, panic beginning to spread through them.

"What shall we do?"

"We need to tell the mayor."

"The mayor's sick. He's got the ague."

"I sense that the mayor has succumbed to his illness, I fear," said Pietr darkly. "You need to listen to me. Charo is here to help you, to guide you on a great quest. Together, we will change the course of this land. If you trust in Mortis, then you should trust in Charo. As I do."

"He was talking about Lunaris, though," called one of the men in the crowd. "Isn't that heresy?"

"No, child," smiled Pietr. "There are many gods. If Mortis wills that we help Charo in his task, then we should do so. Lunaris has given the youth a path to tread, but that does not mean it is not one which Mortis wishes him to tread."

"What about that... abomination...?" cried the man, pointing at the skeletal figure embracing Paull. Their father shot the man an angry look, pulling his wife closer.

"I see only a woman," shrugged Pietr. "A woman reunited with her husband, and with her children. A gift from Mortis, as a demonstration of his support for Charo and his quest."

"Pharma gives life," spat a woman in the crowd, staring apprehensively at Charo.

"And Mortis gives the gift of death," replied Pietr gently. "It would appear that he has taken that gift back from this woman. It is not for us to question his motives."

The crowd were consulting again. Some were still distrusting, but Pietr could sense that he had the majority of them now.

"My lads are good people," called Paull, turning to his fellow villagers. "They always have been. They have more of their mother in them than they have me. And they've brought Raechael back to me. I won't lose my family again. Wherever they are going, I'm going with them."

"You are all welcome," called Charo. "If you do not wish to come with us, that is fine. You may stay here, or you can leave. We will not try to stop you. I hope that you will join us."

Father Pietr smiled at the lad. Most of the crowd were pressing close now, eager to hear the words of the champion of Lunaris.

"What will we do, Charo?" asked his father, moving over and taking his sons in his arms. "I'm yours to command, lads. I've let you down in the past. I won't do it again."

Mathias gripped his father tightly, tears welling in his eyes. Charo moved free from the grip after a second. It didn't feel right. He supposed it was understandable that Mathias had missed the man, they were so alike. Charo was glad he was alive, but it was a muted feeling, distant and intangible.

I think I'm just glad he's here for Mathias' sake...

"We take the baronet at dawn," proclaimed Charo. "The nobles must fall, so that you can stand."

Sounds of approval rose up from the crowd. Not just his own entourage, many of the village people were with him now.

"Charo, please," said his father, clutching at his son's arm. "When I was at my worst, it was the baronet that helped me. He pulled me from the gutter, Charo, gave me money to train as a stone mason. He convinced the artisan to take on a grown man as an apprentice, and a drunkard at that. He is a good man. Please, spare him."

Charo stared up at his father, dark eyes cold and unblinking.

"You did say that Lunaris would be merciful, Charo," said Mathias, looking to his brother. "Not all the nobles are bad, surely? We can't punish one for the crimes of his fellows."

Charo nodded, keeping his eyes trained on his father. "You're right, Mathias. Father, as he knows you, I will give you the chance to talk to him. He must give up these lands to the people, and he must leave. Where he goes is his business. Any of his men who wish to join us should be allowed to do so."

"I'll try, Charo," nodded his father. "He's a good man, but he's proud. I'll do my best."

"You said before you wouldn't let us down again, father," said Charo. "Please don't go back on that vow so quickly. Tell him how many we have behind us now. The baronet must leave, or he will be judged by Lunaris."

Mathias shuddered as he stood beside his father, taking in the dark silhouette of his brother in the torchlight.

Chapter Twenty-Eight

Talia didn't answer the knock at the door to her chambers in the keep. She clung to the bloodstained shawl draped across her lap on the bed, her closest link to the husband she had lost. His things were all still here, of course, but this was the last thing that contained a piece of him. They had taken his body to Kassell, to be prepared for the funeral.

The knock came again; gentle, apprehensive.

She didn't know if she could attend the ceremony. It wasn't the journey to the city. She didn't know if she could physically stand in the temple whilst Tomas lay dead on a slab before her. Watch as they put him the ground. Admit that it was all over, that their life together had come to an abrupt end before it had even really begun.

And they'd expect her to stand there, ladylike and strong, as if nothing had happened. She knew she couldn't do that. She wanted to kill someone, get her hands around somebody's throat and rip it out with her nails. She would want to wail and cry out and grieve, to curse the gods for taking her love from her.

She buried her face in the shawl again, sobbing until she heaved. Her face was puffed and red, her eyes bloodshot, but no more tears came. She wanted to cry, but she had nothing left in her. It made her feel worse that no water fell from her eyes as she bawled, as if she was somehow letting Tomas down.

The door opened slowly, Ivan and Robert stepping quietly into the room. The innkeeper carried a tray of fruit and cheese that he laid down tenderly on the bedside table beside her.

"Brought you some food, Talia," said her old friend, gently brushing the damp hair from her eyes.

"I'm not hungry," she replied absently, her glassy eyes staring past him at the wall of the bedchamber.

"Doesn't matter, love," said Ivan, his heavy body easing gently onto the bed beside her. "You need to eat. Keep strong. Lord Bannar wouldn't want you to waste yourself away, you know that."

"What Tomas wants isn't really important any more, is it?" she said coldly, fighting back the urge to burst into tears again.

Robert knelt down at the foot of the bed, forcing himself into her line of vision. "I think it's more important than ever, my lady. It's down to you to lead the people now, and you need to decide how many of Tomas' ideals you are going to keep."

"Do I look like a woman capable of leading anyone, Robert?" Her bloodshot eyes found his, piercing and angry.

"The wounds to your heart will heal, my lady," said Robert gently. "We have all lost Tomas, although I know your pain is greatest. But we have all lost people in the past. I lost people in the war, and yet I have recovered."

"Did you lose your wife in the war, Robert?" hissed Talia, spit forming on her lip.

Robert looked to the floor, shaking his head gently.

"Easy, Talia," said Ivan, resting his rough hand on hers. "He's trying to help, that's all. You're a strong woman, and we need you. The people need you."

She looked at him, shrugging her shoulders, tears streaming from her eyes as she sobbed. "What do you want from me?"

"We need your orders, my lady," said Robert gently. "Do we raise the taxes? Do we continue with Tomas' plans regarding allowing the peasantry to buy their lands?"

"I don't know anything about all this shit," cried Talia. "Do what's best."

"What's best, Talia, is for you to tell us what to do," insisted Ivan, squeezing her hand. "You're a wise woman. You're kind, you're caring, you know these people. You can rule as you think best. You're the lady of Bannar now. Just tell us what to do."

Robert nodded his support, smiling gently. "Tomas would want it."

Talia pulled herself further upright on the bed, wiping at her tearstained face with her sleeve. "I want the men who did this dragged before me so I can quarter them myself."

Robert nodded, glancing at Ivan. "We are searching for the perpetrators, my lady. The watch is questioning every man, woman and child in Tomas' lands. Someone will give something away, I promise you, and when we find them, we will punish them."

"*I* will punish them," said Talia, her eyes cold.

"We know you will, Talia," said Ivan.

"And Tomas' proposals?" asked Robert. "Shall we continue? Or shall we reverse his decrees?"

"Will the lords not return to punish us if we don't stop Tomas' reforms?" asked Talia.

"It's unlikely, my lady. We have been placed under the direct control of Lord Tremelowe of Kassell. He is our liege lord, and officially he will administer Tomas' lands."

"So you don't need me," said Talia. "I will not be a puppet, especially not the puppet of a man who hates Raskans. Do you honestly think that Oskar Tremelowe will allow me, a Raskan woman, to govern these lands?"

"It is true that Lord Tremelowe is not fond of Raskans," admitted Robert, catching Ivan's angry glare. "But he also loved your husband. And Tomas loved you. He will allow you to govern the lands as you see fit, I assure you. His protection will only go so far, though, if the Lord Chancellor finds out you are still defying him..."

"Then we go on as Tomas would have wanted," declared Talia. "The people loved him. The people agreed to defy the capital, despite the risks. Even you, Ivan."

Ivan nodded meekly, avoiding her gaze. "I did."

"Then it's settled," she said. "Robert, when is the funeral?"

"These things take time, my lady," replied the castellan. Talia caught him glancing at Ivan again. *These men are keeping something from me. Is this what it is, to rule? To be kept in the dark?*

"Let me know as soon as it's arranged."

Robert nodded, heading towards the door.

"Eat something, please," said Ivan, placing the tray gently in her lap. "For me. For the people. For yourself. And for anyone else who might need it."

Robert watched from the doorway, catching Ivan's furtive glance towards Talia's belly.

Oskar Tremelowe sat by the window in the bedchamber in the top of one of the keep's towers, looking out across the city of Kassell. The sun was just setting, the red arch melting down into the horizon beyond the tall city walls.

Oskar gazed through the fading light at the men manning the walls, going about their patrols, honing their weapons, going through their daily routines. *His* men. His eyes turned to the people in the streets below, brushing out yards and gullies, calling children in for their meals, men finishing their toils and heading to the alehouses. *His* people.

It made him proud to watch his people go about their lives. He had a hand in making that happen, in making them safe, in making them happy. It made him feel lucky, too. Not many men got to live thousands of lives at once. He had his own life, and then he led the lives of his people. He made those lives run without fear, without threat.

Oskar stood to light the candles in the room, his heavy frame blocking the meagre light from the window for a second. He moved from candelabra to candelabra, lighting each one in turn. The candles were beeswax, elegantly tall and scented, a gift from one of his people.

From the man in the bed in the tower chamber.

"How is he, father?" asked Oskar, addressing the white-robed cleric of Pharma sat on a stool beside the bed. The priest was dabbing at a deep gash in the patient's upper arm, swabbing at the open wound with a soaked cloth.

"Similar to yesterday," said the priest grimly, inspecting the blood on the damp rag. "This wound will not heal, my lord."

"You haven't even stitched it up, father," shrugged Tremelowe, running a finger through his greying brown hair. "Even I know you need to stitch a wound."

"There is no point in stitching this," replied the cleric, pulling up the bed-bound man's shirt to reveal the black thread binding the deep wound in his ribs. "This wound has been stitched, and it is healing. I do not know how. This poor soul has been stabbed in the heart with a dagger, and yet he has survived. That in itself is not possible. But he still breathes, his veins still throb, and the wound is healing. But this..."

The cleric shrugged, resuming his dabbing at the gash.

"Are you going to finish speaking, father?" asked Tremelowe, pacing agitatedly. "I don't have the patience for riddles and half-sentences."

"Perhaps if I knew what blade had caused the wound..."

Tremelowe reached under the bed quickly, pulling out a curved, thin sword. He held it up to the candle light, looking at his reflection in the polished, perfect metal. It was light as a feather, yet sharp

193

enough to cut a human hair with a flick of the wrist. He span it in his hand, presenting the hilt to the priest.

The cleric didn't take it. His eyes played over it, taking in the razor-sharp edge, the pommel of polished black stone, the tiny ruby in the hilt that seemed to emit a red light of its own.

"This is why the wound will not heal," he said, looking away from the weapon as if it had burnt his eyes. "It is an ancient weapon, made years ago by the most adept worshippers of Sanguis. It was forged in funeral pyres, cooled in fresh blood, enchanted with spiteful magic. You do not see many these days, thank Pharma. It is a Blade of Lament. A wound caused by it will never heal."

Tremelowe scoffed. "Ridiculous."

"I have seen a few cuts from this type of weapon before, my lord. Sometimes they will weep, bleed. Other times they will merely be uncomfortable. They fluctuate between states, ebbing and flowing in severity like the tide. But they never heal."

The man in the bed groaned, the dark eyes opening, peering at the indistinct shapes before him.

"This… This is impossible, my lord…"

"Leave us, father," insisted Tremelowe, ushering the cleric from the room. "And do not speak of this to anyone, as we agreed."

Tremelowe shut the door, turning to his old friend. "Tomas."

"Oskar?" mumbled the martial lord, moving tenderly to stand.

"No, old friend," said Tremelowe, stopping the injured warrior from attempting to get out of the bed. "You're very sick, Tomas. You need to rest."

"Where am I?" croaked Tomas, his throat dry.

"At my keep in Kassell," replied Tremelowe, pressing a bowl of water to the man's lips. "Your castellan and an innkeeper from Bannar brought you to me. You had been stabbed through the heart, yet still you lived. Rose right up from the slab in the temple of Mortis in the town. Scared them both half to death, by the sounds of it. It seems you are a tougher bastard than even I thought."

"There was a fight," recalled Tomas, gingerly touching at his chest. "At the bakery."

"That is where the townsfolk found you. Mortally wounded, or so they thought. A dead man beside you. Do you remember anything more?"

Tomas shook his head, wincing at the pain. "It's very dark, Oskar. I can sense the movement, the fighting. I can't make out the shapes."

"Rest easy, Tomas. It will come with time. Edens is looking into it all in your absence. Nobody seems to recognise the dead fellow. He had this placard on his person."

Tremelowe tossed a carved piece of wood into Tomas' lap. The martial lord picked it up, squinting through his hazy vision at the writing. "This is bullshit. I gave them everything I could."

"You did indeed, old friend," smiled Tremelowe. "Enough to make you very unpopular with the capital, so Edens tells me. But not with your common folk. As I said, it doesn't appear the man bearing this was one of your own, which raises suspicions in my mind."

Tomas nodded gravely. "Who knows I'm alive?"

"Myself, Edens, the innkeeper, the cleric who just left," replied Tremelowe. "That is all. We need to keep it that way for now."

"Talia needs to be told."

"All in good time, my friend. It is bad enough that the innkeeper is a Raskan and knows the truth. I have ordered Edens to deal with him if he speaks a word of it to anyone. Your wife is also a Raskan."

"You aren't trying to insinuate she had some part in this?" growled Tomas, the effort sending him to an agonising coughing fit. Tremelowe gripped his arm reassuringly, his thumb caressing the rock-hard muscle.

"I am saying that we need to find out the truth, that is all. Your lands are under my protection. I have already sent word to the capital to that effect, before the Lord Chancellor attempts to intervene. Your wife is the lady of Bannar, and is ruling in your stead. You can judge a person's past actions, in most cases, by watching their future ones. For now, nobody must know that you live. It could endanger you, your wife and your people."

Tomas' eyes strayed to the wicked blade in Tremelowe's hand. The light glanced off the shiny weapon, seeming to cause a flash of lightning across the murky scene in his head, illuminating the players in a bright, white glow.

"It was Cecil Cramwall," he hissed.

"Tomas, that is a serious allegation…"

"It was his bodyguard, the Q'shari. He ambushed me on the orders of the Lord Chancellor's whelp."

Tremelowe stared long and hard at his old friend, his eyes filled with sadness. He knew Tomas was right. The placard, the dead stranger, and now the martial lord's words. Tomas' memory was bound to have taken a battering during recent events, but he was not one to jump to spurious accusations. Tomas was a soldier; he dealt in cold, hard facts.

"In that case, old friend, it is even more important that you recuperate, and that nobody knows that you still live."

"When do I get to kill the little fucker?"

"I have business in Regalla, Tomas," said Tremelowe, his eyes meeting those of his old comrade-in-arms, trying to soothe his restlessness. "A meeting of the nobility has been called. Rumour has it that there is to be an election. I will gauge the lay of the land whilst I am there. Until then, you must promise me you will not leave this room, and speak only to the priest."

Tomas nodded reluctantly at his liege lord. "You have my word, Oskar."

They were all there. All the people he had killed. They flashed before his eyes, the moments of the killing blows illuminated in a crimson glow as he watched. He looked on through his own eyes, but he could not feel his body, the movements causing the frenzy of death. He winced at each slice, each crunch, trying to turn his field of vision away from the slaughter.

Lord Bannar was last, the dark eyes rolling up into his skull as the dagger grated against rib bone on its way into his chest. The dark sky behind his slumping body was dark, but tinged with red.

Why was this happening? Had he disappointed Sanguis? Had he failed her in some way?

The body of the martial lord rolled off him and he lay, panting, staring at the dark red sky.

Bannar's head jerked back into view, the eyes wide, alive, burning with hatred.

Q'thell woke with a start, pain shooting through his battered body as he banged his head against the wooden wall of the coach. His red eyes were wide as he looked around frantically, searching for the baleful figure of the martial lord.

He found only Cecil, looking disdainfully over at him from the opposite seat as the coach rattled its way along the East Road towards Regalla.

"You fell asleep again," said the noble. "How are you supposed to protect me if you are asleep?"

"I'm sorry, my lord," said Q'thell, working to slow his breathing. He felt the tugging of the stitches in his healing wounds as he shifted, trying to get comfortable. "I am weakened. I need to mend."

"You do," replied Cecil bluntly. "You should be out there on horseback, not skulking in here with me."

"If that is what you wish…"

"No," snapped Cecil, shaking his head. "You are no good out there either. Not in this state. Just hurry up and get better. I need you fit, not broken. I cannot believe you fucked it up so badly out there."

"Lord Bannar is dead, my lord," said Q'thell. "That is what you asked for, yes?"

"I would have liked it a bit cleaner. I would have liked it if the plan had been followed. I would have liked it if one of my men had not been left at the scene. I fear the people of Bannar will see through our ruse."

"How so?" asked Q'thell irritably.

"Well, you left a corpse for them, to start with. And you let Bannar see your face."

"Dead men don't talk," replied Q'thell, trying to push the image of the martial lord's vengeful stare from his mind.

"No, they do not," mused Cecil. "But their identities do. The townsfolk will know the corpse is not one of their own, and that will cast the whole motive for the attack into question. Plus, you appear to have lost a sword."

Q'thell sneered angrily. "Don't remind me. That weapon's been in my family for generations. It's irreplaceable."

"You, on the other hand, are not," said Cecil. "Remember that before you let me down again. I hire you because you are supposed to be the best killer in the land. If you are not…"

Q'thell shifted again in his seat as the noble's words trailed off. "He's dead, isn't he? I killed him, didn't I? He was tough, though. I've never fought a human like that. So strong, so fast, so much stamina."

"It sounds as though you admired him…"

"The wolf does not admire the sheep," snarled Q'thell. "I was just surprised. It won't happen again."

"I am glad to hear it," said Cecil, turning his blue eyes to gaze at the trees passing by through the carriage window. "We are not out of the woods yet, so to speak. We have to get past my father."

"You haven't told him?" asked Q'thell, raising an eyebrow.

"Of course I have," replied Cecil. "I sent a carrier pigeon. I am hoping that giving him as much time as possible to digest the situation will allow his temper to cool before we arrive in Regalla. Even so, it may be that your next task is to protect me from his wrath."

Q'thell smiled.

We shall see if I am inclined to side with you in the that confrontation, pig.

The Q'shari slid across the bench, pulling his backpack up and cushioning it under his head. He needed to rest, to heal. Things were going to get interesting, it seemed, and he would need to be on top form.

Luckily, we Q'shari heal fast. If I can only get some decent rest…

Chapter Twenty-Nine

Charo looked around the assembled members of the group as they picked at the food laid on the mayor's dining table. They were his most trusted advisers, taken from among his followers. He picked at a chicken leg, listening as they talked amongst themselves. It was important to listen. The lords of this land didn't do it, which meant that he should.

His father and mother stood beside him, accompanied by Mathias. They were his family, and that was important. His mother was wearing her hood again; he had told her that the people were finding her appearance unsettling, and she had seemed to understand. Her drew energy from her, a strength he never knew he had inside himself. It only grew when Mathias looked on him with pride. He had always wanted to impress his older brother, to be a man like him.

Father Pietr was there. It had been his idea to appoint a group of advisers in order to channel the feelings of the people through a less clamorous gathering. His initiate, Harat, was in attendance, but merely just to assist the priest in tasks such as sitting and standing. Charo could feel her staring at him now, the unsettling, odd-coloured, crossed eyes focused in his direction.

And the people think my mother's appearance is unsettling...

He shook his head, chastising himself for the uncharitable thought.

Wrathson and Willem were obviously there. They had been with him since the start, and their loyalty was without question. Edgar, by the same reasoning, was a member of the council. They were accompanied by the former head of Baronet Wender's guards, Iain Collagne, a Barralegnan mercenary. Wrathson vouched for him, and that was enough for Charo.

The remaining members were Otho, Helena and Niman, witnesses to the original events at the village that seemed a lifetime ago to Charo. They had become devout followers of Lunaris, taking to wearing dark, home-made, blue robes and insisting Charo showed them the correct ways to pray and preach the word of the God of Fear.

In honesty, Charo did not know any ritual words or incantations. He only knew that Lunaris had granted him the power to defeat the demon and the inspiration to lead these people. He told them to preach from their hearts, to follow a path of respectful veneration of the god that had saved them in their hour of need.

After all, their beliefs should come from what they've seen, not what they are told.

"We should move on," Wrathson was insisting. "If we are going to reach the capital without too much resistance, we will need to travel quickly. Who knows what this Baronet Reinhardt will do? We don't even know if he's fucking left."

"The baronet is a man of his word," insisted Paull, diverting his attention from his family to join the discussion. "He said he will leave. He will do so."

"And we are trusting the word of a drunk?" spoke up Niman, his eyes casting a derisive glance at Charo's father.

"He has cast off his previous vices," insisted Mathias, glaring at the self-styled priest of Lunaris. He turned his attention to Charo. "Surely a man can redeem himself? Lunaris wouldn't condemn a man to perpetual disdain for his past errors if he'd atoned himself?"

"If our father says the baronet has left, then that is so," said Charo, already knowing that the noble had deserted his estate. "Willem?"

"It's true. The baronet left the morning after Paull spoke to him. Took his men and a caravan of wagons and headed east."

"Then he's between us and Regalla," said Collagne, twisting the end of his exquisite, waxed beard uncomfortably. "He'll rally support and be ready to meet us on the road, I'd wager."

"If he has left already, then he will do these things whether we set out today or in a week's time," said Pietr. "We have people who need rest before we head out on the road again, myself included."

"With the greatest respect, father, the longer he has, the larger the force he can rally," said Collagne.

"How many of the villagers are swelling our numbers?" asked Charo.

The three preachers of Lunaris looked between themselves.

"Half will join us," said Helena. "They believe in the cause. They believe in Charo. With time, they will devote themselves to Lunaris. Some of the others left with the baronet. Others headed for different villages. Plenty remain, they are just not willing to follow. They expect you to be true to your word regarding their safety."

"And we shall be true to our word," said Charo. He looked amongst the assembled people, weighing up the possible courses of action. "Perhaps we should stay a while. Gather our strength. Gather weapons. Gather supplies. Train our people."

Pietr called his agreement, the initiate beside him nodding with him obediently.

"If Reinhardt gathers a force of soldiers, we won't be a match for them," warned Collagne. Wrathson voiced his backing.

"Would we be a match for those he could have rallied already?" asked Charo. "How many of our new flock can fight? How many have weapons? We will be outmatched no matter when we leave. We may as well prepare."

"If we're going to lose either way, why head to Regalla?" asked Edgar.

Charo smiled gently at the blacksmith. "I never said we would lose, Edgar. We will win. We must trust in Lunaris. We stay, and we prepare. We will leave when we are ready."

The preachers called out their approval. Charo looked to his family, his dark eyes questioning.

"We trust in your judgement, Charo," said Mathias, nodding encouragingly.

"It is settled, then," said Pietr, the relief in his voice evident. "Let us gather as many supplies as we can. The journey will be hard, and our opposition tougher."

Tayuk watched as the man he was following slid into the alley beside the Bank of the Sun in Regalla. The Knife adjusted the hood covering his face, checking discretely to ensure nobody was tailing the tail. His quarry was a professional, Tayuk could tell by his movements; casual, but taking in everything around him. Tayuk suspected he knew he was being followed. The Knife hadn't seen anyone with the man, but that didn't mean he hadn't let out some discrete duress signal to an unseen henchman.

The man had been asking questions around Little Yanar. Questions that had soon come to Tayuk's ears. Questions about the Wulska family. Questions about Iluma Porwesh.

Questions that made Tayuk ask questions…

The Knife walked casually towards the alleyway, glancing down it amongst the crates and rubbish, searching for the inquisitive fellow. He couldn't see him, but he knew he was there.

A trap? An ambush?

It would be brave in the mid-afternoon, but then Tayuk was planning the same thing. Quick, decisive, silent.

The Knife spotted the tiny movement, the bob of a head popping into view for a split second, at ankle level where nobody would expect it. Tayuk spotted it without looking, continuing past the alley towards the bank.

His prey knew he was being followed. He was waiting to ambush the Knife, concealed behind a stack of packing crates. Tayuk moved to the entrance to the bank, slipping inside quickly. The interior was neat, tidy, furnished well, but not too grandly. It wasn't a good idea for the Yanari to flaunt money, even if they had it. The wood of the tables, chairs and stalls was polished, good quality, but not intricately carved. The counter was the same, opposite now as he moved inside, protected by steel bars that extended from the floor to the ceiling.

A few Yanari were going about their business, talking to the various clerks at desks around the perimeter of the room. Tayuk slipped amongst them, heading for the heavy iron door beside the counter. He caught the cashier's eye as he approached, extending the thumb and little finger on his left hand by his side. He tapped the digits together twice, discretely.

The cashier looked to one side, nodding to an unseen guard. The heavy steel door opened as Tayuk approached, closing behind him as he slid into the back of the bank. He didn't speak once inside, heading through the interior rooms to the side door onto the alley. He slinked up to it quietly, gently sliding aside the slat in the heavy steel.

He could see his quarry, nestled in behind the crates. He had covered himself with a pile of empty, worn sacks that had been cast out into the alley for disposal. If Tayuk hadn't known he was there he would have been difficult to spot. The man was dividing his glances between the alley entrance and the door behind which the Knife stood. Delicate movements, unnoticeable to the untrained eye.

Tayuk retraced his steps, grabbing three of the hired guards relaxing and playing cards in one of the back rooms. They knew him. They couldn't see his face, but they knew him.

"Get into the alley by the bank," hissed the Knife. "Be careful. Enter from the street and have your wits about you."

The men gathered themselves without questioning, heading from the room as Tayuk returned to the door. He peered out through the grille-covered gap, sliding his dagger from its sheath as he waited.

The three bank guards appeared at the entrance to the alley, hands resting on their sword hilts. Tayuk watched as they approached, waiting for the man beneath the sacks to divert his attention to him.

His quarry was a professional. He didn't need to glance, he could hear the men approach. He was up quickly, the worn bags tossed aside as he bolted down the alleyway. Tayuk flung open the door, knife ready, but the man had already passed, scrabbling over the wall at the end of the ginnel. The Knife followed, hauling himself over after his prey, wary of any attack waiting on the other side.

The pursued man wasn't waiting. He was running into the maze of alleys. The Knife dropped down, sprinting after him. As he ran he could hear the guards struggling at the wall. They were out of the race before it had even begun.

His prey had a head start, but that wouldn't help him. Tayuk knew these alleys like the back of his hand. They were his stalking ground, his territory. The only thing slowing him was the need to be wary at each turn, in case the enemy had decided to turn and fight. He made up the distance after each corner, his powerful legs bursting back up to full speed in an instant.

The man wasn't putting any distance between them. He was fast, but so was the Knife. And the Knife could out-last him. His stamina was immense. His mind flicked back to the orphanage, to the endless hours being forced to run in a circle around the perimeter of the large yard, over-and-over, passing the same scenery hundreds of times until he knew the number of slats in each passing barrel and crate, the number of strands on each rope, the number of bricks in each wall.

His prey would tire. But they were heading back out of the maze of alleyways now, nearing the main street of Little Yanar. The man glanced the bustling road to one side, adjusting his path to head for it. It was the right move. Tayuk would have done the same in his situation, hoping his pursuer would want to avoid the throng of people.

But these were the Knife's streets. All of them. He would take the man down in public if needed. Not on the main road, but he needed his prey to think that he would. He slipped a throwing knife from beneath his tunic as they burst out into the street, letting it fly. He knew it would miss; they were running too fast to take proper aim. It clattered to the floor at his quarry's feet, startling him. The man looked back over his shoulder, eyes wide as Tayuk readied another knife.

The fleeing man altered his trajectory, slipping slightly in a pile of dung in the street as he made for the nearest alley, trying to put corners between him and the Knife. Tayuk smiled beneath the hood. His prey was panting now, his chest heaving as he ran. A few more corners and the Knife would take him...

There was a *pfft* of air as Tayuk rounded the next turn. He felt a slight impact in his stomach, a pinprick. His prey was before him, a blowpipe clenched in his fist. Tayuk looked down at the feathered dart sticking in his midriff, pulling it loose and tossing it aside as the tiny wound began to burn.

He crashed into the man, his powerful frame dropping him to the ground, the blowpipe skittering across the uneven cobbles. Tayuk pulled himself up astride his foe's chest, smashing the hilt of his dagger onto the exposed forehead. The blow took the wind from his opponent, giving Tayuk the chance to roll him over onto his back, his arm up behind him, locked in position. The man cried out in pain. Tayuk looked up to the windows opening in the back of the homes surrounding them. The Yanari saw what was happening and closed the shutters. The man heard the sound of blots sliding into place and knew nobody was coming to answer his calls.

"Who do you work for?" hissed the Knife. He shook his head, struggling to focus. He felt the sweat gathering on his brow, not from running but from the poisoned dart. The wound was in the muscle of his stomach, but his heart was pulling hard from the chase, spreading the venom through his system. He shook his head.

"Don't you want to know what I was asking about first?" winced the man, fighting against Tayuk's iron grip.

"I already know what you were asking," said Tayuk. He blinked repeatedly, trying to clear his vision. His heart was thumping in his chest now, rattling against his throat, causing his breathing to become heavier. He could feel his clothes dampening as the clammy sweat oozed from his pores. "I only need to know who sent you."

"You don't have much time to get that out of me," sneered the man, loosening his muscles now, saving his energy. "That venom will see to you soon..."

"You obviously don't know me," coughed the Knife, feeling his head spin. The vomit rose in his throat, watery and yellow. He let it loose, heaving as he spat it across the back of the pinned man's head. Adder venom. Not fatal, he had got the dart out quick. Enough to debilitate him, though. The man wasn't an assassin, then; their poisons were much more lethal. "Even so, we'd best move quickly."

"I'll tell you nothing."

"You won't tell me everything," admitted the Knife, sliding the tip of the dagger under the nail of the man's little finger. His prey screamed, struggling again against the powerful hold. "There isn't time, as you said. But you'll tell me one thing. Who do you work for?"

The Knife prised the dagger up, pulling the nail away from the finger. The man screamed again, shaking his head frantically against the pain. The Knife pressed the blade against the knuckle of the little finger, cutting it off and letting it drop to the ground.

"One finger gone," hissed the Knife. He heaved again, vomit splattering down the front of his tunic. He wiped his mouth on his shoulder, keeping the man locked in his grip. He could feel his heart banging in his eardrums, his vision becoming tinged with sickly yellow. He gasped for breath for a second, composing himself. "That probably doesn't stop the pain though. You can still feel that finger nail, can't you? The finger's gone, but you can still feel the agony. Don't make me do another. Who sent you?"

The man squirmed beneath the Knife, gritting his teeth and thrashing his legs in an effort to dislodge the Yanari. The Knife slid the blade in again, wrenching up another finger nail. The man's howling was distant beneath the sound of the Knife's racing heart. He sliced off the finger.

"You know," wheezed the Knife. "I can cut off a lot of pieces before you die? But I was always taught that if you concentrate on one place, a man becomes numb to the pain. You have to move around. Keep the brain interested. One of these is next..."

He focused, trying to get his vision to line up. He rested the point of the blade beneath the man's buttocks, pressing gently into a testicle.

"Lord Unstead," cried the man. "Lord Unstead sent me."

"Thank you," croaked the Knife. He slid the dagger into the notch between two vertebrae in the man's neck, releasing his armlock and driving it home with a blow of the palm on the weapon's hilt.

He scrabbled unsteadily to his feet, dragging the limp body to the nearest yard wall. His limbs trembling, he gathered the last of his strength, hoisting the man onto his shoulders and tossing the corpse over the wall, out of view. He would have to deal with it later.

He needed to find somewhere safe. He wretched again, bending double in the alley, his stomach knotted in cramps. His home was too far. So was the bank. He knew a place, but it wasn't orthodox.

Tayuk heaved again, vomit splattering across the floor. He looked around himself, his vision a thick blur.

It will have to do...

Esme Wulska looked up from the table, tearstained eyes staring at the insistent knock on the door to their home. She didn't want visitors. There had been so many since their return from those accursed hills. Well-wishers, busy-bodies, people who were both of those things rolled into one. A man from the People's Gazette, preying on the ordeal her family had endured to make money. A man from the Lord Chancellor, offering her gold to keep quiet.

She had thought she had finally seen them all off. It had been days now, sat at the table in her black mourning clothes. Not sleeping, not eating, just crying. And staring. Staring around her at the home... *their* home.

Esme was a strong woman. Much stronger than Alit. She had thought she could cope with anything. But her husband's death had crushed her. She felt more than just loss. She felt angry. Angry at the Castland noble who had killed her husband. Angry at herself for being so weak, for being just like the pathetic women that she despised, for being a typical, tragic Yanari.

And angry that her rage was not strong enough to pull her out of her grief.

The knocking came again now, not the rap of knuckles on wood, the banging of a fist.

"Mother, there is someone at the door," said Alitain, his gentle eyes full of concern as he sat by the fireplace.

"I'll get it," snarled Tanis, whipping a poker from the hearth and storming towards the door. "If it's another one of those bloodsuckers I'll..."

"Sit down," snapped Esme, pulling herself up and heading to the door as the banging came again. "I am the head of this household. Sit down, Tanis."

Esme pulled the door open angrily, her mouth opening to rebuke the visitor interrupting her family's mourning.

She recognised the stocky figure of Tayuk as he slumped forward into the room, crashing to one knee. "I am sorry, Madam Wulska. I know you're in mourning. I had nowhere else to go."

"Tayuk," called Tanis, scampering over to help the Yanari to his feet.

Esme crouched down, getting her arm under his other shoulder. His clothes were soaked with sweat. He was heavy, she noted. She had carried Alit to their bed once when he collapsed with the ague, but Tayuk was much heavier. She felt his iron-hard muscles, knotted with shivering, as he helped her son drag him to the bedroom.

"What happened, Tayuk?" she asked as they laid him down on her bed.

"I won't speak of it, Madam Wulska," stammered Tayuk, curling up into a ball as soon as he was settled. "Do you have kale nettle? And ague root?"

"Why would we have such things, Tayuk?" asked Esme, confused.

"Can you get them? Brew a tea? Heavy with sugar. I'll see to it you're reimbursed."

"You saved our lives, Tayuk," chided Esme gently, placing her small hand on his shuddering shoulder. "Alitain. Get in here."

Her older son was already there, standing awkwardly in the doorway to her room. "I'm here, mother."

"Take my purse. Get ague root and kale nettle from the apothecary. Hurry."

Tayuk nodded from his foetal position on the bed, his hands clenched around his temples. "Thank you, Madam Wulska. If you could send word to Iluma Porwesh for me, I'd see to it that you were again reimbursed for your troubles? Nobody must know of this, though."

"Of course, Tayuk," said Esme soothingly. "His estate is a good distance from Regalla though. Shall we send a rider?"

"He is lodging at the Regalla Rest Inn," said Tayuk, gritting his teeth as though in the grips of some agonising contortion. "Tell him, the weapon has been dulled."

Esme looked to Tanis. He younger son was already out of the room, heading towards the door to their home.

"Thank you, Madam Wulska. I will not forget this."

"Nonsense," smiled Esme reassuringly. "We will never forget what you did for us, Tayuk. Come, let me get a cold cloth on your forehead."

She reached up for Tayuk's hood. His hand snapped out like a striking snake, locking her wrist in a vice-like grip. "No, Madam Wulska. Please, just the tea."

Esme nodded as his grip released slowly. Her hand drifted down to his muscled shoulder, squeezing it gently. "We are here for you, Tayuk. Always."

Chapter Thirty

Lord Oskar Tremelowe of Kassell tried to hide his shock at the proposal the Lord Chancellor had just put forward to the assembled nobles of Castland.

"Are you sure this will work, Lord Chancellor?" asked King Jaros hesitantly, scratching his hooked nose distractedly as he looked around the assembled senior nobles of the realm.

Castland's major lords looked back from around the meeting table in the Lord Chancellor's palace, their moods mixed. They were the rulers of the cities of the realm, charged with cascading the orders of the country's government to their respective lesser nobles.

Lord Gideon de Pfeiff of Westroad was nodding eagerly, so much so that his unkempt white-blond hair was seemingly attempting to invade his eyes. It didn't help that he was inebriated, possibly to the point where he had lost control of his neck muscles. The minor lords he had brought with him were young, men of his own age, similarly drunk on the Lord Chancellor's good wine. Tremelowe suspected this was just a jolly organised by the fat boy-lord for his chums, with no respect afforded to the importance of the event.

Lord Arther Princetown of Snowgate was also voicing his support, but then he would. Cramwall and he were old friends. Princetown children had wed Cramwall children for as long as the realm could remember. It was probably why they were all so insipid. Generations of inbreeding had made nobles ugly both on the outside and in their souls.

Tremelowe eyed the man sitting behind Princetown warily. He knew of Lord Unstead by reputation; a merciless general in the Raskan War and before, shrewd and calculating, but with a fiery temper that matched the red of his hair. A cruel man who had looked positively disappointed when Cramwall had announced that his own son would be enforcing the punishment of any non-conforming peasantry.

You would enjoy that role, wouldn't you, Unstead...?

Tremelowe turned his gaze to Cecil Cramwall, sat behind his father, surprised to see that the Lord Chancellor's son had his beady blue eyes set on him already. The little lord averted his eyes immediately, avoiding Tremelowe's stare. Cecil's small hands settled on the paunch of his belly, the ringed fingers playing awkwardly with one another, obviously uncomfortable.

You did it, you bastard. You set your dog on Tomas...

The youth was sporting a fresh bruise on his shiny cheek. He had tried to cover it with powder, but Tremelowe could see it. Had his father not approved of his actions? Had he struck him? Tremelowe's eyes moved over to the Lord Chancellor. He was shorter than his son, portlier, but then he had had more time to spread. Cecil showed signs of going the same way; the receding hairline, the expanding forehead, the jowls, the weak chin. The only difference between Cecil in a couple of decades and his father now was that the lad seemed to have inherited his mother's, slightly superior, height.

Tremelowe wished he had some evidence. He was trying to think through the variables, assess whether he had the high ground. Matters of court were more difficult than military engagements, in most respects. He did not think like a politician naturally, it did not come to him easily. Outmanoeuvring an opponent was hard if you could not see the movement of their troops, the lay of the land, the turning of the weather. It was difficult because, in the capital, you did not even know who was your enemy and who was your ally.

Would the Lord Chancellor back him if he challenged Cecil? Would the other lords? He trusted Tomas' version of events, but he would be more confident if the young Cramwall had brought his pet Q'shari with him. Tremelowe wanted to look into the creature's eyes. Cecil showed guilt. Would the Q'shari? That would strengthen his resolve.

Did you hit him because he went beyond his authority, Cramwall? Or did you hit him because you gave him a task and he left loose ends?

Tremelowe turned his attention to Lord Garyth Garstone of Port Castor in the south. The city was a fortress, a great harbour at the point where the Regal River met the Jagged Sea. Garstone was a taciturn man who rarely left his home city. In most respects he was left to his own devices. Tremelowe found him humourless, almost empty. He respected him; Garstone was a fearsome warrior. Tremelowe was the victor of countless battles, but he had no knowledge of warfare at sea. Garstone was a master of the waves and of the land. His lesser lords consisted of men who held coastal forts against marauders of the Pirate Coast, whilst keeping their eyes trained on the flat blue horizon for any unwelcome threat from Altanya across the sea.

Garstone looked up for a second, catching Tremelowe's gaze. He smiled mirthlessly, shrugged his shoulders disinterestedly.

I shall get no backing there.

Garstone wasn't interested in upsetting the equilibrium. The realm was at peace, but not in his eyes. The Lord of Port Castor felt under constant attack, and that meant that the only thing he required was obedience and supplies from the cities to the north.

There was only one other senior lord present. Tremelowe knew what he was, even if some of the others did not. Tremelowe knew because he made sure that he knew everything, however distasteful he might find it. Whilst others buried their heads to deny the existence of the Vampire Lords, avoiding the uncomfortable questions it might raise within oneself, Tremelowe recognised their importance. They were old members of the nobility, and they had served Castland loyally throughout its proud history.

Sometimes, in order to keep the high ground, you have to keep friends you would not otherwise keep.

Tremelowe looked over to Lord Drathlax. He was the only Vampire Lord present. He was viewed as their representative, there to gauge their opinion on events that, in the most part, disinterested them entirely.

He took in the slender, white figure across the table. Drathlax's dark eyes remained focused on the goblet of red wine before him, but he shook his head slowly. Tremelowe knew the gesture was aimed at him. He wasn't a superstitious fishwife, he knew the vampire couldn't read his thoughts, but he knew Drathlax could sense his gaze. He would find no support there.

The only other person of note in the room was Iluma Porwesh, sat behind the Lord Chancellor. The old Yanari was paying attention to the conversation with a look of forced disinterest. Tremelowe didn't know why the pale little man was present, which made his attendance more disturbing, in a way. There was no reason to seek his approval or gauge his opinion. He was a Yanari; he neither had any influence, nor craved any.

Tremelowe turned in his seat, gesturing for Lord Mikhel Miller to lean closer. The martial lord from his lands pulled his chair forward, rubbing the ale from his short, strawberry blond facial hair.

"I feel we faced better odds when we fought the Raskans, Mikhel," said Tremelowe, shielding his mouth as he spoke.

"I think you're right, Oskar," replied the short, stocky ex-soldier, a thick-fingered hand running across the stubble of his shaved head. "But then, we've fought against greater numbers and won. That little cunt killed Tomas, and now they're trying to dance on his grave. They're spitting on the graves of all the men who fought the Raskans. Something needs to be said."

"You are right, Mikhel," nodded Tremelowe. "But not in front of everyone. Let us not make the same mistake Tomas made."

Tremelowe turned back to the table as the Lord Chancellor stood to address the assembled nobles.

"It is settled, then. Cecil will travel to Snowgate to ensure that the election goes as agreed. You will all return to your lands to make preparations. I will send word to each of you when Cecil is en route to organise your respective polls."

Nobody protested. The lords stood and began to mingle, calling for more drinks as they gathered together. Tremelowe took to his feet, gesturing for Mikhel to wait as he strode over to the Lord Chancellor's seat.

"Your majesty. Lord Chancellor. I apologise," he said. Cramwall broke away from his conversation with King Jaros. The ruler of Castland shot Tremelowe a disdainful look even as he nodded his acceptance of the interruption. "Lord Chancellor, may I speak with you a moment?"

Tremelowe glanced over the Lord Chancellor's shoulders as the head of the king's government stood, taking in Cecil's body language as he shuffled away from the table to join Gideon de Pfeiff and his entourage.

You did it, you little bastard.

"Of course, Lord Tremelowe. This way, if you will."

Cramwall led the way into a side room, crossing the plush carpet of the room and settling down in a comfortable leather seat behind the elegant desk. Tremelowe took in his surroundings; even the spare studies in the Lord Chancellor's palace were bedecked in more finery than his own, personal audience chamber.

"Have a seat, please, my lord," said the Lord Chancellor, gesturing to the chair opposite him.

"I will stand, thank you, Lord Chancellor," replied Tremelowe.

"Tell me, Lord Tremelowe, what is it that is so important that it could not wait for me to finish discussing business with our king?"

Tremelowe hesitated, mulling over in his mind the best way to word his thoughts. He was on the Lord Chancellor's territory now; politics and diplomacy. "As you are aware, Lord Chancellor, Lord Bannar was murdered in his own town recently."

"A tragic state of affairs," said Cramwall distantly, toying with the gold filigree decorating the desk in front of him. "Murdered by the very peasants he treated so generously. *Too* generously. Perhaps it should serve as a warning to us all. The poor folk do not seem to respect kindness when it is given to them."

"All does not appear to be that simple, Lord Chancellor," said Tremelowe warily, studying Cramwall's reaction. The man raised an eyebrow slightly, nothing more. "It seems that Lord Bannar was not killed by the common folk. Certainly not his own."

"How so, my lord?" asked Cramwall, focusing a little too hard now on showing his indifference.

"Nobody in Lord Bannar's lands recognises the dead man found by his side. He is a stranger. He bore a sign implying he was one of Lord Bannar's people, but he was not."

"Pah," laughed the Lord Chancellor. "You do not expect me to believe that every man, woman and child in Lord Bannar's lands was known."

"Things in the wilder lands are not as they are in the capital, Lord Chancellor," insisted Tremelowe. "If he was a local, someone would have known him, recognised his face."

"A recluse then? A woodsman? A hermit?"

"Why would Lord Bannar's actions raise such anger in a loner who lived so far from the settlements that nobody knew him?"

"I do not profess to know, my lord," said Cramwall, the beady blue eyes fixing on Tremelowe now. "Who of honourable birth can ever understand why the great unwashed would turn on such an overly-generous benefactor? The fact of the matter is that they did."

"With the greatest respect, Lord Chancellor, they did not. A sword was found at the scene. A marvellous blade, not the weapon of a commoner. Not the weapon of a Castlander. Curved, wicked, imbued with unearthly powers..."

"Have you been in the east so long that you have become a gullible child, Lord Tremelowe? Next you will be telling me the fairies took Lord Bannar."

"A Q'shari sword," continued Tremelowe, ignoring the Lord Chancellor's chastisement. "Your son's bodyguard carries two of them, I believe, across his back. Distinctive weapons."

"That sounds dangerously like an accusation to me, my lord," said Cramwall darkly, his eyes narrowing threateningly.

"I know not why your son's man would do this, Lord Chancellor," said Tremelowe carefully. "But he was present in Bannar. Perhaps he did it of his own accord. We will not know unless we question him."

Cramwall paused for a second, taking in the noble before him. "You have your suspicions, Lord Tremelowe. But you have no proof."

"Get the Q'shari in here, then," said Tremelowe, gritting his teeth. He could feel his temper rising. "Let us see if one of his swords is missing."

The Lord Chancellor paused again, weighing up his options. "Q'thell has a task to complete, Lord Tremelowe. He will be instrumental in assisting Cecil with policing the election. These are turbulent times for Castland. Let us get matters of state resolved. I understand that you want what you see as justice for your man. Once the election is completed, we will bring Q'thell forward for questioning."

"Lord Chancellor, I must protest..." insisted Tremelowe.

"And I must insist," snapped Cramwall, the blue eyes flaring. "The election first, then your witch hunt."

Tremelowe opened his mouth to speak before he composed himself. Losing his temper here would cause more trouble, he could not speak rashly. His mind turned, indecision creeping in. He steeled himself, taking a deep breath.

"Then we should get the election over with quickly. I will make preparations on my return to Kassell. Our vote will be carried out as soon as we are ready. Kassell will not be waiting for your son's arrival."

"That is not what has been agreed..."

"I did not agree," said Tremelowe. "The election will be carried out in my lands as normal. There will be no interference on my part, or the part of my nobles. The people will have their say."

"This is dangerous, my lord," said the Lord Chancellor, his gaze heavy on Tremelowe. "Remember what happened to Lord Bannar when he gave too much voice to the common folk. Remember what happened to him when he defied the throne."

"Is that a threat?" snarled Tremelowe, more angrily than he had intended. He felt his hands at his sides, clenched into fists.

"Lord Tremelowe, you are a respected noble of Castland," smiled the Lord Chancellor insincerely. "It is merely a friendly warning, from your concerned superior."

"Your concern is noted, sir," replied Tremelowe.

He did not wait for the Lord Chancellor to stand. Tremelowe turned on his heels and strode from the room, slamming the door behind him.

Cramwall winced at the heavy sound, shaking his head in disappointment.

He wouldn't be so foolish. Surely...

Lord Alain du Chanchat stood up to his full height before his king, watching as the monarch chewed on the greasy turkey leg held in his disproportionately small hand. King Atout the Goldhand was a decent height; not du Chanchat's size, but then few men were. He had perhaps once been a well-built man, but that had long since turned to fat. Du Chanchat didn't know why, but the ruler of Barralegne's small hands also drew his attention.

Everyone knows where a man with tiny hands is also lacking...

He stifled a laugh, waiting for the monarch to speak. It was the custom in Barralegne that nobody sat in the presence of the king. So du Chanchat stood at the foot of the dais leading up to King Atout's golden throne, patiently waiting.

At least, he hoped he was seemed patient. In truth, he could not stand Atout. The man was a fool; vain, ill-tempered, and dangerously ignorant. It was treason to doubt one's king, but sometimes du Chanchat feared the gods had sent Atout into the world to bring shame to the lord's beloved country.

Du Chanchat sighed as the king finished chewing and opened his mouth as if to speak. Instead he took another bite of the turkey leg, the grease running down his flabby chin.

Atout did not even look like a Barralegnan. His skin was a strange orange colour, apart from the milky white bags under his beady blue eyes. His hair was thinning, combed across the top to give the impression of a full head. It was rumoured that Atout's hair was naturally ginger, an undesirable colour amongst the nobility of Barralegne, and that he made it blond using lye soap.

That would explain the thinning...

The king of Barralegne coughed suddenly, choking on the mass of meat stuffed into his mouth. He spat out the contents down his front, struggling to breath as a servant rushed to pat him on the back vigorously.

Choke, you fucking embarrassment.

To du Chanchat's dismay, Atout recovered from the brief interruption in his eating, taking another bite of food as the servant wiped away the mess from his silk tunic.

Du Chanchat shook his head. It wasn't just that the man was an ugly imbecile. It wasn't just the fact that he doubted whether the king could grow a beard worthy of a Barralegnan. What grated on du Chanchat was that Atout did not take to the battlefield in times of war. The first king of Barralegne to never see war. How would the peasants see that? The man was like a fat, spoilt Castlander noble. Yet he talked as if he knew military strategy as well as he knew greasy cuisine and hired concubines.

Du Chanchat cleared his throat, growing more impatient.

"I know you are there, du Chanchat," said Atout, his mouth full of poultry. "You will wait until I am ready. I am the king here, remember?"

He doesn't even use polite terms of address. I am a lord of Barralegne, you arrogant pig.

Atout kept him waiting whilst he finished the chunk of meat. Du Chanchat considered taking a seat, even walking out of the throne room, but thought better of it. The king was a rash man, known to take unwise decisions on a whim. Lords had been executed for perceived slights, their lands given to Atout's lackeys. Du Chanchat wasn't sure whether the man genuinely believed the deluded notion that it was himself who kept order in the realm, or just didn't care.

"Castland, then," said the king, ushering the servant to leave the room with the golden platter from his lap. "How go things in the land of our beloved cousins?"

"I heard hints of unrest whilst in the capital, your majesty," said du Chanchat, looking distasteful at the monarch's ruined silks. "I think the Lord Chancellor is struggling to keep control of his people. It worries me."

"Fuck them," sneered Atout. "Why should we care about their woes?"

"Your majesty," said du Chanchat, summoning the last of his patience. "If the Lord Chancellor is struggling to unite his people, he may take drastic measures. There were intimations amongst the nobility regarding the Marralot region. It is on the border, a long-disputed area."

"It is mine," snarled the king, the blue eyes flashing angrily. "I have the deeds to prove it. Agreements signed after the last border conflict."

"Nobody is disputing that fact, your majesty. I am merely giving you my counsel. If I were in Cramwall's position, I would be feeling under pressure. Nothing concentrates attention away from problems within than a war with problems without."

"Will you stop talking in riddles, man?" snapped Atout, confusion crossing his face. Du Chanchat resisted to urge to shake his head in exasperation.

"The Lord Chancellor is struggling to control his poor folk. They do not know their place. They have ideas above their station. King Jaros is beginning to doubt his competence. The other nobles see opportunities. A cornered boar is at its most dangerous. He may attack our lands as a distraction from his own issues, to unite the country."

"This is what happens when you have democracy," chuckled Atout, wiping his chin on the sleeve of his expensive garment. Du Chanchat's eyes rolled in disgust. "It is lucky we don't have a Lord Chancellor, or elections, or representatives. Just a strong king. Not weak, like that old fool Jaros. A strong and stable king who rules his lands with an iron fist."

Du Chanchat stifled a snigger as Atout banged a tiny hand on the arm of his throne. "Quite, your majesty."

"What shall we do, then, du Chanchat? Invade the whelps?"

"That would be unwise, your majesty," said du Chanchat, realising too late that his wording was poor when the king raised a bleached eyebrow. "It would play into Cramwall's hands. My opinion would be to prepare for attack. Increase training for our troops and our commoners. Discretely move men into position to repel any invasion."

"Sounds a bit weak to me, du Chanchat. Are you a woman or a Barralegnan?"

Du Chanchat felt his hand move to the hilt of his greatsword. He had to force it away with all the inner strength he possessed. "I would nothing more than to wage war, your majesty. But is in our interests to show restraint. We are in a position of strength. We should maintain that position."

"If you say so," said Atout, waving his hand dismissively. "Make the preparations."

"I will move garrisons from the lands in the north to the border regions to the south, your majesty. The border mountains in the north are difficult, an army would struggle to pass through them. The point of vulnerability needs reinforcing."

"Yes, yes," replied Atout, his attention already moving away from the conversation. "Fuck it up and I'll have your head."

"Your majesty," said du Chanchat, his teeth grinding as he spoke.

He bowed as slightly as he dared, turning and striding from the room.

"Fat, useless cunt..."

Lord Unstead sat on his bed in his nightshirt, staring down at his hand, clenching and unclenching the fist with increasing annoyance. He was told it would help control his temper, but it wasn't working. He wanted to lash out, to smash the furnishings in the bedchamber to matchwood. If he was at home in Hearth Hill he would have done so, but the Lord Chancellor would not take kindly to having a room in his palace wrecked.

The spy hadn't reported in. It was late now, almost midnight. He obviously wasn't coming.

Unstead felt betrayed. He should have gone to the Thieves' Guild, the underground worshippers of Larcenara. Professionals who valued only gold. He had plenty of gold, and the best gatherers of information were members of the guild, but they were hard to find, and wary of nobles. He had contemplated the Assassin's Guild, but he had a deep mistrust of any worshipper of Sanguis. Unstead had despatched many men, but these people were different. The kill was the important thing, not the reason for it. Their stealth was beyond parallel, but he suspected a trail of dead men would lead to the information he wanted. If it were linked to him, he was already on thin ice with the Lord Chancellor.

So he had been forced to hire a freelance, known in some circles of the nobility for his discretion and his ability to obtain information. He had paid over the odds to ensure he got the best service. Yet the man wasn't here divulging...

Unstead extended a pale, freckled hand, the palm hovering over the single candle in the room. He left it there for a moment, feeling the heat burning the skin. He lowered the hand slowly, gritting his teeth against the pain until the palm snuffed out the light.

He sat in the darkness of the room, the light of the moon through the window the only thing playing across his scarred face. He reached up, stroking the stitched wound on his jaw.

Why was he surprised? The man was a criminal, after all. He would make sure the cunt never worked for any of the nobility again, though. And if he got hold of him...

Unstead started as he heard a voice, emanating from the shadows near the door to his room. It was quiet, gentle, a soothing lilt through the silence of the night.

"May I speak with you, Lord Unstead? I did not want to startle you by walking out of the shadows unexpected."

"Startle me?" snapped Unstead, pulling his legs up onto the bed and pressing his back against the headboard. He extended a hand to the bedside table, feeling for the dagger he had left there. His hazel eyes peered into the shadows. "Is a voice from the dark of an empty room not startling?"

Unstead's eyes widened as a shimmering shape moved into view. The figure was clad in purple robes, the hood covering the face. The movements were graceful, enchanting, the curves of the woman's hips enticing and soothing. She shimmered as she approached, as if Unstead reached out his hand to touch her it would pass straight through. He almost forgot about reaching for the knife.

"Sorceress!" he called, forcing his hand to scrabble for the weapon again.

The room went black, the light from the window suddenly snuffed out like the candle beneath his hand. He felt a slight rush of air across his hand, heard a dull thud as the dagger dropped to the floor in the blackness.

Unstead looked up, his eyes wide in the darkness. All he could see now was the apparition, silhouetted in the black of the room, slightly fragmented as if viewed through cracked glass.

"What are you?" he called, pushing himself back against the bed.

"I am just a woman, Lord Unstead," said the figure, her voice soothing, her movements entrancing. "A woman with information. You have been seeking information, have you not, Lord Unstead?"

"Did you kill my agent?" asked Unstead, trying to regulate his breathing.

She's just a woman, you fool. She's close. You could reach out and choke the life out of her. Snap her neck like a dry stick.

He didn't want to though. He couldn't see her face, but he somehow knew she was beautiful. Her eyes were concealed beneath the hood, yet they welcomed his gaze, pulling him towards her. He swore he could feel her breath on his cheek; warm, perfumed, sultry.

"No," giggled the figure, sliding onto the foot of the bed. She pulled the robe around her as she sat, tight against her shapely behind. Her body seemed to melt into the sheets, passing through the surface in places as if incorporeal. "But he *is* dead. Killed by a better man. A Yanari."

"Who killed him?" asked Unstead.

"Easy, my lord," said the woman. He could feel the gentle smile on her perfect lips. "I have information, if you want it. But we must have an agreement."

"Who are you? You know my name. We can have no agreement unless I know who I am dealing with."

"You may call me Cinquis," lilted the woman, her hand extending towards Unstead. He wanted to pull away, but found that the muscles in his body had become like jelly. A slender hand rested just above his thigh, almost touching, a warmth emanating against the skin beneath his nightshirt. He felt his loins stir. "I have much I can give you. I think you have much to give me, too."

"What can you give me?" asked Unstead warily, longing to reach out and adjust the sleeping garments around his swelling member.

"You want to know of Iluma Porwesh," replied Cinquis simply. "His involvement with the Lord Chancellor. What he owns. What he does. I can give you that, and much more..."

The warmth on the flesh of Unstead's thigh intensified as the hem of his gown moved up, exposing the freckled skin. Cinquis wasn't touching the garment; it moved of its own accord, as if equally enchanted by her unseen beauty.

"A show of faith?" asked Unstead, watching uncomfortably as his nightclothes moved of their own accord.

"Iluma Porwesh does own the Bank of the Sun. Or, to be precise, he owns enough of it in the shadows to own it. Your man was close to finding that out, before he met an unfortunate end."

"Who killed him? Was it the ugly little milker who killed my son? Who is he?"

Unstead sensed Cinquis smile beneath the hood. "All in good time, Lord Unstead. I can give you that information too, but we must have an accord."

"What do you want?" asked Unstead, flinching as Cinquis' hand moved up his thigh, not touching, but the warmth spreading against his skin as the nightgown receded in its wake, unveiling his erect cock.

"I do not know, yet," said Cinquis. "I may need you to do something for me, in the future. I would hope that you would return my generosity in kind, should I keep you fed with information."

"I am sure I can oblige you," nodded Unstead, his eyes falling to his uncomfortably hard penis as Cinquis crawled up the bed. She straddled his thighs, the robe floating above his legs, avoiding his touch. "Is that all?"

"Yes, Lord Unstead," smiled Cinquis, her hands grabbing the shaft of his cock. The fist clenched around it, not making contact, the burning intensifying on his sensitive manhood. "But know this. If you speak of me, or of our arrangement, I will visit agony on you like you have never imagined. Do you understand?"

The fire in his loins grew stronger, spreading across his crotch, scalding his flesh. Unstead winced, nodding desperately. "I understand, my lady."

"Then we have an agreement," lilted Cinquis, releasing her ethereal grip and floating away from the bed. Unstead watched her mesmerising figure as it slid towards the door. "And I am not a noble woman, Lord Unstead. I am certainly not 'your lady'."

Unstead watched as the purple-robed figure walked through the wall of the chamber, the oppressive darkness disappearing with her. He surged forward on the bed, his hands clasping at his tingling manhood. He looked frantically in the moonlight from the window, searching for any signs of injury from the spectral figure's touch.

There were none.

The hazel eyes looked to the door of his chamber, blinking in disbelief.

Chapter Thirty-One

Baronet Reinhardt sat atop his horse, staring down at the village of Woodhaven. *His* village. The little upstart yokel boy had turned his people against him, but it was still his village. He owned the buildings, the ground they were built upon, the surrounding lands. It was all his, passed down through generations. It was not for any peasant to tell him otherwise.

It was only mid-morning. They had made good time on the return to his lands. The sky above them was solid grey, light drizzle blowing into his face on a gentle breeze. Reinhardt looked around him at the men his liege lord had loaned him. Not a large force, but enough to rout some upstart villagers.

To one side, the group of ten heavy cavalry had dismounted, tying up their horses and stretching their legs and backs after the ride. Their full plate armour was immaculate, their liveried tunics damp but spotless. Reinhardt had always admired the elegant power of Castlander cavalrymen, strong yet graceful. Even just a few of them swelled his heart with pride in his country. If only his lands were big enough to afford to support a unit himself.

Sir Fredrick Yarron led them. The knight rode over to the baronet, the visor of his helmet pulled up to reveal his handsome young face. He brought his mount to a halt beside Reinhardt, gazing down on the settlement in the hollow before them.

"Are you sure we have enough men, baronet?" asked the soldier, his hand resting on the hilt of his longsword.

"Plenty, sir," replied Reinhardt, taking in the rest of the assembled troops as they set themselves down to rest after the journey. "Your cavalry, twenty spearmen, twenty swordsmen. Soldiers versus villagers. We could take five hundred of them if necessary."

The young knight raised an eyebrow. "Five hundred? I hope there aren't that many, my lord. Have you ever been to war?"

Reinhardt avoided the question. "Have you, sir? You do not seem old enough to have fought in the last one."

"I have put down peasant revolts and outlaw bands, my lord. A man fights hard if his home or his family is threatened. Harder than in a noble's war. I do not want any surprises."

"There are far less than five hundred, sir, believe me. We will have a better idea when you ride down to negotiate their surrender."

Sir Yarron laughed, shaking his head gently. "Diplomacy is not my strong point, my lord. These are your lands, and your people. You will need to discuss these matters with them. I will get the men ready. We are giving up enough of the element of surprise by negotiating with them."

"We must try, Sir Yarron," insisted Reinhardt. "Many of my people will, I am sure, have remained loyal to me. You cannot suggest we just charge in and slaughter them?"

The knight shrugged. "I was always taught to err on the side of caution, my lord. If you insist on this talk, I want the men ready when you return. If the news is not good, we will attack immediately."

"Then we shall attack from the north-east," said Reinhardt, pointing out across the land before him. "There are outbuildings there, a pig farm and a mill by the stream. They will cover our approach..."

"With the greatest of respect, my lord," smiled Yarron with feigned sincerity. "I will arrange the military matters. You have requested our help, and my liege lord has obliged. I would like my men to unscathed."

Reinhardt didn't bother to argue. He could see the young soldier's eyes flitting about the landscape before him, eyeing up the terrain.

"I will take a couple of the swordsmen and head down there under a flag of truce, then."

"You do that, my lord," said Yarron absently, eyes still playing across the scene ahead.

"We should have moved on by now," insisted Wrathson, looking around the assembled members of Charo's council, gathered in the main room of one the village's taverns. "We've been here too long."

"I agree," said Collagne. "The weather could become worse at any time. We are betting moving before it changes."

Father Pietr looked at them with sad eyes. He had delayed their onward journey as long as possible. He wondered whether it was as much to benefit his own old bones as those of the tired villagers. He nodded gently as Charo looked to him.

"Have we harvested all the food we can?" asked the youth, dark eyes flitting amongst his group of followers. "Gathered all the supplies we can carry? Made weapons?"

"The wagons and carts will be full when we load them up," nodded Mathias. "It can be done this afternoon if you wish."

"Every man has at least a spear," said Edgar. "Whether they can use them or not is another matter."

Charo looked to Wrathson. The sheriff shrugged his stocky shoulders. "They can carry on training on the road. You can't make a silk purse out of a sow's ear. At least, not this quickly."

"Then we are as ready as we'll ever be," said Charo. "We leave at dawn."

The group murmured their agreement, readying to leave and make preparations. They were interrupted by an urgent knock at the door. It flung open without acknowledgement, one of the villagers stumbling in.

"It's the baronet," gasped the man, pointing out into the drizzle. "He's returned. He wants to speak to Charo at the east of the village."

"I thought we could trust him to leave," snarled Niman, seeking out Paull with angry eyes.

Charo's father shrugged, struggling for words. "I..."

"This is no time for blame," said Mathias. "How many men does the baronet have with him?"

"Just a couple," said the villager, his eyes wild with fear.

"Can we trust him?" asked Charo, turning to Wrathson.

"He won't get far with two men," said the sheriff. "These nobles are cunts, but if he's come to talk I can't see him attacking us."

Collagne nodded his agreement.

"Then let's see what he has to say," said Charo, leading the way from the inn.

Villagers had begun to gather as Charo and his advisers turned up at the eastern track into the village. He took in the baronet, mounted on his horse between a pair of liveried swordsmen clad in chainmail, hands on the hilt of their weapons. Reinhardt himself was wearing damp but pristine travelling clothes, good quality garments but not armour.

Surely he would have dressed to protect himself if he had come to fight?

Charo raised his hand as his group came within ten yards of the baronet, bringing them to a halt.

"What do you want?" he called.

"I wish to offer any of my villagers who wish to leave safe passage," replied Reinhardt, cold eyes taking in the youth before him. "I do not want to see them harmed for your foolishness. Similarly, any of your own who have done no wrong may surrender and be treated justly."

"I would find it hard to trust the word of a man who swore to leave these lands," said Charo, staring defiantly back at the baronet.

"I swore to leave, and I did so," shrugged Reinhardt. "Now I have returned. These are my lands. These are my people."

"The people are not your possessions," snapped Charo. "It is that attitude towards them that has cost you these lands. We have taken them back, in the name of Lunaris, as punishment for the cruelties and injustices you have inflicted upon these folk."

"Cruelties?" scoffed Reinhardt, turning his gaze on Paull. "Injustices? Ask your father who it was who pulled him back to his feet when he fell so heavily to the demon drink."

Paull looked to his youngest son, his head bowed. Beside him, the skeletal figure of his wife squeezed his hand, shaking her head gently at her husband.

"A few good deeds do not cancel out a life of oppressing the poor," said Charo. "You obviously have some good in you, baronet, which is why you were allowed to leave with your life. I pray to Lunaris that you reach deep inside and harness that purity. You must stop being part of the cycle of persecution and recognise that things are changing in Castland."

"Castland *is* the aristocracy, boy. The order of the land depends on the rule of the nobles. Without a strong hand to lead the common folk there would be chaos."

"Lunaris does not agree," declared Charo. "The fear you have sown in the people's hearts makes them strong. It makes Lunaris strong. And he has sent me to harness that power and set them free from your yoke."

"You do not understand..."

"It is you who doesn't understand, baronet," interrupted Charo. "I am giving you a choice. Yet another chance. Leave this place, and accept the change in the order of things. If not, you will die."

Reinhardt shook his head vigorously, his eyes angry now. "Never. I have soldiers with me. Not a ragtag bunch of peasants. Soldiers. It is you who will die. You do not have long to send out any people who wish to surrender."

The villagers around them began to speak up now as the baronet and his men turned on their heels and headed from the settlement. People were gathering in numbers now, desperately trying to gather their loved ones, contemplating their options.

"We are losing control here, Charo," uttered Pietr, watching as the panic began to spread.

Charo looked around the villagers as they moved this way and that, gesticulating and arguing amongst themselves. He turned to Wrathson.

"We need to be ready. This is your area, sheriff. Let anyone who wishes to leave do so, though. I won't force people to tread our path."

Wrathson moved into action, gathering the group together, trying to ignore the clamouring sounds of panic.

"If anyone leaves, they need to go along the east path. That should get in the baronet's way. Maybe it'll delay his move. Willem, gather anyone who can use a bow and get them in the upstairs windows of any building facing east."

The hunter nodded, scurrying off to gather his semi-trained archers.

"If I was them, I would come from the north-east," said Collagne. "Plenty of cover in those buildings."

Wrathson nodded. "Grab some men who can swing a sword and get out there. Try and jump them if you can. Leave the spear carriers here, they won't be any use up close and personal."

Collagne nodded.

"I'll get the spearmen in the street here. The attack will come down this eastern track. Leave me some swordsmen though, Collagne. Some good men, people who can keep Charo safe."

"We do not even know how many of them there are," said Pietr, looking out warily into the drizzle.

"It doesn't matter," said Charo. "We will fight, and we will win. Lunaris is with us."

"I hope to fuck you're right, lad," smiled Wrathson as the group dispersed to organise the defence.

Charo felt Mathias' hand on his shoulder. He looked up at his older brother, saw the barely-concealed fear in his eyes. "Just stay close to me, little brother."

"Any luck?" asked Sir Yarron as Reinhardt approached his vantage point above the town.

The baronet shook his head, bringing his horse to a halt beside the knight. "The little bastard wants to fight."

"So be it," shrugged Yarron. Reinhardt swore he saw a look of pleasure cross the young soldier's face as he reached up a metal-clad hand, slamming his visor shut and turning his horse towards the assembled warriors. "Get ready, you maggots."

The heavy cavalry had already mounted their horses, helped by the young squires scurrying amongst them. The young noble boys were now rushing to one of the supply wagons, bringing forth the long, metal-tipped lances stowed there. It two to carry each of the impressive weapons, straining to get them upright and balanced in the supports on each horseman's saddle.

The infantry were gathering together, the spearmen forming up into two neat lines as their sergeants bellowed orders. The swordsmen formed up beside them, their formation looser, long steel blades drawn.

Yarron brought his mount up before them, snatching his lance from the hands of a pair of squires.

"This should be easy, boys, we all know that," he bellowed, rising up in his stirrups. "But then, over-confidence has turned many a battle the wrong way. Keep your wits about you, and fight like you are engaging the deadliest foes in the Mortal World. Keep the images of your wives and your children in your head. You want to get back to them, yes? You want to get back home in one piece?"

The soldiers let out a roar of approval.

"I want you to. So gather your strength, and follow my orders. Swordsmen, get yourselves into position and approach through the outbuildings to the north-east. I want the spearmen formed up on their flank, tight, like a virgin's cunt. Don't get dragged into the buildings, just keep an eye out for anyone trying to get around the sword-bearers' sides. Once they are through, support them through the village, but keep together."

"Heavy cavalry, we will charge the eastern road. Stop for nothing. Smash through any resistance and then head northwards to meet up with the foot-soldiers. Any resistance should falter by the time we have cut our way through."

"And where shall I position myself, sir?" asked Reinhardt, watching as the men began to move into position, the infantry heading north around the hilltop overlooking Woodhaven.

"Stay at the back, out of the way," replied Yarron. "I do not want you getting harmed. It would be… embarrassing."

The knight bellowed after the infantrymen moving away: "Once you are in position, the horn will sound to signal the attack."

Collagne peered from the window of one of the mill's outbuildings, watching as the pristine swordsmen moved into position, approaching the outskirts of plot of land.

Well drilled. They move like toy soldiers. Rhythmic, disciplined…

He admired that. It showed quality training. His people had the numbers, even out here at the mill. It wouldn't be enough in a straight fight; their opponents were drilled soldiers. But Collagne wasn't intending it to be a stand-up fight. If they could just gain the element of surprise, rush them from all sides out of the buildings, wound a few, that would be the test of the opposition. Drilled soldiers liked things to go to plan. They liked order, regimented fights. Sudden, unexpected carnage might just break them, or at least make them panic enough to gain the upper hand.

If not, we're fucked…

Collagne's eyes strayed to one of the back doors to the outbuilding for a second. Was this really his fight? He was a mercenary, after all, a sellsword. Charo wasn't paying him. Lunaris wasn't paying him. He could just leave, run off into the wilds, find a new life. Go back home to Barralegne, perhaps?

He snapped back to reality as the distant sound of a horn slashed its way through the fine rain. One of the men was watching him, his own eyes turning to the door.

Was Charo really the champion of Lunaris, sent to save the poor from tyranny? He hadn't seen anything, only that creepy skeletal bitch following him around. Any nutcase necromancer could summon the undead, or so he had heard. It didn't make him a fucking hero…

"Did you see it, back at the village?" he hissed, grabbing the man by the scruff of the neck and pulling him close. He could hear the clinking of chainmail as the soldiers moved closer. "Did you see Charo with the demon?"

The man nodded wildly, his eyes wide with terror and confusion. "Yeah. I saw it. He pulled it apart with those hands of his. A fucking creature from the dark."

Collagne steeled himself, releasing his grip on the villager.

Every man has to die sometime…

"Get ready," he hissed. "Pass it on. We attack on my signal. Just hit at the head or the arms, as hard as you can. It probably won't get through that armour, but it'll fucking hurt, hopefully put them down."

The man nodded, his knuckles white from gripping his sword as he turned to pass the message along.

Collagne listened, moving to the side door to the outbuilding, peering out carefully to look into the splattering rain. The first man passed him, the second, the third. He pulled his sword close, tightening his grip, controlling his breathing.

"*Now!*" he roared, charging out amongst the soldiers.

He was committed now, but he registered the sound of the men following him as their feet spattered in the puddles of the narrow yard. It gave him some hope as he ran to the centre of the startled group, bringing his sword down hard on the skull of one of the soldiers. The blade dug deep in the bone, links of mail spraying out from the wound. He planted his foot on the man's body as it fell to the ground, struggling to wrestle his blade free.

Around him, the villagers were not faring as well. Their blows were wild, glancing off armour with penetrating. Luckily, the element of surprise meant that the soldiers weren't ready to retaliate. Some fended off the blows whilst others took them, staggering in the wake of the onslaught. A couple fell to the ground, injured.

Collagne lashed out at the nearest man, catching him in the arm. The blade didn't pierce the mail, but it was hard enough to cause the soldier to drop his weapon. He followed up, the man stumbling away in his wake.

It was enough. Reinhardt's men were caught off guard, taking casualties, and face with superior numbers. The sergeant leading them called out, leading a move to push through the villagers, driving to escape the yard.

"Wait," he yelled, watching as the inexperienced men surged after the fleeing troops. He followed, calling out again. "Form up here. Wait."

It was too late. The villagers charged from amongst the buildings into the heavy drizzle. Collagne watched as the enemy swordsmen parted, revealing two rows of ten spearmen. They were formed up perfectly, tight, their shields covering each other, twenty long, pointed weapons levelled at the oncoming villagers.

The soldiers stepped forward into the first wave of villagers as one, thrusting the spears as a unit. The men couldn't stop in time to avoid them, screams cutting the air as they were impaled. The villagers behind them hesitated, panicking. The spearmen moved forward again, chanting to keep rhythm, thrusting again. More screams. More bodies.

The swordsmen had regrouped now, wading in from the sides, their blows much more efficient against their lightly-armoured, half-trained opponents.

Collagne shook his head. "Run, men. Back to the village. Run for your lives."

Yarron led the cavalry charge, spurring his mount as it galloped towards the village. He could see villagers emerging, forty or so, moving out into the field before his men.

Have they really come out to engage heavy cavalry in the field?

He peered through the slits of his visor. No, there were women and children amongst them. They were all unarmed. They had their arms out wide, shaking their heads, shouting inaudibly.

Get out of the way, you stupid fucking peasants.

"Do not break stride, men," he roared over the thundering of hooves. "Do not waste your lance blows, but do not break stride."

The fleeing villagers noticed too late that the cavalry were not changing direction. They parted before the horses, some too slowly. A young boy's hand slipped from his mother's grip, his eyes wide as Yarron's horse smashed him to one side, his broken body splatting down in the mud.

Willem watched from an east-facing balcony as Collagne's men fled in the face of their better-drilled opponents. The swordsmen were on their heels, the unit of spear-carriers following slowly, keeping their formation. The villagers were less weighed down by armour. The majority were outrunning their pursuers, thank the gods.

There was nothing he and his archers could do to help. At this range, only Willem and a couple of the younger lads would hit a target. Besides, there was a bigger threat. The heavy cavalry were charging across the open ground, heading for the east entrance to the village held by Wrathson's spearmen.

They were in range, at least for Willem. But if he started firing now, the others would too. They would waste their shots, miss. It was better to wait, at least get a decent fall of arrows on the horsemen.

He knew it wouldn't be enough. Both the men and their horses were heavily armoured. It would take a miracle to penetrate all that metal.

Willem steeled himself, uttering a prayer to Lunaris.

We have to try...

"Get ready," he called out, nocking an arrow into his bow. In windows and balconies of the buildings around him, his men followed suit. "Loose. And keep firing."

He released, his arrow flying out to join those of his fellow archers. The shots were good, better than he had expected. The arcing flight of the swarm of missiles came down towards the mounted soldiers, landing in a tight spread. None found a home in flesh, though. The plate armour was just too thick.

The heavy cavalry came onwards. He loosed another arrow. The missiles didn't fly in a swarm now, coming at differing intervals. The level of skill at reloading amongst his men varied dramatically. None of the horsemen fell. None even faltered in their charge.

He readied his bow again. They were nearly at the village...

Wrathson watched the arrows bouncing off the approaching heavy cavalry, shaking his head.

Just one. Even just one would have helped...

He looked to Charo, stood beside him, those dark eyes staring intently, defiantly at the charging horsemen as their mounts thundered towards them, kicking up clumps of mud behind them. His family stood around him, his father and brother less convinced, their fear evident.

The bastards had just run straight through the villagers who had chosen to leave. Not even broken their stride. Rode them down like dogs.

Wrathson took in the spearmen before him, lined up four deep across the muddy street. Resisting a cavalry charge was hard. Strong spearmen could do it, if they were well-trained and resolute. Bind tight, level the spears, hold steady even at the point of impact. Men would die, but it could stop heavy cavalry.

But the men before him weren't well trained. They weren't strong enough. They were too loose, their resolve faltering as the horses thudded closer. Their whole bodies trembled, the grip on their weapons weak. Even if they held rather than ran, they would be run down just like the villagers on the field.

He looked to his deputies, young Ben and Lucas. They stood behind him, their swords shuddering in their hands, their breeches stained with piss. Edgar stood beside them, the heavy battleaxe clasped in his thick fingers, staring past Wrathson at the oncoming enemy. The blacksmith gulped visibly, his Adam's apple sliding up and down his thick neck.

"We need to retreat," said Wrathson, turning his head to Charo. "They won't hold. We'll be wiped out."

"Lunaris will protect us," said Charo, eyes still focused on the nearing cavalry.

"Not against that, lad," insisted Wrathson. "We can form up in the graveyard. Those horses won't be able to jump the wall, not in that barding. They'll have to come through the gate, a couple abreast."

Charo looked to him, his eyes defiant. He shook his head gently.

"Fall back, lads," roared Wrathson, ignoring the youth. "Get to the graveyard. Form up inside the gate."

Charo glared at the sheriff, his eyes dark and angry. The stocky man ignored it, grabbing his collar and dragging him towards the north end of town. The spearmen split as the cavalry reached them, avoiding much of the damage. Long, elaborate lances caught some, throwing them to the ground, their bodies pumping blood from deep wounds. Others were buffeted aside by the powerful horses, thrown to the ground in battered heaps.

"Spread out, boys," yelled Wrathson, looking over his shoulder to make sure the men were fleeing with him. "Get to the graveyard."

"Run them down," roared Yarron, standing up high in his stirrups, his lance pointed towards the grey sky as his horsemen spread around him.

They wouldn't have withstood his charge, so they had broken. Not to worry. Striking fleeing men in the back was less likely to break a lance. He hefted his shield back into position, spurring his mount in motion. He charged down the nearest man, the lance skewering him through the back. As he moved he angled it towards the ground, allowing the corpse to slide off, before re-settling the butt of the weapon in its holder.

He paused for a second, lifting his visor to better survey the scene of the slaughter. Why were they heading to the north of the village? His infantry would be coming in from their flank, hopefully cutting them off.

This is what happens when children play at soldiers with their betters.

Yarron spurred his horse again, slamming down his visor and levelling his lance at his next target.

"Stay here, father," said Willem, running from the balcony and towards the stairs.

Pietr looked up from his chair and nodded sadly. His young apprentice sat beside him, the disconcerting eyes seemingly unconcerned by the sounds of battle outside.

Willem reached the street, his archers from the other buildings gathering around him as he ran, darting north between the structures.

"To the graveyard," he yelled. "Just get to the graveyard."

Ahead he could see Collagne, dragging a man along as he fled the pursuing enemy swordsmen. The man clutched his face in his hands, blood pouring from some unseen wound. Ahead of them ran the surviving villagers, their eyes wild as they fled the professional warriors chasing them down.

214

Collagne was lagging behind. One of the swordsmen was gaining on him, raising his weapon to strike. Willem stopped in his tracks, nocking an arrow and letting fly. He preferred shooting at this range, aiming at the target rather than up into the air. More accuracy. More stopping power. The arrow lodged in the neck of the soldier bearing down on Collagne, piercing the chainmail coif. His legs went from beneath him as he stumbled to the ground clutching his throat.

Willem's men had stopped beside him, loosing arrows of their own into the enemy swordsmen pursuing their fleeing comrades. A couple struck home in soft flesh. No fatal blows, but enough to stop the men in their tracks again. They ran for cover, breaking off their pursuit.

"To the graveyard," shouted Willem again, sprinting forward to help Collagne with the injured man.

Wrathson led the way through the gate into the graveyard, pushing Charo down behind one of the larger tombstones. He turned, watching as the surviving villagers began to stagger in through the entrance. To the east he saw Willem helping Collagne over the wall of the cemetery, their panicked men gathering amongst the graves.

"Keep him here," Wrathson snarled at Mathias and Paull. The men nodded, Raechael's skeletal form settling down to pull her youngest child close. "Keep him safe."

"Get back here, you fools," cried out Edgar, his bald head glistening from the heavy drizzle as he called out to the men fleeing past him.

"Gather round me," roared Wrathson, wiping the rain from his eyes with his heavy hand. "They'll chase you down if you don't fight. We fight *here*. Where we can win."

The men gathered round reluctantly, joined by the archers and Collagne's survivors.

"Spears, form up in front of the gate. Same formation. Nice and tight. Front row kneeling, spears dug in the ground. All of you keep those weapons pointing just below the level of a horse's chest."

"And let them charge at us?" cried one of the men, looking through the hazy drizzle at the horsemen finishing off their straggling comrades. "Fuck that."

"Would you rather they just rode in here and fucking killed us?" snapped Wrathson. "They'll have to come in two abreast. You can hold them."

"Lunaris will protect us," called out Charo, standing up behind the tombstone. "He is with us."

"It's true," shouted Collagne. "These are soldiers, but they aren't invincible. We stuck it to them hard at the mill. They fled. And Willem's bowmen had them running again just now."

The villagers began to nod, their fortitude returning.

"Then form up," yelled Wrathson, watching as the spearmen grouped inside the graveyard gate. "Collagne, your lot just need to stop those foot soldiers climbing over the wall. Don't get too involved, just stop them getting across. Willem, your lads get at close as they dare and stick arrows in them. Make sure they aim carefully, Collagne's boys will be up close and personal with them. But they haven't got any archers, so they won't like it that we have."

Collagne and Willem looked to one another, blinking the water from their eyes.

"Let's get this done," said Collagne. "Fuck the lords. Fuck the baronets."

The men around them roared their approval, readying their weapons as they took up their positions.

Wrathson looked to Charo, the youth staring balefully through the rain at the leader of the cavalry forming up opposite the gate.

I hope you're right, lad...

Yarron threw his broken lance to the ground, drawing his longsword and waving it to direct his cavalry into position. They formed up in pairs, lances at the ready. The little bastard obviously had something going for him. He had convinced his spearmen to form up again, inside the gate of the graveyard.

Will they actually meet the charge this time, though? Cowardly commoners.

He looked over to his infantry, ready to storm the wall from the east side. The swordsmen had taken some casualties, but from the blood on their rain-soaked tunics it seemed that they had dished out some punishment too. After all, the villagers had fled. Yarron was a little disappointed, though. Losing skilled soldiers to yokels was an embarrassment. He would have the sergeant flogged for disgracing his honour.

A hail of arrows sliced through the air over the heads of the villagers manning the low wall, thudding home amongst Yarron's infantry. A few screams rang out where they had breached mail.

Why are they not just charging?

"You," he snarled, pointing his sword at one of the mounted soldiers. "Dismount and get those bastards over that wall."

The man nodded, climbing carefully down from his horse and striding towards the foot soldiers, waving his sword as he boomed orders. The swordsmen and spear-carriers charged as he approached, engaging messily with the villagers. The commoners held their ground, much to Yarron's annoyance.

"Charge," he said, levelling his weapon at the first pair of heavy cavalry.

The men kicked their mounts into action, lowering their lances as they thundered through the gate towards the assembled spearmen. The common folk held their ground. They were trembling visibly as the horses bore down on them, eyes filled with panic, but they held.

The lances were longer than the spears. Two of the men at the front of the line were skewered through the chest, but still they held. The levelled spears dug deep into the chests of the horses, their own momentum driving the points through the armoured barding. The magnificent beasts crashed down amongst the men, breaking their line with their thrashing death throes. One of the cavalrymen landed on his head, the weight of his body snapping it at a sickening angle that made even Yarron avert his eyes for a second. The other's metal-clad body dropped amongst the villagers, heavily winded.

"Draw swords and charge," roared Yarron at the next pair.

The men threw down their lances, drawing their swords and raising them high as they approached. The villagers were struggling to re-form their line, but the soldier who had landed amongst them was up on his feet now, lashing out with his weapon. Their cohesion was breaking down as the next two cavalrymen hit them. The spears weren't levelled properly, glancing off the barding of the horses. The horses crashed down amongst them, their legs twisted amongst the mess of living and dead bodies.

The two mounted soldiers were ready. They managed the inelegant dismounts well. They found their feet quickly despite their full plate armour, their swords lashing out amongst the villagers. The spearmen parted before them, leaving the dead and dying as the only obstacle before Yarron and his remaining men.

The young knight looked over to the infantry. Several were lying on the ground, writhing as they tried to pull arrows from their bodies, but the majority were clambering over the wall, the villagers falling back in their wake. The armoured cavalryman was at the front, slashing heavily at the commoners before him, swatting them down as if they were insects.

Yarron smiled beneath his helmet. "Draw swords and charge."

He kicked his horse forward, leading his men through the gate.

"This is it," yelled Wrathson, bring his sword up and charging forward into the fray, Edgar on his heels.

The armoured soldier in front of him was preoccupied, knocking the spear of a villager aside and thrusting the blade of his sword along the man's neck. Blood sprayed through the rain as the dismounted cavalryman turned, too late to repel the sheriff's attack. Wrathson swung his blade down, severing the hand clutching the sword at the weak point in the armour's wrist. He pulled back to strike again but Edgar was there first, the heavy axe taking the man's head clean off, the weight of the weapon taking it straight through the armour.

The blacksmith charged on forward, the axe crashing into another armoured soldier's chest, sending him sprawling.

Wrathson looked up just in time to see the flanks of the leading knight's horse. The rider was preoccupied cutting down another villager with his weapon, but the weight of the heavy beast threw Wrathson to one side. He rolled over through the mud, coming to a stop on all-fours, winded.

Above him, the knight was swatting away spear-points with deft flicks of his sword, striking out at his attackers between parries. A man's face appeared in Wrathson's view, his head splatting into the mud, blood trickling from his lips.

Wrathson forced himself up onto his feet, just as the knight's sword came arcing down towards him. He deflected the blow barely, the force sending him staggering as the well-trained horse followed him, the knight raising his weapon to strike again.

Collagne came bowling in out of nowhere, gripping his sword in both hands and swinging it at the horse's ankle. The blow cleaved the hoof clean off. The animal staggered backwards screaming, throwing its rider into the mud.

"Get up," urged Collagne, hauling Wrathson upwards and back towards Charo and his family. "We've been broken. We need to flee."

Wrathson staggered into Mathias, grabbing the lad by the shoulders. "We need to go."

He looked around, his stomach sinking as he realised the hopelessness of their situation. The villagers were fleeing in all directions, the enemy soldiers chasing them down. They were surrounded, foes on all sides of the beginning to break off their pursuit and circle the leaders of Charo's uprising. Willem staggered towards them, dragging the heavy figure of Edgar, blood pouring down the blacksmith's face from a wound on his forehead.

"We're fucked," said Collagne, his voice broken. The enemy troops began to gather around them, the cavalrymen still on horseback bearing down menacingly. The dismounted knight pulled himself free from his collapsed horse, clutching his sword angrily.

"Lunaris," cried Charo, tears streaming from his dark eyes as he fell to his hands and knees, his small hands clutching at the mud. It oozed between his fingers as he sobbed. "Where are you? We need you."

The knight laughed cruelly. "Lunaris? It seems you have picked the wrong god, little boy. A dead god."

"*Please,*" hissed Charo. His hands squeezed again, as though trying to claw the ground.

"It is too late to plead for mercy, whelp."

"*Please.*" Charo's voice was almost inaudible over the groans and screams of the dying. The rain was teeming down now, the heavy splattering further drowning out his voice.

A faint purple glow spread across Charo's buried hands, dull beneath the mud. A faint tremble spread across the ground beneath the combatant's feet. The horses that were still standing whinnied nervously, their hooves moving right and left uncertainly.

The knight hesitated for a second, looking about his soldiers. He watched as those that were still mounted struggled to control their steeds.

"Lunaris hears our prayer," smiled Charo, squeezing his hands again. The purple glow seemed to spread, sliding up over his skinny wrists. The dark eyes looked up to the knight, menacing and distant. "You will die."

The knight didn't have chance to respond. Another tremor resonated through his legs, shallower and more insistent than before. He glanced to his side in time to see the first of the horses rear up, unseating its rider. The others followed suit as the mud began to churn beneath the feet of his soldiers, the ground breaking as clawing, skeletal hands erupted and grasped at their ankles and knees.

The men's screams grew louder as the first of the skeletons scrambled into view, pulling itself up a spearman's body and sinking its yellowing dead teeth into his throat. Around him, more of the undead were ripping free of the earth, shaking the dirt from their bodies and setting about his soldiers.

Wrathson watched agape as the skeletons crawled up from the grave around them. The haze of drizzle was tinted purple, a glow that seemed to emanate from Charo himself. He turned to the youth, but his eyes were distant, seemingly tinted violet.

"You will all die," said Charo bluntly. A vacant smile played across his young lips.

Several of the knight's men turned to run. Bony hands flashed up out of the ground, grabbing their ankles, tripping them to the floor. Some died as different hands reached up, clawing at their throats. Others were pounced upon by the undead who had already struggled out from the ground, throttled or beaten to death.

One of the dismounted knights ripped his mace free from his belt, smashing it through the skeletal figure before him. The bones flew in all directions as the undead creature came apart, the fragments spattering into the mud around him. Several of the other corpses grabbed at him, pulling him backwards, wrenching the weapon from his grasp. One of them pulled his head back, exposing his throat, the eye sockets glowing purple as it stared at him, the jaw a macabre grin. Another figure picked up a spear from the ground, thrusting it through the man's neck.

The knight watched in horror as the scene descended into chaos, the undead grabbing weapons from the ground and cutting down his soldiers. He looked down upon Charo, the youth still on all-fours in the mud, the eyes distant and tinged with violet.

"You will die for this, necromancer," he roared, raising his sword and charging forward.

Wrathson reacted quickly, throwing himself forward and knocking the sword from the knight's hand. The man was a warrior though, strong and fit. He twisted Wrathson's sword arm down, planting a metal gauntleted fist on the sheriff's jaw.

Wrathson's head led his body into the ground, his vision hazing over again. It seemed to be a regular occurrence since he had met Charo.

At least it wasn't my nose this time...

He struggled to rise as the knight reached out for Charo, strong hands ready to close around the youth's neck. Collagne and Mathias were moving now, but they wouldn't be in time. The knight was a killer. He would snap the lad's neck like a twig.

Wrathson struggled to stand, but his limbs were heavy, numb. Darkness was beginning to close in at the edges of his vision.

Suddenly a bony hand crept into view as Charo's mother clambered onto the knight's back, ripping back the visor. The other hand clawed into view, gauging deep red lines in the soldier's face, seeking out the eyes. The man closed them, screwed them tight, but the bone of the skeletal fingers was sharp. Raechael's fingers pierced the thin skin of the eyelids, pushing deep into the pulp of the knight's eyes and skull.

Wrathson's view became a tunnel, surrounded by black. As it closed in, the face of the knight crashed into the narrowing circle of sight, mud splattering across the young face, blood streaming down from what remained of the dead man's eyes.

The darkness crept in until Wrathson's vision dwindled to complete blackness...

Baronet Reinhardt watched from horseback as the undead pulled themselves free from the sodden earth to engulf Sir Yarron's soldiers, his mouth agape. He forgot the rain that was pouring down, soaking him to the bone. It had seemed so important a few moments ago, a major discomfort that filled his thoughts.

The weather was nothing now. He had seen something worse, an evil from beyond the grave cutting down good soldiers, and he would never forget it. Tears streamed down his cheeks, mingling with the rainwater.

The boy was evil, a creature of the dark sent to torment the living. He was certain of it. Reinhardt watched in terror as Charo turned his head towards his position, the dark eyes seeming to bore into his soul even from this distance. A shiver ran down his spine, unrelated to the cold and the damp.

His horse reared up beneath him, forcing him to press hard into its back, gripping the reins tightly. He struggled to bring it under control, pulling it round to flee the village.

He had to escape this evil. He had to warn Castland what was coming for them.

Chapter Thirty-Two

"These are dark times," proclaimed Ratcliffe from the balcony to the crowd massed at his feet. The gatherings had been growing. The election had been announced, and he had announced that he would stand. He had similarly-minded men in place in most of the cities and major towns. "The people are not content. *You* are not content."

The crowd roared its approval. At the edge he could see Yarner and his men, watching him speak, keeping an eye on the mass of common folk. Ratcliffe smiled. He felt safer with the watch sergeant around, despite the warning he had been given. He was sure Yarner wouldn't let him come to any harm, despite his frostiness.

"There are rumours of rebellion in the west. Travellers tell of demons stalking the living, summoned by a newly-risen cult of Lunaris. I hear talk of villagers laid to waste, of nobles put to the sword for their crimes against the common folk."

Another cheer. Yarner was looking concerned now. The talk was becoming inciteful. Ratcliffe shook his head at the watchman below gently.

"In the east, a great warrior lord, risen up from the poor folk, has been murdered. Murdered by the aristocracy for giving rights to his peasantry. For giving them value. For making them feel like human beings rather than assets to be abused and spent."

The crowd were booing and hissing. Fists were raised, calls for an uprising were being shouted out. Yarner was shaking his head uncomfortably, looking around for signs of other watchmen.

Ratcliffe raised his hands, calming the people. "There is no need for violence, my friends. The nobility has been forced to hold this election, and they have been forced to allow us to field our own representatives. My People's Party has nominees across Castland. Vote for me, and we can take control of our own lives for the first time in history. No uprising. No revolution. Democratic, lawful rule, where the land is run for the benefit of the masses, not the aristocracy."

The crowd erupted in cheers as Ratcliffe took a bow, withdrawing from the balcony. He headed downstairs into the throng. It took him some time to shake hands with the gathered well-wishers as he made his way over to Yarner and his men.

"Sergeant," he nodded. "I am glad to see you have escaped the sewers."

"Just for the election, I fear," said Yarner. "You need to be careful, Ratcliffe."

Ratcliffe smiled, eyeing Reaper warily as the huge dog trotted over, sitting before him. The agitator reached down apprehensively, scratching the animal behind the ears. "I am doing nothing illegal, sergeant. I am merely standing for elected office."

"Some of what you say is bordering on sedition, Ratcliffe. I told you before, you need to watch your back."

"It seems you are watching it for me," smiled the reporter.

"We're just here to keep the peace," said Yarner. "A lot of folk on the street means the watch need to keep an eye on things. That's all."

"I am grateful nonetheless," said Ratcliffe, nodding his head and moving away into the huge crowd of supporters.

"You need to keep away from him, sarge," growled Magnus, his weasel-like features watching Ratcliffe leave, suspicion wrinkling his face. "He's bad news. I don't want to get dragged down with him or with you."

"Reaper seems to like him," shrugged Griegor, kneeling down to rub the mastiff's nose.

"I like him too," announced Arnie, his young face filled with admiration as Ratcliffe moved amongst the crowd. "He seems a good man."

Yarner pointed at him, speaking more harshly than he intended. "You do *not* like him, boy. Do you hear me? You can agree with him if you like, but you don't like him. He might *seem* a good man. But remember, he's a reporter. He's an agitator. And now, he's a politician, it seems. You can't trust him."

Arnie nodded, his gentle eyes turning to the floor. Yarner felt cruel for chastising him so harshly.

"The sarge is right, kid," said Magnus. "You've got that pretty bird of yours to worry about now. You stay away from that fucker."

Yarner nodded. It wasn't often that he and Magnus agreed on anything. "Come on, lads. Let's get one more patrol done then get an ale or five inside us..."

Lord Perlis sat on the elaborate bone chair, Xavier at his side. His indigo eyes flicked over the letter from Lord Drathlax that outlined the coming election. He passed it to his son dismissively, taking a few sips from the red stone goblet of wine and blood on the arm of his throne.

"Does this mean the Lord Chancellor's son will be coming here?" asked Xavier, running his slender hand through his mane of silver hair thoughtfully. "I cannot imagine the little lord venturing into our bleak lands."

"I am sure he will only monitor events in the major cities," replied Perlis, his eyes gazing down the long, echoing hall. "That is where the power lies."

"Do you wish for me to make preparations?" asked Xavier. "We can be ready, then, when we are told to conduct the vote."

Perlis' eyes turned to his son, anger flashing in them. "*Told?* Are you truly my son, Xavier? The meat does not tell the cook when it is to be eaten."

"But Lord Drathlax is explicit..."

"Do you think he will be waiting? Do you think any of the Vampire Lords will be waiting? They may be cowed shadows of their former selves, but they still have some pride. The details will be worded that way in case the carrier pigeon was intercepted. The election will be carried out in a fortnight. You will need to arrange the nominations of the candidates."

"Will we allow the people to choose representatives?"

Perlis smiled. "Of course, son. Let them do as they wish. The current Establishment Party officials will also stand."

"But father," said Xavier hesitantly. "What if the people vote for other parties? The Lord Chancellor has decreed that we should punish them."

Perlis laughed, the sound hollow as it reverberated around the empty hall. "The Lord Chancellor will sit on my hard, white cock before he decrees *anything* to me. We will not be punishing our people. Let them vote as they wish. Our common folk are happy with things as they are. There are no murmurings of discontent, unlike in other lands. They do not want their representatives to rule. They want *us* to rule. When was the last time one of the mayors came before us to make proposals?"

Xavier nodded. It was true. The people were happy. They were well fed, protected, looked after. There was no reason for them to want change.

"I will make the preparations, father."

"One more thing, Xavier," said Perlis, placing a hand on his son's arm gently. "Was the gold shipped to our friend's partners in the major settlements?"

Xavier nodded. "Yes, father. I have had missives confirming Jaspar Ratcliffe's people are in receipt of the coin. But, isn't this dangerous?"

Perlis laughed again. "For us? Of course not. We have nothing to fear from the humans. The gold cannot be linked to us. Even if it could, what would they do? The only danger is to them, and to the Lord Chancellor's precious natural order. If the agitator's People's Party gathers momentum, the current unrest amongst the peasantry will look like a ripple in the water compared to future developments."

Xavier smiled reluctantly. "If you are sure, father."

Perlis watched as his son strode from the hall. The lad was cautious. That was a good thing. It took centuries to learn what risks were worth taking.

He had had centuries to develop that knowledge...

Iluma Porwesh raised a hand to silence the discussion between the men before him at the dining table in his Regalla abode. They had finished eating and exchanged the necessary pleasantries. Porwesh had proceeded to voice his thoughts, and a clamouring argument had ensued. It was most un-Yanari.

"This is just too risky, Porwesh," said Ceva Mardich, shaking his head as he stifled a belch after the rich food. "I swear to Yanara, you are losing your mind."

"I have to agree with Mardich," spoke up an elderly Yanari, wiping his wrinkled mouth with a napkin emblazoned with the yellow sun motif. His name was Juli Rothisch, the head of the Bank of the Sun in Castland. "It was dangerous enough that you insisted I transfer monies to the Castland Times. It would dire for us all if the donations were discovered. The Castlanders will not accept that their most prestigious news journal is run by a Yanari."

Mardich nodded. "You put us all in danger with that move, Porwesh. I did as you asked because we are friends."

"With the greatest of respect, my friend, you did as I asked because I compensated you handsomely."

"But *you* did not compensate him, Porwesh," insisted Rothisch, shaking his head. "The Bank of the Sun compensated him. You have plenty of funds at your disposal, yet my bank paid the gold to Mardich here."

"Also with the greatest of respect, Rothisch, I own a significant proportion of the bank," said Porwesh gently. "I have my reasons for wishing the monies to be supplied by your institution."

"Would you care to enlighten us?" asked Mardich combatively. "If you could teach me the thought processes of a crazy man, that would constitute my Illumination for this period."

Porwesh fixed the newspaper owner with an icy stare. Rothisch looked to the table, rearranging the knife and fork on the empty plate uncomfortably.

"My apologies, Porwesh," said Mardich awkwardly. "My facetiousness was uncalled for. I merely wish to understand your motivations. Especially since they risk putting us, and the Yanari people in general, in danger."

"This humble Yanari will always accept your apology, my friend," smiled Porwesh, his old face crinkling with the movement of his thick, white lips. "But I cannot enlighten you further on my aims. Some things must remain out of sight. Yanara's light casts shadows for a reason. For you to understand would place you at increased risk. I would urge you to trust me. Have you ever failed to prosper under my guidance? Have the Yanari people done anything but benefit from my actions?"

The two men looked to each other, shaking their heads.

"Good, my friends," smiled Porwesh warmly. "Then we shall donate funds to the People's Party, for us in their campaigning during the election."

"Porwesh, are you aware that the People's Party is run by the same man who publishes the People's Gazette?" asked Mardich carefully. "What if your funds are put into the newspaper rather than the campaign. This could impact on the Castland Times heavily."

"And as before, my friend, the Bank of the Sun will compensate you more than adequately for any lost revenue."

Mardich smiled, looking across the table at Rothisch. The banker shuffled uncomfortably, nodding at his plate.

"It will be arranged," said the old Yanari. "But I am concerned that the bank would be further exposed by giving gold to the People's Party. A Yanari institution giving money to the Castland Times would be a severe blow. If we were found to be donating gold to a party that the Lord Chancellor views as bordering on revolutionary, that would be fatal."

"You are quite right, my friend," said Porwesh, smiling as Rothisch visibly sighed with relief. "If you would, please make arrangements with the Crown Bank in Barralegne. They will, I am certain, be happy to donate funds to the People's Party."

"But the Crown Bank is not a Yanari institution," said Rothisch uncertainly.

Porwesh laughed gently, the sound rasping and wheezy. "That does not mean I do not have a significant interest in it, my friend. Now, if you would excuse me, I am an old man and I need my rest. If you could send my daughter in as you leave, that would be most appreciated."

The two men stood, nodding quickly to the old Yanari and heading from the room. Kalyanit strode in through the doors as they left, gracefully taking her place at her father's side.

"Did you hear anything of our conversation, my dear?" asked Porwesh, smiling at the beautiful fruit of his loins sat beside him.

Kaly nodded timidly, the lashes of her beautiful blue eyes flitting. "The walls and doors are thin in this place, father."

Porwesh chuckled roughly to himself. "Honesty is a good trait in a woman. If a man cannot trust the discretion of his only child, he can trust nobody. Tell me, what did you make of what you heard?"

"I do not really understand it, father," shrugged Kaly innocently. "I find these intrigues confusing."

"Of course you do, my love. You have had a sheltered upbringing. It is time you learned the ways of things out in Castland. It is time you took an interest in affairs of state. You are an intelligent young woman. You have excelled at everything put before you. It is time that you excelled at politics. After all, you are to be the future Lady Chancellor. Tell me, how are things with Lord Cecil?"

"They are well," smiled Kaly shyly, he cheeks tinting red. "He is a lovely man. We have met a few times since he returned from the east. I hope that he is happy with the match."

Porwesh's blue eyes softened as he gazed at his beautiful daughter. "Do you love him? Do you feel you can love him as a wife? Be honest with me, my dear."

Kaly nodded enthusiastically. "I love him, father. Truly."

Porwesh nodded, relief seeming to spread through his frail body. "Excellent. From talking to the Lord Chancellor, his son is very taken with you too. I have arranged for you to accompany Lord Cecil north, to Snowgate. He has a very important task there. You may find some of it distasteful, but it is the way of things. You need to learn about the real world, outside of the bubble within which I have held you so close. You need to give him strength; the fortitude a woman gives a man."

Kaly nodded eagerly. "I can do that, father. I am eager to learn."

Porwesh smiled. "I know you are, my dear. You are your father's daughter."

Tomas sat on the edge of his bed in his nightgown, flexing his arm tentatively. He was getting his movements back slowly. His chest still felt tight, each movement painful, but the wound had healed well. The cleric of Pharma seemed to think it was healing too well. Tomas swore that the man thought he was some kind of abomination.

"I swear that priest would rather I died," he said, smiling at Tremelowe sitting in the chair beside the bed. "For a cleric of Pharma he seems positively disappointed that I've survived."

"You would think he would be glad he was able to bring a man back from such a grave wound," admitted Tremelowe. "I think he is just jealous that he had little to do with it. It seems your stubbornness is what kept you with us."

"It doesn't seem to have done the job with this." Tomas gestured to his upper arm. The wound was bleeding again, the white bed robe stained red with blood.

"I fear that will be with you for some time, old friend."

Tomas sighed, tentatively standing up and pacing to the window, gazing out over the city of Kassell.

"You seem steady enough on your feet," observed Tremelowe. "I wager you will be fighting fit in no time."

"I'm fit enough to get about now," insisted Tomas. He longed to get out of this room, get out amongst people again. He looked down at the figures far below, going about their business. His eyes moved upwards, looking to the horizon beyond the city walls. "I need to get back to Talia. I need to get back to my people."

"Why do you think you are still in that bed shift?" smiled Tremelowe. "If I gave you your clothes back you would be roaming around, letting everyone know that you are alive."

"Do you honestly think I wouldn't roam around naked if I wanted?" asked Tomas, turning to look at his liege lord. "The only reason I'm not out there now with my cock feeling the breeze is because I made a promise to you, Oskar. I waited until you returned. Now it is time for me to leave."

Tremelowe sighed. "These are troubling times, Tomas. I fear it is not safe for you to reveal yourself, with or without your cock hanging in the wind. The Lord Chancellor has called an election. An election like no other."

"How so?" asked Tomas. He listened as Tremelowe divulged Cramwall's plans, shaking his head in disgust at each tawdry detail. "The man has gone insane."

"Quite the opposite, I am afraid," said Tremelowe. "For all these years the people have been happy with the illusion of power. Elected representatives, governing in their name, advising the lords. The lords rarely listen, and the only option is the Establishment Party, but the people accept it. Now they are being given yet more imaginary power. It may well stave off a revolt by the peasantry."

"Don't tell me you are actually going to go along with this?" asked Tomas, his eyes wide with shock. Tremelowe hesitated for a moment, refusing to meet his friend's gaze. "Oskar?"

Tremelowe stood abruptly, striding over to the window to stand beside Tomas. "I am insulted that you asked that, Tomas."

"You didn't seem too forthcoming with an answer..."

"Because whichever answer I give is dangerous, Tomas. Dangerous to me, to the other lords under my stewardship. Dangerous for them..."

Tremelowe nodded out of the window, gesturing at the people below as they went about their daily routines, unaware of the delicate decisions their lord was having to make on their behalf.

"It is precisely because of those people that you must resist Cramwall's call," said Tomas gently.

"I know, old friend," said Tremelowe sadly, his worried eyes turning to the martial lord. "And I will. The election in our lands will be carried out as soon as the candidates have had time to prepare. There will be no coercion. The people will decide, and I will support their choice. *We* will support their choice."

"That's the right thing to do, Oskar."

"You seem so sure," said Tremelowe. "It will lead to conflict with Regalla, possibly with the rest of Castland. There was no support from the other lords."

"Then we'll take the fight to them," insisted Tomas. "Give me the army. We can be at the gates of Regalla before they have time to rally their troops. You and me, fighting side-by-side again."

"Against the rest of Castland?" Tremelowe shook his head. "I will not be a usurper, Tomas."

"The Lord Chancellor is a despot, Oskar," snapped Tomas, punching the sill of the window with a gnarled fist. "If he will not submit to the will of the people, to democracy, he must be unseated."

"And that is democracy? The majority of the country votes for the Establishment Party, and we go against their decision?"

"Is the Lord Chancellor's proposal democracy?"

Tremelowe hesitated, returning his gaze to his people in the bustling streets. "I will not send these people to their deaths fighting the rest of Castland."

"We can win, if we strike first," insisted Tomas. "If we take the capital, the Lord Chancellor, then we take the country."

"I will not start a war, Tomas. I shall resist the capital, but I will not attack it. We do not have the numbers."

Tomas paused, turning his own eyes once more out of the window. He looked to the horizon, imagining the road back home. In his mind's eye he crossed the lands, passed Bannar, moving to the mountains beyond. He thought of the plains on the other side; rolling, barren lands occupied by a vast nation of blond-haired, blue-eyed, hardy men.

"We could get them," he said gently. "An alliance to crush the threat from Regalla."

"Where?" asked Tremelowe warily.

"Raska."

Tremelowe's eyes grew wild, his nostrils flaring angrily. "What did you say?"

"The way we rule our lands is more in keeping with the ideas of the Raskans. We give our people power, self-worth. The Raskans may respect that. Side with us to change this country for the better. It could seal a long-lasting peace between our lands..."

"If you were not an invalid, Lord Bannar, I would smash your head around the walls of this room," snarled Tremelowe, pushing past Tomas and heading for the door. "We fought those pigs, you and I. Do you not the remember the men we lost? Do you not remember the *son* I lost?"

"I remember, Oskar," insisted Tomas. "I remember too that we invaded their lands beyond the Bleakthorn Hills. Our men died taking their lands. Their man died defending them. Defending them from us, from the invaders. Because the Lord Chancellor sent us to kill people over fields and hills and forests."

"Fields and hills and forests that they took from us in the *Second* Raskan War," snarled Tremelowe.

"And how many decades ago was that, Oskar? How long does someone have to own some land before it becomes theirs? Did we have it first, in the dawns of time, or did they? You've said it to me yourself, when you were mourning your lad. He died fighting a war started by the Lord Chancellor because he was losing his grip on the realm at home. He died a hero. All those men died heroes. But they died fighting a war that Cramwall used as a distraction."

Tremelowe stood at the door, breathing heavily, his fists clenched so hard that the knuckles were turning white, the fingernails digging into his palms. A solitary tear rolled down his cheek as he gritted his teeth defiantly.

"I need to get back to my lands," said Tomas softly. "I have preparations to make. I trust you won't stop me, Oskar?"

Tremelowe shook his head, the movement awkward. "No. What preparations? For the election, I trust?"

"That will be conducted first," nodded Tomas. "Then I will gather my troops, and the troops of any other lord who will march with me, and I will bring to justice the man whose son tried to kill me. The man who threatens my people, and your people."

"I will not support you, Tomas."

"Will you stop me?" asked the martial lord gently.

Tremelowe opened the door stiffly. "I have never stopped any of you doing as you wish, within reason. You are lords in your own right. You have earned your lands. If you wish to squander them and the lives of your people, that is your decision. Do not lay any blame at my door, though. Lord Miller is heading back to his lands soon. I will have clothes sent up. You can ride with him, for your own safety."

Tomas nodded. "Thank you, my lord."

Tremelowe paused in the doorway, his eyes sad as he stared intensely at his old friend. "I promise you, though. If you bring Raskan troops into Castland, I will *never* forgive you. A swear it by Guerro's blade..."

Tomas didn't get chance to respond. Tremelowe was gone, the door rattling on its hinges as it slammed shut behind him.

Cecil sat back in the plush chair in Lord Arther Princetown's dining hall, his feet resting on the table beside the silver platter he had just finished. Toby's father looked at him disdainfully from the head of the dining table, plucking a few grapes from the bunch before him and popping them into his mouth.

"The preparations are well under way, Lord Princetown?" asked Cecil, sipping from the crystal wine glass in his hand.

Princetown's dark eyes burned in his pale, chubby face as he addressed the Lord Chancellor's son. "The votes in the northern poor quarter will take place in a week. Once you have addressed any insubordination, the vote in the southern peasant district will be held the following week. Other districts will follow once we are sure that your methods have had the desired effect."

Cecil nodded, smiling at Q'thell. The Q'shari had made a remarkable recovery. The primitive forest-dweller was moving without inhibition now, despite the wounds he had received. Cecil didn't know whether he was just adept at concealing his pain, or whether the healing process in his race really was exceptionally quick.

"Excellent," he said. "Rest assured, Q'thell and his men will ensure that the southern quarter does not emulate the mistakes that the northern peasants make."

"I think you insult the extent of my control over my lands," scoffed Princetown. "The poor know who controls Snowgate. They will vote for the Establishment Party, as always."

"Is that so?" sneered Cecil. "Tell me, Bligh. What rumblings come out of the northern poor district?"

Cornelius Bligh sat opposite the Lord Chancellor's son, a dark-skinned native of the Pirate Coast. His hair was spiked with animal fat, dyed bright yellow, contrasting sharply with his skin tone. He wasn't pitch black like Q'thell, but he was certainly darker than any Castlander. Cecil smiled. If you skinned him and Lord Princetown, you could make a convincing chessboard from their hides.

Bligh was dressed in the traditional, baggy clothes of his race. The shirt was white, loose-fitting, the sleeves frilled. His breeches were similarly ill-fitting, tucked in elaborate leather boots just below the knee. The shirt opened wide below the neck, revealing a toned chest and shoulder muscles. Bligh was a brute of a man, his full strength only slightly disguised by his loose clothing. A heavy gold medallion hung from a chain around his thick neck, matching heavy gold earrings and a gold front tooth that glinted as he smiled widely.

"It isn't good, *machero*," he said, his voice deep and rumbling.

Cecil had had to have the word translated when he met the man, suspecting it was some sort of slight. It turned out it meant 'master' in the Coastman's native tongue, which Cecil deemed near enough to 'my lord' to be appropriate. He had hired Bligh to assist with the task assigned by his father.

"You see, my lord," said Cecil, shaking his head in disappointment. "It seems you do not know your people. How can you control them if you do not know them?"

"I know my people better than this... savage..." spat Princetown incredulously.

"When was the last time you visited the markets in the poor quarter, *machero*?" asked Bligh, turning his disconcerting, light green eyes on the lord of Snowgate. The broad smile remained, wide and goading. "The brothels? The taverns? The poor talk of this People's Party, and they like it. They eye it greedily, like a red-blooded man eyes the arse of a whore."

"I think we can dispense with the unsavoury descriptive devices of a savage," snapped Princetown, avoiding the Coastman's gaze and focusing on Cecil. "I feel like a foreigner in my own country. In my own city. At my own *table*. Tell me, Cecil, why do you insist on hiring outsiders as your retainers? Are native Castlanders not up to your standards?"

"They bring a little variety to the table, Lord Princetown," shrugged Cecil. "And they come untainted by pre-conceived ideas about who they should serve. They natural order is important, obviously, but sometimes, if a man has been brought up within the hierarchy, it becomes a barrier to what needs to be done. These men have none of those preconceptions. They understand our ways, but they are open to any ideas I might bring forth. Their loyalty is to me; the man who pays them, the man who keeps them in their position. They hold no fanciful ideas about what Castland *should* be. The believe only what I tell them it is."

"Is that some kind of veiled threat, boy?" snapped Princetown, his tone incredulous.

"It is a statement of fact, my lord," replied Cecil offhandedly.

"A lord who cannot control his people is a liability," stated Q'thell, the red slit eyes turning on Princetown.

The portly lord shuffled uncomfortably, feeling suddenly outnumbered in his own hall. He opened his mouth to speak.

"Another good observation from the savage," said Cecil, cutting Princetown off. "You see, my lord? They offer an alternative point of view. As my father has already declared, the realm is in the midst of difficult times. Times such as these leave no room for sentimentality. A man cannot rely on the fact that his family has been in the nobility for generations if he is incompetent. Results are what matter in times such as these."

"You forget yourself, Cecil…"

"Not at all," replied the young noble, taking a deep sip of his wine and shaking his head gravely. "You, Lord Princetown, have failed to manage recent events. The Lord Chancellor doubts your credentials. I know this for a fact. In the interests of honesty, I, too, have disappointed him. I accept that my head is on the block. Do you?"

Princetown blustered inaudibly, struggling for words.

"I intend to make my father proud," continued Cecil. "Regain his trust, if you will. Now, being in your position, it would be advisable for you to ensure that happened. After all, it is also in *your* interests. But if you stand in my way… Well…"

Cecil turned his head to Q'thell. The Q'shari flicked a dagger from beneath his armpit, imbedding it into a slice of rare meat still on the plate before him in a flash. The blade pierced straight through the silver, imbedding in the wood of the table. Blood oozed from the skewered morsel, spreading across the platter.

Cecil shrugged, turning his cold, blue eyes on Lord Princetown.

Chapter Thirty-Three

Head Priest Lexis sat on a rock in the small clearing, trying to dry his wet robes out by leaning close to the fire on which a pair of skewered rabbits were cooking. Their guide, a local ranger by the name of Ryn, turned the spit occasionally, charring the animals equally as they cooked on the open flame.

Lexis wiped the hair from the razor-sharp blade in his hand onto a damp white cloth. He reached up again, scraping the implement across his scalp gently, taking off another line of dark hair. Each stroke left behind glistening, bare skin.

"Father, why do you shave your head?" asked one of the initiates from his position close to the campfire. A young lad, enthusiastic, the only one who had not complained yet about the journey. "The Book of Pharos teaches us that Pharma favours the growth of hair to reflect the accumulation of knowledge."

Lexis looked around the group of clerics and initiates. They were glum, their white robes already stained with mud and soaked by rain. They had followed the Low Road south out of Regalla, relying on their position as priests of Pharma to seek lodging in each village or coaching inn from the faithful. Their progress had been slow; even the youngest of the clergy was not used to travelling on foot for such an extended time.

The Low Road linked the capital with the city of Port Castor on the south coast, but they had left the road at the village of Green Hollow. Last night had been their last stay for a while under a roof. Lexis had obtained the services of Ryn and advised the group to get a good night's sleep before they headed out into the forest.

Tonight was their first night in the open. Ryn had been patient, showing the clergy how to erect their tents and get ready for the night. It was obvious to Lexis and the ranger that none of the other eleven members of Pharma's faithful had ever slept outside before.

Lexis eyed each one in turn, making them wait for his response. In his experience, people listened harder if they were left in anticipation first. And they would have to listen hard to some of the revelations in the coming days. Much of the news would be in direct contradiction to their deepest beliefs.

He had chosen each of the group himself. Eleven of the clergy, strong enough to complete the journey. Some fully ordained priests who left their chapels in the hands of their initiates. Five men and the only woman, Mother Elsa. He had not wanted to take any women; the wilds were no place for the fairer sex, and clerics of Pharma of both genders tended to be more fragile creatures than most. But Elsa's knowledge and faith was strong, easily as strong as the men in the group. She was also rumoured to be a good cook.

The remaining five members of the group were initiates, young lads with strong backs to carry the supplies and the tents. The future of the clergy of Pharma. It was important that new, more open minds were in attendance on the quest.

Only the lad who had spoken up, Sewell, seemed to be bearing up. The rest looked broken already. Lexis was beginning to doubt whether they would even complete the first part of the quest.

"The Book of Pharos was not written by the Merciful One's son, Brother Sewell," said Lexis, scraping the knife across his skull and wiping it clean again. "It was written by men. And men do not always impart knowledge exactly as they were told."

"Are you saying that the Book of Pharos is wrong, Father Lexis?" asked Yulli, one of the male clerics. "Is that not blasphemy?"

The Keeper of the Lore fixed the priest with his intense gaze, the flames of the fire flickering in his pupils. "I am saying that there are other tomes in the Library of Knowledge that contradict some of the teachings in the Book of Pharos, Father Yulli. I am saying that, in some areas, the writings in the Book of Pharos may have become distorted."

"So, are you saying that we should be shaving our heads, Father Lexis?" asked Sewell, eager to please the head priest.

"No, child," smiled Lexis absently. "I am saying that it is unclear. Perhaps our mother god has more important things on her mind than our clothes and how we wear our hair."

"If that is the case, Father Lexis," spoke up Elsa. "Why are these teachings not updated? Why are the rest of the clergy not made aware?"

"An interesting question, Mother Elsa," said Lexis, watching as the assembled faithful gathered round like children eagerly awaiting a bedtime story. In all honesty, he would rather save the revelations for another time. He, too, was tired. He was not as fit as he once was. But the discussion seemed to be turning the group's attention away from the day's travails. "The Keeper of the Lore has access to every piece of learning relating to our religion. Each Keeper must assess this knowledge, deciding the potential truth or falsehood or error in each tome and manuscript. Then he must decide what knowledge should be kept withheld, what knowledge should be released, and when."

"Surely the truth is all that is needed?" asked one of the initiates, his young face puzzled.

"That is a youthful notion, Mida," smiled Lexis. "It is admirable, but it is not right. Or maybe it is right, but it is not practical. You see, any religion relies on the faith of its people. The faith is built on the tenets rolled out centuries ago, and then amended a hundred years ago when Pharos was born into the world. Now, that might seem a long time ago, but in terms of religion that is but yesterday. Some of our beliefs changed, according to what Pharos taught us. To change any of those tenets again, so soon, would shake people's faith. They would begin to doubt. Who could blame them? Why dedicate your life and your soul to a clergy that says, 'I made a mistake?'"

"But surely the people will come to accept it?" asked Elsa.

"Would they, though, Mother Elsa?" asked Lexis. "Would the masses keep their faith? Even the most faithful seem shaken by new revelations. When I told the head priests, the most devout of our order, that Pharos still lived, their faith was shaken. Even now, when I tell you there is doubt as to the veracity of tenets as simple and harmless as how to keep our hair, I can see Father Yulli denouncing me inwardly as a heretic..."

Yulli opened his mouth, stuttering, shaking his head. "Head priest, I would never..."

"Easy, father," smiled Lexis gently, the intense eyes settling on his fellow priest. "I do not blame you for being doubtful. It is natural. But please, do not deny it. It is unbecoming. We will travel far together, and we must be honest with one another. I am a man of the world, Father Yulli. I was not always a priest. And I can read a man's feelings as easily as perusing a book."

"I..."

Lexis shook his head reassuringly. "There is no need, father. You must come to see with your own eyes. I cannot force you."

"What else should we know, Father Lexis?" asked Sewell eagerly, kneeling on the sodden ground before the Keeper of the Lore.

Lexis laughed hollowly. "Nothing today, brother. Before we set out, you believed Pharos to be dead. This morning, you thought you should let your hair grow. You thought that everything you had read was set in stone. That is enough for now."

"But father..."

"No," insisted Lexis, his voice harder this time. "When you let a supplicant's blood with leeches, do you drain his body dry to kill the fever?"

Sewell shook his head, bowing his head to the floor.

"Exactly. It would be fatal. And too much new knowledge in one go will kill your faith. You will learn plenty on this journey, I assure you. There is no need to rush."

The howl of a wolf cut through the pattering of the rain, slipping through the thick forest around them and passing over them. Lexis looked out into the darkness, thick and heavy amongst the old trees around their camp. His eyes turned questioningly to Ryn.

"Miles away," said the guide, pulling the cooked rabbits from the spit and beginning to divide them into thirteen portions. He pulled the small iron pot of vegetable broth from the fire, spooning it over the meat.

"How far into the wilds must we travel, father?" asked Yulli, turning his back to the fire to look out into the night around them.

"Into the High Moors, my friend," replied Lexis. "Ryn here knows the place we seek. I have shown him the map."

"But does he know the way?" asked Yulli. "Is he capable of keeping us safe out here?"

"I'm right here," snapped Ryn, standing and handing bowls of food to each of the party in turn. He left Yulli until last. "I can fucking hear you, you know? I do speak Castlander. I know where we're going, and I'll keep you safe. It's what you're paying me for, isn't it? You lot sort out the watch shifts between yourselves. If you see anything, get me from my tent and I'll deal with it."

The ranger tapped the bow slung over his shoulder before returning to his spot, sitting cross-legged on the floor and tucking into his food.

227

"That is settled then," said Lexis. "We shall make sure we rotate the watch each night. I will leave it to you all to arrange amongst yourselves. I will take the last shift each night. I prefer to be up early anyway."

Lexis watched as the clergy tucked into their meal, the distaste evident on their faces. Their temperament would worsen as the rations began to dwindle and the only food was dried jerky and beans.

He began to doubt once again whether these people had the fortitude for the task at hand.

Carilo Tristane plucked another olive from the silver bowl on the table, popping it into his mouth with a smile. It still amazed him when he was called to visit Lord Oskar Tremelowe in his splendid keep. Here he was, a man from the Bandit Country, born on the dusty streets of Matus far to the south, dining with the lord of Kassell.

He looked around the elaborately furnished hall, rolling the ripe green ball around his mouth before stripping it of its flesh, spitting the stone delicately into a napkin. The room was grand. Grander than his own sizeable hall, that was for sure. What astonished Carilo about Castland was that, by all accounts, the homes of the lords nearer to Regalla were even larger, even more flamboyant.

All this wealth, all this opulence, yet they live miserable, serious lives. Always worrying. Always watching for the knife in their back.

Carilo watched his own back too, but he didn't let it dominate his life. Whatever would be, would be. And he was an Illicean. Family was important to the people of the Bandit Country. Family meant you weren't the only one watching your rear.

"This is a good spread, as always, Lord Tremelowe," nodded Carilo, taking a sip of the Panda Port in the crystal glass at his side. "You know how to look after a man."

"I bought it from your people," smiled Tremelowe distractedly. "It ought to be good."

"It still surprises me that you buy my wares, Lord Tremelowe," laughed Carilo. His smile was boyish, alluring. He was a good-looking man, his skin tanned, his hair walking the line between brown and blond, his eyes blue and welcoming. A true Illicean, pure of blood. "A lord of Castland, sampling the illegal delicacies of my home country."

"All the lords of Castland partake in some goods or other from the Bandit Country, Carilo. You know that. The bulk of the country just does not have the right conditions to produce olives, oranges, lemons, grapes, tobacco, coffee, tea. All the good things, really."

Carilo winced slightly. He hated it when Old Illicea was referred to as the Bandit Country. But Tremelowe was his friend. Well, maybe not a friend, but he was a close acquaintance. He let it pass.

"It makes me wonder why our wares are illegal at all, my lord," he smiled, pulling a small, engraved box of cigars from his pocket. He placed it on the table, producing one for himself and Tremelowe. They lit them both from the candles on the dining table, thick smoke filling the air as they tugged the rolled tobacco into life.

"We do not trade with the Bandit Country," said Tremelowe, rolling the fragrant smoke around his mouth. "You are all thieves."

Carilo laughed deeply, smoke puffing from his mouth as he struggled to avoid choking.

An observer who did not know the men might have expected him to take offence. But Carilo could not deny it. Old Illicea *was* a nation of thieves. They produced much, it was true, but the vast bulk of the rough alliance of cities' revenue came from raiding the caravans crossing their lands on the way to and from Altanya. Or making them pay a tithe for passage, which in effect was the same thing.

The journey through the dusty plains and scorched hills was a long one for traders on their way to or from Altanya. The temperature for Castlanders was unbearably hot. Altanyans found it too cold, their alabaster-white bodies shivering at the contrast with their desert homeland.

And when the traders arrived at Freeport, the southernmost city of Old Illicea on the shores of the Jagged Sea, they found many a captain willing to charge exorbitant rates for safe passage. It was the only real choice, though, as a trade route between Castland and Altanya. Some merchants still risked sailing from Port Castor directly, but the city was close to the Pirate Coast. Convoys of vessels banded together to minimise the risk, but there were always casualties. The crossing of goods was financially rewarding, but both routes were fraught with danger.

Carilo wasn't a thief, though. He was a criminal, but not a thief. His family ran much of the illegal trade in Kassell. They dealt in goods from Old Illicea and beyond. Liquor, weapons, delicacies, all fell within their remit. They ran some of the best brothels in the city; the best whores and the best protection for them and their clients.

"And yet you let me go about my business, my lord," smiled Carilo gratefully.

"You help me to keep order in the city, Carilo. The people have vices. I would rather they were satisfied in a manner that does not create chaos. Criminals peddling wares on every street corner and brawling for control of territory is not something I want in Kassell. I would rather things are run... efficiently. In an orderly fashion. Plus, you have an ear to the ground. Tell me, how do things go with the election?"

Carilo took another sip of his port, weighing up his response. Tremelowe was a decent man, he was sure of it. He preferred to hear the truth, even if it was news he found distasteful. Unlike many men Carilo had dealt with during his colourful life, Tremelowe was not inclined to take out his annoyance on the messenger.

But he is a noble. He might not be too fond of this People's Party gaining momentum...

Carilo popped another olive in his mouth, stalling for time. No, it was better to be honest here. His business resolved around Tremelowe being in control of the city. If the election interfered with that, then it threatened the Tristane family too.

"The peasants like this People's Party that's sprung up," he said warily, watching Tremelowe's reaction intently. "Your Establishment Party looks likely to lose a lot of representatives, my lord."

Tremelowe nodded. The lord was weighing up the news, his features knotted in thought.

Is he angry? He doesn't look angry.

"And does this party incite rebellion? Are the people discontented, Carilo? Are they like to take this result as cause to revolt?"

Carilo laughed out loud. "They just want more say, my lord. The people don't hate you, trust me. You're well-loved, for a noble..."

He paused, regretting his words. Had he gone too far?

Tremelowe nodded thoughtfully. "Good. That is good to hear."

Carilo sighed, taking a deep swill of the port.

"And the drugs?" asked Tremelowe, moving on quickly. "The watch reports that there are wicked substances on the streets of our city. People dead. Men with brains rotted by this filth. Any news on that, Carilo? Who is bringing this shit into my city?"

Carilo hesitated. This would be difficult. "Do you mean Gunpowder, my lord? I'm gathering information on the purveyors. Low level, most of them. I can deal with them, if you wish? Would the watch turn a blind eye to a few disappearances?"

"Of course, Carilo," said Tremelowe. "I trust you to purge this menace from my streets. Alcohol and foodstuffs are one thing. This Gunpowder is quite another, a vile concoction. What about the rest of it?"

Carilo hesitated, returning to his drink. His family didn't trade in Gunpowder. It was an abomination, chemicals brewed in secret labs that rotted the brain and body of its users. But he did have a hand in the natural stuff; Pirate Weed from Coastman suppliers, various mushrooms and roots from a few men he knew as far afield as Massapine. Carilo didn't see the harm in it. If people wanted these goods, they should have them. They were just plants and fungus. Anyone could pick them out of the ground. What was the problem?

It was obvious Tremelowe didn't see it that way. The truth was not the best option here. It was a big revenue stream for his family. Cutting it off would hurt him financially. He made a decision, swigging deep on his drink before speaking.

"No news as yet, my lord. I will keep my ear to the ground. Although, it may cause discontent amongst the masses if supply is cut off..."

"I will deal with that," snapped Tremelowe. "Just find out who is bringing it in, and deal with them."

Carilo nodded into his drink, cursing to himself. He would have to think about this, weigh up the risks versus the rewards.

"I need something else from you, Carilo," said Tremelowe, the matter seemingly slipping away from his mind. His face was filled with a seriousness the Illicean had rarely before seen. "I need you to obtain something for me. Several items of the utmost importance."

"Have I ever let you down before, Lord Tremelowe?" asked Carilo, glad of the change of subject. "Food? Liquor? Silks?"

"More difficult to obtain than that, I am afraid," said Tremelowe gravely.

"It isn't going to make me vomit, is it, my lord? You know I don't deal in slaves or corpses…"

"My request is heavier than that, Carilo, but I will reward you handsomely."

Carilo gulped, his stomach turning. He had heard of the depravities of the nobility of Castland. It appeared he had misjudged the man before him. "My lord. I may be a foreigner in your country, but I am a man of principle. My principles may be different to yours. You may class me as a criminal. But I am a family man, and I have to be able to sleep at night beside the mother of my children with a clean conscience."

Tremelowe shook his head, realisation dawning on his face. "Carilo, I do not mean that my request is distasteful. It is difficult. It comes with great risk. But it is not something that would dishonour you or your family. I would never ask that. I trust you, Carilo, and I have a task that you must promise to complete for me if I give you the details. The fate of every man, woman and child in this city may depend upon it. And I will make you rich beyond measure if you obtain what I need."

Carilo paused for a second, draining his glass. He played the rich red liquid across his tongue, sliding it down his throat. It was a risk to get so involved with a noble of this country. To pledge without knowing the detail went against all of his instincts. But Tremelowe was a good man. The lord said that he trusted Carilo, and, against his better judgement, the Illicean trusted Tremelowe.

Carilo placed his glass gently on the table, leaning forward conspiratorially as he met Tremelowe's gaze. "Alright, Lord Tremelowe. I will get what you ask for. Tell me, what is it that comes at such a cost? What is it that requires such secrecy, and involves so much danger?"

Tremelowe reached to his own glass, downing the contents in one and pressing his mouth close to Carilo's ear. "Have you ever heard tales of the Portal Stones?"

Mani Tristane ran into the alleyway, gaining on the Gunpowder dealer with every bound. His younger brother Marito was on his heels, along with a couple of the family enforcers. The drug peddler glanced over his shoulder, immediately wishing he hadn't. Mani bore down on him, and the turn slowed his flight.

Mani lunged, grabbing the man's shoulders and sending him head-first into the alley wall. Behind him Marito winced at the sound, a dull thud as skull and stone connected. The deal slid down the wall, his legs going from under him as he continued trying to flee.

The two thugs grabbed him roughly, hauling him back upright, his head lolling loosely at the end of his skinny neck. The man was pale as a sheet, his eyes red-rimmed and sunken, black bags underlining them. He mumbled incoherently, dazed from the impact.

Mani slipped on a pair of knuckledusters, punching the prone man hard in the stomach. The drug dealer gasped for breath, the intake of air rasping and desperate. He tried to bend double but the enforcers held him upright.

Marito stared as his eldest brother turned to him. They could be mistaken for twins. They both had their father's looks, as did all of Carilo's children. Handsome, tanned, youthful faces, features the right blend of masculine strength and delicate beauty. They had their mother's hair and eyes though; dark, Castlander characteristics mixing with the Old Illicean blood. Mani was stronger built, but that was to be expected, given their differing ages. Marito was the youngest of Carilo's children, and there were five siblings between he and Mani.

"Hit him, then," insisted Mani, gesturing to the pathetic, skeletal figure pinned against the wall, heaving for breath.

Marito shook his head. "I don't want to."

The two thugs looked on, perplexed. Mani turned his eyes on them, forcing them to avert their gaze.

"It doesn't matter whether you want to, Marito," said Mani, planting his fist in the man's midriff again. "Just hit him."

"Why?" asked Marito, his head cocked inquisitively to one side.

"Because you're a Tristane, brother, and this man is your enemy."

"He's not my enemy," shrugged Marito. "He's not done anything to me. From the looks of him, his enemy is the drugs he's putting into his body."

"He's the competition, Marito," said his brother, turning his gaze on the man before him. "And the shit he sells is killing people. Dead people don't buy from us. People who think we're peddling the same shit as this fucker don't buy from us."

Marito stepped forward between his brother and the drug dealer. He wrinkled up his nose, reaching into the man's ragged breaching and pulling out a small jute sack secreted along his thigh. He opened it tentatively, revealing numerous smaller pouches made of soft cloth.

"Is this all of it?" he asked, reading the pitiful eyes of the man before him as he nodded vigorously. "It wouldn't be a good idea to lie to me. Not now. Not with these men around. I don't think they like you very much."

"That's all of it," gasped the man.

Marito nodded to the two men. They released their grip, letting the skinny creature fall to his knees on the alleyway floor. They padded him down roughly, making sure he had handed over everything.

"Right then," said Mani, slipping a long, thin dagger from his belt and placing it under the man's chin. "Time to pay the piper..."

Marito reached out his hand, gently pushing the blade away from the whimpering man's throat. Mani shot him a stare, his eyes annoyed and questioning.

Marito smiled, kneeling down to look the man in the eye. He pulled out one of the cloth pouches, opening it carefully. The powder inside was fine, black granules interspersed with specks of yellow.

"You sell this shit to people?" he asked.

The man nodded warily, blood trickling from his grazed forward down his thin, prominent nose.

"And you take it yourself?" The man nodded again, wiping the red stream from his face. It formed again quickly, dripping to the floor before him. "I can tell. You know, this filth kills people? It's killing you. Do you even own a mirror to look at your face? Do you remember what it looked like before you started using this shit? You know this stuff is death, because of what it has done to you. Yet you take it, and you sell it to others..."

The man nodded, tears mingling with the blood running down his hollow cheeks. "Please..."

"Please?" pondered Marito. "You are asking me for something? You're asking me for a favour? You're asking me not to let these men cut your throat?"

"Yes. Please..."

"I can sort that," nodded Marito, standing and looking down at the pathetic figure before him. "But you owe me a favour. In fact, you owe me two favours. I've saved your life, by not letting these men kill you right here. And I've saved it again, because if I ever find out you have so much as one bag of this shit that's killing you, let alone that you're selling it to others, well..."

Marito shrugged, gesturing to the knife in Mani's hand.

"Now get out of here," said Marito. "And remember, you owe me two favours. One day, I'll come asking, and I want you to return them."

The man nodded, scrabbling to his feet and making his way towards the main street desperately, gasping with relief. The two thugs went to follow until Mani put up a hand, stopping them in their stride.

"Follow him, in a minute," he said. "The rest of the day. The rest of the week. He steps out of line, deal with him and drop him off at the abattoir."

The men nodded, moving slowly after the drug dealer. Mani watched them leave, waiting until they were out of sight. He turned on his younger brother in a flash, grabbing him by the ear, twisting it painfully. "What the fuck was that?"

"He owes us, now," yelped Marito, struggling against his brother's grip. "That's how father said things are done in Old Illicea. Favours. No need for conflict, just favours."

"Between Illiceans," snapped Mani, twisting harder for a second. "That bastard has no honour. He's not one of us. He's barely fucking human."

Marito pulled away as his brother loosened his grip, rubbing his glowing red ear tenderly. "Perhaps we should be educating the Castlanders then? We bring them our food, our drink. Maybe we should import some of our customs, too?"

Mani tried to keep his face angry, but the seriousness ebbed away into a smile as he met his younger brother's gaze. The two laughed together gently, Mani wrapping his arm around Marito's shoulders and gently knuckling his jaw.

"You're an idiot, Marito, you know that? Not a word of this to father. He already thinks you're soft." He led his brother away towards the bustling Kassell street. "For the record, I think you're soft too."

"What happens at the abattoir?" asked Marito as they stepped out amongst the people. Passing peasants nodded to them or smiled a greeting as they walked. They returned each one. People knew them; it was expected, courteous.

"You don't want to know, little brother. A minute ago you refused to even punch a fucking drug peddler in the stomach."

"I know it's where we send the bodies of the men who cross us. I mean... We don't put them into food...?"

Mani let out a laugh. "We're not savages, lad. It's just easier to hide a corpse there. Nobody looks too hard in the offcuts and bones bin. Cut a body up enough, grind and smash up the bones. It could be anything in there, just wastage going out with the rubbish. Anything, or anyone."

Marito looked as his brother. He loved Mani, but he couldn't see how any man could be so flippant about a person's death. He talked of it as though disposing of a human corpse was as easier as throwing away the leftovers of a meal.

Mani had stopped now. His had caught the eye of one of the young women at the laundry. She was a pretty thing, pausing from wringing out clothes into the trough before her and giggling with her fellow washerwomen as she spotted his brother looking over.

"I think she likes you," smiled Mani, nudging his younger sibling playfully. "She's eyeing you up, lad."

"She's eyeing you up, you mean," said Marito. "Why would she be looking at me when you're there?"

"Because, little brother, you look just like me, except younger. And because I look fabulous..."

Marito shrugged awkwardly, trying to move away. Mani pulled him back, his grip strong. "Come on, I'll introduce you."

"No thanks," insisted Marito, wriggling free. "Talk of the abattoir has put me off."

Mani followed, shaking his head. "See? Soft. Not today then. But one day soon I'm going to get you laid, lad. It might stiffen you up a little..."

Mani laughed again, punching his brother in the arm playfully as they moved through the streets of their city.

232

Chapter Thirty-Four

Carilo sat at his table as table as his eldest and youngest sons enter the dining room. He broke off from delicately separating the flesh of the grilled gnasher fish from the bone, placing the flat silver knife down beside his plate and wiping his hands on a napkin from his lap.

"I could have sworn I sent for Marito," he said, raising an eyebrow at the youths as they sat down opposite their father. "I'm not sure why you're here, Mani."

"We've just got back together," shrugged Mani, reaching over a pinching a lump of fresh fish from his father's plate, popping it into his mouth with a smile. "Don't you want to see your eldest son?"

Carilo shook his head gently, returning to preparing his food. "Of course, Mani. Tell me, have you had any luck with the Gunpowder peddlers?"

"We got hold of one today, father."

"Did he tell you where he was getting his wares from?" asked Carilo. "We need to cut this shit off at the source."

"Not yet," said Mani warily.

"What do you mean?" asked Carilo. "I *did* show you how to get a man to talk, didn't I?"

"Yes father. But it's a bit difficult to go to work on a man in the street in broad daylight. He'll tell us soon enough."

"Soon enough?" pondered Carilo, his eyes falling heavily on his eldest son. "You didn't kill him?"

Mani glanced at Marito, warning him to stay silent. "Dead men can't tell us anything, father. The man owes us a favour, now, thanks to Marito. I'll call on him to collect. He can give us some information..."

Carilo tutted, sliding the fish skeleton from his plate into a side bowl. "You're not going soft on me, are you son? It is bad enough that one of my offspring does not have the stomach for the family business."

His eyes turned to Marito, chiding him without speaking. The lad avoided the gaze, looking to his older brother.

"Marito will do fine in the family," said Mani, dragging his father's attention back. "He does things differently. It doesn't mean his ways are wrong. He'll make himself useful, I'm sure."

"He will indeed," smiled Carilo, turning to his youngest son. "I have a task for you, Marito. A difficult task. An important one. One that should toughen you up, teach you the way of the world."

"What task?" asked Mani, speaking for his brother.

Carilo shot him a look before returning his attention to Marito. "Do you know of the Portal Stones, boy?"

Marito nodded, his young face puzzled. "I have read of them, father. Mythical relics."

The lad never spoke much to his father. The head of the Tristane family had a knack of reading into a person's words, finding hidden motives and inferences, sometimes where there were none. Marito believed that the less was said, the less could be twisted within their father's active mind.

"It appears Lord Tremelowe believes they are real. He wants them, and he'll pay handsomely for them. I need you to get them for me, lad."

Why me? He makes it obvious how useless he thinks I am...

"The stories say the Portal Stones were cast asunder, thrown to the corners of the world," spoke up Mani, shaking his head. "It's too dangerous. Marito has never even left the city before."

"Then it is time he did so," snapped Carilo. "A little danger might spark his desire to survive in the world. It might teach him what he needs to learn. Larcenara knows I've tried. You say he can be of use to the family; it is time he proved it. It is time he made me proud."

"He will," said Mani. "I'll go with him. We'll get these stones for you."

"Absolutely not," roared Carilo. "I need you here. We have delicate matters to attend to. Lord Tremelowe is taking a dislike to some of our goods. We need to move carefully to tie up any loose ends in the organisation, ensure our links to the weed and mushroom trades are water tight."

"You don't need me for that," replied Mani, his eyes defiant. "You have Uncle Julio for that, and the rest of them. The family is large, and powerful."

"It is too dangerous, Mani," said Carilo, his face softening. It pained him to row with his oldest child. Mani was headstrong, even when he was breaking his father's heart. He got it from his mother. "You are my eldest son, the heir to the family business."

"You have other sons, father," shrugged Mani. "They'll quite happily step into my shoes. You're right, it is dangerous. That's why I'm going with Marito. To make sure he succeeds. To make sure the family succeeds."

233

Carilo shook his head, his words desperate. "I won't let you."

"How will you stop me father? Lock me up? Beat me, like one of our rivals?"

"If need be," snapped Carilo. His voice lacked energy and conviction.

"You won't," said Mani softly, smiling lovingly at his father. "You've never been cruel to us. You've never laid a finger on any of us. You've taught us, been hard on us, but you've never hurt us. I'm going with Marito. If you try to stop me, then I'll leave once your guard is down. And I swear to Larcenara, I will *never* come back. I will *never* forgive you."

Carilo's handsome features were wracked with hurt, like he had bene stabbed in the stomach. It was useless to argue with the lad. The eyes weren't staring back at him weren't his son's, they were those of his wife.

"You have your mother to thank for your stubbornness," he sighed, smiling weakly. "I've sent word to Matus, to our friends in my home city. They will point you in the right direction, I'm sure of it. The libraries of Old Illicea are rich with ancient tomes. One of them must be able to guide you on your way. Take all the men you need to keep you safe."

Mani laughed, standing up and gesturing for Marito to follow.

"Safe? I'm the most dangerous man with a rapier this side of the old country. The only people in danger are the women of the world. In danger of being pleasured by my other weapon of choice."

Carilo shook his head as his son thrust his pelvis forward, a cheeky smile on his youthful face.

"You can tell your mother," he said, watching the smile ebb away from Mani's face. "It is her pig-headedness that decided this. And you get that from your mother, so it can be you who breaks the news to her."

Mani nodded, grabbing Marito by the shoulder and leading him towards the door.

"Mani. Marito." The pair paused, turning to look at their father, sat at the table. He cut a lonely figure, his eyes sad as he looked at each of them in turn. "Stay safe, my sons. And come back home to us, no matter what."

Mani looked to Marito, punching the cheek of his worried face gently. He nodded to his father.

"We will."

Father Lexis hauled himself up the scree-strewn path, his tired body leaning heavily on his staff as he reached the ledge. A dying fire still smoked, neatly constructed and edged with almost identically-sized rocks. A discarded plate lay on the rocky ground beside it, a few small animal bones the only remnants of a recent meal.

He took in the scene as the others assembled around him after the steady climb, pausing to rest and catch their breath. Beside the mouth of a cave that cut into the hillside was a neatly-constructed drying rack. Rough linens hung on it, the weak sunlight playing across them gently. Near the cave entrance, on a crude stool, sat a set of pipes, fastidiously carved from animal bone.

Lexis waited for the others to gather themselves. The view across the High Moors from their vantage point was magnificent. The barren, rolling heathland spread towards the horizon, the light from the lowering sun casting eerie shadows amongst the bunches of thick, purple heather. Streams criss-crossed the land in deep gullies, blue arteries and veins supplying life-giving liquid to the land.

The scene felt familiar. It was just like the drawings in the book he had stowed in his backpack. The manmade articles had not been present in the picture, but the rest of the scene was identical. He had no reason to doubt the veracity of the tome; the writer was the most trustworthy source one could hope for. But seeing the site, so closely matching the illustration, confirmed to Lexis that the rest of what was written was true; Pharos lived.

"Are we finally there?" asked Yulli, both hands grasping his staff as he regained his breath.

Lexis nodded towards the cave solemnly. "Are you all ready?"

The group rallied quickly, the excitement amongst them pushing aside the thoughts of their aching limbs. Even Ryn seemed interested as he looked up from his position knelt beside the fire, inspecting the scene.

"Lord Pharos," called Lexis, directing his voice towards the entrance to the cave.

They waited, watching the opening eagerly. Minutes passed. They were met with silence, apart from singing of the few birds settling to roost further up the hillside, their whistling voices calling out to the fading sun.

"Is he not here?" asked Mida, bobbing his freshly-shaved head towards the entrance to the hollow and stepping towards it.

"Wait, brother. Patience." Lexis halted the lad in his tracks before calling out again: "Lord Pharos."

Again, they waited. Lexis opened his mouth again to shout, but he was cut off by a deep, grating voice from the cave mouth.

"*Lord* Pharos. Am I a member of the nobility, now?"

A croaking laugh grated from a figure in the shadow of the cave. The outline was of a stocky man, six feet tall, clad only in a loincloth.

"Father, I..."

"Father?" interrupted the voice, cutting Lexis off abruptly. "I have no children, man. You are right, though, I am Pharos. Just Pharos, nothing more. You know my name, but I do not know yours..."

Lexis steeled himself. The voice was penetrating, seeming to reach inside him and grab at his stomach. "I am Head Priest Lexis of the church of Pharma. The Keeper of the Lore."

"Not sure what that is," pondered the figure, a hand running across the bald outline of his head. "I have been away from people for a long time. Make it simple for me. Are you a friend, or are you a foe?"

"We..." called out Elsa, hesitating for a second under Lexis' glare. "We worship your mother, Pharos. We worship *you*..."

The shadowy figure trembling with laughter, a rasping sound that cut the air like a cheese grater. "That could make you a friend or a foe. The last people that worshipped me changed their mind in a most hideous manner..."

The figure stepped forward into the twilight, a pair of near-white eyes taking in the group before him. The iris was the lightest shade of grey, but the pupils still burnt with suspicious fire as they fell upon each person in turn, chilling them to the bone. Every inch of the visible skin was pale, scarred with tight burns that grey into almost a single massive patch in places. The hair had been burnt long ago from every area of skin, even the eyebrows and lashes. Lacerations criss-crossed the flesh, healed but wickedly detailed. The worst stood out on the chest, just beneath the sternum, the scar tissue heavy around a deep indent.

"Pharos, we mean you no harm..." insisted Lexis, in awe of the broken figure before him.

"You could not harm me if you tried," hissed the son of Pharma, reaching out like lightning and snatching the pipes up from the stool. Despite the wounds, Pharos' movements were smooth, quick, dangerous. He raised the pipes to the lips that seemed to melt into the face in places, playing a few delicate notes. "I was weak, then. I did not know what I know now."

"Pharos, we merely wish to speak with you," said Lexis, trying to quell the trembling of his hand.

Pharos played a few more notes, the shrill sound flowing out over the vista beyond the ledge. "Then speak. I merely wished to warn you of what will happen if you go back to your old ways."

"Pharos, we ask for your guidance," pleaded Elsa as the son of Pharma resumed playing the pipes. "We need your help."

Pharos broke away from the pipes, the broken note shrieking as it split the air. His eyes fell on the woman before him, burning with anger. "*Help?* Why the fuck would I help you? The last time I helped you cunts, well..."

He looked down at his scarred body, his arms wide, the muscles flexing threateningly.

The men turned their eyes to Lexis, filled with disbelieving fear. The head priest gulped deeply, struggling to find his voice. "Pharos, I understand..."

"*Understand?*" Pharos surged forward, rearing up before Lexis with inhuman speed. "You do not look like you have ever been set alight. I am sure if I tore off these robes I would not see the mark of a spear in your front. I would not see a scar in the back where it had exited."

"No, but..."

"There is no *but*..."

Pharos raised a fist angrily, pausing suddenly as he felt a hand touch his chest. He looked down to see Mida, the lad's palm resting on the scar where the spear had impaled him. "Does it still hurt?"

Lexis gestured for the initiate to get back. Pharos shoved him away, kneeling down to look to youth in the eye. "What did you say, boy?"

"Does it still hurt?" repeated Mida, his gentle eyes meeting the receding anger in Pharos' face. "Perhaps we can ease the pain. Perhaps we can help you."

235

"You? Help me? No, boy, I am all healed. It took time, but I am healed." Pharos gestured to his chest, jabbing a thumb at his heart. "The only place it hurts now is here. Deep inside."

"What do you mean?" asked Mida, his eyes innocent and questioning.

"In my heart, boy. I was betrayed, you see. Betrayed by the people that I tried to help. They did not like the truths I brought them. They did not fit in with their view of the world."

"I understand why you are angry, then," nodded Mida. "I have never been let down like that."

"Have you not?" asked Pharos, gesturing to the assembled priests. "Were you not let down when these men got you to devote your life to Pharma? To a lie? They told you I was dead, and yet here I am, stood before you. What else are they lying to you about, I wonder?"

Mida glanced at Lexis. "Father Lexis says that, sometimes, people are not ready for the truth."

"And they are ready now?" asked Pharos, reaching out a finger and gently turning the initiate's face back towards him. "They are ready to listen? To let the world listen?"

Lexis nodded, speaking out timidly. "They are, Pharos. The High Priest himself has sent us. The land is in turmoil, and we need your help to stop immense suffering. I believe that they will even allow the truth to be spread, if it averts catastrophe. They are ready."

Pharos stood, reaching out and pulling Lexis closer. The priest looked him in the eye, his hand playing on his ribs where Pharma's son had shoved him.

"It hurts, does it not?" pondered Pharos, sliding his hand under that of the priest. A warmth spread across Lexis' side, the white robe tinging purple for a second as the pain of the blow subsided. "I can make it better. I know the truth now, more than ever. I know how strong I am. I know what I can do. Tell me, what do you know of the truth, *Father* Lexis?"

"I know everything," replied the Keeper of the Lore, keeping his gaze trained on the god-child before him. "I am the only one, but I know it all. The time has come for the truth to be told."

Pharos nodded, reaching up and slipping a strong hand behind the priest's head. He squeezed the vertebrae, Lexis wincing at the strength of the grip. "But I will decide what is revealed. What, and *when*..."

Lexis nodded urgently, gritting his teeth against the pain. It was gone in a second, Pharos releasing his grip and turning as he strode towards the fire. He cast a palm over it, the smouldering embers bursting into light with a violet puff of smoke.

"There is wood in the store," he said, gesturing to a neat stack of stones covering a stack of dried out logs. "Cook yourselves some food, assuming you have brought any. Rest. Tell me, do you have any wine?"

The group looked at each other, shaking their heads.

"Ale? Spirits? Anything? I have missed it, out here in the wilderness."

"We have surgical spirits," piped up Mida, reaching into a nearby pack and producing a phial of clear white alcohol. "For cleaning wounds."

Pharos turned, snatching it from the lad's hand. "That will do."

"But..." called out Yulli, raising his hand in concern.

"Pah," scoffed Pharos, pulling the cork and taking a swig of the liquid. His face screwed up for a second, wincing at the stinging in his mouth. "I have been stabbed through the chest and set alight. This will not kill me. I need to think..."

With that he turned, striding into the cave carrying the bottle. Lexis watched as he went, his eyes drawn to the jagged scar on Pharos' back where the spear had passed through his muscular torso.

Charo sat at the trestle table at the square in Woodhaven, watching as the villages moved about their business. They had been resting for some time now; it seemed like forever. Woodhaven was becoming a new home, somewhere that they were all settled. He understood the need, but the people were perhaps becoming *too* settled.

Will they ever want to move on? That was just the first fight of many, yet they act as if it were the last...

Some of the villagers had left. The battle at the graveyard had unsettled them. They had lost their friends, and they had seen things they would never forget. The dead rising from the grave. It did not matter to some people that the skeletons of the oppressed of the past had risen to save the downtrodden of the present. They could not abide it, couldn't see further than their preconceived ideas of right and wrong.

Most had stayed. Despite the injuries, despite the deaths, they had stayed. They were recuperating. Father Pietr and his initiate were doing a good job at tending the wounded. Most were recovered. In truth, they were almost ready to move again.

"How many casualties are not ready to travel?" Charo asked the old cleric sat beside him.

"Three," replied Pietr, turning his gentle gaze towards Charo. "I do not think Kevyn will make it, I am sad to say. I had to take the leg off, but the rot has already set in, I fear. All are adamant that they do not wish to join the ranks of the undead, should they perish."

Pietr turned his eyes to the street, taking in the skeletal figures moving amongst Charo's followers. The remaining living seemed to have grown used to them as they went about their business. Some of the animated remains sat at tables, sharpening weapons, even playing cards or sparring with one another. Others merely sat or stood, empty eye sockets gazing out into space, waiting to be called upon.

"Nobody will be called who doesn't wish it," said Charo, himself looking upon the undead in the street.

The numbers had been swelled over the days and weeks since the battle. Little-by-little, stragglers had crawled from the graveyard. They moved differently to the yellowed, skeletal figures. The flesh still clung to their limbs to a greater or lesser degree. Their movements were slow and awkward, their limbs uncoordinated and heavy. Some of the villagers had come to Charo in distress, recognised recently-deceased relatives from jewellery or trinkets fixed to putrid, rotting features.

"How do you do it, Charo?" asked Pietr. His tone was gentle, but Charo could see he wasn't comfortable with the dead walking amongst the living.

"I don't know," replied Charo simply, the dark eyes turning to the cleric. A thin patch of white hair had appeared amongst his thick, dark locks, a flash in the black mop on his head. "I don't even know if I *do* make it happen. I know that it drains me. I felt weak for days after the battle. Hollow, almost. If you're asking me to explain, I cannot. Can you?"

"I have studied the theory of necromancy," admitted Pietr solemnly. "A cleric of Mortis must know the enemy. And Mortis' teachings are clear. Raising the undead into servitude is a sin, Charo."

"I have not brought them into servitude, father," replied Charo curtly. "Lunaris has brought them forth to aid the living. I don't control them. They are their own beings."

Pietr nodded. "I think you are right, Charo. They do not seem under duress. Some seem… confused. But not controlled. They just… *are*…"

"The ones with the flesh seem more lost than most," observed Charo, watching as one of the dead approached a horse drinking at the trough outside the nearby stables. It was reaching out clumsily, a brush in its rotting hand, trying to groom the frightened animal as it reared away.

"I have read that the recently-departed do not react as well when their soul is drawn back to the Mortal World," said Pietr gently, gesturing to his initiate. He watched as Harat trotted off towards the zombie, pulling the brush delicately from its grip and leading it away by the hand. "They have not come to terms with their death. They are in denial, it would seem. They cannot control their bodies, or try to control them as if they were still living. All of the undead seem to retain their sense of who they were before they died, unless they are being compelled against their will. It just seems that the fresher bodies have spirits within them that are dazed."

"They are not the only ones, Father Pietr," admitted Charo, his eyes weary. "But we must move on soon. We will never get to Regalla at this rate."

"Perhaps we are not ready yet," pondered the old cleric. "The people are recovering, but the sights of battle scarred them, Charo. They are not trained, and if we move onwards the fighting will get tougher. Mortis and Lunaris will protect us, it seems, but at what cost to those who follow you?"

"What do the others say?" asked Charo, casting a dark, accusing glare on Pietr. "You've already spoken to them, I take it?"

Pietr nodded awkwardly. "I have, Charo. I took the liberty of getting their opinions before raising it with you."

"And?"

"They agree. We need greater numbers, and we need them to be trained. If we re-trace our steps, the hills beyond are on the north-west border with Barralegne. We will be far from the retribution of the lords. We will have time to plan, to train the people. The hills are filled with ancient battlegrounds and burial mounds. You could bring forth more of the dead, to swell our numbers."

"All of the council agreed?" asked Charo. "Even the preachers?"

"Yes, Charo. They agree that we need a greater force. The lords will send a huge force against us now, after what we did here."

"They do not care for the common folk, even their own soldiers," spat Charo.

237

"But they care about their knights, Charo. Collagne put it best. A lord is never someone's son. He has risen to his position due to the fact that his parents have died. But knights are the sons of aristocrats and other noteworthy men. That one man's death will cause more rage than the loss of a baronet or his lands."

Charo nodded reluctantly. "The words are wise. We need to make our preparations, then. As soon as the wounded are fit to travel, we leave."

Pietr nodded, struggling to his feet. "The preachers have asked your leave to remain, Charo. They wish to move onwards towards the capital, to spread the word of Lunaris to the poor folk."

"They are brave," said Charo. "It will be dangerous. Are they certain they want to take the risk?"

"You know them, Charo."

The youth nodded. The priest was right. They cared only for their new cause, for the god they saw as their saviour. "If they are sure…"

Pietr smiled gently, shuffling away to brief the rest of the council members.

Chapter Thirty-Five

Talia beat her hands on his chest, the blows jarring his semi-healed wounds. Tomas winced, trying to rap his arms around her, but she pulled away, striking him across the chin. He raised his hand, tenderly touching the nick in the skin where her ring had split it.

"I thought you were *dead*," she screamed, grabbing a candlestick from the bedside table and hurling it at him.

Tomas moved to one side just in time, the heavy metal ornament crashing against the wall of their chambers between Robert Edens and Mikhel Miller. The pair looked at each other awkwardly, their eyes straying to gaze longingly at the door.

Lord Miller shrugged his powerful, squat shoulders. "You work for them, Robert. I'm a lord. I don't have to watch this."

His bearded mouth curled into a smile as he winked at the castellan before slipping out of the room. Robert considered following him.

"Talia, I'm sorry," pleaded Tomas, trying to grab her. Her blue eyes flared angrily as she upturned the bedside table, throwing it down between them.

"You knew about this," snarled his wife, turning her ire towards Robert. "You watched me cry myself dry in this fucking room and you *knew*."

"It was for the best, my lady," mumbled Robert, avoiding her glare. "It would have been dangerous if anyone found out that Tomas lived. It still is dangerous, in my opinion."

"Who else knew?" she roared. "Have you all been sitting here, watching the stupid Raskan woman cry her heart out, sniggering over your little secret?"

"Nobody else," lied Robert. "Just me and Lord Tremelowe. The Lord Chancellor's son tried to kill Tomas. If he knew he were alive, he might try again. He might have sent an army to raze the town."

Tomas lunged quickly whilst Talia was distracted, grabbing her and pulling her close. He nestled his face into her long, blonde hair, breathing in the smell of her simple perfume.

"By Guerro, how I've wanted to do that all this time," he sobbed as she raised her arms slowly, reluctantly, digging her fingers into his back.

"Is it really you?" she whispered, the tears back now as her anger subsided, disbelieving relief taking its place. "Have you come back to us, or is this a cruel dream?"

"I'm back, lass." He pulled back, cupping her chin in his hand and gazing into those eyes. "It's me. It'll take more than Cecil Cramwall and his lackeys to take me from you."

"Don't ever do that to me again, you bastard." She sniffed heavily, a tearful smile crossing her face.

"I won't, my love. I promise."

"Don't ever leave me again."

Tomas hesitated, his grip loosening. Talia sensed it, her eyes narrowing as Tomas glanced over his shoulder to Robert.

"Are the lords here?" he asked. "I sent pigeons ahead. Are they all here?"

Robert nodded reluctantly.

"Why are they here?" asked Talia, pulling away from Tomas.

"Talia, please don't..."

"*Why?*"

"We have a decision to make," said Tomas. "The Lord Chancellor is tightening his jaws around the throat of this country, trying to wrestle what little control the people have over their lives. His son tried to kill me, Talia. He's called an election..."

"I know all about it, I got the messages," snapped Talia.

"Good. Then you know how he plans to deal with those who defy the will of his Establishment Party."

"Let him do as he wishes," said Talia, desperation gathering in her voice. She had never seen Tomas so angry. It scared her. What he would do scared her. "We will keep to our ways, as always."

"The time for that has passed," snarled Tomas. "The only way there will be justice in this land is to cut off the head of the snake that is poisoning it."

"Tomas..." Talia howled as her husband strode towards Robert.

"Are our other guests here?" asked the martial lord, turning his attention to his castellan.

Robert nodded.

"I'll need you to speak with them, Talia," said Tomas, turning back to his wife as she threw herself down on the bed. "You'll understand when you see them. I need you and Ivan to tell them what happened here."

"You plan on leaving me again, to risk the life you promised to me in another childish war? Then you demand that I play the loving wife and entertain your guests? And bring Ivan into your plots and schemes? Fuck yourself, Tomas."

Tomas bore down on her angrily. She flinched for a second, fearful he was going to strike her. He threw himself on his knees before her, grabbing her hand and pulling it close.

"This isn't some childish war, Talia. This about protecting everything we've built here. It's about protecting *our* people. Because if we don't, the Lord Chancellor will pull it all to the ground after trampling over us. We have to fight for what is right, my love. Otherwise we are nothing but slaves, all of us. And when we have children, I don't want them to grow up as slaves. Do you?"

Talia shook her head reluctantly, the tears forming in her eyes again. She caught Robert's gaze as he looked to her stomach, the slight swelling concealed beneath her dress.

He knows, she thought.

"Tomas…" said the castellan, stepping forward.

Talia shook her head vigorously, her steely glare silencing Robert.

If he has to do this, he mustn't know. It will weigh on his mind, distract him. Distracted men don't come home…

"Better make it quick," said Tomas. He pulled Talia close, kissing her heavily on the lips, before turning towards Robert.

"It… It can wait…"

"Good," said Tomas, striding from the room. "The lords cannot…"

Tomas stood before the assembled lords he had called to Bannar. Mikhel Miller stood beside him, quaffing back the last of his ale as he finished describing the attack on one of their own by the Lord Chancellor's son.

The men before him sat in stunned silence. The majority of them were martial lords, raised to the nobility for their deeds in the Raskan War, just like Tomas and Mikhel. It was not often that these common men raised to lordship sat together in a room without roaring with boastful laughter whilst drinking themselves stupid.

Davyd Kinsman, a man born at the furthest extent of Castland, so far north it was rumoured he had blood in his veins of the nomadic tribesmen who roamed the tundra. He was the only one of the martial lords amongst them who had any skill on the back of a horse. To the rest of them, a horse was a means of transportation from one battle to the next, not a weapon of war. Some of them even struggled to use a mount for that purpose.

Stoddart Ironhelm. It wasn't his birth name, but it was what he went by now. A professional soldier since the day he was born. It was rumoured that an experimental cannon had once misfired right beside him, the massive metal ball of death that it propelled bouncing off his thick skull, leaving him unscathed. The tale was at least partly true, given the huge dent in the crown of his head.

Andor Oxhound, a man who was instantly recognisable due to the network of deep, ugly tattoos that interlinked across his chest and arms, crawling out of his tunic and up his neck, grasping at his eye like a claw. Nobody knew much of the man's history, but he had been stranded between the Raskan lines with a hundred men for almost a year during the way. The damage they did to the enemy back lines was only revealed as the Castlander forces broke through during the retreat at the end of the conflict.

Connor Hawkstone was a scout, the leader of the initial force's outriders at the onset of the campaign. Riding ahead of the Castland army, technically it was his men who were first into the war. Their face-to-face confrontations with the Raskans had been fewer than the majority of the men in the room, but their value was without question.

Deakon Quarry made up the last of the martial lords present. He wasn't exactly a warrior, more an engineer. Tomas had heard tales of the siege towers he could build and the devastation they could bring during a drawn-out blockade, but there had been little need for them when fighting the Raskans. Instead his men had been forced to evolve, digging covered trenches to frustrate the cavalry charges of the numerically superior Raskan forces. It was rumoured that he won the Battle of Ongor's Heath single-handedly, his men digging underground tunnels and then detonating them with deadly effect using gunpowder during the first Raskan charge.

Jeremy Pillory and Vincent Rox were not martial lords. They were from noble families; part of the aristocracy. Tomas trusted them though. They had not waited to inherit titles. They were knights at the time of the Third Raskan War, and their valorous deeds had given them an opportunity to gain a title before the death of their parents. They deserved their lands, and they deserved to hear what Tomas had to say.

"Do we have any proof that it was the Lord Chancellor's son who ordered this, Lord Bannar?" asked Rox, swilling his goblet of mead around and taking a deep swig.

"You have my word, Lord Rox," said Tomas. "It was Cecil Cramwall's bodyguard, the Q'shari, who let the men who attacked me. I'm many things, but my word is honourable."

"Nobody would question that, Lord Bannar," insisted Rox, raising his drink towards Tomas.

"Certainly nobody who has seen him fight," laughed Ironhelm, raising his own tankard of ale. "I'm surprised the Q'shari wounded you so badly. You must be getting old, Lord Bannar."

Tomas smiled mirthlessly, raising his own drink. "We are all getting older, Lord Ironhelm. We would do well to remember our mortality, and the mortality of our people, when we consider our course of action."

"What action do you propose, Lord Bannar?" asked Quarry gently.

"A pre-emptive strike," replied Tomas simply. "I am told by Lord Miller that you all intend to defy the Lord Chancellor's edict, and to let the people vote as they wish, without interference. When Cramwall hears of this, he will throw the weight of Castland against us, I am sure of it. We strike first. We can be most of the way to Regalla before the lords blocking our way have the time to rally their armies."

"My lord," said Pillory. "The articles of war state that it is dishonourable to strike prior to giving your opponent a declaration of hostilities."

"Fuck the articles of war," sneered Oxhound. "Cramwall declared war when he tried to assassinate Lord Bannar."

"It appears that it was the Lord Chancellor's son who ordered his creature to attack Lord Bannar," shrugged Pillory thoughtfully. "Are we punishing the father for the crimes of his child? Is that who we are, now?"

"Lord Miller?" invited Tomas, turning to the stocky man at his side.

"Lord Tremelowe raised the matter with the Lord Chancellor in Regalla. Whether he was aware of the whelp's actions in advance, we cannot know. But he is aware of them now, and Lord Tremelowe believes there will be no punishment visited by Cramwall. That's enough for me, my lords."

Oxhound and Ironhelm banged their cups on the table in approval, joined a second later by Kinsman.

"Will our liege lord back us if we march on the capital?" asked Quarry, weighing up the options in his head.

"He will not," replied Tomas bluntly. "He will not stand in our way, but he will not join us."

"Then we cannot raise enough men to take the capital," said Quarry, looking about his fellow lords, seemingly surprised at the lack of support he received.

"We have enough if we move against an unprepared enemy," insisted Tomas. "If we move quickly."

"Lord Bannar is right," said Rox. Tomas raised his eyebrow in surprise. He wasn't truly expecting to be able to persuade either of the aristocrats. He had invited them out of courtesy. "It could be done. We may even be able to garner support from the lords whose lands we pass through, should they choose to surrender in the face of superior odds. If not, their common folk will likely rally to our cause. My father's lands lie on the East Road. I am sure he would join us, if you would like me to send word to him...?"

"Your support is much appreciated, Lord Rox," smiled Tomas. "But please, do not send word. We need to keep the element of surprise, and an intercepted bird would compromise us. If you think he would join us, it would be a huge benefit to have an ally rather than an enemy between us and Regalla."

"My father has no love of the Lord Chancellor," said Rox. "His lands would provide a good staging post, and his support would secure our lines of communication."

"The plan sounds more viable after Lord Rox's input," nodded Pillory, again surprising Tomas.

"I'm going to be honest, my lords," spoke up Hawkstone. "I'm loving this nobility. I'm loving having a comfortable bed at night, all the ale I can drink. I earned it, just like we all did. I'm not liking the idea of risking it all fighting the capital."

"You'd be risking it all by letting your people vote for their own representatives, Lord Hawkstone," said Miller. "It's better if we all stand together."

"Maybe I shouldn't let them elect them, then," said Hawkstone. The assembled lords broke out in a barrage of noise, some taking their feet as they shouted the scout down.

"Hold, my lords," called out Bannar, raising a hand to bring the room to order. "Lord Hawkstone has a right to his opinion, and a right to speak it."

"I'm just saying, I earned this," said Hawkstone. "I care for my people, and I treat them well. Why should I fight and risk losing what I have? What if some point down the line they lose their respect for me on a whim and decide to take what I've earned away from me?"

"Your people love you, Lord Hawkstone," said Miller, smiling at his fellow martial lord. "You lead your people. You don't drag them, or shove them, or beat them. They follow you because you are a leader. All of us here are leaders, that's how we got where we are. And men will always need leaders. Giving them a decent life and control over their own destiny won't change that, old friend."

Hawkstone nodded, smiling meekly and downing the last of his ale.

"What of heavy cavalry?" asked Quarry, his voice still sceptical. "I know Lord Rox and Lord Pillory have a few, and Lord Kinsman has a unit of light horse. But in the end we will face a fully-rallied army. It will happen before we get to Regalla. They will have heavy horse, and we will not. Certainly not enough..."

There were sounds of approval from the lords. It was a fact that none of them could deny. Heavy cavalry would be instrumental in any campaign, and they didn't have enough between them.

"I am looking to secure us cavalry support," said Tomas, taking a deep swig of his drink. "Not heavy cavalry, but horsemen in enough numbers that it won't matter."

"Where from, my lord?" asked Quarry. "Do you have a secret army that you have been keeping from us?"

Tomas looked to Miller. The stocky warrior ceased playing with his strawberry blond beard for a second, nodding his support to his old friend. Tomas gestured to the guards at the door to his audience chamber. The doors opened as Talia strode into the room, accompanied by a tall man in thick furs. His blond hair was beginning to grey, indicating that he was older than his powerful build and purposeful stride let on.

The pair took a place beside Tomas, the silent hostility in the room prickling his skin at the sight of a Raskan in Bannar.

"My lords, may I present Elder Prilov," announced Tomas, nodding a greeting to the man beside him.

"A fucking Raskan," spat Oxhound. "I should cut him down where he sits."

Talia stood, silencing the calls of approval from the lords of east Castland. "Is that what we have become? When nobles threaten an emissary, a potential ally, with violence, what hope do we have for the poor folk? You sound like Cramwall."

The men paused, avoiding Talia's icy stare.

"This had better be good, Lord Bannar," snarled Pillory, his disdain for the man sat beside Tomas unhidden.

"My castellan has spoken with Elder Prilov on my behalf. It may be that his people will support our war against Cramwall with a significant number of light cavalry."

"How many?" asked Rox.

"It doesn't matter how many," snarled Oxhound. "Lord Bannar, you can't honestly be thinking of forming an alliance with these... savages?"

"*How many?*" repeated Rox, shooting the tattooed martial lord a glare.

"Ten thousand," said Prilov, his Castlander only slightly accented.

"That would double our force," said Quarry, the numbers turning in his head quickly.

"It would," nodded Tomas. The lords had gone quiet, their warrior minds contemplating the implications of such support.

"What would they *want*, though?" asked Pillory uncomfortably.

"Nothing we can't give them," replied Tomas. "They want a border they can rely upon. Nothing new, just to know that they don't face the threat of invasion again. That doesn't just come from giving us support. It comes from supporting those who think as you do..."

"We are nothing like these bastards," snarled Oxhound, gripping his cup so hard that his knuckles turned white.

"It turns out," intervened Prilov gently, reaching out and taking a gulp of the ale placed before him. "That when you speak to a person, rather than engaging them in ferocious combat, you learn more about them. We have been to blame for this as much as yourselves, over the years. Speaking to Talia and Castellan Edens, I have learnt more of your ways in the last few hours than I have in decades of despising you from afar and fighting with you up close. Your ale is much, *much* better than ours, too."

"We are nothing like you," snapped Pillory.

"I apologise, my lord, I do not know all your names. It appears that you are very much like us. Certainly, the way that you have come to do things in the east is very similar. You love the people in your care, you want to make their lives better."

"You control your people and everything they possess," insisted Pillory.

"I am elected to keep them safe. To keep them fed. Life on the other side of the mountains is hard, my lord. You think it is cold here, but it is worse in Raska, believe me. The soil is poor, the food is basic and in short supply. Sometimes resources must be controlled to ensure that everyone gets the same. Nobody starves is Raska, my lord."

"You seem to have some nice furs for a man who is an equal amongst peers," observed Quarry. "And 'elder' does not seem to be a diplomatically-granted title."

"Every man, woman and child in Raska has furs, Lord Quarry," replied Prilov. The engineer's reputation preceded him. "And the title is just our word for someone who is elected by the people. And I *am* elected. More so than any lord in Castland, that is for certain. From what I am told, even your elected representatives are not truly appointed through democracy. That is something where we do, I am afraid, currently keep ahead of you.

"That is not to say there are not things that we can learn from you. I have spoken to the Raskan people here. They do not tell me stories of conquer and subjugation. They have seen both Raskan and Castlander rule, and it appears they prefer your brand of the latter administration. That is something I must take on board."

"And that is all you want from us?" asked Pillory, his demeanour softening at the man's words. "No lands. No gold. Just mutual assurances?"

"And to trade with another," nodded Prilov, draining his tankard at the second visit. "This ale is excellent. My people would like it, I am sure. And to learn from one another. That is all, I promise you."

Rox looked at Bannar, nodding his approval. The former knight glanced at his fellows, sensing the frosty atmosphere begin to recede. Oxblood was not happy, but he wasn't protesting.

"And you can guarantee us the men?" he asked, turning to the Raskan envoy.

Prilov smiled gently. "My lord, I am but the elder of one territory. If I alone had ten thousand horsemen at my disposal, you would not have won the war. It will have to go to a vote, but I am certain my kinsmen will back you."

"Thank you, Elder Prilov," nodded Tomas, shaking the man's firm hand as the envoy stood. "If you would follow my wife, I need to consult with my colleagues."

Prilov smiled gently, following Talia from the room.

"I don't trust him," said Oxhound as soon as the doors fell shut.

"We have no reason to doubt him Lord Oxhound," said Quarry, his logical mind seemingly convinced by the elder's words. "He would be risking much in supporting us. Another war, which his country can afford as little as ours. Should he betray us, the rest of the land would rally and drive his forces back with ease if they stood alone."

"They go in the vanguard," continued Oxhound. "Every battle. I'm not having good Castlander men cut down until we're outnumbered by these bastards in our own camps."

"That makes sense," nodded Pillory. "Not from a vindictive standpoint, from simple practicality. Myself and Lord Rox can bring heavy cavalry, but we have precious few warhorses able to bear the weight of full barding in reserve. Heavy cavalry charges lead to casualties amongst the mounts. If we are not sparing with their use, they will not see the walls of Regalla."

"Then it's settled," said Tomas. "We fight, with the Raskans."

"Is that our decision?" asked Hawkstone, all eyes turning to him. "I mean, like Lord Miller said, we lead our people, yes? And our people are the ones who will bear the brunt of this. We should let them decide."

Tomas nodded. "Lord Hawkstone speaks wisely. We should let our people know that, if they vote against the Establishment Party, that means war. A fight that is for *them* this time, not for the whims of their nobles, but a war nonetheless."

Murmurs of approval spread through the assembled lords. Tomas felt an energy he had not felt since the war; men steeling themselves for a fight, and all the misery that went with it. This time, they would be on the side of true justice...

"I'll be speaking to my people personally," declared Miller, standing up beside him and beating a heavy hand on his barrel chest. "I suggest you all do the same. Tell them what I saw. In Regalla, I saw the face of a Lord Chancellor who would happily fuck the life out of every person in the realm if it saw him cling to power. I saw the guilt on his toe-rag son's face, hiding behind his father's apron after trying to kill a truly noble man. These fuckers want a nation of slaves, even though slavery is supposedly against all of our values. I suggest we show them what true Castlander values are."

Miller turned, wrapping his arms around Tomas and squeezing him tight. Tomas squirmed, the pressure on his wounds causing him to wince.

"Thank you, Mikhel," he smiled.

"Thank you, Tomas," roared Miller, turning to the lords. They were on their feet now, sloshing their drinks down their faces and fronts as they raised their glasses and drained them in a toast to the lord of Bannar.

Chapter Thirty-Six

Pharos watched as the clerics of Pharma gathered around the child's bed, their faces covered with white cloths as they diagnosed his condition. Lexis stood beside him, trying to comfort Ryn and his wife. The woman was sobbing uncontrollable, cursing her husband for leaving them to head out into the hills. She had come running as soon as the party had arrived back at the village of Green Hollow.

Pharos sighed. Their son was ill, some sort of fever by the looks of the sweat glistening on his pale forehead. He didn't quite see how it was Ryn's fault. By her own admission he had fallen sick after the ranger had left with Lexis. How could she blame him?

"What's up with him?" asked Pharos, growing tired of the woman's wailing.

Father Yulli looked over at him, his eyes wide with disbelief over his covered nose and mouth. "Do you not know what this is, Pharos?"

"How the fuck would I know?" shrugged Pharos, now clad in his threadbare clothes, the scars on his body concealed from view. The looks from the assembled clergy had been ones of disgust and disbelief when they viewed him, so the gods only knew what the common folk would think if he didn't hide his battered physique. "It looks like he's got a fever."

"This is the Red Ague, Pharos," said Yulli, shaking his head gravely.

"The Red Ague," agreed Mother Elsa, her gentle eyes filled with sadness.

"The herbalist said that's what he thought it was," added Ryn's wife, her voice breaking as she spoke. Ryn pulled her close, tears forming in his eyes.

"Makes sense," said Pharos. "The spots are red, and he's sweating like a drunkard without a drink. Speaking of which..."

He moved over to the kitchen area of the hovel, opening cupboards until he found a corked bottle of cheap whisky. He opened it, taking a deep swig and sighing. It was shit, but it was better than the last drink he had had.

"This is your fault, Ryn," cried the boy's mother. "You left to help these priests, and Lunaris sent this curse upon us. You aided his enemies, and he has sent his vengeance upon us."

"Lunaris?" laughed Pharos, taking another swig from the bottle. The taste got better the more he drank. "Fuck Lunaris. Fuck all the gods."

"How dare you?" shrieked Ryn's wife. "A trader came through here after you left. Told how Lunaris had sent demons out into the world. He'd seen them with his own eyes. Sent them out to punish the wicked. Punish those who torment the poor. Punish the poor who would not seek his light."

"We are the faithful of Pharma," insisted Mida gently, moving over to the woman and placing his hand comfortingly on her arm. "It is our duty to help the poor and the sick. It is our purpose."

"Look at you," shrieked the woman, brushing him aside. "Your white robes and your silver jewellery. "Lunaris sees through your fake concern. You are as bad as the nobles."

"She's probably right," smiled Pharos, moving amongst the priests to look down on the feverish child in the cot. His eyes were staring and distant, his breathing ragged and strained. "But Lunaris didn't do this. No god did this. You see, they really don't give enough of a shit. Even if they did, they don't really have the power."

"What's he talking about?" asked Ryn, looking desperately at the priests before him.

Pharos ignored him, addressing the clerics. "Look, just cure him, would you? Ryn here's done you a decent job, after all."

"We cannot," protested Yulli, shaking his head sadly.

"They can," said Pharos, swigging from the bottle and gazing at Ryn's wife, his eyes suddenly sad, as though giving terrible news to an unexpecting recipient.

"The Red Ague is fatal in almost all cases involving a child of this age," said Yulli defiantly. "We may be able to make an infusion, but I doubt we have the correct ingredients to hand. Even so, it would be unlikely to succeed. We cannot save him."

Pharos walked away, knocking the priest aside with his shoulder as he looked at Ryn, his wife, then down to Mida. "They can. But they won't."

"What do you mean?" screeched the woman at the daughter of Pharma's back.

"What I mean," replied Pharos, turning quickly on the woman and pressing his face close to hers. "Is that they can use magic. They can call down the power of my mother, channel it through their bodies, heal your son. But they won't."

"It is not true," snapped Yulli. "We can ask for Pharma to grant us the power, but it is unlikely she will answer. Even if she does, the strain on us is too great. It has... detrimental effects."

"They can," repeated Pharos, placing a hand on Mida's shoulder as he stood beside the young initiate. "But they won't."

"How often does Pharma answer your prayers, father?" asked Mida.

The priest looked down on him, his eyes angry and disdainful. "I do not answer the questions of initiates."

"*How often?*" snarled Pharos angrily, his rage seeming to make the loose furnishings of the hovel move slightly.

Lexis stared at Yulli, urging him to answer.

"Rarely," replied Yulli, avoiding Pharos' glare. "Very rarely."

"Because she doesn't care," said Pharos, squeezing Mida's shoulder gently. "She doesn't care, so you need to make her care. Take her power. If you really care, just take it. Don't ask."

"Pharos," insisted Yulli, shaking his head. "It is impossible. The strain would be even greater. It cannot be done."

"Of course, it can," smiled Pharos, moving away from Mida and the boy's parents, staring into space as he approached the bed. "You can see it, can't you? You are trained, aren't you? It's there. You just have to pluck it out..."

He could see it, if he focused. Sometimes it was heavier than others. He let his vision fade, watching as the violet motes of energy around them came into focus. They were distant, ethereal, like specs of dust floating in the air after old bedsheets were changed. Surely they could see them, if they concentrated?

"It is too dangerous..." insisted Yulli.

Pharos knelt beside the bed, reaching out with his mind, pulling the specs of purple energy towards him. He reached out a scarred hand, grabbing the feverish child's skull in his grip. He heard the mother cry out, her scream of panic distant and distorted, as though passing through water. He sensed Mida's hand on her arm, holding her back.

He felt the rush of power coursing through his body, his grip tightening on the lad's head as his vision tinged purple. Yulli stood beside him, his shout of protest muffled as Pharos threw back his head, the eyes clouded and violet. A flash obscured his vision for a second as he threw himself forward onto his hands and knees, releasing his grip on the sick boy.

Ryn's wife broke free from Mida's grasp, shoving past Pharos' weak, prostrate body and throwing her arms around her son. Her wailing ceased as she noticed the boy's breathing becoming more even, his laboured breaths slipping back to normality. The red blotches on his skin seemed to fade, his skin regaining some colour.

Pharos pulled himself to his feet, leaning heavily on the wall of the hovel, breathing heavily. He looked to Ryn, to Mida, to Lexis, his skin pale, faint red marks dotted his features. He grabbed Yulli, pulling him close and ripping off the cloth covering the priest's face.

"It *can* be done," he snarled, breathing heavily on the cleric, even as the blotches on his face began to fade. "You just have to care."

Pharos moved away, his limbs heavy and uncoordinated as he staggered from the hut into the cold evening air. He collapsed down onto the ground in the street, leaning his weary body against the wall of Ryn's home, the bottle of whisky still in his hand.

He took a swig, looking up to see Midas standing over him. The figure was blurred; Pharos didn't know if it was from the exertion or the drink. To be honest, he didn't care.

"How did you do that?" asked the lad, sitting down cross-legged in front of Pharos.

"They can all do it," sighed Pharos. "It takes its toll, but they can do it, if they choose."

"You seem to be alright," shrugged the initiate.

Pharos smiled. "I'm knackered, boy. But it's true, it doesn't seem to wrack my body like it would theirs. There are some benefits to being the son of a god."

"You could cure whole cities, then. Bring an end to the woes of the poor."

Pharos laughed now, grating and cold. "I couldn't, boy. Even if I wanted to, it would put me in a coma before I got past a dozen. No man can fix the suffering in this world alone. It needs everyone to pull together, to see what is really causing the strife and be determined to fix it. It isn't disease that causes so much misery."

246

"What is it, then?" asked Mida, his eyes wide and innocent.

"Men," replied Pharos. "Not gods. Not nature. Simply men. A small number of them. And yet they have the power to do untold damage at the flick of their hand or a switch of their whims."

Pharos swigged again as Lexis emerged from the shack.

"Ryn wants to come with us," he said. "He'll guide us as far as he knows the land, and beyond if need be. He says he owes it to us for saving his son."

"*Us?*" said Pharos, raising his brow.

"Well," smiled Lexis weakly. "To you."

"Tell him to stay. It'll be dangerous, and he's got a family to look after. At least you fuckers aren't allowed to take a spouse. Few people will miss you when you're gone."

"I have tried," said Lexis. "He insists. And we need men like him. Men of the world."

"You're not wrong there, priest," spluttered Pharos. "Those cunts in there are weak. Their bodies are weak, and their souls are weaker. We'll need more than just Ryn to make up for that."

"I know," nodded Lexis. "What do you suggest, Pharos?"

"Mercenaries, I suppose," said Pharos. "We should be able to pick some up before the Barralegne. Then head through to the Pirate Coast, charter a ship."

"We have little gold, though, Pharos. We were sent out to rely on the good will the people bear the clergy of Pharma."

"Good will?" Pharos laughed again. "Why should people show good will to those who will not lift a finger to help a child whilst his parents look on in despair? I'm surprised you've lasted this long, but that shit won't wash with sellswords and pirate captains. You're more naïve than I thought."

"Where can we get gold, though?" asked Mida.

Pharos ignored the disapproving look the senior priest gave the young initiate. "They'll be a chapel of Pharma at one of the villages on the way. We take what they have. It's not like it's stealing, after all. We are on a quest on behalf of the almighty High Priest."

"You are right," nodded Lexis. "The others will not like it, but you are right. I shall have to convince them."

"I'm surprise," said Pharos, cocking his head to one side. "I thought you'd take more persuasion."

"I was not always a priest, Pharos. I understand more of the world than you give me credit for. We will need men who will fight for us. The others will not understand that. They are men of peace. It is written that they should do no harm to any man."

"Not by me," smiled Pharos dangerously. "Tell me, father, what were you before you took your vows?"

Lexis looked away uncomfortably, avoiding the son of Pharma's gaze and focusing on the door to the hovel.

"Come, now, father. Don't make me use my god powers to pull it from your mind..."

"Can you do that?" asked Mida, his face filled with awe.

Pharos turned to the boy, his white, near-transparent eyes locking onto Mida's own, wide and staring. The initiate tried to look away, swearing he could begin to feel his brain grow warm, as if beginning to set alight inside. Lexis looked on, his jaw agape.

Pharos burst out laughing. "No, lad. Of course I can't. Now father, sit down. Tell the son of your god what you used to be."

Lexis sat down reluctantly, folding his long, stained robes beneath him. "I was a field surgeon. I was a soldier, really, but I was trained in basic healing. Cauterising wounds, stitching up cuts, amputating limbs. I saved men on the field of battle."

"Glorious," said Pharos, clapping his hands together, his voice beginning to slur slightly. "A killer *and* a healer. Living proof that the two are not mutually exclusive. You can fight, then?"

"I can," nodded Lexis. "If needed. I have not done so for decades."

"Don't worry," smiled Pharos. "You never forget how. Not if you're good at it. And I bet you were good at it, weren't you, father? You're a killer, aren't you?"

"I could fight again if the situation required it," replied Lexis weakly, avoiding Pharos' gaze.

"Even though your books say you shouldn't, eh? They do say that, don't they boy?"

Mida nodded beside Pharos. "We should not do harm to any man. It is written."

"Is it now?" grinned Pharos wickedly, reaching over and gently raising Lexis' chin with the tip of his finger, forcing the head priest to meet his stare. "You know, though, don't you, father? Tell the boy..."

247

Lexis took a deep breath. "It was written in the old tenets that Pharma forbade us to harm another man. When Pharos came into the world, he told us that this was not his mother's intention. He said that, sometimes, fighting was necessary. Violence, in the pursuit of right, is acceptable. But the priesthood would not change these tenets. Such a fundamental amendment would have made the clergy look weak, directionless. So, these teachings were omitted from the Book of Pharos."

"But, surely, you wrote the Book of Pharos?" said Mida, looking at the god child sat beside him.

"I didn't write it," sneered Pharos. "I didn't have time to write it, did I, father?"

Lexis looked to the ground, dodging Mida's inquisitive eyes.

"What do you mean?" asked the initiate, confused.

"I think that's enough revelations for one day," smiled Pharos. "Father Lexis here needs to convince your fellows, after all, and I need to get drunk."

Lexis stood quickly, dusting off his robes and heading towards the entrance to Ryn's home.

"And father…" called out Pharos. Lexis paused, bracing himself for the son of Pharma's next words. Pharos drained the bottle of whisky, gesturing to it as he tossed it to the ground. "Get some more drink, if you would? This shit's all gone."

Pharma gazed down at the pool, her glass-blue eyes peering into the ripples. She had felt him for a second, she could swear it. The waters had cleared, just for an instant; for a god, an instant was a long time. She reached out a delicate finger, stroking it across the icy waters gently, as though trying to tear a hole in the mist surface.

"What is it, Pharma?" asked Lyricas, the God of Music and Dance. He was stood beside her, his slim form clad in the clothes of a minstrel, patches of vibrant colour now reflecting back on the surface of the pool as he leaned over.

Pharma pushed him away gently, her eyes squinting into the waters. "You are distorting the view, Lyricas."

The Lord of Laughter looked hurt, his usually merry face marred with spreading concern. Pharma was flustered. It was unlike her. She was usually composed, graceful, statuesque.

"Are you alright, Pharma?"

The Merciful One turned away from the pool, her eyes sad. "I thought I saw Pharos. Just for a second, I could have sworn he called out to me. I felt him, pulling at my heart."

"And you saw him?"

"I thought so," nodded Pharma. "Just for a moment. I have not seen him in so long."

"He does not converse with you?" asked Lyricas sadly. "Pray to you?"

"No," she said absently, her eyes staring into the distance behind the God of Music and Dance. "He never prays. I have tried to reach him, but he pushes me away. The demons sometimes sneak in, when his guard is down, but once he realises he cuts them off. I feel like I hardly know him."

"That must be hard for you," said Lyricas gently. He gestured to the lute leaning on the marble wall of the pool. "Would you like me to play for you? Take your mind off it?"

"Thank you, but no," replied Pharma, turning back to the pool. "There is too much on my mind."

"How so?" asked Lyricas, picking up the instrument and strumming gently.

"The Mortal World is unsettled. Some of the others feel it too. The people are praying more. Some of the pleas are despairing, fearful. The tides of energy shift and swell unpredictably. Have you noticed?"

"I cannot say that I have," shrugged Lyricas. "I do not notice the ebb and flow, but then I never have. Not the way that some of you do."

"I do not understand…"

"The stream of prayer is constant for me," he said, caressing the chords as he played. "When people are happy, they listen to music, they dance, they sing, they take pleasure in the arts. When they are sad, they seek these things as comfort in dark times. The flow for me is constant, despite any unrest in the Mortal World."

"You are lucky, old friend," smiled Pharma weakly.

"Perhaps," pondered Lyricas. "I sometimes wonder if I would prefer the surge though. A sudden rush, powerful and gushing, like a mighty river. Something intense, bringing me close to the Mortal World."

"Trust me, you would not want the worry. I fear that there is danger ahead, for our plane at theirs."

"Do not fear, Pharma," smiled Lyricas, looking down at the lute as he broke into a joyful tune. "Fear empowers the Lurker. If what you say is true, the mortals will be feeding the Creature in the Dark enough, without gods adding to the torrent..."

Chapter Thirty-Seven

Cecil stood in front of the lines of gallows, looking out on the assembled crowd in the northern poor district of Snowgate. The commoners were hemmed in by the grim, granite buildings surrounding the square. By the buildings, and by the assembled city watch, supported by Lord Princetown's household troops. The troops were in full battle gear, heavy armour and bearing pikes and spears.

The people were pushing and shoving, roaring threats and outrage. Cecil could understand it. After all, two hundred of their children were stood on crates and barrels behind him on the rows of gallows, their skinny necks snared in thick nooses.

He had brought the structures with him on a caravan of carts, ready for construction, but he was himself surprised that his men had managed to get them all assembled in the square in one night. It was a testament to their dedication. He would have to increase their pay, give them a bonus for a job well done.

The result had come in last night. It had been closer than he had expected, only two hundred votes in it, but the fact remained that the majority of the peasants had voted for the People's Party. He was disappointed, but not surprised. It was the first poll carried out in the country, after all. It would have been excellent to have returned to his father being able to say that his methods in the run-up to the vote had meant that no district defied the Establishment Party's rule.

Only two hundred votes, though. After today, no quarter will vote against us...

Cecil glanced at Q'thell and Bligh, stood beside him on the podium. The front of the crowd was shoving hard now against the troops guarding the foot of the dais, struggling to break through, their fists raised in angry defiance.

"Will they break through?" he asked, the concern beginning to show on his face.

Bligh shook his head first, gesturing a group of crossbowmen forward from behind them. The men lined up, levelling their weapons at the crowd. At Bligh's call they fired, the mechanisms of their weapons clattering as one. A black cloud of bolt thudded indiscriminately into the press of bodies in the square. The crowd faltered, losing its conviction. Screams filled the air as the poor tried to rescue their wounded fellows from the crush.

"Risky," uttered Q'thell, shaking his head a the Coastman.

"Quiet," boomed Bligh, raising a muscled arm in a fist as the crossbowmen strained to reload their weapons. "The *machero* wishes to speak. Be quiet, or we will fire again."

The crowd fell back slightly from the line of soldiers, their resistance waning. Bligh smiled knowingly at Q'thell, returning to his place beside him and Cecil. The Q'shari raised his eyes in exasperation, disapproving of the reckless act.

Cecil smiled as the crowd began to fall silent before him.

This is power. Control. Order.

He took one glance at Kaly, standing well behind the gallows and out of harm's way, surrounded by his best men. She looked uncertain, her shimmering blue eyes timid and scared. She was such a delicate flower. It was one of the things he loved about her. He would explain to her later, but for now it was important that her betrothed remained strong. Looking at her filled him with strength and conviction as he turned to address the crowd.

"People of the Grey Quarter of Snowgate," proclaimed Cecil, his voice carrying strongly across the quiet, open space. "My father, the Lord Chancellor of Castland, has given you the opportunity to vote in free elections. This is a display of trust, a testament to the regard in which we hold the people of this country. You were told prior to the vote that the People's Party was a treasonous organisation, founded by vermin who wish harm upon the great country of Castland.

"This information was given to you in order that you might make an informed decision. Despite this, you decided to vote for traitors. This makes you a party to their treachery. The People's Party, despite being a seditious force, has won the poll by two hundred votes. As such, two hundred of you will be punished for this crime."

"Not the children," screamed a woman, pushing her way to the front of the crowd.

The masses behind began to clamour again, surging forward to join her. Cecil glanced at Bligh, the Coastman gesturing for the crossbowmen to raise their weapons again. The peasants faltered again, their conviction waning in the face of another threatened volley.

"It appears this woman wants to speak," shrugged Cecil. "Bring her up."

Q'thell strode over the edge of the podium, waving the guards beneath him aside and reaching down a slender, powerful hand. The woman took it, the Q'shari heaving her up onto the stage in a strong, fluid motion.

Cecil looked her up and down as she approached. Her face and hands were dirty, clad with whatever filth the common folk crawled in. She was heavily pregnant, her belly swollen with child as she moved awkwardly to stand beside him in front of the crowd.

"The sentence has been passed, madam," said Cecil simply. "In the name of King Jaros III of Castland, Lord Princetown has sentenced these children to death. That is the only penalty for treason."

Toby's father shuffled towards the back of the podium at the mention of his name, joining Kaly in the protective circle of soldiers.

"But look," implored the woman. "They are children. Please, my lord, do not kill these children."

Cecil shrugged. "Do not say we are unjust," he said, the woman's eyes widening as her eyed her swollen belly. "We can execute a different child. That is most brave of you, but the punishment must still be fulfilled."

Cecil gestured to Q'thell as the woman recoiled in horror, her eyes wide with terror. The Q'shari shook his head gently, turning away from the Lord Chancellor's son. Bligh avoided his gaze, moving over to check upon the crossbowmen.

Weak, though Cecil, striding forward towards the cringing woman, his cheeks reddening in anger. *They are all weak. This is why the nobility must step in when the strength of the inferior falters...*

He booted the woman in the stomach, hard. She fell to the ground, screaming in pain, clutching at her womb. Cecil lashed out again and again, furiously kicking as the woman shuffled across the floor, screaming out in agony. He planted his foot once more, sending her crashing to the ground below the podium. She curled up behind the line of guards, sobbing as she grasped at her stomach.

Cecil looked out. The woman's whimpering was the only sound, the crowd silenced by the sheer brutality before them.

"We will honour that sacrifice," he called, turning and gesturing to Q'thell. The Q'shari walked over to the nearest gallows, his head bowed to the floor. He pulled out a dagger, cutting the rope above one of the children and pulling him down from the barrel on which he stood. "Does anyone else wish their child to take the place of one of these?"

Cecil glared, his beady blue eyes angry and challenging. The crowd bowed their heads to the floor as one, a flock of obedient sheep.

Awe. Respect for authority. How does father find this so hard to achieve? Is he weak too?

"Then the sentence shall be passed," declared Cecil, turning as the headsmen took their places at each set of gallows, preparing to kick the supports away one-by-one.

"Please, my lord," rang out a voice from the crowd. Cecil turned in time to see a figure throw himself to the floor on all fours, clutching desperately at the ground. Others followed, shouting out their own pleas for mercy. Cecil watched as the crowd dropped to the floor, dominoes collapsing before him in a tide of imploring hopelessness.

And there we have it. Obedience. Complete, unconditional obedience.

Cecil raised his hand, staying the executioners as they prepared to carry out their duties.

"The Lord Chancellor can be merciful," he proclaimed. He smiled as some of the bowed heads looked up, hope filling their simple eyes. "Perhaps you did not hear that the People's Party was the enemy of the realm before you voted. Maybe you now regret your actions, as you have become aware of the seditious nature of these men, and the consequences for supporting them. Ignorance is not a crime, after all. Certainly not one punishable by death. Is that what you are saying?"

The crowd began to murmur their agreement, heads nodding vigorously on kneeling bodies.

"But you know now, do you not? You know the true nature of the People's Party, and you know the penalty for supporting them. Will you tell your fellow poor folk, now? Help them to avoid the fate that befell you and your children?"

People were crying out now, shouting acknowledgement, hope once more slipping into their voices. They were calling his name, praising his merciful nature, promising to keep faith with Castland and the Establishment Party.

Cecil smiled victoriously, turning to the executioners at their stations. "Cut those children down. Cut them all down."

251

"You are a strong man, my lord," said Kaly, delicately slipping a morsel of food into her mouth.

Cecil smiled. It warmed him inside when she admired him, recognised him what he truly was. They dined alone in Lord Princetown's echoing hall at Cecil's insistence. He wanted some time with his intended. It seemed that the pressures of his duties kept them apart even when they were in the same city.

"It had to be done, my love," he said. "The people need a firm hand, otherwise they get ideas above their station. Sometimes it is unpleasant, but it is our requirement to take the difficult decisions that sets us apart from the poor folk. Sometimes, examples must be made."

"Even so, I am glad that you let the children live."

Cecil's heart warmed at her words. She was such a gentle creature, so beautiful and naïve. "It was the right thing to do. It is important that we show compassion and mercy when required. The people will have seen that. They look up to it. It is what makes a man fit to rule. Rest assured, though, if the execution of those peasant spawn had been required, I would have had the stomach for it."

"I know you would, my lord," smiled Kaly, setting down her cutlery delicately as she finished her veal. "You are so decisive, so wise. I would not have the strength to make such decisions."

"You will learn the ways of the world in time, my dear Kaly. That is why our fathers have sent you with me, I am sure. But rest assured, you will never have to make those difficult decisions. I will shield you from all that."

"I am grateful, my lord," she smiled, the dimples showing beneath her exquisite cheekbones. "You will be good to me, I know it."

"You have no idea, my love. Tell me, was the food to your liking?"

Kaly nodded quickly. "Delicious, my lord. Cooked to perfection. Lord Princetown does have an excellent cook."

"Indeed he does," laughed Cecil absently, reaching out and refilling their wine glasses. "It is probably why he is so corpulent."

Kaly's hand raised to her mouth, unsure whether to laugh.

"Relax, my dear," smiled Cecil. "We are to be wed, are we not? You may laugh if you wish, even if it is at the expense of a lord of the realm. A man and his wife should have no secrets. What they say amongst themselves is the most sacred of secrets."

Kaly laughed freely, her delightful giggle like the trickling of a secluded brook. Cecil stood, pulling back her chair as she gathered her glass and took her feet.

"May I?" he asked, offering his arm. She took it gladly, her touch causing the glow in his chest to swell. "I would like to show you some of the sights of Snowgate, my love. We have had so little time together, after all."

"I would like that. My time with you is precious. It warms me in a way I have never felt before."

"I feel the same, my dear. I cannot wait until this business is done with. I would marry you in an instant, but first I have a very important task to complete. We shall be done in Snowgate soon. When the rest of the elections are complete, I shall formally ask your father for your hand in marriage."

"I cannot wait," smiled Kaly, turning to face him, the light in her sparkling eyes intense and innocent. She moved forward quickly, kissing him gently on the cheek. She hesitated, spotting the shock on Cecil's face. "My lord, I am sorry, I just..."

Cecil smiled, leaning forward and kissing her on the lips. It was not proper, but he did not care. They were alone, and he had longed to be close to her. Her kiss was timid. He pulled her towards him, feeling her comely body against his own. She loosened as he raised his hand to stroke her cheek, kissing her again. Her hand drifted up behind his head, running through his thinning hair.

They pulled away, their eyes locked together.

"I cannot wait either, my love," smiled Cecil. "A man needs a woman to complete him, to make him a whole person. You are that lady, Kalyanit."

They stood for a second, gazing into each other's eyes, Kaly's cheeks blushing gently.

Cecil smiled. "Come. Let me show you Snowgate."

He turned to the doors of the dining hall, leading his betrothed out of the chamber, a broad smile spreading across his face.

Lord Tremelowe sat in his study, perusing the papers laid out before him by his castellan, Stewart Thatcher. The man stood opposite him across his desk, shuffling uneasily from one foot to the other as his lord read the results of Kassell's election carefully.

"It is concerning," said Thatcher speculatively, trying to read Tremelowe's stony features as he analysed the numbers. "Is it not, my lord?"

"How so?" asked Tremelowe absently, continuing to study the results of the poll.

"Well... I just..."

"You are trying to please me, Thatcher," said Tremelowe, looking up from his desk. "I want your own opinion, man. Have I ever asked for anything else?"

"Well, my lord... The people have voted, as you wanted them to..."

"And they have elected representatives from the People's Party," observed Tremelowe. He didn't know how he felt. He was glad they had made a decision for themselves, free from coercion and oppression. But it led them down a risky path. "Every district, apart from the Upper Quarter. The poor, the middle classes, the artisans, all the rest."

"Do we annul the result, my lord?" asked Thatcher cautiously. "Wait until the Lord Chancellor's son arrives to organise the vote as ordered by the capital?"

"How long have you known me, man?" snapped Tremelowe, his eyes angry. The castellan flinched visibly, stepping back from the desk. "We will do no such thing. The result stands. We need to assemble these new representatives. They have important decisions to make. We have to decide how to announce this result to the capital, after all. And we have to plan how we will react should the Lord Chancellor's response be as I expect."

Thatcher nodded. "I will gather them, my lord," he said, eager to leave the room. "At once."

Tremelowe stood as his castellan scurried out, striding over to the window and staring out. His eyes strayed beyond the people below, going about their daily lives, unaware of how their decision might affect those routines. They paused at the city walls, squinting as he surveyed them in detail for a few moments.

Are they strong enough? Will they need to be? We should invest in them, just in case the worst comes to the worst.

He looked out further now, staring into the distance, out in the direction of Bannar and beyond.

"What are you planning Tomas?" he said to himself. "What will you do now, old friend?"

Yarner sat as his table in the Copper Badge, looking over his ale tankard at Ratcliffe. The agitator had become the agitated, twisting the pewter badge on his tunic as he sipped at the drink before him, his appetite for it obviously minimal.

"What did you want to speak to me about, Ratcliffe?" asked the watch sergeant gruffly. "My supper's probably on the table by now."

Ratcliffe didn't answer, taking another sip of his drink. Yarner had never seen the reporter like this. He usually brimmed with confidence, almost to the point of arrogance. But he was pale today, his forehead furrowed into a frown that he seemed unable to control.

"Election not going to plan?" asked Yarner, growing impatient. "Being a politician getting you down? It is a cunt's game, after all, Ratcliffe. I mean, I know you're a cunt, but I don't think, deep down, your enough of one to be a true politician..."

"The election is finished, I fear," said Ratcliffe suddenly, his drawn face turning to Yarner.

"The last I heard it had only just started," shrugged Yarner. "Snowgate first, isn't it? We're next. Nice of the Lord Chancellor to let a different city go before the capital."

"Snowgate has voted," said Ratcliffe miserably. "And the surrounding lands. My representative sent me word via pigeon."

"And you lost?" asked Yarner. He was surprised, if he was honest. He had expected the agitator's People's Party to do well. Maybe not rock the boat too much; after all, change came slowly in Castland. But he had expected them to at least put on a show. From the look on Ratcliffe's face they'd been wiped out.

"One poor district in Snowgate voted for the party," said Ratcliffe. "Everything else went to the Establishment Party."

Yarner felt his mood move from surprise to disappointment. He realised at that moment that he actually wanted the man's People's Party to do well, to send a shot across the bows of the nobles. It would have been especially lifting to have bloodied the nose of that murderous bastard Toby Princetown's father.

"Hard luck, Jaspar," he said gently. "Get some ale down you, I can see it's hit you hard. Maybe the people just aren't ready for change, mate."

"They *are* ready," insisted Ratcliffe. His eyes were dark, wet with restrained tears. "They announced the first result, and Cramwall's son threatened to string up two hundred children in retribution. *Children*, Yarner. My representatives were forced to run the story in the People's Gazette up there."

"They made them write it?" pondered Yarner. "Your lot don't usually do anything they're told."

"They didn't *make* them," said Ratcliffe. "They had to do it. They had no choice. Cramwall threatened to carry out this 'punishment' if any further areas voted for the People's Party. It was the only thing they could do to avoid a purge of the poor."

Yarner shook his head. "I don't know why you're surprised, Jaspar. Did you honestly think the Lord Chancellor was going to let the people have any real power?"

The agitator looked at him, taking a deep swig of his ale now. He shook his head in resignation.

"They'll never let it happen, mate," said Yarner. "If I were you, I'd get word out to the people here before you get them and yourself into deep shit."

"I don't know, Yarner," said Ratcliffe, his features contorted with indecision. "This is the people's chance for justice. They might not get another. Is it right to just throw it away at the first sign of trouble?"

Yarner drained his drink, slamming his tankard down hard on the table in the near-empty tavern. Old Edna moved over to bring him another drink but he waved her away angrily, speaking low to avoid prying ears. "Listen, Ratcliffe. They won't get a chance for anything, do you understand me? Do you honestly think Cramwall won't carry it out next time? You have to tell the people. You're going to fuck up their lives if you don't?"

"But there are always casualties in war," insisted Ratcliffe, seemingly trying to convince himself as much as the watchman. "And this *is* a war, Yarner, between those who have everything and those who have nothing. Surely we can win, if we hold our nerve. We lost men in the Raskan War, yet we still won. Did you serve in the war?"

"No," snarled Yarner. "I stayed here and kept order. I kept things stable, even whilst the poor were starving in the streets whilst the rich stayed fat and comfortable. Food got diverted to the soldiers, and it wasn't the nobles' food, trust me. And when the people rioted because they were dying of disease and hunger, do you know what the Lord Chancellor did?"

Ratcliffe shook his head, his gaze falling to the gnarled wooden table between them.

"He had us beat them into submission, Ratcliffe," growled the watchman. "Starving poor folk, some dragging children along behind them. The Lord Chancellor had us bludgeon them down in the streets. Fuck knows how many died. They never stepped out of line again."

"Why would you do that, Yarner? You're a good man, I know it."

"Because I have a family, Ratcliffe. Because it's my job to keep order. My family got food, because I was a watchman. It isn't right, but sometimes you have to look after your own. There wasn't a day I didn't feel guilty. There isn't a day I don't think about it, believe me. But we kept order that day, and a country with rebellion on the streets of its own capital can't fight a war on the other side of the realm."

"You make it sound like you agree with Cramwall," spat Ratcliffe, shaking his head.

"Of course I fucking don't," hissed Yarner. "Truth be told, I agree with you. I'm telling you because these bastards have done it before, and trust me they'll do it again. You can't take people down that road without letting them make the decision for themselves. You know what's at stake. They should know too, before they go to the polls."

Ratcliffe nodded meekly. "You're right. The people should know. But I won't stand if I'm going to be defeated."

"Damn it, Ratcliffe," yelled Yarner, louder than he intended. He looked around, ensuring they weren't being watched. "This isn't about you and your pride. This is people's lives."

"You think I don't know that?" spat Ratcliffe. "I'm doing this so people have a better life. If I stand and the People's Party gets defeated because the poor are afraid to vote for us because of these threats, they will never get the chance again. The Lord Chancellor will seize on the fact that the people had their chance, and that they rejected their own liberation. I would rather withdraw."

Yarner nodded. He reached over, squeezing the agitator's forearm. "That makes sense. I know it's hard. I know you mean well. It sounds like you have some serious thinking to do. You should get it done, decide whether you're still going to stand."

Ratcliffe nodded, moving to stand. Yarner tightened his grip on the reporter's arm, holding him in place and staring hard into his eyes. "I swear to Guerro, though, if you send those people to the polls without telling them the truth of what happened in Snowgate, it won't be the Lord Chancellor you need to watch out for."

The agitator met Yarner's gaze, nodding gently. The watch sergeant released his grip, watching as Ratcliffe slunk out through the door of the inn into the street. He turned to Old Edna, gesturing impatiently for another drink.

Chapter Thirty-Eight

Marito watched, his young eyes wide with awe as the entertainers swirled around the stage before him and the assembled crowd outside the coaching inn. Their movements were quick and graceful, their leaps and tumbles almost nature-defying. They were short in stature but they flew higher into the air than any taller or more athletically-built man.

Mani looked at his younger brother, catching the lad's eyes flicking between the masked characters' brightly-coloured costumers as they spread out in a kaleidoscope of colour to reveal a svelte figure clad in shining, black leathers.

"What the fuck is going on?" he hissed.

Marito didn't break his wondrous gaze as he replied: "These men killed her lover. Remember, she was the woman in the white dress at the start?"

Mani did remember. The man's death scene had been remarkably realistic, the knife seeming to cut deep into his neck. The tricks these performers could perform really were impressive; better than the entertainers back in Kassell. The wound had looked real. The fake blood still stained the wooden stage where he had fallen, seemingly lifeless.

"I bet she gets a good fucking every night," smiled Mani, nudging his younger brother's arm. "One woman with all these men, travelling the roads. Eh?"

Marito shook his head distractedly. "Women don't act, Mani. Everyone knows that. Her part will be played by a young lad."

"I bet he gets a good fucking then," laughed Mani, swigging from a silver hipflask of clear whisky from their homeland. "These acting types will stick it anywhere, so I hear."

Marito shushed him, focusing on the scene before him. The bereaved woman moved through the crowd of garishly-clothed actors gathered around her, their arms crossed across their chests in disdain. Marito looked hard at their eyes as they looked out from the beautiful masks. They were distant, glassy, seemingly gazing out into the ether.

The men around the woman drew their short swords as one, the blades thin and glinting in the light from the braziers around the stage. The woman amongst them stood her ground confidently, pointing at each one in turn with an accusing finger, the order of the gesture seemingly random as the digit jutted erratically between the assembled men. When she had finished the finger raised to her black leather mask, landing gently on the single, blood red tear below one eye.

The men pounced on her. She jumped lithely, scrambling free from amongst the crowd and clambering over the back of one of her attackers, vaulting nimbly off his shoulders. Her sword was drawn in mid-air, swishing through the air as she brandished it on landing.

The crowd gasped in awe, bursting into applause as she span between them, stabbing out with the blade. Each stroke impaled a man, the tip of the sword protruding through the stricken actor's back before he dropped to the floor, blood flowing from the wound. The sounds of wonder became louder. Marito's jaw dropped at the gory realism of it all. Even Mani clapped, impressed by the parlour tricks as the blood spread across the wooden stage.

The last man was left to face the mourning woman. He was the leader of the men, his clothes even more elaborate and garish than his counterparts. The pair met in beautiful, choreographed combat, their blades sparking as they clashed in elegant, arcing and twisting strikes and counters. The man bore down on the woman in black, using his strength to push her back across the stage. Suddenly she sprang, somersaulting over her opponent seemingly without any tensing of her legs for the leap. She tumbled in mid-air, the sword turning in her hand mid-flight. Before she landed she struck out backwards, the blade piercing the man's back and emerging from his stomach.

The man stood for a second, blood beginning to flow between his fingers as he clutched at the wound, dropping to his knees. The woman in the black leathers performed an elaborate bow as the felled man dropped to the stage floor. Before she stood up straight, the braziers around the stage suddenly died, plunging the actors into shadow.

The crowd sat for a second, gobsmacked by the spectacle they had just witnessed. Marito was the first to his feet, launching into an enthusiastic applause that was quickly taken up by the audience. As they stood, the figures in the shadow of the stage crawled away, disappearing out of sight.

"That was pretty impressive," nodded Mani, taking another swig from the hipflask.

"It was glorious," gasped Marito absently, staring at the stage, a tear running down his cheek.

"It was good, I admit," said Mani, leaning against the large tent the acting troupe had erected in the ground of the inn. It took his weight well, in fairness. It had been put up well. "But we should be drinking with the lads, Marito, not talking to these queers."

Marito frowned at his brother, hesitantly peering through the gap in the flap door of the tent. He wasn't sure whether to knock. Or what to knock on, to be more precise.

He jumped as the flap was pulled to one side abruptly, a figure sliding out and pushing him back gently. The woman before him was short and slightly-built but her gesture moved him easily, almost causing him to stumble. Mani started at the sight of the girl, quickly checking his hair as he moved to stand beside his brother.

Her skin was tanned, like all Massapine. Her features were soft and plain. It was her eyes that caught his attention. They were smouldering purple, their alluring gaze somehow adding to her otherwise-mediocre appearance, tipping it towards the sensual. Her figure was perfect, lean but comely. The tight, black leathers she wore added to the effect, causing Mani to feel his loins begin to swell.

"I knew it was a woman," he smiled, bowing slightly. "My brother here said it was a boy who played the female parts, but I could tell from that figure, from that grace, that it was a woman. The mask hid the true beauty, though."

Marito sighed. His brother's lechery was so blatant, so obvious, but at the same time seemed to charm even the coldest of hearts. This woman wouldn't fall for it though, surely. "I apologise for Mani..."

"Why?" shrugged the woman, smiling at the oldest Tristane lad. The lilac eyes pulsed with sexual energy. "It isn't often a man is forward enough with such flattering thoughts."

Mani beamed, giving his younger brother a victorious glare.

"We have just come to commend you on the performance," interjected Marito. "I've never had the privilege of seeing the Massapine perform. The story was captivating."

"Thank you," smiled the woman, her eyes still locked on Mani as she spoke. "It is an old tale. The Black Woman of Harina. She and her lover came to the eastern lands, to bring the pleasure of performance to the people here. But the local entertainers became jealous. They didn't like that the Massapine captivated crowds in a way that they could not. A band of actors ambushed them, killing the black woman's partner in an alley. She took her revenge."

"A terrible tragedy," said Mani sadly, taking the Massapine woman's hand and kissing the back of it gently. "You played it most aptly."

"The tragedy was their jealousy," shrugged the woman, turning her hand over and tracing it across Mani's face gently. She looked down at his trousers, seeming to sense the bulge there. "The ending is a happy one."

Marito looked puzzled. "But they died, and the black woman still didn't have her lover back by her side."

"True," replied the woman. Her eyes still held Mani, seemingly in thrall. "But Lyricas teaches us to seek the light in every tale. The black woman's sacrifices, and those of her lover and the entertainers, live on forever in the tale. And the story can do untold good, if those who hear it recognise the dangers of envy."

"A deep and penetrating tale," smiled Mani warmly.

The woman laughed, her mirth seeming to sprinkle down gently upon them like a welcome shower in the hot sun of a dry summer. "I am Cat."

"Mani." Marito's brother nodded again, pushing his young sibling aside and kissing the hand once more. Cat pulled him close, kissing him gently on the cheek. She smelled of aromatic candles and seasoned wood. Her firm body against his own caused him to gasp audibly.

"Can we meet the rest of the actors?" asked Marito despondently, sensing he was losing any hold on the conversation.

"Tomorrow, Marito," said Cat. She ran her free hand across Mani's groin briefly, finding his own and leading him inside the tent. The lad swore he saw some of the other members of the troupe for a second, laid out on bedrolls, bloodstained bandages covering the wounds that had seemed so realistic during the performance. "The performance takes a lot out of the actors. They need to recover. Besides, I think Mani has something he wants to give me..."

Marito stood alone in the night, the faint smell of incense hanging on the air after the tent flap fell shut. He stood for a moment, wishing he could just barge in. He had so many questions. The performance had enthralled him; the energy of the players, their glassy-eyed devotion to their art.

257

He was brought back to reality by a long, laboured gasp of pleasure from Cat. He heard his brother, his breathing heavy as he groaned eagerly.

Marito shook his head, walking away towards the coaching inn.

Marito was up early. He had already been awake when the cockerel in the inn's yard began crowing. He was eager to meet the actors. As he trudged through the morning mist towards the tent it seemed to cling to him, dampening his clothes. It added to the ambience, the excitement at meeting these flamboyant, care-free people.

He could have talked to Cat last night, of course, but Mani's cock had got in the way of things, as usual. He loved his older brother, but sometimes his obsession with drink and money and women was a bore. Marito felt sorry for him, in a way. Mani seemed obsessed with the cruder, uglier things in life. He seemed to miss the subtle nuances, the intense flavour surrounding him.

Not that Marito was a man of the world. He just felt that, although he had seen less than Mani, he had appreciated what he had encountered more deeply.

Marito hesitated at the door to the tent. All was quiet within. He considered leaving the troubadours to sleep. It was early, after all. He could come back after breakfast.

He shook his head. Mani would want them to be on the road early, and he had so many questions for them. He steeled himself, teasing at the flap door of the large tent, pulling it aside gently and peering inside.

A hand wrapped around his throat, the grip tight. His was pulled inside, rolling off his feet and onto his back as Cat pinned him to the ground, straddling him. He felt the cold steel of a dagger at his throat.

Marito stared up at her, his eyes wide. She was naked apart from her knickers, and those garments consisted of very little cloth. Her legs crushed in tight around him, her pert, tanned breasts close to his face as she held him down with one arm.

She was strong, especially for a woman. Stronger than Marito. He wasn't sure of her age. Her skin was smooth and unblemished, her muscles thin but toned. Her hair was mousy blonde, hanging down around her soft features as she looked down on him with those violet eyes. It was the eyes that made him doubt her youth. Her body belied a girl no older than Mani, but when he looked into the purple he saw something older, something he couldn't place.

"Oh, it's you, Marito," she said, smiling gently and slipping lithely to her feet, dragging him up with her. "I thought it was a thief."

"How do you know I'm not a thief?" asked Marito playfully as Cat tossed the dagger onto a nearby folding table. "Maybe I've come to steal the gold you earned last night?"

Cat laughed. The sound was almost eerie, like shards of broken glass tinkling to the floor.

"We are Massapine, Marito. We do not perform for gold. We perform for the Lyricas, and a few meals." She smiled at him, those eyes fixing teasingly on him from beneath long, dark lashes. "Besides, I am pretty sure I could best you if you tried anything. If you are looking for your brother, he's over there. I bested him last night. In a different manner, of course."

Marito took in the scene. Mani was lying on one of the bedrolls, half-tangled up in the rough sheets laying on top of it, his cock hanging limply in full view as he dozed. Marito shook his head.

The other actors lay around them, some beginning to come out of their sleep at the sound of voices. The dark skinned, toned men reached for nearby piles of clothes, pulling shirts over their bodies. Marito saw that he had been right the previous night. There were indeed bandages covering their wounds. They moved freely though. The injuries couldn't be real, surely. Their motions were too smooth and easy for men who had been impaled the previous night.

The only sign of weakness was their eyes. They were Massapine, their irises all manner of colours never seen in a Castlander or Barralegnan or Raskan; amber, fluorescent green, dark jade, cobalt blue. But the whites were lined and bloodshot, seemingly through exhaustion from the previous night's performance.

"How do you know my name?" asked Marito, following her as she moved towards the actor who had played her lover the previous night, her shapely behind moving like flowing water in front of him.

"Your brother told me last night," shrugged Cat. She knelt beside the actor, still lying on his bedroll. His neck was bandaged where he had supposedly been slashed during the play. "Not during the sex, of course. That would be strange, even for an Illicean."

258

Marito smiled at her use of the proper form of address for a man from the Bandit Country. "But you knew before that. When we spoke last night."

Cat didn't answer the question. She smiled mysteriously, without looking up at him. She leaned close to the sleeping actor, caressing his forehead gently and whispering in his ear: "Angelo?"

The man groaned, his eyes flickering open. They flitted around, confused, bright orange, bloodshot. His voice croaked as he spoke, his hands reaching up and tenderly touching his throat. "Cat?"

She nodded, reaching for a nearby wooden cup of water. She opened a small pouch beside it, sprinkling a pinch of rough, white powder into the liquid. It fizzed violently for a second, threatening to overflow, before settling back down as she pushed it to the man's lips. He drank delicately, the bandage moving as he swallowed.

"Is he... okay...?" asked Marito, the concern in his voice as he looked upon the youth lying in the bedroll. The Massapine was a beautiful man, his features even more pleasant than those of Mani. His hair was shoulder-length, dyed jet black. It shone in the feeble morning light squeezing its way through the entrance to the tent, wet with sweat but still alluring.

"Who is this?" asked Angelo, a smile breaking gently across his face, the sunburst eyes settling on the lad before him. Marito was as unable to place the actor's age as he was that of Cat. It was the eyes. Wise beyond the body's physical years, the hair-thin lines at the edges the only sign of ageing.

"His name is Marito," replied Cat, carefully pulling away the dressing on the man's neck. The bandages were dark red with blood, but the wound beneath was little more than fresh scar tissue, a neat line slicing across the throat. "He is with Mani."

"And who is Mani?"

Cat wrapped a fresh, white bandage around the raw, pink flesh, securing it gently with a knot behind Angelo's head. She gestured with a hand, pointing past the young Tristane.

Marito followed her finger, shaking his head again as Mani approached, the bedclothes wrapped loosely around him. *Too* loosely. Far too much was still on show.

"Larcenara's tits," proclaimed Mani as he came to a halt beside his younger brother. "What did you do to me, Cat?"

Angelo raised an eyebrow in the direction of the woman at his side. "Indeed, what did you do to him?"

"Nothing other men have been unable to cope with," shrugged Cat, pulling a shirt from beside Angelo's bedroll and pulling it over her head, covering her toned body.

Angelo turned his gaze to Mani, glancing up and down his semi-naked form, the eyebrow still raised.

"Look," said Mani, raising a hand before him. He was looking around, obviously feeling more naked for not having his rapier to hand. "I..."

Angelo threw back his head, laughing drily, his throat obviously pained by the effort. "Relax, Mani. Cat is her own woman. I am sure you know that by now..."

Mani nodded, laughing awkwardly. Marito smiled at his confident brother's new-found modesty as he continued to search for his clothes.

"May I talk with you?" he asked, crouching down beside the actor's bedside. Around them, the other members of the troupe were finishing dressing and beginning to gather their belongings, stowing them in backpacks and jute sacks.

"What about, Marito?" asked Angelo, turning his warm eyes on the lad. Mani skulked away, the quest for his clothes becoming his priority.

"About the performance," answered Marito urgently. "I have so many questions..."

"Ah, questions," smiled Angelo teasingly, glancing at Cat. "If you have questions, Marito, then you did not watch carefully enough. You missed things. Perhaps you need a more practiced eye? Lyricas does not send us to answer your questions. He sends us to help you learn for yourself."

"But Cat told me some of it last night..."

Angelo turned the eyes on the woman beside him, frowning with mock disappointment. "Really, Cat? Of all the beings on this plane, you should know better..."

"I only told him a little," smiled Cat, leaning on Angelo's knee and reaching across to stroke Marito's cheek. Her soft hand moved under his chin, squeezing his cheeks together playfully. "Look at those big brown eyes. I could not resist. He has never seen the Massapine perform before."

Angelo tutted. "Please don't tell me you are going to bed this one too, Cat. It might cause a row between brothers."

"What do you take me for, Angelo?" she laughed, pushing Marito's face away gently. "I would break him like leaf. He is too gentle, too innocent. Too pure."

"Unlucky, my friend," smiled Angelo, turning the warm eyes on Marito. "She is probably right though. You do look... delicate..."

Marito looked away, blushing. "I only..."

"Want to learn?" asked Angelo. "That is fine. I will not show you, though. You must find your own way. Travel with us. Watch the performance again. Pay more attention next time. Look deeper. If you like, we will perform the same story again at our next stop."

"We don't do that often, Marito," said Cat. "You are honoured indeed if Angelo is offering. He must like you."

"Watch," urged Angelo. "*See.* We will not answer questions. But if you wish to give us your interpretation, we will tell you whether you are on the right track or not."

Marito shook his head gently, disappointed. "I would love to. But we have important work to do. I doubt we'll be heading the same way as you."

"You do not know where we are heading, Marito," purred Cat.

Marito looked into those eyes. The purple in the iris seemed to swirl, mysteriously beckoning to him, soothing him as he knelt. He felt himself relax, sliding down to sit cross-legged beside Angelo's bedroll. "We head back to our homeland," he said meekly. "To the Bandit Country. It's not a place for actors."

Cat turned her head, smiling at Angelo. The man returned her stare for a second, as if they were communicating without Marito hearing them speak.

"I have heard Old Illicea is rich with history," said Angelo. "We have always wanted to visit. But it is difficult. We wish to see it, to learn, to experience new cultures. But the place is dangerous, especially for outsiders."

"It would be safer in the company of men of Old Illicean stock," leered Cat. She licked her lips, looking up at Mani as he returned, his clothes hastily slung about his person.

"What are we talking about now?" he asked. "We need to get going, Marito. You know those fuckers will just sleep in until we kick them into action."

"Marito has very kindly invited us to join you on the road to Old Illicea, Mani," said Angelo, taking the light tunic that Cat handed him and sliding it gingerly over his head.

"I..." protested Marito, feeling his brother's angry glare.

"Impossible," declared Mani. "We have important business there. Business that needs to avoid prying eyes."

"We had business last night that needed to avoid prying eyes," smiled Cat, sliding up beside Mani, her hands playing across his shoulders as she circled him. "We could have more business like that on the road."

"And we are not interested in your affairs, Mani," said Angelo. "No Massapine troupe has ever performed in Old Illicea. If you could introduce us, that would be glorious. The roads are dangerous, and there is safety in numbers."

"He's right," agreed Marito, looking up to his brother as Cat sidled to stand before him, staring into his eyes. "They're just actors, Mani. What harm can it do?"

"We are just actors," repeated Cat, the lilac eyes straying down to the nipple that was visible through the thin, white shirt flowing around her slim body, her finger teasing it gently.

Mani nodded with a smile. "Get this tent down, then..."

Chapter Thirty-Nine

Toby walked down the gangplank onto the wharf, the sun beating down on his pale skin. He had burnt already; his nose, forehead, cheeks, even his ears were red and sore. He was not made for the heat of the southern sun, and as the boat had moved further towards Altanya the fiery disc in the sky had grown increasingly scorching. Each morning he had stepped out onto the deck, praying to Argentis that the heat had abated. Each morning it had gotten worse.

And now, on dry land again, the sea breeze was diminished. It had been the one thing keeping him cooler. He dreaded to think how baking hot the desert further inland would be. He was dressed in simple, loose, white clothing. He had shed his warmer attire almost as soon as the ship left Port Castor, heading out into the Jagged Sea. He had tried silks, but as they headed further south they clung to his sweaty body, suffocating him. He had progressed to thin linen, as he was told the locals wore.

Toby waved his hands at his face, trying to cool himself in the heat that beat down relentlessly upon him. His clothes were soaked with sweat already. Any exertion, even just walking, was an effort. His breathing was heavy, as though the air itself was burning his lungs.

"Will this heat never end?" he gasped, looking to the captain of their retinue at his side. "I do not think I can survive in the desert if it is worse than this."

"How do you think I feel?" snapped Capethorne. "Stood here, clad in fucking leathers."

Toby caught sight of his hosts as they walked down the jetty towards him. Their retinue waited on the docks. It was difficult to tell the servants from the soldiers. All the savages wore just a simple white loincloth, their pale, white torsos exposed to the blazing sun. He supposed the soldiers were the ones with the spears.

How are they not red with burns? he pondered. *They are even whiter than me, yet the sun does not seem to touch them.*

The two Altanyans approaching them were better dressed, enveloped in flowing robes and elaborate headdresses. One was dressed all in white. He had more clothes, but he fitted in with the retinue on the docks, with all the other folk Toby could see scurrying about their business. His companion wore garments of fiery red, setting him apart from every other Altanyan in sight.

"Lord Princetown," smiled the Altanyan in the white robes, bowing slightly in Toby's direction. "It is my pleasure to make your acquaintance."

Toby had studied the limited volumes available detailing Altanyan customs on the long voyage. He bowed himself, matching the man's motion closely. The Altanyans did not approve of physical contact during most interactions.

Probably because they are so small and puny...

"Overseer Lysis, I trust," he said. "It is my pleasure, your eminence. Please, though, I am not Lord Princetown. That is my father."

"Nonsense," laughed the Altanyan noble, displaying several shining gold teeth. Each was encrusted with a different coloured gemstone. Up close, Toby could see the opulence that set this man apart from the common folk. It was not just that he wore flowing garments whilst the peasants had little more than a pair of undergarments. His thin little fingers were bedecked with heavy gold rings, set with precious stones. A gold chain of thick links hung round his neck, and his headdress was held in place by a shining pin in the shape of a rearing snake's head. "Your father is not here, so to us, you are Lord Princetown."

"You honour me, your eminence," said Toby, bowing again.

"I have a gift," said Lysis, reaching inside his robe to hand Toby a delicate fan. "I expect the climate is causing you discomfort."

Toby extended the fan gently, clasping the ornately-carved ivory hand. It was adorned with thick, brightly-coloured peacock feathers. For the workmanship of a savage, it was impressive, he had to admit. He wafted it at his face gratefully, rolling his eyes as the cool air washed over his stinging skin.

"Perhaps your servant should do that for you," suggested Lysis, a confused look crossing his lined, white face as he looked to Capethorne.

"Fuck that," replied the soldier, shaking his head at Toby disdainfully.

"Apologies, overseer," said Toby, ignoring the man's glare. "This is Captain Charles Capethorne. He is an honoured warrior of Castland."

Lysis bowed again at Capethorne. The soldier returned the gesture awkwardly.

"It is an honour, captain. I too appear to have forgotten my manners." Lysis turned to the red robed figure at his side. "May I introduce Shaman Xius, my personal priest of Pyra..."

The bowing continued until all were formally introduced. Toby was certain this place would be the death of him. If the heat did not finish him off, his back would break from this constant genuflecting.

"May I ask, Overseer Lysis, where is your palace located?" Toby was hoping it was here, in the port of Kinum. It was, of course, unbearably hot, but at least it was on the northern coast, by the sea.

"I reside in the capital, Lord Princetown," replied Lysis, leading them down the wharf towards the assembled servants on the dock. "That is my place, and that is the place for an honoured ambassador from Castland."

"Oh," said Toby. *The fucking desert...*

"The journey will be long my lord, but rest assured, I shall make it comfortable for you. Come, let us get you in the shade."

Lysis paused before a huge sedan, the sides of the litter swathed in thin, shielding cloth. Toby paused for a second, looking back as Capethorne assembled the troops of his retinue on the wharf.

"They will follow, Lord Princetown," smiled Lysis, ushering Toby into the litter. He followed, Xius sliding in behind them. "I am sure you will want to rest before we continue our journey. I shall show you some of the sights of Kinum. Introduce you to some of our customs. We shall dine tonight in your honour, and that of King Jaros of Castland, our wise friend."

"Quite," nodded Toby, keeping one eye on Capethorne through the opening in the side of the litter as it was lifted off the ground by the servants at the front and rear. The Castlander men were ready now, tramping heavily onto the dock to fall in line behind the overseer's retinue as they moved into the warren of streets.

He watched the buildings pass. They were all painted white, the walls reflecting the bright light of the sun as they moved. The hovels, the shops, the traders, the noble houses, the temples; everything was white. The only thing differentiating them was their grandeur, along with the occasional coloured cloth awning protruding in front of a trader's establishment.

They were different, but he could tell what they were. The goods on sale in the shops were strange, exotic, laid out on the floor rather than shelved neatly, but Toby could recognise the building's purpose. The artisans had different tools, cruder than those used in Castland, but they were not so alien as to be unrecognisable. The one-room hovels were windowless, squat domes, but they were the homes of the poor nonetheless. Virtually every building was ugly though; simple, functional.

The noble dwellings and temples were few and far between. They stood out immediately from the close, crammed buildings. They had gates and high, whitewashed walls, protecting minarets that thrust up towards the sky like neat stalagmites, topped with ornately-tiled roofs.

"Tell me, your eminence," said Toby. "Do they have any taverns in Kinum? I could do with a drink, in all honesty. You know, to take the edge off?"

"Not many, my lord," replied Lysis with a grin, reaching beneath his seat and pulling out a bottle of red wine. He uncorked it, pouring a glass for himself and his guest. "Only from the Bandit Country, I am afraid, but it is the best that gold can buy. There are some taverns, but only for the nobility. We are not a top-heavy society, my lord, so the need for such establishments is scant."

Xius shook his head as the pair clinked their glasses, taking delicate sips.

"Do you not partake, Shaman Xius?" asked Toby.

"It is unwise," replied the priest. His eyes settled on the young noble, the lightest of blue, like most Altanyans. The pupils burnt red though, as if set alight inside his skull. "When alcohol falls on the flame, the results can be violent."

"Quite," said Toby. The man's gaze was unsettling. He turned his attention back towards the overseer, seeking an escape from the worshipper of Pyra. "Is it wise prevent the poor from drinking, your eminence? In Castland they are allowed to indulge. It keeps them happy, or at least content. There would be an uprising if we tried to stop them."

"When alcohol passes the lips of the masses," interjected Xius. "It has the same effect as when it falls on the flame. We keep such things from the poor. They have never known different, so they do not question it. The Three Pillars."

Toby raised an eyebrow over his drink, still avoiding the gaze of the priest. "I have not read of these, overseer."

"The Three Pillars are the basis of our society, my lord," said Lysis. "They apply to the poor, in order that our small number of nobles might rule them for their best interests."

"The Burning," intoned Xius, his voice a threatening hiss.

Lysis smiled reassuringly, spying the concerned look on Toby's face. "It is not as it sounds, my lord. The Burning forbids the poor from engaging in those activities that may foment disorder. Drinking alcohol, the use of intoxicating substances, reading, and suchlike. Then there is the Bondage."

Toby almost spat out his wine. "Slavery?"

"In a fashion," admitted Lysis. "I realise this concept is strange to you, my lord, but you must understand that we are a large country. Much larger than Castland. But our lands are mostly desert. They struggle to be kept fertile. Food and water must be managed carefully, along with every other resource. The Bondage means that the poor are allotted a trade by the nobility. Their role in society is determined by their betters, in order to ensure that the realm runs as it should, according to the needs of Altanya, not the whims of peasants. Once an Altanyan has served in their assigned role for twenty years, they become free to do as they wish. Within reason..."

Toby took a deep swig on his drink. He had been brought up on the importance to maintain order, to keep the balance, but it appeared that in this gods-forsaken desert realm they had taken these ideals beyond the pale. He opened his mouth hesitantly, reluctant to ask the question: "And the third pillar?"

Lysis hesitated, his pale eyes straying out of the window into the street beyond. Toby following his gaze, settling on a queue of women outside a wide, squat building. It was painted black, its windows the only ones he had seen to be covered. There was no glass, just like the rest, but within hung thick, dark drapes. Toby swore he could hear the muted sound of an agonising scream coming from within, stifled by the heavy curtains. The age of the women in the line varied, but seemed equally split between adults and girls of around ten to fourteen. It was hard to tell, not being familiar with Altanyan females. As he looked harder, he observed that it seemed to be a group of mothers, queuing with their daughters.

"The Cutting," said Lysis, looking briefly to Xius for support, scratching at one of the calloused patches of skin on his neck uncomfortably.

"The what?" asked Toby. He drained the wine glass, dreading the answer.

"You must understand, my lord," insisted the overseer, filling Toby's glass from the bottle. "We have a lack of resources. The balance must be maintained. If the population is not regulated there would be famine, drought. A populace without diversions turns to baser means of passing their time..."

"Copulation," nodded Xius solemnly.

"How do you stop people fucking?" asked Toby, regretting it instantly.

"The peasant girls are cut," replied Lysis. "As soon as they bleed for the first time."

"Cut?" Toby was unable to help himself.

"A woman's genitals are complex and sinful," said Xius, leaning forward towards Toby. "They are cut to remove the parts that cause them to take pleasure from copulation. The act becomes uncomfortable. A woman will still want a child, maybe more than one, but she will not breed like a wild hare. The pain would be too great."

Toby's jaw dropped. He felt his grasp on his drink loosen for a second, red wine splashing on the floor of the litter as he recalled the harrowing screams that struggled to penetrate the black building behind them.

"It is difficult for you to understand, Lord Princetown," said Lysis. "But it is our way. I ask that you understand our situation in these lands. Resources are scarce, and we must manage them accordingly."

Toby shook his head, trying to hide the horror he felt within himself from his hosts. "In Castland..."

"You are not in Castland any more, little lord," hissed Xius. The priest of Pyra was still leaning in close to Toby, the flame in his pupils brightening as he sneered. "You are in Altanya. *Remember* that..."

Q'thell watched as Cecil relaxed back in his own quarters in the Lord Chancellor's palace. The shiny-faced little lord nestled into his familiar leather chair beside his desk as he read the papers laid out before him carefully, his beady blue eyes scrutinising every inch of the parchment.

Cecil had to admit that he had not realised the comfort of home before. He had rarely left the capital, and he had begun to find it boring, almost stifling. Journeys back and forth across Castland had instilled in him a previously missing sense of longing for Regalla. It was not until one was away from one's home, from one's own bed, that you realised just how much a part of you it was.

"How has the election gone?" asked the Q'shari, attempting to feign disinterest. "Do we have to beat any more pregnant women?"

"If that is what it takes, then you will do it," said Cecil, not raising his eyes from the documents. "I had to deal with the last one, if I remember rightly."

Q'thell hissed to himself. It seemed Cecil was proud of kicking a woman fat with child to miscarriage, as if it made him some kind of great warrior, something better than the Q'shari. Q'thell had no love for the humans or their spawn, but slaughtering one of their larva in the womb…

He still saw it in his dreams, played out before him over and again. The dead, their faces haunting him as he slept, taunting him. Was he being punished by Sanguis, for failing to live up to all that he could be? He was a Q'shari warrior, after all, Bloodkin. He should be slaying other great fighters on the field of battle. Sanguis could get her fill of the blood of babes and women from the pathetic humans as they fought amongst themselves for what they believed was power.

"It appears the Northern Quarter has voted for the Establishment Party," smiled Cecil, looking up at his bodyguard. "The turnout was low, as the People's Party withdrew their candidate after the Gazette ran those tales of our actions in Snowgate. Disappointing, in a manner. It would have been preferable to beat them at the polls."

"Shall we hang some children as punishment for the poor not voting?" asked Q'thell, the sarcasm heavy in his voice.

"I have a mind to," pondered Cecil. "I do not feel that these people truly know their place. But no, our work in the capital is done, I think. Bligh tells me that the People's Party has withdrawn its nominees in the other wards as well."

"You've won then," said Q'thell with mocking admiration. "Well done to you."

"I do not appreciate your tone, Q'thell," warned Cecil. "But yes, I feel we have succeeded. For now."

"How do you mean?" asked the Q'shari. His interest in human affairs was waning again.

"I hear that Kassell has already held its election. The city declared for the People's Party. This poses a problem for us. The poor will not be satisfied with their lot if they find that others in the realm have successfully defied the Lord Chancellor. This is not over."

"So snide plots and threats haven't worked after all?" pondered Q'thell.

"They have worked for now. But the stability of Castland is still under threat. I have a plan, though. A plan which you will need to execute for me."

"What will you be doing?" asked Q'thell, the red eyes narrowing at the Lord Chancellor's son.

"I shall be arranging the elections in Westroad. You will go to Port Castor on my behalf. See to it that things go as smoothly there."

"So it's the same plan?" sneered Q'thell. "More elections, more threats."

"No," smiled Cecil, tossing the bundle of papers onto his desk. "Once you are done, you will slip away. I need you to gather some artefacts for me. Tell me, Q'thell, were you ever told of the Portal Stones when you were being dragged up in whatever tree you were born?"

"I know of them," replied Q'thell, ignoring the insult. He swore the youth was getting more arrogant as the days passed.

"I want them," said Cecil simply. "Imagine if I could summon Argentis into the Mortal World, to wreak havoc upon the poor and these simple fools who stand for them? It would be a marvellous solution to Castland's problems, would it not?"

"And your father approves?" asked Q'thell, grinning as he goaded the youth.

Cecil shook his head. "It will be a nice surprise for him. His son, the saviour of Castland. Proof that I am the rightful Lord Chancellor-in-waiting."

"You'll need to know the ritual, too."

"Excellent," smiled Cecil. "You know more than I gave you credit for. I have obtained some tomes. The details of the ritual are held in a lost place called…"

"The Library of Souls," interrupted Q'thell, nodding.

"Yes. I take it the savage before me does not know its location, though?"

Q'thell shook his head, looking past Cecil, the blood red slits peering into the distance. "But I can obtain the location."

"How?" asked Cecil irritably. "It is not written in any of the storehouses of knowledge to which I have access. And I have access to a great many…"

"I can find it," replied Q'thell simply. "Tell me, though, why don't you just send your new friend Bligh?"

"I do not trust Bligh as much as I trust you," shrugged Cecil. "He has yet to prove himself. You are tried and tested. And you know what will happen if you cross me."

Q'thell ignored the threat. He was not afraid of many things. He certainly wasn't afraid of any human. The dreams, on the other hand...

Perhaps this is what I must do to rid myself of this curse. Demonstrate my devotion to Sanguis, my skills as a warrior. Truly demonstrate them, instead of pandering to this pig...

"I'll get the location," declared Q'thell. "And I'll get these stones. I'll need to leave immediately. I have a detour to make on the way to Port Castor."

"I shall have a detachment of men ready by the morning," said Cecil. "I have managed to obtain the services of a scholarly member of the Wizards Guild to accompany you. He will be of use. You will need him to decipher the ritual. I want none of these men to know your goals, though, until you are aboard the ship I make ready. From there, they are your responsibility. Their loyalty must be to me. If they falter, you know what to do."

Q'thell took to his feet, looking down on the noble before him. "Send them ahead to Port Castor. I'll meet them there. They can't go where I'm going."

Cecil raised an eyebrow. "Why is that?"

"They are not Q'shari," replied Q'thell simply, turning to stride from Cecil's chambers.

Cecil strode confidently into the Lord Chancellor's audience chamber, Kaly on his arm. She really did set him off perfectly, her delicate beauty the perfect complement to his strong, stable presence. Ahead of them his father and Iluma Porwesh stood on their arrival, waiting as the betrothed couple approached the table. It was laid out with stacks of papers and documents. Goblets of wine had already been poured for the four of them.

Their parents moved to greet them as they neared. The Lord Chancellor reached out, wrapping his arms around his taller son, squeezing him tight. Cecil was taken aback. His father had never displayed such affection, even when he was a young boy. It was awkward. Neither of them seemed comfortable with it.

"Well done, Cecil," said the older Cramwall, a rare smile cracking his old face. "You have done a great service to the realm. You have represented the family honourably."

Porwesh finished embracing his daughter and moved over, extending a pale, wrinkled hand. Cecil shook it. The grip was weak, clammy. "Congratulations, my lord. I have heard of your successes."

"Thank you, both of you," smiled Cecil, bowing slightly as they took their seats around the table.

"The elections in Snowgate were a great achievement, my boy," said the Lord Chancellor, reviewing a pile of documents that Cecil knew had been perused many times previously by the diligent old man. "Only one district voted for the People's Party, and you nipped that in the bud admirably."

"My lord was swift and decisive, Lord Chancellor," nodded Kaly, her eyes fluttering at the youth beside her.

"I was hoping for a clean sweep, father," said Cecil humbly.

"Nonsense, lad," declared the Lord Chancellor, waving his arm dismissively. "With the greatest of respect to you, that was never going to happen. That is why I sent you to Snowgate first. Lord Princetown is weak, his control over his populace is tenuous. I knew there would be dissent. And I knew you would stamp it out. The result in Snowgate and the surrounding lands is excellent."

Porwesh nodded in agreement with the Lord Chancellor.

"The results in the Northern Quarter are favourable too," continued Cramwall, shifting through a new pile of papers. "The Regalla elections will go as planned, I am sure of it."

"The turnout was low, father," said Cecil. "I fear the people harbour resentment."

"Let them," shrugged Cramwall. "We shall monitor the situation, but the dissatisfaction of the poor is perpetual, I am afraid. As long as it does not boil over, it is part and parcel of their lives. As long as we manage it correctly, the order will continue. Tell me, have you planned ahead, lad?"

"I thought that, with developments in the east, we could push the process along, father?"

"How do you mean, Cecil?" asked the Lord Chancellor, his demeanour suddenly appearing guarded. He was a man used to leading, and Cecil knew that unexpected developments were likely to unsettle him.

"I have made plans to attend Westroad, by your leave. Things in the capital seem under control. I have sent Q'thell to deal with Port Castor."

"If you will allow it, I would like to accompany my lord," said Kaly, turning the sapphire eyes on the Lord Chancellor.

"The girl is eager to learn, Lord Chancellor," smiled Porwesh, the aged lips barely moving with the facial expression.

"Of course, that is fine," nodded Cramwall, struggling to re-direct the discussion in the direction he wished. "Are you sure the savage can be trusted, Cecil?"

"He has proved reliable thus far," said Cecil. "He has done the groundwork in Snowgate and in the capital, and he is a quick learner, for a tree-dweller. Lord Garstone is a strong man, he will likely take much of the burden upon his own shoulders anyway. Q'thell will merely need to be available, should he be needed."

Cramwall looked to Porwesh, the pair nodding to one another subtly. "Your words are wise, son. We shall play it your way. I can see that you are maturing into a man worthy of the Cramwall name."

"Thank you, father," nodded Cecil graciously. He reached out, taking a sip from the wine goblet before him. "Tell me, what of events in the east?"

The Lord Chancellor sighed, again glancing to Porwesh. "I have received a bird from Lord Tremelowe. It seems he has defied the orders of the crown and held his election. The people of Kassell have voted for the People's Party."

"And the surrounding lands?" asked Cecil, shaking his head in disdain.

"I have not yet received word," replied Cramwall, reaching out and sipping from his own drink. "Whether they have voted yet or not I do not know. I would be surprised if Lord Tremelowe knows. The man is becoming a liability."

"What shall we do, father?" asked Cecil.

Cramwall paused, gathering his thoughts as he sipped again from his cup. Cecil could see his father's mind was working, weighing up the options, playing out the various actions and potential results.

"What would you suggest?" he asked thoughtfully, his eyes turning to his son. "You have proven yourself astute enough for me to consider your thoughts, after all."

Cecil paused for a second, pretending to weigh up the options. He had thought it through beforehand, of course, in his chambers. The hesitation was merely to show reasoned contemplation. "We should not be hasty. It may antagonise the poor. We should await the rest of the country's results. Lord Tremelowe is not, after all, a traitor. He has fought bravely for Castland. If he sees that the rest of the realm holds a different view, he may well agree to annul the election and re-run the vote."

"Excellent," smiled the Lord Chancellor, his icy blue eyes filling with pride. "I was fearing you would still be hot-headed, demanding we went to war with one of the country's major cities. Your thoughts mirror my own."

Porwesh nodded beside him, bowing his head to the Lord Chancellor's son. "You are indeed wise beyond your years, my lord. Kalyanit is lucky to be at hand to witness your acumen. Hopefully she will learn from it."

"Speaking of which," said Cramwall, his tone lightening as they moved away from affairs of state. "How are things between you two young lovers?"

Their children smiled, glancing between themselves and their parents bashfully.

"They go well," smiled Kaly, the dimples in her cheeks creeping into view. "I hope my lord is as pleased with me as I am with him."

"Nonsense, my dear," laughed the Lord Chancellor. Cecil began to wonder whether the few sips of wine had made the old man drunk. He had not seen him so many jovialities in his whole lifetime as he had seen during today's meeting. "He is lucky to have you. He has my ugly face, I am afraid. His mother was beautiful, but Cecil took after me, unfortunately. Tell me, does he treat you well. Be honest. I shall have him beaten if he does not."

Kaly laughed gently, the trickling notes melting the Lord Chancellor's heart as they had done his son's. "He is the perfect gentleman, Lord Chancellor."

"Excellent," smiled Cramwall as Porwesh nodded approvingly at his daughter. The Lord Chancellor rose to his feet, followed by the rest of them. He raised his goblet high in the air. "I propose a toast. To Castland. To its future Lord Chancellor, may he be as wise as his father. And to his future wife, may she be of as much support as his mother."

The other joined the toast, raising their cups and drinking deep. Cecil turned to Kaly, smiling as he reached out and squeezed her hand tightly.

Chapter Forty

Pharos sat on the ground, watching as Lexis debated with the two Barralegnan guards who had emerged from the border outpost that blocked the road leading west into the neighbouring country. The discussion did not seem to be going in the direction the head priest would have liked.

"I told him that goodwill towards the clergy of Pharma wouldn't get him half as far as he thought," he remarked to Mida as the lad knelt beside him. Pharos looked down at the bottle of rum in his hand and took a swig. "This shit is disgusting. How fucking old is it, do you think? Pirate Coast rum from the cellar of a fucking chapel in Castland. Can't be good."

The young initiate was the only one of the group nearby. The ranger, Ryn, was with Lexis, discussing passage into Barralegne with the soldiers. The rest of the worshippers of Pharma had hung back, distancing themselves from the conversation, and from Pharos. They still seemed pissed off that he had insisted they take all the alms coin from each chapel and shrine of Pharma that they passed on the way to the border.

"What's up with those stuffy cunts now?"

"I do not think they agree with your ways, Pharos," smiled Mida gently.

"Why? What the fuck have I done to them?"

"The coin is sacred, in their opinion," said Mida patiently. "It was given by worshippers to aid the sick, and we have taken it. Some of the way clerics did not seem happy to give it up."

"Why would they be?" sneered Pharos, taking a deep drink from the bottle. He winced, hissing at the burn. "They would use that to buy what they needed. They're just like these insufferable bastards. They look after themselves first, then, if there's anything left, they buy some shit for the poor and the sick. That isn't what being a cleric's about, is it, lad?"

"Of course not. I do not think they like all the drinking either."

Pharos snorted, spitting on the ground in front of him. "They'd drink too, if they had seen the things I've seen. If they'd felt the things I've felt. Being the child of a god is a curse, child, not a blessing."

"Still," pondered Mida. He had come to know Pharos over the journey, and he knew that Pharma's son liked him; certainly, more than he liked any other person. He could push Pharos without suffering his irate outbursts. "You can at least avoid the worst effects of using magic for good. They cannot. Is it any wonder they are reluctant to do so?"

Pharos fixed the lad with his soulless stare. "If they aren't willing to be selfless, why are they clerics of Pharma?"

"Maybe you could teach them?" said Mida. Pharos sneered, seeing he had been trapped. The youth had a cunning that wasn't befitting of a priest of the Merciful One. "You recovered quickly after healing Ryn's son. I could see it pained you, but you recuperated fast. If you taught them, they could be so much more."

"I don't think it works like that, boy."

"How does it work, then?" asked Mida. Pharos looked at him, unable to bring his rage to bear. The lad was young, his innocent questions had no ulterior motive. He still believed in opposing poles, in black and white, in good and evil. The lad reached up, stroking Pharos' bald head gently, his little finger moving down across the lash-less eyes. "How did you recover from your wounds, yet your hair hasn't grown back?"

"You ask as if I should know," sighed Pharos, gulping more rough rum down his throat. "I don't understand it, lad. I know what I can do, and I know what I can't. I know what harms me, and I know how much I can sustain. That came through trial and error. My mother didn't give me any guidance on how this life works."

"Have you tried asking her?" asked Mida.

Pharos glared now, the anger back in his eyes. He clenched a fist, restraining himself from smashing the initiate's face into a pulp. *He's just a boy...*

"That bitch threw me down here to the wolves. I knew what she wanted me to tell them, and I did it. And they fucked me for it. Fucked me good and proper. She did nothing to stop them, because she couldn't. And she did nothing to warn me, because she didn't want to. Pharma is dead to me, boy. Remember that before you try to manipulate me again."

Mida nodded, his head bowed to the ground. "I am sorry, Pharos. But... why are you helping us, then?"

267

"So you can find your own way," said Pharos. "Escape from all this bullshit. All of you, the clergy and the rest."

Lexis was returning now, gesturing for the group to gather together. The priests and initiates came over slowly, their bodies already sore from the journey.

"They will let us pass," he said. "A few gold pieces as a toll."

"A bribe, more like," snorted Yulli.

Pharos took to his feet unsteadily, the rum affecting his coordination. "Bribes make the world go round, priest. You would know that, if you weren't so distanced from reality."

"It does not matter what we call it," insisted Lexis. Pharos was meeting Yulli's disdainful gaze, seemingly daring him to speak again. "It means we can pass. The border guards seem uneasy."

"Very skittish," admitted Ryn. "One of them mentioned Castlander spies."

"Are you glad we waited before we hired mercenaries?" asked Pharos. "Could you imagine them letting us through with a group of armed men in tow?"

"It was a good decision, Pharos," nodded Lexis. "Come, everyone gather your things, before they change their minds."

The group shuffled towards the outpost. As they approached Lexis handed each of the guards a few coins. They bit them, eyeing the robed clergy suspiciously as they passed. At their signal, the portcullis raised in the archway, scraping its way up into the ceiling.

One of the guards reached out a hand suddenly as he spotted Pharos, stopping him in his tracks. "What the fuck have we got here? He doesn't look like a priest."

Pharos looked down at the hand on his chest, clenching his fists.

"He looks like a fucking leper," said the other man, peering warily at Pharos' scarred skin.

"I was punished for the sins and stupidity of all men," said Pharos. His glassy eyes moved up from the man's hand, taking in the bearded face that peered out from the steel helmet.

The soldier's dark eyes met Pharos' stare. He glanced to his friend. "More like you were punished for fucking goats and scabby dogs."

Pharos swung an arm, the movement almost too quick to take in. His fist struck the side of the soldier's head, the helmet dinting inwards wickedly with the force of the blow. He collapsed to the ground, rolling in disorientated agony, blood beginning to flow down his face from beneath the mangled headgear.

"No, no," cried Lexis, pushing Pharos away as the soldier reached for his sword. "The canker has reached his brain. It makes him act rashly. That is why we are taking him to the coast, so that the sea air might ease his condition."

"I can see why there's so many of you transporting him," snarled the soldier, his grip on the hilt of his weapon relaxing as Lexis began pulling more gold coins from his pouch.

"I'm quite a handful," sneered Pharos, the eyes flashing at the border guard.

"Here," insisted Lexis, drawing the man's gaze away from Pharos and pressing more gold into his hand. "For your troubles."

The guard looked down at his comrade, writhing on the ground as he tried to remove the twisted helmet. He pocketed the coins, nodding. "Get that fucking cunt out of my sight. Now."

Lexis nodded, grabbing Pharos by the arm and leading the group through the gate and into Barralegne.

"That was hilarious," laughed the son of Pharma, swigging from the rum bottle with a leer.

"It was uncalled for," snapped Yulli, shaking his head vigorously.

"It was still fucking hilarious," said Pharos, staring at the disapproving priest threateningly. "It's been decades since I punched a man. I miss it. I suggest you remember that..."

Angelo knelt with the other Massapine as they formed a circle in the tent. Only Cat stood, moving around them, a wooden bowl of viscous liquid in her hand. He soaked small balls of rag in the bowl, stopping at each of the braziers around the actors and dropping one in each. The liquid hissed as it struck the hot coals, wisps of coloured smoke wafting out, clouding the space inside the tent.

The Massapine breathed deep, inhaling the heady fumes. Cat placed the bowl down, picking up a tray of simple wooden cups. She handed one to each of the men as they knelt, swaying slightly as the incense filled their lungs. She slid over to one of the braziers, pulling out an iron kettle. The water inside bubbled as he moved amongst the actors, filling their cups one-by-one. Occasionally a slice of soft, stewed mushroom plopped out with the liquid, brightly-coloured and spotted.

The kneeling men hummed a melodic intonation as they sipped from the cups, the drug-infused liquid sliding down into their stomachs. They pulled the mushrooms out with their fingers, slipping the fungus into their mouths and swallowing them whole. Cat could tell the incense was already starting to take effect. The kaleidoscope of exotic eyes looking upon her as she moved were becoming distant, slightly glazed.

She smiled, stroking the hair of one of the men as she moved past him, back to her collection of paraphernalia. She pulled out a small, delicately engraved wooden box, opening it to reveal a pile of tangled, dried roots. She moved amongst them again, handing each of them one of the tubers. The men took them, sucking and chewing as they began to hum.

Cat smiled, her lustrous, purple eyes gazing warmly at the men before her as they rocked, melodic music seemingly seeping from their bare chests. She eyed each one quickly, performing one final check that their wounds had healed from the last performance. They were fine; they could perform again.

She draped her arms around Angelo's athletic, toned shoulders, pressing her cheek against his and closing her eyes. She loved to listen to their music. The range and pitch was beautiful, as ever an admirable tribute to Lyricas. They performed different roles and harmonies each time, but each recital during their preparations made her heart flutter warmly in her chest.

"Do you feel it?" she whispered in Angelo's ear, her breath warm on his skin.

"I see something," he replied, his eyes staring out now into the ether.

"Concentrate on the ritual," hissed Cat gently, her voice soothing. "Welcome them in."

"But I see something."

Cat pulled away slightly, a perplexed look crossing her soft features. "What do you see?"

"The Illiceans," said Angelo, his eyes widening now. His voice was slurred, his mouth moving with difficulty as the combination of hallucinogens took an ever-increasing effect. "We should help them. They seek something of great power. Lyricas wants us to help them. We could use it, to bring peace to the Mortal World. Peace and love. The Great Performance."

Cat stood up, her hand still resting on Angelo's shoulder. "Strange. I have not seen this."

"The Great Performance," repeated Angelo. His eyes were rolling back in his head now as he swayed, his head lolling back weakly behind him, pointed towards the roof of the tent.

Cat looked around. The others, too, were leaning back, their glazed eyes towards the heavens.

"Concentrate," she whispered, nestling back into Angelo's neck. "That is business for the future. Now, we must perform. Concentrate. Welcome the demons. Speak their names."

"Very good, Marito," smiled Angelo, wrapping his arm around the Tristane youth and pulling him close. "It has taken you all day, but you see the meaning of the tale. You have a beautiful soul, my friend. With each performance that you understand, it will grow riper and richer."

Marito smiled, looking over to his brother as he walked beside them, his attention focused on Cat. "Do you hear that, Mani? I have a beautiful soul."

"You have a fucking soft soul," replied his brother.

"I think your soul is softer than you make out, Mani," laughed Cat, nudging him teasingly.

"Not soft enough to be out here at this time of night," replied Mani, pausing to look at their surroundings. "We need to set up camp."

The Massapine had performed last night at the last inn on the road. At least, the last inn on their road. The place was set at a fork, where the main trade route into the Bandit Country branched out east and then south. It was longer, but it was more suitable for wagons and carts laden with goods.

They had continued south. The rough track was already beginning to steepen as they headed up into the mountains bordering the Bandit Country. Both the Tristanes and the Massapine had mules to carry their supplies and trappings, so they could make it through the more treacherous mountain passes along the direct route into the old country.

"Are you scared of the dark, Mani?" giggled Cat. "All the best things happen in the dark."

Mani shook his head. Night had fallen, and they hadn't even set up camp yet. They needed to eat and rest. The forest around the track was thinning as they moved into the foothills, but it was still dense enough to be dangerous if someone with ill intentions decided to sneak up on them. It was time to set up watches, get settled.

269

"Maybe Mani's right," said Marito. "We could be in Illicea by now. There may be raiders."

Angelo laughed gently, shaking his head. "We are not there yet, Marito. Not by a long stride. We have not yet travelled over the Demon's Bridge. You would recognise it, I'm sure."

"He's right," nodded Mani.

The Demon's Bridge was the summit of the pass through the Great Barrier Mountains, a treacherous route that had claimed many an unwary traveller. The scree track twisted and turned up and down. It would be an arduous climb and descent.

"You would have heard the screams of the demons," smiled Angelo. "The souls of the men and women who perished on the trek, their bodies shattered on the rocks below the track, their souls condemned to walk the land of the living as demons, torturing the Mortal World with their harrowing wails."

Mani shook his head, catching the anxious look on his brother's face. "They're just mountains, Marito. Treacherous mountains. Dangerous. But just mountains. Anyway, we need to rest."

Angelo shrugged. "Maybe we could share their fire."

The actor's slender arm pointed past them at the faint glow of a campfire, the light rising up from a rocky outcrop that covered a bend in the track.

Mani cursed, drawing his rapier in a swift, smooth motion, annoyed that he had missed the danger sign.

"Calm down, Mani," laughed Angelo. "I am sure the only person in these hills who needs sticking with your sword is Cat."

Cat wasn't laughing. Her purple eyes glared at him, dark and dangerous in the night. She shook her head, turning her gaze on the track ahead. "Something is not right."

Mani gestured for his men to join them. They stepped forward, weapons drawn, Marito moving to join them.

"Stay back," snapped his older brother, moving forward with the Tristane enforcers.

The actors hung back, beginning to root through the packs on their mules, searching for their weapons. Marito hung behind, trying to keep the others in view as they moved round the bend in the track, Cat slipping onto step amongst them. She was crouched low to the ground like a stalking mountain lion her, movements silent.

Marito watched as the silhouetted figures stood before the campfire. It was dying, having lain untended, but it was still giving out some light. He could see a few pack mules on the edge of the camp, still tied up to a rock. Tents had been set out, but a couple were lying flat, as though disturbed by a commotion. It looked like the camp had been abandoned.

Then he saw it. The corpse of a man, impaled on a long, wooden spike that had been driven into the ground on the opposite side of the fire. The flickering light of the flames played across the man's face, making it seem as if his features were still moving, twisting in agony.

Marito could see them now. Black, slumped shapes on the ground around the fire, twisted and broken. Corpses. Dead traders, cut down and left in the open for the birds. He moved forward, his mouth agape, catching his foot on a sod of earth and almost tripping. As he looked down, struggling to keep his balance, he saw the body of a man, his innards hanging through a jagged tear in his belly.

He let out of shriek, rushing towards the group in the camp, fleeing from the stricken corpse. Cat turned as he approached. Her eyes glowed purple in the dark, like those of a wild animal. She had a knife in her hand, clasped tight to her svelte body.

"Stay back," she hissed.

Marito ignored her, bumping into Mani's back as he reached them. His brother turned around, grabbing angrily at his wrist.

Mani didn't have time to speak. They were around them, shrieking out of the night. Marito had never heard a sound like it; shrill, unhinged cries as robed men and women pounced upon them. The figures twisted through the shadows, armed with knives and clubs, striking out in the blackness. He fumbled for his rapier, struggling to unclip it from the scabbard.

One of the enforcers dropped to his knees as a robed figure threw itself against him. Marito caught the wide, manic eyes as the assailant sunk his teeth into the Tristane man's shoulder, biting deep. The eyes rolled into his head as Cat slid forward, slamming her blade into his temple.

The lunatics were amongst them now, but they were clumsy and untrained. The Tristane enforcers were hard men, armed with swords, axes, maces. Mani slashed at one of the ambushers as he passed,

270

spilling his intestines on the ground. The figure kept on running, slashing wildly, until he was brought down by one of their own men. Mani stumbled back to his brother, pulling him in close.

"Stay behind me."

The pair watched as their men battled the wild, robed attackers. They seemed to keep coming from the night, unconcerned as their fellow assailants were cut down in their stride. Cat moved amongst them, the dagger lashing out, slicing skin and imbedding in flesh. Mani and Marito gasped as he vaulted and pirouetted, her deadly movements as graceful as the choreographed plays they had observed.

Mani span angrily, moving to thrust as he felt a hand on his shoulder. He stayed his hand just in time as Angelo and the troupe joined the fray, moving amongst the Tristane party, their blades less accurate but still deadly.

Suddenly Marito was spinning. A hand had grabbed him, throwing him across the floor. He struggled to come to a halt, sprawled on his stomach, looking up as one of the robed figures confronted Mani. He was dressed in the same rough robes as the others, homespun blue garments that seemed black in the dark of night. His eyes were not wild, though. They were glazed over; purple opening in his face, devoid of white, pupil or iris.

Mani lunged perfectly, the rapier slicing through the man's stomach, protruding from his back. Marito's relief turned to dismay as the robed figure reached out and grabbed his brother by the throat, seemingly oblivious to the wound. He lifted Mani clean off the ground, holding him up triumphantly as he lost his grip on the hilt of his weapon, leaving it skewering his attacker.

Marito struggled to his feet, again fumbling with his weapon. He was too late...

Cat came out of nowhere, grabbing the hilt of Mani's sword and ripping it from the robed figure's body. It spun in her hand like a windmill, slicing down on the arm that gripped his brother. The rapier cut straight through the limb like it was butter, releasing Mani to stagger in an effort to keep his balance.

Marito had never seen such strength. The rapier was a slashing and stabbing weapon. To cleave a man's arm off...

Cat lunged forward, stepping into the robed man's grip as his remaining hand grasped at her throat. He was strong. He had picked up Mani with one hand like he was a rag doll. Cat was stronger. She pushed him back, twisting his grip away from her neck and sliding the blade under his chin, ramming it up into his skull.

The man stood for a second, his body twitching as it realised that it was dead. Marito swore that the purple haze cleared from his eyes as they rolled up into his head, the lifeless corpse dropping to the floor.

He staggered forward, grabbing his brother close, extending his rapier defensively as the night began to fall silent around them.

Cat stood before them, her purple eyes blazing in the night, seeming to bathe them in an intense, violet glow that was brighter than the light of the fading campfire.

"What the fuck just happened?" asked Mani.

Marito sat beside him as they warmed themselves on the rejuvenated campfire. Their men had set to work, pitching the tents and getting pans of food cooking. Neither of them were hungry.

"Will he be alright?" asked Marito, looking over to Cat as she knelt beside their wounded enforcer. She had pulled back his leather jack, revealing the neat, round bitemark in his shoulder.

"It is nothing grave," she smiled, her soothing eyes meeting those of the man. She began to apply a thick, green salve to the wound, massaging it in gently, much to the Tristane man's delight. "We need to make sure it does not get infected, but he will live."

"And the others?" asked Angelo, standing before them, his orange eyes still flitting out into the dark around their camp.

"Superficial wounds," said Cat, pulling the man's leathers back into place and caressing his cheek lovingly. "A few bruises, minor cuts. They will be fine."

Mani stood abruptly, gesturing at the corpses that the actors were removing from their campsite. "Is nobody else concerned with who the fuck they were?"

"Cultists? Lunatics?" shrugged Angelo. "They are dead, are they not? Testament to why only women should fight wearing a dress."

"Some of them were women," reflected Marito, watching as the body of a female was carried by, her head smashed in by a mace, the eye dangling loosely from the socket. He looked away quickly.

271

"Testament to why only competent women should fight wearing a dress," smiled Angelo, winking at Cat.

"I am not wearing a dress," she grinned, looking down at her close-fitting bodice and breeches.

"Am I the only one who doesn't think this is amusing?" asked Mani, his temper beginning to fray. He gestured towards the corpse of the cultist who had picked him up bodily by the neck, booting the corpse angrily. "Who the fuck was that? *What* the fuck was that?"

"Perhaps his mind was addled by drugs," lilted Cat, sidling up behind Mani, her hands playing across his shoulders, moving down to his waist as she pressed in behind him. "You stabbed him good. We all saw it; your manhood is not in doubt. Perhaps he was possessed by a demon. By a god, even."

"Possession?" cried Mani, shaking his head and looking over his shoulder at Cat. "Demons? Listen to yourself. What do you know of these things that are used to scare naïve children?"

"More than you can imagine," mused Angelo.

A wolf howled in the distance, its cry filtering through the night air. The men in the camp paused, feeling anxiously for their weapons, their eyes wide as they stared out into the darkness.

"Grown men, tough men, frightened by a wolf howling at the moon," crooned Cat, squeezing Mani's hips. "We met a traveller from the west not long ago. He said that Lunaris had brought demons to the Mortal World to devour a village and everyone in it. It seems that dark times are upon us, my dear."

"Perhaps Lord Tremelowe is right to seek the Portal Stones," pondered Marito.

He felt his brother's gaze before he saw it, heavy and angry. Angelo raised an eyebrow, his eyes seeking out Cat. She gazed back, nodding gently.

"The Portal Stones?" said Angelo softly, kneeling down before Marito. "Your lord may be right. Perhaps we may be of service."

"We don't need your help," snapped Mani, pushing Cat away and moving to stand behind his younger brother. "This is not your concern. We agreed to take you to Old Illicea, and that is all."

"And why do you head there?" asked Angelo. "The Library of Souls is not in Old Illicea."

"They do not know where it is," said Cat, sliding over and wrapping her arms around her fellow Massapine's shoulders. "They seek its location. Perhaps from the old repositories of knowledge in Matus..."

"So many tomes, though," smiled Angelo, his elegant features turning to sadness in the flickering light of the campfire. "It will take so much time to search them. Assuming the information they seek is there."

"So much time," concurred Cat, staring into Marito's eyes.

"What do you know of the Library of Souls?" he asked, the violet of the Massapine woman's eyes soothing him, seeming to numb his tired muscles.

"*Everything.*" Angelo and Cat replied in tandem as she slid away from him, moving round and sitting cross-legged beside Marito, leaning in against him.

"We are Massapine," she hissed. "We made it. We are the Northern Troupe. We are the most dedicated followers of Lyricas. We flow through the northern regions of the Mortal World, spreading the joy that only Lyricas can bring. We spread the knowledge that can only be found through true understanding."

"And to spread knowledge requires knowledge," continued Angelo. He knelt before Marito, his hand resting on the youth's knee. "We have everything you need."

"You know the location of the Library of Souls?" asked Mani.

Cat nodded, her hand sliding across Marito's thin shoulders as she moved towards his brother. She stood before Mani, wrapping her arms around his waist, pulling him closer.

"And you'll give it to us?" asked Mani as Cat gripped the back of his head, pressing her lips against his.

"We will give it to you," nodded Angelo, his eyes fixing on Marito's, warm and welcoming. "We will come with you. We will give you everything that you need."

Marito smiled timidly, averting his eyes from the fiery orange glare. He nodded gently.

Chapter Forty-One

Q'thell strode through the dense forest, a sneer crossing his face. It had taken them long enough to spot him, but he was being followed now. He could sense them, moving silently through the thick undergrowth around him, watching him from. He was close now, having journeyed into the deep woods, leaving any vestige of human civilisation far behind him.

Too close. They are getting sloppy. Complacent.

The darkness beneath the thick, lush canopy was not a problem for him. His eyes easily adjusted as he walked, flicking nimbly before him, watching for snares, spikes, pitfall traps. The trees around him were old, some of the most ancient living things on the planet. He stopped beside one, pressing a slender black hand against it.

He was no tree-worshipper, but it was difficult not to respect their size, their strength, their durability. His red eyes moved upwards. Tilting his head back he could see the almost invisible outline of a platform above him, high in the branches; a guard post. He could spot it because he knew what to look for. To an untrained eye, it would be impossible to make out.

Q'thell smiled again, turning and resuming on his way through the brush, his carefully-placed feet making virtually no sound. He knew he was getting close, he could feel it. The trees around him became more familiar. Any minute now he would break through into the clearing.

How close are they going to let me get?

His thought was answered as an arrow sliced the air in front of his nose, imbedding beside his head in the thick trunk of a tree. The Q'shari didn't flinch, eyeing the smooth, intricately-decorated wood of the shaft. The feathers making up the fletch were bright, greens and reds interlinking delicately.

She's still here...

"It took you long enough," smiled Q'thell, leaning on the tree as two Q'shari emerged from the undergrowth.

The male was the taller, the same height as Q'thell. His hair was shaved at the sides, dyed blood red on top and spiked up into a mohawk with animal fat. He wore no tunic, his bare, rippling torso and arms intertwined with ceremonial scarrings that traced swirling pink lines across his flesh. He gripped a long, curved sword in one hand, an elegant axe in the other.

The female still held the bow aimed at Q'thell, her muscles taut as she kept the arrow directed at his face. The weapon was beautiful, decorated with the same twisting patterns as the shaft of her arrows. It was almost as beautiful as her. Her eyes were white, peering out from beneath flowing black dreadlocks that cascaded around her face and shoulders as faint recognition crossed her features. She shook her head gently, the red and green feathers mixed in with her locks rustling, the bone ornaments hanging amongst them rattling together.

"Q'thell?" she asked, her grip on the bowstring loosening slightly.

He smiled gently, nodding to her. "Yes, Q'rassi. It is me."

The male Q'shari's eyes met Q'thell's own, equally bright and blood red, glaring out from amongst piercings linked together by fine strands of chain.

"Did you miss me, Q'laak?" asked Q'thell, narrowing his eyes at the warrior before him. "I made you the best fighter in Q'qaara when I left."

"Pah," hissed Q'laak fiercely. Q'thell noticed the envy in the other Bloodkin's eyes as Q'rassi ran forward, wrapping her arms around him.

"*I've* missed you," she said, pulling him close. Her body was strong against his, warm and familiar. He realised he had not embraced another being since he had left Q'qaara. She pulled back, running her hand over his stubbled head. "What is this, Q'thell? Where is your beautiful hair?"

"You have lost the Q'shari in you, Q'thell," sneered Q'laak, flaring his nostrils, his tongue tasting the air. "You look like a human. You stink of them."

Q'thell ignored him, cupping her head in his hand as he stared at those white eyes, his thumb resting beneath one gently. "And you have not decided yet. After all this time."

"It takes time to decide," shrugged Q'rassi, stepping back as Q'laak approached, tucking his weapons into his thick leather belt. "We live long lives, Q'thell. There is time."

"She will choose well, I am sure of it," said Q'laak, sliding his arm around her slender waist, pulling her close. "She will join her mate as Bloodkin, I know it."

Q'rassi pushed him away gently, slapping him across the cheek. "I will do as I wish, Q'laak. You know that. You do not own me. Remember that."

273

"Congratulations to you both," said Q'thell, struggling to contain his disappointment as he clasped hands with Q'laak. His fellow Bloodkin did nothing to conceal his triumphant sneer. "You make a good pairing."

"Thank you," smiled Q'laak, holding the tight grip a few seconds longer before releasing. "Tell us, what brings you back to us?"

"I need to pray to Sanguis," replied Q'thell simply as they moved towards the settlement. The tress parted suddenly, a clearing opening up before them that was mystifyingly concealed until the very last moment.

Q'qaara. The spiritual home of the Q'shari people. The first settlement. Graceful figures moved around them, going about their simple lives in the deep forest. Children darted amongst the adults, playing athletically, lunging with simple wooden swords or firing stringless bows. Animals mingled freely; chickens, boars, sheep, goats. There were no pens, no halters round their necks. The beasts seemed calmed by serenity between the canopy, the thick tangle of branches above them knitting together to almost form a natural, wooden cave.

Most of the adults were crafting weapons or household items or ornaments. To one side the Bloodkin were gathered, training relentlessly before the shadowy tunnel of trees that led to the shrine to Sanguis.

"You do not need to come back to Q'qaara to pray," said Q'laak warily as they moved amongst the people. "Sanguis is everywhere, Q'thell."

"True," admitted Q'thell. "I need a weapon from the priests, though. And I need to speak with the Great Elder."

He turned his eyes to the opposite end of the clearing. It was dominated by a huge tree, the trunk easily thirty feet in wide. The First Tree. Carved into the side was the altar that formed the shrine of Faunis in Q'qaara. An entrance led to the home of the Great Elder, the most honoured man amongst the Q'shari people. Whilst the rest lived in treehouses above, accessible through walkways that snaked around trunks and walkways strung up amongst the branches, the Great Elder resided in the hollowed-out monster that stood over the settlement, tall and proud.

"Why do you wish to see the Great Elder?" asked Q'laak, his red eyes heavy with suspicion.

"That is not your concern, I am afraid, my brother," shrugged Q'thell. "I simply have questions."

"You have been around the humans for too long," scoffed Q'laak impatiently. "Do you forget, there are no secrets amongst the Q'shari? I *will* hear what you want with the Great Elder."

"You will," admitted Q'thell, meeting the other's angry glare. "But only when I ask him."

"I will go and speak with him," intervened Q'rassi, pushing the two males apart as she moved between them. "It is like old times. The two tailed freaks constantly at each other's throats."

Q'thell watched her shapely behind as he moved away towards the First Tree, breaking the deadlock between them. He strolled down to the massive cooking fire before the Great Elder's abode, taking a seat on one of the logs there as Q'laak followed.

"You've still got it then?" asked Q'thell, raising an eyebrow. "Not had it docked?"

Q'laak nodded. "I still have it. It is a gift from Sanguis."

"Perhaps," shrugged Q'thell, reaching to the fire and pulling out a couple of halved chickens. He bit into one, the half-cooked flesh oozing blood down his chin as he offered the other to Q'laak. "I thought maybe you would have gotten rid of it. The bullying when we were children was incessant, as I recall."

"It was," nodded Q'laak, taking a knee before Q'thell as he grabbed the offered food. "When you best those people in combat, they learn to respect you. I am not mocked here, Q'thell. Not any more. Tell me, have you learnt to use your gift? Can you wield a weapon with it?"

Q'thell paused as he bit into the wet meat, his eyes distant for a second. He pulled back without tearing off a chunk, placing the chicken down on the log beside him, his appetite suddenly deserting him.

"I killed a man with it," he said. "A good man. A decent man. And a good warrior, the best I have ever fought."

"A human?" sneered Q'laak. "The best you have ever fought? Pah."

"I know," reflected Q'thell. "But he was brilliant, Q'laak. So strong, so intense, so beautiful. A rarity amongst humans. And an honourable man. That is also a rarity, believe me. And I slid a knife into his heart, so now there is one less..."

Q'laak smiled, his fangs tinged with blood. "Excellent. Sanguis will be proud."

Will she? pondered Q'thell.

His thoughts were interrupted as Q'rassi returned. The Q'shari beside her was old, his tall frame slightly hunched as he leaned on the long, bleached bone staff in his twisted hand. His hair was long and grey, braided and interspersed with decorative black crow feathers. His gentle green eyes fell on the two warriors as they stood and nodded deferentially in his direction.

"Q'thell," smiled the old Q'shari. A few of the people in the clearing had begun to gather around them. A stranger in Q'qaara was a rare sight, and for them to meet the Great Elder was rarer still. "You have come home."

"I have, Elder Q'neipa," said Q'thell. "I have need of information."

"Always so hasty," smiled the old Q'shari gently. "You have not changed, Q'thell. But just because we Q'shari are capable of swiftness, it does not mean that we should always rush. We live long lives. We have time on our side. We should eat, celebrate your return."

"Alas, Great Elder, I have an errand to complete on behalf of a human, and they do not have such a luxury," said Q'thell.

"Pah," spat Q'laak. "A lapdog to a human dog. I knew it."

Q'thell turned on him, his eyes blazing with anger. His rage subsided as he felt Q'rassi's hand on his, squeezing gently. He composed himself, returning his attention to Q'neipa.

"There is unrest amongst the people of Castland," he said gently, his voice calm and measured. "The Q'shari are not a numerous people. Unrest in the country may have implications for us."

Q'neipa nodded slowly, gesturing for Q'laak to be silent. "It is wise of you to note that what befalls the humans eventually affects us, Q'thell. But tell me, what information do you seek?"

"I need to know the location of the Library of Souls."

The Great Elder paused, his old, lined hand straying to his flowing grey hair. He twisted a few locks between his fingers, his green eyes thoughtful.

"Why do you need this information, Q'thell?" he asked softly.

"Do you know it?" responded Q'thell, his tone probing. "There are no secrets amongst the Q'shari. Our knowledge is exactly that. It belongs to all of us."

"That is true," admitted Q'neipa, nodding slowly. "But just as a tree grows upwards, its roots push down into the earth. The path runs both ways, Q'thell. Why do you seek the Library of Souls?"

Q'thell hesitated, considering his response carefully. He felt the gaze of the gathered Q'shari upon him as he thought. He looked up to see Q'rassi's white eyes staring at him, wide and expectant.

"Tell him," she urged.

"The human I work for seeks the power to restore balance to Castland," he said, meeting the Great Elder's gaze. "It is important to the Q'shari people that he succeeds."

"Do you trust this human?"

Q'thell steeled himself, holding the green eyes locked to his own. "Yes, Great Elder."

"Interesting," pondered Q'neipa, his head cocking to one side slightly, almost unnoticeable. "I will give you the information that you seek, of course. It is your right as a Q'shari, after all. I hope that your heart is honest, though, Q'thell. If not, I cannot promise that you will leave the forest with the knowledge that you have obtained."

Q'thell kept his eyes on the Great Elder, pretending not the notice the flashing glance the old man let slip in the direction of Q'laak.

Q'thell stepped out into the twilight from the small, red-wood hut that constituted the shrine to Sanguis in Q'qaara. As he moved into the blackness of the tight, entangled tunnel of branches and foliage that led back to the main clearing his weighed the weapon in his grip gently, giving a couple of delicate slices before him.

The priests had had a Blade of Lament, Sanguis be praised. It had taken them a couple of hours to get it honed to his liking, checking the weighting and grip, but they had worked expertly. He took his other sword the scabbards crossed across his shoulders, swapping the weapons between hands, testing them with a few strikes at thin air.

Beautiful.

He held the weapons up before him, crossed before his eyes. He couldn't tell the difference between the two. He was ready. He slid the swords back into their sheaths, striding down the natural passageway before him.

He had been too preoccupied to spot the black, shadowy figure nestled against the wall of brush. It was too late when he saw the red slits as Q'laak opened his eyes, suddenly finding himself pinned against the thicket, a vicious, curved dagger at his throat.

"Do you think you can come to the home of the Q'shari and pickpocket knowledge for your pig masters, Q'thell?" hissed Q'laak, pressing the blade hard against the surprised man's neck.

Q'thell felt the blade slide in, blood running in a thin trickle down his throat. He pondered reaching for a weapon, but it would be too late. Q'laak was pressed in close against him. He would feel even the slightest movement, the tiniest tensing of muscles.

"I do this for the Q'shari," said Q'thell carefully, conscious that even speaking too heavily might press the blade deeper into his throat.

"Delivering power into the hands of the humans has never ended well for our people," spat Q'laak.

"I never said I was going to deliver it to them."

"Are you saying that you lied to the Great Elder? There are no secrets between the Q'shari, Q'thell..."

"I didn't lie," insisted Q'thell, his eyes narrowing. Q'laak was strong, but he was stronger, he could tell as the warrior bore down on him. If he could just get the knife away from his throat, just for a second... "I didn't say I was going to follow the human's orders. I told the Great Elder truthfully why I needed the location of the Library of Souls."

"So what do you really seek, you treacherous little human-slave?" hissed Q'laak. "And what do you intend to do with it?"

"There are no secrets," whispered Q'thell. "If I tell you, you would be compelled to inform the Great Elder, should he ask. It is best that I keep that to myself, surely? But I promise you, from one Bloodkin to another, I have the best interests of the Q'shari people at heart. I have Sanguis' interests at heart."

Q'laak's posture relaxed for a second, the pressure of the dagger on Q'thell's throat relaxing for a second. He moved like lightning, pressing his head back into the thicket wall, giving himself an inch of breathing space as his hand flashed up, twisting Q'laak's wrist away, the dagger falling from his grip. Q'thell's free hand slipped up to grip the warrior's throat. His nails were sharp, the thumb digging into the windpipe, drawing blood. He twisted the choking man around, slamming him deep into the side of the tunnel.

"How long have these green-eyed Faunis fuckers ruled us, Q'laak?" he hissed, applying pressure to stem his opponent's resistance. "Can you even remember a man of Sanguis leading us? Leading any settlement?"

Q'thell could feel Q'laak's free hand reaching up his back, searching for a weapon. He shoved hard, pinning the arm and his foe's rump into the thick foliage, conscious that Q'laak's tail might produce a dagger and send him the same way as Tomas Bannar.

"*Answer me!*" he snarled, digging his thumb into Q'laak's windpipe.

The Bloodkin shook his head in response, gasping for breath.

"No," growled Q'thell. "Not since we retreated deep into the forests have we had an elder that followed Sanguis. Not one. We have hidden from the humans, slunk into self-imposed exile and let them breed their way across the world. A people who divide their loyalties between Sanguis and Faunis, led for an eternity by cowards and tree-lovers. I intend to bring an end to that. Have you ever left the forest, Q'laak? Do you know anything of the humans?"

Q'laak gasped for air as Q'thell reduced his grip slightly, gulping in deep, spluttering breaths as he shook his head vigorously. "No."

"I know much of them," replied Q'thell, reapplying the grip, being sure not to give his prey too much leeway to mount a counterattack. "I have watched them. I have witnessed the behaviour of those who profess to be the best of them. They are evil, Q'laak. Stinking savages who commit beastly acts that would make animals turn their heads in disgust. And when they see another human who stands up for bravery, for decency, for honour, do you know what they do?"

Q'laak shook his head desperately.

"They kill him," laughed Q'thell. "They are vermin, Q'laak. They are a threat to us. By the blood of Sanguis, they're a threat to themselves. I intend to put them out of their misery. That is why I needed the location of the Library of Souls. Now, tell me, are you ready to meet Sanguis?"

Q'thell's tail unfurled, sliding out and wrapping around the dagger on the ground. It curled up behind him, levelling at Q'laak's face. Q'thell stared deep into his childhood rival's eyes, wide with acknowledgement of his face. Q'laak nodded, gasping for breath.

Defiant. Pious, even in the face of death.

Q'thell released his grip, allowing the Bloodkin to drop to his hands and knees, clutching at his throat as he gasped for breath. He dropped the knife before Q'laak as he turned to walk away, striding towards the clearing.

"Not today, Q'laak," he said. "Sanguis has need of you, I know it. We have a long road ahead of us, you and I."

Q'thell smiled as he stepped out into the clearing at the centre of Q'qaara, the heat from the great cooking fire warming his face.

Perhaps Cecil did teach me something of diplomacy after all...

Chapter Forty-Two

Toby stood in the shade of the oasis, rubbing sweat from his burnt face with a towel. He looked out across the rolling sand, despairing as it extended into the distance. The heat haze blurred the horizon, but he could tell there was nothing out there. Nothing in sight, for days and days. He shook his head as he spied a sidewinder, gliding its way across the scorching dunes.

"This place is nothing but heat and sand and creatures cursed by Argentis himself," he sighed, fanning his face frantically.

Capethorne grunted beside him, easing the collar of his leathers where it rubbed his swollen neck.

"Why are we even waiting around here?" asked Toby.

"It's better here than out in that heat," shrugged the soldier, turning his back and moving into the luscious undergrowth surrounding the watering hole. Toby followed, eyeing the alien foliage as if it, too, was liable to lash out and bite him at any moment.

The pool at the centre of the palms was crystal clear. Toby could not understand how it survived, feeding the tangle of plant life that in turn protected it from the pounding rays of the sun. They had not seen any life that didn't crawl or slither or scuttle for days, and yet here was an emerald and blue patch of sanctuary amongst the hot sands.

"Want one?" asked Capethorne, reaching up and pulling a handful of dates from the nearest palm.

"Are you sure they are safe to eat?" asked Toby warily. "From what I have read, everything in this gods-forsaken land is poisonous."

Capethorne laughed, sliding a date into his mouth. He gestured to some of the Altanyan servants, pausing from taking on water in fat skins to feed on the fruits of the palms. "The locals seem to think they're fine."

"No, thank you," said Toby, moving over to the water's edge and kneeling down to fill his flask. "They look like prunes. I hate prunes. I am merely thirsty. This heat..."

"Do not move," came a hissed voice.

Toby looked up to see the red robed figure of Shaman Xius standing beside Capethorne. His eyes did not meet Toby's, instead focused on the ground beside the young noble, where his hand rested on the bank of the pool for balance.

The priest of Pyra was gesturing to two of the servants. They moved over slowly, quietly, one of them carrying a wicker basket.

Toby caught the look of fear on Capethorne's face. Slowly, he turned his dark eyes down to the ground. He gasped as he saw it, inches away from his hand. A huge, eight-legged creature, the size of a dinner platter. Its body was covered in grey, chitinous plates, bright red hairs spiking out from beneath each joint. Eight, bright red eyes glared up at him from above a pair of vicious, green fangs. Toby could swear he could see the venom dripping from the creature's maw. It could have just an incredibly large spider, if it wasn't for the segmented table that arced up over its back, a vicious barb also directed at Toby's arm.

He went to move.

"Stop," hissed Xius. "That would be unwise, my lord."

Toby kept his eyes on the creature, his heart thumping in his chest. Xius was ushering the servants into position. Toby winced as the barbed tail lashed towards his wrist, striking out over the fanged face. One of the servants pounced forward, dropping the basket into position over the huge arachnid. Toby gasped as he heard the tail strike the inside of the container. The other servant slid the lid into place. As they turned the basket over and moved away hurriedly, the monstrosity could be heard clattering around inside.

"What the *fuck* was that?" cried Toby, visibly shaking as he crawled away from the side of the pool.

"It looked like a half-breed," said Capethorne, looking around himself, watchful for any more of the creatures. "A fucking huge spider crossed with a fucking huge scorpion."

"We have seen these recently," said Xius. "A most interesting creature."

"*Interesting?*" shrieked Toby.

"Another one?" asked Overseer Lysis as he joined them. "How many is that now, Xius?"

"Five in the last month that I am aware of," replied the priest. "It may be a sign from Pyra."

"Perhaps," nodded Lysis, turning to his awestruck guests. "You see, the crab spider is a large creature. It cannot live in the desert. Its shell is too soft, the heat would bake it. A raptor or mongoose would crush it before it had chance to strike. They live in the oases, taking unwary prey near the pools.

278

The grey scorpion is much smaller, its chitin much thicker. It lives in the desert. It would seem that the two have somehow interbred."

"Are they very poisonous?" asked Toby, a shudder running through his entire body.

"Oh, deadly," nodded Lysis. "The venom of either would kill a man in minutes. These hybrids have two methods of delivering such a fatal dose. Very dangerous."

"You see how hazardous uncontrolled copulation can be, my lord?" sneered Xius.

"When your people fuck they don't produce huge venomous beasts," snapped Capethorne incredulously.

Toby looked in the direction the servants had taken the basket. "What will you do with it? Kill it, I hope?"

"By Pyra's flame, no," laughed Xius, the sound grating and uncomfortable. "They will be studied. We need to understand them, find out how they came to be. Study and knowledge are everything, my lord."

"As you shall see," agreed Lysis, gesturing for the men to follow him. "Come, I have arranged a demonstration for you."

Toby looked to Capethorne as they followed the overseer back to the edge of the oasis. For once the captain's eyes were not full of scorn. He shook his head in mutual disbelief.

Ahead of them, Lysis pointed out into the desert. A force of Altanyan troops had gathered, dressed in simple, leather breastplates. The weapons they carried were strange. Toby had seen gunpowder weapons being used back in Castland, but these were much more compact, if that was indeed what they were. There were no clumsy stands to rest the barrels on. Each man seemed to be able to carry his own weapon and aim it by himself. A hundred yards away a group of servants were finishing setting up a line of wooden targets.

"Are those gunpowder weapons?" asked Capethorne, squinting at the men as they formed up into two lines, one in front of the other.

"They are indeed," smiled Lysis. "Rifles. I wanted to give you a demonstration."

A huge crack split the air as the front row of men fired. Toby threw his hands over his ears, watching as the soldiers dropped to their knees to reload. As they did so, the second rank opened fire. By the time they had pulled back their weapons to repack them with gunpowder and shot, the front rank was back on its feet, aiming and firing. As they dropped to their knees again the men behind them launched another volley.

Toby shook his head, looking to Capethorne. The smoke creeping across the improvised range was nowhere near as thick as when he had seen the King's Household Musketeers demonstrating their skills. The time the men took to reload was phenomenally short, an issue that hampered the Castland musketeers in battle. These Altanyans were obviously well drilled, but then so were the king's men.

It must be something else. They seem to be using small paper pouches of shot and powder to reload, rather than horns of gunpowder and bags of bearings...

Toby's eyes turned to the targets. Each volley striking the wood splintered them apart, flying straight through even at one hundred yards and sending up puffs of sand as they landed well beyond. The stopping power at that range was immense. And the accuracy. Every shot seemed to be hitting home.

Lysis raised his small, white hand in the direction of the officer leading the men. The soldiers slung their weapons against their shoulders, standing bolt upright in the blazing sun.

"Impressive, yes?" he smiled.

Capethorne attempted to shrug it off. "We have gunpowder weapons in Castland too, overseer."

"I know," nodded Lysis. "But they are slow to reload. You found that to your peril against the Raskans. Their range and accuracy is inferior also. And they lack penetration, especially at distance."

"They would easily go through wooden boards, even at one hundred yards," lied Toby.

"Those targets are backed with metal, my lord," sneered Lysis.

Toby struggled to hide his emotions. "How have you managed this?"

"Study," croaked Xius. "Knowledge. The volcanoes to the east provide plentiful supplies of raw materials. Pyra gives us her guidance, shows us how to make the powder strong, and yet stable. Less is needed, but the effect is more controlled and deadly."

"Even so, the production of the weapons must be slow," ventured Toby. "The training of the men must take time."

279

"We have plenty of men to make them," said Lysis simply. "We control the people, my lord. We assign them their roles in life. Our men train harder because we make them train harder. Altanya can field thousands of riflemen, and the number grows by the day."

"And the fleet..." urged Xius with a grin.

"Ah, the cannons on our fleet," exulted Lysis. "Similarly superior. Our ships are the best armed in the Mortal World, my lord."

"Why are you showing us this?" asked Toby warily, once again glancing at Capethorne, the soldier looking uncomfortable beside him.

"Respect, my lord," shrugged Lysis. "Simply respect. We respect the strength of Castland and her armies. We sometimes doubt that your king respects our power. True friends are equals, after all. One people should not think themselves superior to the other."

"I assure you, overseer, we Castlanders view the Altanyans as our honoured and noble friends," insisted Toby.

"You do now," bowed Lysis, turning to head back into the oasis. "Come, Xius. We must prepare to move on towards home."

Xius bowed, the flame in his pupils burning bright on mocking as he eyed Toby before turning to follow the overseer.

Capethorne watched them leave suspiciously, waiting for the Altanyans to move out of earshot.

"What the fuck was that all about?" he whispered agitatedly. "Did you see that shit?"

"Their hubris will be their undoing," hissed Toby. "We will send a carrier pigeon to Regalla tonight. The Lord Chancellor needs to know of this. And my father. Will a bird make it across the desert?"

Capethorne nodded. "I brought the strongest I could find. It'll get home."

"Good," said Toby, gazing apprehensively at the Altanyan riflemen as they marched back out into the desert. "I will write a note as soon as we make camp."

"Any luck?" asked Pharos as Lexis sat back down at the table in the inn.

The bar room was quiet. He had been trying to get the attention of the barkeep, but the bastard was definitely ignoring his gestures. The Barralegnans around them talked in hushed voices, glancing over frequently, speaking behind their hands.

The other clergy had gone to their rooms. Mida had stayed. Pharos felt like the lad was his shadow, constantly under his feet, like a faithful but annoying dog. The initiate was eager to learn, and that was admirable, but sometimes he just wanted to get drunk and pass out in peace.

Lexis shook his head. "All the mercenaries say they've been hired already."

"That's the third village in a row," said Pharos, raising his hand to the barkeep again. He punched the table as the man turned away without acknowledging him. "Who the fuck is hiring every sellsword this side of Marralot?"

"I do not know," said Lexis. "We might have to hire when we reach the Pirate Coast."

Pharos grabbed the wrist of a passing serving girl, ignoring her as she winced, trying to pull away. "Three ales, lass," he snarled.

"That'll be three silvers, then," the girl snapped, rubbing her arm as Pharos released his grip.

"*Silvers?*" scoffed Pharos. "Ale costs coppers, love."

"Not for Castlanders," replied the girl. "Three silvers. In advance."

Lexis tossed the coins onto the table, sending a warning glance towards Pharos.

The girl picked the money up, biting it suspiciously as she moved over to the bar to collect their drinks. The barman sparked up a growled conversation with her, his eyes glaring at the trio as he poured.

"I do not think they like us," said Mida, the hurt in his voice evident.

"This might explain why we cannot book passage on a boat, either," nodded Lexis. "The Barralegnans seem to have developed a dislike for Castlanders that surpasses the usual neighbourly rivalry."

"For fuck's sake!" groaned Pharos as the girl returned, slamming the tankards of ale down on the table, the contents sloshing across the wood. "For a silver each I expect a full fucking drink, girl."

"Just get them down you," urged Lexis, ushering the girl away quickly.

"These two are for you," said Pharos, pushing them at the worshippers of Pharma.

"I am too young, Pharos," said Mida.

"Too young?" laughed Pharos, his throat creaking as he took a deep swig of his ale. "These cunts have sent you halfway across the world, probably to die, because they can't be arsed to carry their own shit, and you're too young to drink? I'd say you're more of a man than any of them, lad. Now get it down you."

Lexis nodded gently, reaching out and knocking his tankard against Mida's before taking a long gulp. "Pah! This tastes like horse piss."

"It probably is horse piss, judging by the locals' attitude towards us," sneered Pharos. "So, what about a coach? A wagon? Anything to speed these useless fuckers up on the journey."

"Nothing," said Lexis, shaking his head. He smiled at Mida as the lad grimaced at the taste of his ale. "Go on, Mida. You will get used to it."

"We may as well stay here for a few days," said Pharos, draining his tankard and slamming it on the table. "We'll still catch the bastards up before they reach the border, and at least we won't be waiting around whilst they amble along moaning about their fucking bunions."

Mida chuckled to himself as he brought the tankard up to his mouth in both hands, drinking deep from the ale.

"As much as the idea has merits," said Lexis. "You know they would not get very far alone. Speaking of which, are we to hire mercenaries in the Pirate Coast? Is that agreed?"

"We'll be able to trust them even less than those in Barralegne," shrugged Pharos, raising his hand and beckoning the serving girl over. He reached out, grabbing Lexis' purse and pulling out a handful of gold coins, thrusting them at the wench. "Take this lot, and keep the drinks coming. Full tankards from now on, you bitch."

"I do not think we have a choice though," said Lexis, looking around the bar at the Barralegnans as they eyed Pharos with a mixture of suspicion and threatening greed. "Something is building up here. Tension. Things are amiss."

"You're not wrong there, priest," said Pharos, snatching the drinks from the serving girl as she approached and quaffing heavily. "Having to hand over gold coins just to get a full fucking tankard is as amiss as it gets."

Du Chanchat stood on the hill, looking down on the vineyards of the Marralot, his thick arms folded across his barrel chest. The soldiers marching carefully down the paths formed snaking lines around the valley, an arterial network of contrasting blocks of livery.

Lord Penachal stood beside him, his old comrade-at-arms also watching the hypnotic movements of the troops as they meandered through the wineries towards the mountains in the distance.

"How many mercenaries are en route?" asked du Chanchat, his dark eyes falling on the shorter, stouter soldier.

"My recruiters have not yet reported in," replied Penachal, running a gauntleted hand through his bushy, immaculately-sculpted beard. "Thirty groups was the last count. Varying sizes, of course. Varying quality. Fighters nonetheless."

"They will do as frontline fodder," said du Chanchat, staring across at the Purple Peaks, the mountain range that marked the border with Castland. "Have the funds arrived to pay them?"

"The bankers delivered it three days ago," nodded Penachal. "I have to admit, it concerns me that the crown is not paying these sellswords. Is the king aware of these preparations, Lord du Chanchat?"

"He is aware that we are taking measures to defend ourselves, should the need arise. But it seems that King Atout has spent too much of the treasury funds on food and whores and golden carriages. Rest assured, the bank has no love of Castland if they have given us the gold. It would not be a wise investment to lend money to the losing side, after all."

"You sound as if you have already decided that the Castlanders will begin hostilities..."

Du Chanchat shrugged. "It is best to be ready, my lord. Ready to repel an attack. Ready to launch a pre-emptive strike, if the situation warrants it."

"And the king will be made consulted, I trust, should such a need arise?"

"There would be no need to consult him. Atout will always choose war, old friend. The fat wastrel loves to talk tough. The mighty king and his boastful fantasies about his victories that we all know to be untrue."

"I cannot hear this, my lord," smiled Penachal, shaking his head. "The king is given divine rule by the gods. To speak ill of him is blasphemy."

"Fuck him," declared du Chanchat, slapping the other lord's powerful rump, squeezing the muscular buttock hard. "He does not fight, so he does not care. We have shared the glory of battle, old friend.

Shared a bedroll in the cold. This streak of piss claims he cannot ride to war. His heels are shot, he says. The chubby fool does not even fight in the tournaments. Claims no man would risk harming their beloved king, so the battle would not be fair. I would hurt him, trust me. I would kill him. He is a disgrace to Barralegne. It is time somebody rid us of this curse..."

Penachal looked to his friend, gently moving du Chanchat's hand away from his rear.

"Let us concentrate on defending the realm first, my lord," he said softly, staring at the violet-tinged mountains in the distance.

Chapter Forty-Three

"Well I must say old chap, I am most impressed," said Gideon de Pfeiff, his bumbling voice even more difficult to decipher due to the wine-induced slurring. "You and your Coastman are doing an excellent job with the election. Both of the poor districts so far have declared for the Establishment Party."

Cecil smiled at his old friend humbly, swilling down the last of the cheeseboard set out on the table before them with Panda Port. "I find that I have a knack for nudging the commoners in the right direction, Gideon."

The lord of Westroad paused for a second, a stern look crossing his face. "Gideon? Are you not forgetting something, Cecil? I am a lord, remember? It seems you have lost the knack for proper etiquette."

Cecil looked up, fixing Gideon with an icy stare. The young lord's own blue eyes met the gaze, holding the glare for a few seconds. Suddenly he burst out laughing, running one hand through the thick mop of dishevelled blond hair on his head whilst the other grabbed Cecil's leg jovially, the fat sausage fingers giving the thigh a squeeze.

"I am just kidding with you, old chum," he guffawed, raising his own glass of port in a toast. "To my old friend Cecil, the saviour of our democracy."

"To me," nodded Cecil, clinking glasses with his host and taking another sip.

"But do tell me one thing, Cecil," chuckled Gideon, nudging his visitor conspiratorially. "Why the fuck do you always surround yourself with darkies? First that Q'shari beast, now this black bastard pirate."

"They do as they are told," shrugged Cecil, eyeing Gideon's hand still gripping his leg. "They have no other loyalties, other than to me. And since they are foreigners, nobody will miss them if they let me down and happen to disappear."

"Fair play old chap," smiled Gideon, topping up both their glasses. "Tell me, is that what happened to the Q'shari?"

"No. I have merely sent him on an errand. I have other business besides managing elections for the nobles of Castland."

"What errand is that then, eh?" mumbled Gideon. "Another Cecil Cramwall masterpiece in the making?"

"If I told you, I would have to have you killed," smiled Cecil emptily, gently removing his old friend's hand from his leg. He had forgotten how irritating Gideon's lack of respect for personal space could be.

"Fair enough, old bean," replied Gideon, attempting to conceal his disappointment. His eyes flicked around the dining hall for a second as his mind turned over, trying to find a subject to break the silence. "You have done well with that girl of yours, too, I must say. You will forgive me if I admit that Toby and I were in stitches when we found out you had been matched with a Yanari. It turns out the joke is on us. She is simply divine, Cecil."

"Thank you, old friend," smiled Cecil, his expression softening as his thoughts turned to Kaly.

"A bit older, too. Beautiful *and* experienced. I expect she goes like a charger. I bet she has been round the block a few times, learnt a few things..."

"She has done no such thing," snapped Cecil, his cheeks reddening. The awkward silence returned to the hall, Gideon sulking as if he had been slapped across the face.

"Apologies, old chum," he said eventually, again adjusting the mess of hair. "No offence intended. A toast, to you and your beautiful young lady. Long may you be happy together."

Cecil raised his glass again, taking another sip. "Thank you, Gideon."

"So, tell me Cecil, what are your plans once the election here is done? On to Port Castor, no doubt?"

Cecil shook his head. "Q'thell can deal with that. I have done enough travelling for now, I need to get settled for a while back in Regalla. I intend to formally request Kalyanit's hand in marriage from her father."

"No need, old boy, surely. Porwesh may be rich, but he is just a Yanari. Your father has already made the arrangements, no doubt."

"It is the correct thing to do," said Cecil irritably. "The Yanari deserve the same respect as any other Castlander. I will see to it people learn that. This discriminatory behaviour has no place in modern Castland."

"You are right, of course," nodded Gideon. "I apologise once again."

Cecil shook his head. The man was a hopeless buffoon, stumbling chaotically from one apology for his brash behaviour to the next.

Why does he not think *before he opens that idiot mouth of his?*

"Your apology is accepted, old friend. But you need to understand that things will be changing. Attitudes will be changing. I have matters of state to attend to with my father, and I shall be bringing this up with him. Rest assured, you shall see radical reforms."

"Speaking of which..." Gideon reached over with a huff of effort, sliding his empty glass onto the table before him. "When you talk with your father, would you be so kind as to bring something up with him, old bean? I have reports of activity on the border with Barralegne. Soldiers gathering in the Marralot region. Perhaps the Lord Chancellor could garrison a few troops in the lands around Westroad in case of any unpleasantness?"

"There are always soldiers in the Marralot region," shrugged Cecil. "It is on the border, after all."

"My generals tell me we are seeing more than normal. It would be wise to prepare for the worst, would it not? I could request this myself, of course, but it might be best coming from you. Especially since your comments to Lord du Chanchat may have... precipitated this..."

You fat, sly bastard...

Cecil drained his glass of port, rolling the liquid across his taste buds, savouring the last of it. He smiled at Gideon once he had finished, nodding gently. "I shall ask him, old friend."

"I knew you would, old bean," laughed Gideon, standing up abruptly. He gripped the table for balance for a second, the strong fortified wine having taken effect. "Now, seeing as I will not be in Regalla when you announce your official engagement, I would say a celebration is in order tonight. Let us hit the town of Westroad like the old days in the capital. Drinks, whores, and more drinks and more whores..."

"Just the drinks," said Cecil, joining the lord of Westroad as they moved towards the door to the hall. "I am to be married, after all."

"Fair enough," shrugged Gideon, wrapping his arm round Cecil's shoulders and pulling him close. "More whores for me, then..."

Gideon swayed as he stood on the balcony of his chambers, gripping the parapet as he gazed out over the city of Westroad below. It was the early hours of the morning. The sky was still dark, the lights in the houses below snuffed out whilst the people slept. The only light came from the moon, shining through the clear sky above them, bathing the city and its buildings in its white rays.

His buildings. *His* houses. *His* city.

He smiled as he took it in. It was like a dream. A young man, in control of all this wealth, of all these lives. He had loved his parents, but he was sure Argentis would forgive him for feeling blessed that they had died younger than most. It gave him so much more time to enjoy his own life properly. The Opulent One would understand that, he was sure.

Gideon spluttered suddenly, vomit catching in the back of his throat. He doubled up, gripping the balcony harder as he heaved. A stream of red wine and port issued forth, flowing satisfyingly down into the night, disappearing from view to splatter on the courtyard below.

He finished, shaking his head to clear his vision. He wiped his mouth on his sleeve.

"Delightful."

Gideon jumped at the sound of the woman's voice. She was close, almost in his ear. He span round, gripping the edge of the doorway as he almost tumbled from the balcony into the night after his vomit. She was sitting on the wall of the balcony, her flowing purple robes tucked beneath her shapely rear.

"Who the fuck are you?" he blustered. His eyes strayed into the bedroom, seeking out the large brass bell he could use to summon the guards. He spotted it, sat on his bedside table.

Don't be stupid, man. She is just a woman. You are twice her weight. You could shove her straight off the balcony if she was a threat.

"I am just a woman," lilted the sultry voice from beneath the hood that cast the figure's face in shadow. "I would not try to harm me, though. It would be... unwise."

Can this fucking bitch read my mind? Is she a fucking witch? Gideon shook his head, trying to clear his alcohol-riddled brain. *Listen to yourself. A fucking witch!*

"What are you doing here, woman?"

"I merely wished to speak with you, my lord."

"Audiences will be held tomorrow at..." Gideon paused, raising a bushy blond eyebrow as he tried hopelessly to figure out what day it was. "Later today at... Well... Not now, anyway..."

284

"But I have something to give you, my lord," said the woman, sliding off the parapet and standing before him.

"Listen, I know all you bitches want to fuck a lord, but I am all shagged out if I am being honest. Come back tomorrow and I will be happy to give you a skewering with my pork sword."

The woman laughed. The sound was gentle but dangerous, like the sound of broken glass sprinkling on a stone floor.

"As tempting as that offer is, my lord, I was thinking that maybe I could be of service in other ways." The woman's head moved as she took in the vomit stains on the sleeve of Gideon's tunic.

"Well, it is a woman's place to serve," nodded the lord of Westroad. He was leaning heavily on the doorframe now.

This is fucking surreal. I just want to get to bed. Perhaps I am in bed, dreaming? No, if I was dreaming then I would shag her. Maybe leave the hood on, pull the robes up. Like fucking a priestess...

"Concentrate, my lord," whispered the woman, a slim, ring-adorned hand sliding across the balcony wall. "Do you not wonder how the Barralegnans are funding an army building on the border with Castland? On *your* border?"

Gideon shrugged, his head turning to look inside the room, falling longingly on his bed. "They have gold. Barralegne is a rich country."

"Concentrate," hissed the woman, reaching out a hand and gently turning Gideon's fading eyes to look in her direction as she stood in front of him, close now. "The lords have gold, but they are not willing to spend it freely. The crown should fund a standing army, but the treasury is not adequate. It seems King Atout has rather extravagant tastes."

"Young boys, probably," drawled Gideon. "Country of fucking degenerates if you ask me."

"The Barralegnans are borrowing the money. Men need to be paid, after all. They need to be fed, to be armed."

Gideon's eyelids were heavy now. The figure seemed exasperated, annoyed that the drunken lord was not following the trail of breadcrumbs she was laying down.

"Are you not interested in who is lending them the gold? I have that information."

"I am just interested in getting into my fucking bed, woman," mumbled Gideon, seemingly on the verge of falling sleep leaning against the doorway.

The woman pinched his cheek, a tight nip causing the drunken lord's blue eyes to snap wide open for a second.

"The Crown Bank is funding the Barralegnan army, my lord," hissed the voice. "The same bank that has been channelling funds to the People's Party in Castland."

"Do you have proof of any of this?" slurred Gideon, his drunken interest raised now.

"Of course."

"What do you want in exchange for it?" asked Gideon, suspicion beginning to slide into his impeded speech.

"There is nothing you can give me, my lord," said the woman. "I can assure you of that."

"I could give you my cock, if you stay until morning," sneered Gideon, his chubby, lecherous features cast pale by the moonlight.

"I think I can do without that, my lord." The woman moved away, pushing the young lord away gently. Gideon slid down the doorway, crashing across the threshold into his bedchamber.

"There is a ledger on your bed, my lord," said the figure, a slim hand pointing over his prostrate figure.

Gideon followed the finger to where a thick, leather-bound sat on the blanket. "You have been in my chambers?"

"How else would I get to the balcony, my lord? It is not as if I can fly..."

Gideon looked over his shoulder, his mouth open to speak. He paused, no sound coming out. The figure was gone.

Chapter Forty-Four

Yarner stormed up to the door of the house. It was a decent-sized building in the middle class area of Regalla, nestled amongst the dwellings of merchants and artisans. Easily four times the size of his own, meagre home.

He pounded on the door angrily, waiting only a few seconds before hammering again. The people passing were beginning to stop, their curiosity pricked by a watchman calling on a member of their community in such an insistent manner. Yarner turned his face to the door, pulling his hood up over his head and beating it again.

The door opened slowly, cautiously. Yarner shoved forward, knocking the figure on the other side to the ground. He slammed it shut behind him, pulling a copy of the People's Gazette from under his arm and thrust it beneath Ratcliffe's nose.

"What the fuck is this?" he snarled.

Ratcliffe shrugged, avoiding eye contact as he got to his feet, dusting himself off theatrically. "It looks like a newspaper, sergeant."

Yarner grabbed the agitator's tunic, slamming him hard against the wall. "Get smart with me again and I'll break your fucking face open, do you hear me? It's *your* fucking newspaper."

Ratcliffe nodded, still avoiding Yarner's eyes. "It is. What of it?"

"'The people of Kassell have bravely gone where other cities feared to tread and have voted for freedom, defying the oppressive nobility'," growled Yarner, releasing his grip on Ratcliffe and picking up the copy of the People's Gazette.

"It is the truth," replied Ratcliffe, moving slowly towards the kitchen at the end of the hallway. "Would you like a drink?"

"I'd like some answers," snapped Yarner, following the reporter into the room.

"The answers are in the newspaper," replied Ratcliffe, reaching into a cupboard and pulling out a bottle. He poured measures of pure, clear spirit into two glasses, pushing one across the table to the watchman. "Raskan vodka. Takes a bit of getting used to, but each blend has differing flavours. As many varieties as we have whisky and gin."

"Why the fuck did you publish this? It's going to cause trouble, Ratcliffe. I thought you agreed not to put people in danger."

"I agreed not to stand," snapped Ratcliffe, anger flashing in his eyes as he drained his drink and poured another measure. "I published the story of what happened in Snowgate, so as to warn the people. And then it turns out that I could have stood. That we could have won. Kassell proves that."

"Telling people this will make them angry, Ratcliffe. You know that. You could be starting an uprising with this shit. I thought we went through how many people's lives could be ruined by this."

"The people in Kassell seem to be fine," shrugged the agitator. "Don't the people in the rest of Castland deserve the same? Don't you want the same?"

"It doesn't matter what I think. It doesn't matter what I want."

"It does," snapped Ratcliffe, downing his drink and pouring another. "Kassell proves that, Rollo. What you want, and every other person like you wants, *is* important. This is worth fighting for, surely? If it is what people want…"

It was Yarner who was avoiding the agitator's gaze now. "How did you get this information, Ratcliffe? The watch hasn't even been briefed on this yet. Who told you?"

"Are you asking this in an official capacity?"

"Personal," replied Yarner. "Nobody sent me here. I just wanted answers."

"If you were asking as a watchman, I would tell you that one of my representatives sent word that they had won the election."

"But that isn't the case?" asked Yarner. "I told you, I want the truth. I'm not here to arrest you, Ratcliffe."

"Are you sure you want to know?" asked Ratcliffe. He drained his glass, setting it down gently on the table, leaving it empty, the bottle still in his hand. "I have powerful informants, Rollo. Powerful backers. Powerful friends. Do you really want to get involved? Do you really want to help make a difference to the people of this country?"

Yarner paused, looking at the glass of vodka in his hand. He turned it between his fingers, watching the clear liquid slosh around the sides. His mind strayed to the rebellion during the war, to the starving people the watch had suppressed as they gathered in the streets, hungry and angry. The injustice of it all tore in his chest, ripping at his heart.

Then another image entered his head. His wife. His children. At home, waiting for him to return. Not rich, but getting by. He looked around Ratcliffe's home, at the level of comfort that a lowborn watchman could never aspire to. Nothing would alter that. Rebellion or not, risk or safety, his lot in life wouldn't change. But at least his family was safe as things were.

He necked the vodka, shaking his head as he stared into Ratcliffe's hopeful eyes.

"I don't even want to know," he said, turning and striding from the agitator's home. As he left, he dropped the copy of the People's Gazette on the floor in the hallway.

Ratcliffe poured himself another drink, standing the kitchen, staring thoughtfully at the discarded newspaper.

Tremelowe scribbled on the parchment with the long, elegant quill, scrawling his signature across the bottom of the document and dropping the feather into the ink pot on his desk. He rolled the paper up briskly, lifting a stubby red candle and dripping wax onto the join. He looked up wearily at his castellan for a moment before pressing his ring into the seal.

"Get this sent to the capital, Thatcher," he said, handed the scroll over to the nervous man before him.

"You wish for it to be delivered by a courier, my lord?"

Tremelowe nodded. "The contents will cause a bad reaction from the Lord Chancellor. A delay in delivering the news will buy us some time."

"So Kassell has declared independence, then?" asked Thatcher, his hand trembling as he took the document.

"You heard the representatives," said Tremelowe simply. "It is what they want, and they speak for the people. I am not going to go against their decision. The letter states that Kassell is now an independent city state that bears no ill will towards the country of Castland nor its people."

"What about your subordinate lords?"

Tremelowe shook his head, standing and taking up a position by the window, staring out in the direction of the lands of Tomas and the other martial lords. He found himself there often now, as though glaring into the distance would somehow allow him to glimpse what his old friend was planning.

"Lord Bannar and his band of idealists may do as they wish," he said. "Send birds informing them of Kassell's declaration. As for the other nobles, they were at the gathering. They have agreed to declare non-hostile secession from Castland."

"I will see to it that the communications are sent, my lord," nodded Thatcher, heading for the door. He found that the company of his lord was uncomfortable at present, and each time he was glad to escape the man's presence.

"Thatcher," called Tremelowe, causing his castellan to pause at the door. "Send for the captain of the guard. We have preparations to make, in case the capital reacts as poorly as I expect. You will need to see that food is gathered and stockpiled. We must be ready for a siege."

"As you wish, my lord."

"And get Carilo Tristane for me, please. We will need him to help with our acquisitions."

Thatcher nodded. Tremelowe stared at the door as it slid shut behind his castellan, his brown eyes filled with sadness and trepidation. These were dangerous times, and solidarity would be required to survive them. He needed Tomas. He felt empty without his old comrade, but he would not beg for the man's support. He was still Tomas' liege lord. It was not becoming to ask for assistance when it could rightfully be demanded.

Tremelowe lashed out behind him, striking the window with his fist. The glass cracked, a spider web of lines radiating out from the point of impact. As he looked out at the horizon, Tomas' distant land appeared fragmented, distorted. A solitary tear slid down his face as he turned away, shaking his head.

Tomas stood on a small hillock outside the wooden walls of Bannar, the assembled lords surrounding him. Before him were massed their combined forces; unit-upon-unit of spearmen, swordsmen, archers, light and heavy cavalry, all dressed in the pressed and clean livery of their lieges. They looked like toy soldiers, neat and pristine, lined up in neat rows, their heads held high and proud.

All that will change...

Behind him, outside the gates of the town, the folk of Bannar had gathered to view the spectacle. They in their best clothes, the attire they wore to attend chapel on the holy days. They were murmuring amongst themselves, impressed at the display before them. They had never seen such a gathering.

His eyes strayed upwards, to where Talia stood on the walls above the gatehouse, Ivan at her side. It was too far away for him to be certain, but he knew in his heart she wasn't meeting his gaze. She was staring past him, those fierce blue eyes fixed defiantly on the assembled army.

Tomas turned his attention to the soldiers, clearing his throat.

"The time has come, my friends," he bellowed, trying to project his voice across the cold breeze that was flapping the standards held aloft amongst the troops. "You have all voted. The townsfolk have all voted. This might assembly before me is the result of the decisions that you have all made."

A cheer went up from the crowds massed around him, fists raised defiantly in the air.

"I have, this morning, received word from Lord Tremelowe. I felt it was important to impart this news to you, so that you have the opportunity to change your minds, if you so wish. Kassell has declared itself independent from Castland. A city state in its own right. Lord Tremelowe will not support us on the field, but he has defied the capital. If you wish, we may stay here in silent defiance and stand beside him. The capital will send troops, I am certain of it. They will have time to prepare. But if you wish to stay our hand, now is the time to speak, and I will listen."

He turned, looking amongst the faces below him as an eerie silence crept across the crowd. His dark eyes flicked across commoner, each noble, each soldier and merchant and artisan and farmer. Some faces were looking reluctant, the news causing them to hesitate. But none spoke out. They knew the majority had spoken, and that their minds had not been swayed. They had embraced democracy, and to that end they needed to trust in the wisdom of their peers and stand beside them in solidarity.

Tomas looked to each of the lords stood with him on the hill in turn, meeting their gaze with a grim smile. Each man nodded once before solemnly turning back to face their troops gathered before them.

"Then it is settled," roared Tomas. "We go to war."

A roar split the air as thousands of men let out the angry contents of their lungs, drawing their weapons as though preparing to engage in battle.

"For too long the aristocracy in Castland have oppressed the poor," proclaimed Tomas, pumping his fist angrily. "They have oppressed *you*, and your families. You have been forced to toil, little more than slaves, working on lands you will never own, fighting the wars of rich men for no reward."

"We all know it to be true," cried out Mikhel Miller, beating his fist on his barrel chest. "We all bear the scars."

"Aye," agreed Tomas, pulling off his leather jack to reveal the flesh, pink scar across his ribs and the gaping, bloody gash in his arm. The cold breeze bit at his bare torso, but he hardly felt it. The adrenaline was flowing now, his heart pumping as heavily as if he was in battle. "We all bear the scars. I tried to give you your freedom. We *all* tried to give you the respect you deserve, to allow you to live your lives with dignity and pride. And this is the result. The Lord Chancellor and his spawn tried to kill me. My only crime was to treat you properly. That is the foe we face, a man of pure evil. The fight will be hard, as these vile creatures will stop at nothing to keep what they have. But is a fight we *must* win."

"Death to Cramwall!" screamed Andor Oxhound, the muscles in his tattooed neck tense and powerful. The masses joining in with a chant, thrusting their weapons in the air in time with the call.

"And if that is not enough," bellowed Tomas. "When the people of this country voted freely in an election, they were threatened and bullied into submission. We held our elections, and you chose without the threat of coercion or violence. Others in Castland were not so lucky. Lord Tremelowe is a good man, but by seceding from Castland he has abandoned others. We will not make that mistake. We fight not just for ourselves, but for all the people of the realm."

"For Castland!" shouted Jeremy Pillory and Vincent Rox, raising elegant, gold-filigreed swords to the grey sky in tandem. The men before them adjusted their chanting, crying out assertions of solidarity with the oppressed of Castland.

"Raise it," growled Tomas, pointing to Farrell Ginspot. The captain of his guard stood at the front of the assembled man. He smiled as he hoisted the banner in his hands high, struggling against the gathering wind. Mounted on the crossed poles was Talia's shawl, dark red with blood from that night in the grounds of the mill that seemed so long ago. "We fight. We fight for ourselves and for our families. We fight for our freedom. We fight for the people of Castland. If you ever lose heart, look at that banner.

288

Remember my wife, sobbing as she tried to stop the flow of blood pouring from her dying husband, lying in the mud, murdered by the Lord Chancellor for giving you your gods-given rights."

Tomas turned, thrusting an angry hand up at Talia as she stood on the walls of Bannar. The other lords gathered around him, pulling him close, embracing him one-by-one.

"The Red Banner." The crowd were chanting now, jabbing weapons at the standard that Ginspot held aloft, beating their chests and their shields. "The Red Banner. The Red Banner."

Tomas returned their grips, fighting to keep his eyes on Talia. He swore he saw her nod once in his direction before turning away, her shawl flapping in the wind.

Ivan put his strong arm around Talia as she turned away from the mass of people gathered before the town gates. He adjusted her shawl gently, pulling it tight around her shoulders to shield against the chill east wind.

"Are you alright?" he asked softly, his eyes filled with concern.

"I feel terrible," she said, shaking her head. Ivan could tell she was stifling tears. "You know, I looked at those men, and you know what I thought? I thought that every single one of them better lay down their lives before they let any harm come to Tomas."

"It's understandable, Talia," smiled Ivan, squeezing her shoulder gently. "Have you told him?"

She shook her head gently, wiping the tears away from her eyes irritably. "I swear this child is making me a weak little girl."

"He needs to know," insisted Ivan, looking out at the chanting, bullish mass of soldiers congregated outside the town.

"Tomas needs to keep his mind on what he is doing, Ivan," said Talia, shaking her head. "He needs to keep focused, so that he comes home. You know that men can only concentrate on one thing at a time."

"Interesting." Kennyth Pennant's soft voice made them both start. They hadn't noticed the former mayor standing behind them on the town walls. "I am a man, and I can concentrate on a great many things at once, believe me."

"What are you doing here?" snapped Talia coldly. She had always hated the slimy little man. One of the few benefits of Tomas' rash defiance had been that the Establishment Party representative no longer had any influence in the town.

"Some of the guards still respect the years of public service I have given," replied Pennant, shrugging his thin shoulders as he moved over to the wooden parapet, gazing out over the army below. "I have come to see our brave lord off on his war, just like everyone else."

"Why?" asked Talia, her eyes narrowing with suspicion. "You have always hated Tomas. We all know that."

"Curiosity, partly," said Pennant. "I wanted to see the army he has gathered. It is quite impressive, I will admit that. Nostalgia, too. After all, this is the last time I will see most of these men."

"I think you forget that my husband is a mighty warrior, Pennant," spat Talia through gritted teeth.

"Oh, I do not forget that, my lady," sneered Pennant. "But mighty warriors are two-a-copper in Castland. Even if he were a shrewd general, which I hear that he is not, those too are common in the country. Wars are won on the balance of two factors, as I understand it. Strength of numbers, and heavy cavalry. Lord Bannar has too few of both."

"It seems that you are not in possession of all the facts," said Talia. Her eyes strayed eastwards, towards the mountains that separated Tomas' lands from Raska.

"Well," sniggered Pennant, following her gaze. "It would help a little, of course, if Lord Bannar waited for the horde of Raskan horsemen that are no doubt on their way. I wonder why he has not been more prudent. They may, indeed, sway things in his favour."

Ivan shifted his feet uncomfortably on the creaking boards of the gantry.

"Lord Tremelowe has sent word of Kassell's declaration of independence to Regalla," she snapped, her blue eyes angry at the extent of the former mayor's knowledge. "The Lord Chancellor will rally his armies to take action. Those armies may not be meant to challenge Tomas, but they will be in his way nonetheless. It is better to strike now, and allow the Raskans to join the battle when they arrive."

"Who is to say that word of Lord Bannar's preparations has not already been sent to the capital? After all, do you trust everyone in this town? Everyone in these lands? Do you know all these lords he has called forth to rally behind his cause?"

"The only person in this town I do not trust is you, Pennant," hissed Talia, pulling away from Ivan's restraining hand and moving to stand before the slight, weak-jawed man.

"That is possibly the wisest thing you have said today, my lady," sneered Pennant. "Perhaps I have already sent word to Regalla, in order to limit the bloodshed amongst the people of this town. I am a member of the Establishment Party after all..."

Ivan was too slow to stop her. Talia lashed out, her fist catching Pennant on the nose. The little man's hands clasped around his chinless face, blood oozing out from between his fingers.

"If you have done anything to jeopardise my husband, or these men, then I swear I will gut you like a fish, you little piece of shit."

Ivan had her shoulders now, his strong hands gripping her tightly as she struggled to control her rage.

"I have not sent word to anyone, my lady," mumbled Pennant nasally from beneath his hands. "I am merely trying to teach you the skills you will need to manage these lands whilst Lord Bannar is away. I am a member of the Establishment Party, after all. I care for these people. And at least I am being honest with everyone involved in this unfortunate affair. Unlike yourselves..."

Pennant's eyes strayed to Talia's belly, concealed beneath her flowing dress.

"Perhaps Lord Bannar has a right to know certain things. It may help him see reason..."

Talia felt Ivan's grip loosen. For a second she thought he was releasing her so that she might strike the arrogant little man again, but her old friend had other intentions. He bustled past her, he strong hands grabbing Pennant round the scruff of the neck, thrusting him backwards and holding him over the edge of the parapet.

"Don't you ever threaten Talia again, you little fucking cunt," snarled Ivan, the spit from his angry mouth spraying on the former mayor's face. "Do you understand me? Don't threaten her husband. Don't threaten her child. Don't speak unless she tells you to. Don't piss or shit unless she gives you leave. Understand, you fucking runt?"

Pennant's eyes glanced down at the ground below before returning to meet Ivan's, defiant and sly. "I cannot make those promises, I am afraid. I am a servant of Castland and its people."

"Ivan," said Talia soothingly, her hands resting on her old friend's shoulders. She had never seen him so angry. "Let him go. Please."

The innkeeper looked at her, his blue eyes angry and intense. She met his gaze, rubbing his tense muscles gently. His glare softened, the tensions in his shoulders easing. He nodded gently.

Ivan released his hold on Pennant. The little man disappeared, falling to the ground below. A dull thud sounded as he struck the ground below.

Talia's jaw dropped, her eyes wide and shocked. Ivan turned and pulled her close, his cheek resting gently against her own.

"I'm not going to let anyone harm you while Tomas is away, Talia. Nobody will hurt you. Nobody will threaten you. Nobody will stop you keeping this town together."

She nodded into his thick shoulder, tears running down her cheeks as she heard the commotion below as men clamoured to the gather around the former mayor's broken body.

Chapter Forty-Five

"These events are most disturbing," reflected King Jaros, scratching absently at his beard as he sat on the throne in the palace of Regalla. He looked down, the dark, distant eyes straying to the Lord Chancellor sitting beside him.

"They are indeed, your majesty," admitted Cramwall, shifting in the wooden chair.

He had to admit, the situation irked him. The chair was grand, there was no denying that. The Lord Chancellor's seat at the right hand of the throne was elaborately-carved from the strongest oak, the velvet cushioning easily as comfortable as any of Oliver's own furniture. But still, it felt wrong. It was his seat, that was true, but at the same time it was *not* his seat. He never sat in it. The king had taken little interest in affairs of state, allowing the Lord Chancellor to rule in his stead. Cramwall had only sat in the Lord Chancellor's official position only a handful of times during his lengthy tenure, usually during symbolic events. It felt alien.

"The Altanyans," stated Jaros, shaking his head, scratching at his hooked nose now.

I swear the old man has some form of skin disease, pondered Cramwall. *Scabies. Or at least mites or fleas. He scratches constantly. And he stinks. His perfume does not cover the rank smell of old age.*

"May I ask how you got this information, your majesty?" asked the Lord Chancellor gently, looking up at the elderly monarch. That irked him, too. He was not a tall man, but he was not used to being positioned below *anyone*. Cramwall's blue eyes flicked across the tall, gleaming gold throne. It was told that it was made from gold from all the major countries of the known world. Castlander men in the reign of King Castor I had collected gold on their travels, bringing it before the ruler of their fledgling domain as tribute. Oliver doubted it was pure gold, but it was impressive nonetheless.

"The king knows all," declared Jaros haughtily.

Cramwall's eyes raised indignantly at the ridiculous statement. He was not used to having to stroke the monarch's ego. The Lord Chancellor ruled the realm in the name of the king. It had been thus since the civil war; the last time the commoners had successfully challenged the natural order. To placate them, Castland's democratic principles had been put in place. The monarchy was just a symbol, behind which the people of Castland could rally. The power was given to elected representatives, who in turn influenced proceedings with the nobility.

So why does this pathetic old man feel he can change that?

"Of course, your majesty," smiled Cramwall, the expression barely hiding his annoyance. "But I am the head of your loyal government, and I have only just received word of this myself. I am curious, that is all."

"It does not matter," snapped Jaros. "The fact is, the crown knows, and the crown is not impressed. I want to know what we intend to do about it."

We? When did you ever do anything, *you lazy old bastard...?*

"Affairs of state are complex, your majesty," said Cramwall, resting his hands across the paunch of his belly as he settled down into the Lord Chancellor's chair. "These build-ups are not uncommon. We have never had war with the Altanyans. Our realms are too far distant. Perhaps they are flexing their muscle, demonstrating that they have strength. There is no harm in that. We do the same thing, frequently."

"Do we demonstrate gunpowder weapons of this power?" snapped Jaros.

Cramwall breathed deeply, holding his temper, resisting the urge to reach out and cuff the old man around the cheek. "Toby Princetown is not a military man, your majesty. This is his first diplomatic duty. He would, no doubt, be impressed by an Altanyan who rode a horse instead of a camel. It does not make that Altanyan a threat. I need to discuss this with our generals."

"Then do so. I want to know their opinion."

"I will, your majesty," replied Cramwall, his tone clipped. "But remember, the reasons why we do not invade Altanya work the same in reverse for them. Our climates are too different. Our soldiers would not do well in such differing environments. Our populations are large, the land mass too great. It would be too heavy a strain to support an army so far from home. And the Bandit Country lies between us. They tax and raid our traders, but they would not stomach an army crossing their lands."

"It worries me that you trust our safety to a disorganised land of cutthroats and the weather, Lord Chancellor," said Jaros curtly, still scratching. "I am starting to doubt that you are the man to lead this country."

"I am the man that the people elected, your majesty," replied the Lord Chancellor, standing abruptly and walking down the long, crimson carpet that led to the foot of the crown. He did not bow as he left, his back to the king as he strode from the hall.

King Jaros watched Cramwall walk away, dark eyes stabbing out at his back like daggers from beneath bushy, greying eyebrows.

Overseer Lysis took the gold bowl of soup before him in both hands, raising it up before him. Shaman Xius did the same, the pair nodding to each other before taking a sip from their respective meals. It was a simple dish: thin, chilled vegetable and lentil broth, flavoured with lemon and spices. It was the heat of the day, after all, too stifling for a full meal.

The pair placed their bowls down on the low trestle table between them as they sat, cross-legged on thick, velvet cushions. The tent in which they dined had been hastily set up in the desert by the servants to give some shelter from the midday sun as they ate. The same had been done for Toby and his entourage, some distance away; the Altanyans had matters to discuss.

"Have the emissaries been sent?" asked Xius, waiting patiently as Lysis broke the thin, flat bread on the table, handing half to his guest.

"Fear not, Xius," replied the overseer, rolling up his portion and soaking it in the soup. "They left before the Castlanders arrived. They likely crossed paths in the bay."

"Good," smiled the priest of Pyra, sucking the broth from his own bread. "Then the wheels have finally been set in motion."

Lysis nodded gently. "We must ensure we are ready when the time comes. Men, weapons, camels, ships. All must be brought to bear to schedule."

"Indeed. Tell me though, overseer, are the dukes of the Bandit Country likely to allow us passage through their lands?"

"I am sure of it," replied Lysis. "They have no love for the Castlanders."

"They have no love for us," sneered Xius, the red glow in his pupils pulsing gently. "They blame us for the collapse of the Illicean Empire."

"You read your history well, Xius. But these dukes are not men of the old Illicean Empire. They are brigands and thieves, nothing more. Transgressions of the distant past are of no concern to them."

"I hear they are proud, Lysis," warned the shaman. "The pride of men, even thieves, is never cheaply bought."

"I never said anything about the price," smiled Lysis. "But it *will* be bought, I can assure you of that."

Xius squinted his eyes warily. "Would it not be better to lay waste to the Bandit Country as well, overseer? Secure our lines of communication? Avoid having a potential foe at our back?"

"It has been discussed," admitted Lysis, mopping up the last of his broth with his bread, wiping the bowl clean of food. "But it would take too long. We would lose any element of surprise. The terrain is difficult, the people skilled at ambush and evasion. It has been decided that we will first take Castland. The Bandit Country will be ours too, once we are ready to squeeze it from both sides, like the python."

Xius smiled, his eyes distant as he licked his lips hungrily at the prospect. "May Pyra be proud of her servants."

"May Pyra be proud," nodded Lysis.

Pharos wiped the gleaming sweat from his bald head, glassy eyes looking up at the sun beating down on them as they waited on the docks. The clergy had gathered underneath the shade of a waterfront shop's awning, desperate to get their sweat-soaked bodies out of the sun. Pharos looked down at Mida, nudging him on the shoulder and pointing at the dishevelled clerics. The shop owner had emerged, pestering Yulli and Elsa for coin.

"They are not buying anything, though," said Mida, his young face puzzled.

"Coastmen," laughed Pharos. "You're *always* buying something, according to these men. He's trying to sell the shade of his awning to them."

Mida smiled, looking away to take in the bustling docks around them. Black-skinned men moved about, muscles bulging on their naked torsos as they strained to load and unload cargo from the tangle of mismatched ships that were crammed into the various jetties. The town was little more than a rough settlement stretching along the shore of the cove. The buildings were rough, dishevelled, thrown together from driftwood and salvaged wreckage. Beyond them, the thick forest began immediately, stretching out into the distance to the north.

"I'm actually impressed we made it," pondered Pharos. "No mercenaries, and we still got through."

He turned back to look out over the crystal-clear sea of the cove. He breathed deeply, the salt of the sea air biting at his nostrils. Unfamiliar, clean and yet dirty all at once.

"A party of clerics and initiates of Pharma, bartering for passage in the free town of Naha-ga," said Mida, following Pharos' gaze.

"This isn't Naha-ga, lad," laughed Ryn. The ranger had been quiet since entering the shanty town, the sight of the sea seeming to sap his confidence. "Are you stupid?"

"He isn't stupid, Ryn," snapped Pharos. "I suggest you bolster your faltering resolve some other way, rather than criticising the boy. It's not his fault you're scared of it."

Ryn turned his eyes back to the water, watching the ramshackle boats as they bobbed up and down on the tide. "It isn't natural, that's all. A man floating around on all that water in a wooden box."

Pharos smiled. The ranger was a good man. He shouldn't really revel in the discomfort of others, but he found it difficult to resist.

"But the sign said 'Naha-ga'," insisted Mida. "At the forest's edge, as we came in."

"All the signs say that, lad," said Pharos, looking over to where the shopkeeper was shooing the clergy off his frontage. "Most of them, anyway. Naha-ga is to the west, further down the coast. How would it survive, this close to the Barralegnan border? The forest is thick and unwelcoming, but sooner or later Atout would have ordered it razed to the ground."

"Why lie, though?" asked Mida.

"To confuse the enemy, perhaps. When the pirates get too much of a menace, the Barralegnans or the Castlanders will send a force, burn a few settlements to the ground. Making them think they've razed Naha-ga is more likely to get them to fuck off, I suppose."

"That makes sense," agreed the young initiate.

"Of course, sometimes," smiled Pharos, gesturing to the approaching clergy. "They do it to trick naïve bastards like these into thinking they're in the grand, free town of Naha-ga..."

"This is not Naha-ga?" asked Yulli, looking around as he approached.

Pharos shook his head exasperatedly. Mida smiled knowingly, even Ryn breaking away from his concerned staring to laugh.

"That man wanted a silver piece each to stand in his doorway," said Elsa incredulously. "As if he owns the shade, by Pharma."

"He owns the awning that's making the shade," shrugged Pharos. He glanced over his shoulder to where Lexis and a Coastman were sat on barrels, haggling over passage. Surprisingly, it seemed to be going well. The son of Pharma struggled to hide the fact that he was impressed.

"We are Pharma's faithful," protested Elsa.

"That hasn't really got you as far in the real world as you imagined it would, has it, priestess?" laughed Pharos. "The man owns the property. He can do as he wishes with it."

"This accursed place is bereft of all charity," said Yulli, shaking his head haughtily.

"Really?" asked Pharos. "Tell me, priest, how many of the poor do you share your home with? How many of the sick do you let sleep beneath your roof?"

Pharos felt Mida's hand on his wrist, tugging gently. He breathed deeply, looking down to the lad.

"I think Father Lexis has secured us passage," said the lad, pointing to the wharf. Sure enough, the head priest and the captain were sealing the deal with a shot of rum each. They clasped wrists before moving towards the group.

"I didn't think you had it in you to deal with these cutthroats, father," smiled Pharos as the pair approached. "I'm impressed, I'll admit it."

"*Father*," laughed the sea captain, his dark, weathered face contorting with laughter a few pitches higher than Pharos would have expected. The man was strong, lean, but smaller than most Coastmen. Pharos was sure that didn't mean he couldn't use the wicked, heavy cutlass hanging from his belt. Huge, heavy gold earrings jangled as he chuckled, digging his elbow into Lexis' ribs. "I can't believe these people call you that, *marego*."

"Why would one not called a head priest of Pharma that, may I ask?" snapped Yulli indignantly.

"Well, *marego*," smiled the captain, giving Lexis a sideways glance. "Because I've seen this man splitting skulls with the best of them, *father*. Sure, he could stitch skulls together, too, but I never really thought of him becoming a priest."

Pharos burst out laughing as he took in Yulli's stunned face. "You sly dog, Lexis. You never told me you used to be a field surgeon for pirates."

"I never said that I was not," replied Lexis curtly, avoiding the gaze of the shocked clergy. "What is done is done. That is not who I am now."

"True," laughed the Coastman, shaking his head at Lexis. "Now he wears a white dress and lives as a slave back in Castland. I am Captain Rex Hinnad, your eminences. I will be your host aboard the *Killer Bee*, the finest ship that sails the Jagged Sea."

Hinnad bowed extravagantly, flourishing his arm down the docks.

"I do not see it," said Elsa, peering amongst the tangle of ships. "It cannot be that impressive."

"You are not looking, *marega*," replied Hinnad, the squeaking laugh sounding as he moved over. He grabbed the priestess round the waist and pulling her close. He pressed his cheek against hers, pointing beyond the docks, out into the waters of the cove. "*There…*"

Mida spotted her first, sleek and dark, anchored in the mouth of the inlet. Her hull bristled with openings like gaping mouths, cannons visible like the tongue of a snake, ready to flick out before the strike. The sails were black, striped with vibrant yellow. He could not make out the ensign flapping in the warm wind at the summit of the flagpole, but he knew it would be a cross and crossbones.

"She looks… strong…" ventured Ryn apprehensively.

"She is," nodded Lexis as Hinnad moved over, wrapping a strong arm around his shoulders and kissing him on the cheek with a broad grin.

Mani swaggered down the docks, arm-in-arm with Cat. He ran his hand through his thick, dark hair, feeling the sea breeze against his face as he looked over to Marito and Angelo walking beside them.

"Glorious, isn't it, little brother?" he smiled. "The warmth on your skin. The wind on your face, fresh from the coast."

"It's hot," replied Marito simply, wiping the sweat from his brow.

"We are further south, Marito," smiled Angelo gently, his orange eyes flicking between the Coastmen as they went about their business, absorbing the vibrant energy of the small settlement in the cove. "This is the climate in the Pirate Coast, in Old Illicea, in Massapine. This place is the most like Massapine you will get on the mainland."

"But the trees, the plants, they're so different. They grow so thick, the leaves are strange, even the bark and the fruits…"

"I am not a worshipper of Faunis, Marito," shrugged Angelo. "All I know is that they are beautiful. Castland, Barralegne, they are beautiful too, but sometimes a man needs the feel of his home."

"Angelo is homesick, Marito," tittered Cat, ruffling the actor's hair. "Homesick and tired of the cold."

"How long is it since you have been back to Massapine?" asked Marito.

"A long time," sighed Angelo. "We are the Northern Troupe, my friend. There are four Troupes of Lyricas that travel the world, spreading the joy of dance and performance. We all live to spread love through the Mortal World, but I sometimes feel that we were given the coldest task by the priests in Massapine."

"When will you go home, then?"

"I do not know," replied Angelo, stroking Marito's cheek gently. "But when I do, you may come with me, if you wish."

Marito nodded, looking over his shoulder to the performers and Tristane men following them along the bustling docks. "It sounds safer than here. Are we safe?"

Mani laughed, gesturing to a group of white-robed clerics shuffling down a wharf in the company of a pirate captain. "Safer than these fools. That man will take their gold and cast their corpses overboard before they've been at sea a day. The only people at risk here are those who are not alert. It takes two to make a victim."

"The philosopher speaks," laughed Cat, pinching Mani's rear teasingly. "Where shall we get a ship, knowledgeable one? Are you going to pull one from that firm arse of yours?"

"Nothing has ever been shoved up there," replied Mani curtly. "Let alone a ship. But the Tristane name travels far. People here respect fellow gentleman thieves, I assure you. We are safe. I will charter us the fastest ship in these parts."

"We should get to it, then," said Marito.

"Patience, little brother," smiled Mani, stopping in the street before an inn. Even early in the afternoon the raucous noise from inside could be heard out on the street, the unstable timbers of the building seemingly struggling to contain the frenzy of activity within. "We can rest for a few days. Me and Cat haven't yet had the pleasure of a night in a proper bed."

Cat shook her head, turning her face away in mock shyness.

"We have a long journey ahead of us, Mani…" protested Marito.

"Which means we need to rest up and be ready," interrupted his older brother, pressing a handful of silvers into Marito's hand. "Get yourself laid, lad. You're worrying me. One silver per girl, no more. If she's really good, give her another, but *afterwards*. When we're ready, I promise you we'll make up the time. I'll hire us the swiftest sloop on the Pirate Coast."

Mani dragged Cat by the hand, pulling her towards the inn. She looked back for a second, the violet eyes catching Angelo's. The lead actor nodded gently, smiling as he slid his arm around Marito's shoulders.

"Come, Marito," he said softly. "Whilst your brother is defiling my lead actress we shall drink, and talk of beautiful things…"

295

"How is the food, Tayuk?" asked Porwesh, watching as the stocky Yanari gnawed the last of the meat from the chicken leg in his gnarled hands.

"Good," replied the Knife, tossing the bone down on the plate before him and wiping his mouth on the sleeve of his rough-spun tunic. The hood was still in place, covering his face.

"It pleases a humble Yanari to hear that you enjoyed it," said Porwesh, his old, lined face barely moving as he smiled. "You know, I could get you some better attire for when you visit. It would be the least I could do, considering your service over the years. Would you like that?"

Tayuk shook his head, the face beneath the hood still directed at the table. "No. Thank you. A humble servant doesn't need such things."

"As you wish," said Porwesh.

Tayuk grasped the crystal glass of water on the table beside his plate, draining it down greedily. Porwesh picked up the decanter of wine from his side, reaching over to fill the glass.

"No." A twisted hand flashed out, covering the top of the vessel. "Thank you. It makes you slow."

"As you wish," repeated Porwesh, pouring himself a small glass and taking a sip. "But know this, Tayuk. Any time that you change your mind, I will provide for you. Whatever you want."

"A humble servant wants for nothing," uttered Tayuk, the head once more shaking beneath the hood.

"You have no need to be humble, Tayuk. We are friends, here. You have proved yourself loyal, time and again. This last time you were poisoned, and yet still you served. Those are not the actions of a man who should display constant humility."

"I was weak," insisted Tayuk. "I took too long to recover. I was late giving my report."

"*Late?*" laughed Porwesh, the sound dry and difficult. "You sent word. And barely two days later, you came to me in person. Your legs trembling, vomit on your lips. Yet you came. You gave your report, and then you refused to stay here to regain your strength."

Tayuk hesitated for a second. The strong body was trembling beneath the baggy, sackcloth garments. "A man who fails should not then be a burden on his master."

"You have no master, Tayuk. You choose to do as you do, surely? Because it is right?"

The hooded figure paused, searching for the right answer. The fingers of his hands gripped at the edge of the table, tense and fearful. "I..."

"We are equals in the eyes of Yanara, Tayuk," said Porwesh, his tone gently and soothing. He reached over, his frail hand resting on the Knife's own. "I was born with intelligence, with guile. You were born with strength. Just because I guide your actions on the path of righteousness, that does not make me better than you. It does not make me your master. Is that not so...?"

Tayuk seemed to nod beneath the hood, his body still tense, as though preparing to be struck. "I... A humble servant can't answer such questions. A humble servant trusts your judgement."

Porwesh smiled, squeezing Tayuk's hand before leaning back in his chair.

"Tell me, Tayuk," he said, his voice soothing. "Where did you go? Why not stay here, to recover in safety?"

The Knife's eyes moved upwards under the hood, meeting the gaze of the man across the table for a second from beneath the shadow before flitting down to the table. "A family I know. They are kind to me. They are my... my friends..."

"Am I not your friend, Tayuk?"

"Of course," gasped Tayuk, the grip on the table tightening. "But these people are just... different. They have been through so much, yet they look after a stranger. Just like Yanara would want. The woman, she is strong. She is not a good Yanari, she lacks humility, but she is strong. One of the boys, too. The other is intelligent..."

"You say she is not humble, Tayuk," interrupted Porwesh, sitting up in his chair again.

"No. She is angry. Strong, angry, yet a gentle soul."

"Why is she not humble, Tayuk?" asked Porwesh, the light seeming to gleam in his old, grey eyes. "Why is she angry?"

"The Castlanders." Tayuk paused for a second, glancing up at Porwesh again briefly. "One of the lords. He killed her husband. The boys' father."

"So perhaps she is right to be angry? Perhaps she should cast her humility aside..."

"I do not understand..."

"Do not worry, Tayuk," whispered Porwesh. He pushed his wine glass to one side, leaning forward on the table once more, beckoning. "Nobody here will hurt you. Tell me, what do you think?"

"She has a right to be angry," said Tayuk hesitantly, his body tense. "The Castlander lord, he shot her husband in the back as we fled. He was an artisan. A leatherworker and a taxidermist. Not a warrior, just a father."

"Interesting. I should like to meet her…"

"*No*," snarled the Knife, pulling back from the table, his hands reaching to his chest.

Porwesh raised a wrinkled hand, his palm open, conciliatory. "We are friends here, Tayuk. Your friends are my friends, surely? This woman is right. The Yanari are mistreated. Perhaps it is time we moved to change that. Humility in the face of oppression is weakness by another name, surely?"

Tayuk's muscles relaxed slightly, his eyes once more raising beneath the hood, fixing on Porwesh's own.

"She will not be harmed," insisted Porwesh, the corners of his lips raising. "You have my word. I merely wish to talk with this woman. It may be that Yanara has need of the both of you in the troubles to come."

Tayuk settled into his seat, still meeting Porwesh's stare. "You swear she will not be harmed?"

"I swear it," nodded Porwesh, reaching to his side and taking a sip of his wine.

Mathias shielded his head against the driving rain that picked up through the hills, pulling his hood up to keep the water off his face. Father Pietr stood beside him, Harat struggling against the wind to secure a wax cloak around his shoulders to ward off the rain. Mathias watched as the gawky young initiate fought the elements to protect the senior member of the clergy from the elements. He understood the concern in her crossed eyes. The cleric of Mortis was old, and he was struggling with the rigours of their journey.

"Do you not think we have enough?" asked Pietr, his tired eyes looking through the driving rain at the entrance to the burial mound before them.

Mathias shrugged his shoulders, although he was in agreement with the priest. The north-west hills of Castland were bleak, the nearest settlement far behind them. They had found a rare copse nearby, setting up camp in the shelter it gave from the wind and the rain. They had gathered enough on their journey for the women to sew together tents and awnings of a decent quality. Enough to make them comfortable even in these dismal surroundings.

And around the camp in the copse stood the undead. They waited silently, in numbers so great that Mathias could see them even here through the driving rain. The wind and rain lashed at their rotten figures yet they stood patiently, awaiting Charo's will to drive them. There was nothing for them to occupy their time here, no semblance of their former lives to distract them. But they stood, line-upon-line of dead men, gripping their weapons and waiting for a sense of purpose to fill them once more.

"Charo seemed set on coming here," said Mathias. He did not pretend to know his brother's will. The lad demonstrated an inner strength even he had never seen before. It had taken them a few hours to clear the entrance to the barrow. He looked over to their tools, spades and picks discarded at the rough entrance to the tunnel they had unearthed.

"This could be folly," said Pietr, struggling to be heard above the rain. "The dead on the battlefields seemed happy to follow Charo. The scenes here saw the slaughter of many a Barralegnan soldier. They sought to attack Castland by approaching through the northern reaches of the mountains, to take them by surprise, but the journey took much out of them. The waiting Castlander army slaughtered them to a man with ease. It is not wonder the dead from the battlefield bent to Charo's will. They hate Castland, especially its nobles."

"Do you honestly think these mindless creatures know Charo's intentions, father?"

Pietr nodded, blinking his eyes as a gust of wind threw a torrent of rain in his face. Harat reached up, wiping the water away with the sleeve of her robes.

"These poor souls can tell, Mathias," he said, patting the initiate gently on the shoulder in thanks. "I believe that it is Mortis' will that Charo aids the people. I believe that Mortis is accepting the Lurker's aid in this noble endeavour. But we are taught that the undead are an aberration, especially when a soul is bound into servitude. And yet Charo raises them, and I can sense that they have no binding, no sense of coercion. They *choose* to follow him, just as the living do. They seem to know his thoughts, his aims."

"So what is this?" asked Mathias, turning his head away from another slash of rain, casting his arm in the direction of the burial mound. "Why is it any different? Why is it folly?"

"These barrows were made by ancient tribesmen," replied Pietr warily. "Those buried within were the great warriors of those days. The precursors of the nobility we know today. I fear that the man interred here will not be as in tune with Charo's intentions."

"And you tell me this now?" snapped Mathias. "You let him go in alone?"

Harat's head snapped towards the cleric, anger in her disconcerting, mismatched eyes as she pulled a dagger from her robes. "He could be in danger, father."

"He leads us, children," replied Pietr simply as the pair of youths turned their glare on the entrance to the barrow. "We must trust and follow."

A rustling came from the darkness in the mouth of the tunnel. Harat crouched, as if poised for attack. Mathias drew his sword, gripping it in both hands, trying to put aside his confusion at the young initiate of Mortis at his side wielding a wicked, curved dagger. Their eyes focused on the darkness, trying to make out the source of the rustling.

Charo emerged slowly, leaning on the mouth of the tunnel for support. He seemed wounded, dazed. Mathias moved forward to help him, stayed by the feel of Harat's hand on his forearm. The girl pointed with her dagger into the darkness behind Charo.

Mathias saw it now. A figure behind his brother, tall and gaunt, purple eyes glowing in the darkness. The face was shrunken against the skull; not stripped bare like the skeletons back at the camp, but not hanging in rotten shreds like the newly-dead. It was lined and gaunt, but flesh nonetheless. The rest of the body beneath the simple, iron armour was the same, dried from the grave beneath the earth but not rotting. The figure stepped forward into the rain, its movements clean and smooth, a long, two-handed iron sword gripped by withered but muscular fingers.

Mathias stepped forward, bringing his sword to bear.

"No," insisted Charo, shaking his head. Even through the driving rain Mathias could see that he was weak, dark shadows forming underneath his tired eyes. A faint wisp of purple smoke still gathered around him, slowly dissipating in the rain.

The intense glow in the creature's eyes seemed to narrow as it moved forward, the sword splitting the air as it twisted in an elaborate arc, resting defensively before the undead warrior.

"What is it?" asked Harat, her eyes still focused on the apparition before them, her thin fingers gripping the hilt of the dagger tightly.

"Have you not paid attention to your studies of the undead, child?" replied Pietr, his eyes wide as he viewed the thing from the barrow.

"Assume she hasn't," snapped Mathias. "What is it?"

"*He* is a wight, children," said Pietr, his own grip tightening on the staff on which he leant. "There are many stages of the undead. The newly-dead are slow, confused. They have not had time to come to terms with their... change. The flesh that clings to their bodies holds memories, and those memories baffle them. They feel they should be able to wield a weapon, a tool, hold a child or a cup. They can, but not until they adjust to their new state.

"The skeletal forms have become accustomed to death. It is not just that the flesh has rotted away, although that helps. They know in their minds that they are dead. They have accepted it. When they return, this acceptance means that they adjust to the Mortal World again quickly. They will never be the same, never so strong or so dextrous, but they have more control over their old bodies..."

"But what is *this*?" insisted Mathias, his eyes filled with fear as the apparition before them twisted the blade around again, thrusting at them threateningly.

"As I said, he is a wight. If a corpse is entombed, away from moisture and worms, the skin does not rot. The corpse does not fester, it merely dries out, the flesh becoming taut and hard. I have read that a wight is fast and strong. A soul pulled from the realm of Mortis in this state has been dead so long that it has fully accepted its state, yet its corporeal body is as near to perfect as when it vacated the vessel."

"You are being rude," said Charo, still leaning in the mouth of the barrow, his body limp from his efforts. "He can hear you. His name is Castor the Great, and he is with us."

"Castor the Great?" scoffed Pietr. "King Castor I of Castland?"

The mummified creature's intense, purple gaze fell on the priest from empty sockets as he rose to his full height, gripping the greatsword in wizened, dead hands.

298

"That is what he has told me," smiled Charo, reaching out and placing a staying hand on the undead creature's armoured shoulder. "Do you wish to call him a liar?"

"You can talk to it?" asked Mathias, looking incredulously on the undead form before him as its head turned to him.

"*Him*," said Charo, squeezing the wight's arm reassuringly. "I can talk to *him*. He will fight with us. And there are others in these hills who will fight for us. We, all of us, are the true salvation of Castland."

Mathias watched, open-mouthed, as the wight turned towards Charo. It raised its sword high above its head, the ancient, desiccated muscles in its forearms straining as it brought the blade forward. Mathias moved forward, Harat at his side, but they were too slow. The wight brought the weapon forward, slamming it into the ground at Charo's feet as it bent to one knee before him, its head bowed.

Charo looked to the others, a tired smile on his face.

"The king of Castland is with us," he said, reaching out and gently helping the wight to its feet.

Mortis stood before the pool, blank eyes looking out at the gods assembled before him. They had all attended, light and dark. They formed a circle around the pool, their forms the same; naked, white humans, no gender, no hair, no eye colours, no distinguishing features. Such things were unnecessary when they met. They took them for vanity, to display who they were, what they believed, where they drew their power. But they were unnecessary really. The others were all gods, they could sense each other's presence.

Why do we use them at all? he thought absently.

Another plain white figure strode out of the darkness. The gods moved aside, allowing him to slip in beside them at the marble perimeter around the pool.

Faunis. Mortis felt his presence, the scent of leaves and soil and animals he had never encountered. Even Faunis had attended. Usually so distant, so aloof. Even Faunis was here.

The only exception was Contras. The God of Chaos sat cross-legged on the wall surrounding the pool, breaking the circle. He was in his monkey form, the fur bright orange, the eyes wild cyan. The curled tail clung close to the marble, dangling in the waters, flicking occasionally to send a ripple across the pool.

If I could kill him, I would...

He felt Pharma's hand on his own, squeezing gently. "Tell them, Mortis."

"Yes," sneered Argentis. Mortis could sense it was the Opulent One. The gold flicker at his lips as he spoke, the arrogance in his haughty tone. "Tell us, Mortis."

"You have all felt it," announced Mortis, trying to focus his attention away from the monkey god lolling on the pool's edge. "The turmoil."

"My existence is turmoil," proclaimed Contras, the tail flicking water across at Mortis.

"I can end that for you, fool," snarled Mortis, black smoke issuing from the angry finger he pointed at the God of Chaos.

The gods around the pool flinched, the natural colours returning to their eyes for a second as they looked at the angry form reaching across the water for Contras. Mortis had ended the Great Enemy, after all. Was it an empty threat?

"I believe that Mortis questions your reasons for being here, Contras," intoned Pharma softly, reaching out and lowering the God of Death's outstretched arm. "After all, Light Gods and Dark Gods have come here to talk. These matters are of great importance, yet you do not appear to be appreciating that."

Contras shrugged, his form fading before their eyes. His fur and eyes blanched as they watched, the simian creature on the wall before them now bleached white. "Is this better, Merciful One?"

"I believe Pharma is trying to impart the importance of this meeting," intervened Larcenara, a slender arm reaching out and pulling Contras off the wall. She waited whilst the God of Chaos extended his feet, finding the ground below, before releasing her grip. "Dark Gods and Light, coming together to meet. It has not happened for some time. It must be a matter of import."

"It is." Pharma nodded a grateful greeting to the Goddess of Thieves. "I will be open with you. Mortis is right. I have felt the unrest in the Mortal World. I am sure you have felt it too."

"So what if we have?" sneered Pyra, a flick of flame licking out from her long, white fingers as they played across the marble surround.

"Then we should discuss it," said Mortis softly, recovering his composure. "This threatens our very existence. If the mortals are unsettled, it affects us all. On many matters we do not agree, but as gods we must ensure our mutual survival. The mortals are fickle. It is important that we maintain the balance."

"I have felt it," said Faunis, staring down into the misty waters of the pool. "The Mortal World stands on a precipice. Factions are forming. The people are scared. Their fear seeps into the very fabric of their plane, into the rocks and the trees."

Sanguis reached out a hand, running her fingers softly across the God of Nature's cheek and down his neck. Pharma sent a questioning look in Mortis' direction, surprised at the gesture from the Murderess.

"It is not just the Mortal World that is beginning to shift," hissed Sanguis, looking around the assembled deities. "I know I am not alone in sensing him…"

"The Lurker," nodded Lyricas.

"It is not possible," insisted Guerro impatiently. "Mortis killed the Great Enemy during the last turmoil."

"And yet we feel his presence nonetheless," said Lyricas.

Contras chuckled. "*Did* the great God of Death kill Lunaris, though? Or did he just weaken him? Has he returned?"

"You should know, old friend," said Almas, looking over to Mortis. "When Lunaris killed Termos, he gained his power. Did you feel that, when you struck down the Creature in the Darkness?"

Mortis shook his head slowly. "No. I felt him fade, but I did not gain his strength."

"It seems you did not kill him, then," shrugged Contras.

"Perhaps what we feel is something else," suggested Pharma. "Perhaps the fearful mortals are praying to Lunaris, and that energy has no home in the Astral Realm. Maybe it is flowing free, unharnessed, destabilising the plane."

"It is a theory," agreed Argentis. "But it does not make sense. We all receive energy from the prayers to Yanara. Yanara does not exist, so we each receive the energy sent from the Mortal World. Surely the same would happen with those prayers to Lunaris?"

"Perhaps the worship is forming a new God of Fear," said Almas. "We may be feeling the birth of another of our kind."

"But again, Almas, why has this not happened with this Yanara?"

The gods fell silent, each looking to the others for answers.

"None of us knows," smiled Contras. "Gods who are not all-seeing. Who would believe it?"

"We could open the tomb," said Guerro, trying to stifle the contributions from the God of Chaos.

The others shook their heads warily, trying to conceal the unfamiliar feeling gathering within each of their hearts; fear.

"That would be unwise," said Mortis. "We do not want to upset the balance further. What if the Lurker is within, and we release him back into the Astral Realm?"

"What can we do then?" snarled Guerro.

"Nothing," giggled Contras, hopping back up onto the wall of the pool. "We are all powerless. The Astral Realm stinks of the Lurker, but we do not know how or why. We can do nothing. In the Mortal World, our followers shift their worship, threatening our very existence. And we can do nothing. Perhaps it is us who should pray to the mortals, begging for their affection…"

"A terrifying prospect," said Mortis ruefully.

"No," smiled Contras, dipping a simian toe into the waters of the pool. "It is glorious."

The gods moved away from the pool one-by-one, their heads lowered in quiet contemplation as they retreated to their own domains to mull over the permutations. Pharma once again raised an eyebrow as she watched Sanguis leave alongside Faunis. The Murderess' hand slid down the God of Nature's arm, sliding to lock their fingers together.

Mortis caught her gaze, shaking his head wearily. Pharma slipped her own hand into his, pulling him close in a soothing embrace.

Chapter Forty-Seven

Lunaris crawled across the floor of his tomb, the gold manacles clanking and scraping along the ground. He reached out in the blackness, his weak, skeletal hand feeling for the stone wall of the chamber. He found it, pressing the palm against the rock.

So long in blackness. He was the Lurker, the Creature in the Darkness, but the absence of light was preying on his mind now. He longed for just a little light, to break the tedium.

The effort of crawling along the floor had exhausted him. He leaned against the wall, resting. He felt drained, the way he imagined an emaciated, starving mortal to feel. His sustenance was prayer, and the energy it provided. It had been too long since he last fed on that succulent, nourishing power.

It was worse that he could feel it. The surges were fleeting, gone in an instant, but for a second he could feel the tingle of the power given by his worshippers gathering in his belly. Then it was gone, sucked away by his captor, leaving a vacuum in his innards.

How was this happening? He was so strong once. Older than these foolish little deities, wiser and more adept with his abilities. And yet he had been defeated, and now one of the child-gods had shackled him, leeching his strength. The mortals were praying to him again, and this bastard New God was pilfering what was rightly his.

Lunaris clawed at the manacles trapping his wrists and ankles. He knew it was these infernal bonds that were sapping his strength, but he was powerless to remove them. He had tried, smashing them repeatedly against the lip of the sarcophagus in the dark, but to no avail. The effort was too much, now. Even crawling along the floor like a crippled beast left him needing to recover for a significant period of time.

The contrast with what he once was made him feel nauseous.

"There must be a way," he rasped aloud, the effort of speaking causing his chest to heave. "I must be able to keep just a little for myself."

He closed the pink eyes, reaching down into his chest with his mind. This was the way of things, after all. The powers of a god were simple, in reality. He had made it seem to the others that they were complex and difficult to master, but it was nothing of the sort.

A god just had to *want* something.

"I wonder," he gasped, summoning all his strength and pushing himself upright with his back against the wall. He reached out in the darkness, thin hands playing across the stone until he found one of the torch sconces. He gripped it hard, using it for support as he struggled to keep his legs from folding beneath him.

I just want some light in here...

He worked his hands up the sconce, wrapping the fingers around the tip of the burnt-out torch. He felt another surge of power running through his body, gathering in the pit of his stomach. He screwed his eyes tight together, desperately trying to keep the energy within him, send it arcing down his arms into the torch.

I want light.

He gasped as the energy slipped away, his guts turning over as the nourishing purple wash was sucked out of him.

Lunaris stood in the dark, panting heavily. It was too much. He was trying to keep it all. He didn't have the strength to contain it all, let alone focus it. He felt another trembling through his fragile being as more prayer began to slip into him.

Just a little light.

He groaned with the effort, focusing on breaking off a small fragment of the energy as it began to dissipate within him. His mind chased the tail of the flow, like a predator picked off the weak member of the herd separated from the others. His arms tensed as the energy flowed through them, the torch flickering alive with a fragile, pink flame.

Lunaris opened his eyes, his gaunt face illuminated in the weak light from the torch, the flames licking across his skeletal fingers. He leered for a second, sliding down the wall to collapse in an exhausted heap beneath the solitary, pink light.

"I can do it," he chuckled breathlessly into the dimly-lit tomb, the rasping laugh echoing around the cold, empty space ominously.

About the Author...

Dave Gray was born and raised in Crewe, Cheshire. He studied Law at the University of Nottingham, before embarking on a self-flagellating 17-year management and loss prevention career in retail.

He now lives in Shropshire with his fiancée, Emma, and has a much-improved work-life balance, allowing him to begin producing novels that, hopefully, will bring some small enjoyment to those who read them.

Printed in Poland
by Amazon Fulfillment
Poland Sp. z o.o., Wrocław

50381470R00181